Return to Summ

Joseph Hone has writt
The Private Sector, and
was *Children of the Co*
lives in Oxfordshire.

By the same author

Joseph Hone

Return to Summer Hill

Pan Books
London, Sydney and Auckland

The author gratefully acknowledges the help
of the Virginia Center for the Creative Arts
in the preparation of this book

First published in Great Britain 1990 in a
single volume by Sinclair-Stevenson Limited

This edition of Books Four and Five of the
original edition first published 1992 by
Pan Books Limited,
a division of Pan Macmillan Publishers Limited,
Cavaye Place, London SW10 9PG

9 8 7 6 5 4 3 2 1

ISBN 0 330 32395 4

Phototypeset by Rowland Phototypesetting Limited,
Bury St Edmunds, Suffolk

Printed in England by Clays Limited, St Ives plc

'Audaces fortuna juvat'

For
Tara
and
Philip

Contents

PROLOGUE

It is 1919 – and Hetty, the dazzling, wilful daughter of
Frances Cordiner from the great house of Summer Hill in
Ireland, has decided to go to Hollywood with the young
American picture director Craig St John Williamson. But
it has not been a willing departure. Hetty, as a result of
a fire in the house which killed her grandmother, Lady
Cordiner, and which her mother believes she started, has
been banished from Summer Hill.

However, on the same day as the fire, Hetty meets
Craig again at the house: Craig who has been pursuing
her and her great friend Léonie Straus, when the girls
were touring Ireland with a music hall troupe. Craig
believes that Hetty, with her wonderfully photogenic
features, her mix of vitality and vulnerability, has an
undiscovered talent, which, in his hands, will make her
a great film star.

At first Hetty is uncertain over Craig's invitation. But
finally she agrees to it. There is nothing left for her in
Ireland. Her mother Frances – long embittered as a result
of a disastrous liaison with the Prince of Wales in the
1890s and a subsequently equally disastrous marriage to
Bruce Fraser, a West Indian sugar planter – has become
unbalanced in her hatreds: for her daughter, for everything British. Earlier she joined the Irish Republican
movement, becoming one of the leaders of the Easter
Rising in 1916. Narrowly escaping execution afterwards,
Frances was sentenced to life imprisonment instead, only
to be released in the general amnesty after the war.

But a more important factor in Hetty's decision to
leave is that all her real attachments in Ireland have disintegrated: her love for Léonie and her much older cousin
Dermot Cordiner, and her affection for Robert, childhood friend from the paradise island of Domenica where

they grew up together. Robert's own parents were killed in a hurricane, so that he came to live at Summer Hill when Frances inherited the house – Robert, who has come to love Hetty, but has been rebuffed by her in the cause of Léonie. Léonie is her greatest love, a small, dark-haired Jewish American girl, whom Hetty first met at their convent school together in France. But Léonie, in turn, Hetty feels, has betrayed her – by going back to her parents in Paris just when she most needed her, at a moment in her life when Dermot has equally, as she believes, let her down. All these loves have failed.

Robert meanwhile, despairing of Hetty and the life they might share together, in marriage, as inheritors of Summer Hill, has disappeared into his own life – as Dermot and Léonie have done. And the great house is empty of all that was idyllic there for Hetty – a partly burnt-out shell, inhabited only by her vicious Mama, and her great-aunt Emily, eccentrically happy, alone over her water-colours in another wing.

As a result of all this, and in the light of Craig's seductive assurances, Hetty believes that her connections in Ireland are quite dead, that her true inheritance is not now Summer Hill but her unique talent. 'Fresh woods, pastures new' . . .

And yet, though totally repressing it, Hetty takes with her to Hollywood a whole submerged world – of confusion, uncertainty, of relationships that must be resolved. Though she is superbly confident now, in her new life with Craig, these ghosts are not so easily laid and will continue to haunt her. What of Léonie, the great love of her life, whom she has now so betrayed with Craig? What of Robert and Dermot? Can they be so denied, so forgotten, with impunity? What of Frances's continuing malevolence towards her and the future of the great house – always a fiercely radiant presence, retaining the strange power to preserve or destroy the people who love or hate it? Can Hetty so easily escape its ever-present influence, at however great a distance? Above all, what of Hetty's father? Who is he? – for Hetty is certain that her mother has always lied to her, that he was not Bruce Fraser.

Hetty, believing she has completely escaped her past by going to Hollywood, must one day return and confront it – face her true inheritance, when all these questions must be answered, her real loves resolved.

book one

I

'No! – don't go in!' Craig commanded Hetty, mock-fierce and still panting from their race up the long steps; because of his slight limp, she had beaten him to the great imitation Gothic doorway. 'You just wait here – till I organize the surprises – and carry you over the threshold!' he went on, wagging a finger at her. Craig was willowy, delicately proportioned, with a thin face, full of natural finesse; a neat, quick, contained man, with a darting precision in his movements – an expression steely and dreamy by turns, dangerously chameleon in mood. In the same way he seemed both older and younger than his twenty-nine years. There was a vast maturity some-times in his faraway gaze, an air of contemplative under-standing. Yet just as often he was filled with a dazzling Celtic boyishness, playing the rogue or promoting a biting wit, a deceptively sharp intellect and dominant intent which quite gave the lie to his matinée idol good looks.

'Oh, let me come in, too – I can't wait!'

'No! . . .'

Hetty gave way in the end, as usual, and Craig dis-appeared inside The Wolf's Lair, the phoney Bavarian hunting lodge on the slopes of Mount Lee above Holly-wood Lake, leaving Hetty, in her short silk wedding dress, to twiddle her thumbs on the terrace.

She was momentarily exhausted. It was hot. The air still shimmered and glittered after the long day's heat. Even at this height, nearly a thousand feet above the canyon, the terrace was an oven of burnished wood, spot-lit now by the slanting afternoon sun, a gold-hazy orb dipping into the Pacific away to the right.

It was hot and silent.

A small lizard scuttled across the bogus armorial above

the hall doors. Cortez, the impertinent Amazon macaw, a wondrous blue and yellow, held in a gilt cage under the awning, broke the silence with a guttural murmur. And Hetty, frustrated and impatient to see what the surprises were inside, suddenly started to taunt the bird, prodding the bars, drumming her fingers over the cage, making faces, so that Cortez began to flap and croak, swishing his long tail.

'Bananas! Bananas!'

'And nuts to you!'

Hetty was tempted to continue bullying the bird, but it was too hot. Instead, moving over to the balustrade with its tall scarlet poinsettias and overhanging sweep of jasmine, she leant right out, hoping to catch some air rising from the valley, looking down the almost sheer slope – a treacherous wilderness of scrubby thorn and wild fig – to the groves of old orange and olive trees, the remains of this now-untended Californian mountain estate.

And, suddenly, cool eddies spiralled up to her, the air touched with orange blossom, the desiccated, peppery whiff of sagebrush and wild thyme. And now she basked in the place and loved it, pushing her face out into the evening light, breathing in these wild scents, absorbing the limitless distances, the vast panorama that lay before her – but immune from it, her feelings of power over this reclaimed desert once more confirmed. And power was life now for Hetty – a fact confirmed everywhere in her features: in her risen cheek bones, bold blue eyes, scimītar-shaped eyebrows, the long firm lips, the bobbed silky dark hair, pointed chin. There was a fierce radiance about her now, a startling, almost harsh elegance. She was more than good looking. There was a flush of insolence everywhere in her beauty, a beauty that was both arrogant and divine.

The sagebrush reminded Hetty of the real desert, way

to the east beyond the city limits – of the ravishing heat and the crystal light out there, after all the dark tragedy of Ireland, the chilling mid-winter cold of New York. A month or so after she had arrived in Hollywood, nearly eighteen months before, Craig had taken her up for a joy ride from the little aerodrome outside Los Angeles – just the two of them, Hetty in the front seat of the small biplane, swooping out over the bay, then back round the studio lots, her stomach turning as he banked and switched about, climbing steeply into the blue, levelling out then, breasting the air for a long moment, gliding, stalling, then diving perilously at full throttle – on, on towards the earth.

So that when they landed on a flat patch of quite empty, hard-sanded desert, way to the east of the city, pulling to a stop near clumps of sagebrush and cactus, she was already dizzy with excitement. He had come to her then, raising his goggles, helping her out, holding her in his arms briefly, kissing her chastely. And she had felt the sudden urge to respond, a wild thrill, which she – and he too surely? – had repressed at the last moment.

And yet, in a way, she thought, he had seduced her in that burning empty desert. 'No,' he had said. 'Not yet, Hetty. Not yet . . . Just to see you.' And then, as she had stood there by the plane, he had taken her goggles off, flying helmet, leather jacket and silk scarf, her blouse and skirt.

He had come towards her, so close finally that she had seen the minute rise of flaxen down just below his dark hair line, his eyelids flickering an instant in the brilliant light, his eyes intent on hers, hard, ironic, caring, all in the same glance . . . had seen his hand approach, felt his neat fingers caressing her cheek, lips, neck, touching the first button on her blouse . . . She could have discouraged, stopped him at any point. But the will was never really there, scorched away in that curious gaze of his, both dreamy and wilful – by his hungry, instinctive movements which were yet full of grace, almost mannered. She had been drawn to him, irresistibly, by some strange chemistry she knew nothing of, and had stood there, barely moving, mesmerized, while he undressed her, until she was naked, leaning back against the fuselage, shaking slightly.

He could have made love to her then. In all her new mood – the fire and release she felt in her life now – she would have let him, liked him, to do that. But he did not. Instead all he said was 'You really are – beautiful . . .' – quite simply, before he added, handing her the long white silk scarf she had been wearing, 'Wrap that round your waist, and just stand out there in the light against the desert a moment.' And she had taken the scarf, winding it like a short skirt around her thighs, and walked away, posing in the light against the scrubby hills and dunes that ran away to the horizon, parading briefly, erect against the great burning landscape, stopping, turning back.

'Why? Why did you want that?'

'This Egyptian picture—'

'Yes, but, *which* one? You're always on about it! And it can't be *Cleopatra* – de Mille made that a few years ago.'

'I'll tell you, later – don't want anyone else to get the idea. In Hollywood they really are rogues and vagabonds: thieve a story from you as soon as look at you. But I wanted to see you against that sort of desert backdrop – like Egypt.'

'And?'

'You were perfect!'

'They won't have me half-naked in it, though!'

'Why not? In costume epics, ancient history, they don't mind at all. Just look at de Mille's pictures!'

Later, on the terrace of The Wolf's Lair that evening,

6

she said, 'Why didn't you? – you know – make love with me out there.'

'Ah, you're special, Hetty! – something quite different . . .' had been his only explanation, ironic, still withholding himself from her, mentally now, so that she was tantalized by him in a different way, by secrets, which she wanted to touch in him.

She had no suspicion at that point how Craig had intended just this – to tantalize, to provoke her – by the whole episode that afternoon out in the desert, which he had produced and directed, cold-bloodedly, like a scene from one of his pictures. She had no idea how, in this initial ploy, this feigned restraint, Craig had been baiting a trap for her, allaying her fears and suspicions, encouraging what he sensed was a repressed but rampant sexuality in her, so that in future, goaded beyond endurance by such refusals on his part, she would one day grab the bait, releasing all her sex for him, when he could feed on what would then be a banquet, not a snack.

Hetty had no knowledge of this regimen of sexual denial which Craig had prepared for her and which, indeed, she came to suffer with mounting frustration during the next few months, so that, when at last he sprang the trap, she responded with a fury and abandonment that surprised even him.

He had taken her one night to his 'Astronomer's Lair', a locked room high up in one of the Gothic turrets of the Lodge, a perfectly circular, faintly lit eyrie which he had organized for himself some years before, feeding his passion for astronomy, for peering into secrets unobserved, a wily necromancer, a flawed Merlin in a smoking jacket. Here, with a large telescope, he followed the stars and planets, confirming their courses or plotting deviations in the heavenly bodies, staring past Mars, Venus and Mercury, out into the milky way, and further on, ever questing, identifying distant nebulae.

As he turned a winch and chain, the metal roof slid back, opening the room to a warm, starry night. Hetty had been astonished at the whole set-up – the mysterious stellar maps and graphs and photographs of sunspots on the walls, the great telescope, eight or nine feet long, tilting upwards, as Craig lay beneath it on a sort of steamer chair, his head glued to the eye-piece, turning brass wheels on the pedestal, as if manipulating a great camera, so that the long steel tube, rising into the vertical and already poking out above the castellated turret walls, began to swing slowly round, scanning the velvet sky.

'What? – what is it?' she asked, for want of anything better to say.

'An Engelmann eight-inch refractor,' Craig had told her easily, leaning back into the softly lit room. 'You really want to know? – nine foot focal length, mounting by Repsold's of Hamburg, the glass from Clark's of Cambridge, Massachusetts. Bought it from them in fact, second hand. It's out of date. But it suits me fine. Here, take a look – I've focused on Venus.'

She had taken his place, lying on the cushioned chair, while he adjusted the back, winding her up towards the eye-piece. The view was amazing: a brilliant white crescent, white as the most dazzling snow, with even brighter points and patches, vast snow peaks they seemed, piercing through a covering of milky cloud. Hetty was enchanted. But she could not understand the shape she saw.

'It's not round,' she whispered. 'I thought the planets were all round. This is just like a crescent moon.'

'Venus orbits the sun. So, depending where it is on its orbit, we see it like a crescent, where it is now, almost between us and the sun, or a full sphere when it gets round the other side of the sun.'

'Those huge mountains, they look like . . . as if they were poking up through cloud!'

'They are mountains, maybe. But the atmosphere is much denser on Venus than here on earth. So we don't quite know what's there . . .'

He babbled on. She barely understood him, her whole attention concentrated, spellbound, on the glittering crescent – until suddenly she was aware of him, standing right behind her, his arms on top of the chair. His hands slid down about her breasts, barely touching her, moving lightly, almost imperceptibly. Yet nonetheless she felt his touch like a sharp current, crackling through her thin voile blouse, prickling her skin, coursing on down her whole body.

'We can only see the cold side of Venus,' he said. 'Never the side that faces the sun, the warm part. No idea what it's like. Maybe it's some sort of paradise . . .'

She had begun to tremble then, the image of the planet starting to dance before her eyes, so that she could no longer concentrate on the vision, leaning back in the chair, seeing his face vaguely inverted above hers, letting him fondle her, until he had slipped his hand through and touched her nipple an instant, and she had jumped in the sudden thrill, supplanted by an agony almost, a twisting in her stomach, as he let the back of the chair down, rounding on her.

But she had writhed as he had touched her again, grasping at him, yet pushing him away, tearing at his shirt – so that both of them had suddenly stood up, undressing each other furiously, until they were naked and she saw him standing there in the half-light, alert, his sex risen, a pale figure, his skin a shadowy alabaster, smooth and white, before he had come to her, taking her in his arms and she had felt the whole warm length of his body and they had seemed to dance a minute, locked together, swaying round the great telescope. He had bent down then, knelt, kissing her stomach, her thighs, her sex. She had wondered for so long . . . What was it like?

What was a man like? Now she took his sex in her hand, held it, cupping it, supple yet rigid. It seemed impossible . . . But wonderful.

They lay on the wooden floor. She found herself gazing at the endless freckle of stars, straight above her, just myriad pinpoints of light now, until he leant over, his face masking them, caressing her, putting his hands to his lips, then to hers, taking the moisture there, touching her lower down, so that her legs opened to his fingers, as if he had put some oiled key into a lock – and continued to open as he moved his fingers inside, smoothly, gently, then more firmly, so that she shivered and stretched uncontrollably, raising her thighs, twisting this way and that, as he had knelt between her legs, pausing then for what seemed an age, leaving her in an agony of suspended desire, until she could bear it no longer and had reached out, grasping him from behind, pushing him towards her, pushing him into her . . . And that first long instant of pain had almost undone her when he had come inside and stopped, before gently, insistently, flowing on; then the pain went and he thrust deeper, deeper, far, far up, until he was completely inside her, moving in delirious spasms . . .

And then, minutes later, an eruption – explosions, vast sun spots, flames, on and on, flooding her mind, with a dizzy ringing in her ears, the stars dancing in her eyes: a pleasure she had never imagined possible.

So that afterwards, she turned on him again, feeding on this miraculous source, thinking at last she had discovered the whole meaning of life. Craig – for the first time, the first person, she knew – had found and released all of her, heart and soul, the whole being: he had truly completed her.

She did not see that all he had done, like a canny water diviner, was to tap and encourage a quite exceptional flood of vehement sexuality in her, implicit in her nature, a voracious taste for every kind of exotic sensuality: a thirst for so long denied that thereafter it overflowed with Craig, at the slightest excuse, an explosive chemistry, which overcame them both, often in the least suitable places, so that sometimes, driving home from the studios in his Pierce-Arrow, they were forced to drive off the road and satisfy their cravings.

Hetty became obsessive, adamant in this pursuit of a great discovery: that she could make such thrilling love with a man. It became an overriding imperative in her life. Such a sensational new toy for her, it soon formed an ideal means – one among many – of scrubbing out the memory of her past, her betrayal of Léonie and her own unhappiness there, of beginning life anew in Hollywood, like everyone else in this plasterboard paradise – all exiles, as she was, from the old puritan worlds, all starting again with a clean slate, on which every sensual excess and folly could be writ large. This sex, so right-seeming, so licensed by the world she moved in, eradicated all Hetty's earlier experiences and ideals. She believed the explosive chemistry she and Craig shared was an unavoidable force of nature. And so it was – like an avalanche which might easily engulf her. But she did not see it in that way, spellbound in its path, unable to move, almost unhinged by her passion.

Even though at times, more soberly, she had been touched by vague doubts, and then by direct evidence, of Craig's trickery, this knowledge of his flaws had not affected her obsession with him – had added, indeed, to his mysterious charm. Yet now at last, standing on the terrace in her crumpled wedding dress, she was forced to wonder why she had married him. To make love was one thing – but to marry? For she remembered the party six months after they had arrived in Hollywood, with Craig's friends, his special cronies at Fox, the other members of the Irish brigade there: the production chief

Winfield Sheehan, the directors Walter Brenon, Raoul Walsh and Mickey Neilan.

Mickey Neilan had been in his cups, as he usually was. All of them were celebrating her first real success with Fox, *Faith and Fury*, a four-reeler in which she played the romantic lead as the swashbuckling daughter of a French aristocrat executed in the Terror, whose place she had taken, usually masked and on horseback, avenging his death with all sorts of mayhem against the lower orders, involving scintillating duels and ambushes up and down among the orchard groves and hillocks of the San Fernando valley.

Mickey, congratulating her, had told her how far she could go. 'You were great! Even with that mask on – you have it all in the eyes, where it counts. And, as for the duelling, in God's name, where did you learn to handle a sword like that? That whole athletic thing you have . . .' He shook his head. 'As good as Fairbanks – if you could get a picture with him!' He looked at her wickedly, all curly-haired grace and mischief, one of the most immediately charming men she had ever met.

'What are you doing next, Mickey?'

'A real potboiler – *Don't Ever Marry* – and you won't, will you?' And he had leant forward then, enticingly. 'Keep yourself for me . . . Craig's an old rogue, you know. Love him dearly, but there's more fantasy in his life than any of his pictures.'

'No, I di-di-didn't know—'

'Oh yes – he never told you?' Mickey paused for another drink. 'That limp for example, that famous "war wound" – got it tumbling downstairs in some bordello behind the lines, not falling out of any airplane!'

'But he was in the Canadian Flying Corps out there—'

'Yes – but just as a photographer!'

'But he *can* fly. He's taken me up here.'

'My God, he can certainly fly. Fly you to the moon – in his imagination . . .'

That had been a first dent in Craig's armour. But she had not spoken to him about it. Mickey was probably a bigger liar. But from then on she had questioned Craig – tactfully but in more detail – about his past. And in brief, at least, he had been quite open about it. His family, the St John Williamsons, had been plantation settlers in Ulster – an ancestor had been a commander in Cromwell's Model Army – and his father had been a successful doctor, with a fine white house on the southern shores of Lough Neagh. His mother had died young, and his father a few years later, when Craig was sixteen. He had been an only child.

'Do you have photographs – and things?' she had asked.

'No. They were all lost, when I moved out here from New York in . . . 1915.'

'Didn't your American c-c-cousin – the one you told me about, who brought you up when you left Ireland and went to the art school in New York – didn't he k-keep your things?'

'No, no. Cousin Thomas, I told you – he moved up to Canada, Toronto. That's how I wangled my way into the Canadian Flying Corps.'

'What was it like – in Ireland, growing up on the big lake there?'

'Wonderful. Father took me out with him, most days in the holidays, visiting patients, me sitting up front with him in the trap with the cob, skimming along those little country roads into the mountains. Wonderful collection of old people still living up in the hills there then, mostly too poor to pay, giving him bottles of moonshine instead. Or a bit of mutton. Or a Christmas turkey. Marvellous Christmases by the lake. Frozen over one year, skating . . .' He had made it all sound so romantic, entirely real.

Then one day, as she was taking tea in the Hollywood Hotel with the actress Marion Davies who had become her best friend in Hollywood, Marion had unwittingly torpedoed all these romantic notions. They had been talking about the dancer, Betty Hudson, Craig's first wife, divorced three years before, a platinum, golf-playing blonde from Pittsburg.

'Oh, yeah – I knew her well,' Marion had said in her rowdy New York voice. 'She was in the Ziegfeld Follies with me. That's where Craig met her, when he was playing bit parts with Vitagraph out in Brooklyn – got her into one of the two-reelers he was working on then. But Betty wasn't quite up to it. She could dance, but couldn't act to save her life, couldn't let herself go – know what I mean?' she added, a little wicked edge to her usual great good humour.

'What happened? – the marriage, I mean. Craig never talks about it.'

'Oh, nothing much – other than sink with all hands! You know Craig – all that dreaming he goes in for. And she was rather prim and regimented and on the ball – golf balls, not the other kind. Christ! – they were totally unsu-su-suited,' she stammered, for she suffered from the same hesitancies as did Hetty. 'And Betty was something of a snob, too – father was a big wheel in Pittsburg steel, so when she found out Craig's father ran some crummy f-f-food store in Ireland somewhere—'

'A food store? But his father was a doctor, he told me, with a big house, on a lake up in the north.'

Marion had looked at her teasingly then, thinking she was pulling her leg. 'Hell, that's just one of Craig's jokes, Hetty. Father ran a food store, some smelly little joint he hated, way in the backwoods of Ireland somewhere. And when Betty – and her father – found this out, well, there was hell to pay. But by then it was too late. She was "Mrs Mickey Curtis"!'

'"Curtis"?'

'Why, yes.' Marion had looked at her curiously then. 'Of course. That's Craig's real name – Mickey Curtis – till he came out here to the coast and changed it. That "Craig St John Williamson" bit is just a cover. Didn't he tell you?' Marion had looked embarrassed.

'No – no, he never did!' Hetty had laughed it off. 'Just another of his jokes!'

No, indeed, he had never told her, then or later, Hetty thought, coming out of her reverie on the terrace.

Craig pretended to worthy ancestors, an eminent father, a romantic background in Ireland. But Hetty's own pretences were just as bad. She believed that Craig had drawn out her real nature, the whole person, that he completed her in every way. And in return, encouraged by the reckless post-war mood of the times, by Craig himself and by others she met of the same rash disposition in Hollywood, she acted out that nature accordingly, in all sorts of imprudent ways, taking on, at Craig's skilful instigation, one more role, that of libertine and happy hedonist.

But Hetty's greatest pretence was that she had behaved appropriately with Léonie – which she had not, she knew in her heart of hearts. Léonie, she knew had had every reason to return to Paris, when her mother was ill. It was she, Hetty, who had betrayed her – by going off to America with Craig without a word. But Craig took every opportunity to persuade Hetty that her behaviour towards her old friend had been entirely understandable. 'Why,' he'd said to her one day driving back from the studios, 'there can't really be anything to reproach yourself with there. Léonie, well, she had nothing herself, so she really had to cling on to you, keep herself afloat – and pull you down with her. She couldn't live with the person you really are, the things you had to do . . .'

Craig had become Hetty's Svengali – tempting, promoting her, so much more successfully than Léonie had ever managed, into a far greater variety of exotic roles: liar, mistress, child, daughter, whore and now wife. He saw in Hetty the essence of everywoman – and had drawn these distillations from her in the past eighteen months. And this was the basis of her obsession with him: Craig had become her substitute for real life, offering her false idols, bad faith. He had lifted all the screens in her, released her devils.

Hetty looked down the valley from the terrace. The steep hills around were quite bare of other habitation – until beyond the canyon some new mansions, just white flecks in the violet-tinged afternoon light, glittered on the edge of Lake Hollywood a mile or so away. Beyond that, on the flat valley floor looking south over the dry plain, lay the studio lots, scattered round a wide area on the outskirts of Hollywood, carved out of the scrubby desert in the last few years and practically invisible at this distance.

You could see them if you wanted to, though. Craig had fixed up another big marine telescope on the balustrade – and Hetty, filling in time, played with it now. The view danced violently as she swung it over the horizon. A studio lot appeared as she dipped the lens: shaking plasterboard illusions, shimmer-white fantasies made more fantastic still in the foreshortened optics; a moat and drawbridge, castellated walls and towers with nothing behind them – the Sheriff of Nottingham's castle. Further along, on the old Triangle lot, at the junction of Hollywood and Sunset, the remains of Griffith's Babylon reared up in front of her, the huge sets from *Intolerance* – Belshazzar's Court: an endless waterfall of steps flanked by two immense colonnades, bulbous pillars topped by winged deities and monstrous elephant gods, set beneath even greater walls, triumphant arches, ramparts and towers reaching up into the sky – a Babylon so vast that even at this distance the lens failed to enclose the vision. Yet Craig, whenever he saw these huge remains, had always said, 'My sets, for the Egyptian picture – they'll be even bigger!'

Further across she saw the Paramount lot – Zukor's studio, which she had first visited, with Craig, almost immediately after their arrival in Hollywood: that morning when he had confronted the British director William Desmond Taylor, doing some studio tests for his *Huckleberry Finn* picture. She remembered that first time in a studio so well: the open stages, all in a line, each filled with a different frenzied activity, carpenters hammering, actors acting, little trios playing mood music, a panic of creation, muslin awnings drawn across against the sun, and some other stages with glass overhead, burning hot, with a wonderful smell of pine resin, lime dust, moist plaster, a pear-drop odour of fresh varnish, the acrid whiff of raw film stock.

Craig had simply stood there, at the back of the stage, watching Taylor work, staring at the tall, impeccably dressed, dignified man who looked just like a London stockbroker. Eventually an assistant had come over asking what he wanted.

'My picture,' Craig had told him simply. And Taylor, finishing the test, had walked across then, wiping his hands neatly in a silk handkerchief. 'Well, Craig – how are you? Didn't know you were back—'

'Yes, from a war you should have been in, Taylor, instead of stealing my picture.'

'Now, Craig, that's not so – I did *Tom Sawyer* first—'

'I know, that's the one I meant, the one you stole from me. And what a bloody stodgy, cackhanded job you made of it. And now you'll do the same with Huck – and that was my picture, too. Soon as I went away, you just stepped in and took it all, you bastard . . .'

'Now look here,' Taylor said reasonably. 'That's nonsense.' He spoke softly, in a cultured English accent. 'I was too old for the war, you chose to go away and play the hero—'

'Don't give me that bullshit! – with that phoney accent of yours, you two-timing bog Irishman, you.'

Taylor had been unmoved. 'Just down on your luck, Craig – that's how it is in Hollywood,' he had told him superciliously. 'Someone had to make the pictures around here—'

'I won't forgive you, Taylor, remember that. You can't play the cultured Britisher with me. I *know* who you are, from the New York days – and don't you forget it,' he had told him forcefully before turning on his heel. Hetty had been mystified. 'He's just a shit – that's why I never tell anyone my ideas around here,' was all the explanation Craig had given. And Craig's fortunes at that moment had seemed very low indeed. No one really wanted him back in pictures. But he had taken Hetty to lunch that same day, bribing the maître d'hôtel for a best corner table at the Hollywood Hotel, and Winfield Sheehan from Fox had been there, doing some deal, and seeing Hetty, so young and fresh, so original in a room filled with tired and familiar faces, had come over, gazing at her.

'Hi, Craig – didn't know you were back!' Then he had gazed at Hetty more closely. 'And who's this?' He fished for an introduction.

'Wait and see, Winfield – just you wait and see! I'm making some tests on her – show them to you when they're ready . . .'

Hetty left the telescope, bored with these reminders of her workaday world. She turned and gazed up at the hall doors, willing them to open, for Craig to return. But nothing moved in the stillness. She sighed, leaning back on the balustrade, tilting her bronzed face upwards, closing her eyes – a slim dark figure in the white silk dress, chin tilted, neck arched, as if offering herself to some delicious agony. She had blossomed in the warmth and pleasure of these southern California airs, the attentions of studio make-up men, hairdressers, costumiers – the dark curls straightened now, bobbed and fringed across her brow. There was still the tomboy athleticism, the mischief. But in the last eighteen months, under Craig's direction, and in her own sexual release, there was a quite new poise and sophistication; the childishness had been refined into something sensuous, inviting, knowing. She was a different person, in body as well as thought. Apparently resolving her earlier conflicts of temperament, she combined her previous innocence with a precocious maturity. Only her stammer reoccurred sometimes, as evidence of her former torments, from which she believed she had completely released herself.

Now, she thought herself fulfilled and happy. What did it matter if she had married a liar? She was *who* she was with Craig. That was what counted. She had come into her inheritance, which was not a great house in Ireland, but her own unique gifts, released now in expressing her real nature. And in that cause what did a few inventions matter? They had not lied about their passion, or their success in pictures together. Both these had been very real.

But Hetty, fed on vanities, so obsessed by, so seduced in every way by Craig, had quite blinded herself to the realities of the situation. Now, locked in his orbit, she had no independent track across the heavens herself. She did not choose to see how Craig, from the beginning, had been manipulating her. So intent was she on furthering her own power schemes, on justifying her obsession with him and on repressing her guilt about Léonie, that she refused to acknowledge his own wiles, to much the same ends, with her – had not realized how she had been a key card in his resurgence as a Hollywood director, or seen how he used her voyeuristically, through the camera and in private, unaware that what attracted him as much as anything in her was her love of women, or of one woman at least, a delicious aberration for him, which he had sensed in her from the beginning.

So Hetty, knowing nothing of the picture business – of all its usual great hurdles to success – and caring less, had seen her sudden achievements in Hollywood as simply a natural progression of her talent, a mere confirmation of her gifts.

When Winfield Sheehan had stood up in the small projection room, after he had seen Craig's tests on her, and said, 'Well, Miss Fraser, the camera certainly likes you!', she had taken this praise as almost inevitable, not something upon which Craig's career might hang – for she had not been in Winfield's office afterwards when he spoke to Craig.

'OK, I agree – you've got something quite unusual there. But—'

'But she goes only with me, Winfield. Remember that.'

'Well, I'd like to, Craig – but you've been out of the business quite a while . . .'

'Take it or leave it. Both of us or nothing. Paramount will snap her up, or Universal – and she'll be a star. No doubt of it – see it as clear as the nose on your face. But take us both – and you'll have her with Fox, in on the first floor . . .'

'OK, Craig . . .' Winfield, drumming his fingers on the desk, had unwillingly seen the light. 'Raoul is still held up on location with *This is the Life*. So I'll give you the new Billy Farnum picture to do. Try her in that small part, the sassy, arrogant daughter from Charleston.'

A Family and Its Fortune the picture had been called,

the story of an aristocratic southern household, fallen on bad times after the Civil War, trying to re-establish themselves, in which Hetty, as the youngest of three daughters, falling in love with a Yankee officer, runs foul of her parents, particularly her mother. It was a small role. But it was one which she played to perfection.

She had gone from strength to strength after that – and so had Craig. Their partnership flowered in a succession of swashbuckling costume pictures, some banal contemporary modern melodramas and one or two sentimental love stories – not the sort of picture that Craig really wanted to direct at all. But they had all made money and Craig was on top now again. And Hetty – as Laura Bowen, the stage name he had invented for her, insisting she use it in real life as well – was already a coming star, with interviews in *Photoplay* and an increasing pile of fan mail.

The era of the vamp was fading in Hollywood – as was the taste for Mary Pickford's old-world home-spun childish innocence. Post-war audiences – emancipated, irresponsible, more sophisticated – wanted something different in their dream women: a greater realism, a modern tone of command, a more available sexuality, bounding arrogance, devil-may-care adventure. And Hetty, with her mischievous regality, supplied just this tempting mix.

But more, for Americans, she was a startling face to conjure with – a quite new sort of beauty for them, in which there was nothing cheap or sentimental, the classic features of old European nobility, yet lit by all sorts of contemporary devilment. With its finesse, hers was a unique face in Hollywood pictures, that of a princess who had come right down into the market place, freely available to all, so that a huge audience of clerks and shop girls could feel themselves mixing with royalty on equal terms . . . at least for an hour in a darkened picture palace. For Hetty's availability to ordinary mortals was finally illusory. She was not one of them. She touched their lives with easy grace and command, which they might seek to emulate, but left them at fade-out, elusive in her fiery independence, unobtainable on any permanent basis, leaving her audience only with a tantalizing taste of the power she exuded.

Craig, of course, had seen just these latent images and opportunities in her, and had skilfully promoted them – the right scenarios, parts, make-up, costumes, lighting. But just as much, as she learnt the trade, Hetty had come to inspire him – all her histrionic fancies, so often frustrated before, coming to fruition now, when she could dream in public, licensed in every whim, making love to the camera. There had, indeed, been something inevitable about their professional success. With Craig directing her *sotto voce* on the stages, they sparked off such magic in each other.

But why had she married Craig, she wondered once more, leaning back on the balustrade? Well, she had fallen in love with him – and he with her, or so she thought. She refused for a moment to acknowledge another and deeper reason: that, in marrying Craig, she could prove her love for a man, thus relegating her relationship with Léonie to the status of a girlish crush. She could put the seal now on the tomb of that dead relationship and so forget her betrayal there. And there was a further reason she was not conscious of at all: in her guilt at this betrayal she wanted as much to wound people as to dominate them. Because wounds, she knew intuitively, must be all the more telling in a marriage. Though in both these ambitions she had made no headway whatsoever with Craig.

She opened her eyes, gazing up at the Lodge. Built on several receding levels it was an absurd Alpine conceit in these burning desert airs. No single feature rhymed with any other. It was a complete hodge-podge of conflicting styles and Gothic excrescences – of fairy-tale steeples, castellated turrets, half-timbered battlements, gargoyles, arrow-slit windows, lattice-work wooden balconies, a mix of thin wood, plaster and some brick – a fragile dream in the glimmering light: paper-thin, preposterous.

But Hetty had never been able to dislike it. How could one dislike something so insistently, compellingly bogus? Craig had bought the crazy place early in 1917, before the building had even been completed, after he had been three years on the coast, working on, and finally directing, two-reelers for Jesse Lasky; then he had moved to Fox and had his first big success there, a torrid six-reel extravaganza, supposedly set in ancient Egypt, *Mistress of the Gods*, with Annette Kellerman. The picture had cost an astonishing $40,000. But it had grossed almost ten times that.

Craig had been in the money then. And the man who had originally built the folly, a geologist taking a fortune out of the South Bay oil boom, had let it go cheap. His wife had died just before they were due to move in and the man had jumped at the chance of unloading it. There had been no other bidders. Access was difficult – the geologist had already spent a fortune just grading the site and hacking the road up to it – and it had been miles from anywhere then, from the studios or Hollywood itself, which was exactly why Craig had wanted it. He loathed Hollywood, its vulgar suburban airs, and the brash studio lots growing up all round it. He had wanted just this, something wild and craggy, as far away as possible from all the charlatans, self-styled geniuses, neurotics and hucksters of the plain.

Which was exactly why Hetty had come to like it, too. On this peak, in the limpid air, she could lord it over all the other hazy creations far beneath her, the shallow, dust-dry illusions of the valley. And, though she herself had come to live in a further rackety illusion up here, that was something quite different: the Lodge was an illusion of arrogant European civilization – no matter that the place itself trembled now on the edge of destruction above the canyon, already beginning to split in the fierce heat, wood buckling, paint peeling, the back of the Lodge never completed and still supported by scaffolding and buttresses, just like a set on one of the studio lots.

They both liked it that way. Craig had made no repairs. What was the point of repairing something so insubstantial? You never repaired things out here anyway. The fools on the plain – they just built afresh every time, always desperate for something new. But he and Hetty both cherished the illusion of power and feudal tradition offered by the gimcrack Lodge.

Yes, Hetty thought, despite the fragility, the youth of the building, everything had a memory for her here. She noticed the long, false marble plaster panel, one of three as a surround for the hall doors, through which Craig had put his elbow one night after dinner on the terrace, just to show how skin-deep the place was. Some of the guests had been quite shocked at this wilful destruction of something they took to be precious and genuinely antique. Craig had smiled at them.

'All just phoney! Only a dream palace . . .'

'And you're the dream king, I suppose!' Betty Nansen, the Danish beauty and now a big star, had said drily.

'And you the queen, Betty . . .' Craig had looked at her lovingly. And Hetty had felt a pang of bitter jealousy then, which she thought she had entirely hidden. But Craig, close by, had noticed it and whispered, 'You needn't fret, Laura.'

'I'm not! – don't fool yourself.'

And he had shaken his head in wonder then. 'You don't know yourself, Laura – it's all in your eyes, just as it is in close up. See all your thoughts, clear as day. You can look so jealous or loving, yet your expression doesn't change a fraction. All in your eyes . . . That's why the camera loves you!'

And was this why she had come to love *him*? – because however much she dissembled, disguised herself, he could still see the secrets of her soul? More reason for hating him, surely? – that she could not escape, was held captive in some way by his knowledge of her, his intuitions, which always out-reached what she knew or felt about him.

For the first time in her life she was with somebody whom she could not, in the end, dominate or wound. And there was the challenge. Craig was a tantalizing will-o'-the-wisp, forever dancing away from her, just out of reach, imbued with all sorts of knowledge, secrets, magic – gifts which she longed for herself in the person of someone she could not finally possess. And perhaps she had married him to further that end – as if in such legal possession of him, and of half the Lodge, she might finally command his spirit as well.

Craig confirmed this idea of a shared property, at least, when he emerged on the terrace then, all mysterious smiles, carrying a genuine marble plaque. He turned it round. LAURA'S LAIR, it said, in Gothic characters chiselled deep into the stone. He set it down by the hall door.

'Well . . . Laura Bowen!' He was just in his shirt-sleeves now, sweating, his eyebrows raised. She jumped up and they met in a calm embrace – and she kissed him, half-warily, half-tenderly, brushing the pinpoints of perspiration away from his upper lip. 'You like it?' She nodded as he picked her up in his arms. 'Well, now for the other surprises . . .' And he carried her over the threshold.

As he opened the doors and they moved from the light into the shadows of the mock baronial hall, the music started – a great swirling burst of woodwind, strings and timpani, Lehar's 'Gold and Silver' waltz. In the same instant spotlights illuminated a dais at the end of the hall and Hetty saw the orchestra, some fifteen or twenty men in white tie and tails, with little Eddy Nolan, one of the two dwarf brothers from Fonsy's music-hall troupe, whom Craig had taken with them from Ireland, set up in front, in a miniature dress suit, playing the conductor.

'What on earth . . .' Hetty was enchanted. 'How did you get them all up here?'

Craig still held her in his arms. 'Ransacked the studios – there'll be no mood music down on the plains this afternoon! Sneaked them all up here after lunch – Winfield fixed it for me. Isn't it great?' She nodded again, before he set her down and they waltzed away together, quite alone in the wide spaces, circling round in their tired wedding outfits. Their clothes were sweaty and bedraggled. But the new ring on Hetty's finger, one of Craig's wedding presents, a great cornelian scarab with a strange Egyptian symbol engraved on the flat side, glittered like a dark and pristine moon. She looked at it. Yes, she was married.

'They can't get me now,' she whispered, brushing Craig's ear as he held her lightly. 'However hard they try . . .'

'I'd never have let them get you anyway.'

'Mama might have done anything in her craziness. You'd "abducted" me, don't forget! Remember that detective she sent up here – when I was supposed to be living down at the Studio Club – and you locked me in the turret while he searched the place? And you told him the room there had never been opened, some sort of ghost inside, and he skedaddled!'

'I could just as easily have paid him off.'

'Of course you could. But you invented him off instead! You sweet monster . . .'

Her mother, when she had eventually learnt of Hetty's Studio Club address, had threatened all sorts of woe, legal and otherwise, in several letters, half-dismissive, half-revengeful: '. . . who cares what you do with your stupid life . . . I shall have the police in America apprehend you . . .'

Before that she had written to her cousin Dermot, still in the British army, and to his father Mortimer, of the great beard, lawyer and Home Rule MP in Dublin, and great friend who, all unknowing, had cemented her loving relationship with Léonie by allowing them the use of his Dublin flat several years before. And she had written to Robert, now up at Trinity College there. They had replied in reasonable but concerned tones. Was she doing the right thing? Was she happy? Though they were astonished at her behaviour, she at least felt some contact and understanding there. The only letter which cut her to the bone, so that she afterwards completely eradicated it from her mind, was the one from Léonie, received while she was still at the Studio Club.

'. . . Mama died in the influenza epidemic. Then you disappeared. I thought I'd die myself then. I just can't imagine why you did this cruel thing, without a word of warning or explanation, destroying everything we had in a moment . . .'

The hurt, recriminatory tone had changed then, replaced by apt reflections on Hetty's character and the likely consequences of her actions, yet offering a final understanding, indeed forgiveness, so that it was this last part of the letter which Hetty most completely forgot.

I know you well enough – *so* well, indeed! – to know that with this man you'll just betray your real nature. Oh, you'll think you're fulfilling yourself with him, in his world of nickelodeons or whatever. But it won't be anything of the kind. Don't you see? – with him you'll

lose all that is best and truest in you, your great gift which
is not for acting, pretending, but for being *real*.

I know how you can't face that reality in yourself, because
of your missing father, all the rows with your Mama
and so on. But with this man you'll only be expressing
shallow surfaces of yourself – tricks, vanities, living on thin
ice which will land you in all sorts of trouble in the end.
Yes, that trite phrase – you're running away from
yourself! And don't you see, too, that this man is not the
father figure you've searched so long for, but just someone
out for his own ends, who'll encourage all that's worst in
you? I saw that at once in him, that evening in
Waterford. Really, you shouldn't go on with it. You
mustn't, because one day, if you go on feeding these
pretences, you'll come to hate yourself, for betraying your
real goal, which shouldn't be for impressing the world,
but knowing your true self and expressing that. You gave
that wonderful self to me, often enough. And a thing
like that doesn't just disappear. You've only hidden it
more thoroughly. But you can find it again. Or we can.
I'll wait for you . . .

Hetty had read the letter with angry, tear-filled eyes.
Then, in a fury of guilty rage, she had torn it up. She
had not replied, nor heard from Léonie since. Instead,
asleep sometimes, in nightmares, she moaned her name.
Coming closer to Craig in the waltz, resting her chin
on his shoulder, her eyes circled the hall in all its bogus
splendour. Flowing round in the dance she saw a blur of
hideous sporting trophies – grizzly bear, bison, puma –
high above the collection of mediaeval armour, ghostly
men-at-arms, opposing rows along each wall of dark,
malign figures in visored helmets, great carapaces of steel
and chain mail, with crossed lances set between them,
double-edged swords, Gothic blunderbusses, miniature
cannon . . . Craig had collected these emblems of chiv-
alry and violent derring-do from various studio prop
departments – they were all quite unreal, made of tin,

papier-mâché or wood, just as most of the Lodge was.

But their bogus nature was precisely intended – as a play within the play, further conceits within a greater one, turning the Lodge into a huge toy box for them both to tinker with, room by room, sustaining their own bizarre dreams, their 'games'; each separate space presented a different theme in its décor: a Wild West saloon, complete with bar and pool table; a gilded Versailles salon fit for Marie Antoinette; a drawing room decked out in classic Georgian mode, a memory of great Irish country houses, with hunting prints and imitation Chippendale; and, last and most resplendent of all, an ancient Egyptian room, reflecting Craig's obsessions with the Pharonic period, with coloured tomb murals, hieroglyphics and cartouches, all round the walls, two vast plaster busts of Isis and Osiris at either end, a delicious dancing fountain in the middle, with the anachronistic addition of silken cushions and hookahs from a later Arab period littering the floor: all the magpie collection scavenged from the studios over the years and settings now for their own personal productions, where they returned each night from the studios, isolating themselves from the vulgar crowd on the plains, creating exotic dramas in the Lodge which would never be captured on celluloid.

Hetty remembered one such occasion, six months before, when she and Craig had returned late from a riotous party at the Ship Café, with two young women, bit-part actresses Craig had picked up there. They had all flopped down in the Egyptian room and Craig had masterminded things, filling the hookah bowls with marijuana, so that all of them, in half an hour, were stretched out, dreamy-faced, on the opulent cushions, Craig lolling next to one of the girls, fondling her.

And Hetty, drawing on this narcotic for the first time, had looked over at him, only vaguely surprised, watching the girl wriggle out of her thin dress; the other girl –

called Tansy, she remembered, small, pert, red-haired, adventurous – had leant over and casually touched her lips. Hetty, in a state of happy aerial suspension, had still felt a thump of surprise at this invitation. But instead of resisting it, as she had thought for a moment to do, she had been overcome by a sweet faintness, lying back on the cushions – and the other girl, leaning down, had slipped her hand into her dress, and touched her breast delicately, twitching the nipple. And the sense of rising excitement then, so that she had jack-knifed up, reaching for Tansy, before falling back, stunned almost, as the red-haired girl, kneeling above her now, quickly took off her own blouse, then climbed out of her skirt, and straddled Hetty gently, bending forward, opening her dress wide, kissing her breasts, before running a hand, feather-light, slowly down to her sex. The pleasure, spasm upon spasm, had been delirious.

Though she had considered the whole episode more soberly next morning, she did not allow the idea that she had done anything the least unsuitable to cross her mind. How could there be anything wrong in such pleasure? She had done just this with Léonie many times. The whole business, and its later repetition, she saw simply as a happy extension of their many 'games', all part of the endless tricks and fancies played out between them then, the glorious realization of dreams, in which Léonie in the end had quite failed her. Such escapades were simply other ploys, joyous sexual conceits, in which they could both extend their reach over the common herd. Now, of course, there was a difference. She and Craig were married. Would that change the game? She danced on with Craig through the great hall.

The party to celebrate both her wedding and the release of *Thunder Bay*, her latest pirate swashbuckler directed by Craig, started a few hours later. The boot-legger's van had arrived some time before, filled with crates of Scotch and champagne, which Craig had ordered specially for the occasion, run up the coast from Mexico. The first guests arrived soon afterwards – some straight from the studios even on a Saturday night – roaring up the dark, winding track in their Kessels and Dusenbergs, headlights piercing the night, momentarily illuminating Craig and Hetty as they waited on the terrace – Craig in a white alpaca jacket, Hetty in a sheath dress of black silk, delicately appliquéed with tiny white beads and sequins.

'Hi, Wally! – Dotty!' Craig stepped forward, giving Wally Reid and then his wife a quick bear hug. Wally was smashed already. Was it just drink, Hetty wondered – or had he moved on to the snow? Well, there was that here too, if anyone wanted it.

Wally, with his striking, pretty-boy blond good looks, was with Paramount, the brightest male star in Hollywood just then. And Mabel Normand, who tripped – literally tripped, was she back on the snow as well? – up the steps next with Fatty Arbuckle, was with Goldwyn. But most of the other guests were friends of theirs at Fox – Billy Farnum, Betty Nansen, Virginia Pearson and Betty Blythe, fresh from her success in *The Queen of Sheba*.

Walter Brenon with the rest of the Irish brigade came in a rush soon afterwards – Raoul Walsh, Mickey Neilan and Winfield Sheehan: blond, blue-eyed, flamboyant, with his equally boisterous wife, the opera diva Maria Jeritza.

In couples or excited groups they ran up the steps, pushing into the great hall, hazy with tobacco now, filled with raucous laughter and the sharply syncopated clatter of ragtime – grasping drinks from phoney silver goblets, picking at lobster and bronzed suckling pigs from a mock-mediaeval groaning board. Finally, a vast chauffeur-driven Dodge limousine drew up and the actress Marion Davies, in a long, deep-cut black polka dot silk dress, emerged with her friend William Randolph Hearst, the newspaper tycoon.

Hetty rushed down the steps to greet her. 'Marion!' They embraced. 'How's it going? That director Leonard still murdering you with soft lights and p-passionate romance?'

'Christ! – don't t-t-talk about it! *The Restless Sex* – you can say that again! What a b-bloody picture. Not an ounce of comedy,' she added in her funny, rowdy voice, before they moved away together as Craig welcomed Hearst.

'And the Boss?' Hetty looked back at the tycoon. 'How are things?'

'Always the be-beady eye on me. Never misses a trick.' Then, making sure she was out of earshot, she went on, 'Laura, I could really use a drink.' She looked at her friend, wide eyes flickering, running her fingers nervously through the stiff perm in her auburn hair.

'I've a b-bottle in my room. Come on up and have a jigger while you take your coat off.'

'I ain't got no coat, you nutty—'

'"Powder your nose" then.'

'Powder my ass . . .'

People looked up as Hearst and his mistress moved into the crowded hall. This was a real catch, they thought – almost as good as Fairbanks and Pickford, who certainly would not be coming to this *louche* shindig. Hearst, with all his gossipy newspapers, among these crates of bootlegged drink, would be at risk, while Marion Davies, whom he had made one of the social queens of Hollywood, had a bad temptation that way. But Hetty had insisted Marion come – so that Hearst, ever the concerned jailer in their strange relationship, had had to tag along too.

Marion sat at Hetty's dressing table, settling her hair

with one hand, taking a shot of Scotch with the other. Hetty paced behind her. It was her turn to be nervous now. Drink wasn't her problem. She wished in some ways it was. You could cure it then – by having a few.

'So?' Marion asked, fortified now, even warmer and more scatty. 'What's *your* problem?' She smiled at her in the mirror. 'Marriage – already?'

'Not quite . . .' Hetty, cracking her knuckles, was at a loss.

'Well, it can't be your new pirate p-picture with Craig. Everyone says it's a real wow, held over at Sloans for a second *week*, goddamit!'

'No, not that . . .' Hetty turned, half-smiling, nervous.

'It's the marriage then, when you have him anyway.'

'Maybe . . .'

'Listen, Laura, you're stalling. Either you're nuts about Craig, I mean really c-crackers, or you want to sink the ship without knowing it. One or the other. You wouldn't be m-marrying him otherwise. I tell ya, honey – no surer way of falling out with a guy than getting hitched. And being crazy about someone, *that* crazy, well, that'll have just the same result: *finito*, 'cos no man's really worth it. So either way – you're doomed! Have a drink.'

Beaming hugely, she offered Hetty the bottle.

'P-perhaps—'

'No perhaps about it! Know it myself all too well. Listen, I'm hooked with Randy. But I know *why*. A lot of weaknesses – 'cos maybe I ain't really no actress at all. So I need him to look after me. But if I *m-married* him, why, then he'd treat me like dirt. *I'd* be doomed! So I hold off, for the good of my health.'

'I d-d-don't need Craig to look after me.'

'OK, so you're hooked in some other way – in bed maybe. And that's fine. But you don't need to m-m-*marry* a guy to have that!' Marion took another shot of whisky, looking at Hetty now as if at some new species of woman. 'Ya see, that's what I don't get. Ya gotta perfectly good d-deal going with Craig already, in *every* way. Yet here you are digging your own grave. It's crazy – killing happiness that way.'

'Why should m-marriage kill our chances, though?'

'*Your* chances, not his – and 'cos you don't *need* marriage with him.' She looked at Hetty, shaking her head in wonder. 'So you're really hooked on Craig some quite different way altogether, aren't you? I don't know what. But what's worse is *you* don't know either. And that's crazy! Ya gotta resist the hook, Laura – 'cos it'll destroy you.'

What nonsense, Hetty thought. Marion was lovely – but she really did drink too much.

The evening went from strength to riotous weakness. Drink flowed, the Frisco lobster and the suckling pigs were hardly touched. People danced and hugged and kissed, sometimes in step to the ragtime music, more often not. Some of the guests moved to other rooms, darker corners, for assignations with snow or sex. But most remained in the great hall, a brittle, raucous crowd, mocking the chivalrous men-at-arms all round them, flouncing their short skirts in Charlestons, kicking the papier-mâché mediaeval cannon, while Wally Reid, far gone, aimed an Arab blunderbuss at his wife. Others kept close to the long table with its bootlegged drinks, like desert travellers at some miraculous oasis, laughing like schoolchildren, telling tales out of class.

A drunken minor executive from Fox sidled up to Craig. 'So what's your next picture, Craig? Rumour has it you've got some big costume epic up your sleeve.'

'Rumour's wrong. Got a nice little family melodrama coming up with Laura—'

'You should put her in something big, now's your

chance. *Thunder Bay* – held over for a second week at Sloans, grossed over five thousand bucks there *last* week—'

'I know, I know—'

'But now you've gone and *married* her, Craig! What was the idea there?'

Craig rounded on him then. 'What's the *usual* idea there, you hamhead?'

The man was surprised, swaying about. 'Search me, search me . . .'

Hetty danced with Mickey Neilan, in his cups as usual, but still entirely graceful and charming.

'So, top of the evenin',' he said to her, making jaunty steps, so that they nearly ran over Eddy Nolan, still in his miniature dress suit, dancing with another midget, a little pixie of a woman, part of a troupe working on a Lon Chaney horror picture at Universal. 'Christ, they really get under your feet here,' Mickey went on. 'What's with Craig, that he has to have all these deformed tiny tots about him? – and in his pictures – often wondered.'

Hetty smiled. 'He likes them. And so do I. Eddy Nolan's a sweet.'

'Yeah – but it's really a sort of fetish with Craig. And his friend Von.' He looked over to the drinks table where the Austrian director, Erich von Stroheim, erect in white tie and tails, very Prussian, with close-cropped hair, was lowering a goblet of champagne in one gulp, jerking his neck back, then coming smartly to attention, clicking his heels, laughing. 'Always looking for the perverse side of things.'

'Do they?'

'You didn't see *The Devil's Passkey*?'

'No.'

'Yeah: lust, malice, torture, obsession – that's the Von. And Craig, too, whenever he gets half a chance.'

'And you? You're pure as the driven snow?'

'Well, I *am*! Directing Mary Pickford all these years you *have* to be . . .' He came to her confidingly then. 'Laura, I'd really like to do a picture with you.'

'Me too. But—'

'But Craig's just gone and got you under permanent contract. Why did you have to go and *marry* him, for Chrissakes? I told you, you shouldn't have gone and done it.'

'Second time tonight! Marion said the same thing. What's wrong with you people? A little drink on board – then sour grapes?'

'Oh no, Laura.' He looked at her winningly. 'In Vino Veritas – Vino Veritas . . .'

He was just drunk, too, she thought. Nicely so. But you had to take it all with a pinch of salt, with both of them, because Marion – well, she'd have liked to marry Craig herself. A lot of Hollywood women would have wanted that. And Mickey? – he was crazy about her. Sour grapes all round. But what was a 'fetish', she wondered? She'd ask Craig. He'd be bound to know.

Later, on Von Stroheim's suggestion, a dozen of them made up another party, taking their cars down the canyon, way out east of Los Angeles, to an old barn, with raked benches all round and a cockpit in the middle, made over now as a boxing ring. The foetid, windowless space was already packed tight with fashionable spectators – picture people, gamblers, some of the Mob – coming on here after other parties in town. But it was a very private function in this isolated spot, where normally, most weekends, cockfights were held, run by Mexicans. Tonight, however, it featured a special bill, a series of prize fights – between women.

Hetty was pushed off her feet in the surge towards the ring as the bell went and the main bout started. Two tall, leggy, well-built girls – attractive, though one had a cast in her eye – in singlets and shorts, with mops of long

dark hair down to their shoulders, started to lay into each
other, vaguely skilled in the art, or at least mimicking it
cleverly, leading with left jabs, hooks to the body. Soon
they were in a sweaty clinch, breast to breast, pawing at
each other. The crowd roared.

'Break! Break!' The referee, a lantern-jawed man in a
dress suit, intervened. The girl with the cast tried to knee
her opponent in the groin as they separated. There was
pandemonium.

'Foul! Foul!' The roars reached a crescendo. The girl
with the cast smiled – before suddenly walloping the
other with the side of her glove. 'Foul! Dirty play!' the
spectators shouted. They loved it. Hetty did not. But she
was not going to show it. The girls set to again, gloves
flying, body punching now, getting below the belt, before
coming into a clinch again; this time the girl with the
cast hammered the other on her back, then got a glove
beneath her singlet, trying to rip it off. But the other girl
pre-empted her, pushing her glove inside her opponent's
waistband, ripping it open, so that the shorts slipped
down her thighs and she had to box on, holding them
up, with only one hand.

'Foul! – stop the fight!' Wally Reid roared. And they
did, while running repairs were made, the girl tying up
her shorts with a necktie that had been thrown into the
ring.

Soon, sweating heavily, breasts moulded against their
singlets now, the girls began to tire. The bell went. The
second round was more provocative still. The girls
groped at each other voluptuously in their clinches and
the fight became more of a perverse wrestling match, the
referee trying to part them unsuccessfully. They fell to
the floor, rolled over one another. And now the girl with
the cast took a clear ascendancy, straddling her opponent, while the barn exploded and the crowd bayed for
blood. Instead, the second girl, suddenly recovering,

37

reached up and, taking her opponent's singlet by the neck, ripped the fabric down, leaving the girl naked to the waist, sweat streaming down her breasts.

Hetty could take no more. Overcome with the heat she slumped to the floor in a faint. When she recovered she was outside in the front seat of the Pierce-Arrow.

'What on earth?' she murmured angrily to Craig beside her. 'What *possessed* you?'

'It's all an act, Laura!' Craig was not in the least put out by it all. 'Nobody really gets hurt and they're well paid. Nobody forces them.'

'It's disgusting!'

'Oh, come on, Laura – you're being old-fashioned.'

'It's just . . . degrading.'

Craig started the engine. 'OK, I'm sorry – we'll go home. I've got a special present for you still to come, a surprise.' He turned to her, a shadow in the darkness, touching her lips a moment. 'Sorry – about the boxing match. Just part of this crazy place. One day, we'll get right away from it . . .'

'But you like it, like all that . . . sort of torture, don't you?'

'Hell, no. It's just . . . all part of the scene here. You know that, honey. *You're* part of it, too. Look at those pictures we make together – revenge, lust, violence, high emotion. You'd think they'd work, think the crowds would flock in, if you were just drinking milk shakes in the pictures?'

'Yes, that's only acting, though.'

'That's life, Laura, only most people try and pretend it isn't. But we have to tell the truth in pictures. Least I do. And the Von. And that's what I want to do, with you, in our next pictures. Come on home and I'll tell you about it – your last surprise today!'

He kissed her softly and they drove off.

'What does a "fetish" mean, Craig?' she asked after a few moments.

He laughed. 'A totem pole, or an amulet in ancient Egypt, that's a fetish – something you think has magic in it, that you worship, an inanimate object.'

'And?'

'That's all. A superstition.'

'Are you like that?'

'Oh yes! Got to be. After all, the whole thing's just a charade here, isn't it? You, us, this.' He gestured round the darkened landscape of Hollywood. 'And the only reality in the end – just a flickering image on a screen – is the biggest illusion of all. So of course I'm superstitious. But I don't worship an inanimate object. I'm lucky that way. I have you.' He gripped her knee gently.

Later, Hetty, propped up in bed waiting for Craig, saw him come through the shadows carrying something, a severed head it seemed, and her heart missed a beat. But when he was in the light, and she saw it clearly, she was even more astonished. It was the portrait bust of an Egyptian woman – a slender, unbelievably elegant face, rising from a lotus-stem neck and pointed chin, in a long inverted triangle, up to a flared head-dress: firm swelling lips, perfectly modelled nose, vast, heavy-lidded eyes, sharply crescent eyebrows, the whole delicately washed in soft pinks and apricot, kohl blacks, the head-dress picked out in bands of gold and blue, centred with some great jewel, crossed with a gold band in the shape of a snake's head.

But the woman's expression was the extraordinary thing. Far more than the sum of its parts, it was animate while yet perfectly still. There was life there, a deep, full, sensuous life – but one could not quite touch it. There was profligacy, yet a severe control, great distance, yet intense femininity. She was both goddess and woman. She gazed at Hetty then, as Craig held the bust up to her, with a look of cold, calm, languorous beauty – a perfect balance between the sacred and the profane, a regard that offered everything, yet promised nothing. Hetty felt the eyes drilling into her, through her, something she could not escape – those beautiful eyes, lit with irony, power, wisdom, love – everything she desired in herself.

'It's Queen Nefertiti,' he said quietly, as if the woman was alive with them in the room. 'And it's you,' he added in an even lower voice. He set the bust down, and sat next to her on the bed.

'But who? — '

'Our picture, Laura!' And now Craig was filled with tense enthusiasm. 'The one I've always wanted to do. And we can – soon; Nefertiti, wife of the heretic Pharaoh Akhenaten, eighteenth dynasty, in Egypt — '

'A costume picture — '

'An *epic*, Laura! Bigger than any yet made, bigger than *Intolerance* or anything de Mille ever attempted. Bigger – and better. It's a sensational story, been working on it secretly for years – it's everything that ever mattered to me, everything that ever mattered in ancient Egypt, too. You'll see!' His eyes were bright, almost manic, as he came closer to her.

'It's not just chariot races and battles up and down the Nile out on some tank on the back lot – like de Mille and the others. This is about a whole new *faith*, the first time in history, fifteen hundred years before Christ, that men came to worship *one* god. That's the great thing. Nefertiti married the boy Pharaoh Amenophis the fourth – a dreamer, artist, pacifist – who changed the whole religion of ancient Egypt. Instead of worshipping all the thousands of animal gods they had out there then, he scrapped all that, sacked the priests at Thebes, and worshipped the sun, as the one true god; became the Sun King, Akhenaten, and built an incredible city for the new faith, way up the Nile at Amarna – the City of the Sun, a city of love, not fear, a dream place, with flowers, lakes, pleasure gardens, fountains, great boulevards, vast temples, royal palaces, literally a paradise on earth, till the whole place was razed to the ground twenty years later by Akhenaten's rivals of the old faith back in Thebes. But, for those twenty years, Laura – well, it was the most incredible civilization ever seen, before or since. And Nefertiti, the most beautiful woman. Look at the inscription on the bottom of the bust – one of the poems Akhenaten wrote about her.' Craig read it out:

'"The heiress, great in favour, lady of grace, sweet of love, Mistress of the South and of the North, fair of face, gay with two plumes, beloved of the living Aten, the Chief Wife of the King, whom he loves, Lady of the Two Lands, great of love, Nefertiti, living for ever and ever." And that's her.' Craig glanced over at the bust. 'Had it made up by Leo Kuter, my art director, copy of the real thing in the Berlin Museum.'

Hetty was enchanted. 'It's incredible . . .'

'Yes. And only you can play her. Born for it.'

'Can I?'

'No one else. I have a scenario. But it's all secret – not talked to anyone yet, so you mustn't either. In a few months, I'll move on it.'

'Cost a fortune.'

'Yes.' Craig relished the thought. 'Akhenaten's Royal Palace alone was half a mile long – have to build it. The most beautiful city ever made. And we'll make it even better than the real thing! Fox has all the money. We'll do it in Egypt, the interiors in Rome or this new studio they have in Nice, get right away from this crummy place.'

'They'd never let you—'

'Let *us*, Laura. They'll let us do it. Because they'll see

it, just as clearly as I do: you're Nefertiti, image and spirit. What do you think?'

Hetty looked at the bust again, thrilled by the challenge, the honour, and yet by the rightness of it all. 'Oh, yes, Craig, yes! . . .'

Now at last, she thought, she knew why she had married Craig. Everything fell into place – it had all been ordained. Craig had been secretly working all this time towards this point where her destiny could be fulfilled, where she would become that Queen, not as an actress but as of right. She had felt it ever since childhood – the sense of being a changeling, with royal blood perhaps, a princess. And here at last was confirmation of what Snipe, the maimed fortune teller at Summer Hill, had said. She was about to enter her true estate – as Nefertiti, Queen of the Two Lands.

2

After the war in Europe – and the start of the real troubles in Ireland – the great house at Summer Hill began to languish. Much of the pleasure garden and the terraced lawn, once so meticulously kept, planted, pruned and cut, went to seed. The upper lawns and croquet court, unused, began to seep with moss – and, with the demise of the last of the ferocious Summer Hill terriers, became instead a playground contested between rabbits and moles. The demesne, for lack of milch cows, became ragworty and the high orchards flooded in autumn with unpicked fruit. Moist growths of elder and ivy, the voracious tentacles of Irish nature, began to feed on the ruined north wing, which remained a burnt-out shell. The estate workers, masons and carpenters who, in earlier times, would have at once started to clear the rubble and rebuild the wing, had in many cases never returned from the trenches or had emigrated, leaving their land for ever.

Most of the domestic staff had been paid off as well, for there was no longer the money, either to effect repairs or to maintain such a vast household. Lady Cordiner's considerable fortune had gone almost in its entirety to a Jewish charity in London, while Frances – as an abstentionist Sinn Fein MP in the recently elected, but illegal, Irish Parliament – continuously embroiled now in seditious Republican speech-making and other covert activities about the country was rarely at home, staying with friends and sympathizers, often moving from house to house overnight, on the run from the British forces.

The farm lapsed and the estate rents, on Frances's abrupt instructions, were discontinued. Though Mortimer, one of the last of the old Redmondite MPs, but without any real constituency now in Ireland, came down from Dublin now and then and did what he could for the place, keeping an eye on the dwindling accounts with Mrs Martin, the housekeeper, and old O'Donovan, the farm steward, and selling off, with Frances's agreement, a few of the better antiques – one of the Georgian silver epergnes and a Chippendale table – to pay the few remaining servants and estate workers.

Sooner do this, he had told Frances, than allow the British Army another rout. For in the spring of 1919, searching for Frances, they had ransacked Summer Hill, looting pictures and other valuables. So that afterwards Mortimer had much of the better furniture and effects removed, lodging them with the bank or hiding them in stable lofts and outhouses. This he had done entirely on his own initiative, for in June of that year the police, finally catching up with Frances after a most inflammatory speech in Co. Cork, had arrested her. She was tried in camera, and sentenced to six months' imprisonment in Cork jail.

Apart from Aunt Emily, Mrs Martin, Mrs Molloy the cook, a few maids and Pat Kennedy, the family butler, now returned from hospital after his accident in the fire, the huge house lay empty. Elly, Hetty's nurse in the old days, had long since left the house – marrying out of it, to Jack Welsh, a railway man who lived beyond Cloone. Dust settled on the great reception rooms and then fell on the sheets that had been put out to cover what was left of the furniture. The Cordiner ancestral portraits had been removed from the long dining room. Mice and even some bold rats returned, allowed full play across the hall, up the staircase and along the landings. On the top floor, in Henry's old work rooms, the stuffed crocodile continued its infinitesimal decay.

Only Aunt Emily remained at Summer Hill, a spry, indomitable figure, still at her pen and ink drawings and watercolours, her illustrated Summer Hill journal, retiring more or less permanently upstairs and making a redoubt of her large bedroom overlooking the uncut hornbeam maze, where young Biddy Molloy, Mrs Molloy's granddaughter, ministered to her with endless cups of strong tea and shortcake biscuits. Mortimer, in these chaotic, violent times, when every day brought some new outrage – an RIC barracks blown up or a village sacked and looted by the Black and Tans – had offered Aunt Emily the sanctuary of his house at Islandbridge, in Dublin. But she had adamantly refused to budge.

'*I'm* the family now,' she had told him firmly. 'Excuse yourself, Mortimer. I'll not be moved by a few blackguardly Sinn Feiners *or* the British Army.'

Aunt Emily had refused to move to Islandbridge. But Robert had readily agreed. Since Hetty had left Summer Hill eighteen months before, he had in any case spent more of his time in Dublin – at the pretty, white stuccoed house by the weir, a long tram ride from Trinity College. With Mortimer's kindness, and Dermot's too, when he was back on his leave from England, the house had become a second home to him. Now, with Frances's most recent incarceration, and having just taken his modern history degree at Trinity, Mortimer had invited him to stay there more permanently, while he decided where his future lay. So, in June 1920, down from Dublin with Mortimer to pick up some of his things at Summer Hill, Robert walked through the empty, dust-sheeted rooms now in the bright midsummer light – a tall, somewhat awkward figure, in spectacles, good looking in an unemphatic academic manner, running long fingers through shanks of unruly dark hair.

His life in the great house seemed to be coming to an end, another starting elsewhere. But where, he wondered? For so long he had seen Summer Hill as his permanent home. But some time before he had realized that, without Hetty, and alone with her mother, he could not be happy there. And, yes, the thought had also been there – one day, perhaps, he and Hetty might have married and lived at Summer Hill together. That was obviously not to be.

In his bedroom cupboard, picking through some old school books and papers, he came across the precious cedar-wood pencil box, brought with him from Domenica, the box that Hetty had so coveted then, her mother denying her a similar one, because of her stammer. And he hated Frances as he heard Hetty's anguished stammer again in the silent room – the product of Hetty's rages or just as often of her heart's terror, the hurts she had suffered from her cold and punitive mother, the loss of her father. He had lost both his own parents, but he had never had any doubts as to who they were, or of their love for him.

Hetty: childhood friend, enemy, sister, confidante,

partner over chestnut embers by the nursery fire – and then, later, the longing to be even closer to her, when Léonie had usurped his place. Orphaned, he had surely lacked the loving certainties more than she. Yet it was Hetty who had broken . . . taken to all her self-destructive escapades, with Léonie and then with this man in America, whom she had since married. An adult now, Robert thought he saw why, unable to cope with all those early horrors and indignities in her life, she had done this. He understood what caused her folly, objectively. And yet he had been outraged, made quite desolate, at her final betrayal of him, and thought of her now with more hate than love.

But that was his quandary. He loved and hated her, swinging wildly between the two extremes beneath the outwardly calm and studious surface of his life; he hated her for her cruel arrogance, her callous insensitivity, but loved her, too, for her true goodness of heart.

And he blamed himself then for having lost her. He wished he could have allayed those fears of hers, fought more successfully on her behalf against the wiles of her mother, discovered who, if such a person existed, her real father was. Had he succeeded in any of these causes, he might have possessed her now. But he had to remind himself, once again, how he lacked that kind of rash, intuitive bravery, which was at the heart of Hetty's personality – how he lived with too much forethought, delay, prevarication, seeing too many sides to each question; how he lived, in short, through the ever-twisting ramifications of ideas and books and not in the full flow of life.

He went into Hetty's old bedroom before leaving, looking up at the frieze of primroses round the wall. The room, in the hot sunlight, smelt dead, musty. But then suddenly – and inexplicably, for the windows were firmly shut – the door into the little dressing room beyond swung open and there was a faint odour of limes, a smell he knew so well from his early childhood. And equally suddenly, so that he turned sharply, Hetty was in the room with him, a child, laughing, teasing, stammering – 'You n-n-ninny, Robert! You absolute d-d-dolt!'

He moved into the dressing room and looked vaguely for the source of the bitter-sweet smell. And there, in a soap dish next to the washbasin, he found a tiny lime fruit, desiccated now. He scratched its surface. There was not the faintest odour.

'But if I put it in water,' he said to himself slowly, remembering his science, 'it'll revive . . .' Then he returned it to the table. But finally he took it up again and pocketed it.

Mortimer spoke on the train to Dublin that afternoon. 'So, "Change and decay in all around I see",' he said lugubriously, but with a keen smile. 'But not for you, Robert.' His tone changed, became brisk and encouraging. 'All a wonderful beginning now. You're bound to get a good degree. When will you know?'

'A fortnight or so, I think.'

'And journalism – you really want that?' Robert nodded. 'Certainly, I liked that last article of yours in the Historical Society's magazine, about the Dreyfus trials. Not many of us have faced the implications of all that – the fierce anti-semitism of the French, always pushed under the carpet over there, so that one day the whole thing will blow up in some much worse form.' Mortimer licked his lips. 'Shall we take a little refreshment? Think they still do it on this train. A glass of ale? – go well with this heat.' He mopped his brow. The dining car attendant brought them two bottles of Smithwick's, and Mortimer continued. 'Well, journalism – and France. Two of your interests. No reason why they shouldn't go together. Go over there this summer, why not? See how the land lies.'

'Yes, I'd thought to. But the money, well . . .'

'Nonsense! You have that annuity from your parents' estate in Domenica – and I'll advance you £100 here and now to cover any immediate expenses.'

'That's terribly kind. But journalism – in France? I thought I'd be lucky to get a job as sub-editor or something with the *Irish Times*.'

'Yes, indeed, and you might. I have several good friends there. But why not be a little bit more daring? Start where you *really* want to start – you have good French, know the history there backwards.' Mortimer leant forward now. 'And get out of Ireland for a bit, in any case – all the horrors here. I'm afraid it'll get worse before it gets better.' He looked out at the lush summer countryside. 'The Sinn Feiners won't stop now: the elected government here after all, as they see themselves – as they are indeed. And with these new British troops, these thugs of Black and Tans in the country, there'll be much worse to come. So it's obvious, isn't it? You've got just as good contacts in Paris: your friend, and mine, Ben Straus. And Léonie. Had you forgotten all that?'

'No.' But Robert seemed quite absent. He did not want to admit how he still mistrusted Léonie, did not like her even. Then he gathered himself. 'No, it's just . . .' He hesitated again, rather crestfallen.

'Forgive me. But, well, you've hinted at it before – you and Hetty. I'm sorry, sorry about that. But there's really nothing any of us can do about it. She'll have to find her own level, mistakes, virtues, whatever it is. We all have to. You and I, with our books and training, we take so much support from theory and precedent, you see. But she's never had any of that, only practice – and perhaps that's a better way to learn, one has to give her that. Though it'll hurt more, no doubt.'

'Yes, yes . . .' Robert looked pensively out of the window. Then he turned suddenly, intent, animated. 'You understand her so well. I don't know that I do sometimes: all that business about her father, which made her so unhappy, believing he wasn't her real father. That's the root of her problem, of course.'

'Well, maybe.' Mortimer, with the introduction of this sensitive theme, had already started to temporize.

'But what *was* the truth? She's always been so certain that Mr Fraser wasn't her real father. You'd surely know, if anyone did.'

'No.' Mortimer wiped some froth from his whiskers. 'No, I've never had any reason to suppose . . . otherwise.'

'You see, if she's right – and one could only discover the truth of the matter – well, it might put her on an even keel again, stop all this nonsense in America. I'm *sure* it would.' Robert leant forward earnestly.

'Oh, I don't know about that. She'd retain the same character, temperament, whoever her father happened to be.'

'So you admit the possibility then, at least, that she might be right?'

Mortimer, knowing indeed how correct Robert was in his assumptions, was loath to continue the lie. But he had to. 'It's my view – and I have to say it – that it's her poor mother who's caused most of the trouble in Hetty's life, not her father.'

'Yes, of course. But *could* she have had a different father?'

'It's possible, though I doubt it. Besides, you'd know more about that than me. You knew Mr Fraser after all. I never set eyes on him.'

'Yes, he was a brute. So – so quite unlike Hetty, in looks, everything.'

'I can't say.' Mortimer leant back. 'All theory. Not practice. And I think you, we, have to think in that latter term now. Paris? France?' He raised his glass of Smithwick's.

Robert nodded and they drank to it.

★

Three weeks later, in a new rust corduroy suit, with a good degree, his baggage and French Baedeker, Robert was welcomed under the full-leafed chestnut tree at the door of the Strauses' small eighteenth-century house in the rue Desbordes-Valmore, an old village house once, on the edge of the Bois de Boulogne, now crushed between *belle époque* apartment buildings, off the main boulevard in Passy.

'So! Bienvenu! Willkommen! Step right in!'

Ben Straus, though a little more drawn and elderly, still maintained his brisk and genial air: bushy eyebrows, dark hair silvering at the temples, thin moustache, the busy, quick-thinking, generous American – still the man of the world, still intent, in the most amiable and relaxed fashion, on setting everything to rights.

Léonie, in the shadows behind, stepped forward, wearing a billowy, flower-embroidered skirt and white voile blouse. 'Robert! It's so *good* to see you – really!' She kissed him on both cheeks.

Robert saw her clearly now – the dark, fluffy-haired young woman, shorter than he, the big grey-green eyes, direct and searching in their deep, blue-tinged sockets, the aquiline nose: all the repressed audacity and knowing ardour he remembered coming to the surface then in her quick warm embrace – yet quite grown up now in the eighteen months since he had seen her; a richer, darker, calmer Jewish beauty, the face matured, though touched now with vague lines of hurt, a certain indelible sadness.

'You're honoured, Robert,' Ben told him. 'She skipped singing lessons this evening to meet you.'

'But of course he's honoured, Papa! – my best old friend!'

And Robert, seeing the implications of these last words, felt honoured indeed, thinking a little better of Léonie despite her past relationship with Hetty.

They moved into the narrow hallway, where the evening summer light was reflected and distorted in several mirrors. Robert breathed in a perfumed coolness, the smell of roses – and something else seeping up from the back regions: a whiff of garlic, French mustard? The smell of abroad. He turned back an instant. Léonie was standing dead still, outlined like a statue against the light from the open door, that slightly chunky figure that he remembered thinned out now, the waist narrowing more dramatically, hip bones more prominent, the flat behind – above all that dramatic toss of dark, fine-spun hair, set off by the white voile blouse. She was warm and generous – fruit-filled, somehow. She stood there, looking at him, unblinking, hands clasped together. Then her firm jaw and jutting chin relaxed and she smiled softly – a hesitant smile, imprecise, like the strangely refracted light from the hall mirrors.

'Come on up and I'll show you your room before supper – old Hortense has cooked up something special for us all: lapin à la moutarde, then some Normandy pancakes!'

Ben took him up a winding staircase, past a first floor, then on to a small top bedroom, with a narrow balcony directly overlooking the chestnut tree in the tiny front garden.

'Room's a little small,' Ben said. 'All a little small, if you live in Paris – and no real view. But at least it's a house, with no concierge! – and they're the only grim thing about the city.'

'No – no, it's perfect. Perfect . . .'

Ben joined him at the window. 'Yes, it is, I suppose. One forgets, living here. Then someone like you, just coming to it fresh – well, one sees it through your eyes for a moment, gets that first-time view of Paris all over again, that you thought you'd lost. And then you know – there's never really any end to it.'

Before supper Ben opened a bottle of champagne and they toasted each other in the small first floor salon. He raised his glass to Robert. 'Start of a great career! I had your letter and your College articles – I think maybe I have a possibility for you: Jake Schwartz, business manager of the *New York Tribune* here, good friend of mine, spoken to him and he'll see you, introduce you to the Paris editor. There could be something, sub-editing maybe, or some freelance reporting.'

Robert was impressed by the speed of his host's operations. 'Thank you—'

'Think nothing of it. That article you did on the Dreyfus case – I liked it. And it quite took Jake's fancy as well. You surely seem to know your stuff. And the style was clear – especially after a diet of Gertrude Stein. What do you think, Léa?'

'Why, yes, he can certainly write! He can come and do a review at the Academy.'

'What?'

'*Madame Butterfly*,' Ben put in. 'You're looking at her! Yes, her first big lead at the opera school. Great, isn't it? Both of you starting out.'

Madame Butterfly, Robert thought. He remembered Hetty and Léonie singing passionate duets from it, or guying the arias, in the old days at Summer Hill. Did Hetty still haunt Léonie, he wondered? – as she haunted him. It was a theme he did not care to raise. Yet a chord had been struck already in the salon.

Robert met Mr Schwartz and the Paris editor of the *Tribune* at their business office in the rue de l'Opéra. There was no proper position, but there might be later in the year. Meanwhile they offered him a job as glorified office boy at fifty francs a week, with a promise that they would look at anything he wrote and pay him extra if they used it. He settled into the routine well. At two o'clock he went to the office, often staying until midnight, busying himself in a hundred ways, learning the trade. The mornings he had free to roam the city, looking for possible stories. Often he went out with Léonie, whose singing classes took place at an academy on the left bank, or sometimes, for Léonie was already part of the chorus there, at the Opéra itself, just along from the *Tribune* office.

It was some time before they talked of Hetty. Neither had wanted to broach the subject. Their lives in the city were filled with so much else that summer. But Hetty remained a ghost at their banquet. She could not be denied indefinitely.

One day, in early autumn, walking down the boulevard des Italiens, they saw the huge garish poster of her above the Pathé Cinema: 'Laura Bowen – Dans – BAIE DE TONNERRE – Réalisé par Craig St John Williamson'.

They stood gazing up at the display, shocked momentarily, unable to look at each other. Léonie finally spoke. 'It's extraordinary, seeing someone you knew so well, so completely changed; a different name, not real. Look at the size of her!' They stared up at the vast poster high above them, Hetty in a pirate outfit, tricorn hat, red bandana handkerchief, flourishing a cutlass.

'Yes, extraordinary. Horrible . . .'

Léonie was shaking slightly. They went to a nearby café, ordered coffee on the terrace. Robert was equally shaken, all his hatred and jealousy returning. 'I suppose, one never thought – well, that she'd be so successful.'

'Or never hoped, do you mean?' Léonie said lightly. 'Well, I think I did.' Half-rueful, half-happy, she was unable quite to hide the embers of pride she felt in Hetty's achievements. 'She always wanted that sort of adoring crowd thing, you know. Such energy for it – bound to succeed, quite apart from her looks.'

'She was just ruthless, that's all.' Robert was curt.

'Oh, Robert, it's no use being bitter.'

'It sometimes helps.' He turned away.

'I'm sorry.'

'She behaved atrociously.'

'Yes, she did. But you see—'

'Oh, I may see why – but that doesn't excuse her. I lost my parents, home, everything,' he went on quite calmly. 'But that doesn't mean I have to behave like a cruel idiot.'

'No, you've been wonderful—'

'Look at her!' Robert gazed down the boulevard to where the vast poster was still visible. 'A big "star", don't they call them?' His sarcasm was biting. 'You must miss her,' he went on, trying to console, but distant, remembering Léonie again as his rival and wondering if she still loved Hetty.

'I do miss her. But really – isn't it the same for you?'

'Oh no,' Robert lied. 'All that was just, well . . . just a juvenile thing on my part.'

Léonie reached across to him, breaking the formality of their exchange with a quick warmth. 'Oh, Robert – it couldn't have been! We can't pretend that, it's not true. It *was* a pretty huge thing – for both of us.'

Robert turned away, embarrassed. 'Well . . .' He shrugged. 'Anyway, we'll hardly see her again, except in one of her stupid "pictures" – and I certainly don't want to see them. Do you?'

'No, no. But that's the awful thing though, isn't it?' She glanced down the street again at the poster. 'She's here all the time – seen her before like that about town. And now she'll be posted up all over the place again. Sort of hovering over us, not being able to forget her.'

'But we must. Or we'd better. After all, look what she

did – just walking out on you, on everyone, in a moment
. . . pretty awful thing to do.'

Léonie frowned. 'Yes,' she said at last. 'But there's
always some *reason* for that sort of behaviour. One has to
look for that.'

'"Tout comprendre, c'est tout pardonner"? I don't
agree with that in this case.' Robert was more forceful
now, trying to suppress any possible excuse for Hetty's
behaviour. 'You can't just blame her mother, or the loss
of her "father" for everything she did. It was just . . .
wilful, wanting to hurt, on her part.'

'Yes, of course she wanted to hurt both of us. And she
did – always succeeds in what she sets out on.'

'So why . . . why do you have any more time for her?'

'Because I can't just drop the past and pretend it never
happened. Isn't she still part of you? She's a part of me,
always will be. The things we did, shared, they can't be
"betrayed". They happened. They're still there.'

Robert was jealous again. Léonie, indeed, had shared
things with Hetty, had possessed her no doubt, in ways
he never had. He hid his jealousy but not the sarcasm in
his next words. 'Of course, you knew her so much better
than I.'

'No,' Léonie said dully. 'A different way, not better.'

'Because you loved her in a different way, of course.
I've often wondered . . .'

'Yes, I suppose you did wonder. Well, women can love
each other – just as much as men,' she told him quite
directly.

'Yes.' Robert was non-committal.

'It shocks you?'

'Oh no,' he lied again.

'It must at least have annoyed you. Without me, after
all, she might well have taken to you.'

'Perhaps.'

'You see, that's exactly what made me so unhappy at

55

Summer Hill – for you.' Léonie was suddenly ardent again. Then she was resigned. 'But now I don't think I stopped anything for you. Hetty wanted things in us which neither of us could give her.'

'What?'

'Oh, the slave thing, for one – and that's not us.'

'Or the American she's married. He's no slave, I bet.'

'Ah, but he's the other side of the coin she wants: the king thing, all that power, when *she* can play the slave!'

Robert sighed. 'It's all really so very tiresome and childish in the end, isn't it?'

'Yes. But sometimes we love people for that, don't we? – for their faults, not their virtues. That's sometimes more difficult.'

'You still love her then, don't you? – for all her faults.'

'Sometimes, yes.' She turned then, gazing at him intently. 'Sometimes . . . she sweeps over me again, taking me back, like the sea, when I'd thought I was free of her.'

Léonie sat there quite still, then looked away, unable to face him. And Robert saw how deep her hurt was.

'Oh, perhaps I wouldn't miss the person she's become,' Léonie went on, gathering herself. 'But the person she was – and the person she *could* have been, even more: that's the heartbreak. That's terrible – to think what's lost there.'

'For her?'

'For both of us. I'm not so saintly that I didn't hope to share in what was best in her. I wanted to encourage all that, for myself as well as her. Didn't you?'

'I . . . suppose so,' he said indifferently, unwilling to admit the truth of this.

'Well, then – we can both see how much we've lost, can't we? There was something wonderful there. Such beauty – in so hurt a spirit.'

Robert pondered these comments. They were very

much ones he would have made himself about Hetty – if he possessed more courage and if he did not still feel so hurt by her. It was perfectly true – all that Léa had said: both of them had been deeply scarred by her betrayal. But betrayal it had been: gratuitous, clear-sighted, precisely intended. There was surely no getting away from that. And so he said, again trying to despoil Hetty in Léa's eyes, 'But the glass was flawed. You said so yourself earlier: neither of us could have really helped her in the end, given her what she wanted. That spirit was broken from almost the beginning, the lack of a real father, all those horrors on the island long ago, her mother's cruelties to her as a child at Summer Hill. I know – I was there,' he added, secretly pleased to remind Léonie of his prior intimacy with Hetty.

'Of course, I see why you feel all that. But I think you're wrong – about her spirit. The flaws were part of its beauty. The glass just needed holding together, with love. That's all I wanted to do.'

Léonie looked at Robert again, with a blazing belief in her eyes. And Robert again had to admit the truth of her last words – for this had secretly been his own view – he who had thought, too, that with his love he could have protected that same essential fragility, while sharing in all Hetty's more purposeful, confident ardours.

'The fact is, dear Robert,' she said sadly, 'she's put both of us in the dumps, deep down, because, well – you too, I think – we both more than loved her. We were kind of married to her already – that close, you know? – so that it's not just she who's gone, but a complete civilization, sort of, all the comforts there – a lost language, signs, smiles, everything between people that's beyond words. Don't you think?'

'Well, that's all very fine – but are we to spend the rest of our lives playing archaeologists over her?'

'I don't know, I really don't. I don't *want* to – but how

can one hold back the tide? Because she's not dead, you know,' she went on desperately. 'It's not an altogether vanished civilization. She's over there, large as life, behind that poster!'

Robert saw the truth of this, too, and was at a loss to know what to do or feel about it as regards Léonie. On the one hand – liking and feeling for her as he did now – he wanted to support her, get her out of those dumps. On the other, he saw how Hetty remained a barrier between them, saw how great Léonie's attachment still was to her. He felt jealous and excluded by this and wanted therefore to demean Hetty in Léonie's eyes, expunge every memory of her – as a means of furthering what he took to be their joint cause, which was to forget this cruel woman. So he said, 'But, Léa, if either of us is to have any real life – we'll *have* to accept the fact that she behaved abominably, doesn't care a damn about either of us. We'll have to hold that tide back – together.'

Her reply was only half-confident: 'Perhaps . . .'

Robert's impatience, his frustrated jealousies, rose to the surface. 'But we'll have to, Léa,' he said almost angrily. '*Have* to forget her. And not let her sweep over us any more.'

'Yes,' she said then, almost too forthrightly.

'Well, come on then, let's forget about her – let's go and have a good lunch. The paper's going to use that report I did on Les Halles, so I'll have enough – to go to the Grand Vefour! Remember? – I promised we would, when they first took something of mine.'

Léonie smiled. 'Yes, so you did – always keep your word, don't you?'

She smiled again. But Robert was annoyed now. 'You don't have to – you just think I'm Old Reliable, don't you? That's my problem. Well, I can be unreliable too, if you want—'

She reached across to him. 'Oh, no, Robert – I mean

– I like you, *because* of that. I do! – really do.' She touched his hand, and they got up and walked away from the monstrous hovering vision of their friend.

Was it in the restaurant that Robert first began to fall in love with her? – or afterwards? – as they strolled beneath the arcades of the Palais Royal in the autumn sunlight, round the gardens, and Robert, stopping outside one of the little antique shops, seeing a Japanese fan in the window, went in and bought it for her.

'There,' he told her. 'For Madame Butterfly.'

Enchanted, she opened it at once, fluttering it against her face, not coquettishly, just gently.

Something moved in his heart for her at that moment. But he was wary, taking it no further.

While Robert had to count his francs carefully that autumn, Hetty had begun to spend money with total abandon. *Thunder Bay* had been a complete sell-out. Hetty was now a big star, already beyond that field of gravity which restrained ordinary mortals. Over half-way through her three-year contract with Fox her salary was a thousand dollars a week; Craig's was twice that. Inheriting her grandmother's hungry social ambitions, but promoting these in an entirely eccentric manner, Hetty luxuriated in this new wealth and the power it gave her to express her material whims and her passion, similar to her mother's, to organise and dominate a household.

So she filled the phoney Bavarian *schloss* with exotic European imports – bulbs and shrubs which bloomed in pots with constant care and watering, smoked salmon from Scotland, Bradenham hams, fine wines smuggled in from France – and threw either impeccably formal dinner parties or Bohemian routs, employing a bevy of Chinese cooks, Irish maids, Mexican gardeners; so that the Lodge, at least for the most talented and amusing among the Hollywood community, became a bran tub of bizarre social surprises.

She and Craig, in their free time, rarely ventured down the valley. But, when they did, to attend some première at Graumann's Egyptian Theatre or a party at the Ship Café, people opened a way for them, instinctively, as if touched by fire. If Fairbanks and Pickford, at their dowdy mock-Tudor mansion on the plains, were the formally crowned heads of Hollywood, Hetty and Craig, their raffish but luminous partnership surrounded by an aura of invincible success, were the envied pretenders to the throne. They were envied, feared, even loved but not universally liked – deeply mistrusted, indeed, by some of the most powerful in Hollywood, producers and studio bosses, who resented their European airs and graces, their unconventional life, their culture, talent, their difficult professional demands. But, as long as their success continued, these criticisms were mute. Hetty and Craig were immune from them – as long as their pictures grossed such fortunes. Which they did.

Hetty's only problem was that she, like Craig, longed to be out of the place, this cultural desert, where, with all the money in the world, there was nothing to spend it on. Sometimes, in short breaks between pictures, they drove down to Mexico and once or twice took the long five-day train ride east to New York. But these trips only sharpened Hetty's appetite to leave Hollywood altogether. Unlike Craig, though she worked just as hard, she never came to see pictures as the be all and end all of her life. They were a holding operation of some sort – and the pictures themselves, however successful, were rarely inspiring: costume romances giving way to contemporary melodramas and society extravaganzas. All the time she longed to embark on her great role in the great epic, *Nefertiti*. So did Craig.

'But we can't, not yet,' he had told her. 'We need the

leverage of a new contract for you with Fox. *Then* we can move. Meanwhile, just make as many box office hits as we can.'

Hetty bridled at the delay – became petulant, difficult, demanding, both at home and in the studio. Her attitude towards Craig underwent a change. Unable to dominate him, she started – just as she had with Léonie – to nurture antagonisms, suspicions, hurts. She came to feel that perhaps in some way he was holding out on her over *Nefertiti*, hiding something, postponing the matter unnecessarily, thinking of someone else for the role. More often now he was out in the evening at the studios, in the cutting rooms, or with his friend, the art director Leo Kuter, the only other person privy to the Nefertiti picture, who was already working on preparatory set designs for it. Hetty, on these occasions, left to her own devices in the Lodge, took increasingly to the company of little Eddy Nolan, whom Craig had made a sort of major-domo in the household, and who now became a confidant of Hetty's.

'What's he doing – all these evenings out?' she said to him one night, after the Chinese cooks had gone to bed, and they sat in the kitchen drinking mugs of strong tea and eating slices of fruit cake, just as if they were back in Ireland.

'Working,' Eddy said, at his most direct and laconic. 'The curse of the age . . .'

'I wish I believed that.'

'Drive down and see for yourself then.'

'Oh, I'm not going to spy.'

'Set your mind at ease. Why not?'

'I think he's seeing someone else.'

'Ask him then – put it to him straight.'

'Perhaps. Trouble is, he could just lie, couldn't he?'

'Ah, well, there you have me. Always the problem, isn't it?'

Hetty remained frustrated. That indeed was the problem. Craig, as she knew, had lied about his Irish background. And she had never confronted him over this, anxious to maintain her own deceits inviolate – anxious and secretly frightened of him as well, this man upon whom all her deceits and fantasies rested.

Craig, in the event, was indeed absorbed by something else just then – but not by another woman. While he was researching the Nefertiti material, Leo Kuter had brought him an old copy of the *Illustrated London News*, showing photographs of the German archaeological dig at Amarna in upper Egypt in 1909 and an artist's re-creation of the whole original city. Flipping through the magazine, he was suddenly confronted by a large portrait of Edward VII. He glanced at it idly, before being struck by something in the King's expression. The eyes? The shape of the forehead? The whole cast of the upper face said something to him. What was it? Yes, the shape of the eyes, the hooded lids, the nose and eyebrows, the whole conjunction here, this was Hetty's expression too, he thought – that arrogant, slightly drowsy look she sometimes had. And then he remembered the little brooch-watch he had found in the rubble of the north wing two years before at Summer Hill, with the inscription on the back: 'Frances – from Alix and Edward – Sandringham, Xmas 1898.'

It was not difficult to put two and two together. But did they really add up? Was it possible that Hetty was the old King's daughter, the result of a liaison between him and her mother? And, if it was, did Hetty know of this? Almost certainly not. Should he tell her? Hetty, difficult enough, would probably fly off the handle altogether. So his suspicions would have to be kept under wraps. But it was quite a thought – he, son of a dour, penny-pinching Cork grocer, now quite possibly son-in-law to the old King. He smiled. They might, indeed, be true royalty, he reflected, in their great palace on the hill. One day, perhaps, the family connection might prove a vital counter in their affairs. If it was true . . .

But what was their more likely future? he wondered then. He had spoken to Leo before on this topic, and now he reintroduced it.

Leo had noticed him gazing at the portrait of Edward VII. 'Thinking of doing a picture on him – with Laura as one of his mistresses?'

Craig was momentarily shocked at this incestuous suggestion. 'No. No . . .'

'The Von would get a good story out of it: all that stiff court life, the regalia, then the lusty girls and champagne behind the curtains. They say the old King had dozens of them.'

'Yes . . . No, I was thinking of Laura.'

'Is there some problem?'

'She's getting more and more difficult. And, you know something? – she doesn't really care a damn at heart, whether she works in pictures or not. Doesn't really touch her – all that star thing.'

'What does touch her then?'

'Power, I think.'

'More than you?'

'Oh yes – I'm only a means to an end.'

'That big house of hers back in Ireland?'

'No. She used to want that. But she's broken all the connections there.'

'Listen, she probably just wants *Nefertiti* . . . and to get the hell out of here – like we both do.'

'Yes. Sure. But after that? She wants something else. And it's eating away at her. Oh, it gives her that extraordinary edge on camera – whatever's getting at her, that mix of . . . wistfulness and frenzy.'

'You know something?' Leo looked at him searchingly. 'Often noticed it in her, how she doesn't take compliments, cuts you dead if you try to treat her as a woman. She's got a man's mind in a woman's body. That's her problem. She's going against her real nature all the time – *that's* what's eating her.'

And Craig, knowing full well the truth of this – how Hetty of course, had been the 'man' in her earlier *affaire* with Léonie – had to agree with Leo. But he did so silently, for here was another secret of Hetty's he thought best kept hid.

What Craig refused to see, and Hetty even more so, was the most obvious secret of all in the whole business: how her behaviour, her tantrums, her frenzied sexual and social life, that 'edge' which came across so dazzlingly on camera – all these were the product of her guilt, her betrayal of Léonie, Robert, her family, of Summer Hill.

Craig might well have seen this. But he chose not to, for it was just this fascinating 'edge', inspired by guilt – that mysterious tension, the calm and sudden wild imbalance in her performances – that kept them both so successfully in business. And so he fed all these flaws in her, tactfully, like a concerned zoo keeper, encouraged her illness and her guilt, for without her suffering in this way he felt intuitively that she might leave him and give up the whole picture business altogether. If Hetty held Robert and Léonie in some strange thrall, Craig had just the same power over her; he was the vital link in the chain that kept Hetty apart from her real friends, her real life – the one who, as final puppet master, maintained the hurt and pain for the other three.

3

In Ireland, the Anglo-Irish war deteriorated into horror and atrocity. The Irish Parliament, Dail Eireann, continued to meet clandestinely. But the real management of affairs in this resistance passed increasingly to the Irish Republican Army, and particularly into the hands of its Director of Intelligence, Michael Collins. A large and genial man, behind this façade of Cork bonhomie he was quite ruthless, a born leader and guerrilla commander. Having worked as a clerk in the London post office he had, too, a gift for organization, besides a genius for disguise, concealment, the creation of every sort of surprise. His IRA flying columns, deployed throughout the country, launched almost daily attacks against isolated RIC barracks, coastguard stations and British Army patrols. In Dublin, British detectives, spies and agents provocateurs were regularly assassinated, on the streets in broad daylight, even in their beds.

The British retaliated. But they had little or nothing at which to aim, as their enemy melted into the woods and mountains or city alleyways. As a result the British Army – and most particularly the Black and Tans, a drunken and ill-disciplined group of veterans from the Great War recruited to help the RIC – took to murderous reprisals, gunning down innocent bystanders, roaring along village streets in their Crossley tenders, sacking whole communities and taking over local strongpoints as fortified headquarters.

So that it was not long before a Black and Tan company of some forty men, passing through Kilkenny in the spring of 1921 and moving south along the river towards Waterford, set their eyes on Summer Hill, an ideal site half-way between the two cities, from which they could control the whole middle river valley of the Nore.

Besides, as they soon learnt, the house was owned by Mrs Fraser, one of the most sought-after rebels in the country; they could thus do what they liked with it. At first, they stormed Summer Hill under the pretence of looking for Frances. She was not at home of course, so they commandeered the whole place as their regional headquarters, setting up machine-guns on the roof and in the porch, posting sentries at the gate lodges, sending patrols regularly through the grounds and dispatching all the servants. Aunt Emily initially refused to move. But in the end she was forced to seek sanctuary in Mortimer's house in Dublin.

Pat Kennedy, however, alone among the servants, had been forcibly retained. The Tans needed and indeed came to trust him, for he remained on the surface a man of impeccable credentials – impeccably dressed, too, as the house butler. Almost at once he was in touch with the Kilkenny IRA brigade, who in turn immediately advised Michael Collins of the situation.

A few days later Frances, who had been hiding out in the Wicklow mountains, spoke to Collins in a back room of Vaughan's Hotel near the quays.

'I'm afraid the Tans have taken over your house,' he told her gently. To his surprise she was not in the least put out. Indeed, she saw the whole thing as a wonderful opportunity.

'Since I know the place backwards and Pat Kennedy is still there,' she told him, 'we can storm it ourselves now, make an example of the blackguards!'

'I don't quite see, Mrs Fraser, it's your family home, there'd be terrible destruction—'

'Oh, that's of no account. Far more important to teach those Tans a lesson.'

Collins considered the matter. 'There's some forty or more men there, heavily armed, machine-guns, right up on a hill over the river, as I understand it. A bad position, bad odds, Mrs Fraser – from that height they'd massacre us.'

'Of course, if we made an open frontal attack. But we needn't. As I told you, Michael, I know the place backwards. There are other ways of doing it.'

He looked at her quizzically, quite prepared to consider any scheme proposed by this extraordinary English woman, as he still really saw her, who for years now had defied her own class and nation, with that imperious accent, on hunger strike in prison, or with guns – a woman, indeed, who had outranked him as one of the leaders in the Easter rising five years before. And so he listened to her attentively. After half an hour's discussion he agreed to implement her proposals. They had, he saw, the supreme merits of simplicity and surprise.

A few weeks later, when high summer had come over the land, Pat Kennedy seemed to fall ill, finally taking to his bed in the back of the main house, starting to cough and moan. He asked that a Dr Brennan from Kilkenny be called. The doctor came, examined him, left medicaments and reported to the Tans that it was a case of galloping consumption – an endemic and highly contagious disease, he warned them. There was little to be done.

The Tans, fearing infection, thereafter kept well away from Pat's quarters, where he was tended by young Biddy Molloy up from the village; every day she brought him various balms and foods, including a regular supply of what looked like red candles secreted beneath her petticoats. Pat's condition rapidly worsened and within a fortnight, taking the last rites from a priest one brilliant morning in July, he was dead.

The priest called a firm of undertakers in Kilkenny. A motor van, with two men and a large coffin, arrived in the yard later that afternoon. The Tans' Commanding Officer had the men frisked for arms and checked both the inside of the van and the coffin itself before allowing it into the house. And then later, from a safe distance on the landing, he watched the two men transfer the body into the open box. But, having seen the coffin lid screwed down, he did not linger.

The Tans ate every evening in the old servants' hall, just above the basement kitchens, a narrow room which led via various pantries out to the back yard, forming a natural exit here from the servants' bedrooms above.

But the Tans – some twenty-five of them, for the others were on sentry duty or on patrol – were none the less outraged when the two undertakers appeared in the doorway at one end of their mess room, carrying the heavy coffin.

'Bloody hell! – get that thing out of here,' one of them shouted, before others round the long table took up the same chorus. The two undertakers meanwhile, already in the room, had started to stagger under the weight, twisting and turning, dithering with it, before setting the box down.

'Look at them!' one of the more drunken Tans observed. 'Bloody Irish – can't even carry their dead. Get the fuckin' thing out pronto, you curs!'

'Yes, sir. At once, sir. Paddy!' the first of the undertakers called to his friend. 'Go back and get that wheel trestle.' His companion left the room, while the first man, bending down now over the coffin and fiddling with something at the head of it, said, 'Just a minute now, sir, till we get the oul' wheel trestle.'

'Go on, damn you! – get it out of here *any* way.' Some of the Tans were on their feet now.

'Mick? Where are you at all – with that trestle?' The first man went back to the doorway, standing there a moment, counting the seconds under his breath. 'Six, seven, eight . . .'

Then he stepped out neatly, closing the door, and ran

as fast as he could down the corridor before the tremendous explosion rent the room apart behind him.

Seven men were killed outright and many more wounded. The remaining Tans, none too sober in the first place and now fighting mad, set out to retaliate at once — intent on storming the village of Cloone. But this was exactly what the IRA had anticipated. Two of their flying columns lay in wait, hidden in the trees bordering both the main and the river drive, so that when the big Crossley tenders emerged into the twilight, headlights blazing down the hill, the first vehicle, as it crossed the culvert just outside the main gate, was blown sky high; and the second, racing along the river bank, was raked with fire, so that it skidded, bounced off a tree, then sheared away into the deep water.

The only retaliation the half-dozen remaining Tans could make then was against the house itself and the village, where most of the populace, warned by the IRA, had already made off for the hills. Burning and looting what they could in the village, they returned to Summer Hill and prepared to fire it as well. But half-way through these frenzied arrangements they thought better of the idea. The IRA might attack again, they had their wounded to attend to, were far from any real help just then, and to burn the house down would be to lose their fortified position. So they left things as they were — the back of the house, the old servants' hall, sculleries and pantries, now a blackened mass of debris, windows all blown out, open to the night.

Replaced by another company, who moved into the front of the house, the Tans stayed on at Summer Hill until the autumn, when a truce was called and negotiations began between Sinn Fein and the British government. A month later, in early December, the Tans moved out of Summer Hill altogether, just prior to the signing of the Anglo-Irish peace treaty in London. Apart from the six north-eastern counties, seven hundred years of British domination in Ireland had come to an end.

The burnt-out shell of the Victorian north wing led now to the partly destroyed end of the Georgian house; the rest of it, the great hall, gilded reception rooms, library and bedrooms – all these had been terribly knocked about during the Tan occupation.

Water, trickling through broken gutters, slates and chimney flues, soon made deeper inroads, soot-blackened rivulets coursing down the white walls, bringing mould and damp which rose from the floorboards, mixed with the smell of urine, the rank odour of decay. The tall shutters banged against sandbags and broken window glass in the winter gales. Triangles of gilded plaster hung and spun like glittering kites from the ceilings, then fell, littering the silent, empty rooms. The marble statues of Cupid and Psyche, one bullet-riddled, the other decapitated, stood like frozen mutilated corpses in their niches above the great hall. The heavily sandbagged library, a stencilled sign outside saying 'Armoury', was stacked with empty ammunition boxes, old cartridge belts, pools of oil on the floor, soaking into a detritus of ravaged books. Only the rats and rooks maintained, indeed increased, their tenure about the house.

And now, its sustaining Cordiner presence gone, its nobility destroyed, all its lovely things, the art and thought of centuries quite dissipated – the great house finally promised nothing, drifting rudderless through the months that led into that bright new year of Irish independence.

Frances, with Mortimer, arrived there one afternoon in February, driving up to the ghostly house in a light snowfall, early twilight sweeping in with the cold grey flakes. Pat Kennedy, returned now in full health, acting as caretaker and living in the gate lodge, opened up the house for them, leaving them to walk alone through the dreary rooms, Mortimer carrying an oil light, a beacon illuminating each fresh instance of destruction.

Frances appeared quite unmoved by the havoc. She picked up a piece of jagged plaster in the hall. Part of a gilded harp was clearly visible in the lamplight.

'Well, free at last!' she told Mortimer proudly, holding out the broken harp as evidence of Ireland's release. He did not reply at once, looking round at the obscene graffiti on the walls, the statues of Psyche and Cupid.

'Free,' he said finally. 'In a world hardly worth living in.'

'Your way, though – it was never going to work,' she told him briskly, a harsh edge in her voice. 'Force with force. That was the only way.'

'Force – that only leads to worse.'

'So be it! Were we never to be free?'

'Oh yes – I've fought for just that most of my life,' he told her vaguely, lacking conviction, turning away then, illuminating the corners of the hall; there was a scrawled message on the drawing room door: 'Fuck all Shin Faners.'

'Fought with words, though, all you old Home Rulers – just words,' she added with passionate intensity. 'Words could never have freed us, Mortimer.' She gazed at him, a chilling, mad certainty in her pinched features, pale and lined with prison suffering, but eyes still bright with venom.

Yet he remembered the beauty of that face twenty years before: gypsy-touched, yet regal, wild and free. There was a freedom she might better have fought for, he thought – beauty and right mind and not one filled, as it was now, with bitter, ranting nonsense. She and her companions might, with words, have fought for life and not for death, all about them in the house and throughout the land. Oh yes, Ireland might be free, he thought – but at the cost of all her democrats. And now he faced that freedom: a ruined house and a woman, a political leader, equally destroyed, whose wits had addled, with a voice that only shrieked in the dark.

What use to try and rebut her last words? Words for her and her kind had for so long, under the guise of patriotism, been just a means of rabble-rousing, a coinage of ignorance and self-delusion. And that would be their inheritance now: the mob, the blind leading the blind. Instead of pursuing these grim themes with Frances, he opened the dining room door, finding it half off its hinges.

'But does it mean nothing to you, Frances – this destruction – of *your* house, the one you fought so long to possess?'

'I *have* possessed it, Mortimer, fully. I need it no longer. A symbol of British tyranny.'

'This house has always been Irish.' He was angry now. 'And there was no tyranny at Summer Hill. That was never a Cordiner way. We and the more illustrious of our sort – Tone, Grattan, Parnell – how can you possibly think of tyranny there? Just the opposite—'

'But all that's long gone now, don't you see? – Lord Edward Fitzgerald and the rest of those well set-up Englishmen, really only fighting for their own survival here. Parnell!' she added dismissively. 'That adulterous landlord. *We've* come to rule now, Mortimer, the true people, the real Irish.'

'Yes, the butcher, the baker, the candlestick maker . . .' He remembered how, nearly twenty-five years before, at a dinner party in this same dining room, he had forecast just this – the onset of mindless violence, under the flag of the old true patriots, which would bring just such petty people to rule, and the demise of his own race in Ireland as well, largely self-inflicted, through their brutality, negligence, stupidity. And though, at least, these had not been Cordiner faults then, they were now:

he was looking at a woman who had just casually thrown away her heritage of seven centuries. He found it hard to forgive her for that.

'Who?' Frances was suddenly rigid with annoyance. 'Who are you referring to?'

'You'll see. The gombeen men will come to rule the roost here now. All your "true people" – Connolly, Mac-Donagh and the others – they all went in the Easter rising. And the truest long before that, O'Connell and Parnell—'

'What nonsense!'

'No—'

'Besides, we have some Protestants in the Dail. And there'll be more in the new Senate. You might serve there yourself, instead of carping.'

'I'm too old to serve any more. Besides, was there ever a dog that praised its fleas?'

'Words again. Always so good with them, Mortimer. But you lack humility, the common spirit. You've been defeated, by your wit, your class – along with all the rest of your kind in Ireland. You have no hope.'

Oh my God, he thought, looking at the bitter and disappointed woman staring up at him: where is that bright face of hope you once had, dear Frances? – that I remember so well from your early days with us in London. And then the whole tragedy of her life, once again, fell into place for him. She had fought England for so long, believing that the whole meaning of her life had been released in this fight, so that she could not for a moment accept that England, in the shape of the Prince of Wales, had killed her true spirit long before. Ever since, she had not so much been fighting for Ireland, but more venting her fury on the British crown. She had nurtured a personal vendetta, groomed and inflated it, so that it came to shine forth as martyrdom, honour, in all sorts of righteous violence. The old Prince had much to answer for. But then so had Frances. What could the Prince have done about her at the time, given the child? And surely Frances should have realized this basic incapacity of his – and come to terms with a fault for which, after all, they both shared the blame. But she had not. Instead, a blind obsession and vindictiveness had overtaken her, and destroyed her real nature. And there, he thought, was the banal heart of the tragedy: hell hath no fury like a woman scorned.

He should have shown more sympathy towards her for this very reason, of course. Yet her chilly insensitivity made it difficult. Above all he could not countenance her wilful dismissal of Summer Hill, of all that the house had meant – to him, to so many earlier generations of the Cordiner family, to the local people generally. So that he spoke more acidly than he would have wished.

'I *do* have hope, Frances – for this house at least, if not the political situation. It can be put in hand again, by degrees. As you know, I had most of the pictures, and the better furniture, removed before the Tans arrived. Pat tells me it's all still safe, stowed about the lofts and farm buildings. Some of the land can be sold and the rest put in good heart again. You can't just rid yourself of the whole place, with a shrug, and let it die.'

'But it's already dead, Mortimer. And, even if it weren't, there can be no future here for such places in the new Ireland, such ostentatious show. Besides, I don't need Summer Hill any more. I shall buy that little house in Dublin now for myself.'

'That new bungalow in Rathgar Road?'

'Indeed! And that's the future of Ireland, dear Mortimer!'

She laughed at him, a shrill laugh, turning away from the empty dining room, only dark shadows on the walls where once the Cordiner family portraits had hung. Opening the front doors and clambering over the sandbags, she went out on to the porch, standing in the fluttery snow, before doing a little jig on the steps. Mortimer followed her with the lamp.

'But, Frances,' he called out to her across the great divide. 'Of course, you can live where you will. But all this . . .' He swung the lamp round the great hall. 'It's a *family* heritage. And you're only a caretaker—'

'I have no family now!' she shouted back, clutching the broken plaster harp, as the snowflakes drifted down over her, whitening her cape and straggly hair, giving her the air of an old crone. Mortimer looked at her: Cathleen Ni Houlihan, he thought – the true spirit of Ireland indeed, mad as the mist and snow.

4

Frances was wrong about having no family. Indeed, she was close to becoming a grandmother that winter. However, Hetty's child had miscarried just before Christmas. The pregnancy had not been intended, but the loss of the child had none the less hurt her deeply, greatly increasing her general depression and nervous unease. Craig, secretly relieved, consoled her, as did Marion Davies, during the month she took off from work.

But Craig had been asked to do another picture meanwhile and was not often at home, as Hetty moped or stormed about the Lodge, issuing petulant dictates to the servants, lying restlessly on a day bed on the terrace or drinking endless cups of strong tea in the kitchen with little Eddy Nolan, who was now her constant companion. He was worried for her, particularly one evening when she told him she had a mind to give the whole thing up in Hollywood.

'And do what?' he asked anxiously, flexing his short, muscular arms nervously on the table.

'Oh, go back to Ireland, Europe, anywhere. *Anything!* I can't stand it here any longer.'

This was not Eddy's feeling at all. He had come to enjoy everything of his life in Hollywood – the good money he made now and then down at Universal Studios in one of Lon Chaney's horror pictures, and particularly his role as miniature major-domo about the Lodge, as Hetty's and Craig's particular confidant. He was part of the furniture here. The idea of their giving the whole thing up and his possibly having to return to the cold and violence of Ireland quite horrified him.

'Sure you wouldn't want to go and do that, Hetty.' He poured her another cup of tea. 'It's only temporary. I tell you what! – what you need is a bit of the oul' juggling and cods play we used to do with Fonsy O'Grady!' But she did not respond. 'But you *can't* throw it all up now – what with this big Egypt picture coming up.' Eddy, on the strictest confidence from Hetty, had been told a little of this.

'But it's *never* coming up!' she told him. 'That's the whole problem.'

'It will – it will! Just as soon as you start your new contract. Sure an' amn't I going to play the King's jester in it – cap and bells an' all!' And he did a comic little jig for her round the kitchen table so that she laughed at last. 'Ah, and there's no bad news that you can't do away with a dance,' he told her, finally improving her humour.

But a month later there was bad news. Craig heard it first from Leo Kuter. 'I got rumour of it yesterday from Taylor's art director,' he told Craig. 'Taylor's just asked him to work on some sketches for a new Egyptian picture he's going to offer to Paramount.'

'Just chariot race stuff – on the lot here?'

'Not, not just . . . It's *Nefertiti* – with Mary Minter or

Mabel Normand in mind. Thinking of going over to Europe to do it.'

Craig was unbelieving. But Leo was certain. And Craig exploded then. 'Christ almighty! The thieving bastard. The bloody little drug-peddling womanising bastard! Mabel or Mary couldn't play Nefertiti in a month of Sundays. How the hell did he get the idea?'

'Not from any of us, I assume—'

'Picked it out of the air, did he? Well, by Christ, he'll put it right back there again. He thieved Huck Finn from me. But I tell you – he won't take this one, never.'

'How not? He's made big money for them with Huck.'

'I'll go see him.'

'He hates your guts. He'll just laugh at you.'

'Some way then . . .' Craig stood up, thinking, agitated.

'What?'

'We'll go on it first.'

'But you'll have to see Fox himself for that sort of money – in New York.'

'Some way, don't worry. Taylor will only make that picture over my dead body . . .'

That afternoon, when he returned home and told Hetty, the gloom deepened. Hetty relayed the news to Eddy Nolan.

'Now you see! The picture I've most wanted to do – snatched out of our hands!' she cried out in despair.

'Ah now, don't take on so.' The agile little man comforted her. 'There's always a way out. You'll see. Never so black as it looks.' He put the kettle on then, got the teapot out, and opened a tin of imported fruit cake, almost tearing it open with his vast strength.

When he turned back though, offering Hetty the cake, he saw that she had gone quite still, body rigid, eyes glazed, staring fixedly in front of her, barely a twitch of life in her pale face.

'Hetty?' There was no response. She started to shake then, a minute trembling – grinding her teeth, the jaw bones locked together.

'Hetty – what's up?' Eddy waved his hand in front of her eyes. But she saw nothing and there was no speech, no noise but the pulverizing sound of her teeth – and soon a small trickle of blood fell from her mouth where she must have bitten her tongue. She was having some kind of fit. Eddy ran to call the studio doctor. But when he returned she seemed quite recovered, still dazed, but entirely conscious, wiping the blood from her lip and looking at the red smear on her finger in a mystified way.

'Where am I?' she asked dreamily. 'Oh, Eddy – it's you. Where – where are we? In Ireland, Summer Hill – yes! We're in Summer Hill, aren't we?' For the first time in many months a beatific smile lit up her face, a gentle, loving expression.

'No, no, we're not. We're in Hollywood, Hetty – your own house here.'

She suddenly became agitated, her face clouding over, bunching her fingers furiously. Then she started to thump the table, pummelling on it with her fists, a vicious drumming, a long-pent-up anger released from everywhere in her body, punishing the wood. Some other sort of fit, Eddy thought, when he finally had to restrain Hetty.

The doctor spoke to an impatient Craig that evening. 'Yes, of course I examined her. Nothing physically wrong. Just generally overwrought. Needs rest. And that must have been a black-out she had. *Petit mal*, they call it. A mild form of epilepsy. They don't know what causes it. But she'll need watching. And no driving the car. Just rest.'

'I'll have Eddy with her all the time. And we can get a nurse up.'

'Yes—'

'But what about the other fit Eddy says she threw? – hammering at the table? That wasn't a black-out.'

'Well,' the doctor considered matters, 'that's just some kind of suppressed anger, isn't it?' He looked at Craig carefully. 'Things not been going too well between you both?'

'No – fine. Just the loss of the child some time back.'

'Yes, sure . . .'

'Can she hurt herself like that – I mean, if she takes to it again?'

The doctor nodded. 'Why, certainly she can. And maybe that's what it's all about. She *wants* to hurt herself, for some reason.' He looked at Craig quizzically again.

'God knows why. Unless it's just that she's not working right now.'

'Could be. Or maybe something deeper. She's under some kind of pressure, that's for sure. Find out what it is, get rid of it – and that's the way to a cure.'

Craig knew what the stress was – the possible loss of *Nefertiti* for her. But he was not going to tell the doctor that. And he might have gone on to admit where the real problem lay: the fact that Hetty, at last, was beginning to face the guilt of her behaviour, towards Léonie, her family. As Léonie had forecast in her letter, Hetty had begun to hate herself.

But Craig did not delve into any of these real causes. Instead, over the next few weeks, he consoled Hetty by blaming Hollywood. 'It's time we got out of here,' he told her one Sunday morning, as they sat on the terrace. 'That's the real problem, for both of us. Need to get back to our roots. Your contract'll be up soon. We'll go and see Fox then – and get the hell out of here, make *Nefertiti*.'

'Yes, but what about Taylor?'

'Oh, he won't count.' Craig turned away then so that Hetty had the impression he was avoiding the issue.

'But you said how he'd thieved those other pictures from you—'

'Not this one, though.'

'*How* not—'

'Because we'll move first. And, besides, no one's going to listen to him. Can you imagine? – Mabel Normand playing Nefertiti? Or Mary Minter? The idea's absurd. Zukor wouldn't countenance it for a moment.'

'He might—'

'He *won't*.'

But Hetty was not convinced. 'Who *is* this man Taylor?' she asked then, a sudden hard calmness in her face.

'You know all about him. What do you mean?'

'I mean – why does he exist?'

Craig looked at her carefully, shading his eyes against the harsh, unchanging sunlight, thinking she might be about to have another black-out. But her expression did not alter.

In Paris that September, the flat August light gave way to gusty skies, as the first of the autumn winds, raking across the Ile de France, began to scratch and nose about the city. Stormy sunsets fell from skies of crimson and silver, setting fire to the bridges, touching the arches, one by one, far down-river. The children, back at school, in their black aprons with fresh white collars and clog-soled boots, ran with a great helter-skelter, feet echoing on the cobbles, racing the early twilights, shouting the latest fables. The wind smelt of rain as the city lurched into the dark.

And yet for Robert and Léonie the autumn had no air of ends, much more beginnings, as they easily resisted each item in the slow decay of the year, building castles against the seasons. They took a train out one Sunday morning to the village of Saint-Germain-en-Laye, crossing the great royal hunting forest before walking on and joining the river again on a narrow backwater, taking lunch at a small café-restaurant, the Cheval Blanc, by a bridge below Poissy.

They ate on the open terrace set above the river, on what seemed like a last miraculous day of fine weather, looking through the poplar trees to the river, listening as the leaves rustled and fell, lemon yellow, in the water. It was a day between seasons, bright with a fine sharpness, a little crackle in the air of an Indian summer. And it seemed to them, through the force of their own content, that they themselves had held back the weather, made a truce with winter.

They had pâté, and *goujons* of the local dace-like fish, washed down by Muscadet.

'You do love the food thing, don't you?' Léonie remarked pleasantly to Robert. 'I've noticed it – ever since you've come to Paris.'

'Love French food, yes – because you should have seen what I had to eat at St Columba's for five years up in the Dublin mountains!'

'Yes!' She leant across to him, as he fingered some more of the Brie. 'But it's not a schoolboy greed. You seem to set into it – with a sort of famished tenderness!'

'Another way of loving, you mean?' he said lightly.

'Yes! Something like that.'

'Perhaps . . .' He looked over the water. A few rowing skiffs passed them, skimming lightly downstream, couples out for a last trip on the river. 'Good food – a constancy that doesn't disappoint?'

'Yes. But "another way of loving" . . .' She picked up a pear from the basket, considering it rapturously. 'That was putting it even better. You do say things well, you're really going to be a fine writer. Oh, Robert . . .' She looked at him, her elbows on the sun-dappled tablecloth, head to one side, frowning a moment, but did not continue.

'Yes?'

'You have been . . . so hurt.'

'Not at all.' He was dismissive, taking up a pear himself then, biting into it, leaning forward as the juice dripped on to his plate. 'Goodness me! I'm alive, sitting with you by the river . . .' He looked about him, through the shafts of sunlight, the freckled patterns which no longer moved, for the weather had changed. The earlier breeze had gone, the leaves had ceased to fall, the water was unruffled, like a mirror. The world was silent, suspended in the yellow calm. 'Who can describe the fineness of an autumn day?' he wondered out loud.

'Only Monet . . . We'll just have to sing – and write – for our suppers.'

She picked up her wine and gazed at him through the glass, one of her grey-green eyes magnified in the straw-coloured liquid. A sense of professional companionship, inspired by her last words, bloomed then between them. Their friendship included a shared artistry, an imaginative endeavour. Yet, frustratingly for Léonie, these warm feelings which she felt between them then evoked no words from Robert in confirmation. Léonie longed for just such a response. She was almost certain he felt for her just as she did for him. But he was holding back for some reason. And she thought she knew what it was.

So, leaning forward once more, she said, 'But at least we're lucky – having each other.' Then, changing her tone, she suddenly added, with complete simplicity and directness, 'Let me help you love again. Because I think I know why you sort of . . . hold back with me. Because you feel I can only love – in the way I loved Hetty.' She looked at him uncertainly.

He wiped his lips, not facing her. 'Well, I don't know
. . . But, yes, as I've said, I had wondered—'

'Well, I *did* love her – in that way,' Léa broke in,
almost enthusiastic now. 'And I thought it was the only
way, for me. But it's not – not at all. Or, at least, it
doesn't have to be. I've known that now for quite a while.
Remember that day out on the river at Summer Hill,
with Hetty and Bertie? – when you were in the boat with
me? – I think I knew it then.' She smiled, a hint of
triumph in her admissions. 'So you see!' she added
proudly.

'I thought your feelings then were much more of pity,
at my predicament with Hetty,' Robert said, ironic, still
distant.

'No. I thought that, too – but only to avoid the feelings
I had for you.'

There was silence. A single poplar leaf spun down
towards the table, landing in the fruit bowl. 'Oh, *Robert*!'
She broke the mood with a happy impatience. 'Don't you
see? I *can* love you – it'd be all too easy! That's what I
wanted to say.'

He smiled, glancing at her, but still hesitant, not
entirely given to the idea. 'Thank you,' he said awkwardly at last, so that she laughed outright.

'What a formal response!'

'Sorry—'

'Oh, it doesn't matter – I'm not making any demands.
Just explaining. We'll always explain things – won't we?
So that there's no misunderstanding.'

'Yes, we will, Léa.' Robert was suddenly more confident, involved. 'Absolutely – explain things.'

She took his hand in hers, pleased to have broken the
ice with him, without falling through it.

'*You*,' she said, in a happy, mock-bullying tone. '*You*
– because you're such easy fun to be with and really so
kind and warm and good-hearted – and because we

shared so much at Summer Hill, when we didn't really know each other – so we can talk now and truly explain things. *You*, because . . .' She lowered her voice in mock seriousness. 'You're so lanky and handsome and I like your inky printer's fingers and even that frightful *pipe* . . .' She ran on, enumerating his virtues, still holding his hand, thrusting it down each time on the table.

Robert, bemused, said, 'I like you – just as much – too.' He fiddled with another pear then, as if he had said too much, before handing it to her. 'Fruit-filled,' he added. 'That's you.'

'Thank you,' she said simply.

A skiff passed them on the backwater, one that they had seen with a young couple going upstream half an hour before – floating back now, both oars shipped out of the water, mysteriously empty. 'Oh my!' Léonie was ironic. 'What *can* they be up to – that couple that passed us? Come on, let's grab it!'

Before he could join her Léonie had rushed from the terrace, followed by the *patron* with a boat hook, running down the river bank. Together they caught the skiff just before it passed under the bridge.

'Come on!' Léonie shouted back at him. 'The *patron* says we can take it back to them!'

'Coming!' Robert, leaning on the terrace balustrade, called back to her. Then to himself he said, 'And you, too, Léa – I'm sure I love you, too, because you're easy and warm and beautiful – and everything else nice I can think of. So why can't I say it?' He left some money for the bill; then ran down the river bank to join her.

Hetty, in the hall of the Lodge a month later, was beside herself with anger at Craig. She had been trying, with some logs she had ordered up specially, to get a fire going in the huge mock-baronial fireplace, only succeeding in nearly setting the whole place ablaze, before Eddy Nolan had doused the impending conflagration. Now she confronted her husband, just back from the studios, over the steaming mess of wood and smoking cinders by the grate.

'A *fire*? My God – in this kind of weather?' he asked her, unbelieving, looking out through the open hall doors to where the evening sun shone, as ever, with a flat glare.

'Why not? It's autumn at home!' she shouted at him. 'Just the time for fi-fi-first fi-fires.'

'Listen, honey, we don't have autumn this far down here on the Pacific. Why, it was over ninety degrees out on the lot today.' He wiped his brow. 'Come on, let's have a cool drink on the terrace—'

But she rounded on him again. 'Just because you never had any proper fires, in that miserable shop in Cork where you were brought up.'

'In Cork?' Craig turned to her surprised.

'Oh yes, don't pretend! Marion told me. You never had any fine house on a lake in the north of Ireland – father was some little *grocer* in Cork!'

Fully expecting these arrows to strike home and for Craig to further dissemble or contradict her, Hetty was disappointed. Craig, in his own estimation, had never lied about his dingy, colourless past. He had, rather, done something entirely natural and commendable with it. He had improved, embroidered upon it – had invented it, as he might any of his scenarios. Fact and fiction had never been sufficiently separated in his mind for him to see anything remotely wrong in this re-ordering of his past, so that now he let Hetty rant and simply left her, walking round the great hall, fingering things lovingly as he went, the phoney suits of chain mail, the papier-mâché arquebuses and cannon.

'Yes!' Hetty stormed on at him. 'You lied about all that – and your limp, too: you got that f-f-falling downstairs in some French brothel. You lied about everything – just as you're lying about *Nefertiti*! Taylor's got the picture and you won't tell me – you just let it go!'

Her face was contorted with anger. But Craig was quite calm, saying nothing. 'Why don't you *speak* to me?' she yelled at him. He was down by the hall doors now, a small shadow against the blazing rectangle of sunlight. Then he walked back towards her, slowly, menacingly, in his jodhpurs and riding boots, before finally he faced her, staring at her, as she shivered there with rage in the close air.

'Listen,' he told her, ice in his voice, 'we're not talking about brothels or big houses or grocers in Ireland—'

'*I* am—'

'No, you're *not*,' he interrupted with a viciousness she had never heard in his voice before. 'Because there's only *one* thing we have to talk about – and that's *Nefertiti*. And the one thing you have to remember there is that, without me, you'll *never* make it – *never*. So, if that's what you want, fine. You can walk out that door' – he pointed towards it – 'right now and go back to all the fires you want in Ireland – and forget the whole thing. I'll get someone else to play the Queen – if all you can do is play the fool.'

'You'll what?'

'You heard – and, believe me, I will. So, go on.'

He gestured towards the door again. But she said nothing, rooted to the spot, feet fidgeting in the moist cinders. Craig walked away.

Hetty began to weep, great hiccoughing sobs welling up inside her, exploding. Why had she been unable to walk out of the door just then? That was the crux of the matter. Whether she loved or hated him – and she did both – she saw that she could no longer create a life away from him, without him; that she was drawn to him unavoidably, linked with him inevitably, for better or worse, to the end. That was the final indignity – to see how she had allowed herself to be trapped by him, held by his strange power, how she had as good as thrown her own independence away. That was the worst thing – to recognize now how she needed somebody so obsessively that she did not know whether she loved or hated him.

She tried to staunch the tears of defeat, but succeeded only in smudging her face with sooty fingers. She cried out in anguish, weeping fiercely, clenching her fingers in the sodden debris by the grate, fouling her light white dress with it, like a keening savage, punishing herself uncontrollably.

She wandered into the imitation Georgian drawing room, glancing at the reproduction Irish hunting prints, before sitting down at the piano. Then, very hesitantly, for the first time in years, she embarked on a passage from *Madame Butterfly* – singing one part in a duet quietly to herself, the moment where Pinkerton comforts his weeping bride. There was no answering voice.

She stopped playing. The music only made it worse. She slammed the piano lid down. It was better to be furious than unhappy, she decided, as she had so often decided before. Action – action of any sort – was better than misery.

In Paris that very day, Robert with Ben Straus and a group of friends had gone to Léonie's Academy for the first night of her performance as Butterfly. He listened now to her pure soprano tone as Léonie, in a peacock-hued kimono, sang out the happy words – answer, indeed, to Hetty's cry six thousand miles away. '*Voglia-temi bene, un bene piccolino, un bene da bambino . . .*'

Later, Ben Straus took them on to dine at Maxims. 'You really made me feel for her,' Robert told Léonie, raising his glass. 'Not as some put-upon little geisha girl, but as, well, someone living and loving – and losing – in

87

the here and now: as if it all really *meant* something to you.'

'I did really mean it . . .' She touched his hand, without confirming exactly what she meant. But later, at home, Robert, plucking up courage, asked her, 'When you sang all those passionate duets with Pinkerton tonight – just as you used to do with Hetty at Summer Hill – were you thinking of her?'

'Yes,' she told him with her usual directness. 'That was really the whole point of my wanting to play the thing in the first place: "living, loving and losing" – just as you said. Getting her out of my system.'

'And?'

She nodded vigorously. 'Yes! I've rid myself of all that at last – the slave thing, the servant, the obsession – just as Butterfly does. She's dead and it's dead and I shan't ever play that put-upon little woman again!'

She kissed him briefly then, brushing his lips. He tasted the last trace of her make-up – but it was a taste which seemed to promise a future for them both, an end to the charades and thraldom of their lives, with the woman who for so long had haunted them. And so it was, as Hetty's life in Hollywood became every day more miserable, theirs in Paris started to climb the heights. As Hetty came to hate herself, they – more openly at last – began to love each other.

And yet it was not quite so easy – certainly not for Robert, so inexperienced in love. Now, he had, for the first time, to contend with realities, the delectable but to him unknown actions of the heart, in a love reciprocated.

For Léonie there was a different hurdle. So sensuous in essence, so given to the physical world, its fruits and flowers, winds and weathers, she held ready the same natural inclinations in her sex. But she had never loved a man: she was equally virginal there. And though, as she had hinted by the riverside, she felt ready to embark on the experiment – longed, secretly, at moments, to devour this man – she hesitated, afraid.

Robert equally feared such a confrontation. So they both fought shy of any serious contact or consummation of their affair, fearing they might destroy what they loved in each other, either by witless inexperience or uncontrolled appetite.

In Hollywood as Christmas approached, up at the Lodge, Hetty, despite the fact that she had largely made things up with Craig, became ever more frustrated and unbalanced. She was due to start another picture – her last on the current Fox contract – with Craig the moment he finished the one he was working on. But that would not be for another fortnight. Then they would see William Fox himself, and negotiate a new contract to include *Nefertiti*. Meanwhile the matter of Taylor, and his possibly pre-empting them on the same idea, began to obsess her.

'But he *won't* go ahead with it,' Craig continually told her.

'So you always say. But what have you actually *done* about it? How can you be so sure?'

'Leo Kuter's keeping me in touch. Taylor's art director is working on another picture with him now – some Civil War story. They seem to have shelved their Egyptian idea.'

'But you're fibbing again – I can see it in your face!'

And Craig had indeed been lying. He knew almost nothing of exactly how things stood with Taylor, simply hoping he could complete his next picture with Hetty as soon as possible, then go to see Fox and move first on *Nefertiti*.

'OK, if you want to believe that – I'm lying. Have you any better ideas?'

Hetty had but she did not speak of them. Instead the

idea that she might lose this one great picture came to dominate her – this picture, so far above all others, which would justify the sacrifices she had made, which would assuage the guilt she felt now, the self-hatred, rising up all round her. It was a matter, she knew then, of sink or swim.

In Paris that cold winter Robert heard the latest news of Frances and her visit to Summer Hill in a letter from Mortimer. It was a Saturday. Léonie had persuaded him to go dancing that same evening with her at the Bal Rouge, one of the little *bals musettes* on the rue Soufflot leading down from the Panthéon. And they sat there now, at a table pushed in against the wall, Robert sipping a pastis, Léonie with a cassis-Chambéry, looking out on the small open space, where a few couples – students and scrubbed young workers with their girls – were holding each other loosely, one-handed, waltzing lazily. The accordion music came from a musician on a small platform, set, astonishingly, on top of a stout pole rising from the middle of the floor. The air smelt of cheap brilliantine, anis and burnt French tobacco. Later everything would change, Léonie knew.

'You're a regular here?' Robert asked.

'Once or twice – with friends from the Academy.' She was elated at her success in getting him there. 'You'll see! It's marvellous fun! Get something for the *Tribune* out of it, too.' But Robert maintained his rather glum expression. 'Oh, I know it's tough – about Summer Hill,' she went on quickly. 'But is there anything – *anything* – you can do about it?'

'My home, in a way. Hate to think of it destroyed.'

'But it's not! Only a bit of it. And, besides, you can't live there – *and* make a living as a journalist. Isn't there all your own future to think about? Or did you really hope to live there one day?'

'Perhaps I did, in a way.'

'In the way . . . you loved Hetty?'

He smiled faintly. 'Maybe.'

'Well, that's not going to happen now—'

'Yes, but what happens to the house? Frances doesn't care a damn for it now, nor Hetty obviously.'

'It's only bricks and mortar.'

'Limestone actually. And marble – Kilkenny and Carrara,' he told her lightly.

'Well then, it'll last for ever and ever, won't it? And you needn't worry.' But he did. And she saw it. 'Oh, Robert, don't you see? Summer Hill was Frances and Hetty and all that – horror. You really *should* forget it, as I've done. And have your own life, your own house.'

'Not so easy. It's the only home I've ever really known. The whole place for me – it's something important, quite apart from Hetty and Frances. Feel I should do something . . .'

'Tell you what then!' Léonie was bright. 'When you're rich and famous, then you can *buy* it!'

'Poor and unknown, more likely! The other will be more your department – a great opera singer!'

'Right then.' Léonie was serious. 'Maybe we can buy Summer Hill *together* then . . . some day.'

Robert frowned. 'Oh, that wouldn't really do. The man has to buy the home . . .'

Léonie, though she heard the teasing in his voice, came back at him strongly. 'What a lot of nonsense! Don't believe in that – in marriage, in any relationship. People pay what they can, either way, if that's what they're up to!'

'You, too – all part of the feminine *zeitgeist* now, aren't you?'

'Yes. But part of common sense even more. All that old male-dominated world which Summer Hill epitomizes – formal marriage contracts, strict male line inheritances and so on. All that world is vanishing fast, Robert! Just look around you – those girls, they pay their few sous to dance here just as often as any of the men. And thank God it's like that now. Look at what the old ways did for Frances – that frightful need she had to *possess* everything, Summer Hill, everyone: always to dominate and control.'

'I'd have thought you might have admired that in her – given your own feminine angle on things.'

'Admire the thought, maybe. But not the results. Frances was really looking for some other kind of bondage all the time. Didn't really want to be free – or for any of us to be free either. Just wanted to punish everyone, for something awful in her own life, and wants to punish herself most of all. And that's not the point about "feminism" – just the opposite: it's to release us from all that sort of self-hatred and feelings of being inadequate.'

'Well, maybe you're right – about Frances. And about the world changing for women. Just, I tend to be a bit . . . old-fashioned about all that.'

'So you'd have to buy the house? Wouldn't let your girlfriend – or your wife – help, even if she was stinking rich?'

'No. I don't think I would.'

They were silent then. Robert sipped his pastis. Léonie finally broke the mood, as the accordion started once more, a jaunty waltz, 'Valentine'.

'Oh, *do* dance with me, Robert!' Léonie suddenly asked, head on one side, pleading mischievously to be taken up in the happy swirl of music.

She moved with easy grace. Robert was far less confident. Awkward and gangly, he began to perspire as he swirled furiously round with her.

'Not so fast!' he called out. 'I can hardly see—'

'You're not *meant* to see – just feel!'

'I should have worn my glasses—'

'Gracious sake! – you're not reading a book! Just let yourself go a bit.'

He tried to, but his legs remained stiff and unbiddable, like an automaton toy not properly wound up – until, slackening pace, when the accordionist started a slower waltz, Léonie brought him more firmly to her, resting her chin on his shoulder.

Feeling so close together for the first time, Robert, though fearing the opposite, found himself relaxing. This sort of non-dancing was more within his compass, he decided. Yet in truth there was a different reason for his new feeling of confidence and ease. A scent of warm violets drifted up to him from Léonie's face – from the delicate perfume she used. Encouraged by their exertions, and by their closeness, the perfume seemed to be almost as much a part of his body as of hers: an indivisible odour, creating a heady intimacy between them. And it was this that gave him the sudden confidence, this and the subsequent brief thought of how, if they were sleeping together, the same perfume would so wonderfully cover them both, their whole bodies, skin on skin, all night long.

Rain had threatened for some days in Los Angeles and now the city lay under a boil of humid cloud that would not burst. It was suffocatingly close that afternoon in Hollywood – and later the sky was seared by sheet lightning far out in the bay, an electric storm over the Pacific, with rain and distant thunder, which yet refused to come ashore and cleanse the land.

Hetty, alternating between the bathroom shower and ice-packs in her bedroom for most of the day, had by evening reached a pitch of frustration. She had already found what she needed in Craig's bedroom drawer: the ignition key to her car which, because of her blackouts, he had hidden from her; and the other even more important item in a second drawer. Her special clothes were ready, and Craig had told her he would not be back from the studio until late that evening. Apart from Eddy Nolan, always keeping an eye on her, the situation was perfect. She longed to be off, to break out of this humid carapace, identical to the pall of long inaction which was destroying her life. Now was the moment.

Just as darkness fell, she managed to engineer an argument over menus and provisions between the Chinese cook and Eddy – so that the two of them, disappearing to the larder, gave her just those few minutes she needed. Changing quickly into her new clothes, she ran down to the garage on the lower terrace, reversed her Dodge coupé smartly out, wheels spinning on the gravel, and raced off down the hill into the canyon.

Seeing that there was no one in pursuit she drove more slowly then, past Hollywood Lake, on towards the long suburban boulevards, the twinkling lights of Hollywood in the distance. She was quite calm now. There was no hurry. She knew exactly where he lived, exactly what she had to do. She smiled as she drove.

Coming into Beverly Hills, she took a right by the gas station on the main boulevard, then drove up to the end of a small side-street, and parked the Dodge on some waste ground, leaving it partly hidden in the shadow of an overhanging pepper tree. It was quite dark now, just a few minutes after eight, as she doubled back, walking easily down the street. Wearing a man's light grey mackintosh, felt hat and slacks, with rubber-soled shoes, hands thrust in pockets, she readily mimicked some inhabitant of the suburbs out for an evening stroll. But no one saw her in any case. The street was deserted.

Taylor's bungalow was half-way down, set some thirty yards off the street, part of a courtyard of similar little residences – and the cover here was perfect, all the houses shrouded in trees and bushes.

Turning off the sidewalk, casually she moved up the crazy paving between the other bungalows, before she saw the light in the front window of Taylor's house. Tiptoeing up, pushing in through a tangle of bougainvillaea, she tried to see through the window. But the curtains were drawn and all she could hear were the voices – a woman's voice raised in anger.

'. . . leave my daughter alone . . . hear me! . . .'

'Mrs Minter—'

'You and your drug peddling with her . . . and what else I don't know . . . behind my back. But it's going to stop, once and for all, I can tell you—'

'Mother!' Another woman's voice broke in, younger, in a higher register, even more angry. 'It's nothing the hell to do with you. And nothing of that sort's going on . . . you bursting in here . . . we were just going over a scenario . . . this new Egyptian picture . . .'

Hetty froze in anger. It was obviously Mary Miles Minter, with her virago of a mother having some row with the director – about drugs, seduction, the lot. Hetty was not surprised. It was well-known about the picture colony: Taylor, with his insatiable taste for affairs with young women, had been carrying on with Mary. Mrs Minter had come for a showdown with him now. Taylor deserved no less. But Hetty was frustrated.

She would have to wait, but not here, where it was too exposed. She went round to the back of the bungalow, taking up a position just outside the kitchen door, crouching next to some empty crates of bootlegged beer and spirits. The kitchen door was half-open, she saw, as if one or other of the Minter women had come in by that route. But of course! Mrs Minter had come that way, hoping to surprise the couple at their antics. What a lot of surprising business Taylor had on his plate that evening, Hetty thought. Well, she would not be denied her part in it. She settled down to await developments. The two women could not stay there for ever . . .

Up at the Lodge, Eddy Nolan – hearing the coupé swinging round on the gravel – had rushed down to the lower terrace, too late to stop her. There were several cars in the garage, but Eddy could not drive. Instead he put an urgent call through to Craig at the studio.

'For Christ's sake, Eddy, how did you let her go? – *where* did she go?'

'No idea – I thought maybe downtown to meet you?'

'Like hell she is! Maybe Marion Davies or Mickey Neilan – I'll call them. Or maybe worse . . .' Craig considered something for a moment. 'Listen, Eddy,' he said then. 'Get down here quick, will you? I may need you. Get one of the cooks to drive you.'

Hetty meanwhile was becoming impatient, frustrated in her lack of action, and made more uneasy still as the oppressive sky finally broke in a storm above the city, with patches of vivid lightning, and the electric cables on some small pylons nearby sizzling with blue flashes. She could hear no detail of the argument now, only the raised voices from the front room. And suddenly she thought how, instead of waiting for the Minters' departure, she might better use their presence there instead. She had no need to talk to Taylor, after all.

She moved silently into the kitchen, then on down a corridor towards the front room. Turning a corner into a second shorter corridor, she saw a curtained Spanish archway some yards ahead, light from the drawing room shining through a gap in the drapes, shadows moving to and fro beyond, voices clearly heard now – dominated by Mrs Minter's strident tones.

'Don't lie to me! – that's what you've been doing for years, getting decks of coke to every young girl you could lay your hands on about the studios, then seducing them.

Well, you won't go on doing that with *my* daughter, you creep, you cheapjack . . .'

Hetty took out the Smith and Wesson .38 she had taken from Craig's drawer. It would surely be an easy shot, through the curtains – then back out of the kitchen door. She would never even be seen. She moved forward, hardly breathing, the gun held straight ahead of her, the barrel moving slowly towards the gap in the curtains. Raising the gun and peering through, she saw them all: the two women across the room, Taylor sideways on to her, hardly three yards away, tall and thin, silvering hair, impeccably dressed in his dark English worsted. But, most astonishingly, there was Mrs Minter, at that same moment, taking a revolver from her bag, aiming it at Taylor.

The shot went off with a sharp report which stunned Hetty. Had it come from her revolver, or from Mrs Minter's? Hetty was not sure. Taylor's knees crumpled, then he fell straight downwards, like a tall building being demolished. Hetty, still behind the curtain, saw the look of fear and astonishment on the faces of the two women, standing there for a moment, rooted to the spot, wild-eyed, before they turned and fled, closing the front door behind them.

Hetty went into the drawing room as the thunder boomed over her. Taylor was stretched out on the carpet between his desk and the sofa. He seemed quite unharmed, as if asleep. There was no sign of blood or other injury. She bent over him, a crisis of alarm and guilt threatening her.

Suddenly she felt a sense of fuzzy distances overwhelming her, until she saw nothing, just a warm blackness spreading everywhere round her, the beginnings of some comforting dream forming in her mind, as she fell herself then, to lie stretched out next to Taylor. Soon there was a knock on the door, but she never heard it.

'The lights are on – she must be here.' Craig turned to Eddy on the doorstep. 'That was her car at the end of the street. I'll stay out front – you go round the back.'

Moments later, coming through from the kitchen, they found her on the floor.

'Where am I?' she asked, dazed but calm. 'We were at home, at Summer Hill. I was speaking to Aunt Emily!' She was happy at this thought, as she glanced vaguely around her. 'Where is she?'

'No, Laura, you're here, with us – in Hollywood . . .' Craig told her. And suddenly, at this news, Hetty was on her feet, pushing and shoving at the men, struggling violently, before Eddy, practically leaping on her, like an animal, gripped her fiercely, pinioning her arms. 'Easy, there, easy,' he calmed her, like a tiny jockey astride a racehorse.

Craig picked his gun up from the floor, checked the rooms for any other evidence of Hetty's presence in the bungalow, and they got her out through the kitchen door and back to the car. 'You go with her, Eddy – she'll have to drive, it's the only way. I'll follow.'

As Craig passed Hollywood Lake, he stopped for a moment in the rainy darkness and threw the gun as far as he could out into the water. Back home, he took Hetty to their bedroom. The storm had passed. The air on the mountain was suddenly cool and refreshing for the first time in a week. He embraced her. 'My God, honey – you shouldn't have done it. It was only a picture.'

'Done wha-what?' She looked at him with genuine astonishment.

'What do you mean? Down in Taylor's house – you just shot him.'

'Oh! Was that where we were just now? *Taylor's* house? – but I don't know him. And somebody *shot* him?' She was entirely mystified.

Craig put his hand to her cheek, calming, stroking her.

'OK, somebody shot him. Fine. But, whatever you do, if anyone asks, we *weren't* downtown tonight. None of us. OK? We weren't *in* Taylor's house tonight. Remember that, won't you?' He looked at her urgently. And she returned the look, still curious, but agreeing.

'No, of course not. I w-won't say.'

'Now, get those clothes off,' he told her.

'Yes, of course.' She looked down at her disguise, the men's slacks and mackintosh, suddenly quite bemused again. 'What on earth am I wearing these for? Weren't filming today, were we?'

'No – just some charade we were playing . . .'

She started to get undressed, throwing the clothes about her in a vigorous whirlwind. 'Extraordinary! Don't remember a thing aba-about it all. One of our nice "games" again, was it?' She paused, then turned to him, with a smile of great happiness, like the old days. 'Oh, Craig, it's so long since we played those good games, isn't it? What was it, some frantic party downtown?'

'Yes . . . Yes, but you had a blackout, one of your little turns.'

'Oh, dear. At the p-p-party?' Craig nodded. 'Yes, it's funny, because I remember something now – Mary Minter was there, wasn't she? – with her mother. Some sort of row going on. Anyway, I feel fine now.'

The air had cleared, all the mugginess gone, stars visible in the sky through the open bedroom window, a faint breeze running in from the ocean. She came to him, embracing, kissing him seductively. 'I can't t-*tell* you,' she said vehemently, 'how nice it is – to be playing our old games again.' She licked his ear mischievously. She felt so different now, all the mysterious burdens of the last months quite lifted. 'But *what* a party!' she went on, standing back from him, curious once more. 'Someone *shot* Taylor, did they?' He nodded grimly – and she reached out, touching his cheek briefly. 'Oh my God, but *who*?'

'I – I don't know exactly . . . wasn't in the room when it happened.'

'Well, at least we can make *Nefertiti* now, can't we?'

'Why, yes. Yes, we can, honey.' And Craig kissed her tenderly.

Later he spoke to Eddy in the kitchen. 'Jesus – she doesn't remember a thing!'

'So much the better. And no one saw us. And, if anyone saw her, well, look at the disguise she had on.'

'And nothing to link her with Taylor, she's never met him. We may get away with it.' Craig poured himself a drink. 'It's funny, though, when I spoke to her, she thought she'd been at some downtown party, in Taylor's place – with Mary Minter and her mother there, having some row.' Eddy grunted and Craig continued, 'Funny, because it figures in a way, doesn't it? Taylor's been carrying on with Mary for months now, behind her mother's back. Just the sort of thing she'd do – turn up at his place unannounced and try and crack him one, or even shoot him.'

'Yes . . .' Then Eddy thought out loud. 'Yes, indeed – those two, or Mabel Normand. She's been having a long fling with Taylor as well – while he was two-timing her. Any one of those dames might have shot him – they'll be the first people the cops'll think of.'

'You really think that, Eddy? Or are we just out of the frying pan, into the fire?'

Robert and Léonie had been dancing 'Le Fox' – and then, even more daringly, 'Le Java', the latest craze, a mad dance, stamping their feet furiously, so that by the end of the evening they were both heady-drunk, sweating with exhaustion and excitement.

It had started to snow outside, so that, leaving the *bal*

musette, they walked straight into the delicious, cooling flakes. Lifting their heads, opening their mouths, they drank in the weather, snow melting on their tongues as they walked through the Latin Quarter towards the river.

By the time they reached the narrow medieval streets round the church of St Julien-le-Pauvre on a slight rise above the water, all the traffic had disappeared and the snow had become heavier, colder, falling silently. They stopped a moment by the church doorway, while Léonie adjusted her big red scarf, so that it covered her sugar-dusted hair. Then, looking up at the church, she turned and kissed Robert abruptly, a peck on the cheek.

'Abelard's church!' she told him.

'Oh, I didn't know—'

'Like stations of the cross – one has to mark it!' Robert, stamping his feet, bouncing the snow off his boots on the pavement, had no time to comment on this, before she said, 'Doing the Java again?' She smiled, putting her arm in his, pulling him on. 'You were really pretty good by the end!'

'More the pastis—'

'No! But *no* – it was all you, letting yourself go at last!'

'I'm really no dancer . . .'

'Oh, go on, you old fraud! Do anything if you try!'

She left him then, skipping round him, teasing him, flouncing her arms out in the snow, as he continued his steady walk down towards the Quai Saint-Michel. 'Anything! Anything!' she sang out, lunging at him, tipping at his old felt hat, so that soon they were snowballing each other, both scattering down the street, sliding, and throwing snow, in a great helter-skelter, until they reached the river. They stood by the wall then, at the very edge, arm in arm, watching the white drifts falling, curtain upon receding curtain, against the dark backdrop of Notre-Dame just visible across the water.

'Winter! What a winter!' she said, shivering, wrapping

the scarf tighter. 'I love it – just love it when it snows like this! Wish there was never any end to winter . . .'

'Yes,' he said. Then, quite absentmindedly, apropos of nothing, he went on, 'All wrapped up in the cosy-warm . . .'

She turned, looking at him as he gazed pensively into the snowfall. 'Oh *yes*!' she said, huddling up to him quickly, so that he smelt the damp snowy wool on her scarf then, mixed with the distant odour of violets. '*Yes!*' she said once more. They took a taxi back to Passy.

Ben Straus had long since retired when, opening the door silently, Léonie came into Robert's small top floor bedroom, a wraith-like figure, standing in her cotton nightdress for a moment, vaguely illuminated by the street light outside the window.

'Robert?' she whispered.

Robert, thoughts of the evening's song and dance still churning about his head, was wide awake. But he pretended drowsiness.

'It's so *cold* in my room! Can I . . . come in . . . and share your bed?'

Her voice was entirely sensible, direct, without urgency or passion. Yet Robert felt a complete panic. 'Yes,' he murmured, as if waking from a deep sleep.

'Sorry to wake you!' She lifted the coverlet briskly, and hopped into the narrow space beside him. 'But it was quite *freezing* in my bed.' And she shivered next to him then, a long spasm right down her body, as truthful confirmation. Robert had been lying on his side facing the wall. Now he turned on his back.

'Yes, chilly, isn't it?' he remarked in a casual tone, as if sharing views on the weather with a neighbour. He shivered himself in his warm woolly pyjamas – though not from cold, as he felt the long length of this woman, so close to him, the folds and run of her whole body, just as he had imagined, length by length, so deliciously, perilously close to him. He raised his hands carefully behind his head, and they lay there, side by side, straight out on their backs, still as corpses in the dark, until Léonie chuckled.

'What?'

'Just, it struck me – lying like this – we might be two elderly people, being chauffeured out in a motor, commenting on the weather.' And then she shivered once more, her shoulder throbbing next to him, as if a bitter wind was raging through her, before she turned to him, putting her arm across him.

'Oh, warm me, Robert, warm me – in the cosy-warm!'

He thought of the phrase again. And now he remembered its origins. It had been one of Hetty's in their nursery days together with Elly in Domenica and Summer Hill. He had spoken it involuntarily, without quite knowing why, an hour before on the Quai. But now the words, drifting through the snow of the years, had come home to roost. Of course – he saw it then: the little nursery phrase of the girl who for so long he had loved and wanted had been the key to his bed that night, which Léonie, all unknowing, had picked up and turned in the lock. What irony – that Hetty should so make their bed for them that night, a last gift from her. So that when he turned into Léonie's arms, clasping her, he saw instead that other tall, audacious girl, so full of laughter and shadow, seeing what he owed her then, in the shape of this forgotten nursery fable, saw how he still both loved and hated her.

He felt the thrilling flow of Léonie's body then, soft breasts and thighs, hard hips and knees – and soon he found himself shivering for another reason.

'Violets,' he said as he touched her. 'I had this idea, while we were dancing . . .' He stopped.

'What? Go on!' She encouraged him breathlessly.

'Well, just that perfume you use, smells of violets – I'd

wondered what it'd be like if one was close to you . . .'

'*And*?' She was impatient.

'Well, it's not there now! Just a sort of starchy linen smell—'

'That's just my clean nightdress, you idiot! Here, I'll take it off!' And, before he could do anything about it, she sat up abruptly, pulling the nightdress up over her shoulders in a moment, then lying down with him again at once, hugging him.

'*Now!* – can you smell the violets?'

He sniffed. 'Yes – yes, faintly.'

She laughed outright. 'You are funny.' Then she added, taking up one of her mock operatic voices, 'You and your violets – like an old gardener!'

'Sorry—'

'Oh, *Robert*!' She scolded him kindly. 'Do stop pottering about in the garden!'

'Yes, of course . . .'

And she worried him again, like a terrier, playfully pulling at his hair, pinching his ear, then hugging him to her.

'It's no use – you're tickling me so. You'll simply *have* to take your pyjamas off!' she advised him haughtily, like a duchess in a comedy.

'Oh – sorry.'

She undid his pyjama top then, putting her arms inside, feeling the soft skin there for the first time, before running her hand down to his waist, and pulling the string, so that soon they were both naked.

Robert was astonished at the delicious warmth and pleasure he felt. Their skin together now was like nothing he could ever have imagined: it was a gliding feeling between them, so smoothly tender, and there was a musky sweet smell now with the violets, as he felt his sex rising, surging towards her, so that he tried wildly to withdraw, before she held him.

'No! No – don't go away! That's perfectly *all right*,' she calmed him. 'It's the best thing in the world! Because I love you,' she said as she touched him, leaning over him now, kissing him gently, down his face, his chest, so that for minutes on end then they seemed suspended together, quite weightless – even when she lightly straddled him, opening herself to him, coming on to him delicately, lightly, imperceptibly at first, so flowingly and inevitably that before he quite realized it he was inside her, moving into her, as she pushed gently, drawing back from him, moving to and fro.

'The *best* thing!' she said again, her passion rising, stretching right back, arms fluttering about before she took his hand and put it to her breast; so that, caught in these separate ways, their bodies forming a rough circle, they struggled together in a confusion of pleasure – before Robert suddenly turned over on to her and made love to her, rising to a pitch when he could no longer contain himself, falling then, falling into her, into a great bank of violets.

'I *do* love you,' he said afterwards, in quite a different, more confident voice – the tones of the inexperienced gardener quite gone. While for Léonie the surprise and change was just as great.

'I was *so* scared,' she said, nuzzling him, 'that I – couldn't do it.'

'You didn't show it!—'

'No – no! Easy as falling off a log – because you wanted me! I felt it – the moment you said that about the "cosy-warm" down by the river!'

'Yes – yes,' he said, without elaborating on what he thought to be the key to their success that evening. But Léonie in fact knew the origins of these words, too. Hetty had often used them with her, when they had lived together in Dublin, as a coded invitation to bed. And now, as she had realized by the river, Hetty had used them with Robert as well, long before, as part of some nursery fable in Summer Hill. How strange it was, she thought, that Hetty's words should so bring them together that night – Hetty, still working for her, invisibly, a hand, a voice, a phrase reaching out to her from the past, bringing her the gift of Robert. And for an instant then she saw Hetty's face ahead of her in the darkness, not Robert's – Hetty in all her vivid, tormented glamour.

5

It was the autumn of 1925, and already nearly two months had passed in Egypt. But now at last – with the help of some hundreds of Egyptian builders, carpenters, stonemasons, plasterers and coppersmiths, together with American, Italian and French craftsmen, set-designers and other technicians – the gleaming city of Amarna, the Pharaoh Akhenaten's fabulous 'City of the Sun', was rising up in the desert, beneath a crescent of jagged forbidding hills on the east bank of the Nile, near the town of Beni-Souef eighty miles south of Cairo on the railway.

'Up! Up! *Mein Gott!* . . .' The art director Leo Kuter broke into his Teutonic mode, yelling in tense frustration, his little goatee beard glistening with sweat.

The fifty or so Egyptian labourers in the current work gang – *fellahin* employed from the villages on the other side of the river – tugged on the half-dozen ropes, running down from the scaffold with its wooden pulleys high above them, gradually easing up the vast ornamental plaque, a central altar-piece weighing well over a ton, one among a roughly similar half-dozen, showing Akhenaten, his wife Nefertiti and their three daughters, exultantly happy under the rays of the sun god Aten. The plaque was to be set above the open shrine at the end of the Great Temple, Aten's 'House of the Sun', an immense half-completed construction, three or four hundred feet square, enclosed by high walls, with rows and clumps of columns inside, supporting decorative architraves, or creating little pavilions, sunshades, in this huge mosaic-paved plaza set some way back from the river.

Leo Kuter looked a mess in a pith helmet and sweat-soiled linen suit, and Johnny Seitz the cameraman, flat cap on back to front as usual, was equally bedraggled; both suffered in the intense midday heat, the blaze of light that cast no shadows and seemed to levitate everything in its shimmer. Only Craig, like the sun king Akhenaten himself, appeared to have entered his true element. Perfectly turned out and tailored – in a dazzling white silk shirt, linen trousers, leather-belted, hatless, his smooth dark hair glistening in the light – he drew the sun's rays to him, becoming part of Aten's fire: sweatless, immune, almost inhuman.

The three men stood on top of a thirty-five-foot-high steel scaffold, set on four doubled sets of automobile wheels, sent out from Hollywood and incorporating a camera lift, with which they were experimenting, while at the same time supervising this final construction of the city, which costumed crowds of extras would fill during the first week's shooting. Leo went over again to the huge megaphone, suspended from a bracket on top of the tower.

'Up – and to zee right!' he shouted to one of his half-dozen assistants, on the ground below and on the balcony beneath the dangerously swinging plaque.

'Christ, Leo – don't let them swing it over too far!' Craig warned him. 'It'll hit that balustrade.'

'*Basta*, Luigi, basta!' he called to the Italian foreman high above the altar. Then he shouted down to a second foreman, from the Victorine studios in Nice, who was in charge of the sweating *fellahin*. '*Ça va, Gaston. En haut encore. Mais* doucement!'

The Egyptians, set out in long radiating lines, moved again on the ropes – pulling, heaving, until gradually the great plaque came into position, some thirty feet above ground, opposite the niche in the temple wall that had been prepared for it.

'*Ça suffit, Gaston. Arrêtez! Ne bouge pas encore!*'

The *fellahin* kept the ropes taut, until some of them began to slip on the smooth stone plaza, so that Leo roared at them again like a slave-master. '*Arrêtez, Gaston! Ne bougez* pas!' And Gaston took up the command beneath him, berating the turbanned men in kitchen Arabic, '*Yallah! Ma fische!* . . .' before Leo continued, shouting across the great divide at Luigi, '*Va bene, Luigi!* Take it in now – *ma dolce*, dolce!' The plaque was finally fixed in place.

'My God . . .' Leo wiped his pudgy face with a red bandana handkerchief. 'Verse zan building zee pyramids . . .'

'Yes, but look, Leo!' Craig put a hand on his shoulder. His eyes were glazed with emotion, as he pointed up to the plaque – a spectacular white emblem, reflecting the midday sun, one sun mirroring another, the rays at the end, caressing the five almost naked figures. 'Just look – it's sensational! Better than the original – bigger, better, twice the size!'

Craig was beside himself, his dark sunburned features alive with power and pleasure. Taking over directions with the megaphone, he shouted down to a group of camera grips, standing at the four corners of the steel scaffold beneath him. 'OK boys, take it back now. *Mais doucement pour commencer* – and we'll see how it moves.' He moved forward then, taking up a spare viewfinder while Seitz settled down behind the Bell and Howell camera.

Slowly at first, the pace gradually rising to a walk, the whole steel tower moved back, away from the vast altar, along the centre of the plaza. And Craig, kneeling down, peering through the squared-off glass, suddenly, for the first time, saw the screen shape which would contain this immense vision in these long, high-angle tracking shots. The glass danced in his hand. But it was there all right – everything! – the receding altarpiece, giving way to the balcony, with its steps and pennant staffs came into view, and after that, the great columns and pavilions to either side, as the scaffold drew right back to the end of the plaza.

'Great! Incredible!' Craig stood up. 'What do you think, Johnny?'

Seitz left his camera. 'There's a wobble here and there—'

'Hell, Johnny – with the crowds and all the action going on everywhere, it won't notice!'

'Maybe. But we've not tried the lift yet—'

'We will, we *will*! And look!'

He grasped Johnny's shoulders then, pushing him round. Both men turned in a half-circle, so that they gazed out at a wide street beyond the walls of the temple plaza, the 'Sikket es-Sultan', the Royal Way, crossed by an ornate, covered bridge just in front of them, where men were working on a roof colonnade and a large window at the centre; the bridge leading down the far side to Akhenaten's Royal Palace, an equally vast, nearly completed building, again in glittering white plaster, but here set out with far less austere ornament – a pleasure dome of glinting copper roofs and fountains, palm-filled sunken gardens, lotus flowers, ornamental ponds, two filigreed harem quarters, the whole palace surrounded by walls topped with hanging gardens, fronting on the river bank for nearly two hundred yards.

'See?' Craig went on. 'From here, on the reverse track, when they come across for the inauguration at the temple, we can pick Akhenaten and Nefertiti up, with all the courtiers, moving over from the palace, stopping at the "Window of Appearances", scattering the flower petals, then follow them over into the temple plaza here, right the way through the crowds to the altar – all in one take!'

'Yeah . . .' Johnny was doubtful. 'Maybe. Have to be an early morning shot, though, else we're going to get the sun right at us, like now, reflecting off the river.'

'Jesus, Johnny – we can *do* it, though. The bloody scaffold works! And just look at the view we get from it, up here, over the rest of the city!'

The three men turned about, gazing out over the shimmering bright panorama, high up above the walls and palaces, the streets and houses – here, at the epicentre of this miraculous city risen from the desert, shading their eyes against the tremendous light.

'Jesus! . . .' Craig breathed.

Below them, beyond the palace wall, labourers unwrapped long palm trees, setting them up, boxing their roots in the watered sands of the royal gardens. To their left and right along the Royal Way, painters were decorating the villas of the nobles, setting hanging baskets of flowers above the peach- and lemon-coloured doors and lintels. Further down the street swarms of men made other finishing touches to this enormous complex of buildings.

Yet what was astonishing was not the height or size of the plaster and pasteboard city, but its exquisite detail, design, its perfect symmetry – above all its originality. Designed by Craig and Leo in a new style, it was quite unlike any earlier Egyptian architecture. Here were no heavy repetitions from the old and middle kingdoms at Memphis and Thebes – the bulbous Osirian columns, the monstrous Pharaonic statues of men and beasts, the effigies, obelisks and pylons commemorating all the hundreds of nightmare animal gods. The designs here, in line with Akhenaten's condemnation of the superstitious mummery at the old capital of Thebes down-river, and his departure for the brave new world at Amarna, quite lacked all the earlier doom and clutter. Reflecting his apostasy, his new faith in the one loving god of the sun, the shapes and decorations here had a startling naturalism, freshness, simplicity – straight lines replacing heavy curves, delicate laterals instead of overpowering verticals, the whole city couched in terms of domestic intimacy, an architecture quite new in the world, honouring this warm god, the expression of a free people.

Craig gazed over the palace to the river, watching the heavily-laden barges and feluccas endlessly ferrying across the water, carrying a vast assortment of supplies and props from the invisible wharf, the tented warehouses and railway siding, hidden from view behind an island in the centre of the river.

'And look!' he continued talking to the two men. 'Even from this height – can't see a thing of that messy camp over the water. The palm trees on the island hide it all.'

'Yes,' Leo Kuter warned him. 'And you look after all those damn palm trees! Three dollars a piece, all zee vay up-river!'

'And we can't really shoot the royal barges from the plaza here,' Johnny put in. 'Except as a wide-angle establishing shot – too far away for any detail.'

'I *told* you, Craig,' Leo added. 'Zat Royal Vay is too vide – almost double zee vidth of zee real zing, vhich was only fifty feet, othervise you'd have gotten closer to zee river from here.'

Craig took Leo by the shoulders. 'You know something, Leo – bin on my mind some time. I want you to play Bek, the royal architect. That goatee beard, it's ideal. Put you in one of those Egyptian kilts, knobbly knees and all. Come on, I'll take you to costume and make-up straightaway.'

Leo frowned, taking him quite seriously for a moment. Craig in this mood, he knew, was capable of any brazen conceit. 'I don't know, Craig—'

'Come on, you old kraut! Told you before we started – anything we do will be double the size of the real thing!' He clapped him on the back. *'Double!'* he shouted above the noise of hammering and fervid construction going on all round them.

Suddenly a gong sounded, the reverberation from some distant metal echoing through the midday heat. The men turned back to the great altar of the temple. To one side they saw the huge copper gong, decorated in the pattern of the sun's disc, a tiny figure aiming a second stroke at it with his drumstick.

It was the lunch break – and now the whole busy scene dissolved as everyone downed tools and a silence descended over the city, the last sounds of the gong echoing across the plaza, over the palace domes, setting some doves aloft, to soar into the sky over the dazzling river. And Craig trembled himself with excitement, standing atop the scaffold, lord of all creation, breathing in the smell of warm pine resin and plaster, sensing how, in a few days, all this half-completed artifice, this pasteboard act of faith, would suddenly bloom, become real, filled with the only reality he knew – a world filled with actors and cameras.

'"In Xanadu did Kubla Khan a stately pleasure-dome decree",' he intoned with mock gravity over the magic city shimmering against the arid hills beyond – this myth which he had made flesh. '"Where Alph the sacred river ran, through caverns measureless to man, down to a sun-less sea . . . So twice five miles of fertile ground, with walls and towers were girdled round – and gardens bright with sinuous rills, where blossomed many an incense-bearing tree" . . .'

'What poem is that?' Johnny Seitz asked. 'But I needn't ask,' he rushed on. 'You wrote it yourself.' Craig did not contradict him.

During the somnolent lunch break, Craig took his dozen assistant directors out for a briefing and tour of inspection through the unit's workshops, property stores, dressing and dining rooms – just north of the Amarna sets and hidden from them by a slight dip in the land and rows of imported palms.

And here they entered an even larger city, a vast tented encampment running away across the desert from wharves on the river bank – row upon row of large dun-coloured marquees, army bell tents and scores of smaller haphazard tents dotted about the land, bedouin black, accommodation for the hundreds of *fellahin* who, when the shooting started, would become costumed extras, citizens of Amarna.

The assistant directors, apart from Harry Elmer, the American first assistant and Mark Eldon the second unit director, were all French, Italian or Egyptian, young men taken up from Cairo, or brought over with the unit from the Victorine studios in Nice, where this Fox production had its European headquarters and where most of the interiors would be shot later.

One of Craig's assistants, a young Russian, Mikhail Ostrovosky, was the son of a Czarist exile, Prince Ostrovosky, who lived in a decrepit villa outside Nice – a youth, hardly twenty, who had pestered the company for days at the Victorine studios, asking to be taken on. Craig had finally agreed. Mikhail, or Mickey, had one obvious qualification which he had failed to mention in his earlier approaches. He spoke good Arabic, colloquial Egyptian indeed, for his parents had lived for several years after the Russian revolution in Alexandria, where his father, among many other business failures, had once been director of a now-bankrupt tobacco factory.

Craig had come to like Mickey. He was rather gauche, farouche even – tall and clumsy, like a vaudeville comic with his mobile indiarubber features, gangly arms and legs, his tufts of short damp hair. But, behind this physical awkwardness, Craig soon recognized a fine sensitivity and intelligence, an apparently limitless capacity for hard work and a vast enthusiasm and curiosity for every detailed aspect of the business. At this point, having worked with the unit for nearly two months, Craig had tacitly made him his personal assistant, his interpreter and immediate liaison officer with all the many Egyptians he had to deal with.

Now, in the great silence that had descended over the two cities, the group moved from tent to tent, Craig opening the flaps and ushering the assistants inside with a flourish, like a magician displaying the wherewithal for his tricks, delegating to each assistant his coming responsibilities.

'Costume tents – male, female . . . dressing rooms, ditto . . . stars, feature players, extras . . . Make-up and hairdressing . . . property tents – furniture, jewellery, chariots, horses, barges, armoury . . .'

Moving down the double row of tents he itemised their various concerns, broaching the mysteries, displaying these lavish riches: a dozen spindly chariots flaked in gold leaf, pennanted spears, sling shots, gilt bows and bamboo arrows – 'That's for you, Mario – the battle stuff, against the Theban priests when they come up-river to sack Amarna' – whole chests of sparkling costume jewellery, deep necklace collars, Pharaonic clasps, rings and bracelets, imitation gems and stones, cornelian, lapis lazuli, green and blue malachite, silver and gold. Craig dipped both hands in the studded jewel boxes, letting the glitter run between his fingers. 'Riches beyond the dreams of avarice! . . .' he intoned, and the assistants smiled.

Beyond, in further tents, lay other dazzling or bizarre collections: a stock of ancient Egyptian musical instruments, lyres, and reed flutes – 'For the blind harpists and choirs!' – and a tent next to it, set out as a contemporary band room with music stands and modern instruments – 'Mood music, from half the Cairo Opera orchestra . . .'

Finally, in a boatyard by the river, they saw the two royal barges. It was a stunning climax to their tour. The builders were at lunch and the boats stood empty, buttressed on their slipways, now transformed into delicately sloped vessels, running up to a peak fore and aft, with small gilded pavilions at the back, surmounted by flying sun pennants and ostrich feathers, the gunwales encrusted with decorative hieroglyphics and cartouches, sun discs, lotus flowers, lilies, enclosed in sweeping lines of gold, all set against a Nile-green background.

The assistants gazed on these recreated miracles, glittering in the light, gilded oars rampant, waiting to slip into the river. Craig climbed a step-ladder and stood by the prow, looking down on the men.

'So – here's our first sequence, I think, unless we do the temple inauguration first – Akhenaten and Nefertiti, with all their court, coming up-river from Thebes – from the two camera launches. And that's for you, Mickey – I want you dressed up on the first barge, with Laura and Clive, just beneath the pavilion there at the back, with the drummer marking time for the oarsmen – we'll work out the signals . . .'

Mickey nodded, happy at this honour, looking up at the director, while Craig gazed out on the river – dallying a moment at the end of the tour, delighted by all these paste and plaster props, these papier-mâché toys and baubles, a Merlin once more, turning dross to gold, a lavish spendthrift of the desert.

As they left the boatyard, a man in a heavy suit and homburg, who had been sweating along after the group throughout the trip, now finally closed on Craig, as he walked back alone to his own tent.

'Yes, yes – it's Mr Max Jacobson, our never-to-be-forgotten chief accountant!' Craig told him a little impatiently.

'Yes, Mr Williamson . . .' The man took off his hat as they entered Craig's private tent. 'I had a cable yesterday, from head office in New York – came down from Cairo on the overnight train, thought you should see it at once.' Opening an attaché case, he handed Craig the message. It was from the Fox financial controller. 'ADVISE YOU THAT PRE-PRODUCTION BUDGET NOW OVER-RUN BY ONE HUNDRED TWENTY-NINE THOU-SAND DOLLARS STOP BANK OF AMERICA CAIRO OFFICE CREDIT SUSPENDED PENDING YOUR GUARANTEE NO MORE UNAUTHORIZED PRE-PRODUCTION COSTS INCURRED.'

Craig smiled. Then he tore the cablegram up. 'Well, that's all right, isn't it? Pre-production is nearly over. First day of principal photography in a few days' time. No mention of suspending that budget, is there?'

Mr Jacobson shook his head. 'No. No – but that deposit can't be touched, of course, until you start—'

'And what do we have there – two million dollars?' Jacobson nodded. 'Well, since we're all still technically on pre-production – all you'll need is your train fare back to Cairo . . .' Craig put his hand in a pocket, jangling some piastres. 'Here you are.' He made to hand over some of the coins, then paused, looking at them. 'Trouble is, Jacobson, I don't know about you, but I can never get to trust this Egyptian money – every damn coin's got a hole in it . . .'

Mr Jacobson was unamused as Craig ushered him out. 'Cheer up, Jacobson!' he told him brightly. 'Just wait till we get our hands on the production budget proper – then we'll *really* start to spend money!' Jacobson was horrified, and Craig took pity on him. 'Listen, Max,' he went on. 'You look all done in. Use my steam launch back over the river – take a shower, get them to give you a proper meal, in my *wagon-lit* carriage on the siding. You know the one – the one with King Fuad's arms over the window.'

Craig's tent was sparsely luxurious, set out in the bedouin fashion. Apart from some office chairs and a large trestle table covered in set and costume designs, photographs and scripts, the furnishings were largely hanging silks and exotic cushions, red and cool lemon, with intricate Persian rugs layered over the desert floor and an ornate silver hookah in one corner. Beyond a crimson partition was a low broad bed and a brass-bound army travelling chest. There was an outer hallway, too, and now, as he took off his silk shirt, and his servant Abdullah, a tall Nubian with a red cummerbund, laid his lunch for him, there was a knock on the tent pole outside.

'What is it?' he said impatiently.

'Craig, can I talk with you a moment?'

Christ, he thought – it was Howard Southham, the dull but popular scenario writer, a man he had employed on and off, for over a year, preparing a final blood and thunder chariot racing photoplay to show to Fox and the rest of the big wheels in the company. He would have to humour him.

'Come right on in, Howard!'

'Hi, Craig.' The tall, white-haired man, prematurely middle-aged, looked worse than Jacobson – shaking, bleary-eyed, sweat coursing through a day's stubble on his chin. With Jacobson it had been the heat. But with Howard, Craig suspected, it was drink.

'Some lunch, Howard?'

'No. No thanks. I just came down on the train with Max Jacobson—'

'Great! How are things in Cairo? Brought all the final typed scenarios with you?'

'Yes. As final as we can get them.' He put one of them down on the table. 'The rest are outside.' He lit a cigarette with a trembling hand. 'Trouble is, Craig . . .' He paused, bending his neck to and fro as if to ease a headache. 'Say, Craig,' he went on, 'you don't happen to have a drink hereabouts, do you?'

Craig laughed good-humouredly. 'Wish I did, Howard. But as you can see.' He glanced around him. 'All strictly teetotal here, in the Arab manner! Not a drop this side of the river. I've given strict instructions all round. Got some sherbet, though. Or some iced lemon! Abdullah!' He called his servant. 'Get Mr Southham a glass of that bitter lemon, will you?'

Southham grimaced at the very thought before continuing. 'Trouble is, Craig, as I said before, in this final script, well, the material – apart from the big action scenes – it still doesn't seem quite to fit together, one scene with another. Gaps. Yes, well – just gaps – doesn't altogether make sense.'

Craig, picking at his simple lunch of unleavened bread, beans, sliced onions, tomatoes and anchovies, lifted an onion sliver to his mouth, delicately, pensively. Then he sprang to life. 'Hell, Howard, that's no worry. Lot of it'll have to be changed anyway – and it'll all fit on the day.' He picked up the new scenario on the table, flicking through the pages. There weren't many, barely eighty, for a picture that was planned to run out at eighteen reels, or nearly two and a half hours. 'No, you don't worry. You've done a great job, Howard. I hear you're moving on to Brenon's new picture back home – when do you leave?'

'Monday, from Port Said – Jesus, Craig, I wish to hell I could stay, but . . .'

God forbid, Craig thought. 'Me too, Howard. Never mind. You've done a great job. Great!' He stood up now, taking his hand. 'No, you couldn't have been more constructive or imaginative,' he lied convincingly. 'And I'll tell you what, Howard – don't bruit it around – but if you go over to my *wagon-lit* carriage, you know the one with the Khedival arms, in the siding, ask Mabrouk there, my waiter, tell him I said so: he's got a bottle of brandy – one I keep for emergencies. He'll give you a drink.'

Howard's face suddenly cleared with pleasure. 'Why, Craig—'

'No, no – you go ahead!' And Southham left, offering heart-felt thanks for this impending alcoholic cure in the barbarous desert.

'Jesus!' Craig muttered when he had gone. 'These goddamned rummy writers – nary a one of them ever sober.'

Then he picked up another scenario, hidden on the table, typed, but with very many more additional pages bound in, written in his own neat hand, a scenario nearly 150 pages long, running out at over thirty reels, with dozens of new scenes, which neither Southham nor William Fox, nor Winfield Sheehan nor anyone else, had ever seen. No, not even Laura.

He opened the scenario haphazardly then, reading the handwritten start of one of these new sequences: 'ESTABLISHING MID SHOT: INNER SANCTUM, THE ROYAL BEDCHAMBER: The Queen, half-asleep, without her wig, naked under the diaphanous covers, delicate toes emerging at the end of the bed, wakes to see Akhenaten moving towards her. She smiles dreamily as he bends down, his elongated deformed head and bulbous lips touching the end of the bed in a sort of famished obeisance, before, taking her toes in his hands, and gently massaging them, he starts to kiss them.'

Smiling briefly, Craig closed the scenario and returned to his austere meal.

Way down-river, a day out of Cairo, the teak-decked Nile paddle steamer *Omar Khayam* churned through the water, a contemporary royal barge, one of several belonging to King Fuad, which, along with the Khedival *wagons-lits*, he had lent to Craig and Hetty, as additional accommodation on the picture.

Hetty, in cool khaki bush shorts and shirt, lay out under the foredeck awning on a luxurious steamer chair, drowsily watching the passing scene on the river bank and the water – great lateen-sailed feluccas gliding by, pyramids and ancient temples, *fellahin* in the cotton fields, oxen forever turning *sakias*, irrigating the billiard-table green, the fields of berseem clover.

In her lap lay one of the new scenarios. Eddy Nolan had just brought her out a pot of tea and some of her special fruit cake. But she left it all untouched. Clive Brook, the British actor cast as Akhenaten, was in his cabin resting. She was alone on the great river, moving towards her destiny.

Of her own past now, in this sensuous dream time, she had no memory. Merging with the fabulous landscape, there was only an eternal present for her shaped in these ageless, ancient river monuments, sliding by her in the vivid turquoise light. She was no longer Henrietta Cordiner nor even the famous Laura Bowen. Already lost to those earlier personas, she had entered a pantheon of Gods, impervious to all mortal commonplaces, as Nefertiti – 'Lady of Grace, Sweet of Love, Mistress of the North and South, Queen of the Two Lands, Nefertiti, living for ever and ever . . .' She dozed off in the glaze of heat, already cradled in immemorial dreams. But the dream then was of more recent events.

Dermot – Dermot Cordiner – suddenly came into her suite at the Semiramis Hotel by the river where she had been staying in Cairo, dressed in his major's uniform; Dermot, somehow stationed in Egypt then – Dermot, not seen in years . . . They shook hands, formally, and he did not really smile, putting his cap down on the sofa. 'So, at last . . .' he said awkwardly. 'So many years.' He smoothed his crinkly straw hair, greying a little now. 'Who would have supposed it! Nefertiti! Thought I'd call round – regiment's quartered just next door at the Kasr el Nil barracks. All right, I hope?'

And Hetty wanted to speak in the dream, but found she could not, so that Dermot ran on, in his staccato. 'You used to write, of course. But it's been so long now, since we heard anything. Seen some of your pictures, now and then – even here in Cairo!' But still she could not speak in return, trying desperately to voice her apologies, her guilt. It was torture. 'Hetty?' He came nearer then, wondering at her silence. 'Hetty – why didn't you write? You still have a family, after all. Me and Aunt Emily and Mortimer. And Léonie and Robert, of course – they're married now you know! . . .'

On the foredeck of the steamer, Hetty woke with a start. *Married*? Léa and Robert married? 'Oh, my God,' she said, blinking in the strong light. 'What a nightmare!' But then, gathering herself, she had a worse shock still. The dream had simply been a slight variation of the reality. Dermot had indeed called on her at the Semiramis, and almost everything in her nightmare then – the words, the actions – all had happened in fact a few days before.

She picked up the cooling pot of tea, fiddled with the fruit cake, lit a cigarette, trying again to obliterate everything in her earlier life, the memory of this meeting two days before in Cairo, dispel all her demons once more. Someone moved in the grand saloon behind her. The exotic songbirds in the royal aviary trilled and called. She steadied herself as she drew on the cigarette.

It was all right, she thought then, running her hand along the richly inlaid marquetry of the steamer chair, looking about at the other wonderfully crafted riches and luxuries which surrounded her. Here she was, in the only reality she need consider, regally indifferent, quite insulated from all such nightmares, a woman with no past dooms or connections. Now she remembered her actual words at the meeting in the Semiramis Hotel, her gracious but distant response to Dermot. 'How nice that you should have called . . . But I no longer have any connections in Ireland . . . Robert and Léonie married? How suitable!'

At the memory of these last words, she bunched her fingers and cracked her hands violently on the arm of her chair, stood up and walked about the deck, angry and frustrated. Her stamping footsteps disturbed the after-noon calm, reverberating about the steamer.

Below deck, in a provision hold to the rear of the boat, the snakes stirred, locked in several glass-sided boxes, their keeper nearby, from the royal zoo in Cairo. The reptiles, hired for certain scenes in the picture, had been put on board at the last moment, without Hetty's knowl-edge. They, too, like Hetty – these puff adders and pit vipers – sought some destiny in the paradise of Amarna far up-river.

Robert and Léonie had married earlier that year in Paris at the American church on the Quai d'Orsay, with some thirty guests entertained for lunch afterwards at the Plaza-Athénée Hotel across the river. Robert now had a more secure position as a reporter on the *Herald Tribune* in their main printing office next to Les Halles, while Léonie had joined the Paris Opéra, promoted from the chorus and taking on some small feature roles, keen to succeed there, but more anxious still to make a good marriage with Robert.

For, although she had no qualms or hesitations in her loving there, she feared something in her soul: not so much Hetty, or the memory of Hetty, for there was still that from time to time – but more a resurgence of that kind of love. For sometimes, quite out of the blue, she found herself attracted by other women, by girls in the Opéra chorus or by others – sometimes just seen passing in the street or glimpsed at a café table. She had only to look at such women, and they at her – even briefly, noting a particular fall of hair, a slant of eye, some wayward design in the lips or nose – for a sudden distant echo of that sort of passion to spring from her heart, un-stoppable. She knew how easily she could fall for such women, though it would not take away one iota of her love for Robert, might, indeed, increase it; but she dared not talk to him about, or succumb to, it.

Robert for his part had no inkling of all this. Léonie had got Hetty out of her system; that he knew. And so, he assumed, all that kind of love had died in her as well. It never crossed his mind that Léonie's fervour and devotion towards him, though entirely genuine, was increased by this need to blot out another part of her nature. So Léonie devoured him now, within all the appropriate bonds of marriage, in part to dam up other less appropriate hungers.

They rented a small two-roomed apartment on the left bank, six floors up, on the narrow rue Saint-André-des-Arts, next to the old hotel there, looking out on the rooftops, a crazy chiaroscuro of drunken chimneys, gut-ters, louvred shutters, balconies and geranium pots. Money was short and they were both hard at work. But

Ben Straus insisted they take a proper honeymoon, when they were free to do so, later that year.

'Now, what would you most like to see, to do, in all the world? Go on! Anything! – part of my wedding present to you. May never have the chance again!'

'Oh, I don't know . . .' Léonie smiled. Then it suddenly struck her – they were soon to start rehearsals for *Aida* at the Opéra. 'Egypt!' she said. 'All those temples and pyramids and things – up the Nile in a steamer!'

Her father readily agreed. 'And so you shall – nothing easier!'

Frances, siding with de Valera and the other republicans in their refusal to accept Michael Collins' partition treaty with the British, had survived the ensuing vicious civil war in Ireland largely by dint of spending much of the time in and out of jail, successively sentenced by the emerging Free State government, first under Collins and subsequently, after his assassination, headed by the new President, William Cosgrave.

Finally released, her friends and supporters defeated, at the end of a murderous internecine struggle, Frances had no part to play at all in the new government. She and the other republicans, beaten at arms and discredited politically, returned to a shadow life in the country, under what rapidly became a staid and cautious regime that had no use whatsoever for any of their old republican fire.

De Valera bided his time, repairing old allegiances, mustering new support, generally scheming for eventual power in the land. But Frances, far less politically adept and without de Valera's executive skills and devious acumen, twiddled her thumbs in the ugly little pebble-dash bungalow off Rathgar Road in the Dublin suburbs. She took up good works on behalf of republican ex-prisoners and their families, and the Dublin poor. The bungalow became a clearing and meeting house for these charitable activities, filled with vagabond old suits, shirts, hats and boots. The rooms smelt of damp and stray cats, which she took on in abundance to share her essentially lonely existence.

Emaciated, suffering from intermittent bronchitis, arthritis and other ills consequent on her long and various imprisonments, all her earlier fires, in mind and body, had burned low. She was sustained none the less by her Catholic faith, by a continuing dream of a united Ireland, by the respectful attentions of old and new republican friends and by the ever-increasing admiration of the Dublin indigent – to whom, in a small Ford motor, she delivered sacks of coal at their impoverished tenements, and for whom she rapidly took on all the lineaments of a martyr and saint.

This was precisely the role she had always subconsciously sought, ever since the Prince of Wales had betrayed her, and she played it now with a pale, ethereal vigour, in a submissive yet somehow self-righteous manner, an act which sustained her in a premature old age, for she was still barely fifty. The faith became for her a professional stage on which she elaborated her already-fervent amateur devotions, sometimes now to the point of mania – especially favouring the Virgin, with whom she more and more identified in a flagrant excess of Mariolatry.

In these obsessive activities, spiritual and temporal, she, like Hetty, quite lost sight of her own personal and familial past. Blindly dedicated to God's work – just as her daughter was to the pursuit of false gods – the memory of Hetty rarely clouded Frances's mind. Nor, in any immediate way, did she concern herself with Summer Hill, never visiting the place – though Mortimer, still believing in some possible future there, had prevailed upon her not to sell it, at least, for some nunnery or convent, as had been her intention. Some of the estate she was forced to sell to the new Land Commission, but the house lingered on, under Mortimer's stewardship and Pat Kennedy's more immediate care, with only Aunt Emily and a few maids still living there.

Sun and winter, and long Irish damp, took their toll, together with gathering ivy, lichen, elder. So that when curious village children in summer, pushing through the rampant briars and ragwort of the demesne, saw the house on the hill, it appeared as a green-girt ruin, an enchanted castle, which they dared not approach further; for inside lay no sleeping princess, they knew, only an ugly old witch.

Aunt Emily, in truth, was no such thing, still bright and spry in her mid-sixties, with a remnant of fine looks, she and Pat Kennedy got along famously alone together: she at her illuminated diaries, drawings and water-colours, maintaining every continuity there; Pat ministering to her few needs, taking her out in the governess cart through the lush valley to some choice spot, where she would set up her easel, or sometimes to Stallard's new cinema palace in Kilkenny to watch one of Hetty's pictures when they came to town. Aunt Emily had not forgotten Hetty – had forgotten nothing, by still com-memorating everything.

Pat, who, after the Black and Tan depredations in the house, had retired to the gate lodge on the river drive, now returned to Summer Hill, taking perforce, and for the first time, a room in the main Georgian building. He did so somewhat hesitantly, feeling uneasy in the grand guest room, not far from the great staircase.

He need not have worried about this occupation. A letter arrived for him that autumn from Frances in Dublin. 'I believe,' she wrote, 'that you, as an old Repub-lican and companion-in-arms with me, should now take over Summer Hill on a formal basis – a house which I no longer can, nor care to, administer, but which you do so most competently at the moment. Therefore I intend making over the house and what is left of the land to you, as a legal bequest, as of the first of next month. Of course, you have no family at the moment. But perhaps, with this gift, where you could farm what is left of the estate, you may now consider a marriage? I should so like to think of you and your descendants, people of the real Ireland and not the British usurper, making use of the place . . .'

Frances, with a local solicitor in Rathmines, had quite by-passed Mortimer in the drawing-up and signature of this new deed, one which now revoked her earlier testament, still retained in Mortimer's office, in which she had left Summer Hill to Hetty. Nor did she inform Mortimer of her decision. That task was left to Pat Kennedy himself, on Mortimer's next visit to Summer Hill, when Pat showed him Frances's letter. Mortimer, on reading it, was just as astonished as Pat had been. More, since he wished to avoid any immediate bluntness, he was forced into an unaccustomed speechlessness – since it was obvious that Pat, with no apparent farming abilities, could never in any case keep on such a vast place, and would obviously sell the house, at least, at the first opportunity. When this thought, in the butler's subsequent words, was quite openly rebutted, Mortimer was even more astonished.

'Well, Pat,' he had said to him, 'she has rather put a millstone round your neck . . .'

"Oh, I don't know, sir,' Pat had replied, gazing greedily out over the valley from the butler's pantry window. 'There's more than enough land left about the place to make a fair living out of it . . .'

Mortimer, for once, had misread the man – discounting, in this old house servant, the much older Gaelic land hunger. Still, in this instance, he could not be so stupid. 'But the house, Pat, it's far too big to maintain on just the income from what's left of the land.'

Pat had considered this point, but only for a moment. 'Ah, well,' he said nonchalantly, 'sure there'd be no income from the house anyway. That could go.'

Mortimer saw then the depths of Frances's insane enmity – against her family, her class, her past, against the disaster she and the old Prince had contrived in the shape of Hetty. She would take revenge on all these things through the instrument of her servant who, she must know, would more certainly and completely destroy the place than even the most insensitive religious institution. In Pat's hands, unmarried and likely to remain so, the great house would be guaranteed to end with him, sold to some timber merchant, with the roof off within a year. It was sheer wilful malignity.

When Craig had finally gathered together all the major figures in his cast at the remote bend in the river – far from Cairo and further still from the various Fox headquarters in Nice, New York and Hollywood – he felt safe to hint, at least, at some of the real business in his script. He had already talked to the other principal actors, those engaged to play General Mai, Akhenaten's army commander, Ramose the Grand Vizier, Panhesy the High Priest at the Temple, Huya, major-domo to Queen Tiye, and the devious courtier Ay, whose wife was Nefertiti's royal nurse. Now he spoke to the three stars – Hetty, Clive Brook and Anna Barani, the Italian-American actress who was to play Queen Tiye, mother of Akhenaten – in the great royal saloon aboard the *Omar Khayam* the evening before the first day's shooting.

'What we have to remember, because it's at the heart of the story,' he told Hetty and Clive, 'is that yours is an obsessive, unequal relationship. It starts with love all right, as children together in Thebes and afterwards in

Amarna. But it soon gets into every sort of disaster. You get to hate each other! . . .'

Craig gave his grim résumé light-heartedly. But Clive Brook, flicking through the pages of his own scenario, was puzzled. 'I don't see . . . much of that here, Craig?'

'No, that's only a basic scenario, Clive.'

Clive was equally relaxed, even joky, in return. 'Goodness me, Craig, I know Akhenaten's deformed, epileptic and so on – weak and sickly as a child. But I'd understood that when he takes up with Nefertiti, when he strikes out on his own up to Amarna and becomes full Pharaoh, well, I thought things were really better for him.'

'No. Though it seems so initially. Fact is, people like that, there's never really any final improvement. They're fated from the beginning. And certainly that's the case here, because you see . . .' He turned to Anna Barani. 'You see Akhenaten never really gets out of the grip of his mother, Queen Tiye. You see how she even comes up-river after them, from Thebes, takes another palace in Amarna, just down the road from them.' Craig consulted his own personal scenario again. 'Yes . . . It's one of those fatal three-cornered relationships, Akhenaten caught in his mother's apron strings – and he doesn't *want* to get away. So, realizing his incapabilities, he takes it out on his wife: punishing Nefertiti in a way he'd like to punish his mother, but doesn't dare.'

'So I get the st-st-stick?' Hetty asked brightly. 'That's not really in the scenario either.'

'That's about the size of it!' Craig leant forward, enthusiastic now. 'But there's more to it because, after all, you put up with it, and no one does that unless they somehow *like* it, see?'

'Not really.'

'Nefertiti *enjoys* the pain,' he told her sweetly. 'As I said, it's a three-cornered deal, which never works, always fatal, a cat's cradle, all held together by their vices.'

'And me?' enquired Anna. 'My vice?'

'*Power*, Anna!' He stood up, lit a cigarette, looking out on the violet light of the river, then turned to her. 'Because you're the real power, literally, behind the throne. That's why you follow the two up-river from the old court at Thebes – even before your own husband, Amenhopis III, dies. And when he does and Akhenaten becomes full Pharaoh at Amarna, it's you who try to pull the strings – it's what you've planned all along, from the very beginning, in marrying them off as children, thinking Nefertiti's just a beautiful doll, a Syrian princess of no apparent account. You're the *dea ex machina* . . .'

'God's sake, Craig, speak English!' Hetty interjected. But Anna understood him well enough. 'That's not in the photoplay,' she said.

Craig took no notice. 'Yes, Anna – you're the person that makes everything happen. But what you don't bargain for is Nefertiti as a grown woman, her own tough actions – and reactions. She accepts the punishment from Akhenaten, driven into all sorts of impossible corners by him. But eventually the worm turns – she takes up with Akhenaten's young half-brother Tutankhamun and has her revenge on her husband—'

'Yes, that's in the scenario,' Hetty interrupted again brightly. 'When Akhenaten becomes fre-fre-friendly with his other half-brother Smenkahare – and Nefertiti sets the snakes on him. But what I don't see, Craig, is why she doesn't do away wi-with Queen Tiye instead. *She*'s caused all the trouble.'

It was a good question – and the answer certainly was not in the script. 'Simple,' Craig replied with a note of triumph. 'Akhenaten falls in *love* with his half-brother, more than his mother. So Nefertiti has to kill what he loves most.'

They were all puzzled at this. Hetty finally said, 'I don't quite get it – I thought this whole story was about a w-w-wonderful new religion up-river, doing away with all the old false gods, giving the people real love and hope when everything gets better. Instead, well, with all these de-de-deviants – it's like the Ship Café back in Hollywood on a bad night.'

'But that's the whole point of the story – exactly!' Craig was patient now, quiet. 'How we fool ourselves – because every god is false. And what matters is the truth about ourselves and the fact that we always try and hide this.'

'What – all this punishment, incest, death and sex?' Clive enquired, no longer so lighthearted.

'Well, of course – that's what we hide most! And, unless we first have an insight into people's sexual loves and hates and conflicts, there's no chance an audience can get to make sense of all the otherwise apparently crazy actions in the story. Do you see?'

They did not. But Craig was in charge. He must know what he was doing. They were all somewhat in awe of him. They had to be. *Nefertiti* looked like being the biggest, the most expensive picture ever made – bigger than *Intolerance*, bigger than *Ben Hur*.

Clive and Anna withheld any further doubts they had about this new scenario, anxious not to expose what really worried them then, which was their ability to enact some of these perverse rites. But Hetty, who found these new ideas of Craig's interesting, even titillating, wanted to know more. 'Was all this in the history books, Craig? – these incestuous g-goings on, Akhenaten being a pansy and taking up with his half-brother, Nefertiti throwing him over then and going for the other half-brother?'

Craig laughed. 'Why, of course! And not just in the history books. You can see it all on the wall paintings, the hieroglyphics, in the royal tombs.'

Craig omitted to point out that these were his own

interpretations of the lives of the three royal personages, based on much conflicting interpretations of the wall paintings which, at best, could only be made to suggest the possibility of such decadent relationships. However, given the picture he wanted to present of an ideal love and faith destroyed in Akhenaten's court by ruthless power struggles and by every sort of sexual domination and perversity, he had grasped at any hint of the bizarre or the unusual in those royal cartouches that might confirm his theme, which was really one of hate, not of love.

But he was equally keen not to alarm his cast with any over-emphasis of these depravities, so he continued now in lighter vein. 'And anyway our story is mild by comparison with the real thing. Why, many of the Pharaohs married their full sisters, even their daughters, and had children by them. So we're only touching the surface of what really went on in those days!'

Hetty felt a twinge of disappointment. So much did she trust Craig's inspirations and abilities, so entirely had she come to identify with what she already knew of Nefertiti, that she longed to discover and impersonate these further and ultimate truths of this mysterious, provocative woman, no matter how unsavoury they were.

Impersonate these ultimate truths? Why, no, she thought – *experience*, entirely submerge herself in them. That was the secret – as it had been in all her earlier successes – that she did not act her parts, for she had hardly the formal training or ability, but *lived* them, whatever the emotional challenge or cost. And in this instance she knew intuitively, as Craig had, that the part had been made for her: Nefertiti's steel-tempered will to power, her wily manoeuvrings, above all her skill in deceiving herself and betraying her friends while all the time behaving as the innocent victim – these were some of Hetty's own natural qualities. She would thus, inevitably and easily, be living the part.

What Hetty did not know, since she had seen little of Craig's private scenario, were the other parts in Nefertiti's character, which Craig had contrived for the Queen: the vicious depths she was prepared to sink to in pursuit of her aims, the hatred, misery and degradation she would incur and propagate. And Hetty, in Craig's intent, would not simply impersonate these horrors either. He would see to it that she experienced them in reality as well.

It was blue dark and moonlit with a sharp desert chill at four o'clock next morning. An hour later the sun god would rise over the forbidding mountains to the east, touching his city with the first shafts of pellucid lemon-yellow light. But already, in the tented camp, things were astir for the first day of principal photography – hundreds of shadowy figures moving to and fro by the light of brush fires, hurricane lamps and, in the recreated city of Amarna, under the glare of great Kleig lights set against silver reflectors, supplied from the two mobile generators at the railway siding across the river.

Already, in the previous days, Craig and the second unit director, with crowds of builders and carpenters masquerading as costumed extras, had filmed the final construction of the fabulous city. Now the gangs of property men, costumiers and all the other myriad technicians made ready for the first sequence with the stars and hundreds of extras – the triumphal entry of the royal party, carried in gilded, ostrich-feathered palanquins, into the great temple of Aten to dedicate the shrine. They would move from the palace, over the bridge, stopping at the Window of Appearances, then on across the vast columned plaza, before arriving at the holy of holies, mounting the steps below the great altar to the inner sanctum.

The sequence, they had calculated, would last up to eight minutes in real time – and the cameras, tracking back on top of the steel derrick, would follow every bit of the action. Johnny Seitz was on the derrick at that moment ready to start rehearsals and filming as soon as possible after first light, for this was the sequence which would have to be completed before the sun approached its meridian. Two Bell and Howell cameras, with extended magazines, had been set on top of the derrick, with a third set on the elevator, fronting on to the plaza where, at the start of the tracking movement, the elevator would sink slowly – over the crowds, right down above the heads of the royal party, as they approached the high altar. Half a dozen other cameras, together with a number of small handheld Eyemos, were dotted about the palace, the bridge, the Royal Way, hidden behind columns and pavilions in the plaza, ready to pick up incidental crowd shots.

Assistant directors ran to and fro in the flare-lit shadows of the tented camp to the north, from the costume marquees where the hundreds of *fellahin* were being dressed, to the dressing tents of the stars and featured players, to the armoury and chariot tents, to the main production office by the wharf on the river, where Winfield Sheehan himself, as Fox's production chief, had arrived from New York the previous day to see the picture started.

Mickey Ostrovosky, with a dozen Egyptian prop men, was in charge of seeing to the fresh flowers that morning. They had arrived in hundreds of water buckets, packed in damp moss, a whole wagon-load, on the train from Cairo the previous day – lotus flowers, syringa, elaborate wreaths of jasmine and bougainvillaea, great bunches of gladioli and orchids which would decorate the streets of Amarna and hang in clustered baskets in the temple plaza and above the shrine. And now, as Mickey moved through the streets with his men in the cool desert night, arranging the fragrant bunches above doorways, littering the streets with petals, the air took on a wonderful sweetness, the scent of orange blossom seeping everywhere through the darkness.

Other assistants busied themselves, setting high-backed, gilt-embossed ebony thrones by the altar or supervising the flowing ostrich plumes for the palanquins. The whole river bank, for nearly half a mile, was alive with flickering light, yellow tinder fires and brilliant piercing carbon arcs, the shadows of some strange warrior people, preparing these magic weapons – lights, cameras, props – as if on a night before battle. Yet despite the fact that upwards of a thousand people were on the move that morning, there was a feeling of restraint and order under the waning moon.

But beneath this, and especially among the professional technicians, there was an air of tense, repressed excitement, even fear. They had hitched themselves not to a star here but to some quite unknown comet. A production of this size, so far from Hollywood or any other studios, had never been attempted before. *Ben Hur* had come nearest to it, the previous year in Rome, and that had ended in all sorts of disaster. Now their professional lives were largely in the hands of one man and one woman, sitting then at the centre of this vast web of activity, in Laura Bowen's dressing tent.

Hetty at last faced the moment she dreaded, which she had postponed until these final hours – when all her fine dark curls would be cut to the skull, that being the strict fashion of the time, and replaced in her day-to-day wear by one of Nefertiti's magnificent head-dresses or by a variety of tightly-coiled, shoulder-length wigs. Hetty saw the pairs of scissors laid out on the dressing table in front of her, like instruments of torture. She began to sweat in the chill night air, seeing the scissors rise. She closed her eyes.

The French hairdresser, a Madame Dolores from the studios in Nice, with her assistant, snipped away expertly. Craig stood beside Hetty, watching the big illuminated mirror, Hetty sitting there mute and still, eyes firmly shut. It was just after four in the morning. Craig held his breath.

Hetty, at the end of the hair-cut, with just a dark even stubble erect over her scalp, looked astonishing. She had changed utterly, but was equally striking. She was *gamine*, boyish, looking far younger, fifteen and not twenty-five. Her great oval blue eyes seemed far more prominent; her cheeks more hollow – her delicately shaped ears displaying elfin points, her whole face nude. And yet, despite this brutal cropping, there was no real air of the urchin. What before, with her rich raven curls, had been warm yet formal was now cold and barren but intensely regal.

She opened her eyes, trembling, looking at herself in the mirror. 'Wonderful!' Craig said to her, before she had a chance to speak, brushing his lips over her wounded scalp. 'I'll leave the dressers and make-up to complete the picture. See you in an hour.' Then he bent down, whispering, 'You were born for her. Remember, I told you?' She nodded, and he kissed her again before leaving. But he turned at the tent flap. 'Hey! – don't forget the scent!' he called back and she nodded once more.

Make-up came first with Chuck Stonor, all the way out from Hollywood with his myriad powders, lotions, unguents, lipsticks and eye-liners, an hour's work of infinite care – painting her eyelids with green shadow, her lips a soft raspberry, accentuating her eyebrows with kohl, her cheeks with rouge, dabbing her face and neck with a Leichner apricot powder.

The jeweller had her say then, with pendant amethyst earrings tipped with gold sun discs, ivory bracelets, a girdle and stomacher of gold plaques in the shape of tiny fish, and then the *pièce de résistance*, a magnificent deep-collared necklace, row upon row of lapis lazuli and red cornelian beads held against a filigree of gold wire, ending in a crescent just above her breasts.

Afterwards, standing at a full-length mirror, with the portrait bust of Nefertiti as a model next to it, the dresser put on her the royal gown over a thin, skin-toned elastic body stocking – material in the finest transparent linen, the colour of ripe wheat, loosely pleated over the bodice, gathered under the breasts with the girdle, then running down to her ankles, embroidered with two long panels, threads of pure gold and silver, intertwining every six inches, forming sun-bursts.

Finally the wardrobe mistress took up the magnificent headdress, eighteen inches high, tilted and flared, inset with hundreds of gold rosettes and green malachite stones, ribbed in bands of red and blue, with the royal uraeus, the sacred serpent, mounted at the brow – and placed it carefully on her shaven head.

The effect was stunning. Flaring out like a fan high above her, the headdress dropped in a sheer, unbroken line, narrowing in an inverted triangle, dead straight across her temples, her slanting cheeks, to the perfect base point of her chin.

Hetty smiled faintly as she looked at herself, comparing the vision in the mirror with the bust of Nefertiti next to it. But the others could only look at Hetty, even more striking than the wonderful bust, vividly alive, royal and beautiful beyond all imagining.

Back at her dressing table Hetty picked up the little cut-glass bottle of scent which Craig had given her in Nice. 'Nefertiti'. He'd had it specially created for her at a factory up in the hills near Grasse, asking her not to use it until the first day's filming. 'But the camera won't smell it!' she had told him. 'No, and it won't capture any of the colours in your make-up or costume – or see much of your bare scalp either. But that's not the point! *You'll* smell it, *you'll* feel the stubble, see the colours. And that's what I want – that you feel and see and smell everything, experience *everything*, just as Nefertiti herself would have done, no matter what the cost or trouble.'

She opened the bottle now, dabbing the sun-gold liquid on her wrist, bringing it to her nose. Expecting something rich, mysterious and musky, the perfume surprised her. It was a young girl's scent, delicately fresh: an initial strain of verbena, she thought, but cut with something tart, a hint of lemon – and then, at the back of her nose as she inhaled, a waft of subtle violet . . . It reminded her of something she could not quite place. What was it?

Then it came to her, a swirl of happy memories and pleasures out of the past, that same violet smell, regained now from the little bottle. Of course, it was Léonie's perfume, a scent she had always used, years before, warmed through nights in bed together, spreading from one body to another, shared indivisibly by morning.

Hetty's face, as if the bottle had released an evil genie, clouded at the memory of these old intimacies, thoughts of Léonie again, intruding once more, when for so long she had so successfully repressed them. And now she was forced to remember Dermot's words in the Semiramis Hotel once more, how Léonie and Robert had married. And the outrage of this finally struck home to her then and she was bitterly angry. 'I will wait for you . . .' Léonie had written in her last letter. Well, she hadn't. She had married Robert, and by that act had really betrayed her – their love, their schooldays, their long adolescence, their promises together. She had, as Hetty conveniently remembered it, largely forgiven Léonie for deserting her in going to Paris to see her mother that time. But this was unforgivable, this marriage – a slap in the face – because it undermined her whole earlier life, took the comfort of Léonie finally away from her, set at nought her own dominance over her.

It never crossed Hetty's mind, even at this late stage, that she, not Léonie, was responsible for the real desertion. For, just like Craig in his obsessive fantasies made flesh, she had come, not to lie about her earlier life and behaviour, but simply to deny all knowledge of it, to invent instead a succession of overlaid, alternative lives, false lives, then and now, which she lived and believed in as gospel.

The others noticed Hetty's expression of curdled disapproval. The dresser asked anxiously, 'Is it – is it not all right?'

'No. No, nothing's wrong.' Then she dismissed them curtly. 'Until I'm called, I'd like to be alone.'

When they left, Hetty gazed in the mirror, turning her head, the gleaming gold rosettes in the headdress winking in the bright light. 'I will – wait – for – you . . .' she said, spacing the words out viciously. Then she started to bunch her fingers, cracking the joints. Finally, her face now a mask of rancorous spite, she muttered the words: 'Nefertiti, great in favour, lady of grace, sweet of love, mistress of the North and South, Queen of the Two Lands, all p-p-powerful, l-living for ever and ever . . .'

These last stammered tones were far from suited to such regal testimony. But then they were not meant as such. Hetty, all her earlier fears and uncertainties returned, was voicing a royally vindictive curse. At this moment, just as she was about to set the final seal of power and success on her life, the ghost of Léonie had risen before her, come to taunt and plague her. And now that Léonie's implacable spirit had been so revived in this perfume about her body, Hetty could no longer ignore or repress it. Léonie, she realized, embedded thus in her very flesh, would be a constant reproach to her from then on, mocking her in this happy marriage with Robert.

That was the worst thought of all – how those two, over whom for so long she had held sway, who had both loved her as she well knew, had now quite thrown her over. Hetty longed for some royal sorcery then that would annihilate space and allow her to confront Léonie with her treachery – longed somehow to revenge herself on her.

A few hours later, held aloft in the gilded palanquin, with its canopy of ostrich feathers and translucent alabaster headboard of the sun's disc, Hetty crossed the bridge with Akhenaten, and three of their daughters, stopping at the Window of Appearances; where she and the Pharaoh, alighting, took handfuls of lotus petals from huge faience vases, scattering them over the exultant crowd beneath them.

Mickey, in charge of the extras on the Royal Way at that point and dressed as one of them, stood immediately beneath Hetty, gazing up at her, apparently quite naked beneath the fine cotton gown, every curve in her figure visible and provocative behind the transparent material – the ultimate in cool suavity, arctic-blue eyes in the blazing light, bamboo-thin in wind-drifting voile, an ice maiden in these voluptuous desert airs.

'Nefertiti' – 'The beautiful woman has come'. How exactly she translated her name, Mickey thought – and how he desired her! But her face that morning more than ever confirmed the distance between them, this remote, untouchable woman, this undoubted Queen. Her expresson was more than usually set, he noticed – a faraway smile, circumspect, dilatory, almost blind somehow.

What a fine actress, he thought! – already, in this first sequence, completely living the part, scheming, thinking of the other future machinations in the plot, how she would soon come to manipulate Akhenaten and eventually destroy him.

Looking up at her face then, Mickey entirely believed in the reality of her emotion, her malign instincts and intents – convinced, too, by the veracity of everything he saw before him, the glorious royal panorama on the bridge, the costumed Egyptians milling about, the whole gilt-drenched scene thrillingly alive in the dazzling sunlight, as the petals rained about him, trodden underfoot, the perfume rising. And it seemed to him then, in the thronging excitement, that all of them, by some unexplained magic, had, indeed, returned in time three thousand years.

Then, as the royal party moved on, Mickey turned and saw the great steel camera derrick in the plaza starting to move, Johnny Seitz on top of it, his cap back to front. And he realized how he was caught, not in truth, but in an immense fantasy, a charade of Hollywood props and costumes, a dream of plaster and papier-mâché, all of it skin-deep, insubstantial as the frail zephyr breeze that drifted in from the desert, fluttering the sun-disc pennants. The whole thing was a vast conceit, a glittering contrivance, an offering, not to Aten the Sun God, but to the celluloid recording angel. And this thought, that one could dispense with corrupt reality and recreate the world in one's own image through the incorruption of make-believe, excited him even more.

A month later, far across the Mediterranean in a lurid sunset, the French Messageries Maritimes liner, the *Provençal*, left Marseilles bound for Naples, Port Said and the Far East. Robert and Léonie stood by the after-deck rail watching the coast slip away in the indigo twilight. It had been freezing the day before in Paris that January and almost as cold for most of the train journey down. But now, in this first hint of moist southern warmth rising from the sea, propelled by a dry wind from Africa, they could take off their heavy topcoats for the first time, and breathe a wonderful softness in the air.

'Naples, Port Said, Bombay,' Léonie said. 'We could go all the way to Indo-China!'

'Egypt'll be enough . . .'

'It'll be *everything*!' She hugged him, watching a great lone sea bird hovering above the stern, gliding along, following them, like a lost spirit. Then she shivered involuntarily, as if someone had just walked over her tomb.

6

'Action!'

Craig sat intently behind the lights and camera on a moored raft, on the ornamental lake behind the walls of the royal palace, its water filled with blue lotus flowers and papyrus. Hetty, in a short, tightly-curled wig and another revealing day gown, sat in the bows of a small gilded boat with Clive Brook in the stern.

It was one of Craig's new scenes, set some few years on in his version of the story, when Nefertiti continually taunts her weak and pleasure-loving husband – already, with his harems, epilepsy, drinking and feasting, prematurely aged, going to fat; the elongated skull, sensuously full lips, the deep-set shadowed eyes and generally feminine air turning him into a freak. Akhenaten started to paddle the craft past the camera.

'Right!' Craig went on talking as the camera turned. 'Now, as he paddles, Laura, you're fiddling with that papyrus leaf – yes, that's it – now you reach forward with it, start tickling him – the lips, the chin, go on! – you're provoking, *annoying* him, not playing with him, for Christ's sake! It's *malicious* and he can't prevent you –

yes, that's right, Clive! Keep both hands on the paddle – then you try unsuccessfully to swat the papyrus away.'

The little boat drifted past them, Hetty tickling, taunting the lugubrious figure with unconcealed joy. It passed out of shot.

'OK, cut!' Craig yelled. 'And print it.' He was working fast on this establishing shot, anxious to move on to the closer shots with them in the boat, when he could introduce some real venom into the proceedings.

'Right!' He talked almost aggressively to the two stars beside the lake, while the technicians prepared the next set-up, in which the little boat, tied against the camera raft, would be propelled across the water for the close shots. 'Now we have your title, Laura,' he went on, consulting his scenario. '"You make so much of your new faith, Akhenaten – a whole city built in honour of the sun – yet you've forgotten your old simple pleasures with me, how we used to swim." OK, that's the title here. So we'll be facing you in the bows, Laura, saying this, continuing to annoy him with the papyrus before you provoke him even more, by jumping in the water, swimming away. Of course, what you're maybe hoping here, knowing he can't swim any more, is that he'll jump into the water after you and drown. Well, he does just that – but doesn't drown. We just see you struggling in the water here – the rest of the sequence, the underwater stuff, is for the tank back in Nice. OK?'

'What about the wigs and make-up – in the water?' Clive asked.

'Hell, they'll come off, won't they?' Craig was impatient. 'It's a real struggle. You're all keyed up after that teasing with the papyrus – you know very well she's provoking you, taunting you, questioning your masculinity – so you're blind with rage, with no thought that you can't swim any more – and you *go* for her!' Craig smiled for the first time, happy in the setting-out of this impending confrontation. 'It's a real barney out there in the lake. Jesus, Clive! – this is the vital point, when you *realize* how much you hate her, yet know you can't do without her!'

Clive's sour expression, as he glanced at Hetty, confirmed all this hatred in reality. Having been so tormented by her all morning, he looked as if he could willingly strangle this bitch. Hetty, as she sat on the canvas chair, responded in kind, glowering at him. She and Clive, just as Craig had intended, had come to hate each other.

All actors, he knew, nurtured a secret animosity towards one another. And it had been his intention to unearth and provoke these jealousies and antipathies, so to lend the keener edge to this particular drama, with its alternative slave-and-master roles, its vicious power plays, its sadism and other sexual perversions. Craig had manoeuvred these factors into the players' real lives, so that on camera they would all the more realistically enact them.

Hetty thrived on her part. Clive hated the indignities of his. But he was aware that it would not always be so. The tables would soon be turned once more, as in earlier sequences they had shot, when he would take a cruel ascendancy, inflicting on Nefertiti the various and more intimate punishments the script required for her. And all this Craig had contrived as well – in these see-saw opportunities for domination and degradation the more to enhance his tale of hatred and obsession, of doomed love.

So it was that the subsequent scenes in the water, when Hetty jumped overboard and Clive joined her, were much more vicious than they might have been – the couple nearly coming to grief, though the lake was only a few feet deep, spluttering and ducking, wigs washed away, half-naked in their flimsy linens, as they struggled with each other, first mimicking a playfulness, as Craig had instructed, and then exaggerating his further instructions by really coming to grips with each other.

It was a desperate frolic, and Craig prolonged the cruelty and indignity for Hetty by insisting on several re-takes, with consequent renewed make-up and dressing, particularly in the last scene of the morning, in which the royal couple, back now on the lake shore, indulged in a slapping match, Akhenaten finally in the ascendant.

'Listen, Clive,' Craig said fiercely after the third re-take. 'It's no good – and we can't waste the time now. If you can't do the false slaps, do it for real.'

And Clive did just that, slapping Hetty hard on the cheek, repeatedly, for another two takes until Craig was satisfied and Hetty was genuinely hurt, in genuine tears.

'You *shit*,' she said to Craig quietly, but venomously, as she left the set with her dresser.

'You're welcome!' he called after her, smiling a fraction.

Mickey, watching, was appalled at Craig's cruelty. And when, as was his custom now, he brought Hetty's lunch tray to her tent, he found her with her dresser, still suffering, red-eyed, wiping the make-up from her bruised cheeks, in a bath robe, a towel turbanned round her head, sitting in front of the mirror.

He wanted to say something consolatory, but wondered if he dared. Up to now they had exchanged little more than pleasantries. Finally, thinking of the first thing that came to mind, he blurted out in his polyglot accent, half-Russian, half-French, 'Witch hazel, for bruises. It's an English lotion – my Maman always used it in St Petersburg when I was a child. Will I . . . try to get you some?'

Hetty, who until then had barely noticed him, looked up, seeing his reflection in the mirror. She was suddenly charmed. 'Why, Mickey, what a kind thought—'

'It's just,' he ran on, taking advantage of her warm

response before she changed her mind, 'well, it must have been *pénible* – I was watching the whole thing. All those slaps. I was sorry . . .' He paused. He was sorry that she was married to such a brute of a husband. But he could not say this. Instead, to his astonishment, she said it for him.

'No need to be-beat about the bush, Mickey. I know what you want to say: how can I p-p-put up with such a man? Well, I don't know. I really don't . . .'

There was silence in the tent as she rubbed off the last of her make-up. 'You can go now, Maria.' She turned to the Italian dresser, then back to the reflection of Mickey in the mirror. 'Yes, it *was* painful . . .' She looked at this youth behind her, standing awkwardly with the lunch tray, with his tufts of damp hair sticking up like a mop, his large rather baleful eyes, his indiarubber features. 'But Craig insists on it all that way. Perfectionist, you know!' she continued ironically. 'Do pe-put the tray down.' Mickey did so. 'No, don't go,' she told him, blinking her eyes, swabbing them with iced water.

Mickey turned back. '"Perfectionist",' he said pointedly. '*Oui, mais tout de même . . .*'

Hetty shrugged her shoulders. '*Ça – ça doit être comme ça.*' They talked in French, Mickey more confident now, discussing the morning's work, before Hetty said eventually, 'The point is, Mickey, all great directors are shits – there's maybe no other way to do it, to control things, to get the real pe-pe-performances.'

'*Oui, mais* – all *husbands*?' He looked at her with great sympathy, something suddenly very adult in his eyes: a loving compassion.

'*Touché* . . . You're right. I can't explain that, right now. But what I we-wanted to say, Mickey, was – well, you're far too nice a person ever to make a great director. And that's what you want to be of course. But I tell you what – you should really be an *actor*. You'd make a great comic, with that wonderful face of yours. No! – I've we-watched you. Really!' She swung round in her chair, confronting him squarely.

'Oh, I don't think so, Miss Bowen—'

'Yes! You should.' She gave him one of her nicest smiles, all the more telling in its sadness. 'Think about it. And do call me Laura, not Miss Bowen.'

She felt much better then. She might almost have been flirting with him. After he had left, her eyes remained on the space where he had been standing, so gauche and charming. *Distingué*, that was the word for him. And more, he was somehow so vulnerable and thus provoking. And best of all he adored her. She was entirely aware of that and had felt more than inclined just then to encourage this adoration, for with both the other men in her life, with Craig and Clive, it had been a terrible morning. She longed to call Mickey back and kiss him.

For nearly six weeks' filming now Craig had bullied and punished her, on and off the set, on camera and in his direction of her – all justified, as he had intimated, through the cruelties the script demanded from and for her. And he had laughed at her complaints: 'You're welcome!' Yes, she had finally complained, retaliated, but not truly resisted. And she did not know why, just as she had told Mickey. Logically, she argued, Craig was right: the scenario *did* demand these indignities. And she trusted his interpretations here, knowing, too, how she must live the part. But emotionally the cost of doing this was already high and getting steeper.

Off camera now, her life was in tatters. She was constantly on edge, frustrated, at a loss, almost a nervous wreck – a situation made all the worse by the fact that Craig, from the very beginning of the picture, had left her to sleep alone on King Fuad's steamer, he himself taking up permanent residence in his bedouin tent in the middle of the canvas city.

Their love-making had ceased ever since their arrival in Egypt nearly two months before. And this, too, was very much part of Craig's plan. He wanted, for her depraved role, to sharpen her tastes and frustrations in this quarter, not concerned in the least that he might be playing with fire. For, after all, Craig had never really loved her. From the beginning he had loved a fantasy woman in Hetty called Nefertiti. Craig had always really only loved his picture.

Hetty returned to the mirror, still thinking of Mickey, wanting him again in the tent with her, longing for his kindness and sympathy – anxious just as much to share in this, to return the compliment, to dispense with all this fictitious, tumultuous and hurtful a life. She longed then to live as an ordinary woman, never to have heard of Nefertiti or Laura Bowen. 'Witch hazel,' she murmured the name of the balm to herself. 'Witch hazel . . .' Then she turned away from this hateful, pretentious vision of herself as an actress in the mirror and began to sob.

Then she saw the great gold and blue headdress on the bust of Nefertiti next to the mirror, and looked into those glittering, deep, all-powerful, seductive eyes – and reminded herself how all this power was hers, too, in reality: power in life, in love – vengeance, destruction, as she willed. She had not acted her way to these strengths, she told herself once more. They were her real character, her burden. She could no longer return to the uncomplicated, innocent decencies of her old temperament. She must accept the responsibilities consequent on her present nature – the duties, the unquestioned authority, solemn judgements, just but painful retributions, the ultimate victories of a Goddess, a Queen.

'Nefertiti,' she said to herself in the mirror. 'Queen of the Two Lands, Lady of Grace, All Powerful . . .' And this time she intoned the words without the least hesitancy or stammer. She bunched her fingers together, and soon she had quite pulled herself together, resuming all her old petulant command and anger.

All was not lost yet. She was still the star of the picture. They could get by without Craig at this point, but not without her. 'Craig they can replace,' she said to the mirror. 'But not me, not half-way through the picture. Millions of dollars! – everyone depends on *me* for their future . . . Cards!' she went on quietly. 'I still have all the cards to play.' She would show these men, Clive and Craig – she would show Craig especially – she was not to be treated so. And the answer was quite simple.

She had long wanted to take one of the Arab horses, hired for the production, out on her own – some of them were still stabled on the west bank of the river – and ride forever into the sunset of the Libyan desert. Well, not quite forever. She wanted just to get away alone, with the excuse of visiting some of the ancient Pharaonic monuments west of Beni-Souef, away from the river on the edge of the desert – the ruined temple of Henen-Seten, centre of worship to the Ram God Hershef, and further west in the Fayoum oasis the decaying brick pyramid of Hawara, the tomb of Amenhotep III and the fabulous remains of the Great Labyrinth.

Well, she would do just this, soon, when she was most needed. But she would not tell anyone. Of course not! That was the whole point. She would simply dress up – disguise herself as an Arab, that was an idea! – cross the river, take one of the horses and disappear for a day or two. That would set the cat among the pigeons! – show Craig how indispensable she was. For without her, of course, the whole production would grind to a halt. The plan was all so apt and obvious. She would regain Craig's respect. And even if she did not she would certainly have her revenge on him. It was a splendid idea, for besides everything else she could go back to her old derring-do disguises again, and take to galloping horses, just as she had done all those years ago in Summer Hill with Léonie . . .

Léonie? She thought of her again now, Léonie married to Robert and the insult of all that. Well, that could wait. She had to pay Craig back first. And, besides, she could do nothing about Léonie and Robert in any case. They were thousands of miles away.

That same day Robert and Léonie arrived in Cairo. Embarking at once on one of Thomas Cook's Nile steamers, for their two-week trip to Luxor and Aswan, they had read no local papers, heard no gossip . . . were quite unaware of what lay up-river.

'"The tombs of the Valley of the Kings"!' Léonie read excitedly from her Baedeker as the boat cast off above Kasr el Nil bridge, paddles churning the water, moving upstream towards Roda island. 'Oh, Robert – Tutan-khamun! Remember Howard Carter, when he first got a look inside his tomb? – "Wonderful things, wonderful things"!'

At Amarna next day, they started the sequences with Nefertiti, Akhenaten and his younger half-brother Smen-kahare – at the point when Nefertiti, seeing the growing intimacy between the two men, decides to kill Smenka-hare, kill what Akhenaten loves most, by setting the snakes on him, with the help of her equally malign con-fidant, the dwarf Puthmose, in the shape of Eddy Nolan.

The pit vipers and adders were venomous. But the scene in the royal palace gardens, in one of the little pavilions where Smenkahare is resting on a gilded day bed, was shot that morning through a large pane of glass, set across the floor of the pavilion, the snakes on one side, Smenkahare's couch on the other.

'Action!'

The handler released the snakes, pushing them out on the floor of the pavilion, where they wriggled sleepily, refusing to move. But later, when some field mice were procured and set at the bottom of the glass partition, the reptiles became entirely co-operative, slithering forward malevolently, ominously . . . hungrily.

'Why, of course, Arnold! They're making that motion picture here – *Nefertiti* – some ways up-river.' Robert heard the drawling voice of the American woman, talking to her husband, on the steamer chair next to them. 'I *told* you – had it from the captain last night. We're going to stop by and take a look. Seems they've built a whole new city for it – right in the desert!'

'A motion picture?' Arnold was bored.

'Why, yes, a new Hollywood super-spectacle – with *Laura Bowen*!' She emphasized the excitement of this great name.

Léonie seemed asleep, binoculars in her lap, as Robert turned to her. His eyes were suddenly unfocused. He could barely see her, his heart was beating so furiously. Finally he managed to say, 'Léa? Did you hear?'

She opened her eyes and said quite calmly, 'Yes, I heard.' Then she looked at him, shading her eyes in the bright light. Her eyes – and her mind – were both quite clear. 'Fate?' she asked him lightly. Then she reached out and took his hand, gripping it firmly, closing her eyes again.

That evening their boat moored just downstream of the *Omar Khayam*, on the east bank of the river, below the rebuilt city of Amarna. From the foredeck, as they stood there under the awning taking a cocktail before dinner, the passengers could see the stern and Khedival flag of the royal steamer, not forty yards away. They were all agog now. The travel company, receiving permission to moor overnight, had also arranged for the passengers to visit some of the sets next morning. The Fox production manager had readily agreed. It was good publicity.

'Of course, we don't have to go,' Robert said, biting on his empty pipe. Léonie, cool and fresh in an eau-de-nil silk dress, sipped her glass of iced lime juice.

'Why not? I'm not afraid of meeting her.'

'No, it's not that—'

'But you *are*, Robert—'

'No, I'm not.'

'Well, we *won't* go visit the sets then. Honestly, doesn't really matter to me one way or another. Just I'm not going to worry about it.'

Just then there was a flurry of activity on the gangplank of the royal steamer, a group of people going aboard. Léonie lifted her binoculars. She saw Hetty almost immediately, obviously returning from the set with her dressers – saw her glance imperiously at the distant passengers before disappearing. And Léonie's heart at last began to beat much faster, seeing again this face once so loved, still vivid with all its old glamour.

She had indeed thought it fated – this astonishing conjunction on the river miles from anywhere. Would fate continue its schemes by actually bringing them together? She prayed not. Fate had an awful way of completing its schemes, she knew, and she feared this. Oh, how she feared it. For that glimpse of Hetty through the binoculars had brought back some of her old emotion, a nostalgia that pierced her heart – the clear memory of how she had once loved her and, so much worse, the knowledge that she could easily do so again.

For, of course, Léonie still loved Hetty, had never really ceased to love her – and the feeling had been reborn then. She loved her. And she loved Robert. And in an ideal world she would have loved both of them equally, concurrently, together. So that now she simply did not trust herself and longed to get as far away as possible from Hetty to avoid the occasion of sin, as it were. And, had they not both of them been stuck on board the steamer, she would have taken Robert away with her, there and then, caught a train or simply run from this awful temptation that fate seemed to be planning for her.

'All the same . . .' She turned calmly to Robert, hiding the turmoil in her heart. 'It is uncanny – coming all this way out here, just to find her moored right next to us!'

Robert, wishing that from the start Léonie had shown an obvious distaste at this proximity, had suppressed his annoyance. But now he said rather sharply, 'I just wish you weren't so matter-of-fact about it all.'

Little does he know, Léonie thought. So of course, all the more, she had to respond as if the presence of Hetty meant absolutely nothing to her. 'Oh, Robert!' she chided him, smiling. 'You mustn't be upset. Hetty can't touch us any more,' she lied. 'Why, we should be able to just go across, walk up that gangplank and meet her. It wouldn't matter!' She lied again, putting her hand on his arm. 'Robert? All that's over and done with. There's only you and me now. And, besides, there's no chance we're going to get to meet her anyway. We're only moored here for twenty-four hours – ships that pass in the night! There's absolutely nothing to it. And I tell you what!' she rounded on him enthusiastically. 'Just to make certain, we'll take off in the very opposite direction tomorrow! I was talking to the purser. Anyone who doesn't want to visit the picture sets tomorrow can ride horses out on the other side of the river – courtesy of the company! There are some wonderful old Egyptian monuments the purser told me, which tourists never see, west of Beni-Souef, out in the desert. We'll go there instead. I'd love to ride out into the desert! For ever and ever! – galloping Arab horses!'

'What old monuments? Surely they're all on the banks of the river?'

'No! The purser said – and I've been looking at my Baedeker. There's the ruined temple at Henen-Seten, to the Ram God Hershef, at the edge of the desert. And further on in the Fayoum Oasis even more fabulous things – the brick pyramid at Hawara, the tomb of Amen-hotep III – and best of all the site of the Great Labyrinth! Oh, Robert – let's do that! Let's get away, as far away as possible from here tomorrow, so there'll be absolutely no chance whatsoever of meeting her!'

Robert was reassured at last. Léonie, he saw now, so obviously, strenuously, hated this proximity with Hetty – felt defiled by it, he thought. He had misjudged her. Well, of course, he agreed, they would ride out the next day, as far away as possible from Hetty, so avoiding the remotest chance that fate might bring them all together.

'You're so right,' he said to Léonie, kissing her briefly. 'I'll tell the purser then. We'll need two horses – and a dragoman – tomorrow!'

Hetty, driven beyond endurance by Craig's continued cruelty, decided to disappear that very night. She had the dark make-up already, of course – and had made all the other basic arrangements, collecting and hiding in her wardrobe a dirty turban and an old *jellaba*. Leaving the royal steamer in the darkness, she would cross the river on one of the many ferry barges or feluccas that returned to the west bank and the railway sidings there each evening. Her Arabic was quite good enough now to ask and answer at least all the basic questions. She had collected some Egyptian money as well, concealed in a little drawstring leather bag at her waist. On the far side of the river she would steal one of the Arab horses, or bribe one of the grooms. And then the masterstroke! She had also collected – it had been a relatively easy matter from the company's wardrobe department – all the sartorial items appropriate to an Arab horseman, a sheik of the desert, which she would wear under her dirty turban and *jellaba*: flowing white linen robes, soft leather boots, a crescent-shaped, jewel-encrusted dagger, a dazzling silk headdress with a silver-gilt headband.

In this perfect disguise she would ride away, free of every pain and constraint, out into the desert. As to directions – she had her Egyptian Baedeker, with its maps and routes to these legendary ruined monuments beyond the river. And, better still, she had several times inspected the large-scape map of the whole area set up in the production office. So she knew how the horses were stabled in a long tent beyond the makeshift railway station on the other side of the river, at the edge of the Nile cultivation, giving straight out on to the fields of cotton and berseem clover. A track led through these patchwork fields, beside the railway at first, before turning west towards the temple of Henen-Seten at the edge of the cultivation – and beyond that straight across the desert, for a few miles, she thought, to the Fayoum oasis. There were possible risks, she supposed. But she would take some basic food and water. And her new toy, an ebony-sheathed, ivory-topped telescopic swordstick, that declined to the length of a neat foot ruler, which she had bought from an antique shop in Cairo.

Risks, yes. For what was the point, she had thought from the very beginning, of just disappearing and lurking in some seedy local hotel or back at the Semiramis in Cairo, where they would look for her first in any case. Her plan was necessarily more elaborate. It was not only that she wished to punish Craig. She wanted just as much to break away from these celluloid fantasies, and return to something real in her life, to indulge in some free act of her own unique creation.

And besides, because of Craig, she had begun to think

her reason endangered – not from her old black-outs, which had never recurred once the film had been agreed – but from a simple lack of individual effort. In the vast picture company she lay at the centre – the queen bee – her every whim immediately catered for. And that was part of the problem. She was trapped in the middle of the hive. She longed to fly – longed for some rash individual adventure, to take fate entirely in her own hands once more. And, yes, this entailed risks. But that was exactly her purpose, to test herself again, as she had done so successfully often before, against destiny – this time in the shape of something quite wonderful, she felt, waiting for her, where the green land of the Nile valley gave out, at the edge of the great desert.

Towards ten o'clock, after supper, she dismissed her servants and went below to her cabin. Here she made herself up and dressed carefully, in two layers – as *fellahin* and Arab horseman – then put a headscarf over her old turban and her ankle-length cape over all her other clothes, before taking a final look in the mirror. A little bulky. But everything else was in order. She went up on to the long foredeck, its sun-awning drawn back, and walked to and fro, as she did every evening, taking the air under the open night sky, flushed now with a low moon from somewhere over the hills to the east. She stood watching the ferry lights flicker on the placid water. It was a perfect night: warm, dry, exquisitely soft.

Two royal sentries, in white tunics and red fezes and with ancient rifles, manned the approaches on shore, standing next to a flaring brazier by the end of the gangplank. But, for over a week now, she had prepared her escape, going ashore each evening, strolling to and fro along the bank for five minutes, smoking a cigarette. So she knew already where she could change her clothes – among some scrub back from the river, hidden behind the wooden cabin that had been set up as a barrier and guard post some thirty yards downstream, on the path leading to the ferry wharf, almost opposite the tourist paddle steamer that had been moored there overnight.

She lit a cigarette, drew her headscarf more firmly about her, and walked down the gangplank. The sentries came to attention, saluting smartly. She nodded gracefully and, cape trailing in the dusty path, she moved casually away, thirty yards upstream first, then back, passing the men once more, moving south towards the cabin. She repeated the process again. On her second return downstream, glancing behind her, she saw the sentries, backs towards her, engaged in soft conversation. In an instant she was over the railing and behind the cabin in the bushes, discarding her cape and headscarf, letting out her dirty *jellaba*, and walking as fast as she dared while still mimicking the rolling gait, the casual amble, of the *fellahin*, past the tourist steamer with its sounds of laughter, making for the ferry wharf a few hundred yards away.

It was nearly midnight, with a slight desert chill in the air now, before she took the last felucca over the river, sitting huddled in the stern among a score of others like her, the great lateen sail creaking on its boom, taut against the river breeze, a vast, pale white kite against the velvet sky above her. A *fellahin* said a few words to her, something about the cold on the river, she thought. Lowering her head and wrapping the turban more firmly about her face she muttered, '*Il ham di'illah.*' As God wills. The man said nothing more.

On the far bank, leaving the felucca at the flare-lit jetty, she stayed with the other men until they had crossed the rail sidings and gradually dispersed among the huts and tents of the makeshift village. Then she set off south along the track towards the stable tent, some few hundred yards away, she thought. Leaving the flares and hurricane lamps of the huddled village behind her, she was soon in darkness. But there was enough light in the sky to show her the dust-white path, and she made easy progress.

She stopped suddenly, alarmed. There was another track, immediately to her left now, leading off into the cultivation – and coming along it she heard the rising sound of hoofbeats, some dozens of horses, a clatter in the night with the chink of bridles. The land was quite flat. There was nowhere to hide. And then she saw them, silhouetted against the paler night sky on the horizon: a group of mounted soldiers, some twenty horses, coming towards her at a sharp trot, not fifty yards away.

There was nothing for it. The troop had spotted her, cantering forward now, where they met at the T-junction. She saw the shadows of two men, in the lead, towering above her, then heard the British voice – young, tired, upper class, arrogant. 'All right, Sergeant, ask him where we can stable the horses then, where this horse boss is here.'

The sergeant, an older man with a Cockney accent, relayed the question to Hetty in kitchen Arabic. Hetty, tugging the ends of the turban even more firmly about her face, shrugged. '*Ma fische hosan Reiss heneh*,' she said. No horse boss here.

'For God's sake, Patterson,' the officer remonstrated with the sergeant, 'why *should* there be any stabling here, in the middle of bloody nowhere?'

The sergeant dismounted and grasped Hetty by the throat as if to strangle her. 'Now, you're really going to tell me, you little wog! *Fein hosan Reiss?*' he shouted at her, before pushing her on to the dirt track and prodding her with his foot. Hetty could have killed him, as she felt the ebony swordstick handle pressing into her thigh against the earth. But suddenly, seeing a chance for herself in all these events, she changed her attitude. '*Aioua, Bey!*' she shouted up from the ground, in pleading, low-toned gutturals. '*Aioua! Hosan Reiss heneh! Henak, aho, khema.*' And she pointed up the track towards where she thought the stable tent was.

'He says the horse boss *is* here, sir,' the sergeant translated for the officer. 'Up the road in a stable tent. Knew I was right, the little bastard was lying . . .' Leaving her spreadeagled on the track, the troop moved off. Hetty, picking herself up, stumbled along after them.

The horse tent was indeed there, several hundred yards further down the road. When she got there the soldiers had dismounted, tethering their horses to a rail, while the officer and sergeant, waking the grooms, were berating them in rough Arabic. 'We need fodder and stabling here for the night . . .'

The other soldiers in the troop, taking bags and baggage from their horses, were preparing to bivouac nearby. Meanwhile the Egyptian grooms, awake now, and flopping about in their *jellabas*, had started to lead the horses into the long tent, one by one, before unsaddling them. Hetty, her features barely distinguishable in the faint light of two storm lanterns, and dressed just like the other emerging grooms, stepped in among them, moving to and fro in the mêlée of horses and people, waiting her chance to pick out a suitable beast and lead it inside.

In the half-light she saw a white Arab mare, sharply arched neck, smallish, slightly piebald over its hind quarters, a good-looking animal, from what she could make out, still saddled over a sheep's wool saddle-cloth. It was tethered next in line but one against the rail. She stepped in smartly, untied its halter, took it by the bridle and led it away. But, instead of going through the first of the tent entrances, she took it further along to a second, where there were greater shadows – then straight past that, rounding the tent corner, when she mounted the horse and trotted away.

What a piece of luck, she thought – coming on those British soldiers. It had saved her no end of trouble. But was it luck, she wondered then? Surely it was fate? It had all been meant. Of course! Why else? Fate had obviously stacked the cards entirely on her side, she felt, as she broke into a canter, feeling the pure surge of power then in the lithe animal beneath her, finding all her old riding skills again. Leaving the tent far behind her, she galloped along the moonlit track into the night.

Craig had equally liberating activities in view that same evening, as he'd had on several other occasions since the start of the picture. He had long since stopped making love with Hetty. But – just as in Hollywood with the young girls in the Ship Café – this had not curtailed his particular appetites here. He had discovered, some time before in the great tented city, the existence of several tactful Arab bordellos, catering to every taste, including his own. And in one such bedouin tent, at the edge of the desert, he had found exactly what he fancied – better, indeed, than anything he had fed on in Hollywood – a collection of dusky bedouin child brides, girls of twelve or fourteen, early developers, with whom, for an Egyptian pound or two, he could do what he would. And now, towards midnight, in his own disguise, not unlike Hetty's, of turban and *jellaba*, he made his way swiftly, silently, between the long tented alleyways, flares and brush fires dying as the city slept.

Crouching down at the entrance of the dark tent, and paying the old woman her money, he went inside. The sagging cloth, hardly five feet above him, brushed his rough turban, the space smelling of burst cinnamon, lit by a softly flaring hurricane lamp, the desert floor covered in further sacking. At first he could see little, only the dirty cloth partition a few yards in front of him, and beyond that another fainter light.

Rounding the edge of this curtain, his eyes more accustomed to the gloom, he saw the three girls, in various attitudes of repose, in flimsy shifts, one of them asleep, lying out on cheap cushions. The old woman put her head round the partition. '*Hashishe?*' she murmured. Without looking back Craig shook his head. Two of the girls, sitting up now, gave him glazed smiles. But he wanted the first, who slept, the tallest of them, her back towards him. He pointed to her, then sat down, cross-legged, on the floor to wait.

'*Aioua.*' He nodded at the other two, confirming something obviously expected of them. They woke the third girl then who turned, and seeing Craig smiled wanly, rubbing sleep from her eyes. Unlike the other two, she had a light grey, slate-coloured skin, a high forehead, crowned with fuzzy, tightly curled short hair, like a cloche hat right round – deep almond shaped eyes, thin semitic lips, little of anything negroid in her features – she looked Ethiopian; slim, potentially proud.

Hetty dismounted some miles further on in a palm grove, with the railway on one side and an irrigation canal on the other, took off her old turban and dirty *jellaba* – then flounced out her sheik's dress, the long fine white cotton robes, before adjusting the silken headdress and its gilded headband. There was a patch of berseem clover by the canal. She let the mare graze and drink for a few minutes while she changed, then hid the old clothes, sinking them among some reeds by the water.

It was nearly one o'clock. She could just see the hands on her wristwatch, for the moon was high by now, away to her right. The air, at its chilliest now, was glitter-bright, the mare breathing faint cotton wool fountains on the night. Too bright? – if they were already following out looking for her?

She heard a gasping, bellowing noise in the distance. Turning in the saddle, she saw sparks flying up against the dark sky, heard the rumble on the rail tracks next to her, and finally the great dark shapes of engine and carriages rounded a curve – the night express from Luxor to Cairo.

Spurring her horse, she galloped away, white robes flowing behind her, billowing out in the sharp-aired moonlight, the mare given her head now, neat hooves drumming in perfect rhythm, almost paralleling the train's wheels' clatter as it gradually drew near, creeping up behind her.

Hetty bent low over the flying mane, worried that the mare might swerve and bolt to one side or the other – over the rail tracks or into the canal. Instead the animal seemed to relish the moonlit gallop, spurred on by the engine behind her, keeping to the straight flat path, even when the engine let out a piercing whistle.

Finally, however, the train caught up with her, the engine drawing almost level. Turning briefly, Hetty saw the turbanned drivers and the sparks erupting from the golden mouth of the fire box – before, encouraging the mare to one final effort, goading it with knees and heels, she drew away from the train, Hetty felt the ecstasy of victory.

In fact, the train, approaching a curve, had slowed, brakes squealing – approaching a hazard which Hetty didn't know of.

Suddenly she saw a red lantern on a five-barred gate in front of her, looming up, not thirty yards ahead, in the shadows. A man appeared, waving his arms, as she rushed towards the gate. The train, rounding the curve now to her right, let out another shrieking whistle. Then Hetty realized. The gate was on a railway crossing, already closed for the train to pass – or for her to vault over before it did. There was no chance of pulling up in time, the mare at full gallop – she would simply be

thrown into the gate, or over it, into the path of the train.
She spurred the mare on.

7

Robert and Lèonie, with a mounted dragoman, set off
on the same track, with hired horses, later that same
morning, a faint mist over the river now, an opaque
lemon-yellow dawn, before the heat gradually burned its
way through and the Nile gave up its wispy shroud.

By then they were several miles south on the route to
Beni-Souef, moving over the rich alluvial landscape of
cotton, sugar cane and clover, men and black-shawled
women out working, dotted everywhere. They paused
for a few minutes at the same point where Hetty had
changed her clothes earlier that morning, in the shady
palm grove by the irrigation canal. Léonie, moving away
from the dragoman, took off her pith helmet, kneeling
by the water.

'This is all far too tame,' she whispered to Robert,
scratching her legs, itching now in the unaccustomed
jodhpurs. 'If we stay with this old dragoman all day,
we're never going to get anywhere. Look!' She showed
him the map of the area in the Baedeker. 'We're about
here, this village ahead, it's Barout-el-Bakar. And here's
the temple of Henen-Seten – can't be more than three or
four miles, north-west across the fields, by the edge of
this big canal, the Bahr Youssef – that's the one that
irrigates the whole Fayoum oasis. It'll be easy to find. So
let's just leave the old man! Take off on our own!'

Robert was not convinced. 'We'll get lost.'

'Nonsense. It's all quite clear on the map. Can't miss
it.' Léonie, just like Hetty, was filled with a desperate

urge for adventure; something seemed to drive her away from the river. 'Oh, Robert,' she went on, 'I do so want to have a good gallop, way out there!' She gestured to the west. 'Yes! – get out into the desert.' She felt impelled in this journey westwards – impelled by she knew not what.

Robert shrugged. 'All right . . .'

'Look!' Léonie said suddenly, noticing something in the reeds in front of her – Hetty's old turban and *jellaba*. 'Someone's forgotten their washing!'

Ten minutes later, spurring their horses on, they left the dragoman far behind them, waving his arms hopelessly. Léonie, flushed with excitement, turned to Robert as they took off across a track over the fields. 'I love you!' she shouted. She did. And more: in this sudden freedom from the boat and the river, this certain escape from Hetty and everything to do with her at the film set by the river, Léonie, in celebration, confirming her release from all that surging feminine temptation, wanted to make love with him.

Hetty arrived at the ruined temple of Henen-Seten. The site, on unreclaimed desert by the banks of the wide canal, was quite deserted. The crumbling stone, the vast pylons, Osirian pillars and hypostyle columns, reared up at her through the early mists, as, dismounting, she walked towards the temple down a long avenue, flanked all the way on one side by ram-headed sphinxes. These huge beasts, their eyes and sloping noses emerging from the mist, seemed to study her unkindly. They frightened the mare, they frightened Hetty.

Ahead of her now, the two pylons, one on either side of the first temple gateway, appeared. Passing between them, she entered a long colonnaded forecourt, with vast fluted, bulbous pillars, each topped by a papyrus-bud capital, covered in cartouches and hieroglyphics, supporting broken architraves, the remains of what must once have been a whole stone block roof.

Beyond lay a second smaller columned court, this time partly roofed over, so that the light was frailer, uncertain. Suddenly she turned, looking upwards, at some sound – a bird?

She started backwards, terrified. The huge deformed faces were staring at her, each of them atop fifteen-foot-high statues, the ghostly features coming clear now through the wafts of mist: faces, not of rams, but in some vague human form, with the cold gaze of kings, all in a line, a dozen horribly eroded shapes. For the stone in their lips and cheeks, ears and noses, had been rubbed away by forty centuries – they had great cracks through the eyes, twisted gaping mouths, arms crossed in front of them like crusaders' effigies.

Here, in this early dynastic temple, in these ram-headed sphinxes, these sightless human colossi – so unlike Akhenaten's loving decorations at Amarna – was all the cloudy, superstitious worship of the old Pharaonic kingdoms, offerings for immortality set against the nightmare world from the Book of the Dead – these stone supplications to the animal Gods, to Hershef, Toth, Horus and a thousand others. The threat in this temple was all the malignity of the ages, the power of the underworld, dominated by these fierce gods, where mortals lived in the shadow of every sort of dread and evil, walked at their peril.

Hetty was exhausted. Tethering the mare by some scrubby bushes, thin grazing by the canal, out of sight behind the temple, she sat down, hidden by the vast broken stone columns, eating her meagre breakfast – exhausted indeed, but infused with happiness, satisfaction. The night had gone well. She had achieved her every objective. And what a moment that had been! – vaulting the gate, and the one beyond, like a steeplechaser, barely fifty yards in front of the train. She looked up at the mare, its flanks and muzzle cooling now, as it fed on the sparse dry clover. 'You were wonderful! "Witch Hazel",' she went on. 'I'll call you "Witch Hazel".' As the sun rose behind her, shafts of light burnt away the mists and a flush of pink touched the temple, rising over it, gradually warming her as she ate. Twenty minutes later, in the first of the day's heat, she fell asleep.

Several hours later, the sun full up, a brilliant orb in the lead-blue sky, Robert and Léonie rode down the same avenue of ram-headed sphinxes – marvelling at them, not frightened, in the full blaze of noon. Stopping in the shade of the two pylons at the entrance to the temple, they tethered the horses, sat down for a minute on some stones beneath the monuments, mopping their brows.

'We made it!' Robert turned and gazed at the long cartouche with its hieroglyphics on the pylon at his back. 'Wonder what it says?'

'"No Admittance", I should think. The Baedeker says only the Pharaoh, the high priests and chief courtiers were allowed into the temples in the old dynasties.' She turned to Robert, shading her eyes, gazing at him lovingly. 'Oh, Robert, yes – we made it! Let's find some proper shade inside and eat our lunch – then I can take these damn jodhpurs off as well.'

They walked inside the first of the colonnaded fore-courts, inspecting the vast pillars briefly – then went on into the second smaller court, where they found a huge sloping block of stone, the top of some sarcophagus or altar, partly buried in the sand, half in shadow, near one of the great sightless colossi. Here they laid out their picnic lunches and their water bottles.

Léonie took off her itching boots and jodhpurs, sitting down cross-legged in just her knickers and bush shirt;

opening the picnic lunch: cold delta pigeon, tomatoes, olives, unleavened bread, tepid soda water.

She lay back on the sloping stone, looking up to the top of one of the columns. Then she leapt to her feet. 'It's too damn hot!' She took her bush shirt off, naked to the waist now. 'Robert?' She looked at him invitingly.

He put his head on one side, half-smiling. 'Offend the Gods, wouldn't it?' He looked up at the row of deformed and sightless pharaohs.

'Rubbish! They were always making passionate love – I've read the books. It's even in my Baedeker . . .' She reached over, drew him to the sloping altar, put his hand to her breast, encouraging him gently, feeding on him, undressing him with her eyes, full of audacity and knowing ardour. She leant back then, slipping her knickers off in a rising fever of pleasure, an infection Robert soon caught as she pulled him to her, undoing his belt, seducing him, opening her thighs, moving his hand again, so that he found it between the smooth flesh.

'Oh, Robert – love me, *love* me! . . .'

Hetty, who earlier, inspecting the monuments, had climbed up the interior stairway to the top of this same courtyard, was hidden now beneath the rim of a papyrus-bud capital high above Robert and Léonie, looking down on the passionate scene beneath her.

She was not merely astonished. She literally could not believe her eyes – the vision of this love-making becoming clouded as her eyes glazed over, so that she started to sway, before regaining her balance. She looked up, trying to clear her eyes, blinking out over the vast desert landscapes behind the temple, west beyond the canal, then forced herself to look down again.

Yes, it was all true. It was Robert and Léonie, naked, both of them in shadow, loving each other. Hetty was outraged. Was this the sweet fate that had waited for her at the edge of the desert? But how had the two of them got there? – it was not possible – not just to Egypt, but out here, miles from anywhere, coinciding with her in this temple? No, it must be an illusion in the shimmering heat – an illusion, a bad dream, a nightmare. The two people below her were chimeras: she was seeing things – from lack of sleep and after all the night's excitements. They were mere figments of her fevered imagination in this brilliant desert light, a ghastly sexual fantasy cast on the shadows beneath her. They could *not* be real. She would test the vision. Getting up and crouching on her knees, she saw the huge chunk of cut stone, a great chip from the hypostyle capital, balanced near the edge of the architrave some yards away. Yes, she would test the reality of this vision, she thought, moving towards the stone, set almost immediately above where Robert and Léonie were lying.

At the same moment Léonie, on her back, gazing up over Robert's shoulder, suddenly started up. 'Robert!' she whispered urgently. 'Something, someone's up there – watching us. I saw . . . it looked like an Arab headdress . . . moving.'

Robert turned, leaving her for an instant, so that they both saw the little stone chips and bits of grit scattering around them. They got down at once from the altar stone, and reached for their clothes.

'See! I told you! There's someone up there!' Léonie repeated her assertion while trying to dress hurriedly.

'No,' Robert calmed her. 'Can't be. Just some loose stones in the wind. Or a bird. Look at all those doves flying in and out from the stones, lots of them, all morning . . . It's nothing.'

They were lucky in their escape. Hetty had tried to push the great stone over on to them. But it had refused to move, stuck fast, despite all her efforts.

Robert and Léonie got dressed. 'There was no one there – don't worry,' Robert reassured her.

'All the same, I don't like it. Come on, let's get out of here – give the horses some water at the canal – and get back to the steamer.'

Untethering their horses from the great pylon, they led them round the outside of the temple, clattering over a debris of broken stone, to the greeny, sun-dazzled waters of the wide Bahr Youssef canal. There, where the temple backed on to the water, they came to a sudden halt. In front of them, standing by a huge fallen column, was a white Arab mare, untethered, whinnying gently as the other horses approached it. Léonie felt the back of her neck prickle with fear. 'Oh God, Robert – I was right! There was, there *is*, someone back in there.'

Inspecting the mare, they saw the British royal arms cut into the leathers. And the inscription beneath it: 'Royal Engineers, Abassia Barracks, Cairo.'

'A British soldier – out here?' Robert wondered.

Then, poking out from the mouth of a small saddle bag, they saw something else, the remains of a cardboard picnic lunch box, not unlike their own. Inside were a few crumbs, some olive stones – and a soiled handkerchief, used as a napkin. A woman's fine silk handkerchief. Robert opened it, letting it flutter in the faint breeze off the water. He was puzzled, fingering the delicate material. 'Strange soldier, or maybe it's his girlfriend's,' he said lightly. But when he looked up he saw that Léonie was gazing at something else now, over his shoulder, a look of real terror in her eyes this time.

The two bandits had seen the fine white mare tethered alone in the shade of the broken columns some twenty minutes before. They had stalked the animal down the canal bank, confirming its isolation until, a minute before, they had surprised and then untethered it, before being surprised themselves by the arrival on the scene of Robert and Léonie. The mare meanwhile had strayed out from behind the fallen columns, while the two men lay behind them, peering over.

It had not taken the thieves long to realize that these young *farangis*, quite alone, offered no threat. They would have the mare, and better still the two other horses that had just come into their reach. The older, bearded man stepped out from behind the columns, the hem of his ragged, dun-coloured *jellaba* tucked up into his waist. He held a lead-weighted night stick in one hand. His younger companion, one eye almost completely closed with bilharzia, joined him, carrying a coiled hippopotamus-hide whip.

Robert, following Léonie's glance, saw them not twenty yards away. Their intent was obvious. The older man moved sideways towards the mare. The younger approached Robert and Léonie, uncoiling his whip, flexing his arm, the wicked thongs at the end flicking up little dust storms in the sand.

Léonie shrieked. 'No! No!'

The younger horse thief, his one good eye half-closed in a leer, continued towards them, his other arm outstretched. '*Gib le, gib le hosan . . .*' he intoned in a low voice. He lifted his whip menacingly. '*Gib le . . .*' He seemed to wink at Léonie, mockingly, his good eye blinking repeatedly in the harsh light. Beads of perspiration began to drip down Léonie's forehead, clouding her vision. 'No!' she screamed again. 'No!'

Robert interceded, stepping in front of Léonie, barring the man's path. The thief raised his whip and, flicking it expertly, let the tail thongs open a flesh wound on Robert's neck, three or four livid weals. Robert gasped in pain. The thief advanced towards his horse, with a fuller smile now, hand still outstretched.

Then suddenly he stopped, seeing something over Robert's shoulder, surprise and fear in his sallow features. Robert and Léonie turned. They all gazed, astonished, at the approaching figure.

The Arab, emerging from the shadow of the temple wall in his brilliant white robes, walked easily into the dazzling light towards them. Léonie could make out little of his dark features, hidden behind the cowl of his silk headdress, as he came nearer. Nor did she take in the curious fact that the Arab's right hand, unlike his face, was smudgy white, for all she noticed was the sword he held in it, a very thin, needle-pointed run of steel, metal glittering in the light, as he held the wicked instrument out, gestured for Robert and Léonie to move aside. Passing them, he confronted the man with the whip, who used it at once, the coils shrieking viciously through the air, unleashing their venom at the Arab, but harmlessly, as the thongs caught in the billowing folds of his robe. Once more the thief let fly, but to no better effect, as the Arab sidestepped before continuing his ominous approach.

Then, suddenly, nearing his prey, the Arab took up a position that was vaguely familiar to Léonie, the side-on stance of a fencer, about to lunge with a foil – which he did just then at great speed, stamping his foot on the hard sand, so that now he was well within the compass of the whip, where it could hardly be used against him. Teasing the thief now, circling the blade tip in little provocative flourishes just beneath the chin, the Arab drove him back towards the fallen columns.

It would have been no contest, but for the older man, who joined the fray then with his lead-tipped night stick, waving it about his head, flailing his arm like a windmill, approaching the Arab, and allowing the younger thief to make his escape.

The Arab retreated for a moment, too, letting the older bandit come towards him now, scything the air with his club. The first thief, moving to the side, some way back, was able to use his whip again – and he did so, the coils snaking out, cutting the Arab about his headdress. The other thief closed with him as well, using his stick as a sword.

But the Arab parried the night stick, slashing against it left and right, the thief holding it in both hands now, attempting to use it as a mace, trying to club the Arab to death.

And again he seemed likely to succeed, before the Arab, showing a sudden fevered agility, sidestepped the blows and then, crouching down, made a rush for the thief's legs – cutting at them repeatedly, whipping the bare flesh there, opening little cuts about his ankles, so that the man bellowed out in pain, hopping about on one leg, before stumbling over.

The Arab ran at the younger man now, like a sprinter – went for him with a startling vehemence, sword flashing, circling, boring in towards his chest, where the thief, astonished and fearful at this expert swordsmanship, saw the tip of the blade coming ever closer. Swaying back now, he fell against one of the great broken columns, where the Arab stood over him, about to administer the *coup de grâce*, the needle point an inch from his throat.

The man bellowed for mercy. The Arab pushed him further to the ground with his boot, forcing him to grovel in the sand, before he stepped back and whipped the man on the soles of his bare feet with the blade. Then he gestured away towards the desert. The two thieves needed no second bidding – running, hopping, stumbling away, yelping in pain from the wounds on their feet, disappearing behind the broken columns and along the canal bank.

Robert and Léonie simply stood there, too astonished to be grateful. Robert was bleeding, with a trickle of blood running down his neck, smearing his bush shirt.

The Arab came right up to Robert then, gazing at him

from behind the white cowl of his headdress. Robert, the sun in his eyes, saw little of the man's features, noticing only how the dark skin seemed to be melting somehow, the colour changing, as beads of perspiration ran down the man's face. The Arab reached out suddenly. Putting his hand to Robert's cheek above the wounds, he stroked the flesh there tenderly, almost provocatively, before lowering his fingers and taking some of the congealing blood, rubbing them together, as if testing the consistency. There was complete silence, the others puzzled by these intimate gestures, thinking them part of some bedouin ritual.

'Thicker than water! . . .'

Hetty spoke at last, the cool slightly mocking tones of her familiar voice invading the hot silence. 'It's funny,' she went on before the others had a chance to respond in any way, turning to Léonie, 'seeing you both here. Though now I come to think of it, of course you must both have been on that Nile tourist steamer, moored just next to mine. But why meet out *here*, miles from anywhere, when we could so easily have met at Amarna?' She smiled, an expression of almost cruel satisfaction crossing her features, seeing the quite startling effect her voice was having on her two old friends. But her smile meant nothing to the others. Robert and Léonie, though recognizing her voice, could still not believe it was Hetty in these sheik's robes. They were speechless. 'Yes,' Hetty went on slowly, speaking to herself now. 'What fate is that? – that I should try and kill you, then save you?'

Léonie, aghast, still not taking anything in, looked at the robed figure as at a ghost. 'Hetty?'

'Who else?'

'Oh, my God, no! No, not you,' Léonie blurted out, unable to contain her horror. She put her hand to her mouth as if she was about to be sick.

'Yes, me,' Hetty went on, taking no notice of this

rebuff. 'But why *here*?' she repeated the question, as might an astrologer, pondering some new star in the heavens. 'That's what puzzles me.'

Robert and Léonie remained rooted to the spot. Finally Robert said coldly, 'I don't understand. Can't you leave us alone? – you must have followed us out here.'

'Certainly not! Pure chance.' Hetty moved away then, tending the mare, stroking its nose. 'I was out here, oh, at first light, taking a break, getting away from the picture for a day – or two!' she added, all the old mischief in her voice.

Hetty took her headdress off, the better to mop her brow, displaying her sparse cropped hair, taking the silk handkerchief from the saddle-bag, trying to clear the make-up, walking back to them easily, still entirely relaxed, in command. But then, when next she spoke, her stammer, no longer kept at bay by her role as Arab sheik, returned. 'So why didn't you come and see me on the b-b-boat?' she gasped out. 'I w-was just there, right ne-next to you.'

She struggled so with her words then – her face a mass of chocolate streaks, suddenly a pathetic vulnerable child again, caught at the cake tin – that Léonie, who at first had been angry, quite appalled by her presence, began to relent a fraction towards her, offering her the ghost of a sympathetic smile.

But Robert, finding his voice and wits at last, became more icy. 'It's perfectly obvious why we didn't come and see you. After your appalling behaviour to both of us, years ago, it hardly seemed a meeting any of us would have enjoyed.'

'Still, a meeting was obviously intended!' Hetty, regaining her composure, took no notice of Robert's remarks. Instead, noticing Léonie's slight warmth towards her, she started to play on it, turning, offering her a dazzling smile. 'Obviously intended, because look, here we all are! And be-besides, why did you come out to Egypt in the first place, or at least all this way up-river, if you didn't want to see me?'

'We had no idea you were here . . .' Robert continued his sour response.

'Oh, Robert!' Hetty turned her smile on him. 'You *must* have known—'

'No, only at the last moment—'

'And as to the past,' Hetty rushed on, laughing now. 'That was all *ages* ago – childish rows, mistakes and mis-understandings, all that sort of thing. We're surely all adult enough now not to go on holding all that against each other, aren't we? Can't we just be fre-fre-friends?' She smiled again at Léonie, this time sweetly, quizzically, without guile.

Whereas Robert had obviously confirmed his vast dis-taste at this meeting, Léonie was almost in two minds about it now. Of course, it was a disaster – running into Hetty like this: a real slap in the face from fate, given that she had taken so much trouble to get as far away as possible from Hetty that morning. None the less, her fortuitous intervention with the thieves had certainly saved their horses and possibly their lives. She should at least express some gratitude for that.

'Yes, well, thank you anyway for saving us,' she said coldly. 'They were certainly out to rob us. Even kill us,' she added grudgingly.

But it was Robert who interjected brusquely then. 'Yes, you said a minute ago – that *you'd* tried to kill us. What did you mean?'

Hetty turned one of her most disingenuous smiles on him. 'Oh, not *really* kill you! Just a thought. You see, I was up there, on top of one of those columns in the temple, when you were down below – well, being happy t-t-together. It hurt a little, seeing you both – that way

– because we – were all such close friends, weren't we?' She looked at Léonie, a resonant regret in her eyes. And Léonie coloured, seeing how, from Hetty's point of view, she must have most visibly and passionately betrayed that friendship – with Robert, half an hour before on the altar in the temple.

'Now you're m-m-married, of c-c-course,' Hetty continued, stammering badly once more, but with the hidden intention of doing so now, seeing how this flaw had earlier touched Léonie, even against her will.

'Yes,' Robert said dully. 'Married.' The peeved note had increased. He found it difficult even to look at Hetty, this old robber in his life who had now so conveniently forgotten all her earlier thefts and betrayals.

Léonie, clearly aware of all this rising anger in Robert, followed suit. 'Yes, married – *happily*.' She paralleled her husband's coldness in her voice. But she did not entirely feel the same chilly emotion towards her old friend now. She did not want to be – no, she truly did not – but she had begun to be fascinated by this reborn vision of Hetty: the cropped hair, a Joan of Arc cut above the thin, incongruously chocolate-smeared face, the whites of her eyes dancing with drama, the lizard's tongue, darting to and fro, moistening her dry lips, the old petulant chin, but still the defenceless vulnerability in those blue eyes, so arrogant yet so hurt – this proud but pathetic do-or-die child's face, which she remembered so well, returned to her at last, pleased with herself now at the end of this, one of her most spectacular charades, which yet had saved them, which seemed only to have friendship as an end. Yes, perhaps in the eight years since she had last seen her, Hetty had become truly adult, or at least much more reasonable. Certainly she had lost none of her old extravagance or magic. But this seemed a creative characteristic now – no longer, as in the old days, almost purely destructive. What was the secret behind this happy development? Léonie longed for answers, confirmations here – found herself glancing at Hetty surreptitiously, wondering for the first time if this meeting was entirely an evil chance.

Perhaps, she thought, it had a quite different message, not evil but happy, and she had simply misread the signs, wilfully avoiding fate's true intention here. This encounter – which she had so resisted – was it, in fact, an answer to her deepest, most secret prayer? Oh yes, despite the bitterness of Hetty's earlier betrayal, despite 'getting over her' and being so happy with Robert, she *had* wanted to see Hetty again – once more, to make things up with her, at least. So that now, suddenly believing in a happy outcome, she could not resist pursuing, nurturing the meeting in some way.

Looking into Hetty's eyes, Léonie was certain she saw everything she felt in her own heart reflected there – sure confirmation that Hetty, too, felt some happy destiny was being offered. So a look of wonder, of invitation, a mood of connivance bloomed between them then. Yes, surely that had been the real purpose of their coming together, Léonie thought: that Hetty, finally recognizing all her old faults and betrayals, some fate had sent her out here to make amends, so that they could all at least be friends again. Gradually Léonie's resistance to Hetty weakened.

For Hetty, too, this meeting was a happy fate, but of quite a different kind. Their coming together offered her the chance not of reconciliation but of destruction. Given the brooding, rising anger she had nurtured ever since she had heard of their marriage – a sense of outrage now vastly increased by the vision of their actual love-making – here, she felt, was a heaven-sent opportunity to take revenge on them both. She wanted Léonie again, without Robert. Yet her real aim was even more malign. She only wished for Léonie so as to separate her from Robert, for what she really wanted was to destroy their marriage. Indeed, that had been the real reason she had saved them from the two thieves, so that she could rob them of something infinitely more valuable than their horses – of their love for each other.

'Well, anyway,' Hetty said, finishing her toilet. 'Goodness me! – here we are. Do let's leave bygones be bygones. I was going on out into the Fayoum oasis, see the Harara pyramid and maybe the remains of the Labyrinth. Just over that pa-patch of desert there, can't be more than half an hour away. Coming? Then we can all ride back again to the boats.'

'No. We really have to get back now.'

'Oh, Robert,' Léonie interrupted. 'You did say, I did tell you – how much I wanted to see the remains of the Great Labyrinth. Please . . . I know you're angry with Hetty. And so am I.' She scowled at Hetty then, pretending to a fierceness she no longer quite felt.

Robert, recognizing Léonie's genuine feelings for the antiquities and reassured by her last harshness towards Hetty, weakened. 'Well, if it's only half an hour away—'

'Oh, Robert!' Léonie rushed over to him, embracing him, giving him her most passionate undivided attention, the better to snub Hetty, in the pretence that she felt nothing for her – Hetty, who stood aside and alone now, disregarded. But Hetty was quite content. If Robert had noticed nothing of Léonie's dissembling just then, she had, knowing exactly what Lèonie was up to. After all, Hetty thought, she knew Léonie, knew her secrets, really so much better than Robert.

In these machinations and subterfuges of the heart, they none of them glanced at the distant horizon to the west, where a few dark, pencil-thin dust devils were getting up, little spiralling eddies caught in some encroaching wind far out in the desert, moving slowly towards them.

It was that late winter season in Egypt when the khamseen winds blew in from the deserts, changing the whole air and climate of the country for a few weeks – wicked winds, far out in Libya, gathering up and sweeping the desert sands towards the river, swirls of fine white dust that soon became blinding, choking storms as the winds increased and the air filled with stinging motes.

The khamseen had come early that year. Though in any case, the three mounted figures, single file on the desert track, riding out towards these first intimations of it, knew nothing of this vicious climate, or its sudden furies, remarking only on the strange grey pall that had risen up then, far away on the horizon, obliterating the afternoon sun.

'Clouds!' Léonie said brightly. 'Don't say it's going to rain!'

The atmosphere was suddenly oppressive – the air at that moment being sucked away from them, towards the great feeding spirals of sand, invisible as yet, a mile in front of them. They noticed this impending force only through the rippling top sand on the dunes, wispy rising waves, running away from them, being scooped up by the vacuum ahead.

'Funny – how the sand's all blowing like that, because I can't feel any wind.' Hetty, in front, turned on her mare towards Léonie immediately behind her.

They rode on for another few minutes, the air becoming thinner, with no sound, but for the rustling and skimming over the dunes. Then the mare started to whinny, the other horses following suit, all of them suddenly anxious, starting to prance and swerve, as if refusing a jump. That was their only warning, before, rising over a dune, they saw the first great grey wall of sand, several hundred feet high, rolling towards them. Then it engulfed them, a stinging wind filled with fine white grains, choking them.

Dismounting, they turned their backs and their horses against the onslaught, as the sandstorm roared over them, the force of the wind pushing them back the way they had come, the horses' manes flicking viciously in their faces as they led the frightened animals, struggling at their bridles.

Hetty, with her cowled headdress, was best off, wrapping it about her face, avoiding the worst of the sand. 'Put your hankies round your mouth!' she yelled at the two vague figures ahead of her. 'Or take your shirts off and use them.'

There was no reply. Suddenly both figures were lost, invisible in the sand swirls, which had thickened and darkened now, giving only a few yards' visibility.

'Léonie! Robert!' Hetty screamed above the wind. 'Stick to the track. Or stop! – stop where you are!' But again there was no answer. 'Oh God,' she moaned. Still, she thought, they had been riding for less than half an hour. They couldn't be more than a mile from the big canal. Robert and Léonie would have the sense, surely, just as she had, simply to make straight on until they got back to the water, and wait for her there. Almost bent double now, the better to avoid the blistering sandpaper wind, Hetty led the mare on.

The others meanwhile, having lost Hetty – their calls back equally unanswered in the roaring wind – had waited together a minute; and then, thinking just as Hetty had done, decided to return without her, making straight for the canal.

But all of them were mistaken in their direction. The sandstorm had changed its course, the wind veering southwards. Without appreciating this and quite disoriented in any case, all three turned imperceptibly, continuing to travel with the wind, so that soon they were moving parallel with the canal, away from the oasis, going due south into the empty desert.

It was not quite empty. Half an hour later, the sand-storm abating a little, the air clearer, Hetty saw the vague dark shapes ahead of her – large, strangely crouched beasts, camels, she saw, a minute later, when she came into the impromptu desert caravanserai, stalled at that moment by the storm, herds of fat-tailed sheep and a few scraggy goats corralled in a circle of camels, twenty or so dark robed bedouins, motionless, faces almost entirely masked, shadowy figures, standing with their lances as sentinels right round the outskirts of the encampment.

The first bedouin, alarmed at Hetty's sudden approach, offered his steel-tipped lance to her. A second, sitting cross-legged a few yards from him, stood up quickly, unslinging an old rifle. Hetty stopped, uncertain, forgetting her sheik's outfit. The two men approached her slowly, menacingly.

Meanwhile Robert and Léonie, who had earlier passed invisibly within a few hundred yards of this same bedouin encampment, were now quite lost in the blinding sands, heads bowed, moving in vague circles, but ever southwards into the desert. Their useless progress came to an end, however, when, at the foot of a dune, Robert's horse, alarmed by the looming hill of sand, suddenly swerved, knocking him to the ground, trampling on his foot in the process. Giving one shout of pain, he lay there, the sand whipping round his face, into his open mouth, before Léonie rushed to him. 'Robert! Robert . . .' She brushed the sand from his lips, cradling him.

'It's all right, nothing too bad, not the whole weight of the beast – think I've just twisted my ankle!'

He was just being brave, Léonie thought. His ankle had a bad gash when she looked at it. All round them, the vicious sand-filled dragon's breath seemed set on suffocating them. And they were lost, quite lost. They should have long since reached the canal had they been travelling in the right direction. With only a trickle of water left in their canteens, without food and with Robert immobile, there was no chance of survival.

The bedouin, at first alarmed by the vision of the mysterious sheik coming at them out of the sands, were then unbelieving when they discovered the man to be a woman and a *farangi*, a foreigner, at that. But they were not thieves – far from it: part of the ancient Aneza tribe in these wastes, they had driven their flocks for centuries to and fro across the western desert, between the various oases, Siwa and the Fayoum, and from these to the Nile valley.

So it was that, when Hetty spoke to them in her kitchen Arabic – '*Etneen habib, kitabi hosan,*' pointing out into the sand storm and gesturing hopelessly – they eventually understood her message, that she had lost her two friends, out there on horses. They at once agreed to help her find them.

Hetty tried to cement their agreement by getting out her purse and offering them what Egyptian money it contained. But they looked at her askance, shocked by the idea. They would have none of it, shaking their heads, eyes to the sandy heavens, murmuring darkly. These were true men of the desert – quite untouched by civilization. Hospitality, and every help to a stranger met with in their barren world: this was their immutable law, the vital law of survival for everyone who lived in these cruel wastes.

'*Etim, lel!*' – the dark, the night – Hetty said to them urgently, showing them her wrist-watch which they looked at uncomprehendingly, before she gestured up at the furious sky. 'We must find them *now*,' she pleaded, and they understood.

'*Aioua, Aioua!*' they told her reassuringly. But they did nothing, opening their arms, pointing to the sky. '*Ma Fische . . .*' they warbled on. It was still too black, she understood them to mean, useless to look for anyone as things were.

But twenty minutes later the skies cleared sufficiently as the worst of the storm blew over. And then half the men, nearly a dozen of them, mounting their camels, went off with Hetty, leaving the others to guard the flocks, all of them moving south with the wind at first, before each of the camels started to radiate out in different directions, zig-zagging across the vast desert, visible now for a mile or so under the cover of bruised black, sand-filled clouds.

There were no footprints to be looked for over the sand-thrashed dunes. But these bedouin, alone among all people, knew how to search for the lost in these desolate sands, riding their ships of the desert, which they used as look-out posts every so often, stopping and standing right up on the hump saddles, scanning the horizon, as they moved away from the camp in an ever-expanding circle.

Hetty, insisting on riding out with them, had taken a camel herself, following an older bedouin, their leader, she supposed, an ancient fellow, swathed in a floppy turban, with a scraggy beard, sharply aquiline nose and tiny black oval eyes, who rode immediately in front of her. But they saw nothing.

Finally, almost giving up hope in the darkening sky, from somewhere far away to their left behind a ridge of sand, Hetty heard the eerie whistle, sharp and thin, repeated like a curlew's cry in an Irish bog.

'*Aioua*,' the old man half-turned to her impassively, nodding. '*El ham di'illah*.' They had found them and Hetty's heart soared with relief. No, she had not wanted them lost or dead. Of course not! That would have been too cruel a fate. After all, she had only wanted to punish them . . .

The old man veered off to the left, over the ridge, and

soon they came on them all, several camels surrounding the horses and the two figures lying on the sand beneath a dune just half a mile away: Robert and Léonie, exhausted, shriven, sand-encrusted, but alive. Hetty, dismounting quickly, knelt by Léonie in the middle of the circle of camels and bedouin.

'Léa – are you all right?'

'Fine. But Robert, his ankle, it's cut rather badly, the horse . . .'

Hetty turned to Robert sympathetically, bending down, looking at his ankle. 'I'm sorry. But I'm sure it'll be OK. We'll get you back to the bedouin camp. It's not far.'

'Thanks.' But Robert still regarded her coldly.

The bedouin helped him to his feet. Hetty turned, doing the same for Léonie. As she did so, Léonie murmured, 'Thank you – thank you, Hetty.'

It was pitch-dark by the time they got back to the camp, a dozen goat-skin tents set up, with a few smouldering fires, a stiff wind still blowing and sighing. But the sandstorm itself had gone, leaving only grit in the air, mingled with the smell of food cooking over the stone hearths.

The three strangers were royally treated. Robert had his cut tended with some sticky desert balm that smelt of honey, then roughly bandaged. Afterwards all three of them sat down, Robert on a small stool, leg outstretched, the others cross-legged, on rush mats in the chief's tent, the largest in the caravanserai, some fifteen feet long, lit by tallow flares, spread over half a dozen poles, the chief's lance stuck in the ground by the doorway.

They drank tepid goat's milk from shallow wooden bowls and ate from similar platters – beans and strips of yellowish, sweet-tasting grilled meat, a lizard they were given to understand, served in their honour – the food handed round (to their surprise, for they had not seen them before) by some of the heavily shawled but not veiled women of the camp, wrists and ankles clinking with copper rings and bracelets: small, plain women, quite expressionless.

Hetty talked as well as she could to the chief and half-dozen of his lieutenants grouped about him. But it was hard – her Nile Arabic as minimal as theirs. Instead, they largely contented themselves, each group in its own fashion and tongue, with nods of the head, smiles, guttural murmurs of appreciation, contented silence.

A problem arose only afterwards as to where they were all to sleep. The chief, standing up, beckoned Robert to a rough litter of mats and goatskin cloaks that had been prepared for him in a corner of the tent. Clapping his hands, two women appeared at the tent flap, and the chief nodded, gesturing for Hetty and Léonie to follow them out.

Robert, turning awkwardly on his foot, started to demur, as did Léonie. 'But we're married. Can't we stay together?' She addressed herself to the chief, a note of desperation in her voice. He seemed to frown. She turned to Hetty. 'Can't you explain?' Hetty shook her head. 'No idea what the word for marriage is. The bedouin obviously don't stay with their women at night. Just visit them in the harem.' She shrugged. 'The Arab custom . . .' The chief's frown deepened, thinking the foreign women were questioning his hospitality. 'I suppose we'd better do as he says,' Hetty added. 'He's getting offended.'

'All right.' Léonie turned to Robert. 'Seems we can't stay together – not their custom. Obviously we have to sleep in the harem with the women.' She went over to him, kissing him quickly, tenderly. 'I'll be all right, promise . . .'

The girls left the tent with the two women. Their own

quarters, when they found them, stumbling through the blowing sparks from the fires, were on the far side of the camp, in a smaller and much lower tent, less than five foot high, so that they really had to stoop to get into and move through it. Inside, lit by a single tallow flare, the air was a sweet and sour mix of goat and honey, just like the balm used on Robert's ankle.

'Are there bees in the desert? They seem to use it for everything,' Hetty made inconsequential chatter, though the drumming of her heart belied her easy tones. Then, their eyes becoming more accustomed to the faint light, they saw the vague forms of at least half a dozen women – crouched, kneeling, lying out along the length of the low tent, the whites of their eyes visible now, all staring at them. 'Oh, God,' Hetty said. 'A real girls' dorm . . .'

The eyes followed them as they were led to the end of the low tent. Here, to their surprise, they rounded a corner where the space extended to their left, with rush mats and goat-skins on the desert floor, a bed of sorts prepared for them, beyond the flickering beams from the tallow flare.

Their suppressed excitement at being alone together took the edge off their exhaustion as they sat down gingerly on the skins, preparing themselves for some sort of sleep in the cramped, fetid space, smelling of burnt tallow, and some deep musky odour they noticed now, with which the whole tent seemed impregnated, a smell of cloves, cinnamon. Hetty struggled out of her sheik's robes, making a lower sheet out of part of them, and bundling up the rest as a pillow for them both, a shared headrest in the narrow space, the wind rattling and flapping at the tent just inches away from them.

Their eyes now quite accustomed to the frail yellow light, they looked up as they undressed, only to see all the eyes peeping at them surreptitiously round the corner of the tent pole.

‒ 'On show,' Léonie said, breathlessly, trying to hide her nervous excitement, joining Hetty, lying down as far away from her as the space allowed.

'Shush!' Hetty waved the bedouin women away with her arms, as if they were chickens, and the eyes disappeared. Then she laughed softly. 'Who would have believed it ‒ sleeping in a harem tonight!'

'And all the more extraordinary, because remember,' Léonie murmured, 'if we hadn't met you at the temple, Robert and I, we'd have gone out alone into that sandstorm across the desert ‒ and never been found till we were dead! Fate indeed. You saved our lives . . .'

Hetty did not reply, since for her this fate meant something quite different. Fate had given her the opportunity of saving Léonie only because Léonie was hers, had always been: fate had simply returned her property. Léonie's marriage to Robert was just a dreadful mistake which could now be corrected. That was the true meaning of all this. But did Léonie see it that way?

Hetty, testing the water, reached across in the dark, touching Léonie's gritty cheek, finding her lips, brushing them delicately. Léonie made no resistance. Hetty's confidence rose, so that she said, 'Oh, Léa, I'm just so *glad* ‒ to be with you!' And she was, though thinking more of possessing Léonie now, taking her, dividing her from Robert. 'Of course, all that in the past,' she continued disingenuously, 'my disappearing to America with Craig. Well, I just had to, don't you see? ‒ make a clean break. Things had got too much for me at Summer Hill. And I'm sorry. But it wasn't just childish of me, Léa. You see, I so wanted to grow up, like you always said I should. And I think I have . . . grown up,' she added, allowing the lie to bloom.

Léonie listened to these soft, familiar tones, their pillow talk renewed, excited by this confirmation of her earlier thoughts, that Hetty had indeed matured.

'I'm glad then, too,' Léonie said. 'So that now – well, we can be friends again.' There was still a foot of space between them, as they lay there chastely, talking – both, as Léonie thought, savouring these ideals of maturity and friendship, now held in common.

'Friends, I hope so . . .' Hetty sighed. 'Robert, though – he won't be friends, I'm afraid. He hates me.'

'Yes, because he loved you, as much as I did. And never . . . had you. So he's angrier. And jealous, too. But maybe that'll change.'

'It won't,' Hetty said off-handedly. 'Men are like that. They won't change. Like Craig. I've had terrible trouble – he's been so cruel . . .'

'Yes, I wondered – oh, a thousand things!' Léonie, roused now by a desperate curiosity for all Hetty's lost years, could no longer restrain her emotion. 'So often wanted to know – how you'd got on?'

'Wonderfully, to begin with. Oh yes, Craig was so exciting!' She thought to tease Léonie, make her jealous. 'Then Hollywood and everything – but it would all take *days* to tell – and I will tell. Simply, it's been *such* a life!'

'Yes, I've forgotten – you're so famous!' Léonie, ironic, did the teasing now, turning the tables.

'Oh, the fame – that's nothing. Except that being Laura Bowen – that gave me the c-confidence at last to be *myself*,' Hetty lied. 'It's Craig and his cruelties that have ruined everything. One can't live with that – just as you couldn't live with me in the old days, when I was so beastly to you.' Léonie's heart jumped at this – one more happy confirmation of Hetty's change. 'And you?' Hetty propped herself on her elbow, looking down at Léonie, her hair and nose just visible in the shadowy flare light. 'You and Robert? I've often wondered, too – how you've got on – together?'

'I love him, Hetty,' she told her confidently. 'There's been no problem – that way.' Léonie was a fraction less confident in her last words, and Hetty noticed this.

'But you've not changed completely, have you? I mean, about what we did, l-loving each other?'

Léonie had half-expected this question and decided not to lie about it, not to Hetty at least, for it was something she had longed to speak to someone about over the years. 'No, I've not completely changed, I don't think. I still . . .' There was a sudden frustrated urgency in her voice. 'I still see faces in the street, women in cafés – and I wonder what it would be like, loving them, if I did. Such a secret. No one knows.'

Hetty felt a spasm of triumph drumming through her body. The trap had been set and Léonie was approaching the bait.

'Oh, well,' Hetty said lightly. 'That shouldn't be a problem, or a secret—'

'But it *has* to be, don't you see? Robert would be appalled. It'd be the end for us if he knew, if he found me doing anything like that.'

'Not like Craig! He wouldn't mind, with me.'

'You still have . . . the same feelings?'

'Yes,' she said tenderly. 'I do. But not *with* anyone. Not since you,' she lied once more.

She stroked Léonie's cheek again, then her lips, feeling her tongue momentarily on her finger tips, before Léonie withdrew altogether from her, hurriedly, resisting. 'No, Hetty, no, I can't!—'

But Hetty, aroused now and seeing she was only an inch away from success, persisted – drawing this other straining body to her, kissing her silently, their sand-papery faces rubbing together, as Léonie tried to struggle from the embrace, before Hetty, driven by sheer need, exasperation, frustration, goaded on by an explosive mix of deceit and desire, forced herself on Léonie, crushed herself against her, so that Léonie, her resistance snapping, suddenly gave way, responding.

Hetty drew apart then, the better to touch her else-where, so that she could seduce her, make love to her in the narrow space; which she started to do then, with a shivering delicacy at first, opening Léonie's shirt, touch-ing her breasts, before reaching for her sex, flattering it, slipping her fingers down, easing her knickers off, then her own, tangling with Léonie softly, more feverishly, both of them discovering all the forgotten processes of this love in one giddy-making swoop – this shared, sup-pressed nature reborn in them, rubbing their moist gritty bodies together, coming apart, fondling, stroking, kiss-ing, pushing, feeding this passionate renaissance of desire, their shadow lives touched by flame now, explod-ing everywhere about and inside them in an ecstasy of pent-up liberation.

Here, for long minutes on end, as the wind whipped the tent, they lost all sense, morality, maturity, became adolescent again, as they had been in those Dublin days – Léonie the willing victim once more, helpless, craving this fierce domination from Hetty, with its pain – as, lying above her then, Hetty spreadeagled her, punishing her, with love bites all over her neck and shoulders. But Léonie did not care, was quite oblivious in her pleasure – a pleasure she could not contain indefinitely, gulping for air then, twisting, arching, quite speechless at the last; when later she could only murmur, 'Hetty, oh, Hetty darling . . .'

Afterwards Léonie said, 'Robert, he mustn't know, ever.'

'He won't! Because he won't be there. You'll come back with me, won't you?'

Léonie fondled Hetty listlessly. 'Of course not,' she said. 'You know I can't. I told you – it'd be the end between Robert and me.'

'But you can't live a lie with him, Léa! – for the rest of your life.'

'It's not a lie! I love you both.'

'He won't accept that, though. You just said. So you'll always be unhappy, because you won't really have *either* of us. And sooner or later the whole thing with him, well, it'll just die,' she added, playing the devil's advocate for all she was worth. 'You're not being fair – to him or youself.'

'Maybe. But I'll just have to accept that. I can't leave him. There's no question.'

'No,' Hetty said sadly, giving the impression of accepting this – which she did not, not for an instant. Oh yes, she had loved their loving, really wanted Léonie back. But it was hardly love she felt for her. It was more sex – above all power over her, here so happily renewed – which she wanted. And that power she had not yet achieved. Not final power, not full revenge – for their betraying her and marrying. That would only come in her separating Léonie from Robert. So how could that be done? Hetty smiled in the dark. She had practically done it already, she thought.

Robert only had to know how they had made love that night for things to start breaking up between them – that was perfectly clear. And so she had prepared the evidence of this for him with her love bites, which Léonie in her passion had failed to take account of – love bites, on Léa's neck and shoulders, some on her face, which she had so enjoyed, would now be her undoing. Those fierce little teeth marks of possession – which would bloom in the night into red bruised flesh, clear evidence of their passion, would tell all when Robert saw them.

When Léonie, in her impatience to see Robert, rushed over to his tent next morning, she was quite unaware of the livid blemishes dotted over her neck and face.

But Robert, in the windy dawn light as she moved forward to kiss him, saw them clearly enough. 'What's happened – all those marks?'

'Where?' Léonie quickly put a hand to her cheek, colouring, realizing now, remembering what had happened with Hetty, how she had marked her in their passion.

'There – on your neck, everywhere.'

Léonie swung her head round, tilting it downwards. 'Oh that! Just insects – some sort of awful bedbugs – in those goat-skins. We were eaten *alive* last night, in that squalid tent!' She smiled, yet was unable quite to hide her nervousness, covering the bruises with her hand, scratching them.

Hetty had joined them by now, standing next to Léonie, without her robes and headdress, neck and face open to view, the skin pure and unblemished, something of a contented Cheshire cat smile on her face.

Robert looked from one woman to the other. Hating Hetty, and suspicious anyway of their night together in the harem, some sixth sense was at work in him now, quite against his better nature, anxious to promote and confirm his worst fears. He turned back to Léonie.

'Bedbugs, you say? Both eaten alive? But there's no mark anywhere – on Hetty.' He looked more closely at Léonie's neck, at the tiny intermittent empurpled bruises just beneath the flesh. 'Why wasn't Hetty bitten?'

'Oh, Robert! – you are being a bore,' Léonie said with joking impatience, trying to bluff her way out. 'I don't *know* why she wasn't bitten – though she said she had been, didn't you, Hetty?' She turned, desperately seeking confirmation, which Hetty thought it politic to offer.

'Yes,' she said vaguely, rubbing her untouched skin.

But the poison had taken with Robert now – so that suddenly, sure that he was being cheated, lied to, and unable to contain his frustration any longer, he became enraged, a quite unexpected fury breaking out through his normally kind and placid nature. 'You're lying! – both of you! You take me for an idiot!' he shouted at them. 'As if I can't see what you were both up to last night! Bedbugs indeed, when it was your squalid love-making. How could you, Léa? How *could* you? – on what was supposed to be our honeymoon.' He glared at her, shaking with rage. 'Well, you can have each other, if that's what you want. I never want to see you – either of you – again.'

'Robert, it's not true! I love you!—'

But already Robert was walking away from them, as fast as his leg allowed, making towards their horses. Léonie rushed after him. 'Robert! You *can't* go, don't be an idiot – it's not *true*, I love you—'

'Liar,' he interrupted. 'Liar, liar, *liar*!' He kept on repeating the word, a vicious malediction, pushing her aside roughly so that she fell to the sand, crying out, a mix of sobbing emotion, physical pain, sheer terror at this impending desertion. Hetty, who had watched all this with a faint, wise smile, rushed out to Léonie then, picking her up, consoling her. 'It's all right, Léa – it's *all right*. Just a tiff – he'll get over it . . .'

Léonie did not reply – just pushed Hetty away from her, kneeling now, doubled up with sobs, as the hazy sun rose through drifts of fine sand far above them and Robert stumbled on towards his horse. Hetty gazed out over the wide desert panorama: the figure of Léonie, motionless, quite desolated, in front of her; Robert moving inexorably away, the distance ever widening between them, dividing them.

Hetty savoured what was perhaps her greatest, and certainly most malign, triumph. Fate indeed – at this point and for years, she reflected – had dealt her all the high cards, every one: the joker that had led to her meeting with Craig, who had made her a great star; the glittering royal card which had brought her the role of Queen Nefertiti . . . and now an ace, with which she had regained Léonie. There were many triumphs to savour.

For surely it was obvious at last: fate had nothing but
royal cards and aces for her.

8

Robert, still unforgiving, had taken the train back to
Cairo alone, leaving Léonie with Hetty on King Fuad's
steamer. Léonie had pleaded with him, and – in a calmer,
more philosophic mood at least – he had told her, 'Look,
it's something you'll just have to work out alone. Get it
out of your system. Or not get it out – and take up with
Hetty again. It's no use my being with you now. I can't
help you decide what's your real nature. Though God
knows I've tried, all that last year in Paris . . .'

'But, Robert, it's nothing, *nothing* to divide us. I love
you just as much as ever, promise . . .' She gazed at him,
in so loving a manner, quite without guile, that he was
forced to believe her.

'Perhaps,' he said. 'But I can't share you with Hetty.'

'I'm *not* going to go on loving her, Robert! It's *you* I
want to do that with! You, you, *you!*' She looked at him
challengingly. But he made no response, maintaining his
cold indifference, so that she became quite abject.
'You're only punishing me now, and it's not fair, not
just . . .' And she had started to sob then. 'How could
you do this to me?'

'How could you have done . . . what you did . . . to
me?' he replied calmly, just as unhappy as she was. She
could not answer through her tears. 'I just think it better
we don't see each other for a while. Give us time to think
things over. Only going to make things worse, if we stay
together, rub salt in the wounds . . . You have your
ticket back to Paris. We'll meet there, later, at the flat.

Maybe we'll both be able to think about it more clearly then. For the moment I can't think sensibly about anything. I'm just – so *angry* . . .' And he had left, without admitting how he was simply so hurt, which Léonie understood well enough, blaming herself, as she had to, and so letting him go without further argument or protestation. What else could she do? She had, after all, brought the whole tragedy on herself, and she was mortified.

Léonie, quite drained by all this emotional bloodletting, and by the oppressive, sand-filled heat brought on by the khamsin, had more or less collapsed and taken to her bed in the cabin of the royal steamer which Hetty had organized for her. There, she was tended by the film unit's Italian doctor, given sedatives and cold compresses; an electric fan blew over her bruised and tear-stained face. For Hetty, having regained her possession, this glittering trophy which was Léonie, had other fish to fry, and bones to pick, with Craig.

At first, on her return, he had been furious with her. But, filled with the success of her escapades and conquests in the desert, she had simply mocked him. 'Pe-pe-perhaps,' she told him as briskly as her stammer allowed, 'you'll be more considerate towards me now, stop p-playing the brute behind the camera. You say you've missed two days' filming without me? Just be glad you haven't lost the whole picture! Remember, at this st-st-stage, *I'm* the p-person they need in it, not you.' She glared at him, before striding away to her cabin, walking on air.

Craig had to accept defeat. The worm had turned. He pondered the matter. Hetty had taken up with her old girl friend again – that was what had really set her all cock-a-hoop. Well, this hardly mattered. And it would not last – if he did not want it to. Hetty's cheeky confidence and independence from him, he knew, was a passing thing. Soon, either Hetty would tire of the girl as she had before, or Léonie herself would go scuttling back to her husband.

He still held all the real cards with Hetty – her access to professional mastery in him being just one of them, for she could never make successful pictures on her own since no other director could mimic his unique hold over her, on camera or off. He had created 'Laura Bowen' – a painstaking, lengthy manipulation – professionally, emotionally, sexually. And, for as long as Hetty wanted to inhabit this invented persona, and draw the glittering dividends that accrued from it, then he was her master. He knew he would only ever lose that power over her if she decided to forsake everything in her life as Laura Bowen and return to her earlier character as Henrietta Fraser – that divided, frantically unhappy girl she had been when they had first met.

This she would never do, Craig thought. Who would wish to return to such early horrors, re-inhabit all those bitter familial hurts, enmities, divisions? – all that Hetty had suffered from in Ireland. Above all, what woman, like Hetty, whose problems all stemmed from her lack of a father, would ever willingly return to a fatherless state? He was her father now – that was his strongest suit, the essence of his hold over her. Father, brother, playmate, confidant, friend, lover, enemy – he was all things to her, he knew, but most particularly the first: wise, powerful, all-knowing, ever reliable, for good or ill, there to pick her up from the worst pitfalls and mistakes, punishing yet forgiving, but finally distant, unknowable, not ever to be fully possessed in return.

These were the cards which Craig held – one or all of which he could bring into play at any time, from now on, so regaining control of what he knew to be finally his possession: Laura Bowen.

Why, he only had to make love to her again, for

example, to mimic love to her, as he had done so often before, to regain her. Yes, he thought, he would reward Hetty with that, not at once, something she would construe as a weakness, an admission of guilt or fault on his part, but later when they returned to France in a few weeks' time, for the interior work at the Victorine studios in Nice. Meanwhile, let her savour her illusions with Léonie – while he, once more, would take some final pleasures with the child brides in the black-tented bordello on the edge of the desert.

They were nearing the end of the shooting in Egypt. Only two exterior sequences remained. But they were major ones, which would require all the present fellahin extras together with the addition of a regiment of Khedival cavalry in Cairo, already sent up-river and encamped beyond the tented city. The first was the attack from Thebes, led by the old conservative priests, on Amarna – and the second their subsequent gory victory, when the renegade citizens of Akhenaten's royal capital are put to the sword, the city itself sacked and burnt, the apostasy of these sun-worshippers extinguished for ever.

But these epic sequences were delayed by the cloudy, hazy skies and gritty wind that had come unexpectedly with the early khamseen. Work came to a halt everywhere. Accountants all the way from America, some from Nice and others down from Cairo, loomed ominously in the production office by the river. Invoices and payrolls were mustered and computed, ledgers grimly compared, columns of figures added and subtracted, as vast debts emerged. Urgent telegrams began to move to and fro – between Amarna and Cairo, Cairo, Hollywood and the head office of the Fox Film Corporation in New York.

And it was here, in his oak-panelled office on West 56th Street, that William Fox himself, a sallow, bald-headed, aggressive man nursing a withered arm, came to inspect these same appalling debts, brought to him by his flamboyant production chief, Winfield Sheehan. Worse still, that same morning in March 1926, Sheehan had brought him the latest crop of dailies from *Nefertiti*, over eight reels of film, a month's work in Egypt, including much of the earlier perverse and unscripted footage, which Craig had intentionally delayed sending. The two men had just emerged from the small projection room next to Fox's office. And Fox, so startled by what he had just seen, was speechless with rage, unable at once to comment on these reels of uncut film, so that he tried to distract himself with lesser ills, pawing about among the *Nefertiti* production accounts lying on his huge desk beneath a tall stained-glass window.

'There's nothin', but *nothin*' . . .' Lighting a cigar, he picked up a sheet of figures at random. 'Not a goddamned thing in this production, Sheehan, that ain't a fuck-up of bullshit. Here, take a look at this,' he went on in his strident, lower-East-Side Hungarian accent. 'Twelve thousand dollars – to "palm-trees"! But that country's *full* of fuckin' palm-trees! Seen pictures of 'em, can't move for goddamned palm-trees. So what the fuck is Craig *doin*' – importing palm-trees?' he roared out in sheer disbelief.

'They didn't have any there in the desert, up-river, Bill—'

'And here, even worse,' Fox went on, turning over another sheet in the accounts, 'fourteen thousand bucks for "clover" – now someone must be right outa their mind there, Sheehan, "clover" – that's right! Bloody living in it! *Fourteen thousand dollars* for "clover". It says so. Now, what is this, Sheehan?' He tried to wave his withered arm about, so incensed had he become. 'Palm-trees? Clover? Are we in some big agricultural business out there?'

'It's the grass, the forage, Bill, from the local farmers,

to feed all the horses. It's all desert country up there on the other side of the river . . .'

Fox stopped then, quite motionless, seeming to relax. '"Forage, clover" . . .' he said at last, with an ominous quietness, weighing up these mysterious words, licking his lips, seeming to taste some exotic but unpleasant foodstuff. Then he exploded, his black moustache dancing up and down as he roared out, 'I've been conned, Sheehan! No one's spending twenty-six thousand bucks of my money – on clover and palm-trees – and getting away with it! . . .'

'Yes, Bill—'

'What d'ya mean "Yes, Bill"? They've gone and done it, haven't they?'

'Yes, they have. They *had* to! Even horses have to eat, Bill—'

'And that's only the *beginning*!' Fox started to stride about the office now, his agitation rising. 'Those dailies, Sheehan, we just saw – millions of dollars, and it's all porno-graphy – *porno-graphy*! Cock-suckers, rapists, pansy boys, hoors, deviates, every one of them. Why, ya couldn't show that stuff from one end of the land here to the other, not even in *Mexico*, Sheehan. Over three million dollars already – on cock-suckers! We're ruined, Sheehan, ruined!' Fox started to dance about his office in fury. 'Get me Howard Brenon. We'll have him on the picture straight away. And get that two-timing bastard Craig *right* outa it! And sue him, Sheehan! We'll *sue* him, the fuckin' little porno-grapher . . .'

'But he has a contract, Bill—'

'Yeah, and he's broken that contract! None of this crap was in the original outline – or the scenario – we OKed. He's made it all up as he went along! I *knew* we shoulda never let him out there alone, with all those weird dagoes and wogs, the goddamned little prick of a Paddy! Tossing himself off – on *my* money.' Fox tried to activate his withered arm again, such was his fury. 'And this was supposed to be a *family* picture, Sheehan – a great *religious* picture – with that Pharaoh an early runner for Jesus Christ. And what do we have? A picture ya couldn't even show in a sporting house – in *Mexico* . . .'

'Yes, Bill, but—'

'No fuckin' buts, Sheehan! Get on to it – get Brenon in, and a new editor, and start cutting out all that crap I wouldn't even show my worst enemy.' Fox started to scratch his crotch vigorously.

'But, Bill, if we fire Craig, we'll lose Laura as well. Remember? – we have a deal with them, as partners together on *Nefertiti* – with their company Willbow Pictures. Without Laura we couldn't even begin the interiors in France – whole picture'd be straight down the drain then.'

'Jesus,' Fox said softly. 'I'd forgotten.' Then he burst forth once more. 'The short and curlies, Sheehan!' he roared. 'They have us by them!' He started a series of little jumps then, like a jack-in-the-box, both feet off the ground at once, skipping across the thick pile carpet.

'*Yes*, Bill . . .'

Fox came to a halt. 'Well, I tell ya, Sheehan – every dog has his day. But I'll nail Craig good, one way or the other, believe me. He'll never work in Hollywood again, for *any*one, after this picture. And, as for Laura Bowen, she musta bin in the bag with him over all this, from the very start! Well, she's for the big drop *anyways* . . .'

'What do you mean, Bill?' Sheehan, who had thought he could handle all Fox's earlier bluster, was now suddenly anxious. 'Whatever Craig's done with the scenario, Laura's absolutely sensational in the picture, best thing she's ever done. Just to look at her! – why, there's a fortune to be made out of this picture, if we can just cut the crap out. So what do you mean? – she's for the drop?'

Sheehan, regaining all his flamboyance, was almost aggressive now, leaning across the desk.

Fox smiled for the first time that morning. 'I'll tell you what I mean! For only fifty grand, I just bought all US rights to this new Kraut sound picture process, Sheehan – Tri-Ergo or some cockamanie thing it's called. Going to put a bomb under the whole picture business. Change everything! – a whole new breed of directors, technicians, and most of all stars, Sheehan! We're going to need stars that can *speak*, don't ya see? Not broads like Marion Davies and Laura Bowen – who talk like they had a bag of marbles in their mouths.'

Sheehan was astonished. 'But, Bill, Laura's our biggest money-spinner—'

'Yeah, in *silent* pictures! But with this new Kraut sing-song stuff she won't be! I tell ya, Sheehan, I aim to teach *both* of 'em – a *real* lesson . . .'

The khamseen passed away, the picture started up again and Léonie, physically at least, recovered. But her relationship with Hetty, living together on the *Omar Khayam* now, was cold and strained. So that Hetty, returning each evening from the sets, became frustrated with this toy she had regained but was unable now to play with. Léonie, still exhausted and vastly depressed, looked sourly on everything and everyone, and that included Hetty.

'But it really *wasn't* my fault, Léa!' Hetty told her one evening at dinner, as they ate alone in the candlelit royal salon. 'I've told you, haven't I? How could either of us have known, in the dark, that my . . . loving you that way – that Robert would come to see it all?'

Léonie, as before horrified by the memory of this love-making, made no reply. She did not, though, suspect that Hetty had bitten her with just this end in view, so that Robert would discover their passion and leave her.

For she knew perfectly well that she had shared the passion that night. And now she was simply so deeply ashamed at herself, at this act of resurgent nature that had ruined her life, that she could not speak of it, could not face anything of it in herself. She thought of nothing but how she could regain Robert – and this was all she wanted to talk about with Hetty. So, instead of replying to the question, she said without a glimmer of emotion, 'The only thing I want – is to have him back.'

'But, Léa, if Robert really loved you – he wouldn't *do* this to you, treat you like that and just leave you here. He wouldn't p-punish you – he'd *forgive* you, if he really loved you!' And then she added, most reasonably, 'Because after all it's not as if he never knew about you and me, how we . . . loved each other. So it shouldn't have been such a shock to him, when he found out we'd . . . loved each other again. Don't you see?' she said tenderly, shaking her head sadly in the soft candlelight. 'He's just being childish about it all. Really is. I've known him – really a lot longer than you! If he was grown up, well, at least he'd feel some sympathy or understanding for you. But he can't, you see, because he just wants to pe-possess you, losing both his parents and so on. That's his *real* problem. So he can't really love you – it's just jealousy and spite – *that's* what really dominates in him. Like most men,' she added for good measure.

Hetty, not only playing the devil's advocate again, was presenting much more of her own failings and feelings towards Léonie. And, at last, Léonie began to have suspicions.

'I don't believe all that,' she said evenly. And then, showing some vigour and emotion, 'Oh, I know him, too, Hetty! You forget that! And different things, things you couldn't possibly know about him at all, no matter how long you've known him before. The person, these last few years in Paris – you've never known that part of him. And, besides, it was *you* who simply wanted to possess me in the old days. Remember?' she asked acidly. 'You who always played the childish jealous thing, who wouldn't grow up.'

'Yes,' Hetty admitted, mimicking the older and wiser woman now perfectly. 'You're right, I did. But I've changed. Can't you see? And that's what's so ironic: Robert is doing what I used to do – showing his true colours at last. I don't want to own you any more, or go in for all that juvenile dressing up thing. That was only because of all the bad things I felt then. It's so obvious! I've got all that *out* of me, these last years, in my work, not bottling it up and letting it sour everything in my own life.'

This was an honest-enough appraisal of Hetty's – as far as it went. But it was not the whole story. Hetty lied by omission. She had indeed matured, in so professionally diverting these histrionic frustrations. But she had not lost her will to power, her need to dominate and control. Far from it. This urge had fattened on its appetite, become a vast and greedy thing, which bloomed in the dark, a malign flower. And as before, when she wanted to blackmail Léonie into sharing her fantasies, now she simply wanted to devour her, let loose this voracious hound, which, since Craig no longer fed it, she could not contain within the walls of her temperament.

'I only want you to be happy,' she went on. 'Like me, expressing your real self. Léa. *Our* real selves. That's all.' She was wonderfully meek in this exposition. 'Can't go on telling lies about our real nature, all our lives – that's what I've found anyway, with you the other night. I know it now. Tried to avoid it, just like you. But I can't any more.'

Again, the fair reason here, resonant in her voice, in Hetty's whole candid attitude, could not but affect Léonie. And Léonie had to admit it now: she could, she did, she had loved women – even though of course she loved Robert much more now. She had simply blinded herself to this fact, avoided the issue for so long, for the sake of Robert. She loved men and women – in the shape of Robert and Hetty at least – and could not handle this quality in her nature, as Hetty obviously had come to do. So that the tables were turned now, and it was she, not Hetty, who had the problems of immaturity here – she who might well now be accused of behaving childishly, of dissembling, of avoiding this vital issue: a point which Hetty, with her cunning sixth sense, saw at once, confirming it then, leaning forward, touching her on the arm.

'Because, Léa, you must see – it's not fair to Robert, to lie to him like that – about this, anyway, something so important in your life. After all you told me, that night in the tent – and it was so obvious anyway then – you *do* like women. You like me at any rate! And I love you, not just the love-making thing. And you can't go on having it b-both ways – being secret about that other part of you, with Robert, *and* loving him, as if you *only* loved him, only loved men. I tell you, even if we hadn't met out here, and you'd gone on like that with him, it'd all have come out one day – exploded, with some other w-woman, someone at a café or in the chorus, just like you said.'

And Léonie had to admit the truth of this. 'Yes,' she said hopelessly. 'Perhaps . . .'

'No, it's a certainty, Léa. 'Cos the one thing I do know is that, if people lie about something for a long time, like my Mama – about my father – it all leads to much worse trouble in the end. The tr-tr-truth can't hurt us, I've always told you that, told Mama, too. But she was too far gone to take any notice then. So, you see, the only way you can lose . . . is by going on lying to Robert about yourself . . .'

'And you, with Craig?' Léonie enquired. 'He doesn't mind – that other part of your nature, your expressing it?'

Hetty laughed, huge eyes dancing beneath her urchin haircut. 'Oh no. He's known about you and me all along. I told him. Entirely understanding about it – least he used to be, until recently, before he took to just playing the b-bully boy.'

'But you – you loved him, in that way, too?'

'*Yes!* Of course I did. Because I like men, too, Léa – just as much as you do – sometimes. Because, you see! – we're just the same sort of people in that way, loving men and women. Except the p-point is – and things have rather proved it, haven't they – I think at heart we really like w-women, like each other anyway, better than any man. Don't we? So why don't we live together? Come back with me! We have a lovely villa – one of Napoleon's generals built it – right in the middle of the studios at Nice. Craig wouldn't mind. Don't you see? You could go on with your opera work in the south, at Monte Carlo maybe. Because Craig is going to work in Nice permanently now, take over the little studios there, never going to go back to Hollywood again, which we both loathe. And we're going to do another picture in Nice right after this one. So *do* come back with us, Léa!' she ran on with vast enthusiasm. 'Oh, Léa, there's so much you and I could *do* together again, make up for all my idiocies in the past, now that I'm . . . so much easier with myself and won't b-bully you and be stupid: all the things we *should* have been doing all these years, if only I hadn't behaved like such a fool. Do come!'

Just as Craig, seven years before in the Shelbourne Hotel in Dublin, had offered Hetty the promised land of Hollywood, with all its temptations of glittering self-expression and appropriate happiness, so Hetty offered the same to Léonie now. But Léonie, stunned by the

offer for an instant, said nothing, so that Hetty, misinter-
preting her blank expression, was forced to illuminate
the vision further. 'Oh, I know,' she continued. 'You
think Robert would never have you b-back, if you did
that, came and lived with us for a bit. But, Léa! – that's
the whole point! You mustn't crawl back to him. That'd
be fatal, promise you. Because, after all, you've nothing
to be ashamed of! It's you – your true nature, loving
men *and* women. Your generosity. There's no guilt in
that. So stop all this *pe-pleading* attitude with him. Why
should you be ashamed of what's really you? – that you
love him, but have, well, an affection for women too. If
he won't see that . . . then he's not worth living with.
And if you *do* go on living with him, and deny your true
feelings, then the whole m-marriage is a fraud and a lie.
You have to operate from a position of strength with him,
not weakness, lies or excuses. *Then* he'll have you b-back.
You'll see!'

Again it seemed a fair argument – one which, in many
such emotional divisions, could well have led to a reconciliation. Léonie, by the skin of her teeth, was persuaded by it. 'All right!' she said at last. 'I'll stay here.
And come back to France with you.'

Subsequently she wrote to Robert, explaining her
decision – writing to him lovingly thereafter almost every
day, believing, on Hetty's advice, that she was taking the
correct decision by postponing her return. Which she
was, in a way, for Hetty's advice was valid enough –
though Léonie was unaware that Hetty intended she
never succeed in implementing her proposals.

But Hetty reached the summit of her triumphs the
following day, on set, in her final location scenes with
Clive Brook. As Craig's script demanded, the priests of
the old faith down-river at Thebes, together with the
army of lower Egypt, finally take their revenge on Akhenaten, storming Amarna, sacking the golden city, setting

it ablaze, erasing every image and memory of the sun god Aten and his earthly disciples.

But prior to this, seeing the hopelessness of their position, Akhenaten and Nefertiti choose death in a murder-suicide pact rather than acknowledge any public defeat in their religious and sexual obsessions.

These scenes were shot in the little gilded love pavilion, with its delicate hieroglyphics and cartouches depicting the ideal domestic happiness shared between the royal pair in their earlier lives together – the pavilion perched over the ornamental lake in the palace gardens, where the two had retreated, the army from Thebes already battering at the palace doors, storming the walls.

Hetty – dressed in all her full regalia, the magnificent blue and gold headdress, silver-threaded robes, sun-burst jewellery – gazes at Akhenaten for a long moment, lovingly, remembering the young man there, the days of hope, all the freshness of their love then, their belief in the loving sun god Aten.

Akhenaten, almost an old man now, bulbous and gross in all his increasing deformities, returns the gaze, wordlessly, something of his old fire returning to his eyes at least, before he stares down on the lake water, seeing the reflections of carnage there from the palace gates and walls, then looks back at Nefertiti, pleading now for death.

She kills him, in a murderous embrace, smothering the dagger in his stomach, before turning defiantly on the approaching soldiers, holding the dagger aloft, then driving it deep into her own breast, blood seeping through the diaphanous linen, flooding the robe, as she falls headlong into the lake, floating there among the lotus flowers, head turning in a faint smile, then sinking slowly in front of the astonished soldiers, gathering round now, afraid to touch her, save her, do anything for her – as she disappears, replaced then by a brilliant sunburst on the water, from a great carbon arc suddenly ignited over the set.

Hetty's regality, her courage, beauty and self-belief, had earlier reached an incandescent pitch, which she maintained throughout the day, in a performance that was lived through, barely acted at all. Here was Nefertiti – but Hetty, too – a woman renouncing nothing, standing by her life, every moment of it, every act, good and bad, faithful unto death. It was a sensational performance – Hetty's apotheosis. And the applause at the end of it, when Craig finally called 'Cut!' was spontaneous and unstinted.

Mickey Ostrovosky was quite bewildered by it all. What further triumphs in this art could there be for this woman who seemed now, in the role as Nefertiti, to have exhausted every emotion available to a woman?

And Léonie, too, watching from the sidelines, was equally spellbound, believing she had witnessed a final confirmation of all her hopes for Hetty, in which the evil that was in her character had finally passed over into Nefertiti, had now all been encapsulated and sealed there, dying with the Queen.

Léonie chose not to see how Hetty, in this last act, had forsaken nothing of her divided temperament – that it was just these violent contradictions, maintained and fanned in her soul, which enabled her so wonderfully to impersonate the Queen, in all her good and evil.

Instead, standing behind her at the mirror, back in her dressing tent as Hetty disrobed, wiping her make-up off, Léonie allowed herself to be drawn once more into Hetty's magic orbit, the shining lights round the mirror, a moth to flame – fluffing her short-cropped hair about for an instant, before Hetty took her hand gently and put it to her lips, smiling up at her reflection.

'Well?'

'It was – extraordinary . . .'

Léonie's fingers slipped down and she stroked Hetty's neck, before Hetty caught her hand again quickly and put it to her still damp and bloodied breast. 'It's only the beginning again, Léa – for us.'

Léonie, in a daze of light and warmth, let the intimacy continue, even when Hetty put her hand directly on her breast, so that Léonie felt the heartbeats, strong, vibrant, before the dresser arrived in the tent.

Léonie hurriedly withdrew her hand, smeared with make-up blood. She looked at the crimson on her fingers. And something turned over in her stomach, some strange emotion, deep and happy yet tinged with horror, a feeling she did not understand.

Hetty experienced quite a different emotion just then, which she understood very well: it was a sense, finally confirmed now, of invincible power, which Léa could not resist – that of an animal toying with its prey. She had regained everything, she felt: professionally – and personally, in the shape of Léonie. She had reached the supreme moment in her life.

Hetty turned her gaze again towards Léonie in the mirror, almost exactly mimicking the sum of all this – this expression which for Léonie, as always, remained inscrutable, the central mystery of her attraction, which thus formed the hold which Hetty maintained over her, a mystery which Léonie could never decipher; if she had, she would have found as much dross as gold.

Later, in the days that followed, moving around with the cameras, the women watched the vast action sequences which would complete the picture: the initial battles on the Nile – the surprise attack by the army from Thebes coming up-river, in a collection of adapted feluccas, engaging Akhenaten's two royal barges, putting them to rout with flaming slingshots and arrows; then the long lines of soldiers disembarking on the east bank below the Royal Palace, unloading stores and armaments, commandeering Akhenaten's chariots, before storming through the city.

First they rampaged down the Royal Way, chopping down all the hanging flower baskets, ramming doors open, starting to massacre the citizens of Amarna. Then they entered the great plaza of the temple, where most of Akhenaten's priests, courtiers and nobles had retreated – bludgeoning their way through, laying about them with their short swords, desecrating the sanctuary, blood spilling everywhere on the beautiful mosaic pavements, before launching a final attack on the holy of holies at the high altar, using ladders and grappling irons, climbing up and pulling the great sun disc emblems from their niches; the white bas-reliefs of Akhenaten, Nefertiti and their children crashing down, splintering among the dead bodies of the priests, signifying final doom for Akhenaten's apostasy.

Afterwards, gasoline having been sprinkled in crucial places, the city that had taken so much of Fox's money and Leo Kuter's loving genius to build, was set alight – the pastel-coloured wooden buildings at one end of the Royal Way going first, so that soon, like a long fuse, the whole street took fire, in crackling bursts, fed by its own internal winds, creating explosive vacuums and fire storms, the painted lotus-flowered lintels above the doors smouldering and peeling at first as the heat drew near, then exploding as the fire ran on down the street; costumed extras stumbling, falling with it, before the flames caught the bridge at one end, ripping across it, a great pall of fiery smoke filling the 'Window of Appearances', then rushing on to devour and engulf the Royal Palace.

It was a holocaust of flame, mayhem, destruction – ash and sooty cinders leaping up far above the river into the bright blue dome of sky, so that soon, with the dusk, the city was reduced to red embers.

The heat on the girls' faces, as they watched from one

of the half-dozen camera rostrums, was intense. Hetty was upset at this final destruction of Amarna, this end of Nefertiti's and Akhenaten's dream; it touched her, pricking tears – this violation of their love together as King and Queen in their early days, this destruction of their religious creation, both reflected now in the fiery debris all about them: the end of an age of hope in ancient Egypt, to be replaced once more by the old regime at Thebes, with a further one and a half thousand years of darkness, superstition, evil.

She turned to Léonie. 'An end of love, isn't it? – of what was good. You see why, don't you?' she hurried on. 'Why it's really going to be a *great* picture! Because it really *says* something – how evil always wins out, the urge to destroy! Unless we fight against it,' she added as an after-thought, her moist eyes glittering in the firelight, dazed, mad even.

Léonie nodded, thinking she understood. 'You mean – like you had to fight what was bad in you?' And Hetty nodded vigorously in return. 'But, Hetty, here it seems the other way round – the good is killed in the end. Surely people won't want to see that? – if there's no hope—'

'There's the *truth*, though. That's more important.'

'But lots of people don't like the truth, won't face it – especially not in picture palaces.'

Hetty at that moment, however, felt impelled by it. 'The truth can't hurt us, Léa! I told you. Only our fears of it, our illusions.' She touched Léonie's arm. 'Don't you see? – we're free now. From here we can go *anywhere*!'

What Hetty meant was that this brutal sacking of the city reflected the true nature of things in life for her. In short, this holocaust justified her own continued scheming and destructive behaviour. It reassured her greatly to think that people, even so powerful as Akhenaten and

Nefertiti, had been unable to win over these basic imperfections in humanity – as she had been unable to do. The burning of the city, this triumph of evil, exactly paralleled her own remaining flaws, confirming the validity of all those malign parts in her own quite unreconstructed nature.

Craig, nearby, stood on top of another high rostrum with his cameraman Johnny Seitz, cap still back to front, filming these last images of destruction, the sparks and ashes of Akhenaten's dream city blowing up into the indigo sky.

Throughout these last days of shooting, Craig had watched the destruction of the city with an increasingly exultant expression, a face that matched the fires raging beneath him now – as if, as with Hetty, this end to love and beauty perfectly reflected his own deepest beliefs. He seemed to thrive on this desecration of hope, proof of his own sad philosophy that there could be no lasting happiness, that the malign and the perverse would always triumph in the end. And, in this, he and Hetty were the real sisters under the skin, not Hetty and Léonie.

Now, still immaculately dressed, his white silk shirt smudged with flying cinders, he watched this last grim action with a studied satisfaction, until the flames finally began to wane and he gripped the big megaphone, shouting 'Cut!' – then swivelled the huge cone round to the other cameras – 'Cut!' – 'Cut!' – 'And *thank you*, ladies and gentlemen, all and every one of you. Thank you, *grazie, merci, shoukran* – and that's it!'

He mopped his brow, then turned to Seitz. And suddenly, in the heat of the moment, they embraced briefly. 'Thank you, Johnny. The end, though? Why, it's hardly the beginning . . .'

Léonie glanced over at the two men, seeing this gesture of professional camaraderie, something she was quite familiar with in the world of grand opera. And something touched her then, an emotion about Craig she had never expected: a grudging admiration for his myriad skills, his single-minded dedication, his artistry, his passion to encapsulate all that was vivid and passing in real life, trapping it on these little frames of celluloid, before casting them as mere shadows on a silver screen. There was something heroic in all this, she recognized. And, though she still hated him for his wrong-doing with Hetty, she saw now how Hetty was really a secondary consideration to him. He only lived among, and loved, these flickering emblems of life, invented images quite outside reality. About people, real people, he was hollow. They were just pawns to him on his chessboard of dreams. And she said as much to Hetty later that night on the steamer, in Hetty's cabin, when they were getting dressed for the unit party. 'Just pawns.' And she continued, 'I can see now why you haven't got a future with him, because nobody has, in their real lives: only on the screen.'

But Hetty was surprised at this. 'Oh yes, he's been awful, ghastly, these last months. But that's his work, Léa – all the frightful difficulties of this location. Back in Nice . . . it'll be quite d-different. And even better when the picture's finished. Then he'll be fine – you'll see! Of *course* I've got a future with him. Just as you have with Robert. It doesn't always have to be either/or, you know. We *all* have a future – together. All four of us!'

Léonie was confused by this. She had wanted, in her ideal world, to love both Robert and Hetty, for them to reciprocate. But she had no plans whatsoever in this vague idea for Craig. She could never for an instant – as Hetty obviously did – imagine Craig becoming any sort of friend of hers.

Yet it was not only Hetty's hope that this might happen – it was Craig's, too. Now that the location work was over, it had crossed his mind that Léonie, Hetty's old lover, was an attractive woman, had something about her

. . . Hetty's earlier impertinence, her cheeky independence, had continued to aggravate him mildly. Well, he
would start to draw the kite string now, but in quite a
different manner than he had earlier foreseen.

Hetty's real purpose, he was pretty certain, in this
renewed association with Léonie, had not been so much
to love the woman, but simply to use her as a means of
asserting her independence against him. And more than
that, for he could read her mind like a book, Hetty – to
punish the woman for her marriage – had simply wanted
to divide her from her husband.

Well, he could do something of the same sort to bring
Hetty to heel – divide her from this old love renewed,
separate her in turn from Léonie, by intimating in some
manner how Hetty's love for her was only skin-deep,
which of course was no more than the truth. What would
serve his purposes here? Then it suddenly struck him –
the livid little teeth marks he'd seen on Léonie's neck
and face, when he'd met her briefly on their return from
the desert. And, of course, it was clear to him then – that
had been Hetty's way of taking Léonie from Robert,
of showing him conclusive proof of their covert passion
together that night in the tent among the bedouin
women, by fixing her mark on the girl, something she
had intended from the start – not as true passion, but
simply as evidence of that passion. Well, if Hetty had so
separated these two, he would do the same for Hetty in
turn – separate her from Léonie, using the same lever,
those love bites. The idea had a perfect symmetry to it,
which appealed to him as much as anything.

Craig at the party that evening, with the principal
actors and technicians, was at his most relaxed and
genial. Released at last from months of tension, all his
old boyish charm emerged again, his Celtic roguishness.
And there was drink, too, for the first time on the location
– crates of Gianaclis's red and white wine sent up from

Cairo, so that soon there was an air of conviviality, release, truth-tellings.

Some hundred or so people were on board the *Omar Khayam* that night, milling about the open decks under the stars, trestle tables laden with cold delta pigeon and Port Said prawns — while others chatted in the huge mahogany salon with its opulent *belle époque* décor. And it was here, after supper, with Hetty engaged elsewhere, that Craig, in a white dinner jacket and red carnation, tactfully cornered Léonie, apologizing for not having paid her more attention in the past weeks, his eyes wheeling over her in a gaze that was both contrite yet mischievous.

'Oh no, not at all – it didn't matter.' Léonie tried to be as distant and formal with him as she could.

'Oh yes,' Craig ran on, at his most charming. 'Just I'd not the time. And I'd wanted to . . . to sympathize with you as well, over Robert. Wanted to apologize in general. Knowing how close you were to Hetty, in the old days – well, you must have thought me – think me – a real bastard!' Léonie made as if to concur with this view, before he ran on, 'Yes, you're quite right. Obviously, why wouldn't you think that? When I took Hetty up in Ireland, I left a lot of damage behind. And I'm sorry, truly sorry. But I loved her, love her, just as much as you did – and do,' he added, coming to the point now, in quite a different tone of voice, soft and serious. So that Léonie was involuntarily drawn into his confidence then. 'You see, I wanted to help her just as much as you did then, and now . . . all that unhappiness with her mother. And her father, or rather the lack of one. And I think I have helped her. She's a lot easier these last years, expressing herself, all the things she'd bottled up. We all have to *express* ourselves these days, don't we?' He laughed nicely. 'The curse of the age! But she's done that. And she's a much better person now . . .' Yet as he said this a distinct note of doubt came into his voice, and he broke off in a dying fall, so that Léonie, intrigued, spoke for the first time.

'Better. But you're not quite sure?'

'Well, we all want that for her, don't we? Trouble is, the pressure of her work, being such a big star, it's not easy, being *always* better. In some ways she's worse because she's so successfully expressed herself – worse in her own private life, I mean, because the Laura Bowen part of her leaks into her real life. Do you get me? Being a picture star satisfies all that acting thing in her, but it gets to be quite at odds with her own true personality, gives her ideas she can't, or certainly shouldn't, act on privately, like running away into the desert the other day. She gets to mix the two things up – the public and the private person, confuses them – and that's dangerous, for herself and just as much for other people, her friends, do you see?'

'Yes, I think I do . . .'

In fact Léonie – taking this as a very fair appraisal – saw exactly what he meant. And she slightly thawed towards Craig now, acknowledging his percipience, his apparent care and concern for Hetty.

'So what we have to do,' Craig continued in a more lighthearted manner, 'is to try and see she doesn't go on confusing fantasy with fact like this. And that's been difficult for me, since making pictures with her I naturally have to *encourage* her fantasies! And it's not so easy then to get her back on an even keel after a picture's over. So I'm glad you're coming back with us, for a bit, to Nice, while you get things straight with your husband. And I'm sorry about that, by the way – all this talk of Hetty when you've suffered far more than her right now – truly sorry.'

'Yes. Yes, it was all so stupid. I want him back. Robert

simply . . . misunderstood things . . .' Léonie was confused.

'Well, that's the very danger, you see.' Craig, having carefully laid the foundations and seeing this confusion, moved in for the kill. 'Like I was saying, it's this very problem of Hetty's – that's caused all the trouble, between you and Robert: her playing games, mixing fantasy with fact, so that other people are bound to suffer . . .'

'I don't quite follow. Playing games with me and Robert? What games?'

'Oh . . .' Craig paused, looking at her quizzically. 'I thought you understood. Hetty's games! – how she, well, with you and Robert, she was just playing out some drama of her own – a melodrama! – how she really just wanted to separate you, from the beginning, because she was so damned jealous over your marriage. Oh, yes,' he ran on, before Léonie, whose face had clouded, could interrupt, 'that's exactly the problem we were talking about: making a drama out of other people's lives, as if she was in a picture with them, trying to destroy them that way.'

'But Hetty . . . couldn't have been doing that – with us.' Léonie was aghast at the very idea.

''Fraid she could. I don't want to pry – but, well, why else would your husband just drop you so suddenly and disappear – on your honeymoon?' He looked at her, at his most confiding and sympathetic.

'I don't – well, as I said, Robert quite misunderstood. He must have thought that Hetty and I . . .' She stopped.

'Léonie,' he helped her. 'You've absolutely nothing to fear from me. I've known Hetty was that way, with women, for *years*. And it's never really disturbed me. I understand. So you can trust me that way. But the point is, Robert sure as hell doesn't understand – and he must have thought you and Hetty had taken up again, you know, in that way – that night you spent in the tent together.' He looked at her calmly.

'Well, yes – I think he did. But we *hadn't*!' she lied firmly.

'No, of course not. Just those bites!' Craig introduced the murder weapon tenderly. Then he laughed softly again. 'Hetty – know her of old . . .' He rubbed his neck abstractedly. 'How she likes to mark people that way. Well, that's just her problem, with you two people – little drama she had to create, when her own work wasn't going too well – wanting to wreck other people's lives . . .'

'I still don't follow.'

'Isn't it obvious? She bit you that way – just so your husband would see, just so she could separate you.' He ran on before Léonie could stop him. 'And that's what we have to help her over, the one real flaw she has left, a hangover from the old days, this destructive urge with other people. Look at the havoc it's caused between you and Robert. So it's good you'll be with us for a bit, see if we can help her over this last hurdle. I'm too close to her . . . Though frankly I wouldn't blame you, in the circumstances, if you just dropped her, the way she's behaved to you – trying to destroy your marriage – and went back to your husband straightaway. You'll make things up with him easily enough when you tell him what really happened . . .'

During this peroration, Léonie was backing away from him in horror, digesting all that he had said, seeing, sensing the truth in all this nightmare synopsis of Hetty's actions, her real motives. Now it had been spelt out to her, she could hardly but see it, for it was, indeed, the truth.

'No,' she said, shaking her head violently. 'No, no . . .'

Craig advanced on her, puzzled. 'But yes,' he said, with pained sincerity. 'It's the truth, Léonie, that's the awful thing. And you and I can help her over it, if you'll help me . . .'

But by that point Léonie had turned and fled into the crowd.

Craig savoured his victory – his charity, indeed. He felt no qualms whatsoever at his behaviour. Quite the opposite. Why, he'd done the girl a favour, returning her to her husband, giving her the evidence with which to make things up with him.

Léonie, running to her cabin then and locking the door, was quite appalled. Was Craig lying, inventing, presuming, merely deducing in all this? Possibly. But then why should he do so? As far as she could see, he had nothing to gain. He had obviously been keen to have her come back with them to Nice, to help him out with Hetty. Certainly he had not been trying to separate them again. And, besides, she had no intention of taking up with Hetty permanently. She desperately wanted Robert back, and had told Craig so. Thus he could not have seen her as a rival any more for Hetty's affections.

Had Hetty, jealous of their marriage, simply wanted to separate her from Robert? In terms of the old Hetty – childish and malicious – it made sense. She would have done just that. But the new Hetty? Perhaps there was no such person. That was just another invention of hers.

Léonie put her hand involuntarily to her shoulder, touching the little teeth bruises there beneath her blouse. Had that been Hetty's intention – from the start? Not loving passion, but destruction?

Having mulled over all the evidence, Léonie decided it must be so, just as Craig had said. She stood up, agitated, pacing the cabin, then took her purse from the wardrobe, rifling through it, finding her return tickets, checking them, with her passport, before seeing the photograph of Robert she always kept there. And that finally decided her. Robert obviously was so much more important than Hetty to her. Her sojourn on the boat this past fortnight, as well as her night with Hetty in the tent, had both been sheer folly.

Delving further into the wardrobe she got her suitcase out, starting to pack quickly. If she hurried she could catch the night express from Luxor to Cairo on the other side of the river, without having to face Hetty again. Yes, she'd do just that. Her heart thrilled with the idea of seeing Robert again, as soon as possible, of making things up with him, armed with this evidence of Craig's. Robert would understand, just as she did now.

And besides, even if Craig had invented everything, she suddenly saw how, just as in the old days, anything to do with Hetty was fraught with potential disaster – how she, in these last weeks and in the bedouin tent, had simply blinded herself to this, given in to her wiles. For that was the truth: Hetty – so admirable, brave, talented, lovely in so many ways, also carried within her, like a killing virus, the seeds of plague, of havoc. Her work thrived on and encouraged what was fantastic in her nature, drawing these obsessive fantasies from her, which in turn became dripping acid which would always corrode and destroy when set against the decencies of ordinary life. What was wonderful in her nature depended on what was malign, each feeding on, dependent upon, the other for its movement, its existence. To be with her was an enchantment. But it was a dream from which, at the cost of her sanity, her life, she had to awake.

Léonie left the boat that evening and caught the train, without seeing Hetty again.

9

Hetty, next morning, was beside herself with rage masquerading as grief. 'Why – oh why?' she yelled at Craig.

'I've no idea.' He tried to console her.

'Did you see her last night?'

'Yes. But just to say hallo to.'

Hetty started to sob. Charged with his own successes and conquests, Craig felt free to play the sympathetic father, husband, lover once more, taking Hetty in his arms.

'Don't, Hetty, don't. Things happen like that, and I'm sorry. But you can't just pick up old loves – and think they'll work all over again, as if nothing had happened meantime. It never works . . . And she must have seen that, last night. Don't blame her too much. You love in a way she can't. Remember? I told you just that years ago, in Ireland, when we first met. You have so much more of love. And she only has a little to spare. And, Hetty, I'm sorry I've been so difficult with you. Things'll be easier now, with this location shooting out of the way, I promise . . .'

But Hetty remained angry. 'Léa just disappeared, without a word,' she yelped, conveniently forgetting how she, with Craig, had done exactly the same thing to Léonie eight years before. 'And I loved her, I truly did.'

'I know you did.' Craig, holding Hetty in his arms, looked wisely over her shoulder at the mists clearing across the bronze-blue waters of the river. 'But she couldn't match you.'

Craig – the master of love with Hetty and Léonie, telling to each the story of the other's death – so that their hearts were broken and they died . . .

And he drew Hetty back then, in her silk Molyneux pyjamas, to the big double bed in her cabin, the sheets still tossed about, where she had spent the night alone. And, as the river mists cleared and the bright desert sun streamed through the cabin curtains, Craig gave her that reward he had prepared for her – earlier than he had anticipated.

He began to make love to her, tenderly, expertly, mimicking love, drawing her pyjama top open, sliding the silk across her nipples, bending down, feeding there for an instant, so that she jumped with pleasure, before responding – gently at first, shyly, in a way she never remembered doing before, without vehemence, with a feeling of awkward humility, as if learning this way of love for the first time, returning to her old true self now in a heartfelt process, where there were ends in view beyond mere pleasure. As indeed there were.

'Craig . . .' She looked at him intently. 'Now the picture's coming to an end, and there'll be quite a break after it, I'd so l-l-like a child. So want one. Can't we? Couldn't we?'

'Maybe.' Craig temporized, hoping it would never come to that.

'We'd be easier then, I'm sure we would, you and I, if there was someone else – a family,' she added urgently. With the loss of Léonie, Hetty suddenly felt the unconscious urge for some other quite dependent person. She had not really wanted a child before. Her earlier miscarriage had confirmed this and in any case her career then, and her stark ambitions, along with Craig's, had always been a prohibition. But now she wanted one – as an inviolate security, a salve to her battered pride, to confirm the reality of her marriage with Craig. 'Oh, love me that way, Craig – for that, please do . . .'

She lay back, eyes wide with longing, encouraging him now, as he slipped her silk trousers off, twisting urgently then, suddenly hungry for him, hungry for some vague future mirror image of herself, a toy, her entire possession which could never be taken from her, never betray her, so that now she allowed him full play, provoking him, as he slid over her, into her, lust beginning to rise, so that soon she felt herself sinking – sinking, goaded beyond endurance by wild spasms of joy. Here was a confirmation of all her old happy obsessions, a life renewed with Craig so that, together again, they could don the incorruption of make-believe.

So thrilled was she by this renewal with Craig that the long-delayed letter, sent to Hollywood by Mortimer Cordiner, which she finally received on their return to the Semiramis Hotel in Cairo, barely moved her at all.

'Can you imagine?' She turned to Craig, out on the balcony overlooking the river. 'Think what that old fool of a woman my mother has done: left the entire house and estate of Summer Hill . . . to the *butler*! Mortimer suggests I should buy it off him: buy my own property in effect!'

'Well, why not? You have the money. And it *is* yours, or should be—'

'Oh, what does it matter?' Hetty interrupted as she joined him on the balcony. 'Never really liked the place anyway – or want to live in Ireland.'

'Still, it's the principle – and the family.'

'But I don't *need* it! – the house, the land, my mother, Léonie, Robert . . .' She joyfully enumerated, the better to try to persuade herself how they had no effect, simply did not impinge on her. 'Don't need them . . .' She looked at him, a tender mischief in her eyes. 'As long as I have you.'

But then she looked at Craig much more seriously, intently, trying, as so often before, to plumb the unknowable depths there, seeking some confirmation of her last words.

'Oh yes, you always have me, Hetty,' he lied.

*

When Léonie returned to Paris a week later she had, quite apart from Craig's revelations about Hetty, some other and entirely happy evidence to offer Robert – a confirmation, she thought, of their own real love.

'I'm sorry – sorry I'm late!' she said to him breathlessly, having run all the way up the six flights of stairs to their small apartment on the top floor of the old building on the rue Saint-André-des-Arts. 'You got my telegrams?'

He nodded, not cold, but not warm either. Then she handed him the little bunch of flowers, the bouquet of early spring violets she had bought for him at the flower market in the rue de Buci at the end of the narrow street. He took them awkwardly. 'Thank you,' he murmured rather formally, holding the paper sheath as if it was a bomb. It was nearly eleven in the morning – the overnight train from Marseilles had been delayed – and he had just been about to leave for work at the *Tribune*; the smell of the freshly-ground coffee they always shared together at this time was still in the air.

Léonie embraced him wildly. 'Oh, Robert! – I'm so *glad* you haven't left yet – so glad to *see* you! You can't imagine . . .' She kissed him on the cheek, stroking his hair, flattening it sideways across his scalp, relishing the coarse touch of something missed and loved. 'So glad because I think – *think* I've some wonderful news!' She stood back from him a moment, taking off her headscarf and releasing her hair, so that it crackled with static electricity in the frosty air of a brilliant March morning, sun streaming in through the slanting skylight just above them.

Robert looked at her, overwhelmed, but still doubting. 'What?'

'I'm pregnant! Sure I am! I was due last week – and nothing happened. Oh, Robert! . . .' She came to him again, taking him in her arms, close to him, close to tears. 'And I'm so sorry about everything else. But it was all really . . . *nothing.* I'll tell you later – Craig told me all about it. Hetty was just being a bitch, she only wanted to separate us. And it was all just a brainstorm of mine, with her. Means nothing now. Because, don't you see? – I love you more than anything, anybody else in the world. And now this, I'm sure of it, a child! – that day in the temple . . . So it's all going to be OK.' She clutched him again. '*Oh*, how I've missed you!'

Robert, during all this, had slowly and invisibly thawed. Now he responded more openly, taking her in his arms, leaning over her shoulder, gazing out of the high window at the sliver of blue sky over the crazy paving rooftops, hearing the faint cries of the flower vendors echo up the street in the glittery weather. Mornings with Léonie again, he thought. Bright days in Paris once more. He held up the bunch of spring violets behind Léonie's back, sniffed them a moment, that faint odour of violets which so epitomized Léonie. It was as if, through these flowers, she had given him back the very essence of herself, so that he doubted her no longer. He felt tears pricking his eyes. 'Yes,' he said at last. 'I've missed you, too. Missed – both of you . . .'

Léonie was right. She was pregnant. Her child, in the following months, materialized. But Hetty's never did. Instead of new life she conceived nothing with Craig but misfortune, the first hints of this becoming apparent nearly two months later, just as they were nearing the end of the filming at the Victorine studios in Nice.

She had always slept well enough, even in Egypt, despite the heat and tension there. But now, on her return to the more equable climate of the south of France, she found herself waking regularly at three or four in the morning, unable afterwards to find any release from this hour of the wolf; she lay feverishly, plagued by waking nightmares, delirious abstract visions, tossing about on the bed, seeking relief from the pains that had come to scorch her joints, so that by morning, with a blinding headache, she was worn out and had to miss that day's shooting at the studio.

Yet these bouts went as quickly as they came, so that Hetty thought them no more than a variation of morning sickness, which, together with the cessation of her periods, surely confirmed her pregnancy, so that she bore the discomforts with an unenquiring, almost happy fortitude.

But to the unit doctor these symptoms seemed more those of malaria than of pregnancy. So that initially, without denying the latter, he treated her for the former, with doses of quinine, which left Hetty feeling worse for a time, before her maladies suddenly disappeared and she was able to resume work, finally completing the *Nefertiti* interiors some three months after their return from Egypt.

Subsequently, Craig, moving a bed in, locked himself away more or less permanently with his assistant in the cutting room, on the other side of the lot, editing the picture to show William Fox in New York. He was well aware of Fox's displeasure at what he had already seen of the uncut film. He had expected no less. Equally he had always known that, given Fox's contract with both him and Laura jointly, Fox would never fire him in mid-picture, thus losing all his investment. Of course not. He had the whip hand there. But just as certainly he knew that as soon as he completed the picture, together with the editing and titling, and delivered it to Fox, the latter would then take control of it, try to tamper with it, dictating cuts that would ruin it.

So, like Penelope at her loom, he prolonged and then dallied with the editing, often unravelling at night all that he had woven from the myriad celluloid spools during the day. He took excessive care and time over what in any case was an elaborate process – to ensure as much as anything that the final story line was watertight, that each sequence formed an immovable link with what went before and after, so that any subsequent cuts that Fox might make would make nonsense of the whole. And in this pursuit for perfection nothing else mattered; not time nor cost – nor Hetty, or even her illness.

Craig became more obsessed than ever in this final topping and tailing of the picture, which had been almost a life's work with him in any case. He was determined to complete his vision, to perfection, down to the last tiny detail. No one and nothing would stand in his way, quite sure as he was that, in the end, when Fox and the others saw it in its immaculate final form, there would be no arguments over some of the more bizarre detail: they would be bowled over by the sheer audacity, the miracle of it all, exhibit it in its entirety.

Hetty, given her earlier miscarriage and what she now expected to be another difficult pregnancy, stayed quietly in the ornate villa in the centre of the studio lot She thought herself quite recovered, until one morning she was violently sick. Yet this, too, seemed only to confirm her pregnancy. However, one factor was missing in all this hope, which Hetty chose to ignore. Instead of gaining the slightest weight she had started to lose it steadily. While that night, and subsequently, her draining insomnia and feverish headaches returned, together with the wicked pains in her joints, so that she took to dosing herself with veronal powders, two at a time, which eased the pain, but left her unconscious until midday, when she woke in a state of numb depression – which lasted for days afterwards.

Something was seriously amiss, there was no doubt. So that the unit doctor, before he had to leave, insisted she see a specialist in Nice, a Dr Verneuil, with consulting rooms on the Promenade des Anglais overlooking the Baie des Anges. The silver-haired, somewhat aloof doctor examined Hetty thoroughly, taking blood, urine and other samples for subsequent analysis. To Hetty's impatient annoyance he gave absolutely no opinion then, deferring that until she visited him again nearly a week later.

'Well?' she asked brightly. 'P-p-pregnant? I am, aren't I? I must be!'

'No, Madame. You are not pregnant.' Dr Verneuil stroked his greying moustache judiciously. His blunt reply shocked her; the blood drained from her face, all this hope so abruptly dismissed.

'Malaria then?'

'No, not malaria.' The doctor, just a fraction pleased with himself, stopped dead as if she was playing some guessing game with him.

'Well,' Hetty continued almost aggressively. 'What then?'

'You have syphilis, Madame.'

He was so entirely matter-of-fact that the news hit all the more violently. She felt dizzy suddenly, her vision clouding, shaking. For the first time, after all her recent triumphs, which had seemed to set her so securely on a pinnacle of life, she sensed she had reached some turning point, felt a vague intimation of descent, the barest hint of future calamity.

But she put these thoughts from her mind, seeking to avoid the whole issue and its implications in any way she could. The doctor had turned to the window, looking at the light glinting on the waves out in the bay, beneath a cloudless summer sky. Hetty followed his gaze abstractedly, as if he were indicating that the disease was hardly important, like a cold – that it had come to her from the elements out there, blown on the wind, and would as quickly disappear.

'Syphilis?' She came to her senses at last. 'B-b-but it can't be! I've only ever be-be-been with my husband.'

'Indeed?' The doctor looked at her distantly, as if she had just made some banal comment on the weather. 'Then you have contracted it from him, Madame. Does he know?'

'No. I mean, I don't know. Should he know?'

'There are usually clear signs, in both parties – though not invariably.'

'You mean, he could have known – and didn't tell me?'

'Ah, there I cannot help you. I have no idea. You would have to make enquiries there yourself,' he added delicately, turning again to the window.

Hetty was thunderstruck. 'But he *might* not have known?' she persisted.

'It's possible. Or he may not as yet have recognized the signs. Or have milder symptoms. In any case he should be told. You should both of you seek appropriate treatment at once.'

'Appropriate treatment?'

'Yes.' The doctor spoke more enthusiastically now. 'A full course of it. Not mercury luckily, which is no real cure at all. We have Salvarsan now – the "magic bullet" – a dozen weekly injections to start with, and perhaps intra-muscular bismuth then, for a year or so, depending on how the infection develops. It can change its character, you see, Madame – primary, secondary, tertiary syphilis. There are stages, variations,' he added neatly. 'You are at the primary stage – and one would hope to stop it there . . .' He left the sentence hanging in the air.

'And if not? These headaches, these awful pains in my joints, the nausea, so that I can hardly we-work as it is – it would get we-worse? So that I couldn't we-work at all?'

'Oh, I would hope not.' Again the doctor's gaze seemed distracted by something outside the window. A fleck of cloud, Hetty saw, no bigger than a man's hand, had come to perch over the bay. 'Salvarsan,' the doctor continued, 'has proved effective, in most cases, in . . .' He paused, looking for the right word for the first time in their consultation. 'In subduing the symptoms, Madame.'

But Hetty caught the real gist here. 'So that I might never be cured, you mean?'

'No. I do not mean that. Simply – it's impossible to say, to speak of a total cure as yet. This new drug has not been in use long enough. What we do know is that it can entirely suppress the symptoms. On the other hand we know that the bacterium can lie quite dormant for years, in any case. So it's a matter . . . of time, Madame,' he finished ambiguously.

'A time-bomb, you mean?' The doctor ignored this grim sally. 'And children?' Hetty went on. 'I could never have children?'

'You could, biologically speaking – unless there was some other venereal infection, affecting the fallopian tubes for example. But you would be most ill-advised to do so, whatever the case. There would be very real risks for you and possible complications for the child.'

Hetty at this news bowed her head. She had started to sweat, to shake, almost to cry. Dr Verneuil, seeing this, took her in hand. 'Come, Madame, there is little point in our going into further details at the moment. You must not over-concern yourself there. The important thing is that you start the treatment at once. Will you be staying down here on the coast for some time?'

He stood up, a trifle more considerate now, coming towards Hetty, speaking to her as if she were a wilting flower and not a beautiful woman of twenty-seven, at the height of her powers – a woman, he had naturally omitted to tell her, suffering a painful and debilitating disease, which was likely to develop even more painfully, where there was no certainty at all of any cure. Indeed Salvarsan, as he knew, with its arsenic base, was toxic, so that this cure, if the course had to be prolonged, could be worse than the disease, resulting in agonizing side-effects, even death. None of this Dr Verneuil told her. It had been sufficient simply to break the ice. She would face troubles enough in any case over this disease in the future.

Hetty, driving back to the villa that morning, typically decided there were only two ways of dealing with the problem: either shoot the man or accept her condition. Equally typically she decided more or less on the first course. The problem was that, with Craig incarcerated in the cutting rooms, she rarely saw him these days. Finally she had to beard him in his lair, late that night, when the editor and his assistants had gone home.

She found him, in the stuffy heat of the cutting rooms, dishevelled, sweating in a striped fishing vest, an alchemist once more, now in the final throes of turning dross to gold, bent over a chattering moviola machine at one end of the long room, with high shelves down each side filled with hundreds of numbered cans of film. A long table in the middle held great open wire spools linked together with slack trails of celluloid. Further down, above the cutting bench, dozens of title and leader strips, clipped to the wall, fell in profusion.

He looked up unwillingly, stopping the machine, as she closed the door. 'Christ, honey, I'm pretty busy.'

'I know you are.' She smiled, brushing her short-cropped hair, which was growing again now, an inch or so above the scalp, but still giving her the air of a bright but in this instance a malicious street urchin.

Craig returned to the moviola, setting it chattering again, peering through a lens, as the film sped past beneath him, snapping through the gate. 'Hey, this is the sequence near the end, in the little love pavilion. My

God, it's quite something – you're really good . . .' He didn't look up, preferring the image of Hetty to the reality.

'Yes, I know. I saw the dailies—'

'Nothing like when it's all cut together, though. Here, want to take a look?'

'I saw the specialist today.' Hetty was quite calm.

'Why, yes.' He looked up at last. 'Did he confirm it – the pregnancy?'

'No.'

He gazed at her. 'Oh . . . Just malaria, after all?'

'No, Craig . . .' She paused and he returned to his vision of the little love pavilion. 'You know, you must have known,' she continued evenly, 'that it wasn't malaria, that I wasn't pregnant. It's syphilis.' The moviola had started to clatter away again, so that Hetty shouted now. '*Syphilis* – did you hear me?'

He stopped the machine. 'Yes, I heard you.' He stood up, took a handkerchief out and wiped his brow, then looked at her, his face still damp, without expression. 'Hell, that's bad, Hetty. But what do you mean I knew? I'd no idea.' He looked at her now, without any condemnation, just with genuine puzzlement. 'Who?' he asked her then. 'Who was it?'

Then she erupted. But it seemed to her, as she experienced the sudden anger, to be something quite different – a gradual explosion, as if in slow motion, expanding in waves to fill the long room. '*You*, Craig! – you shit, because I've slept with no one else. *You!* – and you must have it too – you gave it me!'

Her voice rose, before he interrupted her. 'That's nonsense, Hetty. I don't have syphilis. I'd know if I had, wouldn't I?'

'Just hasn't shown itself with you, that's all – can't have d-d-done. But *I* have it.' Hetty went for him then, hammering at him with her fists, before he warded her off. 'And I can't really ever have children now – you've ruined my life – *and* I won't be able to work.'

He stood back from her, holding her at arm's length. 'Now listen, honey, calm down. Can't be that bad—'

'Of *course* it's that bad—'

'And there's a cure these days—'

'Yes, injections – months of them, p-possibly years of treatment, the doctor said. And maybe I'll *never* recover.'

'That's crazy, Hetty. Lots of people get the clap – and recover.'

'It's *not* clap, it's syphilis you've given me! Just look at you, you shit! You've your whole life round you, here, right now, in all this film. But I'll have nothing – won't be able to work, stuck in bed with these aching joints, sick headaches, vomiting. You lying creep. God, how I hate you – your saying how everything was going to be better when we got back to Nice. Instead I can't have children now, never make love again, probably never w-work, ride horses – all that, just gone. The future we had, like you said that morning in Egypt: you and me and – children. And pictures at the Victorine here, when I thought we were both back on the rails. You've killed all that future! And I never want to see you again.'

In default of killing him then, she thought to destroy what meant most to him, in all the cans of film. She turned, throwing herself at the shelves, flinging the cans to the floor, the film reeling out. Then she moved to the big open spools on the central bench, doing the same there, so that before Craig finally got control of her the room was awash in loose film, filled with piles of snaking celluloid, crackling underfoot.

'That's mostly old outcuts anyway,' he said, getting a grip on her. 'But just tell me now – who? *Who* was it you were sleeping with?'

'*No* one. But you, you bastard!' she screamed, before breaking down in convulsive sobs, kneeling on the floor among the serpentine reels of film, crunching it up in her fingers, trying to destroy these images of herself in an impotent frenzy.

Craig looked at her without sympathy. He had consoled her before, many times. But now he made no effort to comfort her. 'You can destroy yourself, Hetty. Or try and destroy me. But you can't kill the real thing in both of us. That's on film now in *Nefertiti*. And it's indestructible, live on long after you and I are gone. Besides, there's a cure for syphilis – if you want it. We're not living in the Middle Ages. You'll get better.'

Well, yes, he thought, she would get better. But something, at last, had finally snapped between them. Something told him this was the beginning of the end of his relationship with Hetty. Timely, perhaps, in that now he had almost completed his long drama with her. All that he had ever really wanted of her lay securely embalmed in the film cans all round him now, in the master print spools of *Nefertiti*, locked in a huge fire-proof safe in the next room.

The culmination of her professional life, everything he had taught her, manipulated and drawn from her, in eight years together, lay there inviolate, captured indefinitely, in long strips of celluloid. So that, even if he lost her, in reality, what did that matter? He would always possess her – at her most perfect, in *Nefertiti*. That was what pictures were, after all – little bits of time, people trapped for ever by a camera, rescued from oblivion, whom other people would never ever forget.

'Listen,' he told her coldly, the image of father, lover, friend melting from his face. 'What happens between us now doesn't matter any longer. Did it ever really matter? What did we amount to anyway? – that wasn't meant for all this.' He gestured round the cans of film. 'You and I and our problems, mistakes, whatever . . .' He smiled shortly. 'Nothing more than a whistle in the dark . . .

But there!' He turned again, looking triumphantly round the cutting room. '*There*, in those cans of film – that's where we really live! That's where our life together begins and ends, where we'll be saved or damned. In *Nefertiti*. For the rest, well, I'm sorry.'

But he was not really, as he offered her this brief apology, a final distant smile from the dandy man with the rogue good looks, his face filled for an instant with all that had made him wonderful to Hetty: power and dreams – the gift of bridging them, in art, in celebration; of giving chaos form, rescuing the passing minute, that magic touch of resurrection. 'I'm leaving for New York in a few days. Show the picture to Fox. That's all that matters now – for you and me.' Then he was walking out the door.

'No, no! . . .' At the last moment Hetty wanted him back. Yet that intensely real but still unknowable image of Craig had gone. And she knew then how she wanted him again, at whatever cost, still wanted Craig – for what she could never possess in him.

It was not until later that evening, going to bed on the couch he had set up in the next room, that Craig, inspecting himself carefully, saw the tiny, slightly pitted white circles on the underside of his penis – quite painless, which was why he had not noticed them before, but none the less evidence of exactly what Hetty had accused him of.

'Jesus . . .' he murmured. 'Those damn bedouin children. Christ!' he added. Should he tell Hetty? What difference would it make, other than to make matters worse – make their parting more difficult, more acrimonious?

In New York ten days later, when William Fox saw Craig's six-and-a-half-hour version of *Nefertiti*, he started by firing everyone in his company who had ever had anything to do with the picture, burning up the Western

Union wires between his office and Hollywood, until wiser counsels prevailed.

'Look, we can get Brenon to re-shoot what we need changed, on the Hollywood lot. Then cut it by half – and more,' Winfield Sheehan told him.

Fox still trembled with fury in his vast and gloomy office. 'OK – as long as Craig has nothing to do with it. *Nothing*!' Fox had refused to meet Craig. 'I'll ruin him, though,' he went on now. 'He'll never work again in Hollywood. I'll talk with Zukor even, and Sam. Never work again, *never!* And from now on it'll be comedies, Sheehan, melodramas, gangster pictures with us – anything – but no more epics, Sheehan, *ever*.'

News of the *Nefertiti* disaster spread quickly in Hollywood. And Fox was as good as his word. Swallowing his pride, he talked with the other studio bosses. Secretly delighted at his epic setback, they were none the less warned now and fearful, too, of Craig's wild extravagances – and, having always mistrusted his cultured European airs and graces anyway, they were pleased to blackball him.

Howard Brenon re-shot many of the scenes, with Clive Brook and some of the other principals. Afterwards a posse of craven editors was put to work on the picture, delving into mountains of celluloid, cutting it to pieces, reducing Craig's masterpiece – for it was that – by more than half, to a banal tale of blood and thunder in ancient Egypt, in which all the cleverly worked psychology in the script, the religious and sexual deviations, the subtle performances, all the obsessions and perverse nuances in the characters, were brutally removed, making nonsense of Craig's original story, turning what had been an artistic epic into an almost incoherent tale of banal mischief on the Nile.

Craig, back at the Wolf's Lair in Hollywood, sacked by Fox and knowing of all this desecration going on down in the Fox studios, fought back vigorously. He instigated legal proceedings against the company, charging them first with unjustified dismissal, then with breaking clauses carefully inserted in his contract which had stipulated that he be consulted over all post-production work on the picture.

Fox counter-sued, charging Craig with gross professional negligence, together with other assorted legal euphemisms covering his various delays and extravagances. Craig employed the best attorneys. It would be a long and costly business, he realized. But then he had the money, plenty of it – over a million dollars cash in WillBow Pictures, his joint company with Hetty, in which his and nearly all her huge earnings over the last few years had been deposited.

Their joint signatures were required to withdraw on this account. But Craig, in his good times with Hetty before leaving for Egypt, had signed a dozen open cheques with her, so that various impending bills in America could be met by the company secretary in Los Angeles while they were away.

Craig used these cheques now, first to transfer half a million dollars into a separate checking account for himself, then to pay the attorneys, then to spend much larger sums in setting up his next picture at the Victorine Studios, a co-production with Gaumont in Paris. For Craig, now increasingly blinding himself to the realities of every situation, saw the *Nefertiti* reception as nothing more than a temporary setback. He would be vindicated there and was perfectly confident of his future, in Europe now, if not in Hollywood. He had long wanted to be finished with Hollywood in any case, so that being blackballed there meant very little to him.

And, besides, he still had a phenomenal record of commercial successes behind him, and a reputation quite unblemished as far as the European producers and exhibitors were concerned; his pictures had always done more than good business in Europe, and they still therefore held him in considerable esteem. Craig had made them a great deal of money over the years and would have no difficulty now in making his own way with them as an independent producer in the picture business outside Hollywood, starting with this first adventure epic, *The Lost Valley* – a tale of an English mining surveyor, journeying alone in the high Atlas mountains of Morocco, coming on a hidden valley there, finding a group of missionaries, together with attendant nuns, attempting to convert and educate the infidel.

Hetty had earlier been set to play one of the young nuns, falling in love with the Englishman, breaking her vows, running away with him – into all sorts of amorous and dramatic disasters. The picture, with its costly locations in the Atlas, had been budgeted at nearly $400,000, and close to half of this was to be supplied by WillBow Pictures. Craig, in Hollywood, had already delved into his capital to pay his attorneys. Now, setting up *The Lost Valley* he went deeper still into it – as well as committing most of the rest of the capital to future co-productions with Gaumont. So that by the autumn of 1927, without Hetty's knowing, the uncommitted money left available to both of them in WillBow Pictures had been reduced, by their standards, almost to a pittance.

These had not been Craig's only activities during his six months back in America. Driving down to Hollywood one summer morning soon after returning he had stopped his Pierce-Arrow at a favourite old picnic spot, hidden by a grove of shady pepper trees right on the edge of Hollywood Lake – stopped because he had been astonished to see half the pepper trees felled, the site levelled and a collection of builders' trucks grinding up the earth, unloading scaffolding, bricks, cement, with other men out and about with theodolites surveying the whole ruined area.

'What's up? What's happening?' Craig had walked over to one of the surveyors.

'What's it look like? New development. New apartment block. Lakeside Court.'

'But, why, you can't! It's a beauty spot.'

'Can't?' The young man was impatient, laconic. 'Well, you go tell that to the boss. He's here right now in fact. That big limousine over there. Mr Borzsony.'

Craig, furious, had walked over to the car parked under one of the last of the pepper trees. He thought it empty at first until he saw something move under a huge mohair travelling rug laid out along the back seat. 'Mr Borzsony?'

The rug moved once more, thrusting, wriggling. And then, like a butterfly emerging slowly from a chrysalis, a girl's face emerged, eyes full of sleep, followed by a neck, then a hand reaching to close the collar of her dress shyly. Finally the whole torso came clear of the rug, sitting up, and Craig saw the full beauty of a young woman, hardly twenty, he thought, the sharply chiselled features, long chin, fine nose, hollowed cheeks, waking now, at first embarrassed, then interested, thin wide blue eyes blinking at him.

'No, it's *Miss* Borzsony. Sorry, I flaked out again. Out late last night – you know . . .' She smiled vaguely. But it was the voice that immediately struck Craig, much more than the pretty face – surprising tones from someone so young: it was dark, fluent, mellow, knowing, the sounds linked together like a rich sigh. It was sexy. Educated, East Coast – some posh girls' school in New England, Craig thought. But with a timbre all its own: autumnal, dream-filled. 'My father's over there, I guess, with the foreman.' She stretched forward, still half-asleep, reaching out towards the window, a long, thin-fingered, sun-browned hand resting on the glass, as she inspected Craig carefully. 'And who are you, may one ask? . . .' Yes, Craig thought again, that extraordinary voice, resonant, full of old music. 'The architect?'

'No. I'm Craig St John Williamson – I make pictures and I'm goddamned furious with your father, ruining this place. Used to picnic here in the old days . . .' Craig gestured about him. 'This was *beautiful* last time I was here.'

The girl leant right forward now, peeking her head out of the window. 'Yes,' she said appraisingly, 'I bet it was.' Her gaze returned to Craig. 'Well, you go over and give him hell then – Mr Craig St John Williamson who makes pictures. And tell him I was due riding at the Country Club half an hour ago.'

'Yes, I'll do just that,' Craig moved away.

'Or wait!' she called after him. 'I've a better idea. Is that yours over there – that Pierce-Arrow? Yes, well, maybe *you* could take me to the Country Club instead?'

Craig looked back at her, the long triangular face leaning out of the window, the fine pointed chin resting on her hand, eyeing him nicely, reasonably. Apart from her voice there did not seem anything terribly special about her – the clear, washed-blue eyes under a swath of corn-blonde hair, not cropped in the current fashion, but long, flowing untended. She was simply . . . pretty.

But at just that moment a breeze off the water raked the blonde strands across her eyes and nose, her mouth. And for some reason this silk-gold curtain, like a gauze front drop lowered against a theatrical set, suddenly entirely altered Craig's perception of her, enhancing the features, highlighting them dramatically, transforming her whole personality. This new view of her excited him – caught his heart strangely, as she let the hair tickle her, doing absolutely nothing about it, not moving a muscle, a still centre amidst the clatter and destruction going on all round them. So that for Craig, too, the world stopped as he gazed at her.

She spoke again, waking him. 'Well, will you – take me?'

'Why yes, of course, Miss Borzsony.'

'Duna Börzsöny,' she said, stepping out of the Dodge. She had on a summer frock, showing long fine legs, as she walked confidently towards him over the ruined site where he and Hetty had once picnicked.

'Interesting name . . .'

'Hungarian. With two little dots over both of the o's.' She cleared her hair away and smiled. They shook hands in the middle of all the disruption – and he took her.

For Craig, just as with Hetty eight years before, Duna in the following months became an obsessive necessity, something offered out of the blue by the gods, a destiny, a happy fate – a woman to love, to mould, someone with whom to renew his old dream of true romance; someone quite untutored with whom to further all his professional dreams; a new photograph in his select album of wondrous women, unmarked, whom he would remake in his own images. And, just as with Hetty, he did everything with and for her from then on, in the way of advancing their personal and professional relationship – teaching her, grooming her, flirting with her, arranging screen tests – doing everything in short except make love with her. It was part of his usual initial way with his conquests, of course – part of the trap, the enticing poison flower he always laid out for these women. But in this instance there was another reason for his restraint – his syphilis.

He had to visit discreet clinics, in Los Angeles and New York, undergoing treatment similar to Hetty's, though for what in his case turned out to be a much less severe infection. He told Hetty nothing of this. He barely corresponded with her in a personal vein at all, merely dictating letters to her about his *Nefertiti* battles – and her new role in *The Lost Valley*.

He told her nothing of how he had spent, or committed, most of their joint capital in WillBow Pictures, nearly two-thirds of which had been Hetty's money in the first place. He told her nothing of Duna Börzsöny either. What was there to say? – other than what Duna herself had said that morning as they drove away from the ruined site: 'Can't stand in the way of progress, Mr Craig St John Williamson who makes pictures!'

Hetty, in these months apart, wrote to him more regularly and personally. She ate no humble pie, yet was conciliatory. Recovering her pride, she none the less wanted to make things up with him – believing that she had, perhaps, over-reacted that night in the Victorine cutting rooms. They had after all – albeit in very different ways – both been unfaithful during their marriage. Her infection had come about simply in the nature of their separate desires – she had slept with women, if not with any other man, while he, no doubt, had made love with other women. Yet it might have been the other way round. So, regretting her initial outburst, she took steps to repair the damage.

For, even if she had lost him personally, she wanted him still for his professional support. She, like Craig, was aware that without him behind the camera she might well make a ham fist of the whole motion picture business – in choice of stories, scripts, costumes, performance, everything.

She needed him again for all that, since despite her setbacks she still had, she knew, one tremendous card left to play in her life. She remained a great star. Her continuing fan mail confirmed this – as did the experience of her immediate surroundings in Nice. She could not walk down the Promenade des Anglais or take tea at the Negresco without being almost immediately recognized, pestered, sometimes mobbed. And her last Hollywood picture with Craig, *Gold Dust*, a costume drama set during the California gold rush, just released in Europe, was doing record business.

So that now above everything she wished to maintain this pre-eminent position in the picture palaces of the world. Her talent, she knew – whatever else happened to her – must remain her saving grace. And that particular talent, of course, lying as it did in her astonishing mix of beauty and athleticism, was what was most threatened by her disease.

So she took to Dr Verneuil's cure religiously, suffering it with quite untypical patience – the continued tests and intimate examinations, the Salvarsan injections, the subsequent bismuth salts treatment. It was a painful business, these weekly visits to his surgery on the Promenade. But the treatment seemed to work. The symptoms disappeared – and, most crucially, did not return when the course of Salvarsan was completed three months later. So that by the autumn of that year, 1927, buoyed up in any case by the balmy southern airs, she thought her recovery complete.

Her dark beauty, apart from the slightest hint of pain wrinkles to either side of her eyes and mouth, was unimpaired. Her body had regained most of its old snap and vigour, so that she felt able to take up riding again at the local Cercle Hippique, often hacking out with Mickey Ostrovosky, returned to his family home now, on the hills behind Nice. Then, in order to test her mettle properly, she started fencing again, at the Foils Club in the rue Gambetta. Here she soon astonished several of her male partners.

So that at a dinner party in October with the Ostrovoskys, she was able to respond to the toast they made to her in full consciousness of health and life regained.

'Th-th-thank you, all of you, ve-ve-very much!' Yes,

she was happy again. Her cure seemed complete, except for her stammer.

And it was then, in that same autumn of 1927, that the sound revolution in pictures began to explode everywhere in Hollywood. Months earlier it had first started to spread like a slow fuse towards a tinder-dry forest. Fox and Warner Brothers, both well-advanced in the development of their own differing sound systems, were in the vanguard of the incendiarists. Warners, indeed, had already embarked on a semi-sound picture, with *The Jazz Singer*, shortly to be released. But Zukor, Laemmle, Goldwyn and the other big studio bosses, already committed to a whole programme of silent pictures for the coming year, were, for the most part, firmly in the camp of firefighters. However, their technical advisers warned them that it was only a matter of time before sound took over everywhere. Sound was the coming thing, they said. There was no way of beating Fox and Warners. They would have to join them.

Craig, greatly taken by all this news in Hollywood and excited by the dramatic possibilities of dialogue, was anxious from the beginning to work with this new sound process. So that when he arrived in Paris that December, just after the sensational release of *The Jazz Singer*, he at once suggested to Gaumont that they film the interiors at least of their new picture in sound. Gaumont agreed.

There was only one flaw in this idea, which Craig had recognized from the beginning: Hetty's stammer. At the very least, he thought, she would have some difficulty in adapting to this new sound process. Quite possibly she would not be able to handle it at all. What then? Should he sacrifice the new sound system – or Hetty? He delayed the decision. She could have voice training, speech therapy, he would test her at the microphone – they would see how it went.

Yet Craig was aware of another factor in all this, which

he kept at the very back of his mind. With *Nefertiti* completed, and after their blazing row, he had clearly sensed an end of things with Hetty. Despite her conciliatory letters their personal relationship was doomed, he thought. She would never truly forgive him – he made the convenient argument here – because in truth he was tired of her. And besides he had taken up with Duna. So that perhaps the arrival of sound had come at an opportune moment. It would allow him to make a final break with Hetty professionally, since she might never adapt to the new system, while he had every intention of continuing with it. Sound, without its being in any way his fault, might offer him what at heart he really wanted: a cast-iron excuse to drop Hetty completely.

And if that happened, well, they would have to look for another star in *The Lost Valley* – Louise Brooks or even Garbo? Or find someone new altogether? Why, of course – and in fact he had thought of this almost from the start: Duna Börzsöny, now already taking small parts in Hollywood, in some of Mickey Neilan's and Raoul Walsh's pictures, under her new name of Diana Belleville. He was a star-maker, after all – and what he had done for Hetty he could equally well do with this woman.

And really, when you thought about it, he continued the convincing argument with himself, that was how it had always been in the motion picture business. New processes, new people. Just as Duna had said – you couldn't stand in the way of progress. Things had always changed overnight in pictures. A chauffeur one day, a director the next – like Mickey Neilan. The cowboy, or the blonde in the drugstore, stars overnight. You could never put a stay on the crazy momentum of the picture business. It had its own unstoppable energies and directions, fuelled in the end by capricious audiences, the fans who paid for it all, driving the industry ever onwards towards new faces, new techniques. He had not invented this new sound process. It was not his fault. You had to ride with change. And so would Hetty.

And so she did – or tried. As soon as Craig wrote confirming the news of the sound revolution (of which, in any case, she had heard ominous rumours at the Victorine) she at once engaged the services of a Miss Dorothea Cave, a retired English actress living in Nice who, rather failing in her earlier career on the boards, had become instead, among the theatrical and operatic community on the Côte d'Azur, something of a specialist in diction, accents, a voice coach generally.

Miss Cave, who turned out to be Scottish, with a startling shock of fuzzy red hair, attended the villa two or three times a week – and, over many hours and sessions, Hetty's stammer improved to the point of being practically undetectable, a mere attractive hesitancy over some few words.

And even this disappeared when, in the spring of 1928, Craig arrived in Nice with the new dialogue script of *The Lost Valley* and Hetty got to work on the actual lines which she would have to deliver in the coming voice tests. However, if her stammer seemed quite cured, Hetty, to her fury and frustration, was now presented with a quite different problem: remembering the lines.

Though in fact rarely longer than a few sentences, they seemed to her great mountainous blocks of recalcitrant, ever-disappearing words, which she tried to hold in her mind, feverishly grappling with them, like great slippery fish, only to have them quite elude her when she came to the point of delivering them. She began to panic at this inability to remember, and the panic made remembering more difficult still. However, as Craig told her, when the time came they would write the words up for her on a blackboard next to the camera. It would be all right on the night.

*

In the stuffy little covered stage at the Victorine studios a month later Hetty, dressed in the all-enclosing habit of a young nun, took the first of her costume and make-up tests for her role in *The Lost Valley*. But much more vitally it was also to be her first voice test as well, since Craig thought she would find the dialogue easier if she were fully dressed and made up for the part, so that she could really believe in it all. And he might have been right but for the furious oven-like heat in the studio, which Hetty's heavy costume and make-up made all the more difficult to bear.

The stage, with a bright summer sun beating down for several hours already, was hot enough in any case. But now it was worse, in that with silent pictures it had always been largely open to the sky, but was now entirely closed, darkened, sealed from every outside sound, so that the heat had become intense.

Hetty, nervous already in this fevered cavernous atmosphere and at a loss without the traditional mood music which Craig had always worked with before, was even more startled, scorched, when the unusually bright stage lights burst upon her and the cameraman began to adjust them – on her face, then over the makeshift set which had been got up as the mother superior's office at the mission.

Now, as the lights played over her, she was sweating profusely under her habit, the make-up beginning to run on her face, half-hidden by the white cowl. The perfume rising all about her was almost overpowering now as well – the little magic phial of *Nefertiti* scent which, as a good-luck charm, she had dabbed over her throat and face before dressing. Craig, she had hoped, might have noticed it. But he had not. And now she felt like a tart, not a nun. She wanted to change everything, go back to her dressing room, start again.

But Craig was waiting to go on a first take – Craig

sitting there, invisible now as he never had been in silent shooting, no help to her at all, somewhere in front of her not next to the camera which, even more unnervingly, was equally invisible – entirely set apart, sealed up in some sort of cubicle with a glass window in front. With the heat and all that was quite new to her in this sound filming, she felt a surge of panic rising in her, like nausea, trying to escape her gut – about to explode out among all the technicians and disgrace her.

With an effort of sheer will she beat the nausea back. For now there was the most important thing of all to attend to: the microphone. Where was it? She glanced wildly about. Yes, there it was, right in front – a large black honeycombed lozenge below her, attached to the side of the desk, facing the hard chair she was to sit on while talking to the mother superior – she was to sit absolutely still, Craig had told her, facing this dark evil thing, this gorgon's eye, a wicked presence which she must somehow outface, which would form her nemesis or resurrection.

That was the microphone. And then there was the blackboard with her lines. Where was that? Again, she glanced around in panic. Yes, there – to the other side of the great black camera cubicle. But in the dazzle of these new strong lights, biting at her all round from out of the darkness, she could barely make out a word of the chalked dialogue.

'Craig! I can't see the lines properly. The lights are blinding me—'

'That's OK, honey. You'll remember them – or see them on the take when everyone's stopped moving and we're all settled. Right, are we all done?' Craig called round the sound stage. 'OK, Hetty, your first position behind the flat . . .'

She rose unsteadily, going behind the wooden flat, and waited, breathing deeply, trying to compose herself.

First, the lines . . . the lines. What were they? She'd have to remember them, for she couldn't see them now on the blackboard. But it was no use. She couldn't remember a word. She said a silent prayer then – not that she remember the lines, for she was certain now that she wouldn't, but that everyone in the studio – the technicians, Craig – would forgive her for making such a fool of herself, for wasting their time. 'Please, God,' she murmured, 'forgive me, I don't think I'm really able for this life any more . . .'

And then, with this prayer, out of the blue, her lines returned to her. Of course! There was Craig's cue first, 'Yes, Sister Martha, you asked to see me. What was it you wanted?' – and her reply 'Mother Superior, I have been anxious. *I am not sure if I am made for this life* . . .' They were almost the same words as her prayer. And then they went on – it was easy now – 'I mean, I want to help others – very much. But in the world outside our mission. I want to help in the *real* world.' Now that she remembered the lines, all would be well. Her stammer had quite disappeared, after all. It was remembering the lines, those awkward bloody lines – that had been the great difficulty. And now she knew them! God or someone had given them back to her at the last instant.

'Action!' Craig called from inside the set. And suddenly, with that old familiar voice and call, it seemed to Hetty that all indeed was well now – that old call to attack, which she had missed, but which gave her a vital thrill of reassurance, reminding her of her power, her beauty, her skills in this business. She opened the door into the set and walked confidently into the light, acting now, transformed from her real self. She took her chair in front of the desk, sitting quite still, not looking at the evil eye of the microphone, but straight towards the glass wall where the camera was. She still could not see the words on the blackboard. But it did not matter. She knew the lines now.

'Yes, Sister Martha, you asked to see me.' She heard Craig's cue from somewhere in front of her. 'What was it you wanted?'

'M-m-m-Mother Superior, I have be-be-been anxious. I am not sure I have be-be-been made for this l-l-life . . .'

She could not believe it. The lines were there – but the stammer had returned. The vital consonants had seized up, bad as ever. The heat was stifling, beginning to overwhelm her. It was torture. It was disaster.

'Cut!' Craig shouted.

She repeated the scene. She did it nearly a dozen times again – relaxing half-way through for a break, cooling her face and throat with iced water, even trying quite different parts of the script. But it made hardly any difference. It was all torture. It was all a disaster.

'I don't understand it,' she sobbed to Craig later in her dressing room. 'It was re-re-remembering the lines I was w-w-worried about. Not the st-st-stammer. And I prayed for the lines to c-c-come back, and they did. But then my old v-v-voice came back as well and ruined every-thing . . .'

Craig considered matters. Then he sighed. 'But maybe that's the whole thing, Hetty. That old voice – that stam-mer – *is* your real voice. And all these weeks we've all been trying to make you into something you aren't. You're a great *silent* star. But not for the talkies. That's all it boils down to in the end. Nothing to be ashamed about. Besides, the talkies probably won't last,' he tried to console her, lying. 'Just a nine-day wonder.'

Hetty did not believe him. And now, in face of this disaster, she wanted, needed, him more than ever. But he wasn't there. He disappeared from her dressing room then – just as he disappeared from the villa the following day, returning to Paris to confer with Gaumont, showing them the voice and costume test on Hetty.

'Well . . .' They were cautious with him. 'Perfect, of course – perfect in every way – except for the voice. But we have to make the picture in sound now, Craig. We're committed to it, everyone is. We'll have to . . . look for someone else. It's tough, she being your wife – and such a great talent, such a great silent star. But that stammer, well . . .' They shook their heads, commiserating with him.

'No, no, you're right,' Craig said. 'Wife or no, she simply can't do it. We'll have to get someone else. There's Louise Brooks perhaps. Or we'll test others. And maybe there's this new American girl, Diana Belleville. She's sensational. I've got some reels of her latest picture with me. Think she'd play the nun perfectly. Naïve yet knowing. Just like Sister Martha. And, as for sound, well, she's got this quite extraordinary voice – you'll hear it: sexy, absolutely wonderful . . .'

Craig called Hetty with the news – that they'd have to look for someone else in the part. He'd been wrong. It seemed there was no turning back with the talkies now: Gaumont was quite committed to doing *The Lost Valley* in sound. Every picture was going to be in sound, from now on. He was sorry . . . terribly sorry, but there was nothing he could do . . .

Hetty was stunned at the news, which soon spread around the Victorine studios like wild fire. Everyone, initially, commiserated with her. But thereafter most people seemed to avoid her when she walked round the lot, or saw her in the café-restaurant – making way for her, giving her space, as if she carried some fatal infection.

Hetty was reminded of something in this behaviour. What was it? Then it came back to her – the incident years before, as a child out at the harvesting at Summer

Hill, when Snipe, the maimed fortune-teller, had seen her as a secret princess in the tea-leaves. And all the crone-ish old tea ladies had been astonished then, gazing at her fearfully, making way for her in awe as she had rushed from the circle. But this time, she realized, it was failure which made the technicians avoid her, a failure which, they thought, might infect their own careers – a failure which made her a pariah now and not a princess. And failure stalked her then, increasing its hold over her now at every step.

A few days after Craig had called she woke at four in the morning, a dull pain in her back, with a feverish headache. Her syphilis, merely dormant, had returned. And several days later, due to a mistake by a new typist in Hollywood, a letter arrived, from the WillBow company secretary in Hollywood – a copy of one sent to Craig in Paris – informing them both that funds in the company had sunk to below $25,000 and would have to be immediately replenished if the account was to be drawn on again over *The Lost Valley*.

Hetty was dumbfounded. Money, at least the want of it, was something which had never crossed her mind in years. It had been a fact of life, like air and water. And she had always trusted Craig with it for the simple reason that she knew how little it had ever mattered to him too – talking of it only in vast sums, half a million or more, the entire budget for a picture. Now this. Craig, she saw then, had withdrawn all the money – mostly hers – in their joint company without telling her. But much worse than that he had been financing *The Lost Valley* with it, a picture she had now been cast out of. It was unbelievable. Craig, who had first given her syphilis, then dropped her personally, then professionally, had now almost bankrupted her.

But worst of all – truly worst of all, like the touch of death – was the sudden loss of power she sensed in all this. Money she could do without – losing Summer Hill, Léonie, Craig, even her health. But power was quite another matter. She could not live without that: the power she had possessed, groomed and refined for years, so that it was instinct now, never performance – a confidence that stemmed not from great houses, from love or money but from her own sheer force of will, character, talent. All this most vital flow, the fountainhead of her life, was suddenly draining away from her. She no longer possessed that quality which was essential to her – of inevitable dominance, which had brought her such success, enabled her to overcome every setback. All this had been taken from her now, like wings clipped from a bird, leaving her earthbound, utterly vulnerable, fallible, fearful.

Now at last the full enormity of what she had lost in the last month dawned on her. Each item in her once brilliant portfolio, all her wonderful shares in the world, stared her in the face then as quite worthless certificates: Summer Hill, Léonie, Craig's love, the possibility of children, her career, money, health – these were gone, but above all power: that sovereign wand, aura of invincibility, that cloth of gold had been stripped from her.

Yet even then, suffering the full horror of this realization, she tried to blind herself to it. It couldn't be true. Craig, for so long needed – as father, lover, friend – could not so betray her, could not be such a monster. It was a temporary aberration on his part. They would come together again. Even then, she could not find it in her heart to condemn him outright. Even then, in the face of all this appalling behaviour, she loved him.

He was still in Paris. She tried to reach him there on the telephone. But each time his new secretary told her he was out. She tried to call the WillBow company secretary, trans-Atlantic, but there were long delays. She called

Micky Ostrovosky. But he had gone to Monte Carlo for the weekend.

Sitting at her bureau then, in the big salon of the villa, twilight coming on, as she gazed out at the line of waving palm trees running down the drive to the studio gates, she started to weep. And now, for the first time in her life, she found no reserves, nothing to halt the flow of tears as the soft, velvet-warm evening descended all round her, sitting there alone, a sick headache coming on, joints beginning to burn, so that first she reached for a packet of veronal powders, then a bottle of Italian grappa, something she had never touched before, washing down the powders with big gulps of the fiery liquid.

Soon she was unconscious, unaware of everything, lying on the sofa – unaware then, as she had been until a few minutes before, how in the space of a few months the tables had finally turned on her – how she had fallen from the pinnacle of every kind of success, and was headed downwards now towards the depths.

Craig himself, of course, was the key to the whole matter. And, when he returned from Paris and they finally met, he played a wily game, allowing her no leverage with him, pretending shame in some matters, none in others – the whole a ploy to be finally rid of her. For his secret use of their joint funds he made no apologies whatsoever.

'Why, listen, honey,' he told her that afternoon at the villa. 'The accountants have all the figures: exactly what was your money, and mine, in WillBow Pictures. And you can have your share back, every cent, if that's what you want, in six months or so when this picture goes out on release. But you ought to see the point. WillBow is a motion picture *production* company, not an investment trust for either of us – there to make *other* pictures, not just *Nefertiti* – to show a profit over the years for both of us, as it has, as it surely will. But you can take all your money out of it if you want—'

'For Chrissakes, Craig – a company to make pictures with *me* in them. Not some other b-b-bloody woman. Not this Diana B-b-Belleville or whoever it is you've got for it.' Hetty flushed then with anger. She had heard rumours of Craig's liaison with this up-and-coming picture actress, heard how she was almost a certainty now for the role of the young nun in *The Lost Valley*.

'We've been through all that, Hetty. The voice test. Talkies. They're not for you.'

'OK.' Hetty climbed down. 'But *you* – you and I? Aren't we – something else? Nothing to do with WillBow P-Pictures? What about us, Craig?' She smiled, an expression that was both meek and passionate, staring at him intently. But Craig turned away from her, gazing out at the palm trees from the bay window of the big salon.

'Honey, you and I have gone . . . our different ways.' He spoke abstractedly, pondering the swaying palm trees, their leaves crackling drily in the moist autumn wind that had come to blow over the coast.

'Craig, I've gone nowhere! Just been here. W-w-waiting for you,' she said evenly, retaining her calm with an effort.

'Well, that's as may be. But . . . I've gone. How could I not? – given what's happened.' He turned then, walking over to the drinks table, helping himself to a Scotch. His slight limp, she noticed, had returned. It always did with the first sign of damp in the weather. She knew so much about him, everything, like a well-thumbed scrapbook. And yet she really did not know him at all. Now she made one last effort to know him, to show herself, to commit herself to him, to touch his heart somehow. She went up to him, holding him gently by the shoulders, speaking softly.

'Craig, it's just not p-p-possible,' she told him. 'That all this, all of us, in eight, nine years – that it just "goes" like that. It can't. It doesn't.'

'It's perfectly possible, honey.' He let her hold him but made no gesture in return. 'I like you, admire you, you're a wonderful actress . . . wonderful times. But times change. And, worst of all, I changed them.' He released himself then, sipping his drink, turning away. Then suddenly he turned again, facing her, serious now, talking urgently for the first time. 'Why, how could you go on loving, living with, someone who's brought you such pain, this syphilis – someone who's taken up with another woman? It's nonsense. Makes no sense, don't you see?'

'I can bear it. Even her.' Hetty played her last cards. 'If we went on together – in some fashion.'

He shook his head. 'You couldn't, Hetty. You'd be denying everything that's good in you, everything that's simply . . . you. Your confidence, vitality, your *brain*. You'd never be any good at playing second fiddle.'

'I might surprise you. Maybe second fiddle could turn out to be my forte . . .'

'No, Hetty. Your music, one way or another, has to be the best. Just going to have to be with a different orchestra. I don't know where, or when, or who'll write the score, who'll conduct. But it can't be me. I'm no use to you any more. How could I be? – failing you so? But at least remember – we'll always have *Nefertiti*. And that was the very best of us. No doubt. Even in the cut version, even how they mangled it, they couldn't destroy you at least. You're sensational. You'll see. They're releasing it soon. And one day – I still have a full print of my own here at the Victorine – they'll show the whole picture, just as I wanted it – and then, why, we'll remember each other even better!'

So it was – neat as ever, with such fine words, truths

and outright lies – that Craig finally dropped Hetty. And when he left the following day, looking for locations in Morocco, Hetty, having played all her most treasured cards with him, did not weep. She showed no emotion at all – simply because she had no decent emotions left, only bitter and destructive ones. She had, she saw now, been finally and completely betrayed by this man whom she had loved, who had meant everything to her.

So, with only those seeds of havoc which Léonie had so well identified in her, she set out then, covertly, tactfully as she thought, to take revenge on life. It would be a punishment which, since it was purely spiteful and vindictive, she came to inflict much more on herself than on anyone else.

IO

Yet to begin with Hetty's descent was not clearly visible as that. It ran in dramatic fits and starts, like a faulty elevator, where there were sudden, startling recoveries, glorious upward flights, followed by steep, stomach-turning drops, juddering halts, reprieves, dramatic ascents, further declines. In this way her fall was even more spectacular than her rise. Initially, for the next month at least, she kept a reasonably even keel, with most of her wits about her, as she started a series of losing battles – with Craig, with WillBow Pictures, with assorted doctors, agents, producers, directors, attorneys, above all with herself.

Moving out of the Victorine, staying with the Ostrovoskys in their villa outside Nice, she soon discovered she had no case against Craig financially. She herself had signed the cheques with which he had partly financed

The Lost Valley. And that was that. Meanwhile she had only some thirty thousand dollars in her own personal account. However, the dollar at that point was ridiculously high against the franc – and this was more than sufficient for her to live on, if on a somewhat reduced scale.

She met various picture producers and directors – in Paris, Berlin, London. Socially, at least, they were pleased to see her – and even more happy to be seen with her. They wined and dined her, at the Adlon, the Crillon, Claridge's, picking up all her bills. For *Nefertiti* was about to be released and a vast worldwide publicity campaign had already been launched by Fox – her astonishingly chiselled, regal face, beneath the dramatic gold and blue Nefertiti headdress, already going up on European billboards, the same regal features appearing in all the picture magazines and popular newspapers. But sound was definitely the coming thing – and these producers merely dallied with her. They saw, they heard, all too well how her stammer now disqualified her – her stammer, which had returned now with a vengeance. They had no real work for her.

She took on a new agent, a balding middle-aged American in Paris, a nice but essentially useless man. She stayed in Paris at the Crillon, conferring in her suite with this Bernie Franklin, who then busied himself on her behalf, but to no avail.

However, anxious to save on expensive hotel bills and drawn by the vibrant Paris social scene, she subsequently rented an apartment, small but rather grand, painted all in stark white, with mirrors, and furnished in the latest art déco style, on the Ile Saint-Louis, the second floor of an old town house on the Quai d'Orléans, with a spectacular balcony view looking straight out over the river and the spires of Notre-Dame.

Here, with her fame and through her contacts in the

French picture business, she was soon taken up and fêted by the smart social and literary sets, both French and expatriate, dining with Cocteau and Colette at the Grand Véfour, at Maxim's with René Clair, the new white hope of French pictures, whose *Italian Straw Hat* had just opened to great acclaim in the boulevard cinemas.

But more often she took casual suppers, sausages and steins of lager at the Brasserie Lipp, with new American friends living in or visiting Paris then – Hemingway, the poet Archibald MacLeish and his pretty wife, the boxer Gene Tunney – going on afterwards to fashionable theatres and night clubs: to see Josephine Baker, sensationally dark and nude in *La Revue Nègre*; to hear Mistinguett at Les Ambassadeurs, the cocky new singer Chevalier at the Olympia Music Hall – or sometimes, from the sublime to the ridiculous, visiting the Folies-Bergère up town, then the Boeuf sur le Toit, with onion soup at Les Halles at four in the morning before a last *café-cognac* back at her apartment.

Hetty knew, of course, that Robert and Léonie were living in Paris then – knew their address, too, not far from her, over the river on the rue Saint-André-des-Arts. At first, quite taken up with her new social life, she did not think of them. Yet, although she repressed the fact, they were never far beneath the surface of her thoughts. They had in fact a powerful existence for her still, in shadow, a life invisible but not forgotten. So that although, when she did come to think of them, she had no intention of making any direct approach, she was left feeling a curiosity which she was not able to repress.

So she took to passing along the narrow rue Saint-André-des-Arts, on her way from the Ile Saint-Louis to the Deux Magots or the Brasserie Lipp, in a headscarf and dark glasses, glancing over at their doorway, sometimes stopping at a café almost opposite, watching, waiting. And one afternoon she was rewarded – and astonished.

Léonie, looking radiant in a summer frock, emerged from the door with a perambulator – a beautiful dark-haired girl, a year old, she thought, sitting up, madly waving a rattle. She followed them across the Boulevard Saint-Germain, up to the Luxembourg Gardens, walking some way behind, past the ornate terrace statuary, until they stopped among a crowd of other children out with their mothers and nannies, spellbound, watching the marionette theatre, the hunchback Polichinelle – tipsy, talkative, quarrelsome – beating his wife with a large stick to the joyfully alarmed cries of all the children.

Hetty, moving tactfully forward, finally got a better view of Léonie and her daughter: Léonie, so happily the natural mother now, had the child in her arms, holding her up to the spectacle. Hetty was quite stricken by the sight, this woman, whom she had loved, who had betrayed her, so happy now, fulfilled – with a child, as she had so much wanted for herself. The vision horrified her. She could not bear the thought, the sight of it all, turning away then and running from the happy throng. So that afterwards she took all the more vehemently to her frenzied social life, hoping to blot out every memory of that terrible vision at the marionette theatre, and the unutterable sense of loss she had felt.

And for Hetty, initially and at least on the surface, these increasingly chaotic, hectic times were happy – happy in that her starved vanity was now so regularly fed, her self-esteem repaired. For most came to adore – or just enjoy and toady – this vivacious, so original a woman, with such a surprising mix of gifts: Irish, Jewish, American all at once, who yet spoke perfect French, and who more surprisingly still, as they had to remind themselves, was a great picture star, talked of in the same breath as Garbo or Gloria Swanson, a woman out of all that Hollywood vulgarity, who yet so obviously was not vulgar herself. Far from it. Just like her dramatically looming presence as Nefertiti going up on billboards all over Paris just then, she had the manners, the hauteur, the whole natural air and breeding of a Queen.

And yet, among these new friends, how often, how splendidly, she climbed down from this pedestal! They loved her even more for that – dancing the can-can or taking two walking sticks and engaging in mock duels at a party, displaying a lovely wit, sometimes lacerating, even coarse, with a mind that could be equally refined or down to earth. Hetty, among these new friends, became profligate with her talents, wasting them, casting them out, words upon the water – all these conflicting dramas in her soul which before had been used to great purpose, absorbed and fixed, in art, on celluloid.

Now, though she could not admit it for an instant, thinking instead how she was regaining herself, she was steadily overdrawing her account, living on borrowed time – on her wits, her nerves, her over-bright looks, her reputation. Now, beneath the surface of her fevered gaiety, there was a festering guilt at her wasteful life, a deep unhappiness. And it was these repressed feelings more than anything else which gave her this brilliant social attack now, this brio – in words, gesture, thoughts. Her friends mistook her irresponsible *éclat* as central to her real nature. But it was simply the product of her secret despair, her sense of betrayal, by all that she had known, by everyone she had loved, in all her previous worlds.

So, trying to forget this, in a whirl of ever more heady parties, chatter, drinking, she launched herself, devil-may-care, on the wild *zeitgeist* of the times, which by that autumn of 1928 in Paris had reached a crescendo of insensate bravado.

This *beau monde* of the city – the shallow, the aristocratic, the genuinely celebrated – did nothing to help her, since they were unaware of her problems, entirely overlaid as they were by what seemed to them a wonderfully genuine *bel esprit*. And this they lapped up, savouring her bewildering mix of wild Irish spirit, Jewish languor, American openness and practicality. They loved her *bons mots*, bizarre Irish twists of thought and turns of phrase, translated into a perfect, if stammering, French. And some of the men were equally tempted by her rash and wind-blown beauty now, by features that were getting thinner, more chiselled, in a way more desperate and so more appealing, with her illness. Or the men were taken by her sly invitations in other moods, her sex, which she promoted now and then towards them, but only as an impossible ideal, a Holy Grail, always finally withheld.

Hetty walked all sorts of tightropes then, a dazzling high-wire act, which her new friends applauded, quite unaware that she was really a rank amateur in these social routs, that this hair-raising approach of hers was a forced performance, so much a lesser part of her nature, the result simply of growing secret despairs which she would not confront.

A few came to know this, though, becoming real friends, among a group of women she came to meet – writers, artists, poets, Amazons of a quite declared sort – who were living in Paris. Initially she had met Gertrude Stein and her companion Alice B. Toklas – and through them a circle of other women friends: the American balletomane and bizarre film director Loie Fuller, the booksellers Sylvia Beach and Adrienne Monnier, the English writer – all the rage then among these women – Djuna Barnes. Above all she met the doyenne of this left bank American artistic set, Natalie Barney.

A friendship ensued here which became close. Miss Barney was not deceived by Hetty's frenetic clamour and social high-jinks – soon sensing the deep unhappiness which lay behind this façade: a surmise which proved entirely correct when Hetty came to explain all that had happened to her in the last year.

And here, with Natalie and her circle, in this gracious and quite open lesbian *milieu*, Hetty found some solace, spiritually, then sexually, involving herself in a number of *tendresses* with Natalie's younger friends and acquaintances, some of which became mild or passionate *affaires*, for a night or for longer engagements, which she pursued vehemently, tasting all sorts of sweet revenge against Craig, against Léonie – and even sweeter, forgotten pleasures, re-animated only so briefly with Léonie in the bedouin tent, but now indulged more continuously and so much more comfortably: a pleasure, she was happy to confirm, still part of her real nature, perhaps the truest part, she felt, in a nature so deeply wounded in every other way.

Yes, there was great happiness for her then in this simple release of a pent-up sexual energy, a loving and a vast need satisfied, which she had so missed, which she could no longer share with men. Above all, naked in these women's arms, she could forget the stigmata of her disease, her syphilis, dormant now again after the last Salvarsan cure, but which she knew was likely to recur at any time. She could forget the disease and its infection, for she did not make love with women in that way, a manner in which, with men, she no longer dared pursue. And besides, with women, she soon confirmed, as she had discovered years before with Léonie in Dublin, love-making was so much longer and better a thing than it had ever been with men.

So, in such loving, throughout wild and tender nights, she found a respite from her social mania, found a liberating contentment. However, in every other sphere of her life she continued to live on frantic tenterhooks, swaying dangerously on her various high wires, always hovering over an abyss.

One such pitfall was drink. As the summer went by, and it seemed more and more that there was no future for her in motion pictures, she took to drink as a stay against admitting this failure. To begin with she drank only socially – reasonably at first, but then overmuch. So that soon, suffering hangovers, she started taking nips of spirit or mugs of champagne with orange at midday or in the afternoons, as a hair of the dog. Then, on the rare nights when she was alone in her apartment, she took to these bottles more vehemently, when she could not sleep or her pains came back, thumbing giddily through old scrapbooks of reviews and production stills from her great pictures.

She never really came to like the taste of drink. But she came to crave first the euphoric release it brought – the illusion of power, dominance, success once more – and then, before she had time to realize how baseless these feelings were, the complete oblivion the alcohol gave her. So that by the autumn, though not a full-time alcoholic, she had started a promising career in the business.

She had, too, among some of her circle, taken to puffing marijuana weeds – some of Cocteau's friends had introduced her to them. But she thought nothing of it – just as she thought nothing of her now considerable drinking. She worried only over the hangovers. But, since these were readily curable with another *coup* of cold champagne or a sharp vodka, she soon ceased to worry about these hangovers too. She was still young enough easily to recover from her excesses, while yet maintaining them.

And then, quite realistically, her circumstances took a turn for the better – and the elevator of her life leapt upwards. *Nefertiti* was finally released – first at Graumann's Theater in Hollywood, then in New York just after Labor Day. Hetty, though she was asked, pointedly refused to attend the Hollywood première – as evidence of her displeasure at this mangled version of the picture. Yet even in its truncated 2½-hour version, some of its glories remained intact, in the huge set-pieces, the battles, and particularly in Hetty's performance in which her regality, together with all her other brilliantly characterized ploys and wiles and final tragedy, overshadowed everything else in the production. Most critics were wild about her, at least, and the public flocked to see the picture. With all this clamour and acclaim Hetty sensed a recovery in the air – the more so a week later when the gilt-edged invitation arrived from London.

Nefertiti was due to open there with a European première at the Empire, Leicester Square – a special charity showing for the British Legion in the presence of the young Prince of Wales as royal patron, in mid-October. And Hetty had received what amounted to a royal command to attend. Craig would not be there. He had already started location work in the wilds of Morocco. Hetty was charmed by the invitation, by the whole idea of renewed public view once more, a fresh start to her career perhaps as well – excited by the idea, too, of meeting the glamorous young Prince.

A suite had been booked for her at the Savoy Hotel. She travelled with her maid, the hairless Mr Franklin and a train of baggage filled with the latest fashionable clothes, for she thought to spend some weeks in London, seeing how the land lay as regards future possible work.

Arriving at Dover after a choppy crossing, they took the boat train to Victoria Station, where to her joy she saw some hundreds – perhaps thousands, she thought – of her fans milling round, cheering and waving madly, beyond the platform barrier as she stepped down on to a red carpet.

The staid, top-hatted station-master greeted her and the head of the Fox Picture Corporation in London came forward, an aggressive, overweight little man in a quite unsuitably loud check suit and bow tie, planting a wet kiss on her cheek, before his chichi, bijou wife presented her with a great bouquet of hothouse red roses.

Hetty stood there for a long moment in her new polka dot Chanel suit and huge cloche felt hat with a dramatically upturned brim, gracefully acknowledging the cheers. Then, taken by this fizzy warmth in the air, and seeing how the drama there might be accentuated, she suddenly removed the big hat, discarding it, as something foreign to her true wild nature, that swashbuckling dare-devil which her fans knew and loved her for – flouncing her dark curls out, eyes flashing, as if she were about to embark on a duel. And in that moment the whole platform seemed to explode, the hurrahs and cheers and blown kisses redoubled.

Hetty smiled wonderfully, sniffing the roses, lifting her huge blue eyes to the crowds, basking in the limelight once more, quite ignoring how this feeling and most of her vivacity, the sparkle in her eyes, the colour in her cheeks, all this suddenly-renewed beauty and confidence, was largely the result of a steady medicinal intake of brandy on the rough Channel crossing, and of the subsequent downing of several large gins on the boat train. She quite put the idea of any such unnatural stimulus from her mind. It was her public, her fans, who had so renewed her spirit. She was herself again. She had found her true position once more. Life was just about to begin all over again for her.

She met the Prince the following evening at the theatre, first in line among others connected with the production, curtsying to him very formally, hardly daring to look at him – then following his retinue of guests, up the grand staircase to an open-topped royal box of sorts that had been set up at the centre of the circle, half a dozen armchair-like seats, specially arranged there for the royal party.

She was to have sat immediately behind this plush corral, with the Fox executives and her hairless agent. But, after the Prince had self-deprecatingly acknowledged the cheers on his arrival, as the spotlights coursed over the royal party, he stood up, turned and gestured for Hetty to join him. There was a spare seat with them, he intimated; the audience, unable to see Hetty, held its breath, wondering what might have gone amiss in the arrangements.

Then, coming forward down the dark aisle, before another spotlight suddenly caught her, Hetty joined the Prince, standing next to him at the front of the circle in the blinding limelight. Then the house erupted, roaring its approval at this unexpected conjunction, the sight of a Prince and a Queen together, both now fulfilling every possible fantasy they might have – a real Prince of the blood royal, linked with something equally unobtainable, a great Hollywood picture star, the two of them standing there, heavenly emblems come to earth, a perfect match, the Prince in tails and white tie, small, neat, charming, outrageously handsome under a thatch of straw hair; Hetty, with amethyst pendant earrings, dressed in a spectacular evening dress, low-waisted, with a scalloped hemline dipping at the back, in fine white tulle, covered in gold and over patterned silver sequins that glittered now in the spotlights. The applause increased. But Hetty knew well what her response must be. She refused the plaudits, curtsying briefly to the Prince, then looking up at him, seeing his face clearly now, staring at him, smiling hesitantly, before preparing to turn away and take a back seat.

Their eyes met – for now he was staring at her, surprised, yet unflinching. He had the same sort of

Wedgwood-blue eyes, Hetty thought, as her own, glittering in the light. And there was something else similar in his features – the line of his chin, his nose, the set of his eyes. What was it? She had seen these same expressions, or something very like them, somewhere, in someone, before. The rebellious air, yet the delicate charm, an attractive hesitancy about him as well, the vulnerability – a sadness too, in the whole expression, which she felt she remembered in someone she had known.

Finally, unlocking herself from the Prince's gaze, she took a seat next to him. The Prince remained standing a few moments longer as the lights faded, a quizzical expression on his face. He, too, had suddenly been struck by something in Hetty – those piercing blue eyes, the pointed chin . . . Who, what, was it, he wondered? She reminded him of himself in some uncanny way. There was the same sadness behind their public façades, a vulnerability – all that he had so clearly sensed in that hesitant smile of hers; all that for so long he had had to repress in himself. The whole sudden confrontation just then had some quite unexplained magic to it. He determined to see more of her, to try to discover the source, the meaning behind this extraordinary sense of affinity he felt with her.

Meeting her properly was not difficult. With the royal party, which included his younger brother George, his equerry Captain Hamilton and several older women, Hetty went on afterwards for dinner and dancing at the Prince's regular night spot, the Embassy Club, a long basement room, mirrors everywhere, with swing glass doors leading from the restaurant to the crowded dance floor.

Here, with small tables edging right out on to the open space, they took seats at another much larger table, always reserved for the Prince, against one wall, opposite the orchestra set up on a balcony at the far end of the smoky, mirror-glittering room. Luigi, the head waiter, ministered with appropriate regality – pâté de foie gras, devilled lobster and jeroboams of Moët champagne. And, very soon after supper, the Prince was dancing with Hetty – first a vibrant foxtrot, then a quickstep, and later, his third consecutive dance with her, a waltz.

'P-p-perhaps, sir,' she said apologetically, glancing over at the other, older ladies in the Prince's party, 'I impose. The others? . . .'

'Certainly not. I'm imposing, if anyone is. Besides, I assure you, my women friends – they will be only too pleased that I dance with someone nearer my own age!'

He smiled, the very slightly hooded eyes narrowing – holding her not too close nor yet too distantly, swinging round in perfect step with the music, as if they had been dancing thus for years. There was nothing the slightest bit shy or risqué in his attitude, his remarks, Hetty thought. He could not dissemble – that was her first and clearest impression of him. His whole attitude – if it was not forthright, almost rebellious – was naïve, willing, simple, utterly straightforward. And so his absolutely magnetic charm – and there was no doubt about that – was something that Hetty could entirely believe in. It was not assumed. It was him.

'I see . . .' Hetty smiled, with a touch of mischief, tightening her grip on his shoulder just a fraction. 'I should have thought – every young w-w-woman in England . . .' She left the idea hanging delicately in the air.

'Indeed.' He came back then with the same amused irony. 'Quite so. That's not the problem – but that there are so few such young women in England – like you!' Hetty demurred, bowing her head. 'No, no,' he ran on. 'I can tell you honestly – few so young in spirit, yet somehow so . . . mature. Regal indeed! But of course I shouldn't be surprised. One saw all that in your performance tonight, as Queen Nefertiti – sensational! You couldn't have played her like that, so convincingly, without having some of exactly the same qualities yourself! Captivating!'

'Thank you.' Hetty, on her best behaviour and having only drunk a very little that evening, coloured quite naturally.

'You surprise me in so many ways,' the Prince went on. 'For of course – I was certain – you were American!'

'No, English—'

'But that slight accent, a touch of something else – Ireland?'

'Well, yes, originally.' Hetty tried to make the least of her origins. But the Prince insisted.

'Irish, indeed! What part?'

'Oh, my family – we l-l-lived at Summer Hill, a house in the south there. My f-f-father, no, my grandfather rather, Sir Desmond – I never knew him – l-l-lived there. But I left years ago, l-living in Hollywood. I married the motion picture director there, Craig St John Williamson, who made *Nefertiti*—'

'Of course, of course – I knew you were married!' The Prince broke happily into this stumbling and embarrassed personal history, unable to hide what seemed to Hetty to be clear relief at her married status. 'I know a little of your public career, of course. Your last picture – *Gold Dust*, wasn't it? – we all so enjoyed that at York House earlier this year. But I'd no idea of all this *other* background, so close to home, as it were! Shall you be staying in London – then visiting home in Ireland?'

'Yes . . .' Hetty was beginning to tread on thin ice. 'Yes, I expect to be here for several weeks, I think. There are p-p-possible pictures to talk about. But Ireland – I don't think so . . .' She smiled vaguely, hoping to drop this whole difficult topic of her homeland.

'Oh, why? I've often wanted to visit. But can't, of

course. Wonderful countryside, wonderful riding – everyone tells me. Why?'

'Well, the house, I believe, is falling down. It's no longer in the family. I live in P-Paris now. And Nice, in the hills outside. I expect you know the area. Nice is really much nicer . . . than Ireland!'

But the Prince, anxiously trying to identify some reasons for his strong emotions, his sense of affinity with this woman earlier that evening in the theatre, was not to be diverted from his enquiries as to her background.

'Indeed . . . But your own family, in Ireland? – surely you shall want to see them?'

Hetty felt herself on very thin ice indeed now. She could not admit to the Prince that her mother – as far as the British were concerned – was the infamous Irish republican and revolutionary, friend to the arch-demon De Valera, sentenced to death with the other leaders after the treacherous Easter rebellion only thirteen years before, and still a well-known name in some quarters.

'Oh, I don't see my m-m-mother. We rather fell out. She lives in Dublin, involved in all sorts of good works. And as for my f-f-father . . .' She paused. 'Well, he died, he was killed long ago, when I was tiny, on the West Indian island where we lived first – killed by a t-tribe of marauding s-savages, can you imagine! I can just remember it,' she ran on, intent now on making an amusing story out of it all. 'There was a stockade of mattresses on the veranda and f-f-flaming arrows and cutlasses and guns going off left, right and centre! An extraordinary f-fracas!'

So Hetty made a joke of her parentage, her own past – hoping thus to dismiss the whole awkward topic. But this only served to increase the Prince's curiosity, increase his sympathy for her as well.

'My goodness me!' He was genuinely astonished. 'I'm

very sorry. But what a tale – more dramatic than your pictures.'

'I suppose so . . .'

'I *am* sorry. How very unfortunate – so to lose, and fall out with, your parents. A father gone so early in life . . .'

The Prince looked at her with something more than sympathy now, with an intense, piercing gaze, as if by such a look he could somehow divine all her secrets without further enquiry.

But he could not, so that finally, seeing Hetty's embarrassment, he mumbled, 'Forgive me for prying like this, about your family. But let me explain – something quite strange, you see – because earlier this evening in the theatre, when I first saw you properly, I had the distinct impression that we'd met before somewhere. Long ago perhaps? Something familiar about your – face, yes . . .'

At this admission Hetty felt the back of her neck prickle. So that, without any restraint now, she said, 'Yes, that's very strange, for I fe-felt just the same myself when we met this evening, in those lights – that I'd met you somewhere before!'

The Prince was wonderfully pleased with this. 'Well, perhaps we *were* together in some previous existence, before either of us was born. And so we may renew the acquaintance, properly now, in reality! If you're here for a few weeks, perhaps you might care to dine with me at York House, or come beagling with us at Lord Carrington's place next weekend? I'd be very pleased.'

'I'd be honoured, sir . . .'

'Come!' He seemed to take her a little more firmly in his grip. 'Not "sir" – Edward, please. And perhaps we can forget the "honour" business too. After all, with our previous incarnation together, we must really know each other very well already!'

And that was true, Hetty felt. She had never got on so

well, so quickly, with a man – not even with Craig. Of course he was royal, heir to the throne, and so charming – the most glamorous young man in England, no doubt. These were not the reasons for her attraction, however, which was so much more due to that mysterious affinity they had talked about – the sense somehow that he was brother to her, or father even, that all-powerful kindred figure she had so lacked and longed for all her life.

But meanwhile they laughed uproariously at other things and danced the rumba.

For the Prince was quite captivated by her, as well – for a lot of other perfectly obvious reasons: her spirit, beauty, her sharp wit and a mind in which, for him, there was nothing clammy or too intellectual. It was a *coup de foudre* of sorts, made all the easier by the fact that his great but unrequited love for Mrs Dudley Ward had, at that point, come to something of a full stop. She had gone away for several weeks, visiting relatives in Yorkshire. And of course in any case, as he knew so well, so sadly, she would have done nothing but tactfully encourage any steps he might take with other younger women – unmarried women, of course. But then that was another of his problems in love. He could not somehow ever get on with unmarried women. So, in the circumstances, he decided he should, and could, get on very well with Hetty.

When they left the Embassy Club early that morning, press photographers were outside. And later that day the early editions featured the Prince and his new friend. Hetty glanced at the papers in bed at the Savoy. At first the whole thing seemed unbelievable. But then, thinking it over, remembering the extraordinary sense of familiarity she had felt with him from the very beginning, it all seemed entirely natural.

Hetty went beagling that weekend with the Prince and some of his friends, house guests at Lord Carrington's place outside Aylesbury – sloshing through the muddy fields in shafts of rainy autumn light, eating late blackberries, sipping cocktails that evening, attending the local parish church next morning. Their friendship bloomed. And the following week Hetty dined alone with the Prince at York House, not in the chilly ground floor dining salon, but upstairs quite informally in his drawing room, decorated everywhere with huge maps of the world, a round table set up by the fire, a simple meal – for unlike his grandfather the Prince was no great eater: soup, grilled lamb chops, a good claret.

The Prince was entirely relaxed with Hetty now – both of them, secure and confident, behaving as old friends. The Prince poured the claret, taking the bottle from his major-domo Finch, who left then, flourishing the wine napkin casually over his shoulder as he went. Hetty loved the informality of it all – the soft lamplight, the shadows running away into the old rambling room, filled with Victorian furniture.

'Your health, Hetty!' The Prince raised his glass. And Hetty hers. But she barely sipped. She had quite stopped drinking. She had no need of that now. She was no longer a failure. She was, in one way, sitting here alone with the Prince, the most successful woman in England. She glanced round, looking at the maps of the world everywhere, looming out from the walls, the Empire, over half the globe, it seemed, coloured red. What were motion pictures, all that fantasy? – when this person, and all this fabulous reality, lay at her feet?

Gradually that evening, as they dined and later sitting opposite each other by the fireside, with her stammer almost disappearing in the extraordinary ease she felt with him, she told the Prince of her life – its beginnings, all the passions and alarms then, in Domenica and Summer Hill as a child, the loss of her father, the frightful rows with her mother. Léonie, too, was described –

though not the full depth of their relationship. And so was Craig. Though here she felt quite free to tell him almost all the worst, everything Craig had done – apart from the disease he had given her – how they had finally separated.

The Prince nodded sadly. 'Indeed, how often it turns out that way. A first marriage . . . If we could only *start* with a second. How much better things might work out!'

And the thought crossed the Prince's mind then: here, here right in front of him, was just the sort of woman he would have wanted to marry – if she were not married already, of course, and if he were not born to be King. And yet he had often wondered about that role . . .

With his lack of stuffy attitude he enjoyed most of his official work as Prince of Wales. But he had come to dread the idea of the throne – the crushing responsibilities, above all the strait-jacket of formalities and ceremonials he would have to take on then, forsaking all his own happy and informal life, which he had come to depend on – to the point of retaining his sanity, as he thought. In his heart of hearts he felt he would be a failure as King. While his younger brother Bertie, so much less restless – steadier, quieter, above all more patient and dogged – would be ideal in that role. Fate had cruelly produced them in the wrong order. And the idea of necessary marriage to some other royal or aristocratic woman – to any of the women he had already met in that line – was abhorrent. But with Hetty, for example . . . Goodness! he thought – how very different life would be then. He smiled at her, thinking these things.

'The awful trouble,' he went on, breaking the silence. 'The way marriage is – we really only have one chance at it. Just like a stupid cricket match, when you're so easily out first ball – and have to spend the rest of your life locked up in the pavilion, as it were!'

Hetty agreed. 'But there is divorce, of course,' she added.

'For you, perhaps. Never for me.'

'No. No, of course not.' They gazed at each other, something passing in the air between them which was more than simple friendship, understanding – a whiff of physical tenderness, the vague smoke of desire. 'You'll have to be absolutely sure – the first time then!' Hetty continued, lightening the atmosphere.

'Yes. But my parents, so many people, want me married off at once, already – willy-nilly, packed up, tickety-boo, out of harm's way . . .'

The Prince galloped through these marital imperatives and they laughed outright at the nonsense of it all, as he eased his legs towards the fire. A sudden wind rattled at the windows beyond the heavy drapes. Hetty turned as if it were a ghost.

'Autumn storms,' the Prince remarked. But when Hetty turned back she found him staring at her, not at the windows.

'Well, of course, you must re-resist being so packed up and put away.'

'Oh, I have! I will . . .'

'A fatal curb. I found it myself with my own M-Mama, wishing all sorts of ridiculous restrictions on me. One absolutely must be one's own pe-person first – if one's to be any real good to anyone else.'

'Of course. But in my position,' he laughed shortly, 'that's not so easy. I'm not my own property, you see – that's the frightful bind. "House of Windsor, the Nation, the Empire . . ."' He intoned the words lugubriously. 'They all have first call on me.'

'Yes!' Hetty leant forward eagerly now, passionate about something. 'Of course. But not yet. Not entirely. *Not yet!*' She smiled at him – forceful, bright and energetic suddenly, her eyes blazing with dictatorial purpose.

Then, equally suddenly, she leant right back on the sofa, hands behind her head, gazing vacantly up at the ceiling. 'Not me-married yet, nor King . . .' She too, in turn, intoned the words mock-mournfully.

'No, indeed.' The Prince got briskly to his feet, as if infected with the energy which Hetty had just then shown to him. He glanced at Hetty, in sudden repose now, lying almost horizontally beneath him – long legs stretched straight out, in sheer grey silk stockings, a pale lilac silk dress riding up slightly over her knees, to a low-belted waist, a lower neckline circled by a single string of creamy pearls, a bloused bodice loosely moulding the shapes of her small pointed breasts. Then, turning away abruptly, the Prince started to busy himself, but aimlessly – looking for a cigarette, then a lighter, kicking the coals with his foot, while Hetty remained there, lost in thought, staring upwards. The Prince finally managed to light his cigarette.

'Shall we dance tonight? The Embassy? Or I have a few records here.' He gazed down on her again, drawing deeply on the cigarette.

'Why not both?' Hetty, without moving, looked up at him. Then, with a sudden spring, she sat forward, brisk and bright once more, keen to promote the Prince's busy new mood, anxious too that he should not think she was being in any way over-familiar with him.

So they danced – to the sounds of the Prince's new electric gramophone: a selection of vivid Scottish dances which happened to be on the turntable – increasingly frantic, far from the proper steps or order, romping about helter-skelter, charging over the great Aubusson carpet, in and out between the heavy chairs and tables, reeling from light to shadow, swinging under the great maps of the Empire: an ever-more frenzied dance, laughing and shrieking as they fell over and into things, picking each other up, jumping round the room like young animals –

until finally the music stopped and they fell into each other's arms, congratulating themselves, enchanted, exhausted, tears of laughter in their eyes.

Then suddenly, drawing apart for an instant, looking at each other in amazement, they kissed.

'Oh my, oh my! . . .' was all Hetty could say, drawing breath, astonished at the end of the embrace – before she moved away from him, putting fingers to both cheeks in happy amazement. 'I see what you mean now – about being out first ball and locked up in the pavilion for the rest of your life!' Then she sighed, turning from him a little despondently.

But he reached for her, gently turning her back towards him. 'Not yet, remember.' He spoke softly, but then suddenly with great brio. '*Not yet!*' And he took her hand then, leading her off to the Embassy Club, both of them imagining themselves as happy as they had ever been in their lives.

Hetty stayed on at the Savoy and in the next few weeks their affair grew in every sort of intimacy, except one. They did not make love. The Prince might have wished it – he did at times. But something – the sense of old innocent friendship with this woman as much as anything – drew him back. As, for Hetty, there was another much more obvious reason for withholding herself.

And yet this enforced restraint did not really cramp their style. They made endless virtues out of the necessity, suspended in what they felt was a delicious balance to their affair, veering towards an even more delicious precipice, over which they might one day launch themselves. And, besides these happy prohibitions, the Prince had come to feel a great respect for Hetty, so spirited and outspoken in one way, wise and calm in another, a mix of sister and potential mistress for him – a variety of conflicting images, none of which he wanted to sully. More and more he saw Hetty not as a passing fancy, but as someone with whom he hoped to have a long relationship, one that might release him from his awful heartache with Mrs Dudley Ward, save him from his consequent restlessness and frustrations there, save him from himself.

So, if not with sex, they satisfied themselves with everything else to hand – and there was much of that: beagling again, theatres, night clubs, uproarious private cinema shows of some of Hetty's old pictures at York House, large or intimate dinner parties, a trip to Brighton, the Prince driving incognito in his open-roofed DeLage tourer.

And it was on this journey, a touch of overnight frost chilling the bright Sunday morning air, the wind bringing tears to their eyes, speeding down the Brighton road at sixty miles an hour, that the Prince turned to Hetty, touching her hand.

'Know something, Laura?' he said lightly. 'If things were different, I'd marry you tomorrow. Would you?'

'Oh yes. Yes, I would!' She laughed, keeping her eyes on the road ahead, thinking the Prince was joking. Then she turned and looked at him – as he turned to her in the same instant – and she saw how serious he had been. And she was sad then, as he was, both of them looking back at the empty road.

'Never mind,' he roused himself, bright once more. 'We'll see each other, won't we? From now on, whatever happens, one way or another – though of course we'll have to be more discreet. In Paris, London, Nice. Won't we?' He looked round at her, anxious again, the small fair face suddenly vulnerable, childlike.

'Yes.'

'Promise?'

'Yes. Yes, Edward – yes!'

Later they dug out the caretaker of the Brighton Pavilion – an astonished functionary, for it was a Sunday morning – who opened the building up for the Prince. And they walked alone through its fantastic eastern rooms, an exotic caravanserai, decorated in every sort of elaborate arabesque and gaudy colour, admiring the set-pieces, the gilded plaster palm columns, with their leaf capitals rising to a blue-domed heaven high above, a fabulous dream of a thousand and one nights here set down by the raw English briny.

'George IV, when he was Prince Regent,' the Prince commented, moving his eyes round the whole glittering extravaganza. 'What a scallywag – and all just for his mistress!'

'She did better than his wife!'

'Mistresses usually do . . .'

They laughed and wandered on silently, arm in arm, thinking now of all sorts of possibilities and compromises which might sustain their future together.

In an office looking out over the royal mews at Buckingham Palace Lord Stamfordham, King George's Private Secretary, glanced once more through the rising stack of popular newspapers which had been collected for him during the past weeks – containing photographs of the Prince with Miss Laura Bowen, gossipy articles linking them together, references and surmises which had already upset both the King and Queen Mary. But the King and Queen had simply been put out by the Prince's indiscreet association with a woman whom they took to be a vulgar Hollywood picture star – and a married woman at that, as all the Prince's women so unfortunately were.

Arthur Stamfordham, however, was horrified by a quite different aspect to the relationship. A man in his seventies now, he had been one of Queen Victoria's equerries and had afterwards worked closely with Lord Knollys, Private Secretary to King Edward VII. So Stamfordham had known Edward well, both as King and before that as Prince of Wales – and now, with Knollys himself dead five years before, Stamfordham, alone among courtiers, was privy to some most dangerous secrets.

Rising from his desk then, he opened a safe in the corner, and with further private keys unlocked a drawer inside. Taking a sealed envelope from it he returned to his desk. Inside the envelope was a hand-written memorandum from Knollys which the latter had entrusted to him, a résumé of several meetings which Knollys had had with Edward, as Prince of Wales, in 1899, when the Prince, on his Private Secretary's stern advice, had eventually and unwillingly agreed never to see again, or correspond with, a certain Irish woman – a Miss Frances Cordiner from Summer Hill in County Kilkenny – with whom the Prince for several years had been on most intimate terms.

The relationship had come to a disastrous head between the two of them, the memorandum continued, as a result of Miss Cordiner's giving birth, in the summer of 1899 in America, to a child, a girl called Henrietta. The Prince had been the father. The woman had subsequently written to the Prince – most indelicate letters which had long since been destroyed – not asking for any financial support, for she had means of her own, but that, to her at least, the Prince should acknowledge his paternity, something quite out of the question, of course. So that subsequently the Prince had cut off all contact with Miss Cordiner. Eventually the woman had ceased to write – and there, quite buried, the matter had rested for nearly thirty years.

But now Lord Stamfordham, remembering very well this ancient liaison and its disastrous results, and having read the popular newspapers over the last few weeks, had that morning suddenly been struck by a brief reference in the social column of the *Tatler* – a note to the effect that Miss Laura Bowen was in reality, and originally, a Miss Henrietta Cordiner, born in 1899 in America, but been brought up in Ireland at the Cordiner family seat of Summer Hill in County Kilkenny. A glance at Burke's Irish Landed Gentry in his office had confirmed the birth of just such a girl, on that date, to a Mrs Frances Fraser, daughter of Desmond and Sarah Cordiner, whom Lord Stamfordham already knew to be the woman's parents.

What followed was all too clear to him. Laura Bowen – this Henrietta Cordiner – was without doubt Edward VII's illegitimate daughter. So that this King's grandson, the present Prince of Wales, was now consorting, and probably indulging in every sort of intimacy, with his aunt. And, almost as bad, Lord Stamfordham suddenly realized, Henrietta Cordiner's mother, this Mrs Frances Fraser, must be none other than the woman who had later become the vicious Irish Republican and revolutionary, a traitor, sentenced to death for her part in the Easter Rebellion of 1916, a fact that the newspapers had so far luckily not yet discovered.

It was all too clear to Stamfordham. If the press were to learn any hint of these familial, sexual or political antecedents, so directly involving the Prince's current friend, there would be a furore of such magnitude as would likely provoke a constitutional crisis and possibly topple the very monarchy itself. The Prince's relationship with this young woman would have to be stopped at once – at any cost.

Lord Stamfordham had asked for a personal meeting with the Prince immediately. And the following morning he was with him, upstairs in his drawing room at York House. At first Stamfordham had hoped not to bring up the matter of Laura Bowen's real provenance, persuading him by other means. So he had started on a line of realistic advice: that Miss Laura Bowen was not a suitable companion for him – simply because she was a motion picture star of such fame herself, and married to boot. Thus there could not but be unsuitable 'talk' whenever they were seen in public together, which must inevitably bring himself and the monarchy into disrepute.

'I am obliged to you, Arthur, for your concern,' the Prince responded nicely. 'And indeed, you're quite right. Given her fame, I have perhaps been too "public" with her. Be assured, I will be very much more discreet with her from now on. Not seen in public . . . Though in any case she returns to France soon . . .'

The Prince stood up and gazed a little sadly from the window at the last leaves blowing from the trees all down the Mall, the beginning of winter. Then he smiled at something. 'So, indeed, I shall see her there, where people are more discreet in such matters . . .'

Lord Stamfordham also rose to his feet. 'I think, sir, you misunderstand me. You must cease to see her altogether and completely. You would, I assure you, be very well advised.'

The Prince turned from the window, a little annoyed, though still perfectly polite. 'Indeed, Arthur, and I'm sure it's good advice – you have never offered me or my family anything less. And I take your point entirely. I must handle the thing quite out of the public eye. But that I should not see Miss Bowen *at all* is surely a quite unwarranted imposition. I am a grown man, neither married yet, nor King. I may surely, if it's handled with suitable decorum, see whom I please.'

The Prince began to fidget, lighting a cigarette, turning towards the door – hoping, intimating, that perhaps the interview might now be over.

Lord Stamfordham saw he had no alternative. 'Sir, you must believe that I should never normally have questioned your right to see whom you please – within the limits of the decorum you mention. But in this instance, with Miss Bowen, there is more to it, much more, and I shall have to tell you now, in the strictest confidence of course. But the reason that you must break entirely with Miss Bowen is that she is the daughter – the illegitimate daughter – of your grandfather, King Edward VII.'

The Prince, who had been moving towards the door, stopped as if he had been hit. He turned, taking the cigarette from his mouth. All the engaging bright sharpness in his face disappeared – all his charm, his natural brio, which this love affair had so increased recently, disintegrated.

'What? . . .' He was stunned.

'Yes—'

'You cannot be serious.'

'Sir, to think that I should ever have brought such a topic up if I were not—'

'I'm sorry, Arthur. Of course . . .' The Prince, ashenfaced now, became extremely agitated, pacing to and fro. 'You mean . . .' He seemed to be counting things in his mind. 'That Miss Bowen – is my aunt?'

'Yes. But her real name, as you probably already know, is Henrietta Cordiner, from Summer Hill in Ireland—'

'Yes, I knew.'

'It was her mother, then Miss Frances Cordiner, with whom your grandfather had this – intimacy . . .'

'You're sure?'

'There is no doubt. I have Lord Knollys's personal memorandum on the whole matter here with me – he was much involved with it at the time. You should read it. It will confirm everything.'

Lord Stamfordham handed the memorandum to the Prince, who read it through quickly. But, thinking of something else as he did so, his eyes soon clouded over. Now he saw the reason for that marvellous sense of ease and familiarity he had felt with Hetty – that surge of natural affinity that had so lifted his heart in her presence, as if they had been related in some way. As indeed they were. He was her nephew.

And yet he had come to love her for all those other quite ordinary reasons for which one might come to love a woman; she had become an adored friend and companion – already, in only a few weeks, supplanting his unhappy love for Mrs Dudley Ward. And now, as he saw equally clearly, he would have to lose all this, that love, give it up at once and completely – lose that excitement, too, and all the possibilities that had waited for them in London, Paris, Nice. A whole happy future was suddenly being destroyed in front of his eyes, as he read through the memorandum. Fate, he thought, could not have played a crueller trick on anyone.

The Prince was quite desolated. But, despite his rebellious nature, he saw how impossibly dangerous and inappropriate it would be to continue the relationship. He had no alternative but to cut off every contact and connection with Hetty immediately.

At first, when the Prince did not call her – as he did every morning at the Savoy – Hetty put this down to some sudden unexpected official business, or absence from London. And then, too, when she could never get through to him at York House, she thought the Prince's secretaries were just being difficult. She sent short notes to him then, by hand. But there was no answer. On two successive evenings, she went with her agent, Bernie Franklin, to the Embassy Club. But the Prince was not there. They had difficulty getting a table. And a group of the Prince's friends, present on the second occasion – people she had met with him – clearly wished not to meet her again. She was being snubbed. By the end of the week it was perfectly clear: the Prince had dropped her.

To her agent the reason for all this was obvious.

'Honey, you gotta see it: you – a Hollywood picture star and married, with the heir to the goddamned British throne – the whole thing was going to run against the grain here from the very start. It stands to reason!'

But for Hetty it did not. This could not be the reason, for she and the Prince, recognizing this very problem, had so clearly agreed that they would go on seeing each other, much more discreetly, whatever happened.

Hetty had no answer as she gazed out over the chilly, windswept Thames from her expensive river suite at the Savoy, no longer paid for by the Fox Picture Corporation. No answer whatsoever, except – and it was there for her in abundance – drink. In face of this appalling turn of events, this sudden brutal ending to something which she knew to have been wonderfully happy for both of them, she took to the bottle once more, hovering over the telephone in her suite, waiting for it to ring, or drunkenly badgering the operator downstairs, attempting to get through to York House, where they no longer accepted her calls, putting the receiver down as soon as they heard her slurred voice.

And it was then, in this mood of bitter alcoholic despair, that she suddenly thought of her cousins in London, Mortimer Cordiner and his son Dermot: Dermot, whom she had last seen in Cairo nearly eighteen months before. He must still be in the army, she imagined, back in England now, in London even, perhaps living at his father's old house in Wilton Place – an address she knew well, number 16, having visited the place and written to Dermot there so often when, as a girl years before at Summer Hill, she had had such a crush on him. Suddenly she felt she needed someone like him – someone of her family. Yes, she needed Dermot. Swaying with drink, and putting a flask in her handbag, she took a cab there straight away that afternoon.

When they turned off Knightsbridge she saw the house

at once, half-way down on the right. It had a big 'FOR SALE' sign outside. Dismissing the cab, she knocked at the door, peering through the downstairs windows. The curtains were half-drawn. A chill bitter wind blew at her ankles, the grey December sky lowering everywhere over the city. But perhaps someone was still there? Perhaps there was a back entrance.

Rounding the first corner, she came into a narrow mews behind, with garage doorways along one side. Establishing what she thought to be the back entrance to number 16, she tried the door there. It was not locked. She stepped into an empty coachhouse. Beyond was another smaller door leading into an overgrown garden. It was the same untended house. She stumbled up between the ruined flower beds and bushes, rustling in the cold wind, until she came to some steps leading to a french window. The windows were locked and curtained. But other steps, she saw, led down to a small basement area. Descending, she found a window, which opened when she pushed the sash. Climbing inside, moving through a dark dank scullery into the kitchen, she saw some shadowy steps leading upstairs. Stumbling drunkenly up them, she eventually found herself in the hall, with reception rooms to either side. Peering into the first open doorway, she was confronted with a shabby and desolate scene – the grey winter light illuminating piles of old newspapers, dry leaves and torn curtain blinds littering the floor; mice droppings, old bottles, broken tea-chests, wallpaper peeling everywhere, the blackened grate clogged with filth, soot covering the hearth, a smell of musty damp everywhere.

Had Mortimer and Dermot ever lived here? The window suddenly rattled, a bitter wind from a broken pane sweeping into the room, scattering the dead leaves towards her, covering her feet like a drift of snow, as she stood there, trembling in the chill, like Rip Van Winkle, aghast at the change in the place – this return to a house she remembered in all its warmth and vivacity. But perhaps it was the wrong house?

She fingered through one of the broken tea-chests. It was filled with old Hansard parliamentary reports. Mortimer, of course, had been an MP at Westminster. And then, certain confirmation that this had been his house, too, that Dermot had lived here, she found an old envelope stuck into the side of the tea-chest, the address written in a youthful hand she knew well. It was her own – one of the many letters, this one forgotten here, which she had written to Dermot years before. Kneeling down, she read it in the waning light. It was headed Summer Hill, the date May 1911. 'Dear Uncle Dermot, It was so bad to have you go. But I am fairly happy, going out and about on my own now, down by the river. At least I was this morning when I saw those otters we discovered together before you left. They're still there! In that hide beneath the willow. And the big one, the dog otter – Mr Mullins we called him, remember? – he was there, just for a moment, poking his nose out and washing his whiskers after some big fishy breakfast! I do wish you had been there to see him . . .'

But her eyes had begun to cloud over and she could read no more – starting to cry, her whole body shaking, before she fell forward, tearing at the dirty floor-boards with her nails, breaking them, spreadeagled there, starting to grovel in the dust and debris, her face smeared in soot, weeping uncontrollably now as unhappiness overwhelmed her.

Neighbours next door, hearing these piercing wails, called the police, who found her there some time later – a drunken, hysterical woman, whom they took to be a tramp at first, putting her into the police car and taking her down to Chelsea Station. Here, identifying her as Laura Bowen, the great picture star, they were astonished, bringing no charges, taking her back to the Savoy.

But one of the constables, in the way of making a pound or two on the side out of such mishaps and misdemeanours involving celebrities, later called the *Daily Mail*, so that news of Miss Bowen's strange escapade in Knightsbridge appeared in the paper next morning. The Prince, reading the same paper at breakfast, saw the item. He bowed his head, closed his eyes, in agony.

II

Dermot had indeed been living at the house in Wilton Place until some six months before, using it as his London base, home on leave from overseas, or more recently – having been appointed to the staff at Sandhurst, lecturing there on military tactics – as a weekend retreat.

But, since his father Mortimer, now in his seventies, had retired several years before to the family home at Islandbridge just outside Dublin, the house in London had been too big, too isolating an encumbrance in a life which, for Dermot, was already – though he rarely admitted it – lonely enough. His father had readily agreed that it be put up for sale and Dermot himself had just taken a small bachelor flat down the road in South Kensington which, together with his similarly austere accommodation at Sandhurst, entirely sufficed for his few domestic needs.

However, at that point, he was not in England at all. Three months' accumulated leave was due to him and he had returned to Dublin the week before, to stay with his father at Islandbridge. Apart from taking a holiday and seeing Mortimer, there were impending problems of all sorts now to do with Summer Hill, with which Mortimer was getting too old and infirm to deal with properly.

Dermot, on the other hand, in his early fifties, with his vigorous outdoor life, had aged only a little. Slim and neat as ever, with a clipped moustache, spruce hair, greying slightly, still parted severely in the middle, he remained a handsome man, albeit in the traditional military manner. There was a calm assurance about him, a kindly confidence in his sharp blue Cordiner eyes. His long military career had not hardened or soured him. Lucky to survive the Great War, he had made a success of all he had put his hand to since – recently promoted to full Colonel, he still loved the army life, the activity and companionship there, and now this lecturing to young officers at Sandhurst.

Yet at heart he remained a lonely man. So that the house at Islandbridge, and the Cordiner family seat at Summer Hill, too, had come to mean more to him than ever, as homes which he wished to preserve if he could. He was quite set on maintaining this brick and mortar, at least, in his Irish background, as a stay and occupation against his isolation in part, but much more with the idea that one day some other Cordiner – Hetty's children perhaps, or other cousins in the far-flung family, or even Robert and Léonie – might take these houses over, particularly Summer Hill.

And there was the very problem about which he had now to talk to his father. Frances, some years before, had left the whole place to the butler, Pat Kennedy. And Pat would have certainly sold everything up long before had not Dermot and Mortimer taken a seven-year lease on the house and lands, a lease that was due for renewal in a month's time.

Dermot spoke to his father now in the bow-windowed drawing room, curtained against the chilly December night, the river murmuring over the weir just beyond the lawn, the faint sound of engines chuffing in and out of Kingsbridge station a mile away, the two men taking sherry in the lamplight by the fire, before Mrs O'Hanlon, the housekeeper, called them to supper.

'So what's the latest position?'

'There's no doubt – Pat Kennedy will sell up as soon as our present lease expires. Married now, you know, with children. The wife wants him to buy a farm near her own people in Tipperary. He certainly won't want us to renew the lease.' Mortimer, stooped and patriarchal in a chintz armchair, sipped his sherry through his still formidable whiskers. 'And, besides, I've no mind to go on kow-towing to that avaricious blackguard Pat Kennedy – or his crooked land agent Cassidy – submitting to what amounts to blackmail, since they both know very well how much we want to keep the place in the family. It'd be different if we had any real income now from the lands. But of course the Land Commission has taken well over the half of it. And there's little enough coming in from what's left in the present agricultural decline. Fifteen shillings an acre at best, when we got two or three pounds there during the war.'

'How many acres do we still have?'

'A thousand odd. Outside the demesne.'

'And the price, at auction, if we had to buy the house and demesne alone?'

'Difficult to say. The house is in bad shape. But the pictures and furniture are worth a bit. Forty, fifty thousand?'

'But, Papa – we can't just let the whole place go, to some timber merchant or institution.'

'May have to. Where's the fifty thousand? And even if we did manage to buy it – what about the running costs? And all the repairs? And the gardens have gone to seed completely. Last time I was down there, this summer, the whole place was sheer jungle – only Aunt Emily really in her element, having a splendid time with her pictures of it! . . .'

'Unless we wrote to Hetty again? . . .' Dermot wondered. 'She'd have more than enough money to buy the place outright.'

'No reply to your last letter! So why should there be now? Tragedy . . . She obviously still loathes the place, the whole idea of Ireland . . .'

'And then, of course, there's the other problem. Hetty and the present Prince of Wales gallivanting about – in all the papers. What should we do about that? Hetty is his aunt, of course. Delicate – to put it mildly.'

'Indeed . . .' He drained his sherry, a little of the old fire returning to his voice. 'Absolute . . .' He shook his head in wonder at the whole thing. 'But what can we do? We can't tell her, at least not while Frances is alive – which may not be long, I grant you. She's pretty poorly by all accounts up in that damp, cat-infested little bungalow in Rathgar Road. Involved in good works for everyone but herself. Probably do for Frances altogether if Hetty were told – since she'd more than likely go for her mother and try and have it all out with her. Anyway, it's my opinion that someone at Court – old Lord Stamfordham for example, who's still alive – knows all about who Hetty is, and will put a stop to her goings-on with the Prince. Besides . . .' Mortimer touched his beard ruminatively. 'Would it really do Hetty any good – telling her now? Years ago, yes. But now?'

'Yes! Yes, Papa – that's the whole point! I'm *sure* it would.' Dermot paced the room restlessly – suddenly touched by his early memories of Hetty, when they had first met, the bruised and unhappy little girl, malicious, withdrawn, whom he had taken in hand twenty years before, showing her all the miracles of life and landscape around Summer Hill, going down to the river bank with her and about the estate, looking for kingfishers, otters, rare wildflowers – teaching her to know and name all these wonders, and so possess them truly – astonished by this wild girl, his heart going out to her, the old King's daughter, yet so dispossessed herself then in every way, being deceived and punished, made an outcast by her mother for her own indiscretions.

So that now, suddenly, apart from saving Summer Hill, he wished passionately that he could save Hetty with it, for it. 'Yes! She should be told.' Dermot turned to his father. 'Because that's the *real* reason for all her hurts, you know, Papa, all her subsequent unhappiness and stupidities – that running off to America and so on, for her hatred of Frances, for Summer Hill, for everything in Ireland. It's because of all the lies she was told then. I'm certain, if she were told the truth now, she'd be a lot easier as a person, perhaps even take up with Summer Hill again. It might change everything for her. She might even buy Summer Hill back for the family.'

'Possibly. But *how* tell her? Where? When? She lives in France now, doesn't she? And our lease comes up with Pat in a few weeks' time.'

'There must be a way . . .' Dermot thought out loud, sitting down again. '*Must* be. Can't see the whole place go . . .'

His father commiserated with him. 'I know how you feel about the place. I feel the same. But this may be the one battle neither of us has the reserves for.' Both of them gazed into the dancing firelight. Mortimer tried to bring some cheer into the sad mood then. 'Let's have another sherry. Rather good, had it from Findlaters. Perhaps we should get a case in for Christmas?'

At that same moment, having returned to Paris, Hetty was taking to stronger drink alone in her apartment – already half-way through a bottle of vodka. Since her return there she had rarely been sober. At first, as Christmas approached, she had launched herself on a series of visits and seasonal parties with her friends, reputable and less so. But quite soon the former found her continual drinking tiresome, her earlier wit and vivacity, once sharpened by alcohol, now quite drowned in it – her beauty dissolving, the chiselled features aerating in a blotched and puffy skin. They tactfully avoided her in public and made excuses when she called. Her louche acquaintances started by encouraging these excesses, in *boîtes*, restaurants or cafés. But soon even they tired of picking up her bills, the mess she made, carrying her out into taxis and seeing her home.

So that now, locking herself away from her maid in her bedroom, Hetty drank alone, often through the night, gazing glassy-eyed through old scrapbooks of her Hollywood pictures, lying senseless in bed most of the day, until the returning pains in her joints roused her in the afternoon and she took to drink once more – to cure the hangover, kill the aches.

Her maid had warned Bernie Franklin. And twice, almost forcing himself into her bedroom, he had tried to reason with her. But she was quite beyond reason. Her life, she intimated drunkenly, was coming to an end. Mr Franklin, having witnessed just such emotional or professional setbacks and consequent alcoholic excess among picture stars in his old Hollywood days, feared this might literally prove to be the case – that she aimed to kill herself.

Well, he certainly was not going to have this great picture star – *Nefertiti* was due to have its French première in a few weeks' time – die on his books. He called the American hospital at Neuilly. A young doctor came to the apartment that same evening. He was probably only just in time. Tapping some secret supply – for the maid had already by then thrown out all the drink – Hetty had consumed a half-bottle of brandy that afternoon and was unconscious on the floor when the doctor and Bernie Franklin broke into the room. Her pulse was faint, breathing weak but stertorous, pupils dilated. They brought her in an ambulance straight away to the hospital.

Here, in the next ten days, with careful nursing and constant supervision, Hetty made a surprising recovery. Her real friends visited her, Natalie Barney, other women, some of the men she knew in Paris. Hetty seemed quite calm now. They complimented her, her good sense on admitting herself to the hospital, they commiserated with her generally – the pressures of her work . . .

They lied to her tactfully, noticing too, but equally failing to remark on it, the deadness in her voice and expression, a chilling vacancy there. She was physically better, they saw, but her mind was no longer that bright thing, full of wit and brio. Behind the big blue eyes there was a void, a brain quite stunned, it seemed, without thought.

Yet Hetty did have thoughts – or one at least – which she nurtured secretly. She had put herself on her best behaviour here since she was determined, at the first opportunity, having allayed everyone's fears, to escape the hospital and resume her deadly life.

It was not that she wanted to kill herself, to kill Henrietta Cordiner. Franklin was wrong there. This vehement drinking, the ever-increasing oblivion it brought, was simply an unconscious means of killing that other overlaid persona of Laura Bowen, an invented character who had betrayed her, that fictional woman with whom the Prince of Wales had fallen in love – and, discovering the hollowness there, had dropped.

Without admitting it – for she could not face the stupidities of her life consequent on this long-assumed role, the cruelties and betrayals she had imposed on Léonie and her own family through it – Hetty desperately wanted to be rid of this other woman now, this false personality, the fatal carapace she had taken on over the years with Craig.

So that now, in this suicidal behaviour, she was acting out the last rites appropriate, as she saw it, to a failed picture star, believing that when she had taken this role to its ultimate depths she would emerge then into a new and proper self, the person she really was, indeed had once been.

This she felt intuitively, the pain expressing itself in drink, the only means of repressing the guilt for all those wrong turnings made long ago. She felt obscurely that, in order to live again, she must first die, must kill that other woman in her, continue to the end of the night, before emerging into a new dawn.

She was right in all these intuitions. But she quite lacked the support and reason then to see how, in the alcoholic means she took towards this happy transformation, she faced literal not metaphorical death.

Of course, as Franklin had warned them and the staff knew well themselves, such ideas of escape were an expected reaction in some of these alcoholic cases. So the nurses kept a constant eye on Hetty in her private room at the clinic, whose windows, though not barred, could only be opened a mere six inches.

However, as she improved, Hetty pointed out that she ought to take some exercise. And so she did, always with a nurse in tow, through the walled garden behind the hospital. And as she walked, in her greatcoat and muffler she inspected the high walls covertly. Recovering as she had, she was sure she had not lost all of her old athleticism. Indeed, it would be a simple matter, she thought – when she saw the low-roofed potting shed, set right against the wall at the far end of the garden . . .

And so it was. Jumping on to the roof here one morning a week later, she easily scaled the remaining four or five feet of wall, before dropping down into a narrow lane on the far side. In a minute she was out on the main road back to Paris – and minutes later she found a cab, directing it straight to the Crillon Hotel.

Here the management, assuming she had come to stay again for the première of *Nefertiti*, welcomed her most graciously, offering her a large suite overlooking the Place de la Concorde. Hetty explained, with a winning smile, how she had arrived early – her entourage, with her luggage, were due later – and could they meanwhile send some iced Veuve Clicquot up to her rooms straightaway?

Several hours later, a hectic party was under way in the suite, attended by her least reputable Parisian friends, drinking fiercely. Later, far gone in drink, when the party had dissipated itself, she made love with one of the men in her bedroom, opening her legs to him vehemently, a vicious love-making; she cared not one whit for any possible infection she might give him, pleased indeed to take such revenge, on Laura Bowen's part, against all men.

A few days later Hetty, having returned to her own apartment, had sobered up once more. Bernie Franklin had seen to it. The Paris première of *Nefertiti*, to which Hetty had of course been invited and was expected, was due to take place at the end of the week. So he had temporarily moved into her apartment, together with a nurse, round the clock, to ensure she took no more drink. They thought themselves entirely successful. Hetty appeared quite sober when she and Franklin set out that Friday night for the Elysée Cinema next to the Rond-Point – to a glittering occasion with a specially-invited audience of the smartest Parisians. Cars were lined half-way up the avenue when they arrived, spotlights picking Hetty out as she stepped on to the pavement. She looked sensational in a superb evening creation by Worth – a black lace dress, with a skin-coloured silk underdress, low square neckline, inset with squares of shimmering satin, a curved hemline dropping to sequinned handkerchief points at the sides and back.

But again Hetty had managed to deceive her overseers. Some time before, she had hidden a bottle of vodka in the lavatory cistern of the apartment. She had drunk a third of it before leaving that evening, then decanted most of the rest into a flask which she carried with her in her purse, gulping this down in the ladies' room at the theatre before the performance, and finishing the flask off there again after the show, just before she was due on stage to receive the plaudits of the audience and to make a brief speech.

Bernie Franklin, smelling nothing on her breath, held her arm as they stood in the wings, before the head of the Fox Picture Corporation in Paris led her out into the dazzling spotlights. She acknowledged the applause in a glazed but steady fashion. Taking the microphone stand then, she leant forward, stumbling a fraction.

'Mesdames et Messieurs,' she started in her perfect French, smiling wanly. 'Je vous remercie beaucoup, mille fois . . .' Then she paused, beginning to sway much more obviously now, before seeming to recover herself again. Then, quite suddenly and spectacularly, she was sick – a jet of liquid spurting out over the orchestra pit. The conductor took cover from the spray, as if from an exploding fire hydrant. Hetty was on her knees, her gown quite soiled, grovelling against the footlights, moaning piteously, 'Oh God, oh God . . . I want to go back to the cosy-warm.'

The spotlights were cut as Hetty was carried off. The orchestra, attempting to cover the disaster, started up with a sudden, ragged *Merry Widow* waltz – more a funeral dirge for Hetty as she was set down, like a sodden corpse, in the wings.

Pat Kennedy, in his wealth, had purchased a small Ford motor. He kept it in one of the old coachhouses, or what was left of these, giving out on to the stable yard, littered with domestic rubbish now, the cobbles encrusted with moss, a thick carpet of ragwort and lesser weeds: a moist green rug spreading voraciously everywhere, climbing the yard walls, giving the place the air of some green-glazed jungle grotto, inexplicably filled with the detritus of hideous civilisation.

Manoeuvring the car out from the smashed coachhouse doors he carefully navigated it round a tip of broken stout bottles, another of old tin cans, before circling a suppurating old manure heap, passing under the crumbling yard archway and down the front drive. The main avenue was almost entirely grassed over, the route only just discernible, a passage made the more difficult by several huge beech trees which had fallen across it, necessitating detours out into the demesne and back. The front gates, with their Georgian pillars and pineapple tops, had been closed and padlocked since one of the pillars had fallen over two years before. So that now, turning off into the demesne again, he left the estate via a jagged entrance broken into the high wall a hundred yards further on.

But Pat Kennedy noticed none of this seedy decay and destruction. He lived here, was too familiar with it, completely unconcerned about it in any case. It was only the farm land that interested him here, not the house and grounds – a house that sat there then on the hill behind him all tattered and torn in the pale December light.

After the disastrous fire ten years before, Lady Cordiner's little study-boudoir at the north end of the Georgian house had never been properly restored; nor had the fire-gutted Victorian servants' wing next to it. Both had simply been patched up with unsuitable brick and weatherboard, which in turn had started to crumble and rot.

In the main house itself several of the tall sash windows on the ground floor had broken clean away from their casements, had been replaced with blind brick, while far above some of the tall chimneys had crashed down on the roof, cannonading into the balustrades, falling overboard together, forming piles of blackened masonry, fluted columns and cornices, lying embedded in grassy hillocks on the lawn beneath.

The roof, holed in several places, had been covered with tarpaulins which flapped now over the gable ends, ominous black triangles, like the wings of monstrous pre-historic birds nesting there. The great porch was fouled with dark rain smears and lichen, while Lady Cordiner's meticulously-kept pleasure garden beyond was now a field of tall rank winter grass and weeds, only the broken astrolabe visible, poking up at the centre, a vision of science and reason quite destroyed everywhere else at Summer Hill.

Higher up, to the west, the ascending lawn terraces and stone steps had become virtually invisible. Here, nearer the real woods, this area was almost a wood itself now, filled with thorn bushes, thick bramble, and vast sprouting clumps of elder, which had spread everywhere, choking the old willow-and-rock garden and almost smothering the trunks of the great trees themselves, the cedars, Spanish chestnuts, the Canadian maple.

In summer all this surging growth, rising up round the house, made it practically invisible from any distance. But now, in bare midwinter, Summer Hill was seen as the wreck of a great ship, driven far inland by some huge tidal wave, foundering in a jungle of ivy, dead nettles, dry thistle, rotting trees.

'No. I won't lease it again to the Cordiners.' Pat Kennedy, arriving in Kilkenny for his appointment, spoke to Mr Cassidy, the auctioneer and land agent, in his musty office. 'I want it sold up, the whole place – house, demesne, farm lands. I have my eye on this farm in Tipperary, near the wife's people . . .'

'Indeed – I'll sell it surely.' Mr Cassidy, slightly hunch-backed, with long strands of wispy hair right round the nape of his neck and a bald crown to his egg-shaped head, had the air of a long-spoiled priest. He leant forward eagerly now, hands shaped as if in prayer, his little eyes glinting at the prospect of the vast commissions here. 'And you'd be well advised, Mr Kennedy – well advised and no mistake. With agriculture the way it is today there's no real money in leasing. But an outright sale – now, that's a different matter altogether. People'll always want to *buy* land here, whatever the other circumstances.'

Pat Kennedy agreed. 'And what would you estimate it all at, Mr Cassidy?'

'Oh, £25,000 or so for the land certainly. And the same or more for the house and demesne. In or about £60,000, Mr Kennedy. So we'll put it all up for auction then, in a month or so, just as soon as I get the par-tik-ulers printed and out. Say in February or March?'

'Right, Mr Cassidy. And you'll let Mr Cordiner know in Dublin.'

'I will indeed!' Mr Cassidy stood up, came round from his desk and shook Pat Kennedy warmly by the hand. 'Ah, sure,' he reassured him. 'Isn't that the best thing to do with the oul' place altogether. Going to rack and ruin as it is. And who'd miss it anyway? Thim big houses of the English over here – no place in Ireland for them now. Hand of the oppressor. Pity the lads didn't burn more of them in the bad times. And then, besides, ye tell me the roof is almost off it already. So ye have a right to sell it now – before the whole place falls down about your ears. And I've a mind who'll buy it, too – the house and demesne, I mean. There's a big timber merchant in Waterford. He'll go for it! Sure, look at all the fine timber about the place. And there's another builder fellow I know who'd take the good stone outa the house as well. Ah, sure there'll be nothing go to waste at the heel of the hunt, Mr Kennedy – nothing! – like a pig at the butchers! *Nothing!*'

Hetty, after the fiasco at the première in Paris, made one last realistic attempt to save herself. She decided, in one of her drunken but more active moments, to visit Léonie at her apartment on the rue Saint-André-des-Arts, and perhaps make things up with her. But, when she got there one chilling afternoon just after Christmas, the concierge told her Léonie had left – for London.

'Londres?'

'Oui, Madame – pour Londres.'

They had all gone there, the old woman went on, aggressively, when Hetty questioned her, not just for a visit, but to live there. Yes, Monsieur Grant had taken up a new position – with *The Times* newspaper, she added dismissively.

Hetty swayed about the street afterwards, drank hot rum in a nearby café and later was nearly run over by a taxi crossing the Boulevard Saint-Michel. Again, as with Mortimer and Dermot in the house in London, her old friends no longer existed – in fact or fancy. They had betrayed her – family and friends – all of them. They had betrayed Laura Bowen, at least. And so, with even more self-destructive energy, she resumed her murderous pursuit of that woman in herself.

Her descent became entirely uncontrolled now. As she made abrupt forays in and out of the clinic at Neuilly, her health seriously deteriorated. Her syphilis, exacerbated by the alcohol, returned to plague her more fiercely. And then, though the fact hardly impinged on her now, her money ran out altogether, large bills could not be met, her credit was withdrawn and claimants everywhere initiated bankruptcy proceedings against her. Craig, still on location in the wilds of Morocco, could not be reached for any help. A few of her friends in Paris did what they could. But Hetty's state was such as to make them quite impotent.

News of her impending bankruptcy and her condition generally appeared in the popular newspapers, whose reporters, after the sensational events in the Elysée Cinema, had come to haunt the clinic or her apartment on the Ile Saint-Louis. They were there on the day that Hetty was ejected by the Paris bailiffs, and returned in an ambulance to the hospital at Neuilly. A number of papers next morning featured this dramatic event on their front pages, including the *Daily Mail*, one of their Paris reporters having been assigned to cover the decline and fall of this once-great picture star.

Hetty, in the weeks after Christmas, had become maniacal in her drinking, alternating between bouts of extreme excitement and fury, a sustained frenzy, when she barely slept or ate, pacing the apartment, shouting, laughing, throwing things about, then suffering sudden black outs of the sort that had overwhelmed her in Hollywood. So that, when she arrived in the clinic again that day in the new year, she had moved to a further stage in her malady: the blue devils, *delirium tremens* – her body shaking all over, making constant purposeless movements, hallucinating, screaming, as she gazed at the terrifying visions materializing all about her in her room, the furniture distorting itself into weird shapes, so that she wrenched her head upwards – only to be confronted by monstrous toads and snakes squirming and crawling all over the ceiling. And, when the doctor arrived in the room, she saw him as hooded and malign, the figure of a hangman come for her execution, so that she leapt off the bed at him, struggling fiercely before they held her down, trying to sedate her.

Failing in this, for she fought so violently, they finally managed to strap her to the bed. Eventually she ceased to struggle; her breathing became quite faint, her eyes stared glassily upwards. Undoing the straps then, they administered what drugs they dared and watched over her.

'Fifty-fifty,' the doctor told Franklin that evening. 'There's inflammation of the lungs. If she develops pneumonia, as quite often happens at this stage of alcoholism, it's usually fatal.'

One who read of Hetty's predicament then – he saw the paragraph in the *Dublin Evening Mail* that same day – was Dermot Cordiner. He showed the Reuter's news item to his father that evening: 'Miss Lauren Bowen, the Hollywood picture star, was yesterday evicted from her Paris home for non-payment of rent. Bankruptcy proceedings have been instituted against her. Subsequently, in a state of collapse, she was removed by ambulance to the American hospital . . . Miss Bowen, until recently a close companion of the Prince of Wales . . .'

'So you see, Papa – you were right. Someone at court has obviously told the Prince who she really is, and he's dropped her. And now she's no money and taken to the bottle by the looks of it. Simply can't let it go on like this. I'll have to go over to Paris, bring her home . . .'

His father agreed. 'That makes two of them,' he said. 'Mother and daughter, both on their beam ends. News has it Frances won't last the winter. She's very low. Bronchitis, pneumonia—'

Dermot was suddenly impatient. 'Papa – so you see now, don't you? – this whole thing is nonsense, gone on far too long. Hetty will have to be told who she is. Perhaps that's the only way to cure her, save her from the same fate as her Mama. I'll tell her . . .'

His father sighed. 'Yes, perhaps you're right.' He sipped his sherry. 'Lies . . . I used to tell Frances in the old days – the truth is the one thing that can't really hurt us.'

Dermot snorted. 'Of course! So what have you and I been doing all these years?' He almost stamped his foot in frustration. '*Why* didn't we tell Hetty long before – so that she might have avoided all this? – this stupidity, this tragedy? I blame myself!'

'No, you shouldn't. We were both of us strictly bound by Frances's confidences in the matter, remember? She asked us never to tell Hetty. Have to remember, too – though it's easy to forget – how Frances was once so much a happy part of our lives, when she was such a different person, before all that ranting political bitterness overtook her.'

'You needn't remind me – I was to have married her!'

'So, we both of us had – must still have – a loyalty towards her, despite the appalling way she's behaved, towards Hetty, over Summer Hill . . .'

'Of course. But, if telling Hetty might save her now, then I'm quite prepared to break that loyalty, Papa.'

Mortimer nodded. 'Yes,' he agreed. 'You're right. The greater good . . .'

'I'll take the mail boat tomorrow then. Should be in Paris the day after.'

Another who read of Hetty's condition was Robert, now working in London as a junior parliamentary reporter with *The Times*. Seeing all along that, as an Englishman, there was no real future for him with the Paris *Tribune*, he, together with Dermot (who had known the editor Geoffrey Dawson well, when Dawson had been private secretary to Lord Milner in South Africa thirty years before), had tactfully lobbied for a position at Printing House Square for some time.

Attending an interview in London the previous autumn, he had been successful, offered work in the press gallery of the House, covering the less important debates, but with a clear intimation from the editor himself of better things to come. Dawson had been impressed by Robert's political acumen, his sober style and general bearing – a true *Times* man in the making, he thought, offering him what was, for that paper, the handsome sum of £650 per annum to start with.

With a first month's salary in hand, together with financial help from Léonie's father in Paris (so that, in Léonie's liberated canon, they could both contribute to their accommodation), they had taken a leasehold on a large, pleasant top floor flat in a Victorian terrace house in Denning Road, Hampstead, just down from the underground station, with views over a pretty back garden, bounded by a row of tall poplars, then a vision of London down the hill beyond – a pearly shimmer in the distance that morning, mists clearing in the bright January sunlight, as Robert read the papers over breakfast, while Léonie tried to feed their child Olivia, fretful and difficult, strapped into her high chair across the table from him.

Opening the *Daily Mail* he had seen this most recent news about Hetty on the front page. Now he tried to read it aloud. But Olivia, refusing her food, had started to whine and squeal, so that eventually he had to hold the paper out in front of Léonie.

'Well?' she asked, harrassed herself now. 'What can one expect? In and out of the papers for months, up to one sort of nonsense or another – oh, do sit *still*, Olivia! . . .'

Robert wiped some crumbs from his chin, sipped at

his coffee. 'Yes, but she's seriously ill now – and bank-rupt. And that letter we had from Dermot the other day, about Pat Kennedy selling up Summer Hill.'

'What's the connection?'

'Well, for one, Hetty might have bought the place. She must have had oodles of money.'

'Spent it all on high living. Picture stars do, you know.'

'She's hardly that any more. They're all sound pictures now. And, with her stammer, she must be finished in all that world.'

'Well, serves her right, for going into it in the first place. I always told her – how it wasn't her.'

'Why have you got such a down on Hetty? Oh, I know – all that Egyptian business. But that's all over. And now, when she's penniless and ill – shouldn't one try and help? Can one just drop someone, someone one was close to, just because one's had trouble with them in the past?'

Léonie turned to him, wide-eyed, astonished. 'But, Robert! – that's exactly what I used to say to *you*, when you were so dismissive of Hetty, in Paris, years ago! How have you so changed your mind about her?'

'I haven't. Still think she's behaved . . . very stupidly. But now it's different, when she's so obviously lost. You, who were her greatest friend after all – why are you so unconcerned about her now?'

'Oh, Robert, can't you remember? What happened between us in Egypt?' She turned away, as if her face might betray her in something. 'Well, I don't want any-thing like that ever to happen again, *ever* – and ruin our lives, you and me, as it very nearly did then. So it's obvious, isn't it? – why I'm not too keen on her. Oh, for goodness' sake – do sit *still* a moment, Olivia!' She wiped the child's mouth and chin. 'Anyway, about Summer Hill . . .' Wanting to change the subject, she turned to Robert. 'There's nothing we can do.' Looking at him properly now, she saw how serious he was, a sad tense face gazing out of the kitchen window on to the garden, lost in thought. 'Robert?' He turned vaguely towards her. 'You *know* there's nothing we can do.'

Robert stood up, going to the window, staring out at the tall poplars. A light frost silvered their delicate branches, the sunlight melting the mists far below, domes and spires in the city gradually emerging. Léonie took Olivia out of the high chair, holding her up in her arms – cuddling, trying to comfort her, joining Robert at the window. 'Oh, that damned house, Robert! I wish you weren't so sad about it. But you – we – we'll have just to accept the loss. We have our *own* place now – here.'

'Yes. But you still have your home in Paris. And Summer Hill was, is, my home,' he answered her rather shortly. 'I'd like to be able to do something about it, obviously.'

'I'm sorry,' Léonie relented. 'It's just that Summer Hill is all tied up with *Hetty* – for both of us. You loved her, I loved her – and it's *gone*, all that, thank God, because it nearly killed us both. So why can't we let the bricks and mortar go, too, of all that past – now that we have all this, *here* in London?'

She came closer to him, Olivia in her arms, the child pressed between them, as she put her other arm round Robert, so that the three were joined in a mild familial embrace. 'We're *us* now, aren't we? And happy. And we can live *without* all that past!'

Robert responded, smiling faintly, stroking Olivia's dark hair. 'Yes. Yes, of course.' But then, gazing over Léonie's shoulder, he returned to his view of the distant city, the rising mists. So that Léonie, despite his warmth and attention just then, knew he was still really thinking of Summer Hill.

'There's always so much there for you, in Summer Hill, isn't there?' She moved away from him, trying to catch his attention again. 'That's the trouble, isn't it?'

'Hardly a "trouble" . . .' He didn't look at her. 'Bit more than that. It's the total disappearance of it.'

'But it's Hetty, too, in some way. Isn't it?' she asked, unable quite to hide the touch of anxiety in her voice. 'So mixed up in the place for you, loving her then—'

'Oh, Léa, no more than a crush.'

She laughed then, sardonically. 'That's exactly what I thought with Hetty first. And look what happened!'

'Well, I don't think I—'

'Things like that, when you're young – first love and so on – why, it can mark you for ever.' She stared at him, suddenly aware, aghast, at how rash this statement might appear to him, applying, as it did, so much more to her than to Robert. But he did not seem to notice.

'That's just operatic of you, Léa. It hasn't marked me,' he went on simply. Yet somehow she felt he might be lying. 'You know very well what I've always thought of Hetty's behaviour.' He had turned to her now, raising his voice over the renewed hullabaloo from the child. 'But now that she's ill with no money – wouldn't you want to help? Just objectively – as a friend?'

'How can either of us ever be objective about Hetty?'

'I can. I thought we both were – have been – ever since that Egyptian business.'

'I wouldn't *dare* help her, Robert. I mean – face to face. Like a bad penny turning up again.'

'That's . . .' Robert hesitated. 'That's nonsense. We've got over all that.'

'We thought just that before – before we went to Egypt.'

Robert turned decisively towards her now. 'Anyway, my real worries are about Summer Hill – if I could do something . . .' Lighting his pipe, he resumed his gaze out of the window.

He seemed, Léonie thought, in this last statement to

have quite dismissed Hetty from his mind. And yet still she refused to believe this – did not really believe in his 'objectivity' about Hetty. It worried her. Had she got over all this business with Hetty – and Robert had not? She, after all, had loved and made up her final account with Hetty in Egypt. But Robert had never successfully expressed his love towards her. Did something of this desire still lurk in his heart, repressed, but re-awakened now in this news of her desperate condition?

So that perhaps Robert's anxiety to preserve Summer Hill was linked with this same hidden love he still felt for Hetty, which continued to frustrate him, which he still wanted to offer her, by saving her in some way now? If this were so she could hardly blame him. Yet the idea posed a threat to her. Léonie had felt it then, the little tremors of insecurity as they had talked – that image of Hetty, come to loom over them once more, as those great cinema posters had done, years before in Paris – so that Léonie longed tactfully to dissuade Robert from having anything to do with Summer Hill now, so to avoid, in that great house, the occasion of sin.

Let the house go, she felt – every last stone of it, levelled to the ground, so that there would be nothing, no evidence or memory, of her love for that woman. Let not one jot remain, she thought, of all that had encompassed that misguided past of hers, when she had loved Hetty, not Robert – whom she so loved now. Let nothing come to disrupt that love again, she prayed.

So it was that Léonie's real reason for wanting an end to Summer Hill, which she could not admit, was that this most recent news of Hetty and the house had renewed her guilt about everything that had happened there. Memories of Hetty, their happiness at Summer Hill, and her subsequent abrupt departure from Hetty in Egypt, crowded back on her now, memories which she had long suppressed in her new content with Robert.

And then, too, what Léonie most feared in all this, equally unadmitted, was something different again. She was not so much disturbed by the possibility of Robert's expressing any great emotion towards Hetty now, but more by the fear, if they met, that *she* might come to do exactly this herself – deeply touched, as she was in her heart of hearts, by Hetty's awful predicament now.

Léonie, in short, feared a resurgence of her old nature, that other nature, in loving women. The past was never really dead, nor one's real nature, she suspected. Both could be buried. One could hold them down successfully for years, as she had done, like suffocating a sweet enemy with a pillow. But the body could go on breathing – she saw that now – could rise up one fine day, come to haunt and destroy again, a ghost at noon. Léonie wanted none of this, was terrified of such spectres. If, even after marrying Robert, she had succumbed once to Hetty, as she had in Egypt, might she not do so once more – if they ever met again? So she prayed for an end to the house, as the site of what she took now to be her own original sin.

Thus for both of them Summer Hill, though for so long unvisited, intangible, remained a secret wound, from which the blood, like stigmata, could suddenly flow again – a place loved and hated: for both, a fiercely radiant emblem, obscured by the years, yet which nonetheless retained the power of resurrection or destruction. The news that morning in the *Daily Mail*, together with Dermot's letter about the impending sale the week before, had uncovered fears and hopes in both of them which they could not fully speak of, nor yet deny. The great house, decaying on that distant hill, reached out to them then, like a mirage hovering over the London mists, touching them deeply, strangely.

Robert finally turned to Lèonie. 'I shall have to go over to Dublin, and see Dermot. It's the least I can do.'

Léonie drew the child closer to her breast, as if trying to muffle the spasm of fear she felt.

Hetty, contracting pneumonia as the doctor had forecast, hovered between life and death for over a week. Dermot, arriving in Paris, saw her at once. Sedated, partly comatose, sometimes delirious now, she drifted in and out of consciousness without recognising him. Taking rooms nearby in Neuilly, he visited her for most of every day, watching over her – sitting on a chair near her bed, reading *The Times* or a detective novel, an electric fire warming the room against the chill dark winter days that gripped the city, rain battering on the windows at first, replaced by frost, and by the end of the week a heavy snowfall which encrusted the edges of the glass, brightly illuminating the room as he gazed at her pale face, lying flat without a pillow, her small pointed chin poking down over the sheet.

He was horrified at the changes wrought here in the eighteen months since he had last seen her – the pencil-thin body, the face emaciated, wrinkled with pain, crow's feet running away to either side of the lifeless blue eyes, whenever they opened momentarily, staring upwards blankly, only to close again – like a marionette dying on the threads.

Was this the same girl with whom he had roamed the land and discovered otters long ago at Summer Hill? Hetty Cordiner, most lovely, wild – and most hurt then, yes, but not like this. He found it difficult to contemplate the change – this vivid past and deathly present of someone for whom he had felt such affection, in herself, through all the letters she had written to him then, letters which he had brought with him from Dublin, kept all these years at Islandbridge, unearthed before leaving, taking them as a talisman of all that happy past, an emblem of some vague hope for the future.

'You see,' the doctor told him the following morning, 'since you are her family, I have to tell you that, quite apart from her alcoholism and pneumonia, she has tertiary syphilis too. *Tabes dorsalis* affects the spinal joints, the digestive muscles, which is why she can hardly take any food. I'm afraid you must be prepared for the worst. There's very little hope – if she lasts the day, even.'

And Dermot thought of this new aspect when he sat with her later – betrayed, even in that deepest part of her, by Craig Williamson, no doubt – the whole disaster of her life with that picture director, that wrong turning, inspired by her mother's lies and coldness, taken long ago. He gazed at her, seeing the damp toss of dark curls falling around the pinched skull, skin set tight against the forehead, a froth of hair like a hat that was far too large for her now, the only remnant of her former glory – raven-dark curls just like her uncle Henry's and her mother's too, both of whom he had so loved – and, now, these same dark curls, the only thing left intact and still beautiful of this family in the wreck and disaster of the years.

He stood up, touching a lock of her hair as she slept. As she lived? As she died? Yes, she was dying, just then – he sensed it, clearly, unable to hear her breathing, even in the utter stillness of the room, as the snow fell in dark drifts outside. She was slipping away from everything. But she must not, she could not die – this last emblem of a family that had meant so much to him; this woman he loved now as well. She must survive, else there would be nothing left of Summer Hill, for Summer Hill, nothing of all that miraculous past, no future.

What could he do? He was not religious. He never prayed. Instead, on an impulse, taking out the envelope of her old letters he started to read aloud from one of them, as he might have read a fairy tale to a child, an account that Hetty had written years before, of her adventures in search of an old badger in Cooper's Wood, on a rise beyond the great house.

'. . . and you know how we suddenly saw him, in the woody dell, snuffling about in the dry leaves that evening? – the big daddy one we called Arthur – well, I didn't see him again until I more or less camped out and stayed there almost into the dark yesterday night – and there were the snufflings and scratching again and I saw Arthur, the huge one, and then the *two* others with him, *much* smaller! His children, I suppose! Or grandchildren. And there they were, *so* near me, until something frightened them and they loped back in that funny bouncy way they have, like waves running, pitter-patter, pushing and shoving each other, back into their set, back into the cosy-warm! . . .'

As he read, the snow fell in lesser drifts outside, shafts of light breaking through from the west, illuminating Hetty's face. And then, almost at the end of his reading, she opened her eyes, turned her head a fraction, seemed to smile, seemed to recognize him.

She had been dreaming, an extraordinary, wonderfully calming dream. She was floating, rising in the room, suffused in brilliant light, suspended in a drift of warm snowflakes, floating above herself, that was the miracle – hovering beneath a transparent ceiling, with a vast blue sky far above her, as she looked down on her own real dying body stretched out on the bed way beneath her. But how could she be in two places at once? – how feel this incredible lightness of spirit, an exhilaration she had never known before, of total warmth, relaxation, a freedom from all pain, floating off high above her old corrupt self, there fading away in the bed below her, drifting upwards among the snowflakes into the glassy blue dome, from where she never wished to come to earth again, so great was her joy, being beckoned, pulled somewhere, into the glorious sky above her, towards some ultimate wonder and release?

Then she heard the voice – well-remembered, yet surprising – and saw the figure of a man, on a chair. She was looking straight down on him: his voice tugging at her, as she tried to resist the pull of it, but somehow could not – unable to resist some other magic here, a voice from the past, her childhood, from a distant country she had known well in some other almost equally happy dream long ago. Again she tried to pull herself away, to float upwards again, but some stronger force, emanating from the man, pulled her downwards and her warm, free floating dream collapsed and suddenly she found herself one with her own real body again and heard the words now – '. . . as they loped back in that funny bouncy way they have . . . like waves running, pitter-patter, pushing and shoving each other . . .'

She opened her eyes then, blinking in what seemed an almost equally blinding light flooding in from the window which illuminated the figure in the chair. She recognized him.

'Dermot?' she whispered weakly.

He stood up, coming towards her, smiling. He had something in his hand. It was the snow-dome, she thought, the little crystal ball with the ivory model of Summer Hill inside. Becoming tiny, it must have been in this, she thought, that she had been floating a minute before. But now, like Alice after the magic potion had worn off, she had resumed her true proportions. She tried to reach out for the little globe but her arms would not move. Yet she suddenly wanted the snow-dome, wanted it desperately then. It was hers. She would stay here, in her own real body, to have that thing, that crystal emblem of Summer Hill, more necessary to her then than anything else on earth.

*

'It was so extraordinary!' she told Dermot a week later, as she began her slow recovery. 'Because, when you came towards me, I was certain you had that old snow-dome of Summer Hill in your hand, not one of my letters. You see, I'd been floating about in it! – just before that – absolutely! – high above my real self, the snowflakes lapping all over me. How can you explain it?'

She tried to push herself up in the bed, then relapsed. Dermot helped her with the pillows. 'I can't. Unless it was some need, something you wanted very strongly then—'

'Oh yes, it was! It was! I *wanted* it, terribly.'

'Well, then – that was it. Something meant. You wanted Summer Hill. After all, I was reading about it, Cooper's Wood, the badgers there, years ago . . .'

'Yes, I suppose so. But I've not really thought about the place – in years.'

'Perhaps you've just been repressing your thoughts about it – all these years!' he said lightly.

'Perhaps. It's all very strange.' She seemed tired then, with the exertion of talking. Dermot stood up.

'Try and sleep, Hetty. I'll come again this evening.'

She put out her hand to him weakly. 'Yes, Dermot, do – please. It's so funny – that snow-dome dream, and coming down to earth again – as if I'd returned from some long journey – then suddenly seeing the actual snow-dome and thinking I was back at Summer Hill again . . .'

'Well, perhaps that's what you want – to be there again – in reality?' He looked at her closely.

'Yes,' she said vaguely, drowsy now. 'Yes, it must be that. Oh, Dermot – let's go back and look for the badgers in Cooper's Wood again! . . .'

She dropped off to sleep then, and Dermot left her – with another letter inside his pocket, one from his father which had arrived that morning, enclosing the catalogue which Mortimer had obtained, filled with all Mr Cassidy's 'particulars' on the forthcoming auction of the house, demesne and farm lands at Summer Hill. He could not tell Hetty about this – it would jeopardize, indeed perhaps prevent, her recovery. Yet now, more than ever, Dermot knew that he must somehow save the place, save it for her. For it was in this house, he sensed then, in the re-possession of it and in knowing who she really was – though he could not tell her that yet either – that Hetty's real cure would lie. Years before, at the very outbreak of the Great War, he had told her more or less the same thing, when she had so doubted her future there, hating the place, the two of them looking down on the house in the August sunshine – how Summer Hill really had so much beauty and promise in it, for her, for everyone. And now, when he next saw her again at the clinic, he repeated the gist of this.

'Yes, I'm sure it's the house you need, Hetty. That's the key to it all – if you can go back there, live there, your own birthright after all – then you'll recover properly, be happy. Mortimer and I can visit. I can help you fix things up – it's in a bit of a state now by all accounts. But Aunt Emily still lives there. And Robert and Léonie can come over. And life can be really good, really wonderful again, for all of us!'

'Robert and Léonie?' Hetty's face clouded. 'I've so fallen out with them, though, been so stupid . . . And what about Mama?'

'She's not well. Lives in Dublin now, you know – and not expected to live much longer. I don't think there'll be problems there – except that you should try and make things up with her . . .'

Hetty was close to tears now. 'But, Dermot, there's *far* too much for me to make up for, isn't there—'

'No—'

'How could I ever *begin* to make things up? I've been

so stupid. I've fallen out with *every*one, so badly . . .'

'You've only really fallen out with yourself, Hetty, all these years. Don't you see?' He reached over, touching her hand. 'And you'll find your own true self again, when you go home. I promise you.'

She clutched his hand weakly in return, breathing faster now. 'Will I, Dermot, will I?'

He gazed at her, staring into her moist blue eyes, life beginning to return there. 'Yes, you will, I promise.'

It was a promise he knew he would have to make good at any cost – the cost of Hetty's life, her future. For she, too, now, at his persuasion, had come to believe that in this house lay her resurrection. But there was only one problem. And the horror of it struck him then: that he had identified the cure for Hetty – this magic elixir of a house that would end all the pain of the years for this family – yet the potion itself, available to them all for centuries on the hill, was about to be snatched from their hands forever.

12

Another who read of Hetty's headlong decline in the *Daily Mail* during those winter months was the Prince of Wales. He was horrified. It was all a sheer tragedy. And he felt himself responsible for it. He had dropped her, perforce – but most cruelly. What more understandable – since she was obviously quite unaware of the reasons for his abrupt dismissal – than that she should take to drink? Now she was ill and bankrupt as well.

He would have to do something for her – on his own behalf, but just as much on his grandfather's account, he felt, the old King, who as Prince of Wales had been initially responsible for the whole calamity and had subsequently done nothing about it. He must therefore try to make up for that appalling lapse, too.

He met with Godfrey Thomas, his Private Secretary, immediately after breakfast one morning in January. 'I shall need the release of some funds, Godfrey – some considerable funds. From the Duchy of Cornwall account, I imagine,' he added brusquely.

'Yes, sir. Some hundreds of pounds?'

'Some thousands, I imagine . . .' His Secretary looked up, surprised. 'What is there available on hand, in cash, immediately?'

'I'm afraid it's not likely to be—'

'I shall need about £50,000,' the Prince interrupted him. He had already decided on a figure commensurate with what he took to be the gravity of his grandfather's fault and his own behaviour. 'If the sum is not available – then things must be sold.'

Godfrey Thomas failed to conceal his astonishment. 'Sir! – that's a considerable sum. If we are to sell from the Duchy estates on such a scale, others may have to be involved—'

'That's quite all right, Godfrey. I shall be seeing Lord Stamfordham this morning. It's a matter of some urgency . . .'

The Prince, in this instance, went round to Buckingham Palace to see the old man, bringing him up to date on the matter of Laura Bowen, explaining his new intentions there.

'But, sir, such a vast sum – there is no need. It is not as if you—'

'Arthur, I have to say – in the light of that secret memorandum you showed me – that there is *every* need. It is the very least I can do in the circumstances. My grandfather appears to have behaved appallingly in the matter.'

'He had no alternative, sir – as you had none.'

'I can't agree. He could have acknowledged his parentage, tactfully, in some manner at least, to Mrs Fraser. So to deny his own daughter in that way – it was shabby to a degree. Because we are royal cannot mean we may simply brush such things under the carpet, as if they'd never occurred. Why, the matter could have been dealt with confidentially years ago, and the whole problem avoided with this Mrs Fraser, long before she became an Irish republican or whatever. Yet here am I, having had to drop Miss Bowen quite against my will, to her great distress, and all entirely on account of my grandfather's, or his advisers', moral cowardice. Well, I shall not be party to the same grubby behaviour.'

The Prince, fuming now, was in his most rebellious mood. 'Yes, remember, I dropped her *most* unwillingly, Arthur! And now, as you can see for yourself' – he flourished the front page of the *Daily Mail* – 'the pickle she is in, as a result of this. Ill and bankrupt! Vast debts apparently – ejected from her Paris home, and so without even a place to live now. I must make amends, on my grandfather's behalf as much as my own – in any way I can. I insist on it,' he added coldly.

'But £50,000, sir – it is a vast sum—'

'Restitution must be made in line with the gravity of the original offence, Arthur. And I hope you will facilitate any financial arrangements necessary to secure the sum. If, on the other hand, you feel you cannot support me in this, well then, I shall clearly have no alternative but to bring the whole matter up – the *truth* of this whole ghastly, underhand business – with my parents, who of course, as you've told me, are quite unaware of who Miss Bowen really is: Miss Bowen, Hollywood *femme fatale* – in fact half-sister to the King, my father. He will be pleased to hear that, no doubt . . .'

The Prince, with what he felt to be this entirely justified blackmail, believed he had won his point resoundingly.

But Lord Stamfordham, canny and persistent, and still determined to forestall these ridiculous plans of the Prince's, had another card to play. 'Sir, there is one point you may have overlooked. Miss Bowen, as I see, is now a declared bankrupt, with very considerable debts by all accounts. Thus any such monies paid to her would immediately be forfeit. So that your purpose here, as I understand it – to effect a rehabilitation for the woman – would not be realized. She would receive very little, if any, of the money. Her creditors would receive it.'

The Prince admitted this point grudgingly. 'Well, then, I shall make some gift in kind.'

'The same would apply. Any such gift, coming into her legal possession now, could – and almost certainly would – be sold off to pay her debts.'

'Indeed, well . . . I am sure there must be some way round that problem. I shall speak to my own solicitors and let you know. Meanwhile I am determined on this course. Miss Bowen – my aunt – cannot be left to languish, penniless, in some hospital ward in Paris, or on the streets. I shall do *something* for her, Arthur – you may depend upon it.'

The Prince at once contacted a close personal friend of his, Montagu Bennington, a senior partner in the firm of Bennington and Peabody, solicitors, at Lincoln's Inn, asking if he could come and see him at the earliest opportunity. Mr Bennington arrived later that afternoon, when the Prince explained the whole situation to him.

'Lord Stamfordham is right, of course. Any monies you paid, or any outright gift, could be forfeit.'

'Is there no other way I could contrive it?'

'Well, really only in one way as I see it. You would have to retain the freehold, as it were, in any gift you made her – just as with Grace and Favour residences belonging to the Crown. A house, for example – might you consider giving her that? At least she would have a place to live, to recover herself in.'

'Indeed . . .'

'You have many such houses, I imagine, in your gift, here in London, or the country, from your Duchy of Cornwall estates.'

'Yes, indeed – I have. An excellent idea. The problem, though, is that I have to make the gift, and secure her future, anonymously, so that nothing could be traced back to me. I'm afraid . . . it has to be that way.'

'Well, that can be arranged, too. You may *buy* a house for her, the deeds retained by you, but under another name or by some holding company. I can easily arrange all that through my office, so Miss Bowen will never know who her benefactor is. The house can be given her from an "admirer" – what more natural? She must have many such, distressed by her present condition – the place to be given her without any legal possession, so that her creditors couldn't touch it.'

'Good, Montagu. Excellent. But a house – where? Not in England, perhaps – too close to home.'

'In France then? Or in Ireland, where you tell me she comes from.'

'Yes, yes . . .'

'Let me have some enquiries made of her, sir. I have a good man – really excellent, entirely discreet – in a firm of private investigators in Jermyn Street. I can have him find out exactly what her present circumstances are, where she might best want to live. Then we can arrange to buy her what she wants there.'

'Excellent, Montagu, excellent! . . . I am most obliged to you.'

'Not at all. Anything I can do – it would be a pleasure. I'll be in touch with you.'

'Really most kind. I only wish . . .' The Prince

paused, a sadness suddenly overwhelming him, clouding his bright good looks. 'Only wish – it didn't all have to be anonymous . . .'

His friend, half-way towards the door, turned back. 'I understand entirely.' Montagu Bennington, of course, had read all about the Prince's association with Miss Laura Bowen – and, knowing him well, realized too – seeing it all confirmed in the Prince's sad expression – how he had so obviously loved this woman and been forced to drop her, of course. Not knowing the real reasons, he simply assumed the obvious: that the heir to the throne could not for long be mixed up with a married, and now alcoholic and bankrupt, Hollywood picture star. But Montagu Bennington would never for a moment presume on his friendship with the Prince by bringing such a topic up, so that all he did now, by way of terminating his part in their interview, was to repeat himself. 'I understand it all completely.'

The Prince, when his friend had left, went to the window, gazing down the lines of frozen trees. 'How I wish you did understand it all,' he said to himself. Then, turning back to his desk, he added, 'And, even more – if she could . . .'

Aunt Emily, standing by an easel at her bedroom window, looked out at the huge crowd assembled for the auction in front of Summer Hill. They stood packed together or in straying groups on the outskirts, several hundreds of them, beneath a blustery March sky – people from all over the country and further afield, rough mountainy men from the hills across the valley, local farmers, great and small, some few Ascendancy landowners, in gaiters and bowler hats, with their stewards; priests, gombeen men, and some professional-looking gents in dark suits and unsuitable town shoes, together with a large assortment of hangers-on and gawpers, come for the sport or to service the multitude – with porter, sweets and oranges: a gaggle of tinkers in damp plaid shawls purveying the latter; their barefoot children pressing in and out between the crush, threatening the mountainy men with this exotic fruit, when they were not trying to lift the wallets from the back-pockets of more substantial prey – portly farmers, big men of the county, who pushed them aside, making for the bar tent, a dank, rain-smeared marquee, filled with barrels of porter and crates of Jameson by courtesy of a shrewd Thomastown publican, set up on the trampled grass in the middle of Lady Cordiner's old pleasure garden, beyond the astrolabe, which stood above the crowd now, a desolate thing, rusty circles of iron, which some thought to be a piece of old agricultural equipment, part of the later sale of such things from the Summer Hill farm. Despite the chilly, unsettled weather there was an air of high festivity and happy expectation everywhere, a holiday mood, with vivid chatter, oaths, backslapping and gossip, wily groups whispering over the sale catalogue, weighing up lots like horses on a point-to-point card.

Aunt Emily's big studio-bedroom, with its *trompe l'oeil* murals of the old Residenz Theater in Munich, had sometime before been tagged and docketed by Mr Cassidy's men – most of the furniture, as everywhere else in the house, numbered with sticky labels, due to be auctioned in the latter part of the sale. She herself, though, had steadfastly refused to vacate the house or indeed leave her room. Quite unperturbed, believing that all this auction was a nonsense and the house would never be sold out of the family, she had locked herself into the bedroom with a supply of oatmeal biscuits, and was set now, as always, on commemorating events – in this instance the whole pulsating scene outside her window: the push and shove of farmers in their bowlers, the shawly travelling people and their impudent children, all this boisterous avaricious congregation come to inspect and devour the carcase of a house where she had spent all her life – a scene lit then by a brilliant sun-shaft which had rushed across the valley from Mount Brandon, illuminating everything in a flush of early-spring light, before the chill wind brought dark clouds scurrying back over the landscape, together with a sudden battering rain squall, driving the crowd to every meagre cover.

As they dispersed then, leaving some of the trodden lawns free, Aunt Emily saw a few first daffodils pushing up from the undergrowth on the lawn terraces to her right. Dabbing her brush in yellow watercolour, she started to sketch in these golden heads on her drawing. But, by the time she raised her eyes again, the shower was over and the crowds, returning, had trampled the little patch of gold into the muddy ground.

She heard the heavy stamp of boots outside on the landing then, unwanted visitors roaming the great house. Her door-handle turned. 'Oh no! You won't get in here, me hearties – you brazen lot of jackals and buzzards.' She picked up a sharp-tipped shooting stick she had with her and advanced with it menacingly, shaking it at the locked door. She had much the air of a pirate then, too – a large red handkerchief as a bandeau round her head, wisps of white hair flying all about outside it, a wicked and yet somehow amused glint in her still-clear blue Cordiner eyes. In her mid-seventies she was a formidable old party, barely one whit less intent, intense, bizarre and cantankerous than thirty years before.

Dermot, surrounded by strangers, stood in the great hall, filled with numbered furniture and with a debris of fallen plaster, the room never properly restored since the Black and Tans had desecrated it. Some of Cassidy's men were there, sitting at a trestle table, noting financial bona fides, letters of credit and such like, from intending bidders unknown to them. Cassidy himself was outside on the porch steps with several other assistants, fussing round his auctioneer's desk, set up high on one of the Summer Hill mahogany tables, getting ready to face the assembly.

Pat Kennedy was nowhere to be seen. Believing that some, at least, of the Cordiner family were likely to be there, and not at all in good odour either with most of the locals now, he had absented himself from the proceedings and was down in one of the basement still-rooms at that point, entertaining a few close friends over a bottle of Jameson's.

Dermot, ten days before, when Hetty after nearly six weeks at the clinic in Neuilly had recovered sufficiently, had taken her back with him to convalesce at his father's house in Dublin. At that point he had, finally, to explain to her how Summer Hill was about to be sold. But by then, too, their house in London had found a purchaser for the long leasehold, paying some £11,000; and a further £15,000 had been realized, between him and his father, by selling stock, through bank loans and mortgages – so that, as he had told Hetty, he hoped to be able to buy the house and demesne at Summer Hill at least, so fulfilling his promise to her. Thus he had with him now a letter of credit from the Bank of Ireland for some £26,000. He prayed it might be sufficient. Taking a last look round the ruined hall, he moved outside among the crowd, pushing himself into a circle of big booted farmers some few yards in front of Mr Cassidy's desk on the porch steps.

A minute later Cassidy, ascending the dais, rapped his gavel on the desk. 'Good morning, ladies . . .' He looked round, there were few such to be seen. 'And *gint*lemen!' He beamed slyly. 'I have here! . . .' He flourished the sale catalogue aloft. 'A sale, by order of Mr Patrick Kennedy – the house and demesne of Summer Hill in the County of Kilkenny, together with all the contents of said house, and of all other farm lands, farm equipment, dwellings and all other rights apertaining to the said estate of Summer Hill in the County of Kilkenny. In short, gintlemen, opportunities of a lifetime!' He looked about him, up at the crumbling portico and façade of the house. 'Five hundred years of history – the sale of the sintury! The lands will be first under the hammer – and some of the finest land in Ireland it is – all noted and itemized in yer copy of the par-tik-ulars: in all one thousand, one hundred and nine Irish statute acres, including, in the main, some of the best of agricultural land, together with assorted woodlands, wetlands, orchards, kitchen and market gardens, river inches, fishing rights, pleasure gardens – ye can see them all about ye!' He glanced over the ruined terraces and herbaceous borders. 'And sundry other parcels. The whole divided into forty-three lots, as per the par-tik-ulers in that first part of the catalogue. Now ye've all seen the lands concerned – I hope – and I want no mistakes as to yer intentions!' He leered out at his audience, continuing his mix of cajolery and threats towards them. 'Gi' me yer bids loud and clear, so there'll be no misunderstandings. And the last man in at the drop of the hammer – has it! Now, then – lot number one: 33 statute acres, the four inch fields on the river Nore, to the north of Cloone village. What am I bid?'

Silence. The crowd, hushed now, was quite still. No one wanted to make a first move. Cassidy, knowing this, addressed himself to one of his plants in the crowd. The man raised his hand. 'Good for you, sir! Put me in there with a bid – good man yerself – £400 – I have £400. £410!' He looked at another and this time entirely imaginary figure. '£420, £430 I have . . .'

Finally a real farmer made a genuine bid. '£440 . . .' The auction was under way. The weather outside continued bitter and squally.

Later that morning, the tenanted farms and other out-lying lands having been dispensed with, they came to the sale of the house and demesne itself. There had been a ten-minute break during which Cassidy had refreshed himself with a large glass of Jameson's with Pat Kennedy in the basement still-room. Now, mounting the dais again and blowing his nose vigorously, he set about promoting the central drama of the day. Straightening his hunch-back, raising his hands, prophet-like, he called for quiet. Then, starting slowly, in a low key, he began his encomium – the pace, the drama in his voice, mounting as he spoke, enumerating all the virtues in the great pile which towered above him.

'And now, gintlemen – the crowning glory, the centre-piece of all our deliberations here today . . .' He lifted his arms up, turning, gesturing to the old stone. 'The house of Summer Hill . . .' He paused for effect, shaking his head, as if in wonder at the vision looming over him. 'One of the greatest Georgian mansions in Ireland, I'll say – without fear of contradiction.' He glowered at his audience an instant. 'Built by Mr David Bindon the great arkie-tect at the height and breadth of his powers. Ye have all the par-tik-ulers in yer hands: three stories over a basement, three wings, eight reception rooms, twenty bedrooms, thirty-two other sundry rooms – smoking rooms, billiard rooms, gun rooms, morning, afternoon and evening rooms!' – he essayed another bad joke. 'And further quarters galore: servants' rooms, laundries, scul-leries, kitchens – old and new – pantries, larders and still-rooms, game rooms, rooms without let or hindrance *ad infinitum*! – inything and everything ye could ask for – together with sundry other outbuildings: stable yards, twenty loose boxes – enough to keep a string of horses! – lofts, haggards, corn stores, kitchen and market gardens. And then the very fine demesne itself: 173 Irish statute acres, filled with the best of mature timber, with a two-mile frontage on the river Nore, to include salmon trapping, and all fishing rights . . .

'And I needn't tell ye—' He paused, blew his nose, coming to his peroration. 'Though there is some very slight dilapidation here and there in the house – nothing ye'd notice – an opportunity like this comes only once in a lifetime. This is no mere gintleman's residence I'm offering here this morning – but a palace, a veritable palace, a home fit for a King! And I have a bid with me already – £23,000!' He smiled ogreishly about.

Dermot's face fell. That was almost all his money on the reserve price.

'£24,000!' Cassidy shouted, pointing at a tall cadaverous figure in a dirty trenchcoat in the middle of the crowd. It was Mr Oliver Mulcahy, the big timber merchant from Waterford, who with his friend Seamus Mulligan, the building contractor, had decided to collaborate in buying the whole place together, so that they could then, at their leisure, gut the house and estate of all its fine stone and timber.

Dermot joined the bidding, raising his hand.

'£24,500,' Cassidy shouted, perspiring now after his whiskey, excited himself at the very idea of dealing in such sums, on which he would take a handsome commission.

'£25,000.' The timber merchant nodded. '£25,500,' Dermot responded again. '£26,000,' Mr Mulcahy increased it. '£26,600,' Dermot raised his hand for the last time. He could go no further.

'£27,000 I have . . . £27,500!' Mulcahy had nodded again. '£28,000 then.' Cassidy looked round the crowd expectantly, taking up his gavel. Suddenly someone caught his eye. 'Yes! – at the back there, you, sir!' A small, innocuous-looking man at the edge of the crush had raised his hand – a city gent in a dark greatcoat, bowler and wing collar, with town shoes covered in mud, carrying a briefcase. People craned their necks round, trying to identify him among the bobbing heads. '£29,000 bid,' the man said in a calm Dublin accent.

'£29,000 I have!' Cassidy roared his approval. But immediately he bent down to his assistant, asking sotto voce, 'Who's that fella?'

'Mulrooney – solicitors from Dublin, Mulrooney and Owen – he's more than all right. Showed a banker's draft for up to £75,000.' Cassidy returned to business. 'And thank *you*, sir. £29,000 I have. It's against you, Mr Mulcahy?' Mulcahy nodded once more.

£30,000, 31, 32, 33, 34 . . .' Cassidy swung his gaze rapidly between the two bidders. '£35,000 then. Any more? Yes, Mr Mulcahy! £36,000, 37, 38, 39 – £40,000 I have. Against you, Mr Mulcahy.' Mr Mulcahy nodded. '£41,000.' Cassidy turned to the little man in the dark coat. 'Against you, sir?' The man nodded, a mild, barely perceptible assent, as if the sum involved was a mere pittance. '£42,000 then – 43, 44, 45 – £46,000 I have. Against you again, Mr Mulcahy.' But Mulcahy shook his head, disgusted.

'Very well then,' Cassidy roared. 'I have it – at £46,000 – for this whole magnificent edifice and pertaining demesne. Do I have any more?' He lifted the gavel. The crowd was absolutely still, but for the cries of a few tinker children playing in the ruined grotto on the high lawn. 'Going, going, *gone*! Sold to the gintleman at the back there in the black coat. Mr Mulrooney it is, sir, isn't it?'

There was a flurry of animated chatter then, heads craned round once more to see who this stranger was in the wing collar and bowler. But the man had disappeared in the crush and was nowhere to be seen. Dermot, also trying to identify him, sighed, finally moving away, biting his lip, looking up at the great house, as a flash of sunlight struck it now – and suddenly he saw the figure of Aunt Emily, spotlit for a moment, standing in the window of her bedroom, motionless, like a ghost. And yet she was smiling, Dermot saw to his astonishment. A happy ghost . . . The poor mad woman, he thought. What had she to smile about? The great house was gone.

Six hundred years of Cordiner history in Ireland, twenty generations of the same family on this hill – first in an old Norman keep at the bridge, then a buttressed castle on the steep side of the hill, finally a lovely Georgian house. All this – and the future, too – Hetty's, Aunt Emily's, his own, all had gone at the drop of a hammer.

Whereas the house and estate had survived the physical attacks and depredations, the familial passions and alarms of centuries, a little blow from a hammer had finally done for it all – in the hands of Cassidy, one of the gombeen men supreme come to power in this new Republic, someone who did not give a tinker's curse for the place: sold to another of his kind, as Dermot thought, some anonymous Dublin city slicker, probably bidding on behalf of a religious institution, who would draw all the warmth and life from the place, turn it over into some cold and ghastly convent or college for the priests. God forgive them all, Dermot thought. Then he changed his mind – God damn them for their meagre souls. He hoped never to see the man with the briefcase and bowler ever again.

And yet, attending the afternoon sale of the house's contents, Dermot did see him again – constantly hovering in the background just as before, making his calm, ever-increasing bids, hammering in the loss that Dermot already felt, buying up nearly all the best items: the Irish Georgian effects – the Chippendale and Sheraton furniture, the silver cutlery, candlesticks and epergnes, the Flemish tapestry in the hall, the better oil paintings, the Cordiner family portraits, the myriad sporting prints, the books and much else – each time outbidding all rivals; including Dermot who, with his money still intact, had tried to secure anything else he could, managing to end up with some few of the lesser pieces, but including at least what in a way he most valued, the contents of Henry's old work rooms on the top floor, and all his equipment there, the butterfly collections and the menagerie of stuffed animals, together with most of the furniture in Aunt Emily's room and a variety of other small mementoes which he would pass on to Hetty, after keeping a few for himself.

Dermot was heartbroken. Moving out of the great hall he stopped by the tall window next to the door, gazing at the tiny inset of coloured glass there showing the Cordiner arms, the great yellow-eyed eagle on top of the visored helmet with the legend beneath – 'Fortune Favours the Brave'.

What a mockery the family motto seemed to him then. The Cordiners had come to the end of the line in this house – through a mix of latter-day arrogance, insensitivity, mismanagement and sheer spite, not bravery. The great fortune had been dissipated by selfish obsession – for all the wrong things. Above all, he thought, in the shape of old Lady Cordiner and Frances, they had, with whatever excuse, promoted pain and not love in this place, and that had really been Summer Hill's undoing. This house, as he knew so well himself, was a warm thing, full of promise. And if you loved it, and the people in it, as he had – if you could love it room by room, every nook and cranny, as he did – then it would have survived, would have avoided its complete physical change or destruction, which was all that awaited it now.

Outside, standing on the porch steps in the late afternoon, he saw how the day had cleared at last, with a stormy sunset, the valley strewn with vivid colours, hints of spring green everywhere, glistening after the rain, budding yellows, patches of white narcissi and golden daffodils, the mountains, Brandon and Leinster away to the east, bathed in a pale-blue evening light. And the light from the west as he turned, clear and rose-tinted, shone on the great façade of the house, gently firing the stone, touching the windows with a soft glitter. So that once more, as he left it, the house was full of warmth and promise. He stood there, as the departing crowd pushed and shoved about him, gazing up and around, trying to imprint this happy vision on his mind, to keep it there as a last treasure. Then someone touched him on the shoulder. Turning, he was astonished to see the little city gent in the greatcoat and wing collar. He had taken off his bowler, deprecatingly.

'Colonel . . . Cordiner?' he asked diffidently. Dermot, too surprised to make reply, barely nodded. 'I'm Mr Mulrooney – um, from Mulrooney and Owen, solicitors in Dublin . . .' The voice, with its genteel Dublin tones, was so mild and other-worldly, frail, full of dying falls. And now, in the silence, it seemed to have given out altogether.

'Yes?' Dermot finally asked.

'I wonder . . . I wonder if you could spare me a little of your time? – er, I have some news . . . some matters concerning this house and . . . Miss Laura Bowen. I understand she is a cousin of yours?'

'Yes.'

'Good. Yes, quite so. I'd be very grateful if . . . if you could, if I could – talk with you for . . . a half-hour . . . confidentially.' He glanced round him anxiously. 'I'm staying at the Club House in Kilkenny. Perhaps? . . . I have a car round by the yard. If you'd like to come with me? – I could give you a lift?' The man smiled, a wan ghost of a smile. He had, Dermot thought, the appropriate air of an undertaker. But he followed him.

'I don't think I entirely understand you, Mr Mulrooney . . . ?' In truth Dermot had been quite unable to believe his ears. Steadying himself now, he lifted his whisky-soda, which Mr Mulrooney, with a lot of nervous footling, had finally managed to order for them both, the two men sitting on the edge of shabby chintz chairs in the residents' lounge upstairs in the Club House Hotel. 'You were instructed to buy Summer Hill, its contents and demesne – on behalf of an anonymous "admirer" of Miss Lauren Bowen?'

'Quite so, Colonel Cordiner, quite so.' Mr Mulrooney sipped his whisky, then eased a pointed corner of his wing-collar away from an old spot on his neck that had been rubbed there over the years. 'And since, as I understand it, Miss Bowen is, er, indisposed at the minute, I took the opportunity . . . the chance of approaching you, as her nearest relative in the matter. I hope you'll forgive me . . .' Again the ever-diffident, apologetic hesitancy of the man, Dermot thought – as if he were commiserating with him after a funeral, and was not, as he seemed to be, the herald of some miraculous birth. 'Yes, Colonel, I was so instructed, by . . . by my client – my clients, I should say,' he corrected himself quickly. 'And I believe I have fulfilled my commission – rather advantageously, perhaps . . .' He allowed himself this tiny congratulation. 'Though the house is not perhaps in the best repair—'

'To put it mildly.'

'None the less—'

Dermot pulled himself together. 'I'm sorry, Mr Mulrooney. Of course . . . it's just that I can't quite take it all in. It's a most generous gift, quite incredible . . .'

'Yes,' Mr Mulrooney assented neatly, with a brief smile. 'There is one point, however. It is not an actual *gift*, Colonel Cordiner.'

'I see.' Dermot did not quite see.

'You will be aware – perhaps? – that, um, Miss Bowen, as of now, is an undischarged bankrupt?'

'Yes – yes, of course.'

'Ah! – there is the point, Colonel Cordiner!' Mr Mulrooney, raising a finger, came to genuine life for a moment, a real smile flooding his wan features, clearly delighted with himself. 'Thus any such outright gift could be forfeit to her creditors. So it is my clients' wish, in the meanwhile, to allow Miss Bowen full occupancy and use of the said house, its contents, and demesne, while retaining the title deeds in their possession . . .'

'I see.'

'Indeed . . .'

There was silence in the lamplit room. A dog barked in the street. The fire crackled and Mr Mulrooney essayed a further smile. 'So, Colonel, tomorrow, at the end of the sale of contents, I shall be meeting Mr Patrick Kennedy's solicitors in Kilkenny and making arrangements for the transfer of those deeds, which will then be held in fee simple by my clients. And after that, in return, I will give you a deed of legal occupancy, made out in Miss Laura Bowen's name, and all we shall need then is her signature to the agreement, which will complete matters . . .'

Mr Mulrooney raised his glass – almost in a toast, before thinking better of it.

'That all seems very fair – more than fair, Mr Mulrooney. There is one point, though – may Miss Bowen never know who her benefactor is?'

Mr Mulrooney fiddled with his glass, seeming to regret his near-celebration a moment before. 'Ah . . . that is, er, quite beyond my brief, Colonel. I am not dealing with any individual in this matter – merely representing . . . legal offices, elsewhere. So I may tell you, in all honesty, that I have absolutely no idea who this benefactor is . . . or might be . . .' He offered another of his wan smiles, becoming almost spendthrift with them now. 'No idea at *all*,' he added, emphasizing a word for the first time, obviously charmed by the neatness of this whole legal conceit, this so-perfectly-closed circle into which no one could ever break.

And indeed Dermot remained entirely at a loss – until just then, easing himself in his chair, his glance fell on one of the Spy cartoons by the fireplace. Part of a long row, it was no more conspicuous than all the rest. But it was immediately clear who it portrayed – the great beard, the aggressive Hanoverian features beneath a grey topper, a portly figure in a morning suit, the suggestion of horses and racing, in the background: it was the old Prince of Wales, some time in the late nineties.

And it came to Dermot then, in a sudden intuitive flash, that this gift of Summer Hill was in some way his, a recompense of sorts – his, through his grandson, perhaps, the present Prince of Wales. Of course! The gift of an 'admirer' . . . Two admirers. Who had admired Frances more – those long years ago when they had all lived at Wilton Place in London? And who since, most recently, had so obviously admired Hetty – and had had to abandon her?

Dermot was almost certain of it – as if the two royal figures were in the room with him then, nodding agreement: the house miraculously returned in all its warmth and promise.

Summer Hill, despite Frances's earlier folly in giving it over to Pat Kennedy, was in Cordiner hands once more. And yet Frances herself remained, if only just: perpetrator of this and other madnesses, but for reasons which Dermot, at least, understood. She had been betrayed, abandoned, exiled – her youth destroyed by Lady Cordiner and the old Prince. And besides, whatever she had done since, one had to take the total life into account. And, if you loved someone, as he had, you loved the whole person, good and bad. And if the faults had come to so outweigh the virtues in that person, so the more must one try and maintain that original act of faith, in loving her. He would have to see Frances now, tell her what had happened over Summer Hill, offer her these last rites of affection. And so would Hetty.

Hetty, if all the ghosts of her past were to be finally laid, if she was truly to start her life anew at Summer Hill, would have to see her too.

Having told her, to her sheer astonishment and delight, how Summer Hill had been regained at the hands of some admirer, he went on to say how this was the moment to make things up with her mother. At first, though she did not refuse outright, there was antagonism everywhere in her face.

'Hetty, she's dying,' he told her bluntly. 'I know how cold and cruel she's been to you. But, unless you can forgive those who've hurt you most, you'll never be able to forgive yourself. Don't you see? Unless you meet, you'll go through the rest of your life regretting it, hating yourself, a secret wound that'll never heal. And it'll poison you, undermine every other happiness you may have. You really have to see her, for yourself as much as for her. Don't you see?'

Hetty, listening intently to this man she so trusted, eventually did see.

Dermot knocked on the bungalow door in Rathgar a few days later. It was opened by a fraught, dishevelled woman – quite young, with a toss of untidy red hair, in a long yellow crochet-work cardigan and wellington boots: a Mrs McDaid, Frances's housekeeper, widow of a Citizen Army insurgent killed at the Easter rebellion, his father had told him, killed accidentally by his own side in the General Post Office – one of any number of Republican friends and sympathisers who had ministered to Frances since her arrival in Dublin, and especially in these last years of her illness.

Once inside the narrow, damp-stained hall, sacks of coal stacked along one side, Dermot and Hetty were immediately assailed by the rank odour of cats – a smell of urine (which perhaps explained Mrs McDaid's rubber boots, Dermot thought) and old fur, mixed with the acrid fumes of a badly drawing coal fire coming from a small sitting room immediately to their right.

Moving through the doorway here, taking their coats off, they started to choke in the foul and sulphurous air, lying in streaky layers, partly obscuring the chaos of the room: a haphazard collection of further half-completed crochet-work cardigans, holy pictures and framed Republican manifestoes, poems and stirring political declarations which covered the walls; yellowing, mildewed piles of Gaelic newspapers with other rebelly and religious mementoes that littered the furniture or had found a home among old blankets on the floor where some great cats lay cushioned, sharing in this warm-moist, festering debris, heads sunk well below the smoky air, and thus impervious to the fumes.

'Surely this isn't good for Mrs Fraser – with her bronchitis?' Dermot gestured through the fog at Mrs McDaid.

'Indeed – an' isn't that just what the doctor's bin telling her Ladyship this long time, and she not takin' divil a bit of notice of him?' Mrs McDaid spoke with an excitable smile. 'How and so ever, she's bein' moved outa here this afternoon, to the nuns in Leeson Street. So ye're only just in time to see her.'

'I'd better see her first?' He turned to Hetty, who nodded.

The woman led Dermot into a much less smoky but no less chaotic bedroom at the back. Frances lay propped up in a narrow iron bedstead surrounded by other cats, a more favoured brood; the animals asleep, Frances gazing vacantly at three sizeable pictures on the wall opposite: a vivid oleograph of the Christ King crowned with dripping thorns, bleeding heart bared, together with two quite contrary portrait photographs, stuffy and retouched, without blemish, formal to a degree – one of Pope Benedict XI, the other of Frances's friend and comrade-in-arms Eamon de Valera. On her bedside table was a plaster statuette, in garish blue and gold, of the Virgin holding her arms out – in a blessing, a supplication or sheer resignation, Dermot could not decide. The Virgin's piteous features, though, could not be misinterpreted – not unlike Frances's own expression a few feet away.

'Frances?' Dermot drew a kitchen chair towards the bed. 'It's me – Dermot.' Silence. 'I hear you're going to the hospital tomorrow. That's marvellous. Should have gone . . . much earlier,' he added diffidently.

Frances wheezed by way of reply, then started a racking cough, her whole frail body heaving in the bed for half a minute, before she eventually turned her face towards him.

He was astonished, appalled by the drawn, heavily wrinkled, emaciated features, the toss of skimpy withered grey hair – the desperate toll that age and illness had taken here. Age? But she was only in her mid-fifties, Dermot had to remind himself. The clear blue Cordiner eyes, however, had survived largely intact in the wreck of the years.

He had to turn away an instant – gathering, controlling himself, so hurt was he by this ruined vision, this ghost of times past, when her beauty had only been equalled by her spirit, both radiant.

'Yes,' she wheezed at last, mucus starting to drip from her nose. 'Hospital – the good Sisters of the Sacred Heart. But I doubt it . . .' Her voice was thin, ethereal, without any timbre to it. 'I shan't leave here alive.'

'Francie! . . .' he said, moved almost beyond endurance, a lump rising in his throat, with that endearment he and her brother Henry had used all those years ago, the three of them, happy together at Summer Hill. 'Francie, of course you will.'

'No. And why should I?' A spasm of coughing took her again. 'You can see,' she went on at last, eyes filled with tears from her exertions, 'I've had everything I want – of this small life . . .' She looked at the statue of the Virgin then before closing her eyes, seeming to sleep.

Dermot took out the little present he had bought at Summer Hill for her – one of the dozen or so of old Lady Cordiner's Baccarat paperweights: a lovely oval crystal with a great, black-hearted scarlet poppy embedded in the glass. 'I brought this for you – from Summer Hill.'

At the naming of the house Frances opened her eyes and gazed at the crystal globe – eyes soon filled with an emotion which Dermot could not quite decipher, a mix of hatred and yet of longing, he thought. He reached out with the paperweight, putting it on the stained coverlet near her desperately thin, blue-veined hands. But she made no move towards it, closing her eyes once more. The glass lay there, next to a big tabby cat, who equally ignored it.

'I've just come up from Summer Hill,' Dermot went on. 'I was there a few days ago.' Frances opened her eyes. But again she made no comment. 'Hetty,' Dermot continued gently. 'You remember? – Hetty, your daughter . . .' She closed her eyes at once. 'Well, some friend of hers – he's bought the whole place back for her, from Pat Kennedy.'

At this news, and at last, Frances, opening her eyes again, spoke with stiff clarity, a glimmer of passion. 'But it *couldn't* be hers. I gave it all to Pat – long ago.' Her blue eyes were sharp then – as Dermot mostly remembered them: sharp with frustration, anger.

'Yes, but we've managed to buy it back. For Hetty – and for you, too. For all of us – Cordiners.'

The family name hung in the rank, stuffy air, isolated in the silence.

'Not for me,' Frances said at last. 'My name – is Fraser. And you should not have bought it back. I'd left it – for Pat, for Ireland, for the Irish.'

'But *we* are Irish, Francie – you and I and Hetty – just as much as Pat Kennedy.' Dermot spoke with a touch of acerbity. 'And Hetty – she's here now to see you.'

Dermot stood up quickly to fetch her. But when he turned he was surprised to see Hetty standing there in the doorway already, quite still, suddenly materialized there, softly as a ghost. Indeed Hetty, after all her illnesses, was almost as ethereal a figure as her mother – tall and thin in a green velvet jacket, lace blouse, long oatmeal skirt, gazing at Frances who, looking up then, recognized her quite clearly.

Dermot, standing between them, glanced at their two expressions. At first, with Frances, there was a dull glower, a dismissive bitter curl to her lips – while Hetty's face, which before had been calm, devoid of any emotion, now reflected her mother's angry distaste. And then, in a moment, having locked horns in this way, exchanged this wordless fury, both their expressions changed to one of supreme disinterest. It was as if two bitter enemies had had the misfortune to bump into each other at a street corner, and having confirmed their antagonism were about to move apart, going their separate ways. And indeed, in the next moment, Frances turned away, facing the wall, while Hetty started to fiddle with her feet, about to move out the door.

But at that moment a big tabby-cat stirred on the coverlet and the crystal paperweight, lying in the folds, fell to the floor, splintering.

The dumb, cold mood was broken.

Hetty, coming forward, picked up the broken crystal, while Frances, alarmed by the crash, turned her head towards her daughter, close to her now, kneeling by the bed. Hetty held up part of the broken paperweight. 'Bit smashed. But not too badly. Perhaps we can get it re-re-repaired,' she added, her expression softening as she looked at the broken paperweight more carefully – the poppy still intact in one half. Of course, she remembered it now – that blazing scarlet flower with its dark heart held in the glittering crystal: it was one of her grand-mother's paperweights which Frances had stolen years before at Summer Hill, as Aunt Emily had told her – and which Hetty, with Léonie, had discovered in the chimney flue: one among dozens of such little objets d'art which her mother had taken in enmity then, in hatred for old Lady Cordiner.

Frances, too, suddenly seemed revived by this vision of the broken paperweight. 'Yes – yes, perhaps we can get it repaired.' Then, in a strangely confiding, almost pleasant voice, she quite changed tack. 'Did you find it in the chimney flue, in the primrose room, my old bedroom, where I used to hide all those little things?' Hetty, not wishing to break this intimate flow of talk, nodded. 'Good . . . Well, we'll keep them all ourselves now.' Hetty nodded once more, happy to collaborate in this imagined conspiracy of her mother's. Then Frances's tone changed again. A look of deep hatred crossed her face and she said with startling anger, 'Whatever you do – don't give it back to Mama – *any* of those little paperweights and things. Never give it back! – to that monstrous old woman, with her pryings and hatreds . . . and killings. It was she who killed Henry, you know, my dear brother . . . So have *nothing* to do with her, *ever*.'

Her voice was cruel and vehement now – just as Hetty remembered it from the old days, when she had so often punished her in just the same tones. But now, in these wanderings, Frances was attacking her own long-dead mother instead. And Hetty was pleased, happy indeed, at this renewal of her own mother's old spirit. For what she had never been able to understand or bear in Frances's latter life was her sudden conversions – to the Catholic faith, to Gaelic ideals, to good works, all her meek and mild renunciations of that previously vibrant spirit, which she thought to be sheer hypocrisy on her part. But now her mother had clearly regained some of that earlier vivacity and ardour which had so characterized what Hetty had always believed to be her real temperament. Now there was a cutting edge to her heart once more, the grandeur of real emotion.

'No, Mama, I won't give any of them back – ever!'

Through these old secrets revived and shared now, the two women suddenly found themselves on easier terms – a secret resurrected from her mother's youth at Summer Hill long before she was born, and confided in her now, so that she and her mother, for the first time in their lives, found themselves on the same side of things, against the world, against others, miscreants both, companions-in-arms in this conspiracy, a solidarity between them which had never remotely existed before; and all created over the memory, the remains, of a broken paperweight.

Hetty, encouraged by this birth of trust between them, was no longer so appalled by the cold and frowsty bedroom – its fearful air of barren nationalism and opiate religion – reflected in the bleeding hearts, lifeless photographs and arid political manifestoes that littered the room. These images faded for Hetty, as she saw her mother revived by this angry intrigue – no longer overwhelmed, deadened, by that timidity of intellect which had taken and crushed her more than a decade before.

Hetty drew up a chair, sitting close to her mother.

The two women gazed at each other in the silence. Now, in this clear regard, they were no longer such strangers. Instead, sharing a complicity over the paperweight, their own long antagonisms had been subsumed in a greater one – against that third figure who stood in the room with them then, the malevolent spirit of old Lady Cordiner who had set in motion this long trail of familial pain and cruelty, and against whom now their own mutual hatreds, dissolving, were redirected. They found some forgiveness for each other solely in this unforgiving of a long-dead woman, mother and grand-mother to them. They were reconciled then as conspira-tors, both their true natures coincided at last, brought together by this whiff of danger, of secrets shared.

Frances moved her lips then, as if about to continue with these intimacies. But instead a frightful spasm of coughing took her and she started to heave to and fro in the bed. Eventually, recovering herself, she fell back suddenly on the pillows, exhausted, eyes gazing upwards, remaining absolutely still.

Hetty reached forward, taking her mother's hand on the sheet. Without her noticing it, the inside of her own middle finger was bleeding, cut by a small splinter from the paperweight, still embedded in her flesh. So that, after she had held her mother's hand for a minute, and still unaware of the cut, the blood began to seep out, a trickle of scarlet falling down Frances's hand – increasing as Hetty took a firmer grip, gazing at her mother all the while, neither of them needing to speak, as Hetty felt, words unnecessary in this vague reconciliation.

Later, when Hetty tried to move her hand, she found her mother's fingers had stiffened in hers. As she released herself, Frances's hand fell limply on the sheet, a red-smeared claw, without life. Hetty, seeing the blood on her mother's hand, thought this was somehow connected with her death. Then, looking at her own palm, she saw the small wound and realized what had happened. The splinter, still embedded there, had cut her mother's hand as well – their blood mixing in the end, as it had at the very beginning, the flow coursing together, uniting them at the last – in birth, death, resurrection. Frances was gone and Hetty thus reborn.

The funeral a few days later was an enormous affair – the largest seen in Dublin since the death of Daniel O'Connell, the Liberator, nearly a hundred years before. After a Requiem Mass in the local church and a subsequent lying-in-state for two days in the City Hall, some quarter of a million people – mostly the poor of the city, the hungry, the cold, the dispossessed, to whom Frances, with her bags of coal and crochet-work cardigans, had so ministered in her last years – turned out to honour her.

They lined all the streets of the three-mile route to Glasnevin cemetery, packed five and ten deep to either side, heads bowed, reciting their rosaries, paying their last respects to this martyr in their cause. It was a tremendous occasion – a mourning, yet a celebration, too; the latter element encouraged by the quite unseasonable April weather, the warm bright day that had flooded over the city almost since first light: a day, as Hetty remembered it, almost exactly similar, green-budding and soft, to that Easter Monday in 1916 when the rebellion had broken out, when she and Léonie had been at the Shelbourne Hotel and had later been trapped with her mother and the other insurgents in the long and bloody battle for Stephen's Green.

Now, following the tricolour-draped coffin in the creeping hearse, with its marching honour guard of young Fianna scouts, Hetty was no longer trapped by her mother, by that bitter intractable enmity that had soured all her early life, every part of their subsequent relationship. She was freed from her and from all the pain in her own disastrous years, as a child, in marriage, as a picture star.

Now, she thought, finally recovered and come to her

senses, she could take up her own real life, before her then in the balmy, summer-like air – a future indefinite, a blank page, a life of unknown adventure. And so her heart was strangely light that morning, a knot of half-fearful excitement turning in the pit of her stomach, that sensuous expectation of youth returned, when there is certain knowledge of a void to be thrillingly filled – as she sat back in the car, veiled, in black, her two cousins on either side of her in dark frock-coats, top hats on their knees.

'What a turn-out,' Dermot remarked, rather shame-faced, for all three of them, seeing this vast crowd of mourners, felt somewhat guilty now at their earlier con-demnations of Frances's passionate republicanism. Lost to them, she had given her life, literally, to these other far more needy Irish people.

'Yes . . . Frances would have been appalled at the show of it all, the grand clerics and dignitaries,' Mortimer commented.

'Another part of her would have loved it, though,' Hetty said. 'That older part of her . . .'

'Yes – that spirited part – slapping Appleton the head gardener in the face and all that. The part she lost . . .' Dermot added, a touch of regret in his voice.

'But she didn't lose it!' Hetty came back, turning to both men, bright-eyed, eager herself once more. 'She was angry and spirited as ever at the end, against *her* Mama. That was what was so wonderful. She *found* all her old self at the end!'

The two men looked at Hetty curiously. They had learnt of Hetty's reconciliation with her mother through the medium of the paperweight. But they had not real-ized how, in this event, Frances in the end had been reconciled with her own true nature as well.

Arriving at the Republican Plot at Glasnevin Cem-etery, a small, ageing, white-haired man who yet still retained the air of a courtly flyweight boxer – Pedar O'Hegarty who had first recruited Frances into the Irish Republican Brotherhood nearly twenty-five years before – gave a short funeral oration.

'. . . She came of the grandest station. In her youth she had every ease that money and civilization can bring . . . She had besides, in herself, great beauty, intellect, wit, a lovely energy for all the distractions of her circle – riding to hounds, music, theatre, dancing. Withal, in that world of her class, she had a future of the greatest privilege, wealth and position. The world lay at her feet . . . Yet she threw it all aside, every worldly prize, to devote herself first to the cause of nationhood – this free Republic, which is her creation, along with those other great Irish patriots whom she is now about to join – and then, in the long years of her own illness, giving what was left of her life, without stint or thought for herself, to those in this city who had less than nothing: the poor, the destitute, the old, the hungry, the uncared-for.

'With these two great visions – the greatest we can know on this earth – of freedom and charity, she brought life, political and material, first to a nation, then to many of its citizens . . . It was a blazing life, in Stephen's Green that Easter week, followed by an equally passionate generosity in all those smaller consolations which she offered to the people of Dublin . . .

'She gave herself utterly, without compromise, to both causes. For her there were no complexities or indecisions, no half-measures or regrets. Hers was an angry passion – for the *right*, and no sacrifice was too great to achieve this end . . . Losing her life, she found it. In suffering she drew happiness. In battle she made peace. So, in death, she has true immortality . . .'

Standing by the graveside, Hetty felt the tears pricking her eyes behind her veil. As O'Hegarty had confirmed it

now, the matter seemed beyond dispute: how wrong she
had been about her mother, blinding herself, through
her own obsessive self-will, to her virtues – and worse
still refusing to acknowledge the validity of her mother's
latter purposes, the different roads she had taken towards
her own salvation. Hetty saw all this at last. Indeed, that
was the final message from her mother as they lowered
her away into the ground: how she herself would now
have to take a quite different route towards the same
end.

Oh yes, her mother had returned to some of her old
spirited ways at the end. But that was no more than a
deathbed conversion, a last acknowledgement of her
earlier glowing but flawed nature. One could not, as her
mother had discovered long before, sustain a whole life
on such false premises. Nor, Hetty saw, could she. The
vainglory she had espoused in Hollywood – rampant
ambition, will to power, the need to hurt, dominate,
betray – why, these had been exactly her mother's old
failings, too, and her grandmother's before her. It ran in
the family. And she had lived just such a life herself –
taken to the brink of death by it, much sooner than
the other two. It was all too clear: she must adapt or
perish.

And yet . . . Now that she was growing stronger, her
taste for life reviving, Hetty saw her predicament in any
such adaptation. She could not become a saint, a martyr,
like her mother, could not renounce all her true characteristics, each and every one – for there was the
hypocrisy.

How then, in what manner of compromise, was she to
survive and yet advance? She had lost her career, her
marriage, and had nearly died. But through Dermot's
intervention she had recovered her health, her family
home, and she was not yet thirty. Was she to renounce
every other possible sweetness in life? – so tempting then

in the balmy spring air standing above her mother's grave. And yet in embarking on that adventure, in tasting that sweetness, had she the self-discipline, above all the new character to savour it without lapsing again – which, if she did, would bring her to the same yawning pit long before her time?

book two

I

Dermot drove down to Summer Hill with Hetty a week later. Though not entirely recovered – she was still thin, weak on her feet and suffered the sporadic backache and violent stomach cramps of her syphilis – she had insisted on it, wonderfully excited by the prospect of returning home after nearly twelve years, of coming, however conditionally, into her inheritance.

Dermot, as yet, had told her nothing of his intuitions as to the identity of her 'admirer' – and now, that bright April morning in 1929, as the car drove up the unkept, grassed-over avenue swerving round the fallen trees, Hetty wondered out loud again.

'Who? – who could it have been? Giving – giving back – all this?'

She gazed around the ruined demesne as the car climbed the slope. Some of the chestnut trees, lower down by the river gorge, were just in bud. Clumps of daffodils, forcing their way up through the rough, thistle-filled pasture, showed as patches of vivid yellow in the winter grass. Across the valley the mountains had a soft blue, almost summery sheen to them in the mild light.

'Who?' she asked again, turning to Dermot at the wheel of his father's old Daimler.

Dermot shook his head. It was not the moment for any such revelations. Later, when Hetty was settled here – there would be time then. Meanwhile he was almost as excited as she when, as they reached the brow of the hill, the house finally came into view.

The rooks in the broken chimneys, alarmed by the engine, suddenly spiralled into the sky, climbing over the half-circle of trees behind the house, cawing raucously, their cries filling the air, an anthem of home-coming.

Hetty gasped with pleasure. 'The rooks! Hear them? They *are* Summer Hill, aren't they?' She watched, wide-eyed, as they tossed and turned beneath an arc of blue sky and puffy white cloud.

Then, careering up the moss-soft drive, rounding the old formal pleasure gardens, stopping on the muddy, potholed gravel in front of the house, they were there. Dermot turned off the engine. There was silence.

'Home,' Dermot said simply, turning to her with a brief smile, reaching quickly for his pipe and matches in his tweed jacket. But before he could get to them Hetty leant across quickly and kissed him on the cheek, feeling the rub of his small moustache an instant, the vague odour of pipe tobacco. Then, involuntarily, she repeated the kiss. 'Thank you,' she said just as simply, leaning away, gazing at him.

This was the man who, nearly twenty years before, had really introduced her to Summer Hill, the wild land-scape, this great kingdom – naming all the parts of it for her, so that she had come truly to possess it – the man who, despite the malign humours of her mother, the dooms she had cast over all her childhood here, had brought her to love the place, to love him too, before everything had changed in 1914: Dermot, for whom she had pined at the French convent school, whom she had thought lost in the Great War, before she herself had been lost, deserting Léonie, family, friends, home, lost in the imbecilities of her marriage, her wastrel career in the motion picture business, those disastrous years which had led to her downfall.

She gazed at him in silence, as at last he found his pipe. She opened the car window, and the drifting odour of an Irish spring came to her then, a damp mossy fragrance, moist with rot, and warm with growth, mixed with a hint of turf smoke from somewhere – a fragrance, sweet and sour, which had been the air of her whole universe once. So that now it was as if, as well as her life, Dermot had given her back even her childhood, returned her to all the innocence and beginnings there.

She loved this man again, as she had years before as a child. And there was the problem. Would he now, as then, prove unpossessable – now as then remain somehow just outside her orbit, the light of her adoration – fond and affectionate towards her, yet somehow distant, always leaving? Could she ever change that? Her kisses just then had changed nothing. She breathed deeply, inhaling the fresh soft air. She wished she could tell him how much she loved him, so far beyond simple fondness and affection. But she could not. Yet words were all she had to express her feelings for him.

'You know, Dermot,' she said intently, still gazing at him. 'It doesn't matter who it really was who gave the place back to me, to *us*. As far as I'm concerned, it was you . . .' She risked a last physical gesture, touching him on the sleeve.

Dermot bit his lip, thought to speak, but said nothing. What could he say? He saw Hetty's love, recognized it exactly for what it was, a woman's bright passion for a man, frustrated. He loved her too, just as he had her mother years before. But he knew that it was a familial love he felt for Hetty, a vast tenderness without desire, an intense concern, filled with every emotion – every hope except that of physical possession.

Her mother was dead. Yet here was Hetty, back from the grave almost, waiting to start her life anew. And, were it not for his nature, she might have started it again with him. He realized that. That was the message in her eyes. Looking at her then – her thin features radiant in the April light – he saw how Frances, betrayed by the old Prince and for lack of just this familial love, had fallen headlong into a career of bitter violence, destroying herself. Would Hetty, though restored to life, come to find just the same sort of betrayal in him, for his inability to respond to her – in that way of desire? It was this thought that made him restrain the kiss he longed to reciprocate with, fearing that she might misinterpret it. They got out and walked towards the house.

A small, rather stout woman in a white apron, with a taller man behind, had appeared on the porch steps.

'A surprise for you,' Dermot said to Hetty quietly. 'I asked them to come here for a bit, as housekeeper and general handyman, until you get yourself settled. Remember? – recognize her?'

Hetty paused at the bottom of the steps, looking at the woman in the apron, a flush of dark, greying hair above a round sweet face, with dimples still there, embedded in her ample cheeks. Suddenly Hetty recognized her.

'Eileen, Elly? – I don't believe it – Oh, Elly!' She rushed up the steps, embracing the woman. 'How on earth? – how did you come?'

'Ah, sure, didn't I come straight up the front avenue, or what's left of it – me and Jack here, me husband, Jack Welsh, from beyant Cloone.'

'And will you stay? – is it true? – really stay?'

'Indeed why not? Sure there was no problem, once that divil Pat was out of the way. And our own children, aren't they all grown up now and we have time on our hands. Of course we'll stay! Once Mr Dermot here asked us and we knew you were coming back, sure there was no question. And isn't it the greatest thing ever? – to see you here again—'

'Yes, yes!' Hetty had tears in her eyes. 'You, though – I never thought – you back here!'

'Why wouldn't I be back here? – an' I with you from the very beginning, out on that island with all them savages! And I'd have been here all along, but for Pat

Kennedy and all the other . . . disturbances . . . And but for Jack.' She turned and smiled at her husband. 'Ye remember Jack? – Jack, up in the garden here?'

Hetty turned, shaking the man's hand. 'Yes . . .' She was hesitant, not really remembering him – a stoutish man in his fifties, strong-looking, with the clearest blue countryman's eyes and reddish cheeks.

'Oh, indeed, I remember you, Miss, Mrs . . .' he corrected himself, not sure how to address her.

'Miss *Cordiner*,' Hetty suddenly and resolutely said. For it was at that very moment – in this meeting with Elly, her old nurse, which finally confirmed her homecoming – that she took the final decision to throw over everything of her past life, resuming neither her married, stage nor Fraser name, but taking on that of her original family. 'Henrietta – Hetty – Cordiner.' She would have that as her name now – and for the rest of her life.

'Indeed,' Jack said, easier now. 'Indeed, Miss – and you up in the oul' walled garden, with Mickey, the under gardener then, remember him? – with that crab apple tree yonder that belonged to the childer here—'

'Yes! I remember! The magic apples – the apples of life!' She remembered how she had taken them for Robert, intent on saving his life, when he had whooping cough, and how her mother had cuffed and slapped her when she found her crouching outside Robert's sickroom door with the apples in the fold of her nightdress.

'The magic apples – and the jam!' Elly came in then, laughing hugely. 'Ye remember the jam-making, Miss? – in the big kitchen below? You and Mrs Molloy – God rest her soul – you were never out of the place in the old days, making greengage jam, I remember it well—'

'Yes, yes – so do I!' And Hetty did – the lovely greeny-yellow fluid, translucent, sugary, dripping from the long wooden spoon over the preserving pan on the great black range, the sticky labels, her neat copperplate writing

357

on the warm jars. The past – her whole childhood at Summer Hill, the joy and the pain there, all the drama which she had repressed or forgotten – was pricked into life for Hetty by these cues from Elly and Jack. These haphazard memorials of crab apples and greengage jam, unearthed from the years, became the emblems now of Hetty's resurrection, spirits disinterred from an autumn twenty years before, miraculously reborn, blossoming on the air of that mild April morning.

Just then a third figure poked her head round the dilapidated hall door – a scrawny beanpole with a quite unruly toss of white hair blowing out from beneath a floppy corduroy hat, wearing a long brown Aran knit cardigan. It was Aunt Emily. Hetty rushed forward to embrace her.

'Aunt! – how wonderful!' She clasped her great-aunt, almost squeezing the life out of her, so that the old lady, eventually disengaging herself, was breathless and more than usually huffy.

'Well,' she said recovering herself with a splutter. 'You're back . . .' She spoke in that harsh slight brogue that Hetty remembered so well, spoke as if Hetty had only been away for a week or two. 'Knew you would be. Had enough of the world, eh? Not surprised. All an imbecility, *tout court*. Heard you were married, too – enough of that, as well?' She looked at Hetty, a dismissive glint in her still-bright eyes. 'Can't say I didn't tell you. Men . . .' Her lined face curdled in deep displeasure. 'Worthless lot, from start to finish.'

'Oh, Aunt, not *all* men. Look at Dermot – and Jack!' She turned back to the others.

'*Excuse* yourself, girl. That's quite different. They're family.'

They all went inside then, through the ruined hall, filled with tea-chests and scattered furniture from the auction, passing beneath the forest of great pillars, beside the tattered Flemish tapestry, down a littered corridor – through the green baize door leading to the servants' quarters: a door which clunked shut behind Hetty in a most satisfying way, the sound risen from her past when, on the run from her mother, she moved across this clear frontier between pain and happiness, from the cold maternal dangers in the front of the house to the warmth, the peace, fun and security of Mrs Molloy's jam-filled kingdom at the back.

Here, in the old servants' quarters where the Kennedys had lived, the Welshes had cleaned up most of the squalor which they had left behind, making over the house-keeper's parlour into a temporary drawing and dining room for Hetty, with a bedroom, within calling distance in which had been the butler's pantry, where Hetty could settle herself and convalesce until the rest of the house was set in some kind of order.

Aunt Emily would not take lunch with them – a hot lunch of roast mutton and a few early vegetables which Elly had prepared. 'Have to finish a drawing,' she told them brusquely. 'That rogue Cassidy – out there on the front steps at the sale and all the jackals he had round him. Doing a series of them . . .'

'Yes, I saw you at your bedroom window,' Dermot remarked. 'Just after the hammer fell, looking pleased as punch. But how were you so certain the place wouldn't be sold out of the family?'

'Out of the *family*?' Aunt Emily looked genuinely puzzled. 'Oh, there was no question. I had a jinx out on that fellow Cassidy from the very beginning. And then, besides, when I was doing the first drawing of it all, that morning, with the vultures out all over the old pleasure gardens, didn't I see Hetty herself out there as well, clear as day, raising her paw, standing by the old astrolabe. Knew the place was coming back into the family then.'

Hetty was astonished. 'But, Aunt, how could you have seen me out there? I was in Dublin—'

'Excuse yourself, girl! I told you once – people are exactly where *you* want them in drawings. That's the whole point,' she went on in her slight brogue. 'I'm in charge when I draw. *I* make the running – not the buzzards and gombeen men.' And she stamped out of the room, rattling her stick against the dining room chair-legs as she went.

As they sat down to lunch Hetty looked round the bare, damp-stained walls. There was just one picture, a Landseer reproduction of 'The Stag at Bay' which the Welshes had rescued from somewhere as temporary decoration, hanging over the small mantelpiece. The horsehair stuffing was coming from one of the leather armchairs. The table they sat at, a mahogany dining table, was deeply scarred at one end, cut by bayonet marks, last used as a table in their armoury by the Black and Tans during their occupation of Summer Hill.

'Oh dear – where does one start?' Hetty, eyes returning, looked across at Dermot now.

'At the beginning . . .' He glanced back at her, struggling with a fatty piece on his chop. Hetty, leaving her meat, only tinkered with the vegetables. 'There's plenty of time. Do it up how you want, room by room. I estimate, between Mulrooney and myself, we must have bought back about half or two thirds of all the better furniture, pictures and things. So you can start out from scratch, painting the rooms, rearranging them, how you want. It's *yours*, Hetty.'

'Yes . . .' Hetty ran her hand nervously over the bayonet gashes in the table. 'But the damp and all the b-building repairs – the windows, the roof, the chimneys. All that w-would have to be done first, before there was any p-painting or rearranging of the furniture.'

'Yes, well, we're going to get a few of the old estate

workers back from the village – and Hoyne, the builder from Thomastown, to do the major repairs. I've talked to Jack about it. He's going to organize all that.'

'But the money. I'm bankrupt – haven't got a pe-pe-penny . . .'

'Yes. But with the money that was left after the purchase of the house and contents – some £20,000 I gather – Mr Mulrooney has given me that to hold in trust for you. So that can go towards the building repairs – if you agree. Then my Papa and I will invest a further £10,000 on your behalf – and you will have the income from that, not much, something under £1,000 a year, for the household running expenses. So all in all there'll be enough to see you started out again here.'

'Oh, Dermot, all that's too much – and too kind of you b-both. But started out on *what*, exactly?' For the first time since her recovery she looked at him almost desperately, the lines of worry and incapacity drawn again on her face, as she raked a thin hand through her prematurely greying curls.

'On change, Hetty. That's the main thing. You have to change your life,' he told her plainly. And seeing her haggard features again he went on even more bluntly. 'You've seen what'll happen if you don't – all that nonsense in Paris. The drinking and so on. Next time . . . it'll kill you.'

'Oh yes, I see that – all too well. And b-but for you I'd be dead already . . .' She gazed at him, head to one side, as if, at this angle, she might somehow wriggle her way into his heart. 'But *how* do I change my life?'

'Well, running Summer Hill, for a start. That's the whole point, isn't it? The house is back in the family now. And you must take responsibility for it. Why, there's some income to be made, too. Some of the trees in the demesne, dead or dying, they can be sold. Farm or rent out the fifty-acre water meadows over the river –

they're still part of the estate. The salmon traps by the bridge, the fishing rights – we still have them. Some money there. Get the vegetable garden going again, as a market garden perhaps. All that, Hetty, in time, when you're perfectly well again . . .'

He smiled at her, one of his short, quick, shy smiles.

'But you'll help me, Dermot? I c-c-can't do it all on my own.'

'Of course! I'll be over as often as I can, any leave I get—'

'But, Dermot, you're not leaving *yet*?'

He nodded. 'I have to, Hetty. Tomorrow on the mail boat from Dublin. I was due back at Sandhurst earlier this week, in fact—'

'But, Dermot . . .' She felt her face about to break into tears. Oh God, she thought, it was just as she'd feared, the same old thing: Dermot always leaving – never there, never permanent.

He reached over, taking her hand, secretly stricken himself. 'But I'll be back in the summer. And listen! – I'm trying to arrange to have the telephone put in, so that you can phone – long distance, to England even! So that I can telephone you as well. And I'll write. We'll both write. Give you all the advice and help you need.'

'But Dermot . . . ?' She had considered posing this question all morning. And now, in desperation at his leaving, she finally plucked up courage to ask it. 'Dermot, how can I manage all this huge place – by myself? C-c-couldn't you live here, a bit, yourself? Live here with me?' she added abruptly, in a startled tone, fearful of her audacity in finally putting her cards on the table.

'Hetty . . .' Dermot, who had feared just this same question all morning himself, looked away.

'Yes!' Hetty interrupted, allowing him no time for a refusal before she had completed her happy theory. 'Live here together. It'd be easy! Near your father in Dublin. Or just down on the train to the Waterford boat – for Sandhurst.'

'Hetty, I can't. I have a full-time job at Sandhurst. And I could hardly cross to and fro every weekend!' He tried to make light of it all.

'Well, give up the army then! And we could run the place together here – what's left of the estate, the market garden, the fishing rights . . .' She looked at him – not pleading, but wide-eyed, with all the clearest evidence, the imperatives of love.

Dermot sighed. 'I'm not really much good at estate management, market gardening . . .' He realized at once how lame this excuse must sound – as Hetty certainly did.

'Oh, damn the market gardening!' she cried. 'That wasn't the real point. D-d-don't you see?' She paused, looking across at Dermot, who had turned away again, as if to avoid some expected blow. 'Don't you *see* – I love you, Dermot. That's why I'd like you here.'

The die was finally cast. There was silence.

'Hetty,' Dermot said at last. 'I have much the same feeling for you—'

'Well, why not then?' She beamed in sudden hope.

'But not exactly the same feelings perhaps . . .'

'What then? You don't really like w-women, in that way?' She rushed on. 'You like men, don't you? I've thought that . . . the only explanation for your never marrying.'

Dermot avoided this issue. 'It's more . . . a familial love I feel for you, Hetty. I'd be no good in loving you – that way, in the expected ways.'

But Hetty was not to be discouraged by this, taking it quite in her stride. 'Well, that would hardly matter. With my problem – my "social disease" as they so politely put it – I can't now expect to love people, in *that* way, either!'

Hetty was bright again, believing that Dermot thought that sex was the only real obstacle between their coming together.

'It's not only that—'

'No!' Again she pre-empted him. 'I know you prefer men. But there's nothing wrong in that, absolutely not, not as far as I'm concerned. Lots of people in Hollywood were just like that – friends of mine, too,' she ran on, even more enthusiastically now. 'So that wouldn't be any problem between us. One can love men *and* women surely? I certainly have. Loving one doesn't have to exclude the other. The *loving* is surely the same, isn't it – whether it's for a man or a woman. And that's what counts, doesn't it? – the feelings, not the goings-on.'

'Yes, perhaps. Ideally. But situations, and the people involved, aren't always ideal. People, in the event, will rarely put up with that sort of loving – concurrently.'

'But I could. I'm sure I could – with you.' She looked at him, a crowd of different expressions crossing her once-more mobile face, a sense of mischief alive in her great blue eyes, compassion in her smile, the actress at large in her again, but expressing things truly felt now.

And Dermot, just as he had been with Frances thirty years before – when she had so consoled him and understood his feelings for her brother Henry after his death – was warmed, amazed by Hetty's almost identical response here. He saw, too, that just as he had once offered Frances marriage – both of them accepting these same conditions consequent on his nature – so, too, he might have embarked with Hetty, under the same equally understood conditions and handicaps.

And once more he was tempted for a moment – just as he had been with Frances all those years ago: to give up this aberration of his, as he saw it, this loving men, a covert passion which he had fed, yet which had haunted him for most of his life. Perhaps with Hetty and even at this late stage, he might cure himself of this sweet disease, find that it was not an indelible part of his nature. Perhaps, as he had helped her, she, in turn, might have the key which would release his spirit, his body, into normality.

He gazed at her: so sympathetic, vulnerable, so much more beautiful now that all her old arrogance and vanity, that fearful dominant regard, had slipped from her features. Oh yes, objectively, there was so much to love in her now, just as there had been long ago in her mother. But to live with her, to marry as he supposed, and thus be responsible for all her daily life and humours, her future? It was possible. But the risks were enormous. What if he failed – and he well might – to satisfy her, even in this sexless loving? And could there ever be such a thing for so attractive a woman as Hetty, who at thirty might one day be cured of her disease – her syphilis – and want that one thing which he could never give her.

As for himself – the leopard who changes his spots, he thought, has no more protection in the jungle. Camouflage gone, the animal, instead of living its nature, must fight every day for survival. Dermot decided then the risks were too great with Hetty and retreated back into the protection of his aberration.

'Well?' Hetty asked again. 'Couldn't I share – in your love?'

'Hetty, you've become wonderfully understanding – and *good*. But that's the whole point. You're recovering, you're already changing – from all that old earlier life that let you down. And you're only thirty. You've a chance to begin all over again. The disease can surely be cured – you're seeing that French doctor in Dublin regularly about it. And there's no reason, in time, that you shouldn't take up with someone else. I'm nearly fifty-five!' he added lightly.

Hetty was crestfallen, shaking her head, wounded. 'As

if that m-m-mattered – your age. As if age mattered in loving either. You're just avoiding the issue – b-bringing that up.'

'No, honestly, I don't think I am—'

'You just don't want to live with me,' she said rather piteously. 'When you know you could, because there *wouldn't* be any demands – and you said you *did* f-feel for me . . .'

Hetty's whole expression had changed. She was heartbroken. But Dermot remained calm. He had to.

'No demands you say, Hetty. No, not now. But do you really believe, at your age, that you're *never* going to make any demands, ever again? No demands now, in your illness, convalescence. But when you're really better – you'll know you are, because then there'll be things you *want* again, badly want—'

'You! I'll want *you* . . .'

'I'll always be there. Promise you.'

'But not here.'

'Not immediately. But when I retire – when Papa goes – I'd always hoped, perhaps, to come back and live here, not Islandbridge. The house is big enough! And I'd be with you then, Hetty. But meanwhile there is another point: my life *now*. You see, I still love the army very much. That's what I've offered to life. And I get a marvellous return. And I want to keep that exchange going a bit longer. I'm sure you'll find something of the same sort to fill your life with – not the cinema, not *people*, but some other passion. We have to have other things besides people in our lives – something non-human to live with, to *change* our lives with.'

'But how? *What* can I change my l-life with? Not by just sitting here for years, doing up and tinkering with Summer Hill. I'm no more interior decorator – or market gardener – than you are.'

'You'll find something – you'll see. It'll come out of

the blue one day, when you've quite recovered. And there's the real point of it all, Hetty – we can only ever change our lives *ourselves*. Other people can be stepping stones. Only you can get to the other bank . . .'

'No, no . . .' Hetty tried to hide her tears, turning away from him – until she saw a furry shape, pushing its way round the door, peering into the parlour. It was a cat, black and fat, with a white bib. 'Pussy, pussy,' Hetty said between her tears, beckoning it – and the cat, tail suddenly erect, came trotting over to her. Turning back to Dermot, still seeing him only as a cloudy shape, she took the piece of gristle from his plate and handed it down to the animal which, reaching up, clutched at it, squirrel-like, before devouring it.

'You see,' Dermot said. 'You've already got company, a new friend . . .' As he spoke, he remembered an almost identical incident, with an almost similar cat, in the crowded saloon bar at the Bear Hotel in Salisbury more than thirty years before when, as he lunched with Frances, she had leant forward to his plate, in just the same manner, offering that other earlier cat a similar piece of gristle. Strange continuities . . .

But that was exactly how it should be, he suddenly thought. The black cat then, and its repetition here – this was surely a perfect omen. That was precisely what all his efforts over Summer Hill had been about – the continuity of family in these three Cordiner women: the first two had ruined or squandered their inheritance and gone, but he hoped this third would in time manage to rebuild herself and the family's fortunes.

And surely Hetty, freed from these two bitter and unhappy women at last, and returned to the soft airs of her country and her home, would do just that – would now truly recover, reanimate all those older and happier Cordiner traditions, when Summer Hill would finally be warmed again, the promise reawakened.

Dermot's was the romantic attitude. And that was the 'passion' – Summer Hill the thing 'out of the blue' – which, though he had not wanted to insist on it, he hoped would come to Hetty, which would fill her life while at the same time giving life back to the great house. That was the non-human pursuit which he had forecast for her, which he hoped she would marry – not him.

A little more understanding of the human heart might have made him see it more realistically. But Dermot – wounded so often before by his nature – had come to love and understand solid brick and mortar better than he did the perverse eruptions, the splendours and miseries of the heart. He did not quite see that Hetty, though longing to change, was no recluse – was not temperamentally built to change her life purely by falling in love with a house. Rather this was Dermot's very nature – a long obsession with renewing old Cordiner certainties and traditions, in the shape of Hetty, a form, he hoped, now undevilled and untinged by aberration.

Dermot pined for an immutable order of brick and mortar, which posed no threat – as women invariably did. So for him this renewal of Summer Hill could not include marriage or any other serious emotional involvement with Hetty. What he wanted of the house was an emblem of restored familial honour, behind which he could the more securely hide his real nature. Hetty would change the house, bring it to order again, when he – indistinguishable once more against this renewed lustre and propriety – could be confirmed in his camouflage. Dermot in this way probably needed Summer Hill more than Hetty – for, though frightened of nothing else, he was horrified by the anarchy which his nature implied, and so had been equally dismayed by the deviations of the lives of both Frances and Hetty, which had resulted in the fall of Summer Hill. Thus to restore the house was to still all such disruption – his own, his family's, the world's.

Only the vaguest intimations of all this occurred to Dermot as he drove away from Summer Hill later that afternoon. He had always lived in action, not in thought – least of all thoughts of this kind, which he had successfully repressed over the years. Dermot, as well as being a romantic, was an honourable man.

Hetty, standing on the porch steps, watched his car disappear down the drive, the rooks screaming again in the late-afternoon light, the great flank of Mount Brandon touched with pale-blue tints of evening, silence descending everywhere as the sound of the engine died away and the birds settled.

Very tired, she knelt on the stone steps, hands flopped in her lap, palms outward as if still waiting for the gift denied her in Dermot, head bowed, kneeling in the dying light, quite immobile, too exhausted even to cry. Elly found her ten minutes later, still crouching there, her cheek touched by the crimson rays of sunset.

'Miss, ye *mustn't* be out here like that in the chill. I've some tea made in the kitchen – jam and a fruit cake I baked . . .'

Elly helped her up. But Hetty could hardly move with weariness. 'Ah, ye'll be all right.' She moved her forward. 'Didn't I know ye'd be tired after all your travels and sickness. So didn't Jack find this old wheelchair up in the attics – and ye can use that!'

Hetty saw the chair in the hall doorway then – the same chair that she and Léonie had used after their accidents years before. She smiled weakly now.

'Why, Elly! – That was Léonie's! Léa's chair.'

Hetty looked round at the shadows seeping forward everywhere, down the ruined lawn terraces, over the pot-holed gravel, up the porch steps, where a last shaft of sunset light caught the wheelchair now, illuminating it, touching the wickerwork with a faint gold. Then, helped forward by Elly, she collapsed into it. Léonie, she thought – Léa, beloved Léonie . . . And all the terrible wrong she had done her. She had come home. And yet she was only at the very beginning of things. It wasn't just the house that had to be repaired – that was almost the least of it, she thought. There was so much else to repair – to atone for – with people.

Jack came into the hall, carrying an oil lamp in his hand. The so-remembered smell of paraffin suddenly filled Hetty's nostrils, the soft light illuminating the torn Flemish tapestry as they passed it, Hetty gazing up at the royal hunt it depicted, stories of medieval kings and queens, a world of violent grandeur. And Hetty thought herself well finished with all that then – that world of arrogance, power, vanity and obsessive self-will where she had lived too long.

She turned the other way, looking up at Elly. 'Yes, Elly,' she said, 'we'll have tea – and jam and fruit cake, won't we?'

Elly nodded, as the lamplit procession made its way out of the hall, along the corridor, and through the green baize door, which thunked behind them, leaving the hall in darkness but for a faint coloured glow, illuminating the little pane of stained glass in the big window – the Cordiner coat of arms, the spreadeagle on the visored helmet: 'Fortune Favours the Brave'.

2

For nearly three months Robert had been totally occupied, to and fro between London and Paris – covering the new Anglo-French trade and tariff agreements – and had thus been quite unable to travel to Ireland, as he had earlier intended.

Now, however, the conference over, he had been given a few days' leave as recompense for his extra efforts. Meanwhile, too, Dermot, back at Sandhurst, had come up to London for the weekend to his South Kensington flat where Robert had met him alone, hearing all the news – first of Frances's death and then of Summer Hill and its conditional repossession by Hetty. This had astonished and pleased him – though Dermot had not mentioned his theory as to the identity of her benefactor. 'Hetty's always been lucky in her admirers,' was all he said tactfully.

'Why don't you and Léa – and the child – go over and see Hetty?' he had gone on to say then, feeling rather guilty for having deserted her himself and hoping for just such a meeting in any case, seeing it as very much part of the whole renewal of things – at Summer Hill and for Hetty: a renewal of friendship between these three old friends, whom he knew to have so fallen out over the years. Such a reconciliation would put the seal on his success in re-establishing the house and Hetty herself.

'I'd very much wanted to go over, when I heard the house was to be sold. I was pretty upset – about the house.'

'And Hetty?' Dermot asked with even more tact.

'Less so, I have to admit.'

'Of course, she behaved very badly . . .'

'More to Léonie than to me.'

'Yes, they'd been such close friends . . .' Dermot left the real nature of their friendship, which he had long suspected and which Hetty had more or less confirmed for him the week before, hanging awkwardly in the air for an instant. He was glad that friendship was over – one more disruptive emotion. 'At the same time,' he hurried on, 'it'd be nice if one . . . could make things up now.'

'Yes.' Robert was almost eager. 'Though Léonie isn't so inclined.'

Dermot nodded. 'And you, you've had your difficulties with Hetty, as well. Not easy. All the same, settled now yourself – perhaps it'd be the moment? And you see!' he had turned to Robert enthusiastically. 'Hetty's quite changed now, setting out on a new life, with none of that old petulance and cruelty, that domineering need to fight and win all the time. You wouldn't recognize her! And I'm sure she'd like to see you, know she had your support – for this new life she's setting up for herself at Summer Hill. You know, she's often told me, since her recovery, how *bad* she feels about the way she behaved to you and Léonie. She really wants to make things up with you now, with both of you. I know she does. So why don't you go? And perhaps Léonie might come to think better of her as well – in time. I hope so. Because you see, Robert, now the house is back in the family again, that's really what Summer Hill must be all about in the future: a place for *all* of you – especially you, so much a part of the family – to visit, live in, whatever. And little Olivia, too! Can't waste it – with just Hetty there in the huge place all on her own.'

Robert, in the light of Dermot's obvious sincerity and enthusiasm, had been largely convinced by these reflections and suggestions. Léonie, when he told her of all this back in Hampstead, had not been convinced.

'The leopard doesn't change its spots,' she said abruptly, on hearing how Hetty had altered, how much she wanted to make things up with them both now.

'Dermot said for us all to go over. Won't you?'

'No, no—'

'Oh, Léa, if Hetty's changed—'

'She hasn't, I bet! It's another of her acts. She did just

the same thing to us both in Egypt, don't you remember?
– when we met her in that temple with the horses: being
nice as anything and pretending she'd quite changed and
how she was *so sorry* for what she'd done—'

'But she's not an actress any more—'

'And you think, just because she's no longer an actress,
that means she's stopped acting *herself*? That's nonsense!
I know her – better than you. Why, acting is the heart
of her nature – and people can't ever really give *that* up!
They'd be dead if they did.'

'But that's just it! Her old nature very nearly did kill
her. Dermot told me all about what happened to her in
Paris, her vast debts, her alcoholism, pneumonia, in the
hospital there. She's bound to change now. Or die.'

'Well, I can't help that. I tried to help her, so *much*,
in the old days. And you know what happened – it nearly
killed *me*. So I'm not going to start on any of that again.'

'Yes, I see all that, Léa. And I was hurt, almost as
much. But she's *family* to me. Can't you see that? Practically my sister. And Summer Hill my home. So my going
over there won't have anything to do with what happened
later between all of us – the rows and betrayals. Only
about now, the *future*.'

'Well, maybe you can forgive and forget that easily. I
can't.'

'Léa, you're being unreasonable. I only want to see the
house – not dig up any rotten old emotions in it.'

'You're being naïve.' She was bitterly sardonic.

'No. Just realistic.'

'About such old emotions? They never really die – I
told you, when we last talked about Hetty.'

'That's what worries me, Léa – with you. Those old
emotions – they've dug in so deep, rotting away. Get
them out into the air – and they'll disappear.'

She had snorted at this. 'That's how old emotions
bloom again, you idiot! – in the air.'

'You know what I mean—'

'Oh yes, I know what you mean: *you* don't know what you mean. You don't know what you're really saying!'

They were fighting now, for the first time since the events in Egypt. So that Robert, suddenly aghast, decided to curtail the whole argument, though his tone remained none the less abrupt, bruised. 'I'm sorry, Léa – if you feel like that. Let's drop it. I have to go to Ireland. I want to go to Summer Hill. I've every perfectly good reason to go – and I'm going.'

Robert, if he was to make use of his short leave, had to take it at once. So he caught the boat train to Fishguard that same afternoon, without having time to warn Hetty of his arrival, quite preoccupied instead by Léa's latest reactions to Hetty's return, thinking of them on the long train journey to Wales. He had been shocked by this re-emergence, after so long, of Léa's bitter enmity towards her old friend – a feeling he had thought quite dead in her, dissolved in the renewal of their own close marriage and her happy absorption with the child. It simply was not like Léa – so open, warm, forgiving, realistic in her American way – that she should still harbour this striking animosity. Was it fear of a return to her own old nature, in loving women? Perhaps. Yet in any case that wasn't the point in this instance, as he had so clearly told her. What really mattered to him in all this was the survival of his home, his 'family' in the shape of Hetty, together with Dermot and Mortimer, and his need to see how things stood now at Summer Hill.

Had she completely forgotten that he was without parents, orphaned years before in Domenica, and how therefore he, at least, had naturally always loved Summer Hill, had been desolated at the news of its impending sale and was now, equally naturally, overjoyed at its astonishing return to the family – which included him?

Yes, she had forgotten. Or, worse still, she had wilfully

blinded herself to all these other facts, so obsessed had she become again with her own old problems over Hetty, when she should have had the courage and the charity – which she showed in every other matter – to face up to her bad feelings over Hetty, dismiss them as the chimeras they were, and support him in all this renewal.

Instead, self-indulgently taking the scabs off old sores, she seemed intent only on running Hetty down, taking no account whatsoever of her vast distress – her near-death, in the first instance – and then giving her not an ounce of credit for her subsequent strengths, her fortitude in recovery, her determination to turn over a new leaf, above all her heartfelt wish, as Dermot had described it, to make amends with them both for her earlier appalling behaviour.

It was all so uncharacteristic of Léa. And, whatever she felt about Hetty, the fact that Léa saw none of his own quite separate feelings in the matter hurt him most of all. After all, in her earlier trouble with Hetty, after she had returned to him from Egypt, he had seen her point of view, consoled, understood, forgiven her. Whereas now, in a matter quite without such blazing emotional overtones, one simply of familial concern, Léa had offered him no help or understanding at all. He felt deeply hurt by this, feeling another clear division between them – a horrifying sense of real absence from her, loneliness, as he gazed out of the carriage window into the dark night.

After Robert had left, Léonie consoled herself with the child, playing with Olivia on the hearthrug by the fire until long past her bedtime.

'He doesn't see, you see,' she whispered to the uncomprehending little girl, as she dangled Thompson, the teddy bear, in front of her daughter. 'He has *no* idea – and I can't tell him,' she went on, handing the bear to Olivia, who took him up vigorously, crushing him to her cheek. Léonie, kneeling on the hearthrug, watching her daughter, but thinking of Robert and Hetty, could make no sense of her conflicting emotions, shared between both of them once more. Now, with Robert's departure for Summer Hill, all her old feelings for Hetty, which she had repressed for so long, came to the boil again.

Before, when Hetty had been so besotted with Craig Williamson, a distant frivolous picture star in Hollywood, she had posed no threat to her. At first, though desperately wanted, Hetty had simply been unobtainable. Then, loving Robert, she was unwanted, almost forgotten. Afterwards there had been the shocking mischance of their meeting in Egypt, all her old feelings for Hetty disastrously renewed. And that, she had been certain, was the final meeting, the ultimate lesson. Making things up with Robert, she was determined they should never meet again, that Hetty would never again threaten their marriage.

But now, with Hetty's fall from Hollywood, rather than just disappearing into anonymity, she had tumbled headlong into their own domestic orbit once more. Having almost wished her dead and Summer Hill destroyed or sold, Léa had instead come to see Hetty not only recovered but in possession of Summer Hill again, so giving life to all the ghosts of their past together there, revivifying their love, which as long as Hetty had remained untrue to herself in another world, pursuing her false life in pictures, she had been able to repress.

Now the past lived, as Hetty did – Hetty who by all accounts had finally gained her real self, that mix of courage, candour, vivacity and deep feeling which she had always known lay at the heart of her character. Hetty had come into this true inheritance at last, in temperament and materially, so realizing all her greatest hopes – which were now fears. Fallen to earth in this true spirit, Léonie thought she could not rest until she had seen Hetty again, confirmed this magic transformation, shared in it. Yet if she saw her she knew not what disasters might ensue. 'I will wait for you,' she had written to Hetty twelve years before when she had first gone to America. And here Hetty was, waiting for her: she, who until a few hours ago, had been so completely and happily married to Robert.

No wonder she could not explain to him her bitter animosity towards Hetty. How – admitting it finally – could one tell one's husband that you loved someone else so much you had to pretend just the opposite, that you *hated* that other person? And yet even that wasn't true, Léonie realized. The violent turmoil in her heart just then made one thing clear to her at least. She loved and hated Hetty equally – wished her dead, yet longed to be with her. How explain such a mix of wicked and tender emotions to anyone?

'So you see,' she said softly to her daughter, words breaking into her thoughts, 'what can I do – loving them both like this?'

Olivia, responding to what for her were just sweet sounds from her mother, thrust the teddy bear at her. But Léonie, just like Robert then on the train, was not to be consoled. Instead she too felt a frightful loneliness, an absence from the two people who, once again she knew now, meant most to her in her life.

Robert, arriving at Thomastown station next morning, found Matty, old Joe Newman's son, whom he had known vaguely as a boy years before – now running the station taxi service, no longer in the shape of a hackney trap but a battered Austin motor. Happy in this continuity of things, in a countryside he had not been in for nearly ten years, he took the taxi straight to Summer Hill, basking in these renewed visions, memories confirmed in a landscape hardly changed at all, he thought, as he drove south, along the twisting river valley road towards Cloone.

Everything seemed more wild and unkempt since he had lived there – the margins and potholes of the road, the landscape: that was the only difference. Or perhaps it was just the brilliant growth of spring which gave this impression – the tall hedgerows ablaze with hawthorn blossom, the budding chestnuts in the village square as he entered seeming vast now, with an almost exotic abundance, spilling right over the railings, huge branches almost smothering the little shops all round. Ireland, in the intervening years, in its new guise as a Free State, had quite gone to seed and run wild, he felt – a world being smothered by moss and dead leaves, disappearing behind tangled briars and great raggedy trees, overwhelmed in drifts of hawthorn blossom, an enchanted kingdom, a lost estate.

With the fine breezy weather, and since he only had an overnight bag, he left the taxi in the village, deciding to walk along the river avenue, then up the hill by the back way to Summer Hill. A minute later, passing through the lower gates, he moved into the shadows of the demesne under the heavy trees, the canopy of great beeches that lined the river gorge here – the salmon traps and the water, high after spring rains, a sun-dappled flow to his left. After a mile, coming to the stone boathouse, he turned right up the steeply-winding track through the birch plantations, emerging a few minutes later on top of the gorge. The house was suddenly above him, a shimmer of stone set against its semi-circle of budding trees, fired by the sun.

His heart beat faster as he neared it along the old beech walk, hidden by these trees – wood pigeons above him, alarmed by his steps making sudden wing-cracking bolts into the sky, pheasants squawking in the undergrowth, a cuckoo calling repeatedly nearby. Home . . .

Crossing the ruined pleasure gardens, he made for the great portico, the battered hall door partly open, welcoming him. But when he pushed inside the whole house seemed deserted. He gazed about at the debris of tea-chests, fallen stucco, furniture piled haphazardly everywhere, still with the auctioneer's labels on them.

'Hetty?' he called out. But there was no answer – no voice but his in the loud spring.

Standing there a minute on the threshold, he breathed the air wafting in behind him, mixed now with the smell of damp and decay from the ruined hall. Turning back, he threw open both sides of the great door, so that the warmer breeze outside rushed in, obliterating the musty climate inside, flowing up the stairs and along the landings, through open doorways, a zephyr of renaissance, flushing the house with its fragrance.

Robert, looking for Hetty, followed the wind up the stairs, the broken glass pendants in the huge Waterford chandelier tinkling in the sudden disturbance. Reaching the first floor he walked round the stairwell balustrade, then down a first long bedroom corridor, back along the second, poking his nose into open doorways, inspecting the cluttered, mouldering rooms, yet light-hearted, walking the marches of his home in his search for Hetty.

Finally, taking the narrow staircase up to the top floor, he found himself opposite Henry's suite of old work-rooms. The door was ajar. Pushing it open, he seemed to have arrived in some tropic jungle – long arms of ivy and Virginia creeper, with the thorny briars of a climbing rose, which years before as tendrils had crept through a broken window-pane, had now expanded vastly about the old rooms, half-filling the space, smothering the work bench by the window, throttling Henry's old bunsen burner, his bell jars and retorts, the glass long since smashed in the ivy's slow grip, before the foliage had swelled onwards, falling to the floor, cocooning the stuffed crocodile, so that the beast looked all the more dangerous, its wicked eyes and snout poking up through the greenery as if from some Nile swamp – until finally, in slimmer tendrils, the vegetation ran out, garlanding the old horsehair sofa by the door with sprigs and buds, as if the seat had been part of a stage set, prepared for some bucolic revels.

'Hetty?' Robert, doubting she was here, looked about him, stepping gingerly through the foliage.

Hetty, who that morning, as on previous days, had been moving up through the house making inventories and taking notes of what might be done in the way of repairs and decorating, was in the next room, the little museum with its glass display cases of Henry's butterflies and stuffed animals. Hidden behind these cases, she heard the briars rustle in the next room. Then, beyond the open doorway, she thought she saw Robert caught in a shaft of sunlight, his figure refracted, distorted in the glass, confirming what was obviously an illusion. The figure turned, retreated, disappeared, so that she was certain now of its unreality. Then she heard the oath.

'Damn it!'

Robert had tripped in the tangled network of creeper. Rushing into the room, Hetty found him spreadeagled on the mass of vegetation, next to the crocodile's snout, the searching knight-errant come to grief in a most undignified manner.

'Robert!' she screamed, as she helped him up, embracing him before he had a chance to resist. They stood there, together, Hetty in a pair of old slacks and floppy pullover, Robert garlanded like a wood demon with ivy leaves and bits of creeper. 'What *are* you doing here?'

'Here?' he asked vaguely, a little stunned, picking a thorn from his hand. 'Yes, here,' he answered himself awkwardly. 'Sorry I didn't have time to let you know—'

'Oh, that's nothing. Just, I meant – up *here*.' She looked at him, perplexed.

'Well, I couldn't see you anywhere else. So I came up to the top—'

'No – it's just that before I saw you, I'd been *thinking* of you – in there by the old porcupine!'

'Yes?'

'Yes! All those sharp quills . . . reminded me of you in the old days.' She laughed, but quite without any of her old cruelty. 'You were so unapproachable then.'

'Oh, was I?' He had remembered rather the opposite – how he had so longed to approach Hetty.

'Yes. But I was such a little bitch then, teasing and getting at you all the time. No wonder you had sharp quills!'

She looked at him with an elation which her fragile body seemed barely able to contain. She was so changed, Robert saw at once. Nothing of the regal, arrogant picture star remained. The imperious vanity, the lines of spite, the fevered dominance – all this had dissolved, to be replaced by a haunting finesse. Her face had undergone a complete distillation, each feature refined, the skin paler, almost translucent, nose straighter and thinner, chin and cheek-bones more prominent beneath a toss of faintly greying hair – and yet, in all, more beautiful, he thought.

'Yes, so strange to see you up here again,' Hetty ran on breathlessly. 'Just look at the place! Talk about going to seed. And yet beneath nothing's really changed at all – all held in aspic – by the ivy!'

Hetty wandered about, stepping carefully over the matted floor of vegetation. 'Look! – even that old snake skeleton in the tea-chest!' She had moved over to the box by the fireplace. 'How you used to tease *me* with it – when we used the place as a secret den.'

'Yes—'

'Where Mama couldn't get at us – and I could take off those frightful ticklish Irish clothes she made me wear.'

'Oh yes . . .' Robert could barely take in all these enthusiastic memories of Hetty's.

Seeing this, she apologized. 'It's just, coming up here for the first time today, I'd been thinking of all these things we did here – and then that *you* should appear at the same moment. Something must be meant!' She laughed easily, rattling the snake skeleton for a moment, then letting it fall back into the tea-chest, closing the lid firmly.

Later, after Robert had seen Aunt Emily and had an astonished meeting with Elly in the kitchen, he and Hetty had lunch alone in the housekeeper's old parlour, when Hetty, in a rush of news, brought him up to date on all her affairs. Robert was more guarded, particularly when Hetty enquired of Léonie.

'She's well,' he said, saying no more, so that Hetty looked at him quizzically.

'Oh, Robert, don't worry, I only asked. Nothing like that is ever going to happen between us again. All that's changed, in me at least. Truly. Quite another sort of life for me here, don't quite know what yet. But *nothing* of that old life. Yet you seem somehow sad – about her?'

'No.' He brushed the idea aside. Hetty had lost none of her old intuitiveness, he realized, in all her changes. But Hetty sensed that something was amiss between them, and thought she knew what. 'Of course, she didn't want to come over, because of me . . .'

'Yes,' Robert admitted. 'She still feels—'

'Naturally. How's she to know there's anything different in me? But I *have* changed, I have to—'

'Yes, I told Léa that – you were so ill . . .' Knowing of her alcoholism and pneumonia, if not her syphilis, Robert was tactful. Hetty was much more forthcoming.

'My actual illnesses were the least of it! I wasn't really

infected by anything except myself. It all came from the crazy way I was living: the picture business, that brute Williamson, my drinking. But I *chose* to live that way. So the real change has to be up here.' She tapped her head.

After lunch, in the bright weather, they took a turn outside, walking up through the long grass of the old terraced lawns – the great exotic trees, the Canadian maple, the Wellingtonia and the cedar towering above them. Hetty, needing support over the matted carpet, took Robert's arm.

They passed the grotto, some of its white limestone boulders just visible, its waterfall now entirely hidden behind a tangle of nettle and ivy. The domed stone dove-cote came into sight, though the doorway and all the lower brickwork were hidden by impenetrable clumps of elder.

'The awful row we had in there,' Hetty remarked. 'When you frightened away my pet dove!'

'Yes . . . You weren't alone, in being difficult.'

Pushing on through a thicker tangle, they came to the line of old wire cages against the kitchen garden wall where Henry had kept his menagerie of snakes and wild animals years before, now almost entirely obliterated. Something stirred in the dank undergrowth – a pheasant or a blackbird – but enough to make Hetty start, gripping Robert's arm more firmly, shivering.

'I never liked this place,' she said. 'Remember how we always kept well clear of it? – after Mickey Joe told us how the snakes got Uncle Henry up here—'

'Yes, and we didn't believe him, because Elly had told us there were no snakes in Ireland. St Patrick had booted them all out—'

'But Elly knew perfectly well he'd been killed by them – just covering up. Everyone covering up everything then. I *hated* that worst of all. Not telling the truth.' She paused, reflecting. 'But then I took just the same line myself later: avoiding the truth. Runs in the family. Oh dear, what a mess we Cordiners always get ourselves into – and now this.' She surveyed the decaying scene. 'A total mess.'

'Well—'

'And all to be put in some kind of order.'

'By degrees . . .'

'You're just like Dermot, saying that!'

But Hetty did not underline the problems ahead of her, as she had with Dermot. Robert was not needed with the same kind of rash emotion. He was more brother to her once more, and so a confidant in quite different, older intimacies.

Passing on into the walled kitchen garden they were confronted by a wilderness, the tall apple and plum trees run riot above a jungle of swaying grass, the once-neat paths now rivers of weed, the old strict vegetable rows, raspberry canes and gooseberry bushes submerged beneath a tide of weeds.

Finally, walking over a scented patch where the old herb border had been, their feet releasing a faint odour of thyme and sage, they came into the smaller walled garden, the children's garden which generations of Cordiner offspring had planted out, and where only the crab apple tree, wizened and raggedy, its furthest branches crackling in the wind high up, still survived, one branch fallen, with several of last year's minute yellow apples still attached to it.

'The magic apples,' Hetty said. 'Remember? When you were so ill with that awful whooping cough and I thought they were the cure – Mickey Joe told me – and I tried to smuggle them up to you, before Mama caught me by the scruff of the neck . . . !'

'Only just. I remember the dark room and the awful smell of camphor oil. And, of course, your Mama . . .

not that row, but all the other fearful rows you had with her—'

'Yes. Because of my Papa mostly – his not being my real Papa . . .' She turned to him. 'There was all that too. Remember?'

'Never forgotten. Does it still . . . worry you?'

'Yes, I think it does – because I'm sure he was someone else. And I've no idea who . . . But then it was much worse for you, knowing but *losing* both your parents. And I was such a selfish, unfeeling prig, taking so little account of all that. Robert, I am so sorry.' She gripped his arm more firmly still. 'All that past, when there was just us – and things only you and I shared. And I wrecked so much of that, for you, for both of us – things that could have been so precious then – and now. I wish I could make up for it all – the cruelties, towards you and Léa. Just awful.' She bowed her head at the memory. 'But I am going to *try* and make up for it all. And none of those old emotional n-nonsenses is ever going to come between you and me again. Robert?' She looked at him, calmly, gravely.

'Yes,' he said. 'I believe you.'

She took his arm again, looking up at him. 'I'm so happy – because you're the person I'm really closest to. I never really stammered with you then, remember? You were the only one. That's how close we were. And I've not really been st-st-stammering with you now, have I?'

They laughed. 'No.'

A bumblebee droned heavily past them, climbing steeply over the high wall. Pigeons murmured in the woods beyond. But the two of them in the hot sunshine, hidden in the secret garden where there was no wind, were no longer part of that other, outer, present world. Instead, drifting back, they were almost children again.

They really had so much more in common with each other than with anyone else – more to remember, more to offer each other now. Robert felt this, so did Hetty, without need of further words. Their arms linked together, without the least embarrassment or tension, said it all. And nothing would have breached this sibling innocence, if Robert had not taken one of the yellow crab apples from the fallen branch beside him, biting into it briefly, before offering it to Hetty. 'Nice. Not as bitter – like they used to be. Try it?'

Hetty, offered the apple, suddenly changed her expression, frowning, downcast. But she took it, biting into it heedlessly where Robert's teeth had been. Then she started to cry.

'What's the matter?'

'Nothing, only . . .' She turned away, her whole frail body shaking with emotion.

She was so piteous a figure that Robert, moving toward her, could not but more openly console her. He took her arm. 'Hetty, what *is* it?' Before he really knew what he was doing, he had taken her in his arms. In another moment, when she responded, he was kissing her, feeling the smoothness, then the slithery damp of her tear-stained face, and then neither of them could restrain this – for Robert – so-long unrequited and repressed emotion, to which Hetty now, for the first time in all their years, responded, fully, warmly, joyously.

Afterwards, both shaken to the depths, they looked at each other.

'Oh God,' Hetty said, her face, like Robert's, a mixture of amazement and horror. This was the last thing they had wanted or expected. And now that it had happened their childhood dissolved, innocent memories shattered. Now, in this admission of love, they were quite new people to each other. And both, though enraptured by the change, were appalled by its implications. So that at first they tried to pretend that nothing of importance had occurred, not speaking of it. But this was a useless ploy.

There was so much at stake now in these restless emotions they knew they could not be held down indefinitely. They had to speak of them.

After dinner, when Aunt Emily had gone upstairs, with a fire in the half-refurbished drawing room, Hetty turned the zoetrope, the old peepshow machine rescued in the auction, gazing through the spinning slats as the little dog laughed to see such fun and the cow jumped over the moon. Then, putting her hand to the wheel, she brought it to a sudden stop.

'What do we do?' But, before Robert had a chance to reply, she answered her own question. 'You can't stay here with me – though God knows that's what I'd love, the most p-p-perfect thing – do up the house together. *Our* house, after all.'

'Yes . . . And, no, I can't stay. There's Léa and Olivia,' he went on, downcast.

'There's no use feeling guilty about it. But I do.' She glanced up at him quickly, looking for some sort of confirmation or denial.

'Yes,' was all he said, equally ambiguously.

'Oh, Robert, you liked me so much – in the old days, and I knew it, and I was so cold to you. Well, I suppose that's just another change in me. I like – I love you now. Don't I? I do.'

'And Léonie?'

'Loving her – that was all part of my past, going down dead ends. The need to win – with everything and anybody, it didn't matter who or what. Léonie wasn't really me.'

'I love her, though.'

'Of course.' She sighed, turning the wheel again, the fantastic, potent, inexplicable life inside set in motion once more. 'Loving two people? – I've known that well enough. Or is it?' She looked up at him carefully. 'Perhaps it was just a fit we both had up there in the children's garden. Thinking of the past, all those old feelings. Just a fit?' she asked, hoping Robert might confirm this so that they could then forget about the whole thing – yet at the same time longing for him to say it had not been; that the whole thing had been wonderfully real. The fire crackled in the silence – Hetty's new friend, the black cat called Ethel, curled up by the fender.

Robert saw the same chance as Hetty. He could easily deny his feelings, and hers, dismiss the whole thing as just a fit, a mere physical consolation, an explosion consequent on all the renewed emotions from their shared past. What more natural than that they should have been momentarily overcome by these old feelings?

But he could not deny his feelings. And he did not want to. Something vital had come into his life then, in Hetty's arms up in the little garden. Something he had longed for all those years ago, had now been achieved, reciprocated, so that he felt transformed, fulfilled. All his anguish in loving Hetty then had now been justified, his suit returned, his life made good. The past, seemingly so completely lost, had now been astonishingly regained. One could not pretend such a transformation had never happened.

'No,' he said. 'It wasn't a fit. And you're right: loving two people. I feel that – for you. And Léa.'

He turned away. Hetty relaxed. 'Well, there's no point getting into the d-d-dumps about it. It's one of the best things that's ever happened to me. This feeling I have for you – makes me the person I know I always ought to have been, going the proper way at last, with *you*, which is what I should have done all those years ago. Yes! – married you! And it's extraordinary, because I wasn't just a cold prig to you then, I *hated* you! Getting in the way between me and Léa, here at Summer Hill, and then when you finally married her, I was absolutely beside myself in hating you! Yet now there's this love of you.

Was it there all along, hidden in what was my *real* nature? Is that how one can love and hate someone at the same time? – because the feelings come from two quite separate parts of our nature, the good and bad? – the bad part which we don't know about, or won't admit to, as I certainly didn't. Do you think that's how it is, so that, when we have a terrible, unreasonably strong hatred for someone, it can sometimes be that we love them just as fiercely?'

As she was speaking Robert suddenly thought of Léonie. And it came to him in a flash. Yes, of course, what Hetty had said was true – for Léonie as well. Because this was just how Léonie was behaving. This explained her bitter animosity towards Hetty. She hated her violently because she secretly loved her just as much. So that now he said, with full conviction, 'Yes, I'm sure you're right. That can happen – exactly.'

But he could not tell Hetty of this new thought about Léonie. The whole idea was too undermining already – this clear intuition he had now that Léa's hatred of Hetty was something from the worst part of her nature, and that at heart Léonie still loved her – as he did now. Oh God, he thought. Where were their bright promises, made but a few hours before, of appropriate, sensible life – all three of them, separately and together? He and Hetty might have saved themselves, escaped their predicament, simply by his departure, his absence on the following day. But if, on his return to London, he confirmed how Léonie had been repressing just the same sort of passionate feelings for Hetty, what hope was there for his marriage? It would be based on a lie.

Had it, in fact, and despite all Léonie's earlier avowals, been a lie all along? Was Léa quite incapable of changing her real nature – as Hetty had done, was doing? Or was it, with Léa, as Hetty had suggested, simply a matter of her loving two people, just as he loved both women, a division in himself, similar to Léa's, which he had only just discovered.

In which case, like musical chairs, only Hetty in her new reformation, loving him alone, was going to be left out. Or a further horror – compounded by his feelings then over Léa's insensitivities about his coming over to Summer Hill: did he now, or would he come to, care more for Hetty than for his wife? The idea of his having married Hetty, which she had just suggested, had been so exactly his own wish years before, when they might both of them have taken over Summer Hill. And now that the idea had been given shape again, entirely at Hetty's instigation, it renewed for him a remote vision – that this might still be possible, creating a stark, unreasonable longing in his heart. If this could happen, then at last he and Hetty could finally still all their old agonies – her loss of a father, his loss of both parents, their general sense of disruption and homelessness.

They could set up a true life for themselves – Hetty had just suggested, well-nigh offered, as much, at Summer Hill, a life which they had carelessly mislaid but which had been their destiny from the very start, since they had first come together as children in Domenica.

This, exactly this, had once been his vision. And now Hetty, so temptingly, had put it just within his grasp again. How might he and Léonie survive together with this vision, this itch, at the back of his mind now? For of course, and he had to admit it then, that had always been his secret ambition, to *possess* Summer Hill, with Hetty.

But then again, he thought, it was all nonsense. He could never desert Léa and Olivia. And yet, and yet . . . Conflicting thoughts stormed about his brain. And, instead of finding all such disruptive emotions over and done with at last, Robert saw then how all three of them were more deeply embedded than ever in potential disaster.

'Yes,' he said at last, 'loving two people. But just as much this house. When you said we'd do it up together, how much I'd have liked to do just that! You know how I love the place.'

'Yes.'

'And if we had married—'

'Don't—'

'How that's exactly what we could have been doing together now.'

'No – don't make it a torture.' Hetty, on the brink of tears, turned away, trying to compose herself, succeeding. Then she turned back to him. 'If my loving you comes from the good part of me, then I can't change it. But I'm not imposing it!' She tried to make light of this promise, but failed. 'And it certainly mustn't come between you and Léa . . .'

'No—'

'Because you and she – that's far more important, with Olivia. And Léa loves you. Of course she does, because she changed long ago – as I have now – to that ordinary, happier kind of loving! And I had the chance of that with you years ago – and threw it away. So I've no expectations. And there's nothing – absolutely nothing – for you to feel bad about. It's just nice that we've found this thing now, between ourselves. And Léa need never know. Go back. And love her.'

'Not all that easy . . .'

Hetty had wanted him to say this, yet she could not openly encourage this attitude in him for a moment. 'Why not? You're just being an old pessimist! It's *nice* – loving people. Shouldn't be stuck in the d-d-dumps about it. There's always a reasonable way out in these things. God, it's hot in here!'

She stood up, moving towards one of the long

curtained windows, pulling them aside to let some air in. But she was confronted by a completely bricked-up space – where one of the windows had rotted and collapsed and had then been repaired in this harsh way. Hetty, hammering on the cold wall then, could contain herself no longer. She started to cry. Robert took her in his arms once more.

In London that same evening Léonie, having thought of little else since Robert's departure, had decided on a complete about-turn over Hetty. When Olivia was in bed that evening she sat down to write a letter to Hetty on Robert's typewriter, keeping a carbon for him.

She had been such a fool, she thought, hating Hetty, when she was really . . . just fond of her. Yes, on reflection, it was simply that: affection, not love. That had been a brainstorm, she felt, the previous night – feeling all those impossible, passionate emotions for her. In the clear light of day she saw it differently. And it was time now that she rid herself of this nonsense in her soul about Hetty – time she set things on an even keel again, promoted a friendly relationship with her, at least, showing goodwill in all Hetty's renewals.

She had nothing to lose. She need not see Hetty, after all. Distance lay between them. And there was safety in that. But she must show willing towards her now, for she saw clearly how she had angered Robert by her fierce reactions towards Hetty – and more still how she had upset him by her stupid insensitivities about his going to Summer Hill, so blinded had she been over Hetty. It was time to mend her fences here. Her marriage was at risk, the child. There was no question. She could show Robert, in the carbon, how she had seen the light, recanted, and was now to be just as reasonably and charitably concerned over Hetty as he so obviously was. Nothing emotional, just care and concern, which she ought to have shown in the first place and so avoided this quite needless row with Robert. Robert, who was so dear to her – so attached to her, trusting, so forgiving: Robert – who would never love anyone else.

'Dear Hetty,' she began. 'Sorry not to have come over with Robert. But Olivia's been a bit difficult lately. This is just a note to say how sad I was to hear of all your awful illnesses and problems and how *pleased* I am that you are back at Summer Hill and how I so much hope that everything's going to work out for you now . . .'

So Léonie lied to herself, once more repressing her real feelings about Hetty – to save herself and her marriage – while Hetty and Robert, at just the same moment, expressed exactly what they felt for each other by the blocked-up window, Robert knowing full well that what they were doing might well come to destroy his marriage.

Only Hetty, after Robert had left the following morning, viewed this new situation with any equanimity. Upset at his departure – this brief taste of loving him had left her with an anguished longing for what could never be – she was happy, at least in that she had made things up with him so convincingly, happy in almost entirely regaining her true self, along with Robert, Elly, Dermot and the house itself. Only Léa remained outside this orbit of happy change and renewal: Léa, and the identity of that 'admirer' who had returned Summer Hill to her – and beyond these, of course, the greatest mystery, which had hurt and haunted her all her life, of who her real father was.

But surely, settled again in Summer Hill – surely, in this new lease of every kind of life, she would come to answers for these matters? – above all make that final identification about her father which would set the seal on her renaissance, give her complete peace at last.

A first step to this end, of course, would be to look through her mother's effects and papers. Several large boxes of these had arrived from Frances's bungalow in

Dublin. And there must besides, Hetty knew, be other older, possibly more relevant papers strewn or hidden about the house: in the old safe, for example, set in the wall of her mother's, and grandmother's, office-boudoir beyond the drawing-room. The keys to this had long since disappeared. But the local blacksmith could soon fix that. So, immediately after Robert had left that morning, she asked Jack Welsh to have the man come up from his smithy in the village.

Waiting for him that afternoon, tense and expectant, she calmed her nerves at the old Blüthner grand piano, bought back at the auction and still preserved in the drawing room, sitting down, starting to pick out a tune. It was nothing from *Madame Butterfly* that came to mind. That, along with all her cruel and foolish passion for Léonie, was long gone.

Instead she found herself playing quite a different melody as the spring afternoon waned and tinges of yellow and gold crept into the sky. She had no idea why the tune had come to mind – half the loss of Robert, half pleasure in this wonderful renewal with him, the memory of their embraces? However it was, the old Scottish melody, 'The Skye Boat Song', ran from her mind then and out over the keys in a delicate thrill of sound. So that soon – while waiting for the blacksmith and perhaps at last an answer to this great mystery of her life – she was humming and then singing this lament for a lost prince, for a king over the water.

> Speed bonny boat, like a bird on the wing,
> 'Onward,' the sailors cry.
> Carry the lad that's born to be King
> Over the sea to Skye . . .

A few minutes later there was a knock on the door. It was Jack Welsh. 'Mick Duggan is here, Miss Cordiner – with all the tools, to open the oul' safe.'

3

The blacksmith hammered and chiselled away at the safe for half an hour making little impression on it, while Hetty looked on in a rising fever of anticipation. But eventually, under the rough pressure of crowbar and jemmy, the door gave way and Hetty rushed forward, peering into the dark cavity.

There was nothing inside. The safe was absolutely empty.

Hetty was stricken. The blacksmith, as though this new châtelaine at Summer Hill were half-witted, offered judicious consolation. 'Ah, an' sure it's the *banks* people do be putting their money into these days, Miss Cordiner . . .'

For the second time in her life – like the hoard of sweets she and Léonie had found in old General Morton's safe in his house up-river – an expected cache had mocked her, yielding nothing. Nor did her mother's papers which had been sent down from Dublin reveal any clues when she went through them. There were some old ledgers, stock certificates, solicitor's letters, other bits and pieces without any value or interest. Hetty had not really expected anything here, for Frances in her will had left everything of any real value in the bungalow to her Republican friends. Even the photograph of her supposed father, Bruce Fraser, which she remembered seeing years before, had disappeared when Hetty, in the following days, had thoroughly searched the other rooms, attics, drawers and cabinets of Summer Hill.

True, she found some things of interest – a collection of old newspapers in an attic trunk marked 'Captain B. R. C. Fraser, Fraser Hall, Domenica, W. Indies' – copies of the *New York Post* describing the Carib attack on their house on the island, an old Webley service revolver still in its holster with two rusty shells in the attached pouch – an object which stirred some memory in her which Hetty could not quite identify, giving her a feeling of unease – together with title deeds and a lot of legal correspondence to do with Bruce Fraser's estate and Frances's subsequent sale of Fraser Hall. There was nothing else – no real letters, nothing intimate or revealing.

Well, of course, she had been foolish to expect anything of this sort. Her mother would long before have destroyed any such evidence, taking every care to hide the truth about who her real father was. So Hetty resigned herself again to living without answers.

But, at the end of the week, in a corner of one of the attics – and entirely out of the blue, as Dermot had suggested – Hetty found another and different answer to her frustrations about the past, and more importantly a quite unexpected key to her future.

It was one of Combridge's artist's sketchbooks, in a chest with some of her old toys and children's books – a cartridge-paper sketchbook which Dermot had given her as a child, just before he had gone away, leaving her heartbroken. In it, as a solace, Aunt Emily had encouraged her to write the story of 'The Magic Jaunting Car', of the man in the Norfolk jacket with the little girl in pigtails – and their adventures with the pony and sidecar, travelling down the railway line, floating over the ocean to the island where the Gobblies lived, prey to the fierce Marshmallows, those blobby, evil, one-eyed beasts, coming out at evening from the mists, the noisome stagnant pools, doing battle with the knight errant in the Norfolk jacket and the little girl, when evil was put down and virtue finally triumphant.

Taking the sketchbook with her into the proper light of the study-boudoir which she had now made over into her own workroom, Hetty gazed through the pages, enchanted now by Aunt Emily's vividly-coloured pen and ink illustrations on one side, her own text in a childish hand on the other.

Had she really been able to invent all that? Well, some of it at least, if largely at Aunt Emily's prompting. The whole thing so sparkled with wit, invention, colour: this magic world, hidden for so long, preserved in the pages, and released from them now, leaping forth mint-fresh, exciting, disturbingly potent, telling Hetty something which she could not at once quite interpret.

Then it came to her. Of course! Here, in her present reclusive circumstances, was the obvious manner of expressing herself – by writing, inventing in this way again. But instead of a child's book she would do one for grown-ups. Why, it was a perfect idea, she thought, rushing upstairs to tell Aunt Emily about it at once.

'Aunt – I've thought of something really good.' She showed her the old sketchbook. 'I'm going to try and write something, like we did here, but not for children.' As she leant over her great-aunt's shoulder, they looked through the sketchbook together, commenting, laughing over it.

'Indeed, why not?' Aunt Emily said eventually.

'Of course, it was all really you – in that b-b-book.'

'Oh no. I just did the drawings. You had the ideas, I remember. That fat old pony with its ears through the straw hat for a start – *you* called him "Awful". So of course you can write. Best thing ever books – and drawings and paintings. I've hundreds of old sketchbooks here.' She gestured round at a pile of them in a corner. '*You're* in charge, you see, with books and drawings and the like, not the other imbeciles . . .'

'Yes, of course. Like motion pictures . . .' Hetty spoke more to herself then, gazing round at the high theatricality of the room, remembering her own similar power in acting, how it was she, when the cameras rolled, who imposed the initial order on the celluloid. If she had done that so well once in the crowded picture studios, she could surely do the same again, alone, on paper.

'But what'll I write about?' she mused. 'You do all your drawings – from what's *real*.'

'Excuse yourself, girl!' Aunt Emily was huffy. 'That's only the *start* of it all in my drawings. It's the invention that counts. After I've got the background in I've no interest at all in *reality*. That's a mug's game, just painting what you *see*. The last thing you want to bother about – reality . . .' She curled her lips in vast distaste.

So it was that Hetty started writing for grown-ups – taking as theme and background her own life, the story of her childhood in Domenica, growing up with Robert in that island paradise: the pellucid, dew-drenched mornings in the old citrus groves, the dazzling rainbows spotlit against the plum-bruised skies over the thunderstruck mountains, the fantastic lemon and crimson sunsets, the great python in the Emerald Pool, the voodoo ceremonies with Cook and Big Jules the sailor behind the laundry, the dismembered chicken in the flare light, the drunken father, the hurdy-gurdy music machines in the hall, the battle with the Caribs, the hurricane . . .

It would be the tale of a girl cast out of this strange Eden, with her orphaned friend – exiled to a cold and fearful house in Ireland, the years of pain there, with her cruel Mama and wicked grandmother, locked away in the Gothic wing of the house: the meeting with the man in the Norfolk jacket, and her consequent joys in discovering the world outside the house with him, running free and wild, looking for otters and kingfishers, before his sudden, awful disappearance in the war. Then her years at the convent school in Normandy, the meeting there with that other person, the girl who was to dominate her subsequent life . . .

My goodness, Hetty thought, there was no lack of

interesting background. All that was needed was an invented foreground – the drama, conflict, dialogue. And that would come. After all, she had read or acted through scores of every sort of dramatic motion picture photoplays. She knew what was required there. It would be a novel – perhaps a series of novels, in which she would delve through all her past, feeling intuitively how in this way she might finally take the sting out of it, by mapping all its fears and wonders, so capturing the imaginative truths of her life, as consolation for all its folly and loss in reality, a balm in such fiction for all that had wounded and defeated her in daily life, a redemption for all the wounds she had imposed on herself and others.

Above all, perhaps, she might in this writing achieve what she had quite failed to do in looking into the safe and through her mother's papers – might, in these fictional recreations, come to some peace, make terms with that ultimate loss, that deepest intuition of hers that she had another and quite different father.

So she sat down that same morning – just as the builders from Thomastown arrived to start on the major repairs to the house – opening a fresh sketchbook which Aunt Emily had given her, considering how she might best begin.

What would she call the book? She remembered the rippling play of light and shadow, the endless sea glitter, the crystal drifts, the prisms of colour slanting off the Atlantic waters below the cliff in front of Fraser Hall: iridescent green and blue and deeper purple. Yes, she might well call these first adventures *Aquamarine*.

And then, as she thought of her early life on the island, basking in those ever-changing colours, the first paragraph, after half an hour's work, came to her fairly easily:

> Running through the coral-walled garden, she stopped to pick a little hard green lime, sticking her nails into it, scoring the skin deeply, putting it to her face.

Immediately the sharp, tart smell fizzed up her nose. She loved this limey essence of the island. Taking the fruit, she danced on across the lawn, dipping her nose into various flowers – roses, orchids, heliconias – comparing the flavours, darting from one to the next, savouring each bloom, just as the humming birds were doing. But soon, sated and confused by the different odours, she ran on around the house to her look-out point, a raised flat rock on the cliff above the cove, a crow's nest high above the bay, where she could wait for the first sight, the twirl of dark chocolate smoke on the horizon, which heralded the arrival of the weekly packet steamer . . .

As she wrote, correcting, changing, becoming completely absorbed in the work, she smelt the tart odour of limes invading the air around her once more, felt herself sitting on that same rock, as if on the bowsprit of a ship held far out over the ocean, the waves rolling towards her, so that she seemed to be moving herself, pushing away from the island, a strange sinking feeling in the pit of her stomach. As she wrote, testing this alchemy of invention, adventuring into these miraculous caves of the imagination, the temporal scene before her faded and she found herself launched forth, as over the waves, into a magic restoration.

Robert, returning to Hampstead, found no such inspiration. For the first time with Léa he was forced to live an outright lie with her and it hurt him deeply – the sense of betraying her, made all the worse when he saw the carbon of her letter to Hetty: Léa was rediscovering a true perspective over Hetty at last, while he was cheating her, just at the very point when she had seen this light and was being so particularly loving to him.

'Oh, Robert, I made such a fool of myself before you left,' she had started out straight away, standing in the hall. 'About Hetty, about your going over to Summer

Hill. Forgive me. I was just frightened about the past.'
She had kissed him sweetly as Olivia clawed at his
trousers, reaching up, insisting on her own embraces.
But Robert was depressed.

'So, how did it go? How was she?' Léonie asked later
when Olivia was in bed. And Robert told her everything
that happened, except the most important thing. Later,
when they were in bed themselves, she wanted him and
they made love together, and Robert, trying to forget his
feelings for Hetty, almost punished Léa in his love-
making – bringing an anguished, unaccustomed vigour
to it all, to which Léonie responded just as vigorously,
trying in her case to expunge all memory of her brainstorm a few evenings before: the thought that she might
still love Hetty.

Later still, just before dawn, Robert had a dream. He
and Hetty and Léonie were at some party in a huge house
of endless rooms. Both women had left him and he was
searching frantically for them, through room after room
filled with strangers.

'Léa? Hetty?' He was running, shouting out for them
both desperately now. Then he woke with a start. Léa
was awake beside him in the half-light of dawn.

'Yes, I'm *here*,' she reassured him. 'What's the matter?
– your calling out for me and Hetty like that? *I'm* here!'

God, he thought, am I to betray myself like this, even
in my dreams?

Meanwhile Hetty got over Robert's absence more readily
– by turning her thoughts of him into fiction, starting to
commemorate him there, as the companion in her story,
so that she could hold him in these pages, if not in her
arms. So the novel flourished each morning in the little
office-boudoir, while the builders got about their restoration on the roof, tugging rotten rafters out, renewing
slates, rebuilding balustrades and chimneys. Jack and

Elly began to sort out the furniture, while men from the village, stripping the tattered wallpaper and plaster, set up ladders in the reception rooms prior to redecorating them. A man came down from Dublin to see what he could do about repairing the delicate Italian stucco work, the bas-reliefs of cherubs and cornucopias and gilded harps. Aunt Emily sallied forth with her easel into the overgrown, daisy-filled gardens, where some half-dozen other local men, glad of the casual labour, were attacking the overgrown wilderness there, the briars, nettle and elder, with scythes and saws.

Hetty continued to visit her doctor in Dublin, Dr Langlois, and, on his insistence that she take up some form of regular physical exercise, began some gentle horse-riding with a quiet mare called Buttercup, purchased from a livery stable near Thomastown; moving about, rediscovering, inspecting the ruined demesne. So, too, gathering strength in the spring days that followed, and largely due to the enthusiastic suggestion of Major Ashley who came to visit, she thought she might well repair her reflexes with some fencing, getting out Henry's old foils and laying the marked hessian carpet again across the hall. Here, once a week or so, she and the Major indulged in some mild bouts, with masks and padded vests – the Major, still spry, glorying in these renewed jousts, much laughter between them, so that Hetty, taking to this old sport and aiming to maintain her fitness when he was not there, had a big leather punch-bag set up in the hall, hanging it from the first-floor balustrade. She lunged and parried at the swinging leather for ten minutes each morning, before settling down to work on her book.

The whole house became a hive of activity, life renewed, inside and out, in the warm spring weather. Hetty finished the first chapter by the end of May, reading it aloud to Aunt Emily on the porch one afternoon.

She came to the final paragraph, where the women and children, left alone in the coral-walled house on the cliff-top after the battle with the anaconda at the Emerald Pool, decide they must leave at once for the capital before the August storms set in.

> Almost as soon as her Mama had finished speaking they heard the first faint thunder, a long gathering rumble out over the bay, which ten minutes later had moved over the house, in withering explosions and spits of blue lightning. Afterwards the rain fell in solid curtains. During the night a fierce wind came which lasted for days, the sea rising in vast breakers, dashing up over the cliff beneath the house, rattling the green storm shutters, every room tight shut now against these searing gales. The packet from Roseau was cancelled. All of them were marooned then, as the wind and rain shook every fibre of the house, so that it seemed to lurch and fall in the great storm like a ship at sea about to founder.

'Not bad,' Aunt Emily said grudgingly at the end. 'You've got the girl – it's you I suppose. And those awful women – and the feel of the whole place – pretty well. I can see it, almost as good as a painting . . .'

Hetty, with this faint praise, felt a thrill of pleasure. Everything was coming right. Her world was being put together again, bit by bit, inside and all about her; all the failures of the past banished in this restoration of the house and in this bright pure light of her imagination. 'I'm glad you like it. Really so happy!' She leant across, touching her great-aunt's hand.

Just then, in the silence, they heard a car coming up the avenue. A minute later it drew up by the porch. Hetty, remembering her bankruptcy, thought the casually-dressed stranger who stepped out then must have come about her debts, since he addressed her at once as 'Miss Laura Bowen'.

'Yes?'

He was American – baby-faced yet cumbersome, over-weight, in ill-fitting clothes, with a loose necktie and fedora hat tilted back, which he took off now, displaying an almost shaven head, hollow eyes that had dark circles round them, giving him a theatrical air somehow, the eyes staring out from their dark rounds, like a clown's face, only half made up. The effect was almost comic, yet inquisitorial, vaguely sinister.

The man hitched up his baggy trousers – a further clownish effect – his stomach bursting out over his belt. Yes, Hetty thought, there was something both farcical and dangerous about him. Could the man have to do with her financial affairs in America? He reminded her of Fatty Arbuckle. And this memory of the doomed comic with his disastrous taste for young girls at once triggered an unease in her, a feeling immediately strengthened when the man introduced himself.

'I'm Carlo – Charlie – Mariani, detective, Los Angeles Police Department.' He produced a card identifying himself as such. 'Could I talk with you privately for a few minutes?'

At first Hetty had no idea what this might mean, until they were both alone in the drawing room and the man continued very evenly, while gazing at her all the while with his deep-set, questing eyes. 'We've been investigating the murder of William Desmond Taylor some years back, in Beverly Hills. Could I ask you a few questions on this – I believe you knew him: you and your husband, Craig St John Williamson?'

At the mention of Taylor's name, Hetty froze inside, something deeply hidden in her past striking back at her now which she could not immediately identify. But something quite fearful, so that she knew she must at all costs maintain her composure with this herald of danger, which she did almost at once by resuming some of her histrionic skills.

'No, I never knew him,' she said off-handedly.

'Oh.' The detective was not in the least put out.

'My husband – we're separated – he may have known him, b-before we married. Directors together in Hollywood.'

'Yes. Yes . . . They were on pretty bad terms, I gather.'

'Were they?' Hetty shrugged, getting into her role now. 'I've no idea.' She was lying now, for she remembered it all then: Craig's bitter antagonism towards Taylor for stealing his Huck Finn picture; the row they had had over this at the Hollywood studio that morning soon after she and Craig had arrived there after the war. 'As I say, I never met the man. You'd need to talk to Mr Williamson about that.'

'Yes, yes . . .' The man had wandered over to the piano, admiring a vase of narcissi there.

'I can't see why you've come all this way just to see me about this.'

'Oh, just a few points – I have to see if I can tidy up.' He fondled one of the narcissus cups in his powerful hands. 'Wonderful flowers you have in this part of the world – never see the like of them out on the coast, Miss Bowen!'

'Yes, wonderful.'

'I'm sorry you left the motion picture business. I was a great fan of yours!'

'Thank you.' Hetty was impatient now – her role demanded that. 'But Taylor died years ago, didn't he? Four, five years ago?'

'Oh, yes.' Mr Mariani smiled, his clown's face lighting up – apart from the dark orbs, which retained all their ominous gravity.

'And wasn't it – I seem to remember – something to do with the Minters? Mary Miles and her mother? I remember all the gossip. Weren't they supposed to have been in his b-bungalow that night?'

'Bungalow?' Mr Mariani asked nicely. 'You knew Taylor lived in a bungalow?'

'Well, I heard he did – saw it in the papers, the photographs.'

'Of course . . .'

Hetty still showed no sign of fluster. But her heart was beating wildly now, as memories flooded back to her, so that she hoped to keep her distance then as Mariani approached. She stood up, moving easily towards the window, while he stopped by the fireplace, looking after her intently. 'Yes, the Minters,' he went on easily. 'But there was no proof, no final proof.'

'So?' Hetty turned back to him. 'I don't see how I can help you. If you couldn't p-pin anything on anyone – surely the case must have been closed?'

'Well, it *was* closed, Miss Bowen. Until a month ago, when a hand gun turned up in Hollywood Lake. They were emptying it, dredging the shoreline for some new apartment development. A Smith and Wesson .38. We checked the serial number. They still had the records at the Hollywood police station – you know how fussy they used to be about guns there in the old days. The gun had been licensed out to your husband. And the shells that killed Taylor came from the same gun . . .'

Mr Mariani smiled faintly. Hetty was dumbstruck for a moment. But again she recovered herself. 'Well, you'd better ask my husband about that.'

Mr Mariani sighed. 'I have, Miss Bowen. I met with him last week in France. Told me the revolver had been stolen, about six months before Taylor's death, from a drawer in his bureau. One of your servants, he thought, maybe. Or a party guest. And that's what I wanted to ask you – the servants – who did you have up in the Wolf's Lair just then? Can you remember?'

'Barely. We had a Chinese cook and his wife – a Mr Chen. And half a dozen others, inside and in the gardens – they came and went. But they're not very likely candidates, Mr Mariani.'

'No.'

'More likely a party guest. There were a lot of them, when we first lived up there. Some total strangers, too. Anyone could have taken the gun.'

'Indeed. And you yourself, Miss Bowen – I have to check·out everyone who was living up at the Wolf's Lair then – what were you doing, on the night of the murder? Can you remember at all?' Mariani, still gazing at her carefully, took out a notebook and pencil.

Hetty laughed. 'No, of course I can't remember. But I guess we were both at home, Craig and I. Because we very rarely went out evenings – when we were both at the studios all day.'

'Of course.' Mr Mariani consulted some earlier pages in his notebook. 'Except – I have a record here, from the Fox studios. In those weeks before and after Taylor's death – nearly six weeks in fact – you weren't working at the studios. You were indisposed, as I understand it.'

'Or between pictures? I don't remember. You may be right. But, whether I was working or not, we always stayed in evenings anyway. Didn't have much to do with the social goings-on in the valley, Mr Mariani.' She gazed at him, regaining some of her old imperious hauteur. 'So you can take it – yes, we were in the house, *all* that evening.'

'I see, Miss Bowen.' Mr Mariani made a note of this in his book. 'Well, maybe that clears everything up, doesn't it?' He gazed at her in a way that suggested rather the opposite. 'And now we're back to square one again. Like looking for the proverbial needle in a haystack, isn't it?' He smiled knowingly, getting ready to leave, gazing at her intently once more. 'A needle in a haystack . . . A shame you gave up the picture business, Miss Bowen. I was crazy about you – in *Nefertiti*.'

407

'Thank you.'

Mariani, at the doorway now, fiddling with his fedora, suddenly turned back to her. 'Oh, by the way, that reminds me, *Nefertiti* – extraordinary coincidence, wasn't it? – how Taylor was all set to make that same Egyptian story. Bungalow was full of notes and drawings about it, photoplays we found afterwards. Funny coincidence, two directors – Taylor and your husband – having just the same idea at the same time. But of course it was Miss Minter Taylor had in mind to play the Queen. Lousy casting, Miss Bowen. She could never have played it the way you did – that ruthless lady!' He smiled a last time, the dark-circled eyes full of irony, knowledge, some sure appreciation, as it seemed, of the truth in the whole Taylor situation. 'We'll be in touch, Miss Bowen, if there's anything else,' he added finally, rather emphasizing the provisional tone, before closing the door.

After he had gone Hetty paced the drawing room in something of a frenzy. Here was something which, above all else in her life, she had completely repressed: the business with Taylor. At the time, suffering those recurrent epileptic fits, complete black-outs, when she forgot everything that had happened immediately beforehand, the whole thing had been entirely vague to her. But something had gone very wrong in Taylor's house that night, there was no doubt about that, and she had thought herself somehow involved. Dressed as a man, she'd been to a fancy dress party there – wasn't that it? – and there'd been some sort of awful row, between the Minters and Taylor. But her involvement, she'd thought then, had simply been part of those nightmare fits, a fantasy, a bad dream of the times, which she had completely forgotten afterwards.

But now, at Mariani's enquiries and promptings, most of the reality of that evening had come back to her. She had not gone to any fancy dress party at Taylor's bungalow. She had taken that same revolver of Craig's and driven down to Beverly Hills alone, not in fancy dress but *disguised* as a man. She remembered waiting outside the bungalow, seeing the lights on in the front room, the sound of raised voices, arguing – then going round to the back and coming in through the kitchen, seeing the Minters through a curtain in the front room, Mrs Minter threatening Taylor with another gun. She remembered all that now, before the shot had gone off. Then nothing. She'd blacked out and the next she knew she was back at the Wolf's Lair with Craig and little Eddy Nolan.

The papers then had been carefully vague about motives and suspects in the killing. But the Hollywood gossip had been entirely to the point. Everyone came to know how Mary Minter and her mother had both been at the bungalow that same evening: Mrs Minter surprising her daughter there, and killing Taylor for his affair and drug peddling with her.

But now, with all that time unearthed again by Mariani, Hetty had to face the fact that she, and not Mrs Minter, might well have killed Taylor. She certainly must have had something of that intention, taking Craig's gun with her. And her motive was clear enough – that had all come back to her in Mariani's remark about how Taylor as well had been preparing to make *Nefertiti*. She had been determined to stop him doing just this, obsessed as she had been for months with playing the Queen. And then there'd been that last knowing look of Mariani's, his remark about her being so ruthless a lady in her role as Nefertiti. And in reality, too, he'd implied. It was clear – he suspected her of the murder.

But was it true? Was it possible? All her new-found contentment disappeared. Evil shadows sprang up from the past, infecting her thoughts, putting her off every kind of balance – that so hard-won equilibrium which she had achieved in these last months – confronted now with the fact that, quite apart from all her other old faults and cruelties, she might well be an assassin, a killer. One person alone might confirm this or allay her fears: Craig himself, whom she thought she loathed above all people.

A week later Craig, as if sensing from afar this vast alarm of Hetty's, turned up in a hired car at Summer Hill. Hetty was fencing in the hall that morning when he arrived, lunging at the punch-bag. In any other circumstances she would have shown him the door at once. But now she did not do this. Instead, after Elly had let him in, she viewed him coldly in the hall.

'Hi! . . .' He stood there, in a soft Donegal tweed jacket and flannels, well-dressed as ever, quite unabashed, even the hint of a smile crossing his still-boyish good looks, tints of grey at the temples creeping over his darkly brilliantined hair. 'How are you? Glad to see you back with the foil!' He seemed particularly pleased over this. 'Quite recovered?'

'Recovering. No thanks to you.' Hetty glared at him, so angry that she could barely restrain herself from throwing him out. But she had to keep control. And Craig sensed this clearly.

'I know . . .' He took off his tweed cap, fiddling with it humbly. 'You'd like to boot me out of here. And I deserve it. I'm sorry. Truly.'

She made not the slightest effort to forgive him. 'Why did you come?'

He walked away, gazing round the pillared hall, fingering objects, as if this huge space might form an ideal setting for some epic motion picture he was preparing. He turned back to her. 'Oh, several things – when I heard you were settled back here, I thought we should meet anyway – talk about our finances. I guess you want a divorce?' He smiled. 'And what about that gumshoe

Mariani . . . I expect you've had a visit from him?' He looked at her easily.

'Yes. He did come to see me. You'd better come into the drawing room.'

Ten minutes later, having described her meeting with the detective, Craig said quite simply, 'Well, they can't touch us. Not a shred of evidence – other than that revolver – to link us with the slaying. And, as I told Mariani, some party guest stole the gun at the Wolf's Lair some months before.'

Against her increasing agitation, he looked at her calmly. 'Yes, but me – what about *me*? Because I remember m-most of what happened now. I *was* down at Taylor's house that night, with your gun, and there was a shot, just before I blacked out. Did I kill him? And how did I get out of the place?'

Craig, drawing on a cigarette, waited a moment before replying. 'Yes, honey, I know you were down at Taylor's place. Me and Eddy Nolan – we followed you – found you in the passageway, behind the curtain there. You'd blacked out, one of your fits. So we picked you up and got you out of the place – *quick!*'

'But did I *kill* him?' Hetty's face was a mask of anguish.

'No, honey. That's what you had in mind maybe. But it was Mrs Minter who shot him. Everyone knows that she was there before you with a gun—'

'Yes!' Hetty was suddenly bright again, for the first time in a week. 'I remember seeing her, from the curtain, threatening Taylor with it just before I blacked out.'

'Of course! She'd been gunning for Taylor for months, ever since she'd found out he was having a heavy affair with Mary, as well as giving her snow and decks of coke. And there were half a dozen others in Hollywood then who'd have done just the same for Taylor. He was the worst, peddling drugs to all those little girls, debauching them – Mabel Normand, Mary Miles, there were dozens of them. He got exactly what was coming to him.'

'You *are* telling me the truth, Craig?' She addressed him by name for the first time. 'You know I couldn't live with the idea—'

'Of *course* I am, honey. Why, that revolver of mine – none of the shells had been fired. I checked, before I threw it away in the lake.'

'So what's this Mariani up to – saying the bullet that killed Taylor came from the same gun?'

'Trying to set us up, that's all. You see, we were suspects, once we'd started out on *Nefertiti*, since they'd found all those notes and photoplays about the same story in Taylor's bungalow. Then, when they found my gun in the lake, they guessed it might have been the murder weapon. Well, the serial number was maybe there, under the rust. But they couldn't possibly have matched the bullet with the same gun after it'd been in the water all that time. They're just trying to close the case, that's all – since they never managed to pin it on Mrs Minter. But everyone knows it was her.'

'You're sure? Because I have to know – and I'd never have let you in here today, not for a moment, but for this Taylor business cropping up with that detective.'

For the first time Hetty forgot her antagonism against Craig as he approached her now, allowing him to put an arm on her shoulder for an instant. 'Laura, you just believe me. That's all you got to do . . .' His tone had quite changed, lulling yet imperative. Hetty relaxed.

But Craig did not press his suit – his various suits, for such they were. He was happy the way this first hurdle had been taken. He was a step nearer getting Hetty back, to dominating her once more, to working with her again and eventually, perhaps, achieving what he had longed for all his life: a great house in Ireland, when he could at last take revenge on his own banal upbringing in this land, the mean streets of Cork, the cold threadbare rooms above the shop, the penny-pinching grocer who had been his father. Here, at Summer Hill, he would come into his true inheritance.

But Craig had another even more important card to play with Hetty now – one which he had kept up his sleeve for years, since he had never been quite certain of its value. Now he thought he was sure. And, in playing it with her, he would win her back. He turned from the window, standing quite still, silhouetted against the light, jangling some loose change in his pocket. Then the sound stopped.

'Forget all about Taylor, Laura. Because I've got something much more important for you to think about.' He took a small glittering object from his pocket, holding it up, walking slowly towards her across the length of the room. Hetty remembered just the same dramatically charged approach years before in their bedroom at the Wolf's Lair when he had first brought her the portrait bust of Nefertiti.

'What? What is it?'

'Your father, Laura. It must be. Look on the back.'

He handed her the little brooch watch with its diamond-studded clip which he had found in the rubble after the fire at Summer Hill and kept all these years.

Hetty, not yet following anything, turned the watch over.

'You see,' he said. '"Frances – from Alix and Edward. Sandringham, Xmas, 1898."'

'So?' Hetty was still quite bemused.

'Your mother, Laura. And Edward, the old Prince of Wales. *That*'s where you came from.'

Hetty felt the back of her neck prickle. 'How?'

'You never knew? – how they must have been pretty close friends, for him to have given her that.'

'No, never. No idea they even knew each other.'

For Hetty, receiving this gradual information was like unwrapping a fascinatingly shaped present when the final gift was not yet visible. A strange thrill coursed through her. She felt herself shaking.

'Well, they *must* have known each other. And more than just a little, if she'd been asked to stay with them over Christmas. Besides, have you never looked at yourself? Here, look at this.' He took out a portrait photograph of the old Prince of Wales in the 1890s, torn from a copy of the *Illustrated London News* in Hollywood years before, handing it to her. 'See the resemblance?'

Hetty gazed at it. 'No. No, I don't.'

Craig laughed. 'I've been looking at faces very closely all my life. It's my business! It's there, I can tell you. Shape of the eyes, run of the eyebrows, the forehead . . .'

'It couldn't be!' Hetty decided not to tempt fate by opening the package any further. 'M-m-must have been some quite different Frances he gave it to. Where did you find the watch?'

'Here. Found it right here, in the rubble after that fire, the day I came to see you and we went off to Dublin together. It's your mother's watch, no doubt about that.'

'Well, maybe. But that's no real proof. They could have been just friends. My Mama did the London season after all when she was a young w-w-woman.'

'OK: the watch and the looks – maybe both just circumstantial evidence. But there's one more thing . . .' He had come close to her now, gazing at her intently. 'Which pretty well convinced me of it – when I read about it in the social columns last year: all that business between you and the *present* Prince of Wales . . .' At mention of this Hetty started again, as if, with this hint, the final wrapping on the gift was about to be discarded. '*Why* did he drop you?' Craig continued firmly.

But still Hetty would not take the final step. 'Oh, because I was a p-picture star. And a bankrupt drunk as well,' she continued, lying now, for she had never been remotely drunk with him and money had been absolutely no object between them in any case.

'You don't think there was any other reason?' Craig asked lightly. 'Like maybe someone at Court told him, or he found out, that you were his *aunt*?'

'Me? His *aunt*?' She laughed, thinking then how it must all be nonsense, that Craig had gone too far.

'Yes, illegitimately, of course. But the same thing. And that's why he dropped you. A real skeleton in the closet. Just think of it! – if the papers had gotten hold of that: the glamorous young Prince carrying on with his *aunt*! So you see, it fits, doesn't it? – the watch, the looks, the Prince dropping you like that . . .'

Hetty, feeling herself sway, sat down on the sofa. Her head was swimming. Because she saw now how it might well all fit. And certainly it at last explained how the Prince, when they had been so close and happy, had suddenly and brutally cut her off.

Then another distant memory came to her, filling in one more bit of the puzzle. She remembered Snipe, the maimed fortune-teller out at the harvesting years before in Summer Hill, and how he had clearly seen her as a princess in the tea-leaves. She had a sudden feeling that Craig must be right – so that the shock mixed with relief was intense, as the gift was finally unwrapped and displayed before her.

'There's no real doubt in my mind, Laura. This explains it – your mother's hiding everything from you about your father. Because you're not a Cordiner or a Fraser, nor even Laura Bowen. Your father was Edward VII – you're his daughter, daughter of the old King.'

He turned away, jangling the coins in his pocket once more.

'Yes . . .' Hetty said more to herself. 'M-m-maybe I am.'

Craig, at the window again, turned back to her, smiling. 'Changes everything, doesn't it?'

'Yes, I suppose it does.'

Craig, she felt then, had brought her another gift, greater than Nefertiti, greater than any she had ever received before. It seemed he'd confirmed her birthright, brought her finally home again. And yet, because the gift had come from him, it was somehow poisoned. She felt that just as strongly. For Craig personified everything she most hated, a whole way of life which he had imposed on her, cruelly and almost fatally – nightmare years from which she had now recovered. She might accept his consoling evidence over Taylor and his other astonishing deductions about her real father. But she could never have anything more to do with him again.

Craig had a quite opposite aim in mind. His last picture, *The Lost Valley*, with his new girlfriend Duna Börzöny, had not done well. Always a great pictorial director, he had not yet successfully adapted to sound filming, where the dialogue, which had always to be shot in close-ups, gave no play to his real gifts, which were for the depth of crowd scenes, great perspectives, subtle lighting, elaborate props and scenery. Now, with the camera immobile in a sound-proof cubicle, his hands, his eyes, were tied. And all the money he had invested in *The Lost Valley* – mostly Hetty's share in WillBow Pictures – had not been returned. He, like Hetty, was now bankrupt, living on fees, advanced in cash by his producers in France, while trying to set up another picture there. But not with Duna Börzöny who had left him for another man some months before. His future had looked bleak, until he had met a new producer with his own independent production company in Hollywood – Howard Hughes, a young multi-millionaire, who had just completed *Hell's Angels*, a tremendous flying picture with

Jean Harlow, and who was now anxious to invest in another equally grandiose project.

Craig had met with Hughes in Hollywood. They had talked. Craig had a particular picture in mind. Hughes had liked *Nefertiti*, liked Craig as well – two men, rebels outside the Hollywood system. Laura Bowen had been the key to Craig's idea, and Hughes had immediately agreed. After all, Laura Bowen was still remembered everywhere. She had been a great silent picture star, along with Pickford, Garbo, Harlow. *Nefertiti* was still doing the rounds, making money all over the world. So that Craig, after his failure with Duna Börzöny, saw the opportunity now to resuscitate his career, just as he had done before – with Hetty. And surely, with these consolations over Taylor and this vital information about her father which he had brought her, she might well be persuaded?

He broached the topic very gently at lunch. 'Had you ever thought . . . of pictures again? I mean, maybe only as the means of getting rid of all these debts we have?'

'Your debts, not mine,' she told him shortly.

'My debts, yes, and I'm sorry. But, hell, Laura, I've spent the money making pictures, not living in the Ritz.'

'You said *The Lost Valley* would p-p-pay all those debts back.'

'And it *will*, in time. It'll be in profit soon. But I meant a much bigger picture, Laura. Where there'd be *real* profit – for us both. I have a producer now, young millionaire quite outside the system, Howard Hughes, just finished a great picture with Jean Harlow. Got a lot of money he wants to invest. In me – and you. Something really big . . .' He gazed over at Hetty. There might, he thought, have been just a flicker of interest in those blue eyes. 'Yes, a big picture, with all the finance we want, where I could get you all your money back – profits later maybe, but a guaranteed salary anyway – which would more than pay off all your debts. That's the point. You had $10,000 a week on *Nefertiti* as I remember. Well, this guy Hughes would pay you that as a *minimum* now. On a sixteen-week schedule, say, that would be close on two hundred thousand bucks. Cover your debts four times over. And, even if you never did another picture, you'd have $150,000 or so to put in the bank here – put it towards running this place.'

Hetty, watching him equally carefully, let him run on. It was all nonsense, of course, but the idea of all that money, for Summer Hill, did vaguely tempt her. At one fell swoop she could put all her financial worries behind her, pay Mortimer and Dermot back, set the house in real order, be secure financially for the rest of her life. But it *was* all nonsense, of course, for there was one point at least which Craig had taken no account of.

'Look at me, Craig! Doesn't your pre-pre-producer friend know what I *look* like now? As if I'd been dragged through a ma-ma-mangle. And I have. No resemblance to that other w-woman, Laura Bowen, who played Nefertiti . . .'

'Yes, I told Howard that,' Craig came in brightly. 'Told him how you weren't the same, how you'd gone through a pretty rough time recently. But that's exactly the whole point of the story we're going to do, Laura! This woman in it goes through a pretty bad time as well. Worse than you in the end. So for a lot of the time she *has* to look like you do now!'

Hetty, at this continuously proffered mystery, could no longer restrain her curiosity. 'What? – who is she?'

'Joan of Arc,' Craig said simply.

And Hetty, just as she had when Craig had first suggested Nefertiti to her, bringing her that portrait bust from the darkness into the light of their bedroom, felt a thrill rising in her, which she wanted to repress, but could not.

But, thinking of something, she finally did resist it. 'Joan of Arc? But that Swede – Dreyer, wasn't he? – he made that picture only two or three years ago, I remember. You can't do it again – so soon.'

'A Dane, not a Swede. And of course I can make it again. Carl's version was only the trial and execution – done as a silent, a small-scale picture. Shot largely in close-ups, with only a limited exhibition, cinema clubs and so on. This'll be in sound, starting from the beginning – the wars against the British, the storming of Orleans, you dressed up as a man like Joan herself, the riding, the sword play – and you can do all that again. I've seen you. A popular epic, honey! The whole works, Laura. Like *Nefertiti*. And filmed in France, not back in that dreary Hollywood. Don't you see? OK, forget it all between you and me personally. I don't expect anything there. I behaved like a shit. I know that. But this'd be just a professional relationship, to recoup our losses *and* make a great picture. You know I can do that, too, don't you?'

Hetty, glimmers of all that old exciting life coming alive in her again, nodded. 'Oh yes – I know you could do it . . .'

'We can do it, honey. Only *we* can do it – just like only *both* of us could have done *Nefertiti*. Because, don't you see? – this is a story about suffering, like you've suffered. Not scheming vengeance. But sainthood. And just as only you could have played Nefertiti, only you can do Joan now. You've just lived through something like she did. I've got a draft photoplay with me. Just look at it at least.'

Hetty looked at him instead – the devil tempting her again. But again she resisted. 'And my stammer? Wha-wha-what about that? Remember the test at the Victorine?'

'That was my fault much more than yours. I rushed

it. If I'd been more patient with you, it'd have been OK. This time we'd get it right. Promise.'

And looking at him, his face lit up with all that old surging confidence, she had to believe him. The whole thing *was* possible. Certainly she felt much better physically, what with the horse riding and fencing. And her syphilis had indeed once more responded to the Salvarsan treatment which Dr Langlois was giving her. The violent aches and stomach cramps had disappeared. Perhaps, as Dermot had suggested, she was going to be cured. Or at least the disease was once more entirely dormant.

Why not? Why not at least consider the idea? As Craig had said it would be purely a professional relationship. She needn't forgive him his earlier behaviour. But surely she was composed, wise and sure enough of herself now, just to collaborate with him, drawing on his undoubted professional gifts which, as in the past, had drawn such magic from her.

'Well,' she said. 'No promises. Leave me the photoplay. I'll consider it.'

'I'll be back – at the end of the week! . . .'

Craig left that afternoon, thinking how almost certainly he'd hooked Laura again.

Hetty, when he had gone, considered these extraordinary results of his visit. Change of all sorts – way back before she was born and in the future – was in the air. And she was suddenly revivified by it all. Instead of settling down to a reclusive, semi-invalid life at Summer Hill, it seemed she might be about to embark on the great world again: a woman with a future – and a father. She would move forward not in her old false persona, of course, but as the new and responsible person she now was, and therefore as quite another sort of actress, too.

Then, as well, and much more importantly, she was embarking on a startlingly fresh character in reality – as the old King's daughter. Was it true? She looked at the portrait photograph which Craig had left behind, holding it up to a mirror, gazing at it. Yes, she thought, there might be some resemblance. But how on earth had it all come about? – when her mother had been a débutante at the London season in the 1890s? But, checking the dates here, they did not fit. She had been born in May 1899, in New York – and therefore must have been conceived the previous August. Her mother, by that date, had long since finished her London season – had been living in London with Mortimer and Dermot before going out as a nurse to the Boer War. So it was then – and there in London – that she must have been conceived. But the Prince had lived just down the road at Marlborough House, so that was quite possible. She would ask Mortimer about it when she next went to Dublin for her medical treatment – for surely he, if anyone, would know of her mother's associations then?

However, a few days later, she received another unexpected visit – from a small man, in a slouch hat and wearing a rather shabby trenchcoat despite the warm weather, who had driven up to the yard entrance, knocking on the kitchen door, before Elly had brought him into the drawing room.

'Yes?'

'Ah, Miss Cordiner – I'm sorry to trouble you. Detective Sergeant O'Reilly, from the Kilkenny barracks.' The man had a soft brogue. He stood there awkwardly in the great room.

'Sit down, Sergeant. What is it?'

He remained standing. 'It's just – I've been asked to make inquiries, from police headquarters in Dublin, Ma'am . . .' He opened a notebook. 'An American, a Mr Marian. I wonder did he come to see you here, about ten days ago?'

Hetty's heart started to thump, so that once more she

immediately resumed a role, detached, distant to begin with. 'Yes. A Mr *Mariani* I think he was called.'

'Ah yes, Mr Mariani . . .' Mr O'Reilly made a correction in his book. 'Do you remember – anything about him, Miss Cordiner?'

'How do you mean?'

'Did he – did he identify himself to you?'

Hetty could not lie here. 'Yes – as a detective, from the Los Angeles Police Department. He showed me a card in his wallet saying so.'

'Ah, good, quite so . . .' O'Reilly made a note of this. 'Did he issue any threats? Was there anything missing from about the house after he left?'

Hetty was astonished. 'No, nothing. Why? Why would he take anything here, if he was a detective?'

'Ah, well, now that's the whole thing, d'ye see, Miss Cordiner. He wasn't a detective. He had an accident, like, in the oul' car he hired in Dublin. They found that wallet on him – and the police card – and your own address down here. So the Dublin police sent a telegram to Los Angeles informing them. But they had no one on their force of that name, nobody at all. And never had. So the fellow was an impostor, Miss Cordiner, and that's why we had to check up with you, in case he'd thieved anything here or issued any threats, like.'

'An impostor?' Hetty was suddenly shaking – not with fear now, but with rage.

'Indeed. That's what he was.'

'Was?'

'Oh yes. The car he was in ran into the back of a cart on the Naas road, a terrible mess be all accounts—'

'But he must have come from somewhere in America?'

O'Reilly consulted his notebook again. 'No, ma'am. I have it here. He had another address on him. Headquarters are investigating it now. He lived in Paris. Some class of an actor,' O'Reilly added dismissively, before realizing his gaffe, looking up at Hetty. 'Well, now, I didn't mean that derogatively, Miss Cordiner – I meant he was nothing like the class of an actress you are yourself . . .'

But Hetty, her mind crowded out with astonished rage, did not take the compliment. Of course, she thought. Baby-faced Mr Mariani: she'd felt there had been something theatrical about him from the start – a made-up character, disguised, with those hollow eyes ringed with dark circles, the shaven head, the little moustache, the baggy trousers. But Craig had made him up. Mariani had been his production – another of Craig's lying ploys.

And, then, she saw how Craig's whole visit had been a ploy of some kind. So that everything had been untrue about it – not just Mariani, but Craig's consolations about Taylor and his idea that the old King had been her father. Craig's behaviour had been a malicious, evil charade from start to finish. And all her happy release in knowing who her real father was had gone now. That was the worst thing – that Craig had lied to her, betrayed her over this most important thing in her life.

She was astonished at the fury she felt then – an anger against Craig, which did not subside after O'Reilly had left, but became the more intense the longer she thought about it. She saw it all now: how Craig had done this simply to ingratiate himself with her again, to secure her agreement to return to pictures as St Joan – for of course, as she had said to him, she would never have let him in the door if it had not been for Mariani's arrival the week before.

Yet how could anyone have been such a savage as to impose this pain on her, in the shape of that phoney emissary, then turn up himself to capitalize on her fears, before going on to tell such lies about her father? Since he knew how she would always feel about her empty background here, this was unbelievable cruelty, Hetty thought, beside herself with rage.

Craig returned to Summer Hill that Friday morning while she was exercising with the foil, chaffing and parrying the big leather punch-bag in the hall.

'Hi!' he said again, coming in, closing the door, watching her lunge. 'Getting in shape for St Joan? How did you like the photoplay?'

Hetty paused, dropping the point of the foil. 'You shit,' was all she said, not even turning towards him. 'Mariani,' she went on with chilling emphasis, 'was a fraud. A lie, just like everything else you told me . . .'

Craig coloured, looked grim for an instant, but regained his composure at once. 'What do you mean?'

'I mean your Mariani was some bit-part actor in Paris you set up to come here and torment me, so you could get me back into pictures. *That*'s what I mean.'

'That's crazy, honey—'

'No, it's not. Mariani died in some car accident here ten days ago. A detective came out from Kilkenny and told me so – Mariani was nothing to do with the Los Angeles police.'

Craig had begun to walk towards her now across the great hall. 'That's nonsense, Laura – the guy from Kilkenny must have been the fraud. Did you see his card?'

'Didn't need to. The man was real. I checked. And everything you told me was a lie: about my father being the old King, everything.'

At last she turned to face him, looking at him, shaking her head in amazement, the volcanic anger she had felt in the last few days beginning to erupt.

Craig continued his progress towards her, aiming to console her, allay her fears, then control her again with that old fierce chemistry of his.

'Look, honey, you just *believe* me . . .' His eyes never

left hers, full of blazing intent. 'The guy from Kilkenny was lying . . .' He took another step towards her.

'No! Get away! *You're* the liar, everything you told me.'

But still he approached her, so that she lifted the foil simply to make him keep his distance. But he took the buttoned blade easily in his hand, pushing it gently aside. 'No, honey, no. You just listen to me . . .' His voice was slow, hypnotic.

But Hetty was not to be enslaved this time. Raising the foil, she struck him on the arm with it. But the blade slid along the shoulder of his tweed jacket and opened a weal on his neck. Gasping in pain, he put a hand to the wound, before launching himself forward, trying to disarm her.

Hetty struck from the side again, this time on the brow, so that, enraged, he lunged at her once more. But this time Hetty had the foil straight at him, so that he rushed blindly on to the button point, the blade buckling against a rib, before the rusty button snapped off – and the sharp steel pierced his shirt over his heart and went deep into the flesh behind.

Crying out in agony, he tried to pull the foil from his chest, before falling to the floor. Hetty, standing above him, pulled the blade out herself. Then she called out 'Jack? Elly? Quickly!'

Her tone was one of command, not panic or fear. In those manic instants of the fighting she had quite lost herself, thrown away all her good resolutions, all the happy changes in her months of recovery, regaining her old character: bitter, raging, dominant – as she stood over Craig's body, triumphant for a long moment in this vengeance.

Then, nervelessly, she dropped the foil, letting it clatter over the marble flagstones, standing quite still, head bowed, vacant-eyed, placid.

The doctor came and Craig was taken to the county hospital in Kilkenny. Later that day Detective Sergeant O'Reilly, with another officer, paid a second visit to Summer Hill.

'I'm sorry for your trouble, Miss Cordiner . . .' He was diffident, humble as before. 'But I'm afraid you'll have to come with us to the barracks. A few questions . . . The matter of your husband.'

'Is he dead?' Hetty was still entirely calm, resigned, had entered a nightmare, where all was lost and where there was nothing she could do to retrieve the situation.

O'Reilly did not reply. Instead he led her gently away down the porch steps and on to the gravel, where the builders on the roof and the casual labourers clearing the lawn terraces looked down dumbly on the little procession. Elly was in tears on the front steps, but Aunt Emily wasn't standing beside her as Hetty was helped into the car.

'Men . . .' Aunt Emily said, scowling at the motor wheeling round the old pleasure garden, disappearing down the avenue into the bright summer light.

4

Léonie came forward to the wire grille separating visitors from prisoners in the grim room at Mountjoy Jail in Dublin. She had not attended Hetty's trial a month previously, though all the others had been there – Robert, Dermot and Mortimer, who had organized Hetty's defence. But now Léonie, leaving Olivia with Robert, had come over to Dublin, seeing her old friend for the first time since the events in Egypt nearly six years before.

Taking a hard chair, she watched anxiously as the group of women prisoners were admitted to the space beyond the partition. At first she could not see Hetty, who was standing in the background, uncertain where to go. A wardress led her forward, pointing out her seat, her visitor. And when Léonie did see her then she barely recognized her: the vague, emaciated figure in a coarse, ill-fitting grey flannel dress almost down to her ankles, the wan features, short-cropped greying hair, the whole impression quite colourless.

This was not the glowing woman Robert had told her about, the woman who had rediscovered herself, in beauty and true character – with whom she had so feared to fall in love again. This was someone, she saw at once, quite broken in spirit, a lost soul, and Léonie's heart went out to her, not with love but with a sudden overwhelming pity.

'Hetty!' Léonie reached forward impulsively, only to knock her hand sharply against the grille. Hetty did not reply, just looked at her with a frown, vaguely puzzled about something quite unimportant in her vision. 'Hetty! It's me, Léonie . . .'

'Oh . . .' Still the quite vacant look.

'Are you all right? You got my letter? I'm sorry I couldn't get over before.'

'Yes. Yes. I'm all right. I suppose . . .' Hetty spoke slowly, the words unfelt, unconnected. There was no real response – as if, with the grey of her clothes and skin, all the spirit had been washed out of her as well. And Léonie was stricken by the idea that Hetty, though physically alive, was dead in every other way. So that she wanted to revive her now – reach forward through the wire and warm her somehow, rub her hands, bring her back to life.

There was silence between them; the long room loud with country brogues and raucous Dublin tones as the other prisoners chattered with their visitors. Léonie had to raise her voice when she next spoke. 'Did you get my letter?'

'Did I? A letter? I think so . . .'

Oh God, Léonie thought: she doesn't know me, remembers nothing. She's lost her mind. So that again she took the initiative, more forcefully this time. 'Hetty, it's been so awful for you. I do feel – I wish I could touch . . .' Moving her hand forward, but finding the barrier once more, she turned away, tears beginning to prick behind her eyes. Then, regaining her composure, she decided on a different, consolatory line. 'Craig – he must have behaved terribly that day at Summer Hill . . .' Her voice trailed away unconvincingly, for Léonie had no real evidence for saying this.

Hetty had said nothing, to anyone, either before or at her trial, about the Taylor business, or spoken of Mariani from Los Angeles nor told of how Craig had led her on and lied to her about her father. From the moment she had killed Craig she had been indifferent to her fate, already in that vague, unresponsive state which had now almost overwhelmed her.

So that her defence had had to rest on her husband's many earlier cruelties towards her, in Egypt and the South of France, when he had punished and lied to her, bankrupted her, then taken up with another woman before finally abandoning her. In France murder as a consequence of such repeated betrayals of fidelity might well have been viewed as a *crime passionnel*, with the lightest of sentences or possible acquittal. In Ireland no such worldly attitudes obtained.

However, Hetty's senior counsel, an old friend of Mortimer's, a Mr Archie O'Grady, with several crucial witnesses brought from overseas, had pointedly and very successfully illuminated Craig's long provocations, the general appalling stress he had imposed on his wife, resulting in her bankruptcy, alcoholism and near-fatal illness. Then, too, in Hetty's favour and hovering radiantly above the whole sensational trial, there was the halo of her illustrious mother – heroine of Easter Week, Republican martyr, saint of the Dublin poor, only recently interred among Ireland's greatest patriots at Glasnevin cemetery.

The court, disposed towards leniency in any case, and covertly taking this last matter into account had, on Archie O'Grady's initial plea, reduced the charge to one of manslaughter (the foil wound had been a complete accident), eventually sentencing Hetty to a minimum term of five years' imprisonment. So that Léonie, remembering this, and for lack of anything better to say, thought to console Hetty with this fact.

'Anyway, Hetty, it won't be too long before you're out, Mortimer said. With good conduct, you'll be out in two or three years – even less perhaps, on parole . . .'

'Good conduct?' Hetty was puzzled.

'Yes, of course.'

'Oh, there'll be no problem about that.' Hetty at last put a coherent sentence together, so that Léonie was encouraged.

'Yes, of course—'

'No problem at all!' Hetty was almost bright now. 'The nuns are very strict here. We even have to bathe in our shifts – just like I had to . . . do years ago, at a convent school in France. With someone? . . .' Hetty's voice trailed away. She was puzzled again, gazing round the crowded room now, as if trying to locate that person.

'Hetty! It was me – *me*! I was with you then – at the school in Normandy. The Château de Héricourt – remember?' Léonie asked desperately. Hetty's blank gaze returned to her.

'You?' She was not put out, just genuinely mystified, gazing at Léonie for a long moment before turning away, distracted by some other thought, starting to crack her finger joints, clasping and unclasping her hands nervously. At this point Léonie could barely restrain her tears and had to turn away.

'I couldn't believe it,' Léonie told Mortimer that same October afternoon at his house at Islandbridge, where she was staying. Dermot was there as well, over on leave from Sandhurst. 'She didn't really know me at all.'

All three were in the pretty, bow-windowed drawing room, looking over the darkening lawn covered in swirling drifts of autumn leaves, the river running high over the weir beyond, squalls of rain thrashing against the glass. The mood among them paralleled the sad weather.

'Sometimes she's better,' Mortimer murmured through his whiskers, trying to make the best of things. 'Depends on her mood . . .'

Dermot stood up, offering Léonie more tea. But, before he had time to pour it, Léonie had burst forth once more. 'I really can't *believe* the whole thing – when everyone said she was so improved: then killing Williamson like that.'

'Could have been so much worse.' Dermot tried to console her. 'Charge reduced to manslaughter—'

'Of course! But why that sort of violence in the first place?'

Neither of the men replied at once. Then Mortimer said, 'Like mother, like daughter . . .' He sipped his tea. 'One has to remember that, perhaps. Frances had just the same sort of violence in her.'

'Yes,' Dermot broke in, 'and one assumes there must have been some terrible provocation that day Williamson turned up at Summer Hill.'

'OK. But why can we only *assume* that? Why did Hetty never tell the court – or any of us, at least – what exactly happened that day, what the provocation was?'

'Oh, just all Williamson's cruelties towards her, as the defence showed. And, when Hetty saw him again, she lost her head.'

'But if that's the case why didn't she kill him the *first* time he showed up at Summer Hill? After all, he'd been there several days beforehand, hadn't he? Why didn't she kill him then?'

The men had no answer to this. 'Who can tell?' Dermot said eventually.

'But that's the whole point!' Léonie burst out again. '*Why* can't Hetty tell us? Privately, at least. When she saw you both – or me this afternoon. Why is she like a zombie, ever since it all happened?'

'She's trying to forget the whole thing, that's why.' Dermot attempted to speak with some consoling authority now. 'I talked to her doctor about it all. This French chap, Dr Langlois. He's some sort of . . . "psychoanalyst" he calls himself. As well as a doctor. So that she can survive, he says. In order to live with what she's done, she's burying everything that happened that day with Williamson – killing him, then the trial, being in prison, everything. Sometimes happens, he says – people like Hetty, imaginative . . . They blot it all out, pretend the whole thing never happened—'

'All right. But what do we *do*?' Léonie almost shouted. 'We can't just let her stew there, getting crazier every day.'

'No,' Dermot responded, in his optimistic mode once more. 'Said just that to Dr Langlois. And he's going to see her, on a regular basis – if the authorities allow it, and I think they will. Talk to her. That's what he does. This psychoanalytic stuff. That's what it's all about, apparently. Talking about the past, dreams and so on, so he told me—'

'I *do* know what psychoanalysis is all about.'

'Yes, well – that's the point: to try to get her to

confront reality, he says. So . . .' Dermot gestured vaguely, rather losing his optimism. 'That's really all we can do.'

Léonie slumped dejectedly. 'Oh God, it's just – I wish *I* could do something . . .' She looked up suddenly. 'Because *I'm* her past, more than anybody really.'

Mortimer glanced at Dermot an instant before turning to her. 'Yes, of course you are, Léa. So let's hope you can see her as often as . . . as you can get over . . .'

When Léonie had gone to bed that night, the two men talked, taking port together in the storm-buffeted house.

'Léa was right, of course.' Mortimer gazed into the ruby depths of his glass. 'She'd be more help to Hetty than this psycho – what is it? – chap.'

'Yes. They were close – years ago.'

'They were in love.' Mortimer, remembering all the emotional turmoil he had been indirectly part of then, corrected his son rather bluntly. 'That spectacular business when they had my flat here, and Frances found out they were up to something "unsuitable" together before they ran off with that theatrical troupe. That's obviously why Léa is rather more than just upset by the whole thing.'

'Yes . . .' Dermot turned away, dropping this topic of improper love. 'Though their relationship can't have anything to do with her killing Williamson.'

'No. All the same, you and I know, at least, that something spectacular must have happened again with Hetty that week when Williamson visited her. Frances's little brooch watch from Sandringham. And that photograph you found on her desk when you went down there after she'd been arrested – of the old Prince of Wales. She must have found the stuff about the house somewhere, found out she was his daughter.'

'Yes. But is that linked with her killing Williamson? And why did she never mention finding the watch and so on to any of us?'

'Simply because she's buried it all, like this French chap says.'

'And yet . . .' Dermot was thinking along another line now. 'As Léa said, why didn't she kill Williamson the *first* time they met?'

'Something changed her opinion about him – between the first and second meetings. That's why.' Mortimer spoke emphatically, pleased to resume his old courtroom attitudes.

'Yes. But *what* changed her opinion?'

Mortimer shrugged. 'Who knows? And we may never know now.'

Dermot drummed his fingers on the chintz arm of the chair. 'The old King,' he said impatiently. 'Something to do with her finding out about him, I'm sure. All Hetty's problems go back to him, her not knowing. We should have told her the truth years ago – and none of this would have happened.'

Mortimer grunted. 'Perhaps just the opposite. Perhaps she killed Williamson *because* she found out who her real father was. Unhinged by it in some way. Some things are better hid, Dermot – for ever.'

'I still think all this would have been avoided if Frances had been honest with Hetty, years ago.'

'Sins of the mother . . .'

'Exactly.'

'And what of Summer Hill?'

Dermot shrugged. 'Back to where we started. Place will collapse again.'

'But it mustn't.' The old man was decisive. 'You've put so much effort—'

'I can't look after it now, though – not with this Sandhurst job. And I may be posted to India. There's the hint of a brigade command there . . . .'

The two men sipped their port without further words, hearing the storm rattling the windows, rushing up from the south – sweeping up the Nore valley as they imagined it, over Summer Hill and the demesne which they both loved, a place which seemed barren to them once more, all the promise they had nurtured there, first with Frances, then with Hetty, destroyed again.

Then Mortimer, still set on finding some hope in the whole disastrous business, said suddenly, 'Robert. Robert and Léonie – and the child. Had you thought of them? He loves the place.'

'Yes, but his work in London—'

'Of course. But he could come over regularly, keep an eye on it. And holidays there with the child. Why not give him the authority at Summer Hill, while Hetty's . . . away. I'm sure he'd jump at the idea.'

'Maybe.' Dermot considered the point. Then he nodded. 'Why not?'

Mortimer smiled, fluffed his beard, licked his lips judiciously. 'Why not indeed?' He lifted his empty glass. 'Shall we have a last one? This is Taylor's Imperial – rather good. No? Got it from Findlater's last week. Think I'll get a case in for Christmas . . .'

Léonie, when she returned to London, repeated to Robert, in the same vehement tones, almost exactly what she had said to the two men.

'Yes,' Robert said. 'Hetty was in that same unresponsive way, more or less, when I saw her, too.'

In this he lied. For Hetty had been only intermittently vague when he had seen her – and certainly she had recognized him. She had said to him, 'Oh, the children's garden, Robert . . . And now all this. What a rotten, stupid thing to do – when there was so much we might have done.' And she had looked at him intently, entirely aware, almost passionate. Had she meant things all three of them might have done, Léonie included, with Mortimer and Dermot? Robert thought not, because just then she had reached forward, trying to grasp his hand, before finding the painful barrier of the wire grille.

'But what can any of us do about it now anyway?' he continued with Léonie. 'The whole thing . . . hardly bears thinking about.'

'But that's just the point! We *have* to think about it. Can't let her go quite mad there,' she added loudly.

Robert was surprised at the passion in her voice. 'You've rather changed your feelings about her, haven't you?' he asked cautiously.

'Yes. How could I not?' She was defiant.

'Well – just before, when she was in almost as much trouble as she is now, you couldn't bear the thought of her, of helping her.'

'Seeing her – it changes things.' Léonie turned away.

'Yes. Yes, it does . . .'

The thought came to Robert then: did they both love the same woman once more – just as they had all those years ago at Summer Hill? Well, if so, it hardly mattered. Hetty was quite beyond the reach of both of them now, untouchable, existing only as a wraith. But then, he thought, perhaps loving a ghost could become just as disruptive a passion as any other.

Dermot visited them a week later, pleased to dandle his god-daughter Olivia on his knee before supper. After the meal he said to them, 'Papa and I have been talking. Now that Hetty's away, would you like to take over the running of Summer Hill? Be responsible for it – whenever you can get over, I mean – and for holidays and things.'

Robert was astonished – this dream, this longed-for possession, offered to him now, albeit temporarily. He looked over at Léonie before replying. She said nothing. Her answer lay in her smile.

'Yes,' Robert said. 'Yes, I suppose—'

'Good, good.' Dermot leant forward enthusiastically.

'Olivia would love it, I'm sure. Jack Welsh has got the old pony and trap out again. And there's the river, fishing and everything—'

'Yes,' Léonie interrupted, equally enthusiastic now. 'Olivia'll love it.'

But Léonie's enthusiasm was due in part to her entirely unadmitted feeling then that, at Summer Hill, as well as having readier access to Hetty, she would be living in her aura – that passionate spirit, now lost again, but which might yet in some way be regained, returned to her. Robert, equally repressing the fact, felt almost the same thing: Hetty, not dead but sleeping; Summer Hill – an advance position from which he might better rescue her.

Hetty in her present incarceration had come to haunt them both again – just as she had years before when they lived in Paris. But now there was a difference. Then, after her callous betrayals, they had neither of them wanted her. Now, in this tragedy of her finding and so falling from grace, they both did. Both of them hoped to save her – save her sanity, her future in a world in which she had come down from her pinnacle as cold goddess to their own warm, fallible, mortal level. Ideas only of charity, of objective concern, motivated them, as they thought – hoping to restore Hetty to a free and unencumbered life, to that stance of right true character she had herself regained before meeting Craig again.

In truth, they also hoped to restore her to this spirit so that they might once more love her in some manner, a feeling they could not admit to for a moment, since once again now, as after their divisions in Egypt, they had come to love only each other. Robert, after Hetty's mental paralysis, had found it easy to repress his re-awakened desire for her, which appeared almost obscene then, like thoughts of seducing a child. And Léonie, too, had come quite to disregard that brainstorm of emotion for Hetty which had overwhelmed her six months before.

Now, by going over to Summer Hill from time to time, by simply concerning themselves with the place while Hetty was away, they thought themselves involved only in good works, as neighbours might tend a vacant plot of ground in winter, so to ensure spring growth for the absent owner; neighbours expecting nothing more than traditionally temperate growths there – daffodils, narcissi – but harbouring the vaguest, secret hope that some much more exotic flowers might bloom from the cold earth.

Hetty lay on the cell bed staring up at the ceiling. Her vagaries had changed so much for the worse that she had been moved a month before to the women's section of the criminal lunatic asylum in Dundrum, a village suburb on the south side of the city in the shade of the Dublin mountains. Dr Langlois, disappointed again in his efforts, turned away from the bunk, opening his attaché case.

A small neat man in his mid-thirties, compact and muscular, with tortoiseshell spectacles, he had delicate features and a noticeably fresh-complexioned skin, both at odds with a shock of unruly hair, thick and dark and crinkly, that leapt straight up from his scalp, giving him the air of someone permanently startled – for which he then apologized with his eyes, which were mild and kind, almost childish.

There appeared to be two quite separate people in Pierre Langlois: in his hirsute body there was a thrusting, self-confident character, limbs aggressively poised over the main chance. But, in his pale skin, the finesse of his mild blue eyes and delicate features, there was a mood of the artist, the contemplative. He was like a double-headed coin: Caesar on one side, Christ on the other.

He had qualified in Paris, specializing in venereal diseases. But, with an increasing interest in psychoanalysis,

he had gone on to study the subject in Vienna, under a
Dr Fischer, a friend and colleague of Dr Freud's. Some
years later Dr Langlois had come to Dublin at the invitation of an Irish doctor, much taken with the same
movement, a Dr Harry Craig with a practice in Fitzwilliam Square, whom Langlois had met at a conference
of the International Psychoanalytic Association in
Vienna.

Pierre's mother had been English, originally a nurse
who had married his father, also a doctor, when he had
been posted – in effect exiled – as a junior physician at the
French Hospital in London, forced there by the gentile
French medical establishment as a result of his so
favouring Dreyfus during the scandal and subsequent
trial of that officer in Paris thirty-five years before.

So Pierre spoke English almost perfectly. His father
was dead. His son had not got on with him – familial
disagreements largely, which culminated in his refusing
to join his father's practice in Paris. Six months later his
father had suffered a stroke. His mother had been taken
ten years before in the influenza epidemic in Paris. Medicine in France thereafter had not greatly appealed to
Pierre – particularly since it offered little scope in what
had become his main interest, psychoanalysis.

Fresh fields, pastures new, Pierre had thought. And,
besides, he believed English was the coming language in
both medicine and psychiatry – and thought he should
capitalize on his natural gift in that tongue. So he had
taken up Dr Craig's invitation gratefully.

Subsequently, while working under Dr Craig, who was
an old friend of Mortimer's, he had been given the task
of treating Miss Cordiner – or Laura Bowen as he knew
her better. Indeed, he was something of an admirer of
hers, having seen most of her pictures as they had
appeared in France, so that the chance of dealing with

her problems – first medical and now psychological – had appealed to him.

Hetty would have been allowed books and writing materials had she wished them. But she was beyond all that now, so that her cell contained only the very fewest personal effects and was without any decoration whatsoever. For Hetty, if she had a life at all, lived it only somewhere deep within her soul – a closed mind, which Dr Langlois, with little success, had been trying to prise open for some time.

But today, with the first hints of spring, a few light fluffy clouds passing across the blue space of the tiny window giving out on to the mountains, Dr Langlois had decided to take a quite different line with Henrietta. Opening out half a dozen travel posters which he had taken from his attaché case, he started to decorate the cell with them. They were French and German State Tourist posters, which he had obtained from Hewett's travel agency in Dublin, beautiful things, strikingly designed, vividly coloured: a skier leaping into the blue above the French Alps; an onion-domed Baroque church set against the other side of the same dazzling snow-peaked mountains; a gingerbread hostelry in the midst of the Black Forest; Mad Ludwig's Gothic fantasy castle set high on its crag above the pellucid blue waters of the Bavarian lake. Soon most of the walls were covered by these romantic visions, an air of dramatic liberation invading the cramped grey space of the cell.

It might have seemed a cruelty so to impose these dreams of escape on someone who had no chance whatsoever of indulging in them. But this was exactly Dr Langlois's intention. Having failed to elicit a response from Hetty by any conventional psychoanalytic approach, he had thought to introduce these posters as a shock treatment – a sort of cinema show as he viewed it, which, promoting these romantic visions of all the happy drama in the world, might tempt some reaction from his patient.

At first, as he hung the posters, Hetty had taken no notice. But when he came to pin up the last of them, Ludwig's castle on the crag, he saw her sudden agitation – eyes flickering as she pressed forward, half-sitting up, seeming to understand something at last in this mountain view and becoming rapidly more alarmed by what she saw.

'Yes?' he asked quietly, standing quite still at the far end of the cell like a fisherman giving the hook free play, waiting for the fish to take it firmly before striking. 'You see something . . . here?' He gestured to the fairy-tale castle.

'I . . . I l-l-lived there.' Hetty's face was angry now as she leant further forward, stabbing the air with her hand. 'Hateful . . . horrible.' She turned away, slumping back in the bed. 'Horrible, horrible . . .' she murmured, facing the wall now.

'Why? Why horrible?' Dr Langlois advanced, taking a chair by her bed. He was happy at his success here. Henrietta had not managed such a definite response in weeks. But why had this particular poster drawn it forth? Hetty cracked her finger joints in feverish annoyance, humped up, writhing in a foetal position. She made no reply.

'When did you live there, Henrietta?'

'Laura Bowen – lived – there . . .' She spoke slowly, in harsh, unnatural tones, like a medium in the voice of another woman.

Dr Langlois tried to remember a Laura Bowen motion picture with such a fairy-tale castle in it, but could not. She was fantasizing, he thought. But at least she was voicing the fantasy, speaking whole sentences now. That was something. 'When did Laura Bowen live there? *When?*' Hetty, her back towards him, continued her writhing, hunching her knees up, then down, seemingly in pain, as if struggling to force a birth. 'A castle, looking over a lake,' Dr Langlois continued. 'But where? *Where?*'

'A lodge,' Hetty replied, in that same harsh tone of another woman, Laura Bowen. 'A hunting lodge. Looking over a lake. But it was all phoney!' She screamed then. And then, just as suddenly, she sprang round in the bed, reaching out with her arms and pummelling the doctor with her fists. '*Why?*' she shouted. 'Why have you – why torture me – with *that?*'

Dr Langlois resisted her blows, while still allowing her the satisfaction, the release of hitting him about the chest. He knew well of this violent reaction. It was usually a good sign. He had experienced it several times before in sessions with other patients – how, at a certain point, a real nerve touched, the patient may literally attack the analyst, so signalling the release of some nightmare pressure, a dark secret, a long-festering mental boil, now lanced, signifying the beginning – or sometimes the end – of a cure. Yet he remained quite mystified as to why this Bavarian castle should so evoke this violent response. He was not left in doubt much longer.

'But why?' he asked, warding off her blows. '*Why* is it a torture, Henrietta?'

'Craig!' she screamed at him. 'Craig Williamson – we lived there, in Hollywood. The man I killed.' And then, just as suddenly as she had started the attack, she stopped it, dropping her arms, blinking, as if waking from a deep sleep, looking round her, dazed.

Dr Langlois smiled faintly. At last, he thought: reality. A clear, fierce, first admission of the real world which she had buried for months. She and her husband Craig Williamson – they must have lived in some sort of Hollywood imitation of a Bavarian hunting lodge, he thought. But he could not let the moment slip. 'So, you lived in a place like that—'

'Put it away – away – the picture,' Hetty interrupted

him, not looking at him or at the poster, but calm, insistent.

Dr Langlois did nothing. To remove the poster might be to let her sink back into her mute world. 'It's only a picture, Henrietta. If you face it, it won't hurt you—'

'No,' she said urgently. 'I won't – no.' She shook her head vehemently.

'But you *have* faced it – already. And you got rid of the hurt, didn't you? – here, with me. Here, look.' He reached forward and took her arm, placing her hand on his chest. 'Here – the pain is in here now, with me, not with you. I have it – see?' He kept her hand over his heartbeat. 'It's here – and it's gone. Because I've thrown it away, too. I don't need it either.' He looked at her easily, then dropped her hand. 'There, it's all gone. Disappeared.' Hetty, at this, finally turned her head and faced him.

'Is it? Really gone?'

'Yes.'

Hetty looked at him clearly for the first time in months, her vacancy dissolving, a puzzled but intelligent look on her face. 'Your hair,' she said at last. 'It stands up, doesn't it? Straight up – as if you had an electric shock. Funny . . .' She reached forward, running her fingers over his hair with the entirely unselfconscious gestures of a young child. Then, retreating, she gazed over his scalp in wonder, like someone viewing the Alps for the first time.

'Yes,' he said brightly. 'My hair – it goes straight up. Just like an electric shock. That's where the pain went out.'

Dr Langlois – he took it from his witty English mother – had an inventive humour. And he was lighthearted then in any case. Not only had Hetty seen him properly at last but she had looked at him, made comments, exactly as a young child would, quite uninhibited and naturally curious – exploring the physical attributes of a visiting uncle. She had, in this reawakening, even lost her stammer. It all added up, he felt. She was coming back into the reality of her childhood, not her maturity. And this was something he could put to good use in his future conversations with her. For it was in childhood, as he well knew, that such traumas and repressions had their origins. He would develop, open up, this distant country. Hetty was more or less a child again – returned, hovering over a violent land, which was yet the only place where she might find a cure.

When Robert, Léonie and Olivia came to Summer Hill on those earlier occasions they gloried in the place: Olivia, nearly eight, revelling in all that was new and wild; the other two remembering old emotions between them there, initial covert affections out on the river or on the croquet lawn – affections which had bloomed elsewhere, in love and marriage, which had withered in dispute several times, but which now, to their surprise, they found wonderfully revived and cemented at Summer Hill.

So that the June airs of their first holiday there together seemed to gild the lily of their content, zephyr breezes through the chestnuts increasing their ardour for the place and for each other. The great house, smelling of new paint and renewed plaster, doors and windows open to the weather, dazzled in the summer light – the old timbers cooling later when they sometimes took supper alone out on the porch, the house unbending with slow creaks and murmurs behind them.

The midsummer twilights lasted forever, as they sat without lamps on the steps, watching and waiting, silent or talking, until stars pricked the gloaming. Then, as they took candles for bed, the moths badgered the flames before the lights were doused. To their happy astonishment they found they had come into a new country of the heart at Summer Hill – two unique emigrants, for whom the house was a tender empire all round them, peopled only by benevolent spirits. Their love, which had been so fraught and divided a few months before, was nurtured here and mended.

Olivia, released into proper country for the first time, roamed free beyond all cars and streets and tall red buses – her fall of dark hair bobbing and flying as she ran into every distance: down to the salmon traps by the bridge which Jack Welsh had got working again, or standing on the look-out post with him over the river waiting for a run, seeing the fish trapped once more in a tremendous flurry by the opportunity netting; limpid dawns with her father tucked in a hide spying for otters, or out with him in the midge-veiled evenings as he waded for trout over the shallow water. Olivia was living just as Hetty had, years before at Summer Hill, but sharing it all with a father.

Sometimes, thinking of Hetty in her prison cell, Robert's thoughts ran along these lines: Hetty, then as now, lost to this world of fathers and daughters – when a moment's passion and sadness for her struck at him, so that he tried not to think of Hetty at all afterwards, both to avoid this sickening resurgent emotion and because, though she was lost to him in prison, he would also lose Summer Hill on the day of her return. If she returned? Or might she, with her lunacy, be incarcerated indefinitely? Here was a worse thought which he suppressed – for, if this proved to be the case, then he and Léonie might in some manner come into Summer Hill as a permanency. And he secretly longed for that.

Léonie, on the other hand, at least during those early holidays, was more open in her feelings about Hetty. While still firmly maintaining her charitable approach, she visited her every time they came over, finding her improved on the first occasion, but astonished at the form this had taken. Hetty seemed a child again. She talked now, more or less. She responded, but with the confused stops and starts, the bizarre logic, of childhood, in the voice and manner of someone Léonie had never known. She spoke, apropros of nothing, of her early years on the island of Domenica, of a time when only Robert had really known her.

'The island,' she had said wondrously, 'rising out of the sea from all that fluffy cotton wool mist in the mornings . . . Then the air so sharp and clear, running through the lime groves. Robert – and those rainbows . . .' She had looked at Léonie so happily then, wanting her to understand it all, and disappointed when she did not – seeming to remember nothing of their own subsequent life together at the convent school, the loving days in Dublin, the magic of Fonsy O'Grady's theatrical troupe. And this hurt Léonie to the point of jealousy almost, realizing how only Robert could join her along these paths of island memory.

So that on her return to Summer Hill she barely mentioned the substance of Hetty's talk, simply telling Robert rather abruptly that he ought to go and see Hetty instead, since she spoke of nothing but Domenica, the life she had shared with him there all those years before. But Robert was unwilling.

'Oh, Léa, I can't. There's so much to do here. And Hetty'd want me to get on with that, rather than chattering about our childhood. It's *now* we have to think about – both of us.'

And indeed Robert had much to think about and execute in this direction. On Dermot's authority, through Mr Mulrooney the solicitor in Dublin still acting on behalf of Hetty's unknown admirer, Robert had taken up on all the repairs and renovations of the house where Hetty had so suddenly left off, putting these suspended effects in hand again. For he had financial control now as well, over the various budgets for household expenses and the major repairs. And he greatly enjoyed exercising this power over a house which, though not his or his inheritance, he more and more regarded as his birthright, his home.

At first he quite accepted the temporary nature of this possession. But, as the months of Hetty's imprisonment drew on, visiting Summer Hill over long weekends, Christmas, spring and summer holidays, Robert came to forget how he was tenant here, not freeholder. Léonie, too, came vaguely to assume the role of châtelaine. This was natural, they thought – when they thought about it at all. For it was so obvious: without their practical concern over the place, their ever more frequent visits, the house would have lapsed again, decayed, lost without a purpose. It was almost inevitable, given their own growing ease and content about the house, that they should gradually come to play the part of owners, not of visitors.

They saw how Summer Hill, with its aura of grace and tradition, its spacious air and setting, had cemented their marriage, given it a real foundation, which the little flat in Hampstead had somehow not quite done. And so, in the nicest possible way, they gradually took to forgetting Hetty – unconsciously seeing how their content depended on her continued imprisonment – feeling too, in the same unconscious manner, how that happiness could be shattered by Hetty's recovery and return, when they would both once more have to confront their buried emotions for her. So, for the same reasons, they no longer had quite the same firm thoughts of saving Hetty. Rather they came to hope vaguely for her continued childish incapacity. Their happy cat's cradle at Summer Hill, seemingly so firmly held between them, was in fact a delicate thing, depending for its stability on the absence of that third hand, Hetty's, which would immediately disrupt the strings.

But Hetty, under Dr Langlois's clever intuitions, his sympathetic but insistent enquiries, was not to be so innocently childish for ever. As the months went by, turning into years, feeling for her secret wounds, he found them, one by one – exposing them, often explosively, painfully, when the long-suppressed corruptions burst forth, exhausting Hetty, but bringing her one step nearer to recovery. Through these tender probings she was not to be held in limbo indefinitely.

'But who, Henrietta? Who was it you saw upstairs that night at Fraser Hall coming out of your Mama's bedroom?' Hetty shook her head, refusing all reply. '*Who?*' Again, the ever-gentle insistence.

'A man,' Hetty said finally, almost petulantly.

'A man. Good, Henrietta. What was he doing – what was happening?'

'A row. A terrible row, in their bedroom . . .'

'And what sort of row?'

'I . . . I didn't see. But Mama ran down the landing with no clothes on – down to Elly's room where they slammed the door and he tried to break it open. The man, he'd been drinking. Rum. Always drinking rum.'

'Il était soûl?'

'Oui, il était ivre mort.'

Sometimes, knowing how her French was almost as good as her English and as a means of perhaps plumbing deeper depths in her, Dr Langlois would suddenly break into his own language.

'But who was he, this man? He cannot have been some stranger in your Mama's bedroom—'

'He was – he was,' she interrupted loudly. 'He – he was r-raping her.'

'But *who*? You must have known.' Hetty shook her head once more, dead to all his entreaties. 'Who? Who?'

Dr Langlois, stopping his slow pacing of the cell, sat down now, facing Hetty.

'My f-father,' Hetty said at last. And then she shouted, coming alive with fiery anger. 'But he *wasn't* my father! Never, ever.' And now she was shouting, weeping almost, about to attack the doctor once more – her screams reverberating about the cramped space.

Well, there it was of course, Dr Langlois thought: the loss of her father, who he knew had been killed on the island when Hetty was six or seven, so that she had, for this loss, to denigrate him subsequently, make him out to be a drunk and a rapist, a monster for betraying her with his death. So, too, because of this, she had eventually come to see him not as her father at all, which had created all the later patterns in her life, as he had learnt or guessed from her in the last months; her frantic search for a father and her consequent failures with men when they did not live up to that paternal image. It was so frequent a reason for a wounded psyche, one he had met with often before in his patients, that he was almost disappointed that such a commonplace neurosis should be Hetty's.

'So,' he asked her, as if talking to a child again. 'This man – Mr Fraser it must have been – was not your father, Henrietta?'

'No.' She was sullen now, head bowed, leaving her tear-streaks untouched.

'Who do you think was, then?' She shook her head. 'No ideas at all?'

'The old King,' Hetty said at last, almost off-handedly.

'Who?'

'Edward – Edward VII, King of England.'

Dr Langlois was properly disappointed now. After nearly two years in prison, Henrietta had been improving recently, getting out of her childish stages. Now, in a typical regression to childhood, she was fantasizing again.

So that, when he next saw Mortimer and Dermot at Islandbridge, as he did from time to time to give them news of Henrietta's progress, he had no very favourable report to offer.

'I had thought she was getting better,' he told them that summer evening in the drawing room, the river invisible behind the heavy shroud of trees. 'More reality in her mind, more coherence in her ideas, her speech. But now – inventions again, sheer fabrications.' Dr Langlois had moved to the window. He turned, gesturing hopelessly. 'For example, when I saw her last, she told me – she believes her father was the old King of England, Edward VII.' He was about to turn away again when he noticed a look of triumph on Dermot's face. And what he heard him say then kept him rooted to the spot.

'Well, doctor, that's precisely the truth. The old King was Hetty's father. Her mother never told her. It was the main reason for Hetty's hatred of her, I'm sure – suspected she was always lying to her. And she was. But we knew. Both my father and I – we were both very close to Hetty's mother when she was young. And perhaps we should have told you before. But there were – there still are – problems.' He glanced at his father. 'However, now that Hetty has told you, you ought to know the whole truth.' Dermot proceeded to tell Dr Langlois of Frances's liaison with Edward, Prince of Wales – a story which Mortimer had to confirm in every detail.

'So, Henrietta was speaking the truth.' Dr Langlois, having been astonished, had a defeated air about him now.

'Yes, absolutely.'

'She *is* improving then. But how could I? – I was so sure. Such a common fantasy: a girl's traditional father image – a King. Or the Prince of Wales . . .'

'Well, Hetty had both in a way,' Dermot broke in with some satisfaction. 'Her Papa *was* the old King. And, as you probably know from the papers, Hetty herself had a close relationship with the present Prince of Wales.'

'Yes, I remember reading of that—'

'So, you see, that's part of her problem too: the Prince had to cut her – when someone at Court, obviously, told him she was his *aunt* . . .'

Dr Langlois shook his head, astonished once more. 'Yes, of course. But the point is she has told me of this at last. And I didn't believe her. What a fool . . . She is improving. I am failing.'

'Oh, I wouldn't say that, doctor. Anyone would have thought that a complete fairy-tale.'

'Does her particular friend know this? – Robert, who she talks so often of, their life on the island together. A sort of brother to her.'

'No, he doesn't know,' Mortimer said. 'He's married to Léonie now. They look after her home at Summer Hill. Léonie was an even greater friend of Hetty's, later . . .'

'She has not spoken much of this Léonie. Though I know she comes to visit her.'

'An American woman. They were very close,' Mortimer went on. 'When they were younger. In fact – they loved each other,' he added, determined not to beat about the bush.

'I am surprised, then, that Henrietta has not spoken of her. But perhaps it will come. We are barely out of her childhood at the moment. But, if neither of them knows, how the old King was her father, they should be told, if they are to help her, now and when she is released. It would help when they visit her – for them to confirm this reality about her father. Because that's the heart of all her problems: never knowing. And Henrietta in my opinion will never completely recover *until* she knows these truths, everything that was hidden from her. Only then does she have any good chance of facing reality, of

450

properly taking her life. It is all these lies, more than anything, which have put her in the state she is in.' He looked at the two men somewhat critically through his tortoiseshell spectacles.

'Indeed,' Dermot said. 'That's always been my opinion, too. But there have been many difficulties over the years in telling her the truth. Most particularly her mother, not to mention Hetty's own often rather unbalanced state . . .'

'Well . . .' Dr Langlois spread his hands in a Gallic gesture. 'It's as you wish. But if Henrietta is to be cured the truth should be the first, the only, consideration here.'

'I'll tell Robert and Léonie then,' Dermot said with military precision. 'When next I see them.'

Dr Langlois, when he left, was incredulous at these revelations. He had begun to think Hetty's problems commonplace. Just the opposite. It was obvious now that he had only touched the surface of her many traumas. Her mother had lied about everything important to her. Without her knowing, her father had been the King of England. She and her girlfriend Léonie had been lovers, it seemed. She had had some sort of very possibly intimate relationship with her nephew, the present Prince of Wales. She had murdered her husband for some not entirely explained reason. Good God, he thought, a commonplace neurosis . . . After nearly two years he had hardly begun to plumb her depths.

This, for Henrietta, was parental deprivation and betrayal on the grand scale – mixed with subsequent sexual aberrations, combinations both within and outside her family, that he could hardly have dreamt of. No wonder she had so searched for a father figure. No wonder she had so successfully impersonated the revengeful, murderous Queen in *Nefertiti*. It was not surprising that she should have come to kill her husband in reality.

Yet, for all these appalling mental bruises and sexual bizarreries, he saw how, in Hetty's calmer moments at Dundrum, there was a firm shadow of sanity in her, a reasonable person, trying desperately to overcome these huge handicaps and escape back into reality. Indeed, he had known something of just this other woman in her earlier visits to him in Dublin over her venereal disease. And now, with this new information, he felt touched by Hetty. Her suffering to some extent at last explained – why had these men so long delayed the explanation? – drew a new and personal response from him. She had been badly misused by her family – as of course most of the patients he saw had been. Yet this woman had obviously once had such courage, gifts, beauty and spirit that her tragedy seemed the worse, so that he was all the more determined to restore these virtues to her. Henrietta was no longer just a professional challenge to him.

5

'But would it really have made any difference to Hetty?' Léonie asked disingenuously, talking to Robert in their flat the morning after Dermot had told them of Hetty's real father. 'People are what they are – whether they know who their father is or not.'

'Would have made all the difference to Hetty. It's incredible. Astonishing no one ever told her – or us.'

'But Dermot said how Frances came to forget, to deny everything about the old Prince. And now it's so clear – Frances's life, all that violence – against the British, against the *Crown*.'

'And Hetty's violence too . . .' They sat in the kitchen after breakfast, Olivia away at her school down the road in Belsize Park.

'Does it change anything, though, for us?' Léonie wondered aloud.

'I can still hardly take it all in. I don't know. Just feel . . . *angry*. So much of Hetty's life wasted, ruined, and all probably because of this. I remember . . . so wanting to help her, in the old days, about her father.'

'Me too. Always her great theme. The tears she went through. But she wouldn't have been the person she is, then or now, but for the lies. That's what made her — good and bad. Anyway, it doesn't really change anything. She's still there, the same person, locked up.'

Despite all these theories and denials, however, this news had changed their view of Hetty.

For Léonie, the knowledge of who Hetty's real father was had given her a full definition of her at last, as if someone had finally drawn the missing head of a mysterious character in a game of Consequences.

It completed Léonie's view of her after so long, filled in vital gaps, explained so much. It brought to Léonie a whole new person, someone she had never met, and wanted to meet now — just as she had so wanted to meet her before, on hearing how Hetty had regained her true self. Hetty, chameleon-like, had transformed herself once again for Léonie.

And all that Léonie felt in this manner Robert felt as well. He saw how, years before and more recently, he had only loved a part of Hetty. Now there was a final reality to be discovered, to be seen in her, a full extraordinary photograph come clear into the light, which again attracted and repelled him.

Though unable to admit it to each other they both now wanted to see Hetty again. Admitting only to a natural curiosity in all this, their knowledge of who her real

father was had stirred up embers of their old fascination
and love for her, as the startling discovery of a masterpiece under a cleaned canvas, signed and entirely auth-
enticated, will send people scurrying to view again a
favourite but neglected picture in a gallery.

'So, your Papa . . . was the old King . . .' Léonie said
diffidently, trying to catch Hetty's attention as she
walked ahead of her, preoccupied, the two of them strolling the narrow prison gardens of the women's wing in
Dundrum prison. Half a dozen other inmates wandered
in the high-walled space, safer lunatics, yet none the less
disturbed, sometimes grotesque figures: one jumping
repeatedly back and forth over a minute hillock, shouting
'Hannibal! Hannibal!' – another down on all fours
meticulously shredding and chewing individual leaves
from a pile which had blown into the garden from a row
of chestnut trees beyond the walls. The sun that autumn
afternoon was low in the October sky, so that it cast a
long shadow across the exercise yard, leaving only one
side of it in light, as the two women stood together, backs
to the wall, heads raised, quite motionless, gazing into
the sun, like fire-worshippers longing to be consumed in
these faint and temperate autumn beams. Léonie had
special permission to see her friend in this way, Hetty's
patriot mother casting privileges on her daughter from
beyond the grave.

'My Papa? – the old King?' She was entirely unconcerned.

'Yes. Dermot told us.'

'Oh. I thought you knew already . . .' Hetty had
stopped and was gazing up at the Dublin mountains.

'No, of course we didn't know.' Léonie looked at
Hetty, who was still absorbed in the mountains. Hetty
spoke now in a less childish way. But there was still
some strange vacancy, a hole deep inside her. Though she

clearly recognized her – even called her by her name now and then – her whole attitude towards her was one of dealing with a kind stranger, someone recently met. She still wasn't *there* for her, Léonie knew, as a person in memory. Their earlier life together didn't seem to figure at all in Hetty's mind. And Léonie found this unnerving. Worse, it was like the chill of death – this complete erasure of their shared past, all that they had done, all that they had felt for each other. But perhaps these meagre responses were better than nothing. Perhaps at any moment something would jog Hetty's memories of her back into life, Léonie hoped.

So to this end she said then, 'It's funny, you know – it kind of dominated all your life in the old days. Your not knowing, about your father.'

'Did it? Yes . . .' Hetty turned from the hills but did not look at Léonie, still preoccupied. They walked forward. But another young woman – hawk-nosed with some old wound running in a scar across one eye, twitching her shoulders uncontrollably – was on a collision course towards them. It was clear she would give no ground – and Hetty did not seem to see her. At the last moment Léonie took Hetty's arm and pulled her out of the way.

'Yes,' Léonie went on. 'Don't you remember? – in Dublin, at Mortimer's flat, those evenings, when you used to get into such weeps about it!'

'No?' Hetty was genuinely astonished.

'Yes!' Léonie continued rather desperately. 'And at Summer Hill – I remember one morning – you were in the old wheelchair when the postman came up the avenue—'

'A wh-*wheel* chair?'

'Yes. After your accident with Robert down those awful caves!'

'Robert!' Hetty suddenly came alive, beaming, as if

she had at last identified her earlier preoccupation. 'Oh yes, I remember Robert. On the island. And Robert – in the children's garden at Summer Hill. That was w-wonderful . . .' She nursed the memory, turning away.

'What was wonderful?'

'You know – the little garden with the old crab apple tree – the magic apples of l-life that I wanted to cure him with. And then – we so made things up there! Oh, that was really happy, kissing there. You see, I knew he always loved me. But I'd been such a beast to him – I've been talking about all that with Dr Langlois – and then we made it all up so wonderfully!'

'When?' Léonie tried to hide her sudden agitation.

'When? Oh, when he last came to see me there. When was it? Sometime – lately, wasn't it?' She rushed on, seeming in full sane spate now. 'I'd been so awful to him. But then I loved him too. So much, in the garden . . .' Her voice trailed away as she walked on ahead, counting out something on her fingers now, muttering. Then Léonie saw she was pulling petals from an imaginary flower. '"He loves me, he loves me not. He loves me, he loves me not" . . .' Hetty suddenly turned to her. 'Wh-*why* doesn't he come and see me?' she asked piti-fully, agitated, cracking her finger joints. 'It's been so long, hasn't it?' She spoke to Léonie, as if she were a confiding mother. 'Wh-why has he gone away from me?'

Léonie so wanted to think these words the ramblings of a mad woman, among the other obviously mad women about them. And at first she thought just this, until Hetty came to her then, touching her arm delicately, with the hesitant gesture. 'Do ask him. Oh, do!'

Hetty seemed so sane and open in her request, then, that Léonie felt she had spoken the truth about her extra-ordinary coming together with Robert. And she was suddenly stricken by the hurt that overwhelmed her. Why had Robert never told her?

'It was nothing,' Robert told her later, at Summer Hill. 'She was exaggerating completely. Madness. Nothing at all – that thing in the children's garden.'

'What "thing"?'

Robert sighed. 'Just old affection, goodness me! When she was so happy and restored in herself that first time I came over – I kissed her. Just an impulse. What's so surprising about that? – Good God! And now she's built it all up, poor woman – locked in there with all those other mad women, inventing things with men.'

Robert hated the lie, all the more so for knowing how reasonable it must sound. And indeed at that moment – because she so wanted to – Léonie did believe him. 'It's funny though . . .' She was pensive. 'When everyone said she was getting so much better.'

'Doesn't look like it.'

'No. Well, you really had better go and see her. Even if she's only pining for you in her crazy imagination.'

'Yes.' Robert, as a result of this revelation, was now not at all anxious to see Hetty. To do so, and because of these lies, he felt he might find himself in ever deeper waters. But this was true already. For Léonie, almost immediately, did not entirely believe him. Robert, she thought, with his restraint and formality in such matters, was the last person to kiss people impulsively – unless he loved them. And, if he had done this with Hetty, then she knew it must have been more than just friendly attention.

For the first time her image of Robert as the entirely faithful husband was dented. A small, cold sliver of doubt about him came into her heart then. While for Hetty – well, now there was something else in her feelings about her. She felt betrayed again by her in some way – and this because of Robert. She had a firm intuition of it: Hetty and Robert had found some special bond at last in the children's garden, achieved an intimacy there of some sort from which she was excluded.

When Robert, to maintain face, finally did go and see Hetty during that Christmas holiday, visiting her in the Governor's parlour with a smouldering coal fire beneath a large oleograph of the Christ Crucified, she was almost passionately forthcoming towards him, embracing him.

'Hetty—' She had nearly smothered him.

'At last – you've come. I've so missed you!' She stood away, both arms on his shoulders the better to see him, to hold him more firmly in her gaze, which seemed quite balanced now, without vacancy. 'I – I've be-been waiting for you. So m-much!' Her sanity shone out in her stumbling words. She cradled him with her eyes. 'You've no idea how much better it makes me feel – your coming . . .'

Her eyes sparkled – with tears perhaps, Robert thought. Yet all he could find to say was, 'Yes. Yes . . .'

But she noticed nothing empty in his tone, running on. 'Oh, when I'm out of here, *out* – why, then we can take up again, just where we left off – in the children's garden. We will, won't we?'

Her smile was so reasonable, as though she were speaking to her husband and such an expectation was the most natural thing in the world. And it was then that Robert realized that she was still quite mad – that she had entirely repressed the fact, which had formed such a block after their earlier coming together in the children's garden, that he was married to Léonie.

'Hetty,' he said as gently as he could. 'Of course we'll see each other. But Léa – I'm with her, you know. Married. Remember?'

'Léa?' she asked curiously.

'Of course – Léonie.'

Hetty seemed to rummage then in some dark basement of her mind, among long-forgotten things, picking them over in the dust before finding an object all tattered and torn, of no use whatsoever to her now. 'Oh, her,' she said, discarding the dull relic.

'And Olivia. Remember?'

'Who?'

'The – our child.' He tried to smile.

'Well, of course.' Hetty was almost bright again, before she hesitated. 'But we can't have children. I've s-something wrong with me . . .' She sighed, hurt by her inability to remember what was wrong here, before turning back to him. 'But we'll have each other. And Summer Hill.'

Then she embraced him again, while Robert stood in her arms, unresisting but quite unresponsive, so that she withdrew, first in sadness, then in tears. 'But wh-why?' she said at last. 'Why is there no more fe-fe-feeling for me? When you fe-felt so much before, in the children's garden?'

She shook her head in anguish – a feeling which Robert shared but gave no indication of, standing there mute, quite overcome with guilt, watching her cry, before a wardress, entering the parlour, took Hetty away, when Robert found himself alone for a moment staring at the vivid bleeding oleograph of the crucified Christ.

From then on, with this guilt, Robert started to nibble away at his marriage to Léonie. At first he was merely increasingly distant with her, as a means of hiding his feelings, repressing the whole substance of his last meeting with Hetty. But soon the sore of his deceit with both of them began to fester beneath the skin of his life – starting to erupt in little poisonous explosions.

He became short-tempered, irascible with Léonie, his old inner calm disrupted. Indeed, he thought – it was just that disruptive passion for a ghost that had now come to him. For he had to recognize it, he loved Hetty once more – and yet had so betrayed her at their last meeting. And betrayed Léonie as well, with his lies to her. Two entirely guilty loves now which, like opposing chemical elements forced together, set up an explosive turmoil, seeking release from the sealed confines of his soul.

At times, the pressure becoming almost unbearable, he thought to tell Léonie, to bring it all out into the open, to take his chances with her. But he could never finally bring himself to do this, fearing the loss of everything dear to him in her and Olivia. Instead, he began a fatal undermining of his marriage, transferring his own guilts, in shabby bits and pieces, on to Léonie, starting to blame and find fault with her over failings which were his own.

Yet Léonie, as regards Hetty, was not faultless either. So that, as a result of this distancing, these pressures that built up between them in the following months, Robert's guilts did indeed take root in her. For she, too, like Robert, still nurtured secret feelings for Hetty. While Robert was trying to repress his love for Hetty, Léonie had an unconscious hope that she might regain with her what they had once shared.

So Robert and Léonie were not so much at cross purposes in this matter. Rather they were both on the same path: one seeking surreptitious retreat down it, the other poised for an equally secret advance. They became in these covert manoeuvres confused figures to each other, alternating between performer and spectator, watching a shadow play with hands behind a lit screen, where simple fingers create demons, promoting nightmare dramas from a secret text hidden in the flesh and bone beyond the curtain. They started, turn about, as audience and shadow-master, to torture each other – never quite understanding how they had brought each other into this chamber of horrors.

Léonie asked him one day a few months later at

Summer Hill why he never saw Hetty now at all. And he had responded sharply, 'Why me? It's you she loved. As you loved her,' he added accusingly.

'Robert, that's all over and done with years ago.' She looked at him, believing the surprise she felt to be quite genuine.

'It's never over – those sorts of emotions. You said so once. You should go and see her, not me.'

'Oh, Robert.' She leant forward in the deck-chair on the sunny porch. 'What's the matter? These last months – you're so difficult. Nervy. Is it the work?' She took a convenient side-track away from what she sensed might be his real problem. And Robert took the same opportunity to follow her down it.

'Yes. I'm so tired of *The Times*. That dreary sub-editor's room upstairs. Every time I go into it – I can hardly face them all, at the long table, all dry as dust.'

'Well, move then! That man in the *Express* said they'd take you – said how much Beaverbrook liked your articles.'

'Maybe. But travel, right away somewhere – that's what I need. Then you can see Hetty without let or hindrance,' he went on acidly.

'I don't understand, darling . . .' Léonie was truly upset, alarmed.

'What's the point of pretending?' he asked wearily. 'You have this thing about Hetty. Always going up and seeing her—'

'But I don't! Haven't been for ages—'

'Then you *want* to and you're hiding it. And that's what makes me nervous.'

'It's not true! There's no "thing" between us now. None at all. Just the opposite. She hardly recognizes me. It's you who had those goings-on with her, not me. In the children's garden!' She had raised her voice now. 'And you're the one who's pretending – that "impulsive

461

kiss" you told me about. I bet! It's you two who have some secret goings-on between you now, not me.'

Soon they were fighting – just as they were both lying, for both had a hidden 'thing' about Hetty. And Léonie was unable to make any honest reckoning with herself or with him over her feelings for Hetty – and yet felt more and more helpless in the face of Robert's withdrawal from her.

Finally, in desperation, looking into her heart of hearts, she wondered if there might be some truth in what Robert had said. Did she still harbour any such emotion for Hetty? She had done, she knew, with that brainstorm over her nearly three years before. But now? She could identify nothing here – nothing but the dead coals of a fire, quite burnt out. Were there hidden embers? Perhaps. She was not going to finger through the ashes. But what if she at least spoke openly to Robert of this possibility, making such admission simply as a means of achieving a reconciliation with him? No. Such an admission, she felt, might well sink their boat in open sea. As it was, with both their ditherings and navigational deceits, their boat was heading for the rocks in any case.

Robert soon after this responded to Beaverbrook's overtures and took a position as roving political correspondent with the *Express*. With his particular knowledge of France and Germany he was soon ferrying between London, Paris and Berlin, covering – in a much freer way for the *Express* – the increasing tensions between these three capitals, a situation now exacerbated by the advent of Hitler as German Chancellor in the spring of 1933 – triangular tensions in Europe which came exactly to parallel those which grew in him, in his frustrated inability to sort out his own emotions between the two women who, like persistent tides undermining a cliff, had come to eat away at his own life.

*

Hetty lapsed badly after Robert's visit. When Dr Langlois saw her next she had gone right back into her wan vacancy and despair. And the reason soon became obvious.

'But your friend Robert,' Dr Langlois said, 'he is married, with a family. It is unreal of you – to have this . . . so strong feeling for him.'

'*Who* am I to feel for then?' she asked bitterly. 'Must fe-feel for someone . . . And him – I feel for *him*.' She was petulantly childish now. Yet Dr Langlois had to concede her point.

'But of course . . .' Yet having said this he felt at a momentary loss. For whom indeed could she properly feel, incarcerated in this asylum? 'But you must first feel for yourself, Henrietta – realistically,' he went on, finding an appropriate way out. 'You must feel well about *yourself*. And distant people cannot really help you in that.'

'Oh, but they can! Here.' She tapped her head. 'I think about him here. And wha-what a help that is.'

Again Dr Langlois had no ready answer. It was a fair point, if one were completely balanced. So that he said then, by way of diversion really, 'Why do you not think of Léonie? You have other friends. And she was a great friend, I know. And comes to see you much more often than Robert does.'

Hetty was puzzled. 'But Léonie . . .' She dried up.

'Yes?'

'Why, she's a *woman*,' Hetty had a startled look now – a child caught with her hand in a sweet jar.

'Yes?' Dr Langlois said evenly.

'I can't think of a woman in the same way.' Hetty turned her face to the cell window. There was the finger-cracking again. Dr Langlois saw how, inadvertently almost, he had raised this repressed trauma in Hetty's life – her love of women.

'Why can't you think of a woman in that same way?'

'It's – it's disgusting!'

'Is it? Why is it?' Hetty shook her head violently. 'It's not disgusting – if you face it,' Dr Langlois went on. 'Only hiding it makes it disgusting. Don't you see?' Still Hetty refused any response. 'One can love men and women, Henrietta – if that is how you really feel. And you have, have you not? – loved both?'

'No! No!' she shouted, turning to him.

He smiled a fraction. 'But of course you have. Why not? – if it is natural to you. What is *not* natural is to hide from it. You are trying to love Robert too much, so that you may pretend that you don't love your old friend Léonie at all. But admit them both, Henrietta, love them, think of them both, *reasonably* . . .'

She looked into his eyes at last. 'Yes?'

He nodded. 'Yes . . .'

Hetty was relieved, a clarity coming into her own eyes then, as if she had suddenly seen an old and well-loved landmark coming into view at last after a long and perilous journey.

'Léonie,' she said. 'So loved—' She clapped her hand to her mouth as if she had said something obscene.

But Hetty was recovering. At first, though, there was a great block over Léonie which Dr Langlois at once started to try to clear. It took him months. Hetty had forgotten Léonie, put her right out of mind, simply because, once again but more thoroughly, she needed to repress the terrible guilt she felt over her earlier behaviour towards her, all her betrayals: leaving her without a word for Hollywood, seducing her so as to take her from Robert in Egypt. Now, under Dr Langlois's careful probings, she had to face, to admit, these betrayals all over again. But now, in her unbalanced state, the guilt lay at a much deeper level. It was a long excavation.

'So,' Dr Langlois said one squally spring day, 'you

were in Egypt, with Léonie. And Robert – when you were making *Nefertiti*?'

'Yes. They visited . . . the location,' she said quite reasonably. Then silence. The rain battered on the cell window.

'Of course. They would visit. You were old friends.' Dr Langlois eased himself on the hard chair. 'Except, as you've told me – how originally you went to America without telling Léonie. So she cannot have been too pleased to see you in Egypt . . .'

'No. But she was – later . . .' Hetty spoke with a small note of triumph.

'Later, she was friendly to you?'

'Yes.'

'How?'

But Hetty closed up then, quite unable to face the facts of what had happened 'later'. She gazed vacantly out at the rain. So that Dr Langlois, seeing these usual signs of a complete refusal to respond, took a stab in the dark. 'You met later out there, alone. You made things up. You loved her again—'

'No, no—'

'Yes, Henrietta. You made love with her – you loved her again.' Hetty shook her head. 'But she was "friendly" to you, you admitted that. What *made* her so suddenly friendly to you again?' he ran on, insisting. Still she shook her head. 'And if she was friendly, then it must have been because she liked you once more. And if that was the case, you loved each other again, didn't you?'

Hetty had started to weep now. 'No, no!' she said desperately.

'Yes, Henrietta.'

'All right!' she suddenly screamed like a cornered animal. 'Yes, yes, *yes!*' Then she broke down helplessly.

'So . . .' Dr Langlois had calmed her slightly after a

minute or so. 'You made it up. But what about Robert? He was out there too.'

'Of course,' she gasped between her sobs. 'And that was what was so awful. I – I made love to her really only for that re-reason. To get her away from him. No, it was so awful . . .' She shook her head violently again, trying to push the memory away, to repress it once more.

'Face it, Henrietta. *Face it!*' he told her urgently. 'Keep it there. Don't bury it again. Here . . .' He took her hand and placed it on his head, on his wiry stand of hair. 'Put it all away here, let it escape.'

Keeping her hand there for a minute, Dr Langlois saw her relax, just as she had done on that first occasion with him, through this same emblematic transference, as the pain drained away from her and into him.

So that, when Léonie next came to see her, while Robert, after the last in a series of quarrels, had gone away for a month to Europe, the air was quite changed between the two women. Hetty entirely recognized Léonie now, was sane and confident about her once more.

Léonie was astonished and charmed by the transformation. Here indeed was the return of right, true character in Hetty, which she had heard about before her imprisonment. Here was the woman she had so longed to meet – the masterpiece restored. They, too, met in the Governor's parlour. But it was almost spring, not winter, and the crucified Christ seemed a wan and unthreatening figure over the empty grate.

'Léa, dearest, it's such ages . . .' Hetty gazed at her friend, having embraced her gently. 'Such a foolishness, all this time, about you. Not – not knowing you. But I'm so much better now, with Dr Langlois. Now I can see you properly. I *know* you! Oh, for so long . . .' She shook her despondently. But then she suddenly brightened. 'Yes, now I *know* you!' And she laughed outright.

'Yes. These last years – the coldness – I didn't quite understand . . .' Léonie was tactful.

'Of course not!' Hetty stood up and wandered round the room. 'I didn't myself. But now – it's going to be all right. With us.' She turned to her intently. 'And, when I'm out, we can be proper friends again, can't we?'

'Well, of course . . .' Léonie temporized, still somewhat distant, still trying to suppress her joy at this turn of events – trying to hold down the swarm of sudden emotions re-born for Hetty then, feelings she had for so long repressed. But they bloomed in the spring light streaming into the room, an irrepressible harbinger of renewal, which warmed all her old thoughts for Hetty, so that she said, 'Why, of course, Hetty. But we can be friends like that *now*, too.'

And something impelled her then – the last rows with Robert, the sense of how some long emptiness might soon be filled, a streak of her real nature rising into the glittering light – to move towards Hetty. She kissed her.

Later they talked. 'Oh, Robert,' Léonie said. 'It's not been easy. It's – it's gone bad. I don't quite know why.'

'Why? You must *feel* why?'

'Rows. And things . . .'

'About me?' Hetty asked sadly.

'Sometimes.'

'My fault, too. I had such a thing about him – he must have told you, when he came to see me here, and before at Summer Hill.'

'No. No, he didn't. But I thought – something was going on.'

'Well, it was. When he first came back to see me at Summer Hill, I sort of – well, I fell for him. The past and everything. It caught up with us. Then it all became a m-mad obsession. He did – for me – here in prison. But Dr Langlois has put all that away. I'm clear, I'm in control of it. It's all *raisonnable* now – that's his great word!' She

467

laughed and Léonie believed her. 'Oh, Léonie, it's so good to have made things up again. And I'll tell Robert when he gets b-back, when he comes to see me again – that I'm over all that nonsense for him. And then you and he'll be fine together again. You'll see! – You will be, because it's all going to be *reasonable* from now on.'

Hetty's blue eyes were locked in Léonie's. And something quite unreasonable passed between them then – old nature, old times, old emotion – all reborn: a flood which they could not resist, which they hoped only might support and not drown them. But they did not speak a word of it in the long silence – this love between them flowing again in the spring light.

One by one Hetty's fears and phobias were brought to the surface, admitted, released – until she and Dr Langlois came to that day nearly three years before when Craig had first arrived at Summer Hill.

'How could you have let your husband in? You told me how you hated him for all he'd done to you.'

'Another man – had come the week before . . .' She described the visit of the bogus detective Mariani. 'But Craig had set him up, just so I'd do another picture with him, *Joan of Arc* . . .'

'I'd like to have seen you in that . . . But how would this Mariani have helped towards that?'

Still there were the remnants of refusal in Hetty's face. 'That's – that's a d-different story . . .'

'Well?' Dr Langlois said conversationally. They were much easier, calmer together now.

'Another murder – in Hollywood. A director called Taylor. I thought – I still think – I killed him . . .' Hetty told Dr Langlois of the incident years before in Taylor's bungalow. 'So you see,' she went on, 'Craig sent this Mariani to scare me, so he could turn up later and console me by telling me I *hadn't* killed Taylor – and get me to work on this new picture with him. And that's why I let him in, so he could tell me all this, that of course I *hadn't* killed Taylor – which is exactly what he did!'

She continued her tale of all that had happened that week at Summer Hill: how she had discovered Mariani was an impostor, seeing then how Craig had lied about the detective, about her not killing Taylor, about who her real father was. All lies – all the most terrible, despicable, hurtful lies. So that when he had turned up again – well, she had killed him.

'I see . . .' Dr Langlois sighed. He had the truth now at last, as the court at her trial never had.

'So you see how, don't you? I *must* have killed Taylor – and the old King wasn't my father. That's what I had to believe afterwards.' Hetty bowed her head, vacant again, seeming not to care one way or the other about the implications of these truths for her.

But Dr Langlois, watching this stark depression overwhelm her, saw full well how Hetty had another and perhaps greater problem on her hands now. He fidgeted a moment, uncertain how to proceed. 'Well, we know the King *was* your father. That part was true.' He offered her this consolation.

'Yes, but I killed Taylor. I must have done. And ce-ce-certainly Craig. I killed b-both of them.' She was quite dulled now, careless, hopeless in her response. Her stammer had come back badly once more.

Hetty had been stricken by these final admissions of the last weeks, which she had come to face without hiding from them, without taking refuge in her earlier imbalance. Now she had nowhere to retreat to. Now, in her sanity, she saw how she was a double assassin.

Yes, Dr Langlois thought, as far as plain balance went, she was almost cured. And there was just the problem – another task they had to face, just as difficult: Hetty's cure-in-life. She had come to admit the worst, to face it.

But this had left her, as he had seen in these last weeks, quite drained, hopeless. Finally admitting everything, she had now to face the open guilt for these acts – acts which were real, not fantasies. How was she to carry this burden with her into freedom, when she was released, as she might well be, at the end of the year?

What use curing someone, dispelling their traumas, all those dark deep-sea repressions, only to leave them beached, immobile, manically depressed, prey to marauding reality? To leave Hetty like this would be to have her regress at the first pressure, taking on the camouflage of fantasy and madness again, to slip back into those murky depths where she would no longer have to confront these terrible facts.

Henrietta now had to live with cold truth. And that, left alone in her present state, could be just as much a threat as her madness had been. She would not survive in the real world outside. Dr Langlois was certain of that – not without watching, care, above all company. Of course, as he had come to see, that had been Henrietta's problem all along: she was simply unable to live alone.

But even these were not to be the worst of Hetty's problems. Robert, taken abroad by his work, stayed away from London and Summer Hill more often in the ensuing months of 1935. So that Léonie, coming over on her own with Olivia, had indeed more frequent opportunities to see Hetty without let or hindrance.

These first meetings, on the surface at least, seemed only to cement their friendship. But that did not last. Soon they came, if they could in no way speak about it, to admit their love in a variety of other covert ways: a brief touch, a happy gaze, the joy and hurt at meeting and departure – those irrepressible marks of the heart coming clear into the light without words.

Léonie, so aware of the fire, kept her distance from it, yet could not turn away from its warmth – a temptation encouraged by Robert's cold silence and increasing absences. Hetty likewise – seeing all the dangers, how she might once again disrupt Léonie's marriage in this renewed *tendresse* – took a firm rein on these emotions, quite determined that the horse should not bolt. Yet she too, equally aware that she was saddled on a dangerously exciting beast, did not dismount. Both women in their separate ways were playing with fire.

Yet, even so, things might have been saved if Hetty, one day in midsummer and feeling so depressed, had not written to Léonie while Robert was still away in Berlin – a mild enough letter, speaking of this and that, of her depression, but ending with a rash postscript. 'I can't tell you, Léa, what it means to me in these awful dumps to have you again – thinking of you.'

This, too, would have brought about nothing if Robert, finishing with the Berlin conference early and travelling over to Summer Hill unexpectedly, had not taken the post first the following morning and seen the envelope from Hetty with its Dundrum postmark and had afterwards enquired about its contents. Léonie had no alternative but to show it to him.

'So,' he said shortly when he had read it. 'Just as I said. You and Hetty – all the old business again. All the while I've been away.'

'No.' Léonie tried to bring some conviction into her voice.

'But of course!' He was sardonic. 'As I said – the leopard not changing its spots!' There was a harsh, unreal triumph in his voice. 'Well, so be it. But don't expect me to tag along with your life any longer. We went through all this before in Paris – after Egypt. And I'm not going through it again. You have her. But not me.'

Listening to this, Léonie bowed her head, paralysed. Once before, indeed, in Egypt, she had protested how this was not true, how she loved only him. And he had

471

believed her and they had made things up. But he would not believe her again. For what could she truthfully protest now? – that she loved both of them, then as now, and that for Robert it was the same, she was sure, except that he would not admit it, his old morality keeping him in a straitjacket – so that rather than relax these strictures he would sooner lose both of them, because he could not share love in this way, as she would so willingly have done. Léonie sensed all this clearly, but was afraid to talk of it directly, thinking this would only incense him further.

'You've not seen the whole thing, Robert,' was all she said.

'I see it too well. This last year everything, growing between you and Hetty again. Besides, it's all there in the letter, in black and white.'

'The letter, the postscript, only says the half of it. The other half is *you*.'

'The other third, you mean, if I'm in the equation at all. And I don't want to be, in any case,' he added sagely, a man supposedly free of all this messy emotion.

'If only you realized how you *are* in it, so lovingly – how all three of us are part of the same thing.'

'Three's a crowd, Léa. It's lucky I'm going to Abyssinia,' he went on curtly, 'to cover this fascist war.'

Léonie, quite desolated, was left alone in Summer Hill. And when next she saw Hetty she could not refrain from telling her a little of these events with Robert. Who else could she speak to? – of something that had come to tear her heart out. She did not want Hetty's sympathy, just her response as confidante, for Hetty was that third in the magic equation.

Had Hetty been less depressed, had she been free and stronger, she would certainly have taken on this role, listened to, consoled, her friend – and more perhaps. But as it was, imprisoned still in every sense, behind walls and with her own guilts over Taylor and Craig still fresh, it was she who really needed help even more than Léonie. So that her reaction on hearing this news was to dismount that wild horse at once, to stumble away from Léonie, taking with her a further burden – this time of intolerable guilt.

'Oh God,' she said towards the end of their short meeting, agitated again, cracking her finger joints. 'I can't – I can't bear it. Because it's all my fault again. And I truly didn't mean it this time—'

'But it's *not*, Hetty!' Léonie was suffering agonies at this unexpected reaction. 'Not at all. No one's to blame. Who's to *blame* – for loving.'

Hetty shook her head violently, turning away. 'Of course there's blame – *me*! Without me, this would never have happened—'

'And me!'

'No,' Hetty almost shouted. 'I'm the outsider. Had no right to this – loving you again. And you must make it up with Robert, as soon as you can—'

'What's the use? He won't believe me any more. And, besides, why should he?' Léonie was brutal in her truth-telling now. 'It's true. I love you and him – both of you.'

But Hetty could face none of this. All she saw then was that once more she had destroyed Léonie's – and Robert's – marriage, their lives, the life of their child. She in her madness – for she must in some way still be mad, she thought, so to let this love for Léonie escape into the open – had betrayed these two friends once more, ruined their lives and so again ruined herself.

The scalding meeting ended in tears. Hetty rushed from the room. Léonie was left alone – totally thereafter, for Hetty refused to see her again at Dundrum and Robert was somewhere far up-country in Abyssinia, where she heard nothing from him and could not reach him.

★

Dr Langlois, in the months after this terrible meeting, had to start with Hetty almost all over again. Her despondency, though she was sane – at least for as long as she saw him every week – seemed fathomless. And soon Dr Langlois learnt the reasons for it. Indeed, he thought, hearing Hetty describe her last meeting with Léonie: 'The heart has its reasons, which reason knows nothing of.'

Hetty, though he believed her when she told him how hard she had tried to prevent it, had fallen back into her old nature with her girlfriend. As Léonie must have done, too. And yet of course, with the men in their lives, this, though the deepest part perhaps, was only one aspect of their natures. These two women had struggled for years – in sharing their affection between men and women: two who could not determine love by gender; women who simply loved. What more natural? What better? But of course the world would not accept that – and they were forced to repress that nature – with all the consequent disasters.

But it was precisely his job to confront just such *bizarreries du coeur*, to disentangle them, let his patients live with them – however deep and grievous the wounds imposed by others had been. There was nothing in life, no psychological horror or aberration, which could not, he thought, be brought to light and dispelled. For these were the world's impositions, misguided men and women punishing others, refusing to see how their strictures were more aberrant still. And to clear all this brutal undergrowth – this was the promise of the new science of the mind. And he would fulfil this promise with Henrietta, from her imprisonment and beyond into freedom if necessary, for she was to be released before the end of the year.

So, in the succeeding summer and autumn months, he talked to her week by week, and sometimes more

often – digging, listening, questioning, consoling or sometimes more forcibly trying to get her to see the innate
philosophy of human life, what was tragic and joyful at
the same moment – which was exactly Hetty's predicament in that she could not face the dichotomy.

He told her one day, as hints of autumn crept
over the faded chestnut trees beyond the prison walls,
purple-cloud shadows sweeping over the mountains
above them, 'Your friend Léonie was right, from what
I can gather. You cannot blame people – for loving,
Henrietta. And there can be, there often is, pain for
others involved.'

'But *that* is the b-b-blame then. *Me*.' She sat on the
cell bed, hunched up, arms fiercely wrapped about her,
as if she were freezing. But the room was warm, almost
muggy, in the hot afternoon sun. She stood up quickly,
fanning herself, seeming to change her suffering from
cold to warmth in an instant. She was almost feverish
now. 'One mustn't hurt people. Everything, as long as
you don't do that. And look what I've done.'

'Yes. And that's a fine "rule of thumb" as you English
say, Henrietta. But none of us is actually made that way.
Nature is not subject, I'm afraid, to such morality. We
are thinking animals. There is the division. The problem.
Try our best not to hurt, of course. But in the end we
remain . . . animal. And we have to accept – or painfully
learn – this. That gulf, that flaw in all our lives. Accept
it, when we have to – and not blame yourself or others
for it. And Léonie's husband Robert, from what you tell
me – he especially will have to realize this. We never stop
growing up, you know – doing battle with our nature.
Blame . . .' He waved his hands dismissively. 'In these
matters of the heart there cannot be blame, for there is
no law.'

He looked up at Hetty, standing by the cell window
now, gazing out at the cloud shadows sweeping over the

yellow gorse on the hills – and saw the animal longing in her gaze then, a bird that would fly. There, outside the window, was the freedom she longed for but most feared. For she, like him, knew how she would drown in life alone.

He felt stricken by her predicament – her closest friends both gone, her cousin Dermot away in India; husband, lovers, friends, family, parents – all that makes for stepping stones in life disappeared in the flood. Hetty could see across the water once more. But there was no one to take her over to the other side.

Yet he had to say it then, how she must move forward somehow, into that life beyond the cell window. 'In a month or two,' he said almost desperately. 'We've heard the news – you'll be free, Hetty. You'll find it easier—'

She turned to him then suddenly. 'You – you called me Hetty. You've never called me that before.' Seeing his puzzled face, myopic eyes enlarged behind the tortoiseshell spectacles, his shock of unruly hair seemed all the more rampant, giving him a really farouche air. So that she had to smile. Then she laughed. 'That's nice – that's wonderful! "Hetty" . . .' She tested her name against him, enjoying the informality of it, the intimacy which it implied. Taking his spectacles off, wiping his face in the muggy air, Dr Langlois laughed as well.

Hetty, he saw, in these last turmoil-filled months of analysis, had been brought to life again not by any of his psychoanalytic probings but by an inadvertent human word, a diminution of her own name, which he had heard her friends call her. Her nature had at last been touched by this – quite by mistake, he thought. But it was no mistake. Dr Langlois had lapsed into the personal with Hetty, his professional objectivity towards her beginning to crack.

Hetty walked over to him. She put her hand on his crinkly hair. 'No,' she said after a few seconds. 'I d-d-don't think I need that sort of release any more. Somehow, you've done it all – just then, calling me like that.' She brushed the prickly strands. 'It's just nice – to touch your hair.'

When Hetty was released a few months later, it was Dr Langlois who drove her down to Summer Hill in his new Wolseley motor. But now she called him Pierre. It was December when they drove through Naas and Carlow towards the great house. In the early twilight the cold turned to snow, a few light flakes, spiralling into the windscreen, the wipers nudging them aside. Soon the leafless roadside trees, caught in the headlights, had gathered a carapace of astonishing white as they sped into the night. She touched his arm now and then, for comfort, against the huge dark outside.

They flew down the trail between the pines, one ahead of the other, skis hissing over the snow, the pass of trees ringing in their ears. The sun had dipped over the Col Marmontan to the west and it was almost dark as they came out into the open, moving through orchards and hillside farms now, a silver-and-red-streaked aura in the sky above them, with the cold creeping in everywhere. But they were still warm, the inn less than a mile away, the lights of the village of Marmontan twinkling here and there between the pines as they rushed down the valley.

Later, at the bar of the logwood inn with its fine trophies of chamois horns set round the polished wooden walls, they sipped hot chocolate in the sudden dark, their faces glazed with heat and sunburn.

Hetty touched his peeling nose. 'You'll need some more cream . . .' She kept her finger there, before taking a minute piece of skin off, gazing at it. 'They say we shed our skin completely, every seven years,' she said. 'Become new people.'

Pierre put his glasses on. He needed them only to read.

He read Hetty then. 'Yes – yes, something like that. Every seven years!'

But Hetty had changed in far less time than that: in barely three months since that day when he had brought her back to Summer Hill, when he had spent Christmas with her. Then they had come on six weeks later, he taking leave from his practice, for this skiing holiday at Marmontan in the high Savoy. He looked at the change now – her own sun-frazzled face, the blue eyes heightened against the silver-brown skin, the lines still there, small crow's feet running away from eyes and mouth, but only as archaeological remains, already softening in the growth of new life which she had found with him.

Later, at the far end of the big wood-floored room, scarred from hob-nailed boots, they sat over a red-checked tablecloth, eating cuts of venison in a chestnut sauce. And she said, 'You like that new wine – so have some. Don't be stupid. I need only smell it! The wine breath . . .'

'I don't suppose it would hurt you.'

'No. Probably not. But why tempt fate? – with all this.' She cradled her arms on the table, head down, then to one side, gazing at him. And her way of looking at him now was only the repetition of a common gesture she made towards him, confirmation of a happy certainty and fidelity between them.

'Such a day! . . .' she said.

'Such a two days.'

They had left the village early the previous morning, climbing the slopes with rucksacks, sealskins attached to the bottom of their skis, towards the higher passes, making long runs there over the untracked snow – marked only by the spoor of hares and foxes in the high world at the edge of the treeline, moving from one peak to another across country, sleeping the night in an empty woodcutter's hut on a mattress filled with beech leaves, leaving a few francs for the wood they burnt in the open grate, grilling cuts of venison, warming the bread, before travelling back next day, their own tracks still in the snow, without any others, making great glacier runs, smooth and straight and seemingly for ever over the bright slopes in the winter sun. They had barely spoken in all this exaltation. And now, in their fatigue, it was the same – only a shorthand on these wonders available to them.

'Oh, such days,' Hetty said, sniffing the carafe of new wine. '*All* such days.'

'Yes.'

Later that night they lay together under a feather quilt in the big bed upstairs, a window partly open to the starry night, star bright without a moon, skin to skin. It had not been easy, the first time – making love. Hetty, for her disease alone, had not wanted it. But her syphilis had been long dormant now. And Pierre took the risk in any case. Now they made love easily. She said afterwards, '"When the day breaks, and the shadows flee away."' And soon it was morning, glitter-cold and bright, when the maid came in to light the big porcelain stove, bringing them breakfast afterwards, the fire crackling and the room smelling of coffee and burnt pine.

Hetty reached out, touching his hand on the coffee pot. 'I didn't dream again last night, did I? – a nightmare or anything? You didn't hear anything?'

'No. And not any night here. I told you.'

At first, when they had slept together, a month before at his flat in Fitzwilliam Square, there had been nightmares, a continuation of those she had had in prison and later, on her own in Summer Hill: fearful dreams, of running, but not running, of being caught, pursuing Léonie or Robert, or being pursued by them, monstrous visions of Craig. But, for as long as she had slept with

Pierre, in these last weeks, they had not returned. As long as she was with him, she was free.

Pierre finished his coffee. Then, with a gesture of formal decision, he wiped his mouth and put on his spectacles. 'Will you – will you, do you think, marry me?'

His voice was calm enough. But with his hair on end, tousled with the night, he had such a more-than-usually startled look that Hetty had to laugh. She laughed outright. 'But would you have me?' she asked eventually.

'Oh yes,' he said more cheerfully. 'I don't see why not.' He pondered the idea with Gallic thoroughness, as if trying to find a flaw, any at all, in the proposition. 'No, I can't see why not.'

'Who's to object?' Hetty said. But the joke did not quite work, so that they clasped each other suddenly, in a moment's sadness, as the fire roared in the tall stove, hugging each other. But then Hetty brightened. 'My!' she gasped. 'What a cosy warm this is!'

Two days later they took the train back to Paris and from there they returned to Summer Hill.

6

The starting flag dropped and the crowd started to bay almost at once. The half-dozen hunters, jockeys crouched over their necks, thundered away between the gorse bushes, over the first of the hedges, before they were lost to sight in a dip of the hill. Hetty and Pierre, surrounded by some hundreds of other vociferous and rather bibulous locals, rushed across the track and up the slope to where they had a vantage point over the circular course: nearly three miles, marked by yellow flags, running away through rough pasture, over banks, fences, ditches, and hedges, behind coppices of elm – all in the lee of Mount Brandon across the river from Summer Hill.

It was the high season for point-to-point racing in Ireland. So it was a bitterly cold and rainy March afternoon. They shivered in their hats and mackintoshes as they shouted, Pierre watching the disappearing colours of the jockeys as the horses stretched out in a line now, the bright golds, reds and blues of the racing pullovers strung over the sodden grey landscape like a vivid beaded necklace.

'Come on, Nickelodeon!' Pierre shouted. He had backed this grey mare, ten shillings on, to win. But at ten to one it was almost the rank outsider. 'How is she doing?' he asked Hetty, who had the binoculars.

'It's nowhere,' she told him happily. 'It's last! My horse is second,' she added with sweet malice.

'Here, let me see – give me the glasses!' She handed them over. '*Mon Dieu!* It *is* last.' The horses were making a gradual circle now, disappearing behind slopes and spinneys, before re-emerging. 'And your horse, Mooncoin, is third. Come on, Nickelodeon,' he shouted despairingly. Hetty took the glasses back.

'No hope, Pierre. I told you – an old mare.'

The horses disappeared again for half a minute. But, turning into the home stretch, when they came in sight once more, Hetty saw there were only three horses left in the race. At the last hedge before a ditch, Nickelodeon, to her astonishment, was leading, with Mooncoin nowhere. Then the mare, tiring, stumbled on the far side, landing awkwardly – and the other two horses passed her. But, recovering wonderfully, Nickelodeon made ground in the last few furlongs, overtook the second horse and was only beaten to the post by a length.

'See, I told you!' Hetty said, breathless with excitement and happy now at Pierre's justified choice of a nag. 'If only you'd backed it *both* ways. Then you'd have had your money back – and some winnings!' She tore up her own betting slip.

'Both ways? – I don't understand you.'

'Yes – you back it to win, or for a place, second or third. You don't have to go for bust on every race, like I told you.'

'"Go for bust"?'

'Yes – I mean risk everything on a win.'

'Well, why not?' he asked, putting his spectacles on, looking at her.

'Because a clever gambler hedges his bets . . .'

'"Hedges his bets"?'

'Yes, you idiot! That means you do things *both* ways, to cover possible losses.'

'Oh? Why should I do that?'

'It's safer, that's why. You can get to keep your money that way.'

'I'd prefer to "go for bust".' He smiled, taking his glasses off, blurred with raindrops now, and then his tweed cap which had come to perch dangerously on top of his unruly hair.

He looked naked. Hetty could have kissed him. Instead she said tenderly, chanting her mocking tones, humbled by her feelings for this humble man, 'Well, all right. But you can tear your betting ticket up now as well.'

Responding suddenly, he tore it with a dramatic flourish, then threw the pieces in the air, laughing, as the tiny bits of coloured cardboard spun away like confetti in the squally wind.

Across the river they could see the bare winter trees around Summer Hill, the house itself, with an inviting curl of smoke rising from a chimney, visible behind.

'It'll be dark soon.' Hetty shivered in her mackintosh. 'Only one more race anyway. Teatime? There's fruit cake. Elly made it specially for you – and strong tea,' she added with exaggerated relish. 'Strong enough to trot a mouse across . . .'

'What? A mouse in the tea? What is—'

'Just an expression. Irish . . .'

She took his arm and they went back to the car. It stuck in the muddy gateway as they were leaving. But a big carthorse was on hand for just such eventualities, pulling them out with ropes.

'Ireland, indeed,' Pierre said, rather morose behind the wheel. It had started to rain in earnest now. 'Strange being pulled by a horse – in my new Wolseley . . .'

'It's wonderful,' Hetty said as they moved sluggishly forward.

'Yes. Yes, I suppose it is.'

And it was, for both of them in the ensuing months, when spring and summer came – great deep drifts of daffodils spreading over the lawn, followed by the high green of the chestnuts in early June round the edge of the demesne.

Hetty recovered herself once more at Summer Hill. Pierre came down from Dublin every weekend. Elly and Jack Welsh took to him – seeing not only how he was Hetty's cure, but now her friend – and more than that perhaps. They had separate bedrooms, for propriety – Pierre along the landing from Hetty's primrose room. But late at night he came to her, leaving at dawn, before Elly brought Hetty a cup of tea at eight.

Aunt Emily still occupied her bedroom-studio. But at over seventy she was finally frail. Age, stalking her in the last years, had suddenly taken her by surprise, bowing her head, withering her neck and leg muscles, so that she stayed indoors mostly, working at her immemorial sketchbooks, drawing and painting from the memory of things. Sometimes, on a fine day, she would go out in the wicker wheelchair, Hetty pushing her down the avenue and back.

'So,' Aunt Emily said one brilliant June morning. 'You've taken up with men again. I'd have thought you'd have learnt your lesson there.' She was grumpy, sitting under a patchwork quilt rug.

'Yes. But not men. A man. Pierre.'

Aunt Emily sighed. 'All the same. There's no teaching you, is there?'

'Yes, there is! I've learnt. Pierre is a good man.'

'Oh, they all make themselves out to be that. Clever that way, you know. But just look at you – with men. Taken in by every one of them.'

Hetty laughed. 'No, Aunt Emily. One can be lucky, you know. At last.'

Aunt Emily humphed. 'Here – stop here. Give me the sketchbook.' She raised a gnarled, arthritic hand from beneath the rug. Hetty handed her the Combridge's sketchbook and a big carpenter's pencil. Aunt Emily put the pad on her lap, holding the pencil awkwardly. But she could still move it about the paper deftly, almost at once finding the essence of the sketch, filling in the rough outlines, as Hetty watched over her shoulder.

'What is it, Aunt Emily? What are you looking at? There's nothing there.'

They had stopped at the first of the white gates, near the house, with tall chestnut trees to either side. Aunt Emily had drawn one of the trees. And now she was sketching something in the branches. Soon Hetty saw what it was – a tree house high up among the leaves, with a little pagoda roof, all in the Chinese manner. And inside it, soon emerging, Hetty saw two figures – a man and a woman. One was obviously her, the other, with a shock of dark hair sticking up like a crop of bad thatch, was Pierre.

'What is it? Why are we up there?'

'Excuse yourself, girl. Men . . . It's all a childish game, don't you see? Playing houses.'

'But why is it a *Chinese* house?'

'Oh, it's *fun* – while it lasts.'

For Léonie and Robert meanwhile things had not lasted. They had come to the beginning of the end. Robert had spent months away reporting Mussolini's war in Abyssinia and when he returned to London late the previous year he and Léonie had not managed to make things up. Léonie had tried – vaguely. But she was depressed and bitter over many things: his lack of communication with her ('How could I? – there were no posts out of Addis Ababa'), but for a few messages passed on to her and Olivia from the *Express* newsroom – while her break-up with Hetty continued to hurt, to obsess her.

She felt deeply that both Robert and Hetty had let her down. She was sullen, unforthcoming, on Robert's return. What was the use of explaining things to him, she thought? He had gone from her, in body, but much more in spirit. What was there to explain that wouldn't appear either self-justificatory or give him further ammunition against her?

None the less she was honest enough and still at that point just sufficiently anxious to make things up with him, to tell him how her relationship with Hetty had come to an end.

He seemed unconcerned. 'Well, it was all a crazy thing from the beginning. I'm not surprised.'

'It came to an end because she didn't want to break things up between you and me,' she said dully.

'No doubt. But you love her. You love women. What use is that – for our marriage?'

'You loved her, too.'

He shrugged. 'A long time ago.'

'In Summer Hill as well, last year. She told me.'

He poured some more coffee. They were having breakfast. Olivia, at a boarding school now in Kent, was not with them – due back for the Christmas holidays in a few days' time. 'Summer Hill,' he said, sipping his coffee. 'Yes. But that was impulsive. I told you. A passing thing. And it's not my nature, to love *men*. That's the crucial difference.'

'I wouldn't have minded, if that were the case.'

'No. But that's the whole point. We're built differently. And I do mind. Anyway . . .' He remained aloof. 'There's Olivia. I'll pick her up in Maidstone. There's Christmas. Let's make the best of it.'

There was silence until Léonie said, 'Robert, what is it that's got into you? You were never really like this. OK, we have these differences. But for you to be so *cold*, impersonal, unconcerned.'

He stood up, draining his cup. 'The war, maybe. Ethiopians strung up with piano wire in the main square in Addis. Or flung from aeroplanes, alive, and finding them spattered about in the valleys.'

'Yes, but to be so hard as this, now that you're home—'

'Well—'

'It's so much not you!' She was her old concerned self again for a moment. 'This time last year – we were happy, going to Summer Hill for Christmas . . .'

He turned to her bitterly. 'I loved Summer Hill. That was my home. Don't you see?'

'Well, yes, I *do* see. But we both knew Hetty was going to be free one day, that she'd take over again there. And if only you'd been a bit more understanding about all of us . . .' Léonie had started to shake with suppressed anger. 'You wouldn't have lost Summer Hill. And nor would I. And I love it, too.'

'Well . . .' Robert had no real answer.

And this was exactly what made him hard. He had lost Summer Hill because of his own intransigent attitude – a fine nature become bitter and self-righteous because of his inability to share Léonie with Hetty. Had he been able to yield on this, the prize would have been Summer Hill – and the two women. But to these ends he could not sacrifice what he saw as a paramount morality. And so he had to be hard – to defend the stockade he had set up to protect himself against his own, and the other two women's, marauding nature.

So, too, the real reason for Léonie's lack of ardour in regaining him – her creeping dislike for him indeed – was that she saw all this in quite a different way: how for the sake of dull principle, as she viewed it, he had wrecked their marriage, lost them both Summer Hill and Hetty as well. And, since she was angry then at his inability to admit anything of this, she told him as much.

'You know the *real* reason for your coldness, Robert? It's not the war, or my loving Hetty – but simply that you can't relax, over your real nature, or mine, for we *both* love Hetty. If you could just stop playing dog-in-the-manger – you could have Summer Hill. And me. And her. Your principles are killing you.'

He left for the *Express* office without another word.

And Léonie was able to confirm her thoughts on Robert then. It had not been Hetty who had destroyed their marriage. It had been Robert with his unyielding nature. What Robert had as a strength in his character, Léonie could only see as weakness. It was something which he must always have possessed, she thought. Before, she had seen this only as a rather stuffy European sense of duty, something which had amused her, even endeared him to her. But, now that it had so destroyed things between them all, she could only abhor this in him. It was not now a sense of honour which he harboured, as she had earlier seen it. It was a façade, hiding an essential immaturity, an inability to adapt, sheer jealous childishness. Whereas she at last fully admitted her own divided nature, and was prepared to face and grow with it, Robert, the child, could not do this.

Robert's charm, balance and good sense had been destroyed, she thought, by this fatal weakness, this intransigence in his soul preventing him from seeing the real nature of living, loving and giving. So, after he had left that morning, she believed she might better survive without him – better swim alone than sink with a wounded man, pulling her down.

Yet Léonie in all this failed to see the truth, just as Robert had. Anger, hurt and high emotion had blinded them. For they were both of them, in their opposing attitudes, entirely true to their natures. Robert's beliefs were not a weakness. They were the product of his old-fashioned Victorian background and a temperament that happened to match this. And so were Léonie's beliefs – moulded by her father's always very liberal ethics, her own sexual characteristics, her modern and relaxed view of things. Robert would and could not for a moment give substance to the animal in him, to what he saw as aberrant. Léonie could not accept this denial in him of what to her was entirely natural. They both remained, according to their lights, honourable people. Their incompatibility lay in their strengths, not in their weaknesses.

So that their separation, when it came a few months later, was all the more tragic – two people who, through their hurt, could no longer see the virtues in each other. And perhaps it was hearing of Hetty's marriage to Pierre in that summer of 1937 which brought about the final rupture between them.

Hetty and Pierre were married in France at a civil ceremony outside Paris, at the Mairie of the village of Saint-Germain-en-Laye, where Pierre had relations, cousins of his, who lived in a small *manoir* there. Hetty had told only her most immediate circle of her plans. But some of the French press got wind of the event the day before the wedding, and a paragraph on it came through on the tape from Agence-France-Presse to the *Express* newsroom in London where Robert, checking through that day's news from France, spotted the item: 'Mlle Henrietta Cordiner, qui était autrefois la vedette fabuleuse Hollywoodienne Laura Bowen, fut mariée hier à Docteur Pierre Langlois, à Saint-German-en-Laye . . .'

He told Léonie when he saw her that night. She barely responded. She had been busy arranging their summer holiday. She and Olivia were going to Paris first for a few days, visiting her father who still lived in the old house in Passy, before all three of them went on for a month to the seaside, where they had rented a villa near Carteret in Normandy. Robert, who had conferences and interviews throughout most of the summer, in Paris, Rome and Berlin, was to join them there as and when he could.

'So,' Robert continued rather sourly that evening, 'you won't have to worry about Hetty any more . . .' Again Léonie made no real reply. And they left it at that.

But Léonie no longer saw the pretty gingerbread villa above the cliffs over the beach which they had rented once before; she could not remember the details of picking Olivia up the following day from the school in Kent – had no mind for all the other business of tickets and travel. She saw only Hetty – a sudden sharp vision: the slant of blue eyes, the particular smile, shy yet audacious, the run of lips, a face she had kissed. All this now quite lost to her. Then she saw Robert standing in the kitchen doorway, a hint of triumph on his face. And she thought afterwards, journeying to Paris with Olivia, how it was just then, as he stood in the kitchen doorway, that she had ceased to love him.

Hetty meanwhile crossed over the Channel on that same day, but in the opposite direction, returning with Pierre to Summer Hill, while Robert a day later took the train to Berlin – and the day after Léonie and the other two made the journey north-west to Carteret. Each of them travelled in a quite different direction, all three of their lives now irretrievably broken and separate.

And, because this was so painful a thought to them, they took care not to think about it. Léonie exhausted herself in holiday activities with Olivia and Ben Straus, her father. Robert pursued his featured news stories throughout Europe that summer with incessant attack – while Hetty buried any thoughts she had of the other two by throwing herself, with Pierre's active help and money, into the life of Summer Hill, once more starting to redecorate and repair all that she had had to abandon there six years before. A proper bathroom was at last installed and electric light finally brought to the house, by means of a windcharger, a tall metal pylon set on top of the hill beyond the orchard, a sinister whirring device as she thought it, so that she was secretly pleased when it broke down, as it quite often did, and they had to return to oil and candlelight.

These frenetic activities successfully held the past at bay for all three of them. And then, as the months went by, they began to bury it, like the ruins of a lost city, which started to sink below ground, overlaid by layer upon layer of current life, the detritus of time, expunging the memory of that once-fabulous civilisation all three had shared in. The past, which had indeed been merely sleeping between them all, now seemed quite dead.

But, as an archaeologist can see in the vague ridges of a grassy hillock the lines of old walls and buildings far beneath, there emerged a vibrancy sometimes, emanating from somewhere, which brought the three of them back to each other when they least expected it.

At odd moments in the following months, years, they were linked in this way – a sudden spirit arriving in a room or from an open sky, making its presence felt as a spine-pricking air wafting through a closed door or an odour of violets in midwinter, which would immediately bring one or other of them together again, in that sealed room or frozen solstice of the year. The ghosts of their former selves walked, meeting across the ether, each wraith identifying the other in their old manner.

One autumn evening, when the windcharger had failed again, Hetty was lighting a tall oil standard lamp in the airless drawing room at Summer Hill. Her eye caught by some movement, she looked over at the small drum table some distance from her. On it the zoetrope, the magic wheel of life, was moving slowly, the strip of coloured paper inside beginning to animate the cow jumping over the moon. And then she thought of Léonie.

The memory was startlingly clear, though she had quite forgotten about it in the intervening years. She and Léonie had been sitting there, next to the same small drum table, years before, Léonie reading *Middlemarch* to her, while she sat in the wheelchair after her accident in the caves, spinning the same wheel of life, repelled, yet attracted by the moving images, which had seemed to beckon her, away from Léonie, her future staring at her somehow in that wilful machine.

Robert, walking alone one evening along the Unter den Linden in Berlin, was suddenly assailed not by the smell of lime trees in blossom, but by an odour of violets, almost sickly-sweet, so that he hurried on, as if pursued by some horror.

Léonie, standing on the porch of the villa above the beach at Carteret in the dazzling sunlight on the last day of the holiday, suddenly thought she heard a voice behind her, so that she swung round. The voice said, 'Hallo! What on earth are you doing here?' The tones were unmistakable. It was Hetty's voice; Hetty, inside the villa soon to emerge and welcome her on the porch, as if they were about to begin everything again.

All three of them immediately re-buried these vivid intimations of each other, like undertakers returning to a grave, secretly at night, determined now to do the job properly, to hammer longer nails into the coffin of their past, prevent any further release of these tormented spirits.

Dermot returned from India on leave that December in 1937, staying first with his father at Islandbridge, before both of them came down to Summer Hill for Christmas. Mortimer, at eighty-four, with painful arthritis and a touch of gout, was a little feeble, so that he, rather than Aunt Emily, sometimes used the wheelchair in the house and down the front drive. But his mind – and his great beard – were both as stately as ever.

All five of them celebrated Christmas with dinner in the great dining room. Though Aunt Emily, her moods ever more bizarre, insisted she ate separately, having a small round table to herself, set next to Hetty, sitting there with her back turned to the company, apparently intent only on her private *dégustation*, but in fact, like a nosey-parker in a café, eavesdropping sharply on everything that passed at the main table.

The dining room had at last been redecorated, a dozen Cordiner ancestors cleaned in their portraits. These gallants, more gallant still in the flickering light from the great candelabra on either sideboard, seemed poised to launch themselves from their wire trapezes hanging from the picture rails. The ceiling bas-reliefs, already gilt, were yet more golden: risen angels, swaying vines, soaring strings – all starting to sail across the oval blue which was their usually windless empyrean, seemingly stirred now by the candle flames far below them. What was shadowy and inanimate on the walls and ceiling came to life in rising waves of light, breathing motion into this lifeless art, returning the room to all its old familial vivacity – bonds of blood, elegance and wit, a calm certainty in the order of some heavenly host.

Elly had done a splendid turkey and a flaming plum pudding; and, when this last arrived, Pierre had raised his glass to her, proposing a toast. Elly, in her long white apron, blushed.

Later, when port and nuts were passed round and some crackers pulled, Mortimer, in a funny paper hat, turned to Hetty. 'Thank God women don't have to leave the room these days, least not with us . . .' He gazed at her. Hetty, in a dark, loose-flowing Paisley dress, with her amethyst pendant earrings, looked back at him fondly. 'Without you, Hetty, none of us would be here now.' He raised his glass to her. 'To your return to Summer Hill – to your most happy and welcome return . . .' Then, gesturing his glass towards the portraits, he added, 'Among your ancestors.'

And it seemed that these Cordiner grandees responded to the toast, drawing life from the flowering light, the wine's breath; that the presence of these five people raising their glasses – for even Aunt Emily joined in this toast – had revivified them in their gleaming colours, their white cravats, stiff gilded coats and breeches, wigs and rouged cheeks.

Mortimer, encouraged by the port, went on. 'I remember a great dinner party here at this same table – oh, it must be forty years ago now, with your grandmother, Hetty – old Sir Desmond and Sarah, Henry, Eustace, your mother Frances – and Humphrey Saunders, that theatrical rogue who was such a friend to us all. And Bunty and Austin . . .' He seemed to half-raise his glass as he spoke, acknowledging if not toasting the memory of all these Cordiners dead and gone, while the table remained silent. 'All the women left the room, of course, with the port, and we started to talk of Home Rule . . .' Mortimer smiled, then cleared his throat. 'Or rather I must have started it. None of the men – except Humphrey of course – had the least idea of what was upon them in Ireland – that Home Rule was inevitable and would come soon or else come violently. I told them so. And it did both . . .' He looked about him with as much awe as his patrician features allowed. 'So that I never thought to sit here again like this – among Cordiners. With all those other Cordiners.' He tipped his glass in their direction. 'Yet here we are!' He brightened. 'By the grace of God – for whom I can't say I've ever had an over-abundance of time. None the less, he must have had a hand in this. But may I say, if I be not struck down in the saying, that the bigger hand is yours, Hetty, and you with Pierre.' He turned to the doctor, then back to Hetty. 'Let me honour your fortitude, in survival – and simply your being here this Christmas, and many more to come.'

They drank her health.

'Th-th-thank you . . .' Hetty was nervous. 'Thank you all. I s-s-survived only because of all of you here, no other reason.'

And then, having raised her glass to them in return, Hetty, quite inadvertently it seemed, raised her glass once more, offering the traditional Christmas toast. 'To absent friends,' she said.

One of the candles started to gutter and complete silence returned. Silence, for there was nothing anyone cared to say about these absent friends – and enemies – dead or alive, or in the family portraits, all of whom, taking their cue, spirited themselves into the room then, invading the silence, like latecomers gate-crashing the feast, the welcome and unwelcome together, seeking their rights, to share in this living toast, to answer it in their own coin; to reprimand the present company, to plead their case, to justify, explain, redeem or just to express their love again, of all that they had once loved in this great house – speaking from whatever distance or tomb they occupied, calling voicelessly from afar or from the Cordiner vault in the little family church over the river, actors in a passionate dumb crambo condemned to wander for ever, seeking their true theatre, which was here at Summer Hill, among these other living Cordiners.

The following evening, on Boxing Day, Hetty, renewing the old custom at Summer Hill, had invited Jack and Elly, together with the new maid Bridget and the half-dozen other people of the village who were now working again on the estate, with their families, to take their presents from the tall Christmas tree set up in the great hall. She and Dermot, with a step-ladder, had been preparing the tree for the last half-hour. And now, half-way up the steps, Dermot started to light the candles one by one about the tall fir. Soon, the candles all lit, the hall began to smell of warmed pine and burnt wax, a smell that Hetty so remembered from her childhood here. So that when Dermot came down from the ladder she took his hand involuntarily.

'What?' he asked.

'Just all this! Can't believe it. All . . . How much! – returned to me.'

'But it's yours, Hetty. Always has been.'

'No. I lost it all. You know very well. All this: the gift of some "admirer".'

'Yes . . .'

'Some rich fan. But who, Dermot? Who, I've often wondered. Do you think Mr Mulrooney could ever be got to tell?'

'No.' Then Dermot, deciding on something, changed his tack. 'But I've had my ideas – and why shouldn't you know them now? Now that you're settled.'

'Oh, do tell!' Hetty was all enthusiasm.

'I – I can only think it must have been your friend David, seven or eight years ago, when he was Prince of Wales – before the abdication.'

Hetty's face clouded suddenly. 'David? But why?'

'Making amends. For his grandfather. And his behaviour to you.'

Hetty's face, lit by the myriad flickering candles, was ghostly bright now, a mix of awe and hurt. 'You *think* so?' The candles stirred in some faint breath coming down the stairway.

'I can't think who else. He would have had the motive, above all the need – once he'd been told who you were, as somebody must have done – remembering how he'd had to treat you then, dropping you completely. And with his impulsive nature – it's just the sort of gesture he'd have made. I feel it.' He looked at Hetty. Head bowed, she was agitated, cracking her finger joints. 'But you mustn't get all fraught about it, Hetty.' He put his hand on hers.

'No, I'm not. It's just all that r-r-royal business. I still haven't really come to terms with it – be-be-being the old King's daughter.'

'Well, that's true. There's no doubt—'

'And now this, that his grandson – poor David – might have given me back all this.'

Dermot, using the last of his Swan Vestas, lit his pipe, letting a curl of rich smoke drift in the air. 'The past sometimes has a way of settling its bad debts, Hetty, of paying for old wrongs. Sometimes. And I think that's what's happened for you. Goodness me!' He swung his pipe in the air. 'All those years ago, when you and I first met – that day you sent me over the weir in the boat, remember? – you were such a put-upon child, all those lies . . . Your Mama's hurt – so that she hurt you. Remember that so well – and wondering if anything would ever come right for you.'

'And it didn't – went from bad to worse.'

'Yes! But that's just what I mean. There was Pierre at the end. And all this.' He gestured round the great hall. 'All this, waiting for you. A reward. Sometimes things do end well, you know. And you, and the child I knew – no one could have deserved it more.'

They heard the others moving in the drawing room and the footsteps of the estate workers coming along the passageway behind them. Hetty kissed Dermot quickly on the cheek. 'Thank you. But you're my best reward.'

Dermot turned, almost embarrassed, fearing he had said too much. And Hetty thought then – loving Dermot in that old familial way at last, which she could not do before – how her life was filled with every sort of love.

Yet something still irked her, stirred in the very corner of her mind, an itch, a loss. She knew what it was, but refused to touch the dead pain lest she might re-awaken it. She was complete in every way at Summer Hill that Christmas – but for the lack of those two others, her contemporaries, who had made up all her young life in the great house. And these two she had lost, irretrievably. But they lived, she knew. They were alive somewhere at that very moment – just as they lay dead in that sealed cupboard of her mind – as in a hidden sarcophagus, embalmed, surrounded by the grave-gifts they had all shared in a previous life together, funerary emblems, cartouches, mysterious hieroglyphics – all the texts of a lost language whose Rosetta stone had been smashed and buried as well.

The company arrived in the hall. Dermot put away the stepladder. Hetty stood alone by the sparkling Christmas tree, a tall frail figure in a quiet dress, amethyst pendants motionless at her ears, the parcelled presents lapping round her feet in brightly coloured waves: the châtelaine resurrected, who would now dispense these gifts, supported by everyone and everything that was most dear to her. And yet, standing there alone, before Pierre joined her, she had the air of someone quite lost.

*

Robert and Léonie had separated. Robert's political commentaries for the *Express*, featured on the leader page now, had brought him more money as well as prominence, so that he had the income to set himself up in a small top floor flat in John Street, up from High Holborn, not far from the *Express* building in Fleet Street. Léonie retained the pretty top-floor flat in Hampstead, while Olivia, now nearly fourteen, remained at the boarding school in Kent, returning sometimes at weekends to Hampstead, where Robert, when he was not abroad, saw her.

But he was in Europe much of the time now, reporting on the ever-increasing political tensions consequent on Hitler's aggressive policies – his open demands for the Sudetenland, his covert intent to annexe Austria, his harrying of the Jews in Germany. So that although Robert saw as much of Olivia as he could when he was home, and sent her postcards from everywhere he went, he saw little enough of Léonie. However, that Christmas at least, they were all together in Paris with Léonie's father at the house in Passy.

Ben Straus had aged well. At nearly seventy-five his hair had barely thinned, was all a rich silver now, and he still possessed his old mix of wit, bustling American ease, above all his liberal man-of-the-world stance. He had continued working part-time for the American Marine Insurance and Salvage Company in the Avenue de l'Opéra until only the year before. And now he spent his leisure strolling the city he loved so much, taking a cab or the air on the open deck of the number 63 bus down the Avenue Henri Martin, going to the Café de la Paix or the Crillon bar next to his embassy, passing the time with his old cronies.

If Olivia was confused and hurt over her parents' behaviour and problems, Ben Straus understood most of it. And Léonie had filled in some, if not all, of the obscurer details. She did not tell him how she had wished that all three of them, she and Robert and Hetty, could have shared Summer Hill together. She told him nothing of her hopes here and of how Robert had destroyed them. She hid these longings from him, for she could not face them in herself.

Instead she said how they had come apart in dribs and drabs – Robert's work taking him abroad so often, an incompatibility of character – how they could no longer supply anything of each other's needs. And her father accepted this, if not entirely. For he sensed there was another reason, and that that was Hetty. He knew well how his daughter had loved her, and supposed she might still in some manner. And that here, perhaps, was the greater reason for things having come apart between her and Robert. But he said nothing of this, only consoled her as he could.

'Things, well, they get to be like that between people,' he told her on Christmas Eve, as they sat alone together in the small upstairs salon, after Robert had taken Olivia out to the Cirque d'Hiver, the two of them sipping flutes of Veuve Clicquot. 'There's little to be done about it. And, once it gets beyond a certain point, there's no retrieving the situation. Though people often kid themselves they can. Only start out to save the marriage – when it's already dead.' He smiled faintly. 'Glad at least you haven't done that. A clean enough break. And don't feel blame. Because there's little point in that either. It's the fate of people – to complicate their lives. And few can get to untangle it afterwards.'

'Yes. But I'd like to have done just that. Because it *could* have been set straight.' Léonie spoke with barely suppressed passion.

'Of course! We Americans, we believe in that more than most. Setting everything to rights! And you can sometimes do that with a wrecked ship. But, if it's a marriage, well, you usually can't – and there's no insurance policy that'll cover it.'

'I still think Robert and I could've stayed together, if – if he hadn't been so *stiff*, unyielding about things . . .'

'What things?' he asked gently.

'Oh, so many things.'

Ben Straus played with the stem of his glass. He thought he knew what these things were, but could not say so directly. 'Yes . . .' he said. Then, changing tone and tack, he asked brightly, 'And Hetty? Do you have any news of her?'

Léonie responded in the same casual tone, but it was not easy. 'No, nothing on what I last told you. She's cut off everything completely, with us, me and Robert – living with some Frenchman at Summer Hill, like I said.'

Ben Straus shook his head, making nothing of this response, staring into the champagne bubbles. 'Extraordinary girl. Quite extraordinary. Always saw it in her, that mix of Jewish and Irish – the magic people . . . But dangerous, volcanic. Lucky there aren't too many of them around!'

'Yes,' Léonie said dully, head bowed, before she stood up and walked to the curtained window. Her father knew she was trying to hide some emotion, tears even – and knew almost for a certainty then what must have taken her and Robert apart. But he left it at that.

'So, what will you do now?' he asked, bright once more, much in his old get-up-and-go mode. 'Ever thought of taking up the singing again? Your voice – it's still lovely.' He smiled at her, loving this hurt daughter of his more than ever.

'Too old – and too late.'

'Oh no! It's never that. That's nonsense, Léa, from us Strauses. At thirty-eight, why, things need only be starting for you.'

'What things?'

He leant over and touched her hand. 'You know something, I was all of thirty-eight and more before I married your mother.'

'But I'm a woman.'

'So? That's no bar. There are other fish in the sea.'

He smiled again, raising his glass. But it was quite a few moments before Léonie finally raised hers, and then with little conviction.

At Summer Hill, after the presents had been given out and the estate families had gone home, the others gathered round the tree, Dermot up on the step-ladder again, extinguishing the higher candles, snubbing out the little dancing flames one by one.

'Well – *voilà un Noël!*' Pierre said.

'And the next – and the next!' Hetty said with vast enthusiasm. 'We'll meet here every year like this – won't we?'

'Yes, I hope so,' Dermot called out, licking a sooty finger, extinguishing a top candle, before climbing down to them. 'Except my brigade's being called back from Delhi—'

'Well, that's even better! So you'll be much closer to home anyway.'

'Yes. But it's because they really need the troops back here at home – Auchinleck, our C-in-C in Delhi, told me privately.'

'So what? What does that mean?' Hetty asked.

'Hitler,' Pierre put in quickly, snuffing out one of the lower candles. 'War,' he added abruptly.

'But I thought we – I mean the British – we weren't going to have any trouble with that little moustache. Everyone, Chamberlain, says so.'

Mortimer humphed in his wheelchair. 'All the fools and the appeasers say so. Dawson of *The Times* and his fatuous cronies. But the more we kowtow to that little moustache the more trouble we'll have from him.'

'Exactly,' Pierre said. 'Though the French, we think we can hold him on the line – the Maginot line.'

'Possibly.' Dermot wiped his fingers. 'But in my view the French Army won't hold him there at all. Because he won't come that way. Hitler's armoured divisions will go straight through – right to the north, through the Low Countries.'

'But that's Holland, Belgium,' Hetty said.

'Oh, the Germans will eat them as a snack – for breakfast,' Dermot, quite unusually for him, was terse, his wit mordant.

The company was silent.

Hetty, wanting to break the suddenly glum mood, said, 'I know! Let's sing some songs, a few rousing carols and things – "Good King Wenceslas" – we've not played a thing on the p-piano here, not for years! And it's still Christmas!'

They went into the drawing room, where Pierre opened the whole lid of the old Blüthner grand for Hetty, taking out a pile of music which had been stored there, lying over the strings, and putting it out for her on the music stand.

'There,' he told her. '"Oodles" of music for you. The right Irish expression?'

'Oh, I can play it all from memory.'

Some books of music fell from the stand before Hetty could start. So that when she finally looked up she suddenly saw a score of Puccini's confronting her: *Madame Butterfly* – the same score which she and Léonie had used, guying all that emotion, years before at Summer Hill. She stared at the prelude. The music came back to her. The sweet, plangent notes struck in her heart. The past was in front of her once more in all its loss. And the future was suddenly indefinite.

Upstairs Aunt Emily, by an oil lamp – for she refused

to use the electric light – was at work on a drawing. It was another of her vivid natural history pictures taken from memory from about the demesne. It showed a dead rabbit lying on the snow, brilliant meringue folds running down the lawn to the river gorge, with the bare winter trees and house in the background. The rabbit, its bloody entrails splashed in the immediate foreground, red against white, was being devoured by black crows.

Downstairs she heard the faint music and voices. '"Good King Wenceslas looked out, on the feast of Stephen, When the snow lay round about, deep and crisp and even" . . .'

7

After Christmas Robert took Olivia back with him to London while Léonie stayed on in Paris with her father until the new year; he had suggested she might come with him to a dinner party celebration with Ambassador Bullitt at the American Embassy on New Year's Eve. So that it was not until early in that January of 1938 that Léonie finally returned home. Despite all the festivities, she remained low in spirits. So much had ended for her and the new year promised nothing. To cheer her up, Ben Straus had bought her a return trip to London on the Dunkirk–Dover night ferry.

'I couldn't reserve you a bunk. Booked up. But they told me you'd be almost sure to get one on board – cancellations, or a little money to the conductor. Anyway, it's all first class, so you'll be *comfortable*.'

He came with her to the Gare du Nord, kissing her at the entrance to the green and cream Pullman carriage;

the big engine letting off steam, mushrooms of smoke spiralling up into the freezing air.

'Yes, comfortable . . .' He repeated the thought idly. 'Because in the end, when things go adrift in one's life – there's always a solace in comfort. The little things – Veuve Clicquot, first class sleepers . . .' He smiled and they embraced again. 'You'll see,' he told her as she climbed on board. 'Next time we meet, when I get over to London with the better weather, you'll be a different person. Know you will. We Strauses – we're never down for long!'

He prayed she would meet some other man. He was not the least censorious of what he had long before recognized as his daughter's divided sexuality and, for the most part, he had always liked and admired Hetty. But there was no doubt that Hetty had finally been a disaster for Léonie, and that she had been the real reason for the break-up of his daughter's marriage. And, since he loved Léonie more than anyone, he said to her then, as a last word, 'Seriously, though, bound to be other fish in the sea . . .'

Buffers clanked. The long train stirred minutely. Late-comers shouted and rushed along the platform. A signal turned from red to green out in the bitter night. A whistle shrieked and in a minute the train started to move. Léonie waved to her father for as long as she could see the crown of his silver head on the disappearing platform. Then she turned into the dark corridor, unable to restrain her tears.

There were no sleeping compartments available. She might possibly share one of the double compartments, the conductor told her. But, in her present mood, she did not want this. She had a seat, though, a veritable armchair in heavy maroon plush, once she had mopped her eyes and tidied herself in the Ladies. She had a copy of that evening's *Paris-Soir* and a fashion magazine, too.

But she could not concentrate on either. She was depressed at leaving her father. And the chic advertisements in *Elle* depressed her further. She felt frumpy, fat and sad. She had put on weight in these last months, eating too much, especially chocolates, as some sort of recompense, she supposed, for her various losses. And now she felt hungry again. She would take dinner at the first sitting.

Arriving in the dining car, she saw the soft pools of light from the coloured scalloped shades over little silver table lamps, set on every gleaming white tablecloth. The head waiter brought her to a table for two right at the end of the car.

'*Si vous voulez partager?*'

No, she did not mind sharing – not the meal at least.

Another woman was already sitting there. Léonie could not see her head, hidden by the lampshade. But her hands were visible, embroidering or repairing a sequined Victorian envelope purse, a needle being thrust deftly to and fro under the light. An older woman, Léonie thought, who might not care for company.

'*Si cela est égal à Madame?*'

Léonie spoke to the hands, assuming they were French. And then, to one side of the coloured *art décoratif* lampshade, the woman's face appeared, sharply triangular, pastel-coloured, brown and rose, the red-tinged hair, parted exactly in the middle, sweeping straight down past wide brown eyes behind glasses, a competent but withdrawn, preoccupied look.

'*Non, pas du tout,*' the woman said. '*Soyez la bienvenue.*'

Léonie, sitting down, was surprised. Far from being old the woman was about her age: a pretty mouth that turned down slightly on each side, eyes that slanted upwards in balance, it seemed, giving her face a strange symmetry, a vaguely oriental air. Yet she must certainly be French, Léonie thought. Her clothes confirmed that. She was beautifully dressed in a three-quarter-length cotton gaberdine coat with patch pockets and a wide roll collar over a high-collared shirt, striped in red and white, an ivory cameo brooch at the top stud. A low-crowned wide-brimmed stiff felt hat with a bow trim lay on the table beside her. She put it beneath the table, allowing Léonie more space, then passed her the menu.

Léonie gazed at the choice for a minute before peeping over the top of the card at the other woman, now entirely absorbed in her needlework once more.

She was smallish – rather her own build, Léonie thought. But she had not let her body run to an inch of fat. Léonie saw that, too – the sharply narrowing waist, hugged by the candy-striped shirt, behind the open coat. And Léonie envied her that – but even more her complexion and her hair. Her cheeks in the soft light had a peachy opalescence, which was not from the lamp or any make-up – simply a bloom of youth retained, the skin everywhere absolutely unflawed. And her hair was that perfect wavy brown colour, ripening into red, ending in a flutter of curls about the nape, under the ears – again nature's work, not that of any hairdresser with curling tongs or tints. That was obvious. Only her nose might have been criticised. It was very straight and pointed, but ended too soon – abruptly, in a sudden *retroussé* – as if the designer had lost his nerve at the last minute in this otherwise heady creation.

She might have been a mannequin, Léonie thought, in her chic clothes, with her upright carriage. Yet she was surely too small, and perhaps too old – and somehow too distant, formal, even severe. So that Léonie feared to open any conversation with her. 'Do Not Disturb,' the woman seemed to say, totally absorbed in her sewing.

And indeed they might never have spoken if another

waiter, assuming they were together, had not arrived at their table with his note-pad.

'*Mesdames? Vous avez choisi?*'

He looked expectantly at them each in turn – and the two women regarded each other an instant. Léonie forced a smile. '*Nous . . . nous ne sommes pas ensemble.*' She offered the menu back to the woman. '*Madame – elle était ici d'abord.*'

'*Non, non – je vous en prie.*' The woman, refusing the menu with a delicate gesture, offered Léonie first choice.

'*Non, pas du tout.*' Léonie in turn tried to hand it back. The waiter, confused now, was becoming impatient. Léonie was nervous, in a panic almost. 'Oh God,' she said. 'I don't know . . .' The waiter fidgeted. She scanned the menu furiously.

'Try the veal escalope.' She heard the voice opposite. 'I've had it before on this train and it's good. They do it without too much batter.'

'Oh, thank you.' She turned to the waiter. 'The veal, please.' She spoke in English now herself, before looking back at the woman, astonished. 'I'd . . . I'd no idea you were English.'

The woman smiled for the first time, then nodded, so that her curls danced. 'Yes, English. Or half so.' She left the other half open. 'And I thought you must be French, too.'

'No, well I . . . I've lived in France a lot, went to school here. But I'm actually American.'

'Of course – there's that slight intonation. I couldn't spot it at once.'

The woman's tone was outgoing and direct. But Léonie felt she was not really seeing her, was looking through and not at her – her calm grey eyes unfocused, vague. But then she took her glasses off and the effect was startlingly different. 'Sorry,' she said. 'I hadn't quite seen you. I've been so tied up with this sewing. Forgive me. I can't see anything much beyond my nose with them on!'

She looked at Léonie properly then for the first time. 'I'm Jennifer Bryden.'

'Léonie – Léonie Straus.' Léonie wondered immediately afterwards why she had given her maiden, not her married, name.

With the crush of people and the steaming dishes, it was becoming warm in the dining car – so that Jennifer had to take off her coat half-way through the meal. Léonie saw the vague imprint of her breasts through the striped shirt, as she moved her arm across the table, pouring from the bottle of hock they had decided to share.

Léonie raised her glass. 'How nice to have some company on these trips,' she said casually, trying not to notice how her heart had started to thump.

By the time their dessert arrived they had become only a little better acquainted. Despite the relaxed mood in the dining car, the touch of alcohol, their exchanges remained strangely stilted, formal. Something – something wary and unspoken – seemed to prevent them falling into any true ease of communication. And yet, as Léonie felt, it was not any coldness between them. Rather the opposite. Perhaps it was the heat of the dining car which kept them at such an arm's length, which made them both stick to banalities in their conversation: talk of the weather, the Christmas holiday, the Paris fashions, together with the briefest exposure of their separate backgrounds.

It seemed as if they did not want to know – at all costs must not know – too much about each other; that they should strictly maintain their role as polite strangers, forced together at a dining car table, who would very soon go their separate ways. Léonie was perplexed by this barrier, for it was obvious that they had much in common – a natural fluency in French and English, a life spent moving between the two countries, an intimate knowledge of Paris and London, same age, same sex, an interest in clothes, even in sewing, for Léonie remarked on Jennifer's skills here, wishing she had more time for it herself.

And yet they persisted, both of them, in talking only of formal commonplaces. Léonie gave only the scantest details of her life – how her father lived in Paris, had been an attorney in marine insurance, that she was married to a British journalist, had a daughter of fourteen, lived in Hampstead. While Jennifer, in her résumé, was equally restrained and far more mysterious. Her mother was French, worked in some capacity for a Paris couturier, her father lived somewhere near London – the 'home counties' – a retired Army man, while she herself was a secretary in Whitehall and had a flat somewhere off the Edgware Road.

She did not explain the very disparate backgrounds of her parents, or why they lived apart. Nor did she enlarge on her job in Whitehall. So that Léonie, a little frustrated at this constraint, thought to lighten the mood and prosper some greater friendliness by saying brightly, 'Oh, Whitehall! What do you do? Something exciting or dreary?'

Jennifer sipped her coffee guardedly. 'Nothing – nothing really. At one of the Ministries. Just typing, letters and things.'

But Léonie, smiling now, was not to be deterred in her lighthearted mood. 'I suppose you think I'd tell my journalist husband! Well, I won't. Because he and I are separated, I'm afraid.'

Jennifer looked up, concerned at once, though only formally, it seemed. 'I'm sorry . . .' She looked at her. But it was not a warm look, Léonie saw. Jennifer seemed agitated by something in her last statement.

'Well, yes, it was . . . all rather tough.' Léonie avoided any suggestion of the crestfallen. 'Are you happily married? I hope so!' she added brightly.

'No. No I'm not – married, I mean.'

'Oh, should I be sorry?' Léonie was confused. 'No, I mean – did you, were you, did you want to be? . . .' She left all these possible permutations hanging on the close air. A man at the table behind had started a cigar, the smoke drifting over their heads.

Jennifer started to cough. 'No, no . . .' she spluttered. Her face, her eyes, were more than ever alarmed now. She was shaking with mild paroxysms – from the effects of the smoke, Léonie supposed. 'No, I'm not married,' she added with finality, a cold aggrieved look masking her warm features, as if Léonie had verged on the impertinent with these enquiries.

'I'm sorry. I didn't mean to pry—'

'No, no. It's just – I can't stand the smoke any more.'

They had settled the bill. They both stood up. Jennifer held out her hand, offering a formal goodbye. But a group of people for the second sitting were pushing behind them, so that they had to walk the length of the dining car together, before they could stop at the junction of the two carriages, both of them swaying over the jolting couplings in the half-dark, Jennifer still coughing, a handkerchief over her mouth. At last she held out her hand again. 'Well, goodbye. I hope you have a good night.' She seemed so anxious to escape. But another coughing fit took her then.

'Are you all right?' Léonie asked, putting her hand out, steadying the other woman over the swaying junction.

'Yes – yes. Fine, thank you. I'm this way.' She gestured towards the engine where the wagons-lit were.

'Lucky you,' Léonie said. 'I couldn't get a sleeping compartment, all booked up . . .'

Jennifer, who had turned away, half-opening the door into the next carriage, turned back.

'Oh dear . . .' Her voice was resigned. 'You could share my compartment. I've one all to myself.' Her tone was filled with such an air of defeat that Léonie said at once, 'Of course not! I've got a perfectly comfy armchair – the other way. Sleep like a log in any case – after all that hock! Goodbye.'

She had half-turned, leaving Jennifer, before she felt a hand on her shoulder and heard the suddenly urgent voice.

'No! No, I meant – I'm sorry – I meant, *please* share my compartment. There's plenty of room.' She touched her shoulder again, a gesture in which there was a whole surge of informality, of need. 'Please, it's this way. Just up here.'

Together this time, they opened the door into the next carriage, moving into the smooth-carpeted, tactfully lit calm of the wagon-lit carriage.

The moment they were inside the compartment and she had locked the door, Jennifer embraced her – delicately, urgently, apologetically. 'Oh, you poor thing . . .' She kissed her on one cheek. 'I'd no idea, not having a berth . . .' Then on the other. 'Just one of those stuffy armchairs . . .' She kissed her on the nose.

So formal in her speech, distant in attitude a few minutes before, she had now run to the opposite extreme, was utterly informal – childish almost, in her excited tumbling words, her nervous, unresolved movements, fondling Léonie's ears with her lips, standing away a fraction, gazing at her happily, sadly, her grey eyes dancing with concern, ardour.

Léonie for a moment pretended not to know what to make of this sudden onslaught of passion. Yet from the start she had made no attempt to resist it, so that she saw then how something had snapped between them the moment they had entered the compartment, saw how willing a partner she was – had been all along in this meeting – in this now equally irrepressible, unquestioning feeling she had for Jennifer. Embracing her, kissing her in return, she sensed a great well of long-suppressed physical desire rising in her, for this total stranger, who was holding her, facing her, chin slightly tilted, lips apart, speaking to her again in that startlingly different voice, soft, capricious, yet almost desperate, stammering: 'Oh, I can't . . . can't tell you how awful I felt, all the time at dinner, being so cold to you, because I *knew*, I just knew—'

'Yes, yes!' Léonie put her fingers to Jennifer's lips. 'But don't. It doesn't matter now . . .'

The dross, the hurt and pain of the last months – the last years, indeed – started to drop away from Léonie then, like weights, and she seemed to levitate with joy, felt herself rocketing upwards in the compartment, stomach churning, head swimming about the ceiling, so that she was surprised at her own tears, unaware of them until she felt them trickling down her cheeks. Jennifer, hugging her once more, brushed the tears away with her nose, and they stood apart again, holding each other at arms' length. Then Léonie laughed. But her mouth was strangely dry, her throat constricted, so that the laugh emerged as more of a cackle. She reached out for Jennifer, about to hug her once more.

'No, let me—' Jennifer struggled out of her cotton gaberdine, then tugged at her cameo brooch, hurriedly opening her shirt all the way down the front – 'These buttons – they're so twisty!' – climbing out of her pleated beige wool skirt, standing there in a silk petticoat with a low neckline, a tie belt at the waist, her hand on the bow.

But, before she could pull it, Léonie, reaching forward pulled it for her, and the petticoat flowed freely out about her waist. Lifting it by the hem, Léonie drew it right up over her small breasts, her head, knelt down, head against her chin, her neck, running her lips between her breasts, over her stomach, clasping her round the middle, nibbling at the elastic rim of her knickers.

Then suddenly they both seemed furious with each other – in their delay, delight, the urgency of their desire. So that Jennifer tugged at Léonie's clothes in frustration – pulling at her collar, the shoulders of her navy cardigan, as she knelt in front of her. Léonie, standing up, made a huge effort to be calm. 'Here – they're here – the buttons.' She brought Jennifer's hand to the top of her blouse. 'They all unbutton . . . quite easily!'

Jennifer, making an equal effort to control herself, undid them one by one down to the waist. Léonie, releasing the belt, stepped out of her skirt and took off her blouse, standing there in her black satin petticoat, garters and silk stockings. Jennifer took her then, arms linked round her waist, pulling at the crinkly satin, lifting it over her behind, finding it caught between them then, so that Léonie moved away and, crossing her arms, herself lifted it off.

They hugged each other, finding their skin together for the first time, a velvet burning all the way down to their waist, standing half-naked together in their knickers, suspenders, garters, silk stockings – swaying suddenly as the train rushed over a curve of points, so that they fell on to the bunk in a fever, writhing and twisting, pushing and pulling, tearing, tugging and arching.

It was making love to a stranger, Léonie thought. And it was intoxicating – just because this woman was so entirely unknown, so that she felt quite without any inhibitions, her appetite correspondingly increased, so that she was almost brutal in her desire. For she was a stranger to herself now as well, liberated, a dare-devil adventurer. A feeling of sheer irresponsible abandon swept over her:

there was no past or future, in either body caressed; no questions, fears or obligations, no dross of yesterday or tomorrow – as she discovered this woman, nameless almost, sweeping into virgin country, reaching a hand down her smooth flank, stroking it, then moving inside her thigh, caressing the smoother skin there, until she touched her sex and Jennifer shuddered an instant, arching away, then back, offering, opening herself to Léonie's hand.

Jennifer touched her in the same place, supple questing fingers – and Léonie felt that choking sensation again as her stomach rose and churned before she killed the feeling by giving, thrusting herself vehemently at her: the start of a pulsing rapture in their love-making now, when time disappeared, as she felt the bolts of pleasure, striking her, one after the other, a near-painful ecstasy, as Jennifer discovered her – bolts that came like lightning now, a sharp searing joy, remembered and regained from a lost time, her old nature re-affirmed in rising spurts, a gulping famished bliss, as of two strangers, dying of thirst, met at the same water-filled oasis.

'Oh God!' Léonie almost shouted, towards the end, as Jennifer so held and felt, touched and moved with her, then lifted herself above her, hands to either side on the berth, arching over her, moving to and fro, before Léonie hugged her down on to her, taking her breasts, widening her legs. 'Oh God!' she breathed, violently, on the edge of an abyss, gulping thin air.

Léonie seemed to black out for several moments, as the berth tilted and spun and she saw Jennifer arching and shuddering above her, curls dancing, eyes shut tight, her face a creased mask, almost of pain, before suddenly everything flowed and rushed between them and they fell together, half-laughing, half-crying, in a tumbling flurry of intertwined arms and legs, heads and clenching toes.

Later, as a tired calm descended on them, Léonie saw

all the reasons for Jennifer's earlier formality and restraint – how she had wanted her almost from the beginning, when she had somehow sensed their similar natures, but had bitten this knowledge back, withheld herself in the dining car, been brief, even brusque, fearing to involve them both; until, seeing the end of this chance-in-a-lifetime meeting over the swaying carriage junction, she had dived in recklessly, asking her to share the compartment, rescuing their joint needs at the last moment.

'Thank you,' Léonie whispered, touching the lobe of her ear with her tongue, 'for finding me.' Jennifer turned on the pillow then. 'You see . . .' Léonie was about to start again. But, this time, it was Jennifer who reached out, putting a finger to her lips, shaking her head in loving astonishment. 'No, no need to talk,' was all she said. 'Each other – we found each other.'

They slept then, oblivious to the vague noise as the train pushed on board ship, slept in each other's arms, the sleep of the just in their true nature. But Léonie woke later in the early dawn, feeling the boat swaying beneath her and, seeing the other woman next to her in the vague light, thought for a moment that something terrible had happened to her.

Where was she? Who was this person? – gently asleep beside her, the long curls twisted round, falling across her cheek, the small, half-bared breast lying over the sheet, the sweet smell of warm linen, and of something else . . .

Then, as she came to her senses, it all returned to her. Jennifer. Jennifer Bryden. Léonie tried to cling to the mundane name – like a life raft, something just out of reach, unpossessed. For the name and all that lay behind it in the workaday world had meant nothing to either of them last night. They had lived in a different country then, under all sorts of aliases.

Oh, the sheer release, the joy of it . . . And yet it all frightened Léonie now. Their love-making, thinking of it, seemed too vehement, too abandoned ever to be a part of the real world. It was a temporary fever, a moon flower, that bloomed and died in a night, an extravagant creation dependent on their being, remaining, strangers.

Léonie remembered how Jennifer had put her fingers to her lips. 'No need to talk,' she had said. And Léonie was terrified then, for that was what Jennifer must have meant. It was, it would be, all over by dawn. That was the unstated agreement. Ships that pass in the night. And she longed to wake Jennifer then – to promote reality between them, to talk and talk and talk – for she longed for a future with this woman now. Yet here she was gone away from her, fast asleep, already forgetting her, the widely spaced, slanting eyes now blind.

She need not have worried. When Jennifer woke half an hour later, just before they docked at Dover, she reached out for her quickly, touching her cheek, taking her hand, kissing it. 'Léonie . . .' She was quietly astonished. 'You're still here. I thought – thought you mightn't be. That you'd have left, without saying anything . . .'

'No.' Léonie was almost shocked. 'No, of course not. I'd never do that.' The two women gazed at each other gratefully in the cold morning light.

A thin fall of moist snow slanted across the docks as the train left for London. They had breakfast in the dining car. The waiter asked if they were together. They nodded, smiling.

No, neither of them need have worried. In this *coup de foudre*, somehow knowing intuitively that they were meant for each other, they had simply reversed the usual processes of loving. From then on, having first come together with such unthinking fever, they worked backwards – gradually, carefully, like explorers – into all the other usually undiscovered tributaries of blind passion: the deeds of association, the revealing texts of domestic enquiry, the set books of care beyond intimacy, friendship.

'You want to know what I do in Whitehall? – something *terribly* secret!' Jennifer stood by the tall first-floor window of her flat in Connaught Square, just off the Edgware Road. Léonie gazed at her, as Jennifer gazed out of the window – seeing her in profile, exploring a face that was still new to her, noticing how the point of the chin rose a fraction, as if to parallel the tip of her nose. Another discovered symmetry in the geography, new bearings in the map of love.

Léonie sat on the sofa, stroking Brewster, an ageing corpulent springer spaniel belonging to Mrs Ogilvy, a rich widow wintering in Monaco, from whom Jennifer rented the flat, and looked after the rest of the house while she was abroad.

It was a week later, a Sunday afternoon, under a frozen sky. Snow had fallen thickly for three days, drenching the plane trees in the square with a heavy powder. Some branches had fallen. People walked the half-cleared pavements along narrow trenches, dodging little Matterhorns. 'But it isn't really, the job – just letters and things, in French, for the War Office.'

Jennifer, in a plain beige skirt, patchwork-quilted waistcoat and bright red stockings, came over and sat beside Léonie for a moment, ruffling her hair. 'But *do* come and look. Some boys in the square, behind the bushes, getting snowballs off at the old dears and major-generals! A bit cruel, I know – but funny.'

Léonie went with her to the window, gazing down at the sporadic ambushes – some elderly pedestrians all in a rage, ducking the powdery cannonades. With their faces glued to the chilly window, two of the small panes in front of them were soon clouded over by their warm breath. Jennifer drew some letters with her finger on the glass. 'EMIA'T EJ'

Léonie was mystified. 'It's a secret code,' Jennifer told her gravely.

'Oh, what does it mean? Do tell!'

'Read the letters backwards, you ninny!'

Léonie was momentarily surprised at their childishness, for they were both of an age – she at thirty-eight, Jennifer a year younger – when maturity might have tempered, even prohibited, such juvenile responses. Instead she saw how this surge of loving had released a whole lost innocence in them, youthful conceits – flooding their adult reserve, promoting these games, floating them out on a second childhood.

'ISSUA IOM.' Léonie, after some hesitation and several corrections, wrote her message on the window-pane. They laughed and hugged, before Jennifer put some more coal on the small grate behind them. 'You're pretty quick and clever with words though – writing backwards straight away.'

'Ah, the War Office – codes and things,' Jennifer joked.

Léonie looked at this woman, the flow of tawny-red curls fallen right over her face, glinting in the firelight – incredulous at her new possession: neat, so accomplished, contained, someone who knew who she was and yet was hers. Here, Léonie was sure, they would neither of them have to search furiously for an identity, dress up and swap clothes, as she and Hetty had done. Jennifer was already so entirely herself – dressed or undressed.

'Oh, so it *is* exciting work that you do.'

'No. It's deadly dull.' Jennifer stood up from the fender. 'Come on, before it's too dark. Brewster needs a walk. And after we can go and eat at that little Italian place on the Edgware Road.'

*

'I'm sorry – all that about your friend Hetty . . .' Jennifer, gazing down, picked at her spaghetti.

'Yes, well, it's all over now anyway. And Robert, too.'

'A sort of whole family to you really – Hetty and Robert, with those two other Cordiner cousins, all those servants, that huge house.'

'Yes . . .' Léonie for a moment considered the world she had lost. 'But I still have my own Papa. And now . . . you.'

Jennifer looked up at her suddenly. 'I was to have married – oh, ten years ago. The son of a great friend of my mother's. Frenchman. But when he sort of realized, about me, well, it was nonsense. He became flustered – and chilly.'

'Yes, I did wonder.' Léonie's lips opened in a half-smile. 'You're, well, obviously so . . . "marriageable" – is that the word?'

'And another older man at the War Office . . . I liked him very *much*. And he liked me. But he was married, of course . . .'

'*Would* you have married though, if he'd been free?' Léonie asked, a trifle anxiously.

Jennifer sighed. 'Yes. And no. Don't really know.' She put on her glasses as if the better to consider the problem, then took them off again. 'He was so tremendously kind, understanding. I might have done, a sort of companion-ship marriage. But that wouldn't have been fair – because he wouldn't have entirely wanted that, I'm sure . . . Anyway, then I met Mary. Not at all plain, like the name. Very startling looking, dramatic. Long golden tresses, like Rapunzel. Worked in the Zoo here of all places. But that came to an end, last autumn. She wanted to go out and live in Kenya, Uganda – study, deal with the animals there, the baboons up the Ruwenzori mountains, and so on. Wanted me to come out with her. I couldn't.'

'Because you didn't want to?'

'Oh yes, I did, as far as she was concerned. Just, I knew Africa wouldn't work for me – out there in the colonies, all that Happy Valley crowd. I just wouldn't have felt *responsible*, do you know what I mean? I'm something of a home-lover, too,' she added a little ruefully. 'Spent such a time getting the flat right here—'

'It's lovely, those Liberty fabrics – and your sewing! I *like* your being a home-lover!'

'And London,' Jennifer rushed on enthusiastically. 'I *love* the winter walks in the parks, round Regent's Park. And Paris – my Mama, and the shops there. And the Opera! How could I have lived in Kenya?'

'I used to sing at the Opera there years ago.' Jennifer was astonished. 'Yes, I was trained as a singer.'

They took coffee. 'Next weekend,' Léonie said, 'come up to Hampstead – and we can go for a long walk on the Heath!'

'I'd love to!'

Jennifer came up to the Hampstead flat with Brewster next Sunday morning, and they all walked up to Whitestone Pond next to the Heath. The snow had been replaced by a sharp frost for most of that week and the shallow pond was frozen solid. Children in bobble hats and red mufflers, taking long slides over the ice, laughed and shrieked. A few adults were majestically skating. They watched the animated scene, the figures waltzing and sliding under a freezing grey sky.

'Come on!' Léonie, stepping out on to the ice, beckoned her. Jennifer, in a long green woollen coat and even longer striped college scarf, stood on the edge, nervous. Léonie went back, holding out her arms. 'Come on, I won't let you fall!' Jennifer put a foot on the ice, gingerly, holding on to Léonie's shoulder.

'It's just . . . I'm not so . . . athletic as you . . .' She put her other foot on the ice and, with Léonie holding her arm, they paraded very gently, Jennifer making tiny slithering steps, out towards the middle.

'You home-lover, you!' Léonie told her. 'I can see why you wouldn't have been much good storming up mountains looking for baboons in Uganda . . .'

Jennifer stopped, her peach complexion reddening now in the cold, breathing fast, the chilling frost bringing tears to her eyes. 'You are an awful tease, Léa.' She looked at her weakly. The same tears of cold had also come into Léonie's eyes. She took out a handkerchief, holding Jennifer with one hand, while she dabbed her face with the other, then wiped her own cheeks.

'No, not really a tease, Jenny. It's just . . . that I'm teasing because I can't . . .'

'What?'

'Because I so want to kiss you! Come on, we'll go for a walk round the Heath . . .'

Far down the Heath, where there was no one about, they ran to keep warm beneath the frozen beech glades near Kenwood House, digging up snowy sticks and throwing them for Brewster. But the old dog made a mere pretence of chasing them – ambling a few yards before turning back, sitting firmly down on the snow and looking at them with infinite regret.

'And Olivia?' Jennifer asked, when they had slowed to a walk. They had been talking of Léonie's affairs.

'Well, she likes the boarding school in Kent. And I like to think she hasn't been hurt too much by all . . . this separation business. She's very quiet and resilient. But she must have been.'

'Better the separation than tensions and rows.'

'So one would like to think.'

'I'm sure it is. Which is why my parents live apart. Mama still sometimes does work for Coco Chanel.'

'Why didn't it last – between her and your father?'

'Oh, Daddy met her years ago in Paris – he was at the Legation there, junior military attaché. "Love at first sight" business. But it didn't work out when they got older. He was too British and she just the opposite . . .'

They walked on to the edge of the empty lake in the lee of the great house. It was chilling cold, but they did not mind, watching a group of mallard standing motionless far out on the ice.

'Anything's better than rows and tensions,' Jennifer said. 'Your living with Robert – it simply couldn't have been you.'

'More, it simply wasn't *him*, I'm afraid. Couldn't accept – me and Hetty. And he loved her too, after all. But *she* couldn't be doing with me in the end anyway. So it didn't much matter . . .' Léonie turned impatiently away from the lake. 'Better get back and have that hot lunch.' But Jennifer stayed where she was by the edge of the frozen water. 'What's the matter?'

'Just – all these separations and leavings.'

Léonie walked slowly back to her, fiddling with a snowy twig. 'We needn't have them. We *won't*,' she added very firmly. 'I've had all and enough of that. But not this time, not with you. I'm not going to lose my life with you, Jenny. So let's be open and honest – and I'm not going to be ashamed of anything – so you'll meet Olivia and Robert and my Papa and anybody else in my life. I'm not going to lose this chance with you, ever.' She kissed her then, a kiss full of purpose, a kiss with a future.

'Me too,' Jennifer said.

As they walked back, the sun emerged strangely as a pearly halo through the clouds, casting their pale shadows ahead of them on the snow. 'You see!' Léonie said. 'A future! . . .'

*

In the ensuing months they were as good as their word. They usually spent only weekend nights together, at one or other's flat, and went out mostly then, too. They tended to save each other up for weekends. They went to the Everyman cinema in Hampstead or the Academy in Oxford Street. Carné's *Quai des Brumes* and Eisenstein's *Battleship Potemkin* made them feel sad and serious. But, listening to the Savoy Orpheans on Jennifer's wireless, they danced the tango; and had a sweet martini round the corner afterwards at the Duke of Kendal pub.

They visited Keats's house in Hampstead one day in March when the first warm hint of spring was in the sun, tiny buds on the cherry trees down Frognal.

'Look – in his own writing! Part of his "Ode to a Nightingale"!' Jennifer gazed into the glass case. She read out the fragment.

> '". . . the viewless wings of Poesy,
> Though the dull brain perplexes and retards:
> Already with thee! tender is the night . . ."'

The next weekend they persuaded Brewster on to a Green Line bus, out to the beech glades near Aylesbury, an ancient forest, bluebell heads nudging up through the leaf mould. Kew Gardens offered them more exotic spring blooms a few weeks later.

Once, for no reason, they gave a grand tea party for themselves, with Mrs Ogilvy's best Spode china. Jennifer made cucumber and sardine sandwiches and a sponge cake with cream and raspberry filling. Brewster, taking vaguely ill on the remnants later, was excused his walk that evening.

Sometimes, in placid diminuendo, they stayed in most of the weekend, one or other of them writing letters, reading, sewing. Or both of them making love.

Through these idle or intense preoccupations, their lives had come to a balance: a caring give and take, making or not making love, Jennifer standing vacantly at a window, spellbound by some lines in Keats's hand, long red knitted stockings on the white bedspread, Léonie allowing herself the one cigarette of the evening, before dragging Brewster to his unwilling duty in the square. Trips to the local Odeon, sausages and chips, a shared bedsitter, an Ascot heater spuming water. Diminuendo and crescendo. A London romance.

It was an attraction of equals and opposites, where neither was the lesser or greater: Jennifer the frustrated home-lover; Léonie the wounded explorer. They met now in the middle of their lives together, fulfilling longed-for needs in the other: Léonie so wanting this balanced companionship, never discovering it with Hetty – but finding such an anchor in Jennifer. While Jennifer at last possessed in Léonie a vital spice in her domestic adventures.

They did not advertise the nature of their relationship – nor yet make efforts to hide it. A life which soon became so natural and happy for them radiated an ease towards others. Except for Robert.

He met Jennifer one weekend at the Hampstead flat. He was distant. But that was his usual attitude towards Léonie now. And seeing almost at once the nature of their friendship made him no more or less so. He was, perhaps, secretly pleased to confirm his opinions about Léonie once more, how he could never have led a real life, or made things up with her. He left immediately after tea – to catch the night ferry to Ostend, going on to Berlin and Prague. He had an article to do, with a series of interviews, he hoped, on Hitler's latest plans to annexe the Sudetenland.

Afterwards Jennifer said, 'It's funny, because he doesn't seem the sort of person who'd make a fuss – over all the things he did. Seems so gentle.'

'Yes. He is. He was. Just, there's some poison – that's

got into him. Oh, a self-righteousness. Nice, gentle people – they can fall ill that way, sooner maybe than others.'

'Other women – do you think? With all that travelling?'

Léonie shrugged. 'I doubt it. That's part of his self-righteousness. He doesn't want to risk being proved wrong over me – because I'm not really so very different from many women.'

Olivia came home for the spring holidays from Kent: rapidly growing, slightly gauche in pigtails, beautifully dark, nervous, trying to find herself in all sorts of covert ways. She had, with the pressures of the last years, developed something of a stammer. At first things were a little awkward between all three of them. But Brewster marvellously eased matters, making a beeline for Olivia, resting his head on her lap, gazing up at her lovingly, wagging his tail.

'He is a sw-sweet dog!' Olivia stroked him. 'I suppose he really only wants me to take him for a w-walk.'

'Oh no, he doesn't. He *hates* walks!' Jennifer told her. 'He's the soppiest, laziest old dog ever. All he wants is a cuddle and then for you to *stop* us taking him out!'

Olivia quite took to Jennifer. Unaware of the real nature of her mother's relationship with Jenny, she came to regard her as a sophisticated, interesting aunt. 'Such smart clothes she wears,' she remarked to her mother. 'I do rather envy her.'

'Yes, so do I – sometimes.'

Léonie, though far less frumpy now, had not quite the same delicate figure.

'I bet she's pretty in a bathing suit,' Olivia went on.

'Yes, I should think so. But we'll see anyway – I've made arrangements, like last year. We'll all spend part of the summer together, at that seaside villa in Normandy.'

Ben Straus arrived for a holiday in London, staying at

the Hampstead flat, early in May. Léonie had dinner with him alone on the first evening.

'So who's this great new friend of yours?' he asked expectantly.

'You had my letters—'

'Yes, but you didn't say exactly—'

'Jennifer – Jenny Bryden. I hope you'll meet her tomorrow.' Her father was put out – only for an instant, but Léonie noticed it. 'Oh, I didn't tell you all the details in the letters, Papa – wanted you to see me, and her, first. I'm afraid . . . it's not a man!' She looked at him, smiling a little wanly. 'But it's even better!' she rushed on. 'I'm really so happy.'

He gazed at her. 'Yes, I can see that. All the depression gone entirely. Lost weight, too. I've not seen you looking so good in years.'

'It's true! It's – she's changed my life. Couldn't be better. And all because of you!' Her father looked doubtful again. 'Because I'd never have met her, if you hadn't given me that first class ticket back on the night ferry. I've never ever had a better present.' She kissed him on her way to the kitchen.

The following evening, when he met her, he had to agree with his daughter's luck in meeting Jennifer. As they sipped drinks together before supper in the Connaught Square flat he saw everything: the gleaming reddish hair in the lamplight, the delicate lively eyes, faint blue, widely parted, slanted, the small mouth, full lips, the perfect symmetry, the neatness everywhere, the Paisley blouse and skirt and bright red stockings – above all the obvious happiness of the two women together.

He raised his glass to his daughter's new friend.

Good God, he thought afterwards – what could it possibly matter? People surely had a right to love in any combination of gender. They could fail or succeed in one permutation just as much as another. But at least it was blindingly clear here for the moment – the success of this arrangement. His daughter was transformed. That was what counted. Nothing lasted for ever.

He stroked Brewster, who had come to him lovingly, chin nuzzling his knee, paying him almost unbridled attention, huge liquid eyes filled with a worried, hopeful emotion.

'Your dog – he seems to have taken quite a shine to me!'

'Get down, Brewster! Do push him down, Mr Straus. It's entirely feigned. He courts every stranger, in the hopes of enlisting support against his evening walk . . .'

Ben Straus decided he liked a relationship which included such a percipient, right-thinking dog.

8

At Summer Hill meanwhile Hetty and Pierre lived a life of equal content. The house and gardens had now been restored to something, at least, of their former splendour. Even the many unused, dust-sheeted bedrooms and reception rooms did not depress. Summer Hill had a heart to it again, a body without the tensions, or suffering the prohibitions of old, so that the house came into its own once more, breathing freely in the summer sun.

But even in this remote rural paradise by the river, circled by rooks and water, where growth, decay and the weather were the only dictates, the war clouds in Europe could not be kept at bay for ever. Other dictators would now have their say over the chestnut-shrouded house, as the buttercups faded and the climate dipped to stormy, then fell beyond the measurements of the barometer. In late September 1938 the stockade of Summer Hill which enclosed their happiness began to tremble.

The postman brought the letter from Paris. Pierre showed it to Hetty on the porch as they took coffee after lunch – a letter from the Medical Adjutant General at the French Ministry of War.

'The French Army – about to be mobilized?' Hetty was calm enough at this idea, though not at the next. 'But why *you*?'

'I'm on the reserve – of the Army Medical Corps, Hetty, that's why. I'm still a French citizen, you know.'

'Yes, but there isn't going to be a war. Chamberlain, Daladier – they've all said so.'

'Wishful thinking, I'm afraid. Chamberlain – "J'aime Berlin" we call him – and Daladier . . .' Pierre scoffed. 'Both of them just postponing the inevitable. Hitler has Austria, he's as good as taken the Sudetenland, Prague. Next he'll turn on Poland, France, the rest. I'll have to go back to Paris—'

'But, Pierre!—'

'Even if the Army hadn't been mobilized, Hetty, I'd have to go. I'm French. I couldn't stand apart and see France go down.' He stood up from the wicker chair, taking the letter, draining his coffee, looking out over the landscape – autumn tints, browns and reds and golds creeping over the valley.

'But if all of us – the French and the British – if we make a show of p-power, as Daladier's doing now, Hitler'll climb down.'

Pierre shook his head. 'Chamberlain won't make any show. And Daladier'll climb down, not Hitler. Daladier will always compromise, I know it. Hitler never will. I'll have to go over to Paris more or less at once.'

'I'll come with you of course.'

He turned to her. 'If there is a war, Hetty, you'll have to stay here.'

'No. No, I won't.' Hetty was suddenly her old vehement self again, dictatorial, imperious. 'Let's not even start to argue about that – because I *won't*. I won't be apart from you. Or from France for that matter. There's no question.' She looked at him steadily. He said nothing. 'I'll tell Elly,' she went on, 'to get some clothes and things ready.'

Pierre, with a gesture of resignation, let the letter drop. A breeze took it and it sideslipped like a leaf down the porch steps, blowing with the other falling leaves over the gravel.

Hetty took Pierre's arm and together they walked up the lawn terraces, past the maple tree, the big cedar, to the little limestone grotto with its waterfall, now all restored. The water murmured in their ears as they turned round, gazing back at the placid vision below them, the house with its brilliant red creeper gleaming in the sun, the purple hills way across the valley, the murmur of the hidden river, the stillness of an autumn day.

'Such peace,' Hetty said, gripping his arm tighter. 'Neither of us . . . can let anyone destroy it.'

On just such a day, almost to the month, twenty-four years before, Hetty had stood at this same spot with Dermot gazing down at the house: August 1914, a few days before he had left for the Great War. She remembered the moment: Dermot puffing his pipe, blowing smoke rings over her, trying to cheer her up, saying – after all the rows with her mother, when she had come so to hate Summer Hill – how the house was really so full of peace and promise, how they could all be unimaginably happy there in the future. Now, through Dermot, through Pierre, that promise had been fulfilled. Lost before to her, through her own stupidities, this time she was not going to lose it.

A week later, at the end of September, after his

meeting with Hitler in Munich, Chamberlain returned to Croydon airport with a piece of paper. It was 'Peace in our time'. By then Hetty and Pierre were in Paris, staying temporarily at the Hotel Rond Point just off the Champs-Elysées. From their bedroom balcony they watched the vast crowds, ten deep on either side of the great boulevard, welcoming Daladier home from Le Bourget to the War Office. He, too, had been with Hitler in Munich – and, just as Pierre forecast, had compromised. For France, as for England, it was peace with dishonour. Having promised to go to war over Hitler's rape of Czechoslovakia, Daladier had done no such thing. Prague had been thrown to the wolf.

But Hetty, taken by the joyous surge all about her in the city, saw it differently. 'Look!' she said. 'It's peace. It must be!'

Pierre sighed. 'Daladier's Munich accord is nothing but a diplomatic Sedan—'

'Oh, do stop spouting history at me!—'

'A disastrous climb-down then,' he said irritably. 'Daladier's delivered us over to Hitler all in a neat parcel. And we won't see that. Just look at them out there on the streets, women and children crying for joy. And where are the others, the men? Do you notice? So few of them. Because they've drafted every man under sixty, half a million Frenchmen under arms, up to the Franco-German border – where I have to go tomorrow.'

'But isn't that exactly the point? Hitler won't fight France – or Britain – now. Not with all this show of force.'

Pierre laughed. '"Force"? France is a second-rate military power now. They're all up there on the border just "twiddling their thumbs" as you say. They're not a fighting force. Their heart isn't in it. You can see that, out there, all those wives, women and children. The political issues are all far too confusing for any of them to feel any anger or threat. The men don't know what they're *doing* up there on the border! They won't *fight*. They want peace. Everyone wants peace, which is fine. Except you have to be *really* prepared to fight for peace. And none of us is. Which means war – sooner or later.'

In London Léonie and Jennifer heard Chamberlain's thin voice on the wireless: 'Today I have met with Herr Hitler . . .'

'Well, that's that all over at least,' Léonie said joyously. 'All those elaborate preparations for air raids last week, the sirens . . . We can sleep easy at nights.'

But Jennifer was not so reassured. 'At the War Office . . .' she said.

'What?'

'Some people are not at all certain.'

'Well, that stupid little moustache of a Hitler isn't going to bomb London tonight anyway. "Peace in our time"! We should celebrate. Let's go – let's have a splurge at Kettners!'

Brewster, asleep on the carpet, stirred at these lively tones, then whined unaccountably, some canine nightmare oppressing him.

These celebrations, many in Paris and London thought subsequently, had been entirely appropriate. There was no war that month, or the next – and the coming season of Christmas goodwill would surely set the seal of the peace. 'You see!' Hetty spoke in French. 'All that Munich business – just a war scare.'

It was mid-December. She looked down the dining room table of the furnished apartment they had taken in a modern block on the Avenue Mozart in Passy. Pierre had returned the previous week from the Army medical headquarters at a hospital near Lille. Most of the French forces on the border there had been stood down as well, returning home. Hetty and Pierre were entertaining an old and close friend of Pierre's from his medical student days in Paris, a Dr André Vonot, and Eve his wife.

Pierre, as usual on this topic – and becoming generally depressed by the continued political cowardice of the French and the British – disagreed with Hetty. 'We've compromised with Hitler to such an extent that even his greed is temporarily satisfied. Now it's the lull before the storm. I went over the border a few weeks ago to see a friend of mine in Osnabrück – a German doctor I know there, met him when I was studying in Vienna. He takes the worst possible view of things. Clearing out of Germany altogether, can't practise any more of course, because he's a Jew,' Pierre ran on before he could stop himself.

Dr Vonot looked at Pierre an instant, something wary, protective in his expression. Hetty noticed it, this worried look – so directed at Pierre. She asked him about it after the guests had left.

'Yes.' Pierre was resigned. 'He was thinking of me. Because I'm Jewish – half-Jewish – as well.'

'You?' Hetty was more mystified than astonished.

'I should have told you about it before.' Then, in his frustration, he turned to her. 'Can't you see?' He took off his spectacles, then ran a hand through his thick spiky-dark hair, before moving to the bedroom window, drawing the blinds.

'But your name is Langlois?'

'My real name is Neymann. Jewish family, settled here years ago from Alsace. But my father changed the name – after the Dreyfus trial, when he couldn't get any preferment in medicine here. That's why he went to London to the French hospital. Afterwards he changed his name to Langlois – the most *petit bourgeois* name he could think of – when he came back to France, starting up afresh.'

'But why didn't you tell me before?' Now Hetty was

truly surprised. 'Nothing to be ashamed of. Just the opposite – I'm half-Jewish after all. We're both Jewish that way!'

'No. Nothing to be ashamed of. Except the fact that I've always been ashamed of my father for changing the name in the first place. And Vonot knows I'm Jewish. Known since we were students together. That's why he looked at me. He was worried for me, I suppose.'

'But the Jews aren't being persecuted in France now.'

Pierre turned from the window abruptly. 'Oh, you don't know. They were, they are – and they certainly will be if Hitler gets his hands on France.'

'Pierre, darling, he *won't* get his hands on France! You're far too pessimistic about the whole situation. You must get out of yourself a bit.' She stood up from the bed, kissed him, then ruffled his hair. 'Of course, I should have seen it! . . . But your skin is so pale.'

'My mother's. Pale as snow.'

'How *good* you're half-Jewish! Brother and sister under the skin! Always felt we were.' He took off his spectacles again, scratched his nose, gazing at the delighted, optimistic Hetty. 'So don't go on anticipating war. It's nearly Christmas. Come and we'll do nice things – go to the Cirque d'Hiver, see Chevalier at the Casino, have a treat at Maxim's!' Hetty was determined to float Pierre off these shoals of discontent.

'But I thought you didn't want to go to any of those smart places, from your old days here. Might be recognized. The old Laura Bowen . . . which is why we took this quiet place in Passy.'

'Yes, I did think just that, to get as far away as possible from all those old dives of mine on the left bank. But I'm cured of all that now. And no one's going to recognise me as Laura Bowen now – an old hag of nearly forty!'

'Far from it, Hetty, far from it . . .'

They went to bed then, and they were happy.

Pierre, though released from the front, was still retained on the active service reserve. He had to remain in France. However, he was given a week's leave over Christmas and both of them returned to Summer Hill, spending the holiday there, as on the previous year, with Aunt Emily, Mortimer and Dermot.

Dermot, returned from India six months before, at nearly sixty-five, was just too old to be appointed to an active service command. Instead, with a promotion to Major-General, he was put in charge of Home Defence – the Territorials and a mooted Home Guard – for south-east England. His temporary command headquarters outside Maidstone in Kent had taken over a defunct girl's school. 'We'll be fighting them with hockey sticks,' he told the assembled company over Christmas dinner. He, like Pierre, was in no doubt that war would come, and soon at that. His father Mortimer, frail now, agreed. 'Churchill,' he said, 'knew him a bit in the old days at Westminster. An awful rogue in some ways. But the only one of them with any guts, only one who'd give Herr Hitler a real clip over the ear. And where is he? Building garden walls somewhere down in Kent!'

Only Hetty remained resolutely hopeful. 'You're all just a lot of warmongers,' she told them, rather hurt. Not wishing further to offend or depress her, they kept off the topic, in her presence at least, for the rest of the holiday. Privately they were blunt.

'Peace – until he addresses the Reichstag?'

'Till he can get the rest of his Axis war crew into the fighting line?'

'Till the Balkan wheat harvest is in? . . .'

Hetty and Pierre returned to Paris immediately after Christmas. Pierre, who by this time had had to relinquish his medical partnership with Dr Craig in Fitzwilliam Square in Dublin, resumed his negligible duties with the Army Medical Corps. But soon he, too, was stood down from active service. However, he remained on the reserve and had to stay in France. Anxious to continue with his medical work, he took up his practice again, joining his old friend Dr Vonot who had a private clinic and dispensary on the Avenue Foch, not too far from the Avenue Mozart.

Hetty in the following months, as the cherry flowered in the Bois de Boulogne, moved between the apartment in Paris and Summer Hill. She came to enjoy this alternating change of scene: Summer Hill, but above all Paris again, where she spent most of her time, in the comfortable modern apartment in Passy where there were no memories – so different a Paris from the one she had known, and ruined for herself, ten years before: a city always loved, but so lost to her then, in which she now lived soberly, happily, gradually coaxing Pierre out of his depression as the spring burst over the city.

She took him to Serge Lifar's 'Ballets Russes de Diaghilev' exhibition at the Louvre, to the Théâtre-Français revival of *Cyrano de Bergerac* with Bérard's fantastic Gothic costumes and décor, persuaded him to Maxim's, to dinner in the Bois de Boulogne – took him here, there and everywhere, discovering the city anew with him, without that overwhelming vanity, that idiocy, arrogance, that stammering fury of heart: free now of all that had nearly killed her, with the man she loved who had given her this new life.

She had as well, while Pierre was out of work, another more intense and private pursuit. With Pierre's encouragement, at Summer Hill, and now in Paris, she had taken up her autobiographical novel again, *Aquamarine*, which she had started and dropped nearly ten years before. She continued with it now, remembering her past once more – the years in Domenica, the deadly hurricane, coming to the great house in Ireland, the shadows, the cold terrors there, her stammer, her punishing Mama, the magic apples, the old witch hidden in the Gothic wing: she remembered it all, and wrote with some fluency, until she came to that part of the story where the girl Alice, sent to the convent school in France, meets Sarah, embarking on a friendship which would dominate all her young life.

But there, having completed a few paragraphs, Hetty stopped. To write of Sarah was to remember Léonie – every emotion, every detail of their first experiences together at the convent school in Normandy. And this Hetty felt quite unable to face. She was surprised, upset – for surely she had recovered from Léonie, had confronted, with Pierre, all the hurt and damage she had done there?

But now, with this literary impasse, she wondered if, in her heart of hearts, she had really recovered from Léonie at all. Remembering the adventure of the holy relic in the convent chapel, the trout-fishing with a bent pin, the mysterious emotion she had felt in placing the snail on Léonie's forehead – in writing of all this the past returned and struck her viciously once more.

She had, she saw then, not only so hurt and lost Léonie, she had thrown away her own youth as well, debased the unique emotions there, sabotaged that unrepeatable adventure which they had shared, sullied everything they had experienced, hoped for and found together – all the mystery, beauty and imagination which life had offered them then.

She had betrayed more than human flesh, she saw. She had broken with the spirit of existence itself. And so, in writing of these early years with Léonie, which should have been a commemoration of happiness, she saw only her responsibility in a terrifying loss – the gift of faith, so that she had dropped the pen half way down the page. Such fictional atonement could only be a pale shadow of what was required here. And what was that? She had no idea – but that such atonement would have to equal what she had destroyed: the spirit of life itself.

'How can I ever really make it up to her?' she asked Pierre when she had explained the whole matter to him that evening. 'All those early things she gave me, that we had together, that I killed – in her and me.'

Pierre, worried at this turn of events in someone he had thought long cured, had no ready answer, seeing how, in this area of supposed sin and redemption into which Hetty had moved, science had no reach or cure. So he fell back on vague proverbial wisdom. 'You can't make up for things that happened that far back, Hetty – first love and such like – unless perhaps through your writing, which is exactly why I suggested you take up the book again.'

'Yes, but I can't face it – all those early days, now I'm remembering then, and knowing how I treated her later.'

Pierre made a vague gesture. 'Well, drop it then. Accept the fact that none of us can make up for the past that far back.'

'Yes, but I so *want* to make it up to her – now that I'm quite better.'

'But you can't . . .'

'No.'

'Why can't you?' Hetty shrugged despondently. 'You can't face the complete dissolution of the past,' he went on. 'Few people can. And psychoanalysis isn't much help. It can disentangle – clear the fears and horrors there. But it can't set the past right. God, if you like . . .' He smiled. 'Or art. But if you can't do it in your story, Hetty – what other way is there?'

'There *ought* to be some other way. There's still this huge gap in my life, about Léonie, I see it now. Of things – undone.' Hetty was more downcast still.

And now it was Pierre's turn to coax her out of her depression. 'Well, drop the book for the moment.

Because I've got a surprise for you this time. One of André's patients – I've been dealing with her, too, she's a hypochondriac – the Comtesse Etienne de Beaumont, she's giving a *bal costumé*. And she's asked all of us, all four. What about that?'

'Where?' Hetty was doubtful, seeing in this something frivolous, a temptation, something out of her old louche Parisian life.

'At one of the Versailles pavilions, Madame de Mury's. And you needn't worry. It's all awfully proper. The *ancien régime*, Comte de Paris, Maurice de Rothschild. None of your old friends from the left bank! . . . And all of us to be dressed as characters from the plays or the period of Racine. And each partner to be dressed in complete opposition to the other!'

With the arrival of the better weather, Paris celebrated peace all the more vigorously, in manic fits of gaiety, the city *en fête* all that summer – music and dancing everywhere. Lady Mendl gave an international garden party for seven hundred and fifty guests and three elephants, all of which refused to be ridden. Mrs Louise Macy hired the empty Hôtel Salé for the night, installing temporary furniture and plumbing with a mobile kitchen. But greatest of all the receptions was the de Beaumont costume ball at Versailles.

It was held early in July – an aristocratic *fête champêtre* at first as the several hundred guests took a buffet supper on the lawn surrounding the lovely pavilion which Louis XIV had built for his mistress, milling about in costumes of every conceivable extravagance, wit and splendour, before going inside the long marble-floored *salon*, now cleared and made over as a ballroom, lit by some thousands of candles in silver sconces and candelabra, a Paris chamber orchestra at one end, harpsichords, violoncellos and little tambourines playing minuets, sarabands, gavottes, pavanes and quadrilles.

Marie-Louise Bosquet went attired as La Vallière, with a pale chiffon mask painted in the likeness of the nun that she was to become. Maurice de Rothschild was the Ottoman Bajazet, wearing the famous Rothschild diamonds in his turban, the family's Cellini jewels across his sash. Hetty and Pierre, dressed more soberly in Grecian robes, went as the lucky lovers Iphigenia and Achilles, an appropriate mix of the noble and the chivalrous.

The air was heavy with the scent of orange blossom and crushed bay leaves from the miniature trees set up at intervals along the gilded walls, the *salon* filled with the sound of the delicately fingered music as the bewigged and doll-like figures made their stiff peregrinations about the marble floor. They were like automata – the men retreating, advancing, arms held high to the proffered hands of the women, linking, turning in the stately dance.

'Strange,' Pierre said to Hetty from the sidelines. 'The essential immobility of everyone. Straitjackets. Blind. Mad.'

But Hetty loved the formal drama of the ball – the wild contradictions of time and place and costume reawakening something in her histrionic soul. 'It's all a *jeu d'esprit*,' she told him. 'There has to be that in life, you know – as well as reality,' she added sweetly.

But that was exactly the trouble, Pierre thought. There was neither here, because there was no life at all in these dancers. They were people on strings, erect but dead behind their wild disguises, Meissen figurines moving through a flood of archaic golden light. The effect was eerie: an arcadian shepherdess circling a lascivious Ottoman prince; a masked nun in a saraband with a cardinal-archbishop. Bérénice with her flaming hair, turning, ever turning, only just at arm's length from the chilly figure of Death. Phèdre herself, the epitome of human agony in a torn Grecian robe, dancing with the court jester.

Here, in the clockwork movement of these bizarre conjunctions, there was a perfect order, but no rhyme or reason. These dancers fled away, retreating into chaos. And time was not reclaimed by those who would not seize the day or set one finger out to save the future.

9

There had been no sirens that night in the area, so that the first in a stick of bombs fell quite unexpectedly behind the Cumberland Hotel not a quarter-mile away from Connaught Square.

Léonie woke with a frantic start. Beyond the black-out curtains the bedroom window rattled from the blast, as the other bombs fell in quick succession, moving away from them along Oxford Street. She clutched at Jenny, awake beside her now. 'It's all right,' she reassured her. 'When you *hear* the explosion you're not going to get hit—'

'That's nonsense!—'

'And anyway that must have been a mistake. They're bombing the City now, the East End, or the docks.'

'We should have been in the shelter – or Hampstead.'

'I'm only frightened of one thing – being buried alive. Besides, we can't sleep together in the shelter – and, I've told you, it's so much easier for me to get to work in Whitehall from here. Léa, it's just a matter of *controlling* yourself.' She touched Léonie's shoulder and they lay back together as the bombing disappeared in a sharp thunder down-river over the docks.

But Léonie could not sleep. It was true – Connaught

Square was much nearer to Jenny's office in Whitehall than Hampstead. When the buses were re-routed, as they often were now, taking long detours round the blocked streets, Jenny could safely walk straight down to Whitehall, across Hyde and Green Parks, in half an hour. She was a great walker. And sometimes, too, she kept odd hours at the War Office, working at weekends, or going out early and returning late, when public transport had stopped, so that being able to walk to work was all the more important to her.

Léonie, returning to Hampstead by tube, had made the first part of this journey with her on many Monday mornings beneath the silver barrage balloons, walking along the sandbagged streets, glass crepitating beneath their feet from blasted houses, the air full of greasy dust, floating motes of ash, snowflakes of plaster, the debris of disaster settling in their hair, aggravating their eyes, itching the skin, so that she and Jenny, along with other women, often wore turbans now, putting on any extra lipstick and face lotions they had against the insidious dust and grit.

But in Hampstead, which had hardly been bombed at all there was none of this. The streets and houses were still intact on the high hill in the spring weather of 1941. How she wished Jenny would come and live with her and her father, whom she looked after now, in Hampstead. Oh God, she prayed silently – *do* have her come up and live with me and Papa safely, and not this living apart, my coming down here just at weekends. Let her live with me so that, if we are killed, we'll be killed together.

When the blitz had begun on London the previous August in 1940, people took it almost as a relief from the tensions of the long phoney war. They had not expected such intensive bombing to last. Yet now, over six months later, the bombs continuing to fall almost every night, the self-control and good humour of the populace had increased, not diminished. It was phenomenal.

And Léonie, too, who had become a fire-watcher in Hampstead, was normally part of this impeccable British self-control – except in so far as Jenny was concerned. Personally, at least, she had little else to worry about. Olivia's school in Kent had been evacuated to a country mansion near Cirencester in Gloucestershire. Her father, putting the house in Passy under wraps with a French caretaker, had left Paris just before the Germans moved into the city the previous June. Robert, too, covering these climactic events for the *Express* – the German Panzer *blitzkrieg* through the Low Countries, the fall of France, the British Expeditionary Force's retreat to Dunkirk, the Nazi occupation of Paris – was now back in London, still in his Holborn flat, as safe as anyone could be in the increasingly broken city.

Léonie saw him rarely: a visit together to see Olivia at an inn in Cirencester on one of her half-term breaks, odd London meetings when the telephone wires were cut to discuss their daughter's affairs. But otherwise they remained apart – and distant together, preoccupied in their own worlds. Robert was vastly stimulated, engrossed in his work. Some people had come to flourish in the war, Léonie realised. There were many whom this climate of danger suited, who took to the razed streets at dawn or walked the nightly black-out of the city like excited explorers adventuring into undiscovered territory. Robert was one. Jenny another.

Yet Léonie was not so sure of things in herself – not so certain, as an American non-combatant, of her part in this war at all. Certainly she was not excited by it, like Robert – nor so icily self-confident and fearless like Jenny. She feared the war, not so much for herself but for Jenny, who was so much more involved in, and exposed to, it in the city centre. She had put so much of her life into Jenny in these last years – relied on her so completely in return – that she had little heart left over to maintain her own sense of self-preservation. Her real fear was that, without her friend, she would be nothing.

So that at night, up in Hampstead when she heard the bombs falling all over the city below her and saw the fires raging in the lurid sky, she lived in tremulous fear, until she could confirm Jenny's safety the following morning. They telephoned each other as often as the connections allowed. And when the telephones were out she usually travelled down to Connaught Square during the day to see that the house was still in one piece.

Léonie lived on tenterhooks, impotent, unable to do anything which would stop these raids which on week-days so threatened her sanity, longing above all that Jenny would come and live with them out of harm's way in Hampstead.

Hetty and Pierre meanwhile had stayed in Paris. Hetty initially, on the outbreak of war in September 1939, had refused all Pierre's pleas that she return to the safety of Summer Hill. And she did the same, when she might still have escaped the chaos of the city in face of the German advance, in June of the following year. Hetty, too, with her Irish passport, was a non-combatant – and she made much of this to Pierre.

'Ireland's neutral,' she told him forcefully. 'Quite a few people over there are even pro-German! "England's difficulty – Ireland's opportunity." So the Nazis won't – they *can't* – touch me here. I'm staying – with you.'

Hetty, like Léonie with Jenny, depended for her very life on Pierre. She, too, had invested everything in her companion. She, too, would survive the war with him or not at all. But unlike Léonie she lived with Pierre all the time, and so had a blinding sense of self-preservation – as long as that included their both being preserved

543

together, in the same place. Without him, she knew, all the chasms in her life would open again. And so that was her only fear – that they should ever, in any way, be separated. Dying together, if it came to that, would be relatively easy. Living apart, so that he was lost to her, by distance or in dying alone – that would be the only death for her. She had seen that clearly when he had been away from her in the first months of the war.

Pierre had been at that time with the French Army, along the Maginot Line. But the Germans, just as Dermot had forecast, had run their Panzer divisions well north of the line through the Low Countries. In the subsequent collapse of France, the signing of an armistice with Germany in 1940 and the appointment of Pétain as Prime Minister with his supposedly independent administration at Vichy, Pierre was released as a medical officer from an army that no longer existed, resuming his partnership with his friend Dr Vonot on the Avenue Foch.

Pierre, like so many others in that June of 1940, had thought to escape the city with Hetty before the Germans arrived, going south – and thence perhaps over the Pyrenees, getting back to England, and joining the Free French there with de Gaulle. But André Vonot had suggested otherwise.

In the silence of their consulting rooms, late one evening in early June, when the daily panic outside on the streets with the vast exodus of people fighting to get south had subsided, he had said to Pierre, 'With this practice on the Avenue Foch – and all our right-wing "clientele" – we might serve France better by staying put, here at the centre of things, when the Germans take over the city.'

Pierre was appalled. 'You can't be serious! Stay here just to minister to those French traitors. I hate them! – the cowards, turncoats. That's one reason why I want to get out of France and back to London – so as I can see those people finished with—'

'Yes, Pierre.' Dr Vonot stood up quickly. 'Exactly my own feelings. But think of it another way. When the German high command arrives in Paris, the senior officers – some of them are bound to come to us for consultation. If we play our cards properly, pretend we're turncoats, too, we'll be in a position to learn from these Germans. Their troop movements, dispositions, other goings-on in Paris. It could be vital.'

Pierre was not clear about this. 'What good will that do *us*, you and I—'

'*Others*, Pierre, in London. And in France. They'll want to know.'

'What others? Who? France has collapsed – totally. There are no others.'

'But there *will* be others – soon. There'll be a resistance. There's one already. Me.' He looked at Pierre carefully.

'I *see* . . .' Pierre nodded. Then, after a long moment, he said, 'Yes. Well then, there's me too. I'll stay.'

'Good. But say nothing of this – to anybody. Not even our wives. Nobody must know, except us. Safer that way. Agreed?'

Pierre nodded again.

In the summer of 1941, when Léonie wanted to visit Olivia for her half-term in Gloucestershire, Jenny offered to stay in Hampstead and take care of her father while she was away. 'And I'll be safe up on the hill, too.' She smiled. 'So you won't have to worry about me when you're gone!'

When Léonie left Olivia after the long weekend in the country she caught an afternoon train back from Kemble junction. But the train was endlessly delayed – first by military transports, then by another train derailed outside

Reading and finally by that night's bombing, when the Luftwaffe chose the north Paddington area again as their target, so that Léonie's train stopped short at Southall station in the London suburbs at three in the morning, and it was not until dawn that she arrived in Hampstead.

At once she realized there had been a raid somewhere in the area. The High Street was alive with emergency traffic – fire engines and ambulances, bells ringing, streaming up the hill and turning into Willoughby Road some way below her. Over the rooftops a pall of thick black smoke rose into the crystal air of the summer dawn, bits of charred paper and soot spiralling about, an acrid smell of gas, scorched paint and burning wood everywhere.

She went down the High Street, turned left into Flask Walk, running fiercely towards her house in Denning Road. But at the end of the Walk she had to stop. The junction here, which led down towards her street, had entirely disappeared, replaced by a crater, a sheet of yellow flame leaping upwards from a broken gas main; the whole area was roped off, so that Léonie had to turn away.

Retreating back to the High Street, she tore on down the hill, turning left again, taking another route home. But here, in Willoughby Road, there was worse chaos – numbed victims picking their way between fallen rubble and household debris. She pushed through the scurrying crowd of ambulance and firemen, police, ARP wardens, first aid and rescue workers, moving between dazed groups of civilians, in blankets or pyjamas, sitting on the pavement, some still bleeding, others being bandaged, given cups of tea, or taken off in ambulances.

But the really wounded – and the dead, she saw – were being carried out on stretchers from behind another rope barrier which led into her street. There was a stench in the air here – of broken drains, sewer pipes, a smell of suppurating corruption.

Léonie ran on desperately through the crowd, getting right up to another rope barrier. Beyond her the entrance to Denning Road where she lived was partly blocked by smoking rubble, some houses with their windows blown out along either side. But, further, almost two houses had simply disappeared – leaving a great gap in the Victorian terrace – with their back gardens exposed, giving a view clear out over the Heath.

These flattened houses lay to the end of the street where she lived. But from this distance she could not make out if her own house was still standing or not. Running furiously now, she made a second detour, via Pilgrim's Lane, coming back to the south side of Denning Road. But here was another rope and a policeman. She tried to pass.

'Sorry, miss. No entry. None of the houses is safe. It's been a dirty night here. There may be more time bombs in some of 'em.'

'But I must! My father, my friend – they live, I live, half-way along!'

But now, from this new vantage point as she spoke, Léonie saw the familiar porch, the steps, the hall door of her own house – all intact. She felt a surge of relief. It took her an instant to realize that only the far side of the house was still there.

The building had been cut sheer down the middle, the inside exposed like a doll's house neatly sliced open by a huge knife. She looked up at the top floor where their flat was. Her bedroom was still there. But something was blinding her. She moved aside. It was the big dressing table mirror, she saw then – the one she'd bought at Heal's last year – glittering in the rising sun.

The mirror seemed to have been smashed in half. But why was it moving about like a semaphore mirror – glinting malevolently in the rising sun? Stepping back she finally saw what had happened. The mirror was suspended on a swaying floor joist sticking right over the empty space which had been the other half of the house. And next to it now she saw half her bedroom carpet lurching out into the void, moving gently in a spume of dirty smoke rising from the basement area.

Léonie looked across to the bathroom, where her eye was caught by a tall white shape. Then she saw it was the bath tub itself, but upended against the interior wall, standing vertically, its four clawed feet facing out into the air.

'Your father, miss?' The policeman had continued talking. 'Well, they've all been evacuated from those houses or – removed . . . You can't go in yourself. Go round to the first aid people in Willoughby Road. They'll know, give you all the names . . .'

Léonie rushed back to the ambulances and first aid post in Willoughby Road, finding a first aid post in a caravan. The door was partly open. Inside a doctor was bandaging a man's torso, the partly mummified figure groaning. A nurse pushed by her.

'My father – and a friend – they were in one of those bombed houses,' she said to the woman as she passed.

'Not here – this is only for the worst cases. Ask Sister – down there, the other first aid post.' She gestured back down the street. Running up and down the street then, Léonie looked at the faces of the stunned civilians, some sipping tea from the mobile canteen, others smoking, their hands shaking, eyes quite blank. Léonie recognized a neighbour of hers, a Mrs Cowdrey, who lived two doors up, sitting there, a blanket round her shoulders. 'Mrs Cowdrey?' She looked up but said nothing. 'Mrs Cowdrey – it's me, Léonie. Did you – did you see my father, or my friend, a woman with reddish hair? Half our house, the whole side of it has gone.'

Mrs Cowdrey shook her head vaguely. The man sitting next to her said, 'All her house went. Lucky she lived in the basement – they just dug her out.' Léonie knew what she had to do then.

A few minutes later, having run right round behind Denning Road on the Heath side, she was climbing over the rubble of her own back garden, dodging a fallen poplar tree, stumbling across the smoking debris scattered over the lawn, making her way towards the garden entrance to the house. This door, to one side, leading into the ground and first floor flat where the Morsebys lived, was still more or less intact. And so was most of their drawing room inside, and the hall, and the flight of stairs leading up to their own hall door. On the way up she found an ARP warden's helmet.

At the top, pushing open the remains of the shattered door, she stepped straight out into bright sunshine, pulling herself back at the last moment, gasping. Only half their hall corridor remained, floorboards still running along one side against the wall, but the other half was empty space, smoke drifting up, dark spumes in the crystal light, from the basement area.

Very gingerly, hands clutching the wall, she moved along this perilous bridge towards the first bedroom door on her left, where her father slept. The door was wide open. And since this bedroom was on the intact side of the house the room seemed largely unscathed. The blast had tipped the furniture and a chest of drawers over, scattering her father's clothes everywhere. But his bed on the far side was still in one piece – and empty. Her father was not there.

Moving on along the swaying floorboards of the corridor she passed the small kitchen and dining room, both damaged, but both empty, then rounded the corner and saw the drawing room in full view ahead of her. There was no door here now at all. It had been blasted clean away. And half the room itself had gone as well, but down the middle, the rest of it a mess of smashed debris and charred furniture.

Beyond it lay her bedroom, the door gone here as well, so that she could see straight into it. Crossing the remains of the drawing room she stood at the threshold. There, to one side by the wall, was her white divan bed, the coverlet all a rumpled mess, smeared, and filthy, but otherwise undamaged, just as her father's bed had been.

Beyond lay the bathroom, the door quite disappeared here too. Hugging the one firm wall, she moved along it into the bathroom. The tiles and washbasin were smashed, the lavatory cistern leaning out into space, and the bath tub itself upended against the firm wall to one side. But the bathroom was quite empty, too.

The whole top flat, or what was left of it, was empty. Above all the two beds where her father and Jenny must have been sleeping when the bomb had fallen were quite intact. And there had been the ARP helmet on the hall stairs . . . They had been saved, miraculously saved – both of their beds against the walls on the side of the house that had survived the bombing. Then, just as she was about to turn and leave, she noticed something on the bathroom floor, a red stain, a pool of liquid, oozing over the remains of the white tiling. It had come from beneath the rim of the upended bath tub. Léonie thought it nothing at first, the water reddened by soil, she imagined, which had come up through the pipes from a broken water main.

Then she started to tremble.

It was too thick for water, the liquid congealing round a mess of glass splinters, broken tiles, familiar cosmetics, old sponges, toothbrushes lying on the floor. She dipped the tip of her shoe in it. It was sticky.

She felt dizzy then. She was dreaming, living out of time now as she moved forward, putting her hand out, grasping one of the upper foot claws of the tub, pulling at it.

A moment later the tub reeled forward and then, gathering momentum, spun outwards, crashing down on the remaining floorboards, where it lay for an instant exposing its contents, before it slipped away over the edge of the broken joists into space, falling out into the sunny morning air, landing with a crash on the rubble beneath.

But in that instant Léonie saw everything – the naked, mangled, bloodied remains of her friend Jenny, entombed in the white enamel tub.

Robert was away, reporting out of Cairo on the Eighth Army's campaign against Rommel in the Western Desert. So he had no immediate knowledge of this appalling tragedy, or of Léonie's stunned reactions to it and her subsequent stay at the New End Hospital in Hampstead, suffering acute shock. There was only her father as immediate consolation – and Olivia who came up to see her for the day.

Ben Straus had survived with a nasty gash and some other minor cuts and bruises. He had gone to bed that evening after Jenny had told him she was taking a bath and had been asleep when the bombing, quite unexpectedly and without any sirens, had started – a whole stick of bombs from some Luftwaffe pilot off-course or, possibly hit by ack-ack fire on the Heath, intent simply on dumping his load anywhere. Stumbling out of bed, Ben Straus had luckily been crouching down, near the inside wall, looking for his dressing gown when the second or third in a series of bombs had exploded, slicing off one side of the house. The blast had hurled him against the wall so that he had been knocked unconscious, lying there for an hour or more before an ARP warden had found him, rescuing him. But the same man had seen nothing of Jenny, hidden in the bath tub.

Now, a week later, recovered and staying with a family temporarily across the High Street, he could say little to Léonie – except, as he did on his first visit to her in hospital, 'I only wish it had been me, dear Léa . . .' And she had looked up at him blankly, saying nothing.

All she could think of was the hideous irony, the malign fate of Jenny being up in Hampstead that weekend, a safety which she had longed for but which instead had resulted in her death.

And Léonie felt responsible for this. So that a sliver of ice grew in her heart, soon becoming a glacier. A cold passion for retribution, or for sacrifice of some sort, came to her then. She was part of the war now, with a vengeance. And the only thing she felt which might release her own vast hurt and guilt would be to punish the Germans somehow, punish fate for its cruelty, punish herself.

By the end of her few days in hospital Léonie had become a different person – hard, bitter, cold. Without Jenny her own life meant nothing. At first, in bed, she had thought simply of killing herself. But then, as she recovered her senses, she changed her mind. She would maintain her life now, but for one reason alone – that she might in some way make amends for Jenny's death.

It was Robert, when Léonie left hospital at the end of the week, who ensured their immediate survival in London. Ben Straus, through the *Express* office, had managed to get a cable through to him in Cairo, giving him the news. And he had replied almost at once, saying they should both move into his empty flat in John Street near High Holborn.

And it was from here, almost immediately after they had moved in, that Léonie went across London one morning on her own to Jenny's flat in Connaught Square. Jenny's father in Camberley had been in touch with her after the funeral – she had been buried in the local churchyard there – offering Léonie what consolation he could and suggesting that she might like to go to the flat herself and take any small mementoes she wished.

Léonie still had the key of the house which, apart from Jenny, had been unoccupied since the start of the blitz, when Mrs Ogilvy had removed herself, with Brewster, to her daughter's house in Yorkshire. Walking into the familiar square where the plane trees were full-leaved in the summer light, Léonie's heart ached. She wondered if she could face it all. But she would, she *must* . . . Jenny would want that. 'It's only a matter of *controlling* yourself, Léa . . .' Jenny's confident voice came back as she walked round the square, the railings all gone, where Brewster had exercised so unwillingly. And she could hardly bear the memories, so that when she came to the sandbagged steps leading up to the front door she was almost in tears.

She wiped her nose. The milkman was coming towards her. Léonie knew him from her own frequent visits to Jenny, leaving with her on those early Monday mornings.

'Mornin', miss,' he called out brightly. 'Another dirty night . . . Glad to see you're still in one piece. And Miss Bryden?'

Léonie could say nothing. Shaking her head, putting her key in the door, she rushed inside. And now she cried – all the way up the darkened stairs, until she got to the door of Jenny's flat, bursting it open.

She pulled herself up, quite horrified. A man was standing by the window where the black-out curtain had been drawn apart – next to Jenny's bureau, which was open, papers scattered about, which he had obviously just been going through. A burglar. Léonie stood rooted to the spot.

A burglar? He seemed far too well dressed for that – a small, neat man in his early forties, fastidious-looking, with a tiny moustache and sleek black hair, wearing a sharply cut brown suit and expensive dimpled leather brogues, almost a dandy.

Léonie was speechless. But the man was not at all put out by this discovery of his presence in the flat. More surprising still, for Léonie had never seen him before in her life, he knew who she was – calling her by her married name then, which she had not used in years.

'I'm sorry – Mrs Grant, isn't it?' He dropped the folder he had been looking at, came towards her, taking a white silk handkerchief from his breast pocket, offering it hesitantly. Léonie refused it. 'Your great friend Jenny – what a blow. What a blow for all of us.' The man used the handkerchief himself now for an instant absent-mindedly, dabbing his nose.

Léonie stirred at last. 'Who? What? – "All of us"?'

'I'm sorry . . .' The man smiled a fraction in the half-light, before turning and opening the other black-out curtain so that the room was flooded in sunlight. 'I'm Swanning, the War Office, Jenny's department. I've been in touch with Colonel Bryden, of course, who knows all about it – my being here, I mean.' He gestured towards the bureau. 'Just in case, to check Jenny didn't leave any War Office papers here.' His tone was clipped, but soft. There was something sensitive about him, and yet dynamic.

'I see.' Léonie was a little more at ease, wiping her own nose, recovering. 'But how did you know my name?'

Swanning smiled quickly again. 'Oh, Jenny told us about you, Mrs Grant.'

Léonie was annoyed as much as surprised. 'Did she? Why?'

'A close friend . . . We're a small department. You met each other in Paris, I believe?'

'No.' Léonie was abrupt. 'On the train from Paris actually. The night ferry.'

'Of course.' He wiped his neat hands on the silk hanky. 'You've both spent a lot of time in Paris.'

'No.' Léonie was pleased to contradict him again. 'We were never there together.'

'I meant separately. She said – how your father lived there—'

'I was born and brought up in Paris, Mr Swanning,' she told him abruptly.

'Of course—'

'But why should Jenny have told you all this? What's it to do with you?'

Swanning, looking at her carefully, made an apologetic gesture. 'I'm sorry. It must seem like prying. It's just – that Jenny always spoke of you so highly. I was going to write to you – when you got out of hospital,' he rushed on.

'About what?'

He seemed surprised. 'About the possibility of our meeting. At my office – if, if you could spare the time.'

'Yes. But *why*?' Léonie was increasingly impatient.

'Well, I'd wondered if – if you might consider doing something with us for the war effort.' He turned, looking out at the blitzed view – the sandbags, a fallen plane tree in the square, a shattered house on the other side, the silver barrage balloons floating over Hyde Park in the pale summer sky. 'You see . . .' He turned to her, picking up a framed photograph from the bureau, so that Léonie glowered at him and he put it down again. 'You see, we can't just let the Germans go on killing innocent people like this. We've all got to help stop it.' He looked at Léonie. There was silence.

'Yes,' Léonie said at last, but without interest. Then she added, but with no more enthusiasm, 'Yes, I'd like to help.'

'Good. Very good.' Swanning took no notice of her

dulled response. 'I thought you might. When would suit you to meet me more formally – next week?'

'As soon as possible. Tomorrow?'

He seemed slightly put out by this eagerness. 'I'm afraid . . . I'm away tomorrow. Would next week suit? Friday, ten o'clock? Here's my card. We're at the Victoria Hotel for the moment, the Quartermaster-General's H.Q. in Northumberland Avenue. Ask for me with the commissionaire. He'll show you straight up.'

After Swanning had gone Léonie picked up the photograph he had been looking at. There were two separate photographs, joined together in the same frame – both taken at the same time several years before, in the beech glades near Aylesbury when she and Jenny had gone out there with Brewster on the Green Line bus. Léonie pulled out the one of Jenny, sitting against the bole of a huge trunk with Brewster. She left the other happy vision of herself, in the same position, behind.

'It's a matter, Mrs Grant, of causing maximum discomfort and inconvenience for the Germans in France . . .' Mr Swanning spoke in an off-hand way, as if these Germans were unwelcome guests in an hotel and Léonie was simply to help in persuading them to leave.

'Discomfort, inconvenience – I see,' she said with some irony. Swanning was gazing absent-mindedly up at the ceiling.

'Well,' he pulled himself together. 'I meant sabotage, physical disruption of every sort – trains, factories and so on. That's what our work is all about. And the Germans don't like it. They react savagely, brutally.' He looked at her carefully.

'That would suit me fine,' she replied immediately.

This seemed to bother Swanning. But he continued with his initial résumé. 'There are a number of French resistance groups involved in just this sort of sabotage at the moment – but with too much uncoordinated enthusiasm, I'm bound to say. It's our aim to help them – actively on the ground, as well as supply them with arms, ammunition and so on. So we're going to need people over here – French people, or people like yourself who can pass entirely for French – to help us in this. How would you like to go to France?'

He stood up from the plain table with just a green folder on it, offering Léonie a cigarette. Apart from a notice about air raid precautions, the room was quite bare, high up in the Victoria Hotel, all the windows shuttered, just a naked light bulb illuminating what had once been a single bedroom, a dusty washbasin in one corner.

Léonie refused the cigarette. She was quite calm already, icy calm. 'I don't know whether you're aware of it, Mr Swanning, but all the Channel boats have stopped . . .'

'Ah, yes . . . But there are other ways of going to France – other than by the night ferry, Mrs Grant.'

'The War Office can send people to France?'

Mr Swanning was shocked. 'Goodness me, no! Far too proper an organization. Just accept that we could get you to France, if you were absolutely sure that this was something you'd be prepared to risk. This would be dangerous work – and entirely voluntary.'

'Who is "we"? I thought you – you and Jenny – worked for the War Office.'

'Another and quite separate department of it, Mrs Grant. But just accept that we could get you there. Would you go?'

'Yes.' Léonie responded at once. 'I'd be quite prepared to go.'

Again this immediate agreement seemed to worry Mr Swanning. 'Why, Mrs Grant?' He looked at her closely.

'Why have you asked me here, suggested I go – if you didn't think I would?'

'I just wonder about . . . your motives.'

'Well, the Germans obviously – as you said the other day – killing innocent people. Jenny . . . I wouldn't mind dying, the way she did.'

Swanning looked even more worried now. 'This work is about living not dying. We'd want you to *live*, Mrs Grant. That would be the whole purpose of the work. This could be no personal vendetta against the Nazis, or gone into with any idea of self-sacrifice—'

'No,' Léonie interrupted him. 'I just meant I was quite prepared to face the risks. You said the work was dangerous. If that includes dying, well, I'm prepared for that, too.'

'The risks are very real. We've already lost quite a few of our agents and wireless operators over there. And by lost I mean almost certainly dead – and cruelly tortured by the Gestapo before that—'

'Shall we talk about the work involved, Mr Swanning, not the risks,' she told him brusquely.

'Yes, of course.' He was almost apologetic. 'You would have to be trained for what we have in mind, several months at least, before being sent into the field.'

Again Léonie was impatient. 'Yes – but what kind of work, and where in France?'

Mr Swanning sighed, leaning forward. 'I don't want to go into details now. I want you to think about the general idea very carefully, before committing yourself. As I've told you, this is entirely voluntary—'

'But I've *said* – I'm quite prepared to go.'

'You have a daughter, Mrs Grant.'

'She's at boarding school, safely in the west country. And, if anything happened to me, my husband would be there to look after her.'

'Yes, your husband – Robert Grant, the *Express* war correspondent—'

'We've been separated – nearly four years.'

'Yes, we knew that. I'm sorry . . .'

Léonie was surprised how much he knew about her. 'But, you can see, there's nothing to stop me in that direction.'

'All the same, give yourself a week, be quite sure.' He stood up. 'Get in touch with me again. Here's my card.'

'You've already given me your card.'

'Another card.' He handed it over to her. It gave quite a different name and address. 'Capt. Selwyn Jepson, Ministry of Pensions, Sanctuary Buildings, Northumberland Avenue, W.C.'

Léonie looked at it. 'My, is that your *real* name this time?'

'Yes.'

'What a lot of cloak and dagger . . .'

'Yes, Mrs Grant. That's exactly it. And I have to tell you that's the very basis of all the work we do. So you will remember, won't you? – "Careless talk costs lives." In our business – literally and most painfully. You must mention nothing of our meeting – to *anyone*.' Captain Jepson had quite lost his vagueness now, was direct, steely.

'Of course. I can keep secrets.' She stood up and Jepson went with her to the door, before she turned to him. 'All the same, you must have been very sure of me, to ask me here and tell me all this secret stuff in the first place.'

'Jenny was very sure of you, Mrs Grant.' He looked at her now in his old vague sensitive way. 'And Jenny was one of the mainstays of our organization.'

'*Was* she? How? What did she—'

He put a hand on her shoulder, then took it away

almost at once, embarrassed. 'Not just now. *Think* about it all first.'

'I *have* thought about it, believe me. I'll be in touch with you. Goodbye.'

He opened the door for her. 'Well, Mrs Grant – *au revoir* perhaps, rather than goodbye.'

Returning to his desk, he opened the dark green folder, making a note at the end of a long typed memorandum, which included a great deal of personal information on Léonie – her family background and much else – which had been supplied to him during the past ten days by MI5.

'As far as I can tell at this juncture,' he wrote, 'Mrs Grant would in many ways be an ideal recruit for us. Her French is practically flawless, as is her knowledge of Paris and much of Normandy – two of our main target areas. There seems a steely purpose in her temperament – to the point of truculence almost. And here is one of her problems. I fear that perhaps her motives in so readily accepting our offer to join us (in the main, I am sure, due to the death of her – and our – close friend Jenny) may lead her into a quite unwanted mode of impetuous self-sacrifice, of personal revenge indeed, in any work she might do for us.

'The other problem is her age. At 42 she may be too old for the rigours of training, not to mention the physical requirements and dangers of life in the field. However, she certainly looks fit enough – and I believe her other merits outweigh these possible disadvantages. I shall be seeing her again, I am sure, and will make a final recommendation then.

'Meanwhile, it is my feeling that she would make a first-class agent. She sees the alternatives, yet the *heart* in every matter. Above all she has the *intelligence*, in every sense, which is so essential in this work. On the other hand, as I have suggested, she is a woman of very strong emotions, not always kept under control. There is a core of explosive personal venom in her which she must suppress, or redirect towards the common ends of our work. In short, she must temper this emotional imprudence, become more self-aware, objective, cold, calculating, more concerned with her own preservation. If she can achieve this I believe she would confirm all Jenny's high recommendations of her.'

He put the memorandum into a TOP SECRET manila envelope, addressing it to a Colonel Maurice Buckmaster, at premises in Baker Street.

10

'So, Mrs Grant, you have thought about it. And so have I. You are quite certain about it all. And I think I am as well.'

Captain Jepson smiled his vague smile, then offered her a cigarette. The mood between them was easier now – a week later, in Jepson's equally austere, unused room in the Ministry of Pensions. 'Now we can start on the details. You'll have to enrol first as an officer in FANY. It's necessary under international law—'

'FANY?'

'Yes. First Aid Nursing Yeomanry. A fine body of women – they run ambulance units, work in forces canteens, act as chauffeurs for senior officers—'

'But that's not the sort of work I expected—'

He raised his hand. 'No, no, of course not. Just a necessary, indeed an excellent, cover while you're in training here. You'll be commissioned as a subaltern – you'll even get to wear a red "raspberry" on your shoulder strap! Once we get through with that I'll take you to our HQ, introduce you to the man in charge of all these operations.'

'Some other room tucked away here?'

'Oh no. We have quite separate premises – just north of Oxford Street.'

'Where Jenny worked?' He nodded. 'But I thought she was in Whitehall all the time.'

'No. She was closer – to home . . .'

'What did she do? You said you'd tell me.'

'She would have been doing just what we hope you may do – an agent in the field. She very much wanted to. But her short sight prevented her. She worked on codes with us, Léonie. Codes – and clothes . . .'

'Clothes?'

'Yes. French clothes. And all the many accessories. Everyone we drop into France has to be kitted out in exactly the current manner over there. Right labels, stitching, linings, buttons, clothes coupons, and so on. Women's jackets, for example, are eight or ten inches longer over there now than here.'

'I see. Of course . . . Clothes, all Jenny's sewing and so on. All her experience with her mother working for Chanel.'

'Exactly.'

And codes, too, Léonie thought – seeing then how Jenny could so easily write 'Je t'aime' backwards on the clouded window-pane. Their life together returned to her, heart-rendingly. But she would make up for that loss, she thought with a bitter certainty, in one way or another. 'But "dropped" into France?' she asked.

'Parachute, Léonie. I told you – we can't send agents in on the night ferry now. That'll be part of your training, too. At Ringway, Manchester. They say it's wonderful – floating down in the blue . . .'

He smiled, his nice vague smile.

★

A week later, enrolled in FANY and wearing a smart new uniform, Léonie was taken by Jepson not to Baker Street but to a luxurious private apartment nearby at Orchard Court in Portman Square. Here she met Maurice Buckmaster, a willowy, sparse-haired, pipe-smoking Colonel, out of uniform now, with a notably mellifluous voice quite at odds with his austere, sharp-eyed military bearing. He treated Léonie as an equal, from the moment she sat down on a deep-cushioned sofa in the drawing room.

'Léonie . . . Léonie Grant.' He looked at her appraisingly then continued in French from then on. 'Good to have you with us – in Special Operations Executive – more usually known as "the Firm", "the Racket", "the Org" – and sometimes, indeed, as the "Stately 'Omes of England"!'

He laughed, tipping his chin up in the air and lighting his pipe. Léonie was surprised at this sudden jocularity. The Colonel continued more soberly: 'Forgive me, but absolute trust, confidence, mutual understanding is, must be the basis between all of us at HQ and anyone we send into the field. We're equals here. No standing on ceremony. Everything, at Orchard Court at least, in the open.' His eyes twinkled. 'A cup of coffee, Léonie? Selwyn, would you do the honours? It's in the kitchen. We have some *real* coffee – sent over by our man in New York. Now where was I?'

'Confidence, Colonel.'

'Ah, yes – absolute mutual trust and confidence. We depend on you, as you do on us. That's the first thing to realize. Without this feeling of close partnership the whole enterprise collapses. And the second thing to remember, Léonie – if and when you succeed in this training and go into the field – is that your life, the life of your contacts, comrades, will always lie on the tip of your tongue, on your *silence*. "Upon these two commandments hang all the law and the prophets!"' He laughed uproariously again.

'And – what else, Colonel?'

'Yes, indeed . . .' He leant forward briskly in his arm-chair by the marble fireplace, then paused, setting a flame to his pipe once more, puffing vigorously. 'A hundred and one things, which you'll come upon in your training. But, first, your name . . .' He took another match to the recalcitrant pipe.

'A name?' Léonie asked in the silence.

'Yes,' he said at last, now garlanded in smoke. 'From now on, and through each stage of your training, you will have a different name, a French Christian name only, and you will be known by no other, so to make it the more difficult for other agents, or nosy outsiders, to keep track of you. May I offer you the name "Lise" to begin with?' he said with a touch of irony, the mock knight errant.

'If you like.'

'Excellent, Lise. This will only be the nursery slopes of your aliases. The Everest, if you complete your training satisfactorily, will be the name you take up before you actually go into the field. Not only a new name but a whole new identity, as a French citizen, living – who has *always* lived – in France. And before you leave you will have to know everything, but *everything*, about an entirely imaginary person, who will be *you*. You'll have to eat, sleep and dream this person – at the cost of your life, if you slip up on the picture.' The Colonel was entirely serious now. 'That's really the third law, Lise: an absolute belief in this mysterious other person whom you will inhabit when the time comes.'

'Like being an actress?'

'Yes. But dramatist as well. You'll have to write the text here, too, as you go along.'

'I think I could do that well enough.' Léonie

remembered her years with Hetty, playing just such games, swapping clothes, roles, getting in and out of new characters almost every day.

The Colonel nodded, but then was gently dampening. 'Indeed, Lise, I hope so. Your audience and the critics, will be made up of the Gestapo or their French lackeys. And the subsequent notices – quite possibly death notices.'

'Yes, of course.'

There was a moment's chilly silence, until Jepson returned with the coffee.

'Ah, Selwyn! – *real* coffee. You can always rely on that here as well as in Orchard Court, Lise.' And again there was the soothing, confident laugh.

Ben Straus was pleased though surprised when Léonie joined the Nursing Yeomanry. It would get her out of herself, he thought, occupy her after the brutal shock, the tragedy of Jenny's death. Yet he was taken aback by the speed with which she had started on this fresh war work – surprised, too, by a whole new air of cold decisiveness now in her character. He had expected a dumb depression, for he had seen just this in her before, for months on end, when her life with Hetty and Robert had come apart. Instead, almost as soon as she had left hospital, there was this hard streak in her, a ruthless intent which he did not understand.

After all, she was only going to drive ambulances in England, work in canteens or as a chauffeur – mild enough war work. Yet here she was behaving like a combatant about to go into the front line. It disturbed him so that, when she told him she was going to be away for a month or more at a FANY training course, somewhere in the country, he could no longer restrain some of his feelings.

'I thought they'd train you here in London? You have

an address for this place? So we can keep in touch?'

'No, no. I don't. I'll be moving around, different places, all over the country apparently. And that's what really worries me – you. I don't think I'm going to be able to get back to London at all, even weekends.'

'Oh, I'll be fine. The bombing's stopped by and large right now. And I can manage the stairs here, not in my dotage yet, you know. And I've all these new friends over here now at the Embassy in Grosvenor Square. It's you I'm worried about, Léa. You've gotten so . . . preoccupied, hard, lately. Not like you. Oh, I know it's one way of dealing with tragedy—'

'Yes. Yes, it is,' was all she could say.

'But this going away, to some unknown address, Léa. You're not doing anything stupid?'

Wearing her smart new uniform, she turned to him from the window, smoothing the lapels out, brushing down the skirt. 'No, Papa. Not stupid. Just necessary.'

She stood against the light streaming into the Holborn flat. She had almost entirely lost her slight plumpness, he noticed. That soft mellowness had quite disappeared, the friendly, candid air. It seemed as if the warm heart had been torn from his daughter and replaced by a cold pump. She was harsh and military as she stood there in her uniform. Léa, his dear daughter, had grown away from him – embarked on something he knew nothing of. For he knew with some certainty that she was lying to him about going off on some innocent nurses' training course in the country.

'Well, you're no fool, Léa . . .' He came to her, touching her cheek an instant. 'You'll know what you're doing. But I hope – I know you're up to something out of the ordinary, probably dangerous, not just driving superannuated colonels round the parade ground – I hope you're not thinking of doing something rash, because of Jenny.'

She turned to the window. A taxi crawled along High

Holborn – making a complete circle round an old bomb crater, before returning the way it had come.

Did she know what she was doing? Was she really prepared to go to France – to shoot and kill and very possibly die herself – simply on behalf of Jenny?

Did she owe Jenny her own death?

No, it wasn't that. It had been – initially, when she'd first met Selwyn Jepson. But she saw clearly that she owed Jenny, owed everyone, her life, not her death – just as Jepson had told her afterwards. Her hardness was for that now. She would survive this work, this war. Certain before that she could not live without Jenny, she saw now how the only way to do this was to survive for her – and to fulfil what Jenny had not been able to do because of her short sight: go to France for the same organization as she had worked for. This way, at least, she would remain with Jenny in a sense – linked with her, not through death but in this future life. This way, however tenuously, she would keep faith with her, preserve their love.

She turned back to her father then. 'No,' she said. 'It *was* that feeling, that I didn't want to live, wanted to die like her, just in any violent old way in the war, it didn't matter. But now it's different. I want to live for her – and you. And Olivia.' She looked at her father. 'But I can't live any more just twiddling my thumbs in London. I have to do something – as Jenny did.'

'Which I bet wasn't driving decrepit old colonels about . . .'

'No. But I can't tell you what, exactly—'

'No. You don't have to. I can guess – something secret, and therefore dangerous. So – I just hope you don't see this work as a simple way out.'

'A way back, Papa – I hope. For me, to her – to all of you.'

*

With half a dozen other girls Léonie, as Lise, started her first month's training at Wanborough Manor, a rebuilt Tudor country house in a heavily-guarded estate outside Guildford in Surrey. The place was as comfortable and well appointed as Orchard Court – antique furnishings downstairs, large chintzy bedrooms, special rations, a French chef, tennis courts and a swimming pool among the pines. The mood was one of a pre-war country house party.

They were not told, of course, but this luxury was intentional – intended to get them all at their most relaxed, the better to put them off their guard, so that the training officers and NCOs, under the elegant Major Roger de Wesselow, might spot any character faults, lapses, gauge their true spirit and outlook.

Léonie came through with flying colours in this respect. Unlike some of the other girls from suburban backgrounds, she, with her long experience of just such elegant living, in Paris and at Summer Hill, found nothing tempting or extraordinary in this mode of existence.

Nor – soon getting back into the way of her circus experience with Fonsy O'Grady's troupe in Ireland years before – did she find much difficulty over the initial physical training – or in the various tumbles and painful falls which she had to undergo in her unarmed combat course.

So, too, the evening indoor games – played to sharpen their wits and memory as when they were given a quick glance at a laden tray and had to itemize all the objects on it afterwards – posed no problems for her. And the charades, which she had indulged in so many times – publicly and privately, with Hetty – were almost too easy: these theatricals designed to prepare the girls for the new identities which they would have to assume in the field.

French was spoken at all times. And Léonie thought her grasp here was as good as any, until Major de

Wesselow remarked on her slight American intonation in some words.

'You must remember,' he told her in his own perfect French. 'Some of the Gestapo are the world's best interrogators. And certainly all the ones you meet, if you have that misfortune, will speak and understand French like natives.' The shadow of the Gestapo was never far from the Major's presentations and lectures. This, too, was intentional. Fear, he knew well, was a great aid to self-preservation.

All mail sent or received was censored. And telephone calls either way were strictly forbidden. But here, like the other girls, Léonie was able to keep in touch with her father via letters written on a number of differently headed sheets of Army notepaper, addressed from various barracks and military depots throughout the country, and posted from there, so that relations and husbands might be reassured as to the girls' well-being and whereabouts.

In the other training activities Léonie was less adept. Morse code she found difficult. Hand grenades and explosives alarmed her far more than they might any enemy. So, too, the use of weapons – Tommy guns, rifles, revolvers – was something she did not take to easily. She handled these violent lengths of metal clumsily, afraid of them, afraid of her ability to control them.

The Major watched her one day at the indoor shooting range in a barn behind the house. Her first four shots from the Beretta automatic had all gone wide, outside the circle. She paused, in frustration.

'Two hands, yes, but hold it more *firmly*, Lise! And you really have to *look* at the target, not turn away at the last moment.'

'I wish I could use a foil – I used to fence a lot . . .'

'Indeed . . . But I fear the days of the Three Musketeers are over in France, my dear.'

'Or a knife. Couldn't I just use a knife to kill them?' She was entirely serious. And the Major saw this.

'Yes,' he said. 'In certain circumstances. And you will have training in that later, if you pass on from here. But, for the moment, let us concern ourselves with your just *shooting* your enemies, Lise . . .'

The Major watched her. She raised the Beretta again. And this time, with a vehement look in her eyes, clutching the automatic fiercely and without turning away when she fired, she let off the remaining bullets, two of them finding the circle. The Major congratulated her. 'Well done,' he said. 'Two Germans down the hatch.' She would just about pass the initial course, he thought. More likely to wound, rather than kill, in her small arms ability. On the other hand her intelligence work, her memory, her impromptu charades, her gift of taking on new identities, her quick-thinking responses under questioning – all this was superb.

In the far north of Scotland, where she went for a second month, after a week back with her father in London, Léonie's training was far more rigorous. They were camped in a small, partly ruined farmhouse at the end of some five miles of tortuous, bumpy tracks, way out on the wildest part of the Inverness coast.

The food consisted largely of herrings, stale bread and weak tea. The broken windows rattled in the autumn storms. It was wet – and cold, especially at five in the morning when they set out on their daily treks and training sessions over the bare mountains rising steeply up behind the farmhouse.

Here, throughout the autumn, the girls were put through an entire commando course at the hands of various instructors, both military and civilian, experts in small arms fire, rock-climbing, map-reading, judo, close-armed combat, sabotage – involving mock attacks with live ammunition, the use of explosives of all kinds. Even a royal gamekeeper from Balmoral had been engaged to teach them how to stalk, to avoid being stalked, how to live off the land.

Léonie, under the new name of Céline, was twelve years older than the next oldest girl, and did not bear up well to this punishing regime. The forty-eight-hour treks over the stormy hills, sleeping rough at nights, getting lost in the freezing mists, falling into ice-cold burns, climbing almost-sheer rock faces, live ammunition whistling over her head as she crawled across a sodden bog – all this, despite her very best efforts, very nearly undid her.

And her instructors noted these disabilities in their reports. So that when, after six weeks, she returned to London, Colonel Buckmaster, having read the reports, spoke to her in Orchard Court.

'So . . .' He looked up from the papers. 'It seems the hard life is not quite your forte, Céline!' There was still the musical voice, the laughter there. But a note of regret now as well.

'I didn't do too badly, surely?' She knew from his tone that he was going to turn her down.

'No. Indeed not. For someone your age – if you'll forgive me – you did remarkably well. It's just that, in France – this is rough work, Céline. No two ways about it . . .' He glanced back at his papers. It was a cold, depressing November day. Léonie felt the chill of failure then, as well as of climate. He had not offered her any coffee either. But she was not to be put down. She was not out of it all yet.

'But I did well in the close-armed combat, didn't I?' She referred here to her vicious exercises with a short-bladed knife, first against a suspended sack of straw, then against a rather surprised young man, a commando

NCO. Her fencing experience with Hetty had served her well in this.

'Yes, I see that. Full marks!—'

'And surely this work in France won't be all physical. Won't it be just as much *intelligence* work? Walking the streets, sitting in cafés, eyes and ears open, taking trains and buses, knowing the routes and timetables and so on. And not being *noticed*, living the part. Isn't that so?'

'Yes, quite so – when the work is going well. But if it doesn't – as will quite likely be the case – then you have to be entirely competent in the other, more violent aspects of the job.'

'Well, I'm obviously better at the first part. But I can do both. And, besides, my age may be a disadvantage for sabotage work. But in another way it's an advantage. The Germans won't expect someone my age to be a British agent!'

'Possibly, yes—'

'And then, couldn't you give me – won't you need people in *Paris*, not in the country? Because Paris I know like the back of my hand.'

'Yes, that's possible . . .'

'Please, Colonel – you know I so want to do this, to go to France.' She looked at him, without pleading, without any expression of bravado, totally controlled, sincere.

The Colonel, seeing all this – this calm passion – suddenly knew he must take a chance on this woman. On physical grounds he ought to have turned her down. But she had so many other gifts – of imagination, adaptability, quick verbal response – all so ideally suited to some of the work involved, that he knew he could not let them go to waste. And, besides, she was right – there was, he thought, likely to be most vital work required in Paris . . .

'All right,' he said finally. 'I take your points. What name would you like – for the last part of your training – the "finishing school"? Michèle?' She nodded. 'Right,

Michèle. Now what about a cup of real coffee before you go?' She smiled for the first time in weeks.

Léonie woke with a violent start, the torch light directly in her eyes, before two shadowy figures in trench-coats pulled her up from the bed and pushed her violently out of the room, rushing her down the stairs, taking her at a run down to a bare, cold, cell-like room in the basement.

A plain table was set in the middle, chairs to either side, with another much brighter light shining straight into her eyes. The two men sat opposite. She was still half-asleep. The first man, quite invisible now behind the light, started to question her aggressively in French.

'Name?'

'Yvonne . . .' She hesitated, wiping the sleep out of her eyes. 'Yvonne de Sertigny.'

'Your father?'

'Jean de Sertigny. And my mother was called Claudine—'

'We didn't ask you about your mother.' His tone was vicious, spiteful. 'What does your father do?'

'He's dead—'

'How, when did he die?'

'Killed. He was a Captain in the 54th Regiment of Infantry. Killed just a year before the armistice at Verdun – in the Great War.'

'And your mother? – what did she do?' The questions, switching suddenly and irrationally, came staccato from both men now.

'My mother disappeared—'

'I asked what she *did*?'

Léonie shook her head in confusion. 'She – she didn't do anything. She was just married—'

'How did she disappear? When?'

'On the route south from Paris, in June 1940. We were

just outside Rambouillet, all the crowds on the roads. I think – she was killed, in the strafing.'

'Where were you brought up as a child?'

Léonie hesitated again, wiping her eyes. 'We lived – number 12 – no it was 14 – rue du Dragon, eighth *arrondissement*. An old *hôtel particulier*. A big ground floor apartment, through the arched doorway, right at the far end of the courtyard. There was a little bell over the side-door, the servants' entrance – and we used to eat sometimes at the Restaurant du Dragon, just a little way up—'

'The Chinese restaurant?'

'No, of course not. It's French – just a bourgeois family restaurant – Madame Galliard runs it.'

'And when you lost your mother outside Rambouillet – what happened then?'

'I came back to our apartment in Passy. Number 27, Avenue Henri Martin, just up from the Cimetière de Passy.'

'Not married? Why is that? – a woman like you.'

'My fiancé, Richard Bouvrier, a Captain in the Fifth Armoured Division – he was killed on – on 29 May, 1940, near Lille, during the Panzer *blitzkrieg* there.'

'Convenient, isn't it, Mademoiselle de Sertigny – your father and your fiancé both dead, your mother "disappeared" . . .'

Léonie shrugged. 'I don't know what you mean "convenient" . . . It's a tragedy. The war. Two wars.' She glowered at the two men beyond the bright light.

'What did your mother do – between the two wars?'

'Nothing. I told you. She was a widow. She bought our apartment on the Avenue Henri Martin – and lived there. With me. I looked after her.'

'Is that *all* you did?' The question was derisive.

'No, I taught the piano, and singing, privately, in the apartment. I'm a music teacher. You've seen my Carte d'Identité.'

'And your grandparents? Who were they? Where did they live?'

'My mother's parents, the de Bellays, came from Chambrais near Lisieux—'

'And your father's father?'

'The de Sertignys – they lived in the Château de Courcy, just south of Coutance in the Cotentin peninsula. My great-grandfather bought it in—'

'Where was your fiancé educated?'

'Here, in Paris. The Lycée Henri Quatre.'

'He was clever then?'

'Yes.'

'Why did he join the Army, when he could have gone on to one of the *Ecoles Supérieures*?'

'He disliked . . . bureaucracy. He wanted something in the open air.'

'What was your grandfather's château like?'

'Small, in the Louis XIII style, two turrets at either end. There was an old dry moat, the ruins of an Abbey just behind it. Mama and I used to come up on the train for summer holidays there – the branch line that runs south of Bayeux, up to Carentan—'

'We don't want to know about your summer holidays. Where were you at school?'

'At the Ecole Sainte-Mathilde, near Bayeux, at the Château de Héricourt. It was a convent. The nuns were *soeurs sécularisées*.'

'An expensive establishment, in another château . . .'

'Yes. The school no longer exists. Closed years ago.'

'All these châteaux, Mademoiselle de Sertigny – *la vie grande luxe*. Châteaux and apartments in the *seizième*. Well, we'll soon take you down a peg or two from all that.' The man stood up. 'Your *Carte d'Identité*,' he shouted now, coming round to her side of the table, laying her *Carte* in front of her. Léonie looked at it in the bright light. 'It's out of order,' the man continued grimly.

'Out of order?' Léonie felt herself tremble with fear.

'And you cannot see it yourself?'

'No.'

'Your hair, Mademoiselle. Black, it says here. But your hair is obviously brown . . .'

'Oh, I had it dyed,' Léonie said immediately and quite evenly.

'And your photograph – it shows you wearing spectacles. Yet you have none on. And none with you.'

'I only wear them for reading,' she retorted equally quickly. 'But they broke, just the other day.'

The bitter, brutal interrogation dragged on for another thirty minutes – in the cold little basement still-room at Beaulieu Manor, before Léonie was finally released and returned to her comfortable bedroom in the huge house in the New Forest.

'So, Yvonne – flying colours, on all your finishing school reports.' Colonel Buckmaster congratulated her as she entered the drawing room of Orchard Court a week later. For the first time she saw him in uniform – both of them in uniform, standing at the doorway, exchanging smiles.

'Thank you, Colonel. A month's parlour games in the New Forest . . .' she added a little ruefully.

'Your forte, Yvonne – as I well knew!' The pipe was not in evidence today. He was brisk, pleased. 'And it's the most vital part of the training. All these psychological games, taking on an entire new life – every detail, every *potential* detail, living it, dreaming it, day and night. Not easy. But the reports—' He moved over to the marble mantelpiece, picking up a folder there. 'Superb – by and large.'

'By and large?' They sat down.

'Difficult to fault you. Except that you had a tendency

in the interrogations to be a little *too* forthcoming, inventive. Watch that. Remember, you're a woman of the French upper classes, of the *seizième*, the *ancien régime*. They would not be so forthcoming, more *de haut en bas*!'

'Yes.'

'On the other hand your hesitancies – they were fine.' He opened the file. 'Forgetting the number of your old apartment in the rue du Dragon – and contradicting them about the Chinese restaurant. Very quick of you!'

'Who *were* those men?'

'Clever, weren't they?' He smiled.

'Especially about the *Carte d'Identité*. The wrong hair and no glasses. That nearly threw me completely.'

'As was intended. But your responses were just the ticket.'

'Thank God! I certainly don't want to wear glasses and dye my hair . . .'

The Colonel looked up at her searchingly now. 'That is exactly what you're going to have to do, Yvonne – on your first mission, after you complete the parachute course at Manchester.'

'Oh, no—'

'Yes, Yvonne. Because we're sending you to the same *quartier* where you lived in Paris – Passy, the *seizième*. And although you've only been back there to your father's house irregularly over the years, it's just possible a concierge or someone might recognize you – on the street or in a café. And then, of course, Yvonne de Sertigny herself had brown hair – and wore spectacles . . .'

'Yes, but *Passy*?'

He nodded. 'It's vital work. There's a French resistance network operating there. One of the most important we have connections with in France . . .' The Colonel paused. And now he took his pipe out and started to fiddle with it.

'And?'

'We believe it's been penetrated by the Germans. Various suspicions. They transmit on the usual short-wave circuits, from various parts of the western suburbs and further out. But several times in the last month or so, the WT operator's call-sign – his "fingerprint" – has struck us, not as incorrect, but "smudged".'

'But if he was under any sort of duress there'd be the other signal – the intentional mistake in the message itself.'

'Yes. And there's never been that. Which makes us think that either the WT operator has been turned, or that the network recruited a French traitor from the word go.'

'But you've no other direct evidence?'

'Well, we may have, I'm afraid. We've sent two of our agents from Normandy into Paris in the last two months, to contact the head of this circle to check on his WT operator. The idea was to get him to transmit some false information, which, if he was a double agent, would get back to the Germans, of course – which they'd act on and which we'd know about then, proving the operator was a traitor.'

'And did the information get back to the Germans?'

'No. It didn't. Because both our agents, either before they got to Paris, or as soon as they arrived there, got picked up by the Gestapo.'

'Who in the Paris network knew they were arriving?'

'No one. No one from this Passy circle anyway – as far as we know. So it may be just coincidence they were both picked up. On the other hand we can't rely on that. The head of this Passy circle – code-named Michel – may have betrayed them. Or French resistance groups in Normandy, where they went in, via Gisors, part of the Centurie network. Some of these French resistance networks are not at all secure.'

'You mean this man Michel may be a double-agent as well?'

'It's possible. And that's exactly what we want you to check out: him and the WT operator, code-named Louis. They may be working this together. And your job will be to contact Michel without his having any idea that you're with us. And, having contacted him, stay with him, find out all you can, above all try and join his resistance group. We have to be sure of this network, one way or the other. Because the information we're getting from them is grade A stuff. But this could well be a ploy, their offering us genuine information, so as to trap more and more French resisters as well as our own SOE agents, before they entirely bust the circle.'

'Fine. But there's the problem, isn't there? – if I contact this man as Michel he'll know at once I'm an agent myself, with SOE or a French group . . .'

'Yes, but we've been doing some work on our own over there, Yvonne. We now know who Michel is. We have his real name and his business address in Paris. You'll be able to contact him quite openly and directly there.'

'Who is he?'

The Colonel demurred. 'It'll all be in your operation instructions. When you get them, read them here, memorize it all, after the parachute course at Ringway. What I want to impress on you now is that this is important – and dangerous, of course. Because, if one or other of these two men is working for the Germans, and for a moment suspects that you're with us, you'll go the way of the other two agents we sent in. Because they'll do anything to maintain the fiction of their running a genuine resistance circle. And we'll be none the wiser. So we have to know.' He stood up, opening Léonie's finishing school file. 'I'll see you again, of course, before you leave. But you're happy about Yvonne de Sertigny?'

'Yes. Yes, I'm her all right, top to toe. Apart from the hair and glasses . . .'

'The relations, your fiancé – the addresses are all covered – because they're nearly all true in fact. And your Passy address, where you live now, well, it's as clear as we can get it. The apartment's been unoccupied since June 1940, as you know – ever since Madame de Sertigny got out of France and came over to London. You're her daughter of course . . .'

'Of course. Yvonne de Sertigny – who died in the Luftwaffe strafing on the road near Rambouillet.'

The Colonel nodded. 'But you are her – reincarnate.'

'I hope so.'

'Oh yes, Yvonne. You *are*. That's your great gift. Yvonne de Sertigny, to the manner born . . .'

'I sometimes think it might have been easier if I'd taken over some completely fictional identity.'

'Perhaps. But how could we have turned down the chances offered here? You know the whole *real* story of your mother Madame de Sertigny – to put it mildly.'

'Yes, indeed. And the whole family. By heart. Spent days with the old lady . . .'

'And, remember, she's totally secure here in London. Under surveillance day and night – not that she isn't entirely on our side anyway, what with losing her daughter that way to the Luftwaffe.'

'Yes – I'm not worried about her. It's the others in the apartment block.'

'I know. But that chance was too good to miss as well – a "safe house" right at the centre of things, which if all goes well we can use indefinitely.'

'The neighbours, though—'

'Your immediate neighbours, on that third floor of the building, have gone. Two of them to Vichy, the other man died. Those three apartments have been sold to new owners. They won't know you. And the other occupants downstairs won't know which apartment you're going to – because you'll be using the lift. The only problem is Madame de Sertigny's brother-in-law—'

'And the concierge.'

'Yes . . .' The Colonel paused. Then he stood up briskly, confidently. 'As for Edouard de Sertigny living in the château in Normandy – well, Madame assures us he never comes to the apartment in Paris, which of course is no guarantee that he won't.'

'No.'

'But, if he does, then you show him Madame's ring, which you'll be wearing. And tell him the story we've prepared. Her brother-in-law is a patriot, we know that. And he knows Madame de Sertigny escaped to England – and that Yvonne died. If you do meet him, he'll put two and two together – and say nothing. No, the only real problem may be the concierge, Madame Bonnot – quite a different breed. Likely to be nosy – and quite possibly a collaborator, at least with the local gendarmes. On the other hand, you have all the right keys – and she's new. She won't know what the real Yvonne de Sertigny looked like. However, if she does show any suspicions, asks questions, then you'll have to take steps accordingly. The mission is too important not to . . .' He did not elaborate on what these steps might be. But Léonie knew exactly what he meant.

11

The war had not touched Summer Hill. Only nature – and the absence of those who loved it – had done that. Ivy gripped the stones. Lichen climbed the porch columns. Elder, nettle and briar sprouted round the walls. Moss grew in thickening carpets up the terrace steps and made little rugs over the cobbles in the back-yard.

The tentacles of voracious Irish nature, no longer held at bay, began to rise and feed once more, creeping over the house and demesne, strangling and flourishing. The war, diminishing human life in the house, gave it another – a creeping vegetable animation, which soon held the place in a green calm, the great house adrift in a sea deep jungle, so that there was something eerie in this wilderness and the village boys thought twice about raiding the old orchards, hesitating at the walls, fearful of being set upon or lost in this enchanted kingdom.

The house itself, at least, was not empty. Aunt Emily survived with her sketch-books, coloured inks and oat-cake biscuits in the studio-bedroom. Elly and the young maid Biddy looked after her, while Jack Welsh maintained the fires and logs in winter and swept the chimney flues in summer. John Hennessy's son Michael, from the grocer's shop in Thomastown, now that there was no petrol, had got his father's old horse-drawn van out again and rattled down the high lane every Friday with the groceries. The wind-charger had broken down completely. Spare parts, in the 'Emergency' as the war was mildly termed in neutral Ireland, were unavailable. They lived by oil and candle-light again.

The house survived, in itself and in the memory of those others overseas – Dermot, Hetty, Pierre, Robert, even Léonie. And yet, in the potent damp-dry air of the rooms, against the unchanging décor of generations, there was still a sense of performance postponed, some few pages lost in the text of a play that would surely be resumed. For Summer Hill maintained its own secret life, a murmur beneath the dust-sheets, the stir and vague rumour of spirits past, an invitation for those to come, who would some day return, at curtain up, as audience and players, taking their seats and cues, giving voice and laughter, part once more of the house's immemorial drama.

Summer Hill did not readily give up its ghosts – either the dead or the living. Mortimer had died the previous autumn and his funeral had been held there with Dermot and Mortimer's many friends down from Dublin: Mortimer, returned at last to the family home, lying in quiet state in the great hall for a September morning, a day filled with showery golden colour, before the horse-drawn hearse took him down the back avenue and all the way along the river, to the Cordiner family vault in the little church across the valley. The house waited, faithful in life, in death.

'So, you've memorized your operational instructions?'

'Every bit. "Operation: Café Noir. Name in the field: Yvonne. Destination: Paris. Date: 16 March."'

'Good,' the Colonel said, sitting across from her in Orchard Court. 'So then,' he continued, 'let us see, let me play the ogreish examiner!'

He opened the operations file at random. Then suddenly, his jocularity over, he was serious in his ecclesiastic manner. 'When you need to send secure messages to us in Baker Street, or if you have any difficulty with Michel after you've contacted him – what then?'

'I contact our SOE circle for the Seine-et-Oise region. Their courier, Louise, comes to Paris every Tuesday, goes to the Café le Prince outside the La Muette Métro station between twelve and one o'clock. She always sits inside, at any of the vacant tables to the left, reading a copy of *Le Matin*. I identify myself as Yvonne from London by taking the *last* cigarette from a packet, then putting the empty packet on the table and saying, "What are the trains from Versailles running like today?"'

'Fine.' The Colonel turned to another page, then spoke

enthusiastically. 'At what point do you identify yourself to Michel, as an SOE agent?'

'Not initially at all, of course,' Léonie was very prompt. 'Having made the appropriate professional contact with him I'm then to try and join his French network, get his WT operator to transmit particular information to Baker Street which, if he's a double-agent, will get back to the Germans, who will act on it, proving—'

'Fine. What if you fail in this – and yet come to know or suspect that Michel himself is a traitor?'

'Break all contact with him and his network. Contact Louise—'

'Yes – yes, indeed. Get out quick.' The Colonel put the file down. 'Because of course we've lost two agents already, Yvonne – quite possibly in this spider's trap. You'll be going in via Beauvais, the French resistance network there will look after you initially. But, even so, say the *least* when you arrive to any of these French people. This is vital. Trust no one in your reception committee especially, because it may be one of them who's working for the Germans, not anyone in Michel's circle in Paris. All right?'

'Yes.'

Suddenly, without dropping his gaze, the Colonel switched track completely. 'Where do you live – as far as Michel is concerned?'

'In Normandy – near the Château de Balleroy, the manor there. But I'm up in Paris, staying at the Hotel Meurice, on the rue de Rivoli.'

'Indeed you are. Because you'll take a room there initially to establish your rich and aristocratic bona fides with Michel who, unless and until you become quite certain about him, is not to know of your "safe house" in Madame de Sertigny's apartment on the Avenue Henri Martin. We have to preserve this safe house at all costs, both for yourself – and for others coming after you. You have your money? The Meurice isn't cheap and you should take a decent room there.'

Léonie nodded, patting the money belt round her waist. 'Two hundred thousand francs . . .'

'About £1,200, Yvonne. Because, remember, you're *rich*. You're part of the *ancien régime*, you favour Pétain. The Germans by and large for you are a "good thing" in France – you're almost, but not quite, a collaborator yourself. All this is very much part of your general cover, so don't forget it. Additional funds are always available through Louise at the Café le Prince. Though of course, if you meet her regularly, you'll have to change the rendezvous each time.'

He paused, lighting his pipe. 'So, now – to the details. I can't say I think much of your parachuting reports from Ringway . . .'

'I didn't break my leg.'

'Very nearly did, by all accounts. However, on this occasion, it won't matter. We're sending you in by Lysander tonight, or tomorrow night, while the moon is full. A landing somewhere near Beauvais, I gather, because we've some urgent and breakable medical equipment going in as well – and one of our SOE men to take out. And talking of medical equipment . . .' The Colonel stood up, going to the mantelpiece, picking up a number of small French aspirin bottles, returning with them, commenting on each as he handed them to Léonie.

'Some medicinal aids for you. Remember what each bottle contains – this is vital, too. Literally! They are clearly marked by the little numbers in each corner here. One: these will give you very nasty stomach pains – and all that goes with it – for twenty-four hours. Not very pleasant. But it will fool any doctor – which of course is exactly what you'll need to do when you make your first contact with Michel in Passy. Clear?'

'Yes.'

'The pills in this box – number two – have just the opposite effect: stimulants – keep you going like a Derby winner for twenty-four hours. These, number three, are knock-out pills. One in a cup of coffee or a glass of wine – and the person won't know what's hit them, unconscious for up to six hours, with no after-effects. Finally this single pill . . .' He held up a brown sphere the size of a pea. 'Your "L" pill, Yvonne. Stands for lethal. And it is. If you get in a jam, you'll be out of it – permanently. Takes about five seconds. I can't tell you whether it's painful or not. But it's likely to be much less painful than the attentions of the Gestapo. Always keep it with you, the hem of a dress or some such . . .'

He handed it to her. But she did not take it. 'I won't need that.' She was matter of fact.

'You should.'

'I must?'

'Well, no, because you can throw it away when you leave here, and I'll be none the wiser. But you *should*.' He looked at her evenly.

'You don't trust me to resist – interrogation?'

'Not a question of trust, Yvonne. We know – you know – that very few people with the Gestapo, under torture, can keep their mouths shut for more than twelve hours, twenty-four at the most. Just enough time for their colleagues in the network to get well out of the area. The pill is for that – if, or before, it gets unbearable.'

'You're not like Captain Jepson, are you?' She looked up at him, almost angry. 'Think I need that pill for some sort of glorious self-sacrifice – because of Jenny?'

The Colonel was taken aback for a moment. He knew of just this possibility from Jepson's original report on her. 'No, I don't think that. How do you know – that Jepson thought that?'

'Because I thought it myself, when I first talked to

him – and I know he sensed it. And I did have something just like that in mind. But not any longer.' Léonie stood up and went over to the window, lighting a cigarette, one of the few she allowed herself each day, just as she had when she and Jenny had been together. Memories flooded back as she gazed out on the blustery March weather, the plane trees in Portman Square so like those in Connaught Square. Her breath clouded the window-pane as she stood there – just as it had when there was peace and Jenny lived and had written 'Je t'aime' backwards on the glass.

The Colonel sensed her thoughts. 'You were very close to Jenny. I know that. Closer than any of us here at the Firm. But, believe me, she was such a great friend to all of us here, too. I miss her particularly. So I know your feelings. And I understand that original feeling of yours as well.'

Léonie turned. The Colonel, by the mantelpiece, looked across at her, a clear sympathy in his gaze. 'Thank you,' she said. 'Yes, I've felt that understanding in you, Colonel, and in all the others ever since I came to Orchard Court, to Baker Street, which is why I won't need that pill. I want to live now – for you, the others – just as much as for Jenny.'

'Yes . . . Good.' The Colonel lit his pipe, at a loss for a moment. 'Well, on a more cheerful note.' He reached into his pocket, producing a silver powder compact, from Cartier in Paris. 'A much happier going-away present, Yvonne. With love from the French Section.' Léonie admired it, opening it, glancing in the mirror. 'Ideal for seeing behind you, too,' he added drily.

'You think of everything, Colonel.'

'Of course! And now your clothes – let me have a look at you.'

Léonie came forward, parading, turning round like a mannequin. She was wearing a superbly-tailored grey woollen coat and skirt, the hem of the coat low beneath her waist in the current French fashion.

'Everything been checked?'

'Every stitch. It's all from Paris – chose it myself. The stuff only came out a month ago. French dressmaker's labels, everything. All from Molyneux in the rue Royale, Colonel. Even the knickers . . .'

The Colonel nodded appraisingly, with the hint of a smile. 'You've thought of everything, too.'

'Of course,' she said neatly.

'Yes, I think that's just the ticket!' He stood back, admiring her. 'Yvonne de Sertigny – from the Manoir de Balleroy, the Hotel Meurice and the *seizième* . . . And of course you'll have all Yvonne's real clothes and her other knick-knacks once you get to the apartment. She's almost exactly your size . . .' He had a serious air as he gazed at her. Then he brightened once more. 'And your new hair – and your glasses. You mustn't worry about that. You look *most* becoming, with both . . .'

Léonie doubted him. She had seen herself this way in a full-length mirror. As far as her new role went, her hair, now dyed brown, did indeed go very well with her tortoiseshell spectacles – giving her a distinguished, more mature air, an almost middle-aged hauteur. On the other hand, these props and changes, together with the lines of pain and sadness that had creased her face in the last nine months, suggested to Léonie all too clearly how her youth was over.

'Anything else, Yvonne?'

'One thing, Colonel . . .' She produced a number of postcards from her bag. 'I've written to Olivia, my daughter – ten of these. I've told her I'm being sent to Scotland for several months – on special war work. Could you have them posted from there, every week or so, so that she knows I'm all right? To the school in Gloucestershire, then the Holborn flat?'

'Of course. And we'll see that she's fine in any case. And your father. As you know we have several FANY liaison officers for doing just that.'

'Yes, I know. And if anything should happen to me, more permanently—'

'They'll both be taken care of, in *every* way. I can promise you. But, Yvonne, that won't happen. You'll be back. You're too good to lose.' They stood up, shook hands. '*Bonne chance – et au revoir*, Yvonne!'

She turned back at the doorway. 'Oh, by the way, Colonel – why is the operation called "Café Noir"?'

'In your honour, Yvonne. As an American – and because you were always so appreciative of our American coffee here.'

Dipping through layers of silvery cloud beneath the large moon, the Lysander circled several times over the landing zone, before the pilot, coming right down to 400 feet, finally saw the 'All Clear' code, a flashing morse from a strong beam, and then the half-dozen flares in a line, with another smoky reddish flare set out at an angle beyond them, giving the wind direction. Rising up then, and banking very sharply so that Léonie's stomach turned a somersault, the little plane swung right round, flew on for half a minute, then turned again and dipped equally sharply, before the pilot, cutting the engine, glided over some trees, then hit the frozen pasture with a thump, running on for a hundred yards before turning and taxiing to a halt near the woods at the top of the field.

Everything happened very quickly then. Léonie almost fell out of the plane, seeing the men running towards her in the half-dark, moonlight glittering on the frosty earth, hearing the sound of voices, shouted commands in French, urgent messages.

A small, broad man loomed in front of her as she ran

from the slipstream of the roaring propeller. '*Bonjour, Madame. Je suis Marc – venez, venez vite!*' Another taller figure rushed past her, climbing into the seat next to the pilot which she had just left. Several others in the French reception committee were already lugging boxes of medical equipment away from the plane, running with them towards the trees – before Marc, tugging at her arm, pulled Léonie away in the same direction. She heard the plane door slam behind her – the engines roar as the Lysander took off again, rising steeply before disappearing into the moonlit, cloud-mottled sky.

Less than four minutes had passed since they had landed. And now, the flares doused and the others in the reception committee having joined them from all over the field, they took cover in the wood, crouching down in the frozen undergrowth. There was dead silence before a dog barked not far away.

'*Ça va?*' The man in the leather jacket, lying right next to her, asked.

'*Oui. Ça va.*' Léonie barely felt the cold in her fur-lined boots and thick zippered flying suit – the pockets stuffed with emergency equipment: iron rations, maps, a compass, a collapsible spade, flask of cognac, a six-inch sheath knife, the Beretta 9 millimetre automatic.

'There's an Abwehr Field Security patrol out tonight – between here and Beauvais. So we're going to take you out in the opposite direction, to Gisors, a forest near there – a forester's hut for the night. It's safer.'

Léonie was at once on her guard with this mention of Gisors. 'Safer? But I'm to come in by Beauvais. It was all fixed.'

'I know. But we can't risk it tonight. And this other way is fine. We've used this forester and his hut quite often before. You can get a train from Gisors instead of Beauvais in the morning. There's no problem. Several of your other agents have gone this way.'

Indeed, Léonie thought – but she could do nothing about this now. Marc was in charge.

After ten minutes lying in the undergrowth, hearing no further sounds, the dozen men in the reception committee dispersed silently with their guns and the medical equipment, leaving just Marc and another man to accompany Léonie. They led her, unerringly, south-east in the shadowy, quicksilver light – across rough pasture, along wild lanes, skirting apple orchards, through ever-thickening woods and then into a deep forest. An hour later, at the end of the track, a logger's hut came in view in a wide moonlit clearing and Marc introduced her to a tall, burly figure in a huntsman's cap, wearing gaiters.

'*Voici Claude.*'

'*Excusez moi.* But it is safer for you not to be in my hut.' The man spoke in a broad Norman patois. 'I have left everything – food, some blankets – in the wood store, here.' He pointed to a low wooden building, open on either side, at the edge of the trees some fifty yards away. They walked over to it, and Claude with a torch showed her a hidden nook completely surrounded by a huge pile of stacked logs. There was some hay, blankets, food.

'*Excusez moi, Madame . . .*' Claude gestured again, apologetically. 'It's not too comfortable. But it's safer . . .' He seemed to want to insist on this idea of safety, which puzzled Léonie, for surely in these deep woods his forester's hut would be as safe a place as the log store?

Marc was behind her. 'Your other arrangements,' he said. 'For the morning.' Claude was next to them. Léonie had to avoid talking in front of him. She moved out into the moonlit clearing. Marc followed her. And so did Claude, before he saw their confidential purpose and stopped, leaving them alone, rather unwillingly, Léonie thought.

'Your train from Gisors,' Marc asked. 'Which way are you going?'

'North. To the coast.' Léonie lied. Then, half-turning, she saw Claude in the background watching them.

'Fine. There are trains quite often. But be careful. They're full of German officers, going up to the coastal defences, the Atlantic wall.'

'Of course.'

'A man will take you to the station—'

'One of your men?'

'No, from the Gisors network. But we know him. I told you, he's taken quite a few of your people out through Gisors already. At first light walk down the track here, past the forester's hut, then straight on for a kilometre or so, until you get to the wooden barrier on the main road. Wait in the trees there, hidden. Then, if all's clear, sometime between seven and eight, this man will pick you up – in an old black Peugeot breakdown truck – he runs a garage in Gisors, so he has petrol. And you'll bury your flying suit carefully, won't you?'

'Naturally.'

'Because Claude is a vital link for you people coming in via this sector – when we can't take you in through Beauvais.'

'Yes, I understand.' Léonie understood all too well. As Colonel Buckmaster had told her – at least three SOE agents, including the two who had been sent to investigate Michel's circle in Paris, had come in this way, via Gisors, and had subsequently been picked up almost at once by the Gestapo, either on the train to Paris, it was thought, or soon after they arrived in the capital.

'*Alors, au revoir, Madame. Et bonne chance.*'

'*Merci. Merci beaucoup.*' They shook hands firmly. Marc she felt confident about. But when he left she turned and saw Claude still watching her at the edge of the clearing. Seeing him now, vaguely silhouetted in the moonlight, something struck her about him which made her uneasy. What was it? Of course – it was his gaiters, the tightly-sheathed leggings all the way up to his knees – gaiters which, in the shadowy light, looked just like Nazi jackboots.

Perhaps it was all nonsense. But this image, together with the man's exaggerated concern for her safety and the feeling she had had of his wanting to eavesdrop on her conversation with Marc, made Lèonie decide there and then not to spend the night in the log store – to get away from the place as soon as she could without his knowing.

But get away – out of the frying pan, into the fire? There were problems. Claude, for example, might be entirely loyal – and the man giving her a lift in the Peugeot breakdown truck could be the traitor, delivering her not to the station, but to the Gendarmerie or the Gestapo in Gisors. Then, too, if she left the log store secretly now, got to the road, hid there, but did not take the lift in the breakdown van – how was she ever to get to the train in Gisors? With all her smart clothes under the flying suit she was obviously no country woman. She would stand out like a sore thumb, either walking into Gisors or hitching a lift later in the morning. Besides, taking a chance lift could be suicidal. With the lack of petrol, nearly all the vehicles on the roads these days, she knew, were run by the Germans or the Gendarmerie. On her own, out in the country, she would be easy meat for any of these patrols.

Then she saw a way out. There were risks. But there would be those however she handled it. And at least, with this plan, she might kill two birds – get to Gisors station undetected and possibly find out who was the traitor in the Gisors resistance network.

Ten minutes later, just after two o'clock, she crept out from the back of the log store into the woods, then made a big half-circle round the clearing until she came to the logging track on the other side, making off down it in the chilly half-light, for the moon was on the wane now below the trees.

An hour later she struck the road, quite suddenly, the wooden barrier looming up in front of her. Finding a hiding place in the undergrowth, she settled down to wait – shivering in the cold, dozing for odd moments through the rest of the night.

Dawn came just after seven – the low sun, quite hidden by the tall trees everywhere, only illuminating a long path of sky above the straight road, gradually rising then over the woods, touching the frosty tarmac with glittering diamond points, a pale-blue sky emerging far above her. It would be a fine, tingling-sharp day.

She had buried her flying suit back in the forest. Now, in her elegant clothes, with her suitcase, she got out her new compact – tidied her face, combed her hair, put on her spectacles, checked everything in her handbag: Carte d'Identité, clothes and food coupons, pills . . . She was ready.

A farm labourer on a bicycle and two cars passed her in the half-hour she waited. The second car was the black Peugeot breakdown truck. It slowed as it approached along the straight road, then stopped just beyond the wooden barrier into the forest. A man got out, checking the back wheel as if for a puncture, looking up and down the road as he did so. Léonie did the same. There was no sign of traffic in either direction. Running out, she jumped into the other front seat of the truck, as the man joined her.

'*Bonjour, Mam'selle! Je suis Albert.*' He plunged the gear forward and the truck gathered speed down the road. He smiled at her. He was youngish, early thirties, good-looking, with an open face, blue eyes, fair hair – and surprisingly well dressed for a garage man, in a new sports jacket and tie. 'All went well on your drop – I hope? Didn't break your ankle or anything!' He was easy, jokey and quite without any of Claude's suspicious airs.

'No, all isn't well.' Léonie put her plan into operation at once. 'The drop went all right. But I have to tell you – from the chief of the Beauvais network – you are not to take me to the station at Gisors. They've had word. The Gestapo are planning a big check there today. You're to take me to Gournay, up the line, or to Chaumont below Gisors.'

The man's happy features clouded. 'But, Mam'selle, I've just left Gisors – indeed I was at the station there only an hour ago, with a taxi fare. I spoke to one of our network people who works in the ticket office. There's nothing on in the station – and nothing planned for today. I assure you, I'd be one of the first to know if there was. There's a train to Paris at 10.15.'

'Fine. But I have to catch it either up or down the line, not at Gisors. Besides, it's not much further from here – to Gournay or Chaumont.' This insistence on a change of plan clearly worried the smart young man. Léonie saw his deep concern for an instant in his pale-blue eyes. 'Gournay or Chaumont,' she said with finality. 'I must insist.'

The man was equally determined, shaking his head. He would not contemplate any change of destination, despite Léonie's apparent orders, from the head of another network, to change it. 'I can't – look at the petrol gauge, Mam'selle. Nearly empty. Only enough to get back to Gisors. And, besides, I can't risk travel outside the Gisors area. The check-points: if they ask me what I'm doing in Gournay or Chaumont – I've no cover, no clients in those towns. This morning, for example, if we're stopped on this road – I've got cover behind me: a farmer who will vouch for the fact I've been trying to repair his old tractor.'

They drove on to Gisors. His excuses sounded reasonable enough, Léonie thought. Yet she was pretty certain they were false excuses. She had seen the spare can of petrol in the back of the truck. And it was perfectly clear from the map of the area she had looked at earlier that both Gournay and Chaumont, only ten miles north or south, were very much in the Gisors area. He would be sure to have some clients, at least, in and around both of these villages.

It was clear that he was absolutely determined to take her to the station at Gisors. And there could surely be only one reason for this, Léonie thought. In order to maintain his role as a double-agent with the Germans, and to trap future British agents in the same manner, Albert himself would never be directly involved in any trap. Having warned the Gestapo in advance, he would simply take her to the station – which would have to be Gisors station – where they would be waiting for her, at the entrance, easily identifying her as she stepped out of the breakdown truck. The Gestapo would then pick her up at the ticket barrier, or more likely follow her to Paris, to see what contacts she made there, before they took her, along with anyone else she might have met there clandestinely. This, indeed, must have been how the other two SOE agents had been picked up so quickly. What was essential now, Léonie saw, was to get to Gisors – the centre, not the station – then drop this suspicious blue-eyed garagiste.

'A coffee? Something to eat? – I'm absolutely famished,' she asked him as they came into the outskirts of Gisors.

'You can have something at the station. There's a buffet there.'

'I can't wait – I'm dying – to get to the lavatory.'

They stopped in the main square of Gisors. There was a café on the corner. Albert did not move.

'Won't you come, too? It'll look better, if I'm not alone. We have plenty of time – and there are a few things about the trains I want to ask you.' Léonie held her breath. He remained unwilling. 'Please.' She gave him her nicest smile. Finally he agreed.

When she got back from the lavatory she had the knock-out pill hidden in her hand. There was no real coffee, just a chicory extract, with a roll of hard bread. They sat at a table by the steamed-up window, a crowd over by the zinc bar lowering nips of Calvados and cheap *rouge*. Albert fiddled with his spoon impatiently – there was no sugar – his cup in front of him, looking straight down on it.

Léonie wiped the clouded window. 'Which way is the station?'

'Left, at the bottom of the square.' He did not look out.

'Which way?' Léonie cleared his side for him and now at last he peered out.

'There,' he said, pointing. 'Just a few minutes' drive.'

Léonie's right hand was already lying on the table, over by his cup. As they both peered out of the window she slipped the pill into it.

Then she groaned. 'Oh God, this diarrhoea again. Stomach's been upset. Excuse me a minute.' She stood up and made for the lavatory once more.

'Don't be too long,' he called after her, looking at his watch. Then, just before she got to the door of the *lavabo*, she glanced back and saw him drain his small cup of ersatz coffee in one gulp.

When she came out his head was slumped in his arms – but quite comfortably over the table, as if he were asleep, so that no one had yet taken any notice of him. She left the café and walked away, hurrying towards the station.

Along the road and outside the station there was quite

a crowd of other people making for the booking hall –
and a few hangers-on standing by the entrance, among
them two men to either side, obviously Gestapo who,
rather than looking at the passengers passing them, were
gazing out on the road, waiting for some other arrival –
someone getting out of a black Peugeot breakdown truck,
Léonie was sure.

She walked past the two men, quite unconcerned,
going on to the booking office. But instead of buying a
ticket to Paris she took one to Gournay, on a train out of
Gisors in the other direction, north, leaving before the
Paris train.

She crossed over to the other platform. Ten minutes
later the Gournay train pulled in and she took a seat – a
seat offered her very readily in a reserved compartment
full of Wehrmacht officers.

They helped her with her suitcase, putting it up on
the rack. 'Why, it's heavy enough to have a radio trans-
mitter in it!' a young Oberleutnant joked in bad French,
before offering her a cigarette as she sat down next to
him – pleased, as they all were, to have the company of
this attractive and distinguished-looking woman.

A few minutes later the Paris train arrived on the other
line, just across the tracks from her. Almost at once she
saw a disturbance. The two Gestapo men, accompanied
by the guard and ticket collector, were going through
every compartment, checking each passenger. Then she
heard the shouts – 'Out! All out!' – as everyone was made
to disembark from the train. This was going to be a most
thorough check, luggage and everything else. Her own
train pulled away a moment later without being checked
at all.

It was clear what had happened. The Gestapo at the
entrance, failing to see the breakdown truck arrive at the
station, but assuming the British agent they had been
warned to expect had arrived there in some other way,

had decided to check everyone on the Paris train, leaving the earlier train, the one going north filled with Wehrmacht officers, alone.

Léonie was pretty certain she had the answer then. Albert was the double agent – not, she thought, someone in Michel's circle in Paris. Her work had started well. She would get a message as soon as possible, via Louise in Paris, about Albert. The Normandy networks would use him no longer. No one would deal with Albert much longer, she thought, except the undertakers and the local curé. She looked forward to Paris now with an easier heart, arriving there that same day without incident, having changed trains at Gournay and taken a later train back to Paris in the afternoon.

Dr André Vonot prodded about over her naked stomach in his consulting rooms on the Avenue Foch. 'Nothing much wrong, as far as I can see, Mademoiselle. Not appendicitis. A virus of some sort.'

He moved out of the cubicle in his white coat. Léonie had taken the pill for this stomach upset the previous night, having made an appointment with Dr Vonot from the Hotel Meurice a few days earlier.

'It's just – I feel so dreadful.' And she looked it, too, as she got up, dressing herself behind the curtain, before emerging into the bright first floor room looking over the narrow gardens to one side of the Avenue.

'It's a bug going round, Mademoiselle de Sertigny. The food these days,' he told her easily, at his desk. 'And there's not much I can prescribe for it either, with so few drugs available now. Best cure is just rest in bed – not to eat for twenty-four hours, and then only some toast. And come back and see me in a day or so. You're staying at the Hotel Meurice?'

'Yes – just up from the country for a week, from Normandy. I have a place there.'

'Fine. Well, come and see me in a day or two.'

Their eyes met. He gazed at her appraisingly, and she liked the look of him, too – this tallish man, with a firm open face, a hint of laughter in his brown eyes. Dr Vonot – Michel, chief of the Passy network – seemed a most unlikely traitor. But one could never tell. She would have to put him to the test.

'Dr Vonot,' she said at the end of their second consultation a few days later. 'I wonder if you'd mind giving me some advice on another matter . . .'

'Of course, Mademoiselle.'

'Not medical. But I believe I can trust you – and there's no one at home I can trust.'

'I hope so, Mademoiselle.'

'Last week, before I came up from the château, a man arrived, some time in the night – I found him in one of the stables at dawn before I went riding: a British officer, a pilot – shot down somewhere in the area . . .' She looked at him. His expression had not changed.

'And?' he said evenly.

'I wondered – wondered what I should do with him?'

'Mademoiselle, you should have reported him at once to the local *Gendarmerie*. You have put yourself at great risk,' he added firmly.

'Yes – but I couldn't hand him straight over to the Germans.' She looked at him carefully. 'And see,' she went on. 'Now I've put myself in your hands.'

'Mademoiselle, I am a doctor. Anything you say in this room remains entirely between you and me. No one else. But my advice is that you should report him immediately you get home.'

'I can't do that. I hate Pétain – and the other collaborators. I hate the Germans. I couldn't possibly hand this man over – one of our allies after all.'

'That must be your decision. But, as I say, you should do so. Have you told anyone about him?'

'I've told no one.'

'Nonetheless, you've not only put yourself at risk, Mademoiselle – but also your servants, friends and neighbours. If the authorities find out that you've been harbouring this airman, they'll round up all of you, with the gravest consequences. You should get him out of your house at once.'

Dr Vonot stood up. The consultation was clearly over. But Léonie was entirely satisfied. She had put her cards on the table – making it abundantly clear to the doctor that, not only was she a staunch French patriot, but she was also aiding and abetting a British airman.

If Dr Vonot was working with the Germans, then the Gestapo would be coming for her at the Hotel Meurice that night. She would not be there, of course – she had checked out that morning. But she would know if they had called, by telephoning the hotel and asking for any messages. If the Gestapo had been there, the management would make this clear, one way or the other, either by hinting at their visit if they were patriots, or by enquiring as to her whereabouts now if they were not, for she had given the hotel an entirely false address in Normandy. Dr Vonot would clearly be the informer then. But if no one turned up looking for her at the Meurice, then he – and she – would be in the clear.

Moving into the apartment on the Avenue Henri Martin without incident that same day, she let a week pass, telephoning the Meurice several times for messages. There was none – and not the slightest hint of any enquiries made of her. Finally, at the end of the week, to be quite sure, she put her head in the lion's mouth – going down to the Meurice in person, making the same enquiries at the reception desk. They were polite – there had been no messages or enquiries for her whatsoever.

Without making an appointment, simply going to the Avenue Foch and waiting for him, she finally saw Dr Vonot again. He was not entirely pleased to see her.

'Dr Vonot, I must apologize – but I had to be sure.'

The doctor, for the first time, looked startled. 'I don't understand? . . .'

'I'm not Mademoiselle de Sertigny – someone quite different, from London. May I explain everything?' She had lowered her voice from the beginning. Now she looked round at the walls, the door.

'I don't understand. I've no idea what you—'

'May I tell you *everything*? Are we – safe here?' she interrupted him, before she uttered the single word 'Michel' very quietly.

He gazed at her for an instant. There was no alarm on his features, which neither admitted nor denied this last appellation. 'I'm listening, Mademoiselle,' he said. Then he added, 'And, yes, it's entirely safe here. As I said before, as my patient anything you tell me in this room is entirely between us.'

'So you see,' Léonie said, having told him who she really was and coming to the end of her account of what had happened to her in the past ten days in France, 'it seems the double agent is Albert in Gisors – and possibly your WT operator here. As I've said, his call sign has appeared smudged in London.'

Dr Vonot shook his head, gesturing dismissively. 'Simply the hurry he was in, to get off the air. We've had to transmit from dozens of different places these last months. The German detector vans are much more numerous now, patrolling everywhere. And, besides, our WT operator is completely reliable – I'm in no doubt. I've known him for years, since long before the war. It can only have been this Albert in Gisors who trapped the other two agents you sent in. Your story about him all fits. I'll get word to the Beauvais network at once. They'll deal with him. Meanwhile – thank you . . .' He stood up, coming round his desk towards her. 'Mademoiselle de Sertigny.'

'Yvonne.' She took his hand.

'You played your cards well.' He smiled. 'That château in Normandy, the British airman . . . I quite believed it all. I hope you can equally convince your chiefs in London that this Passy circle is entirely secure.'

'Yes – at once.'

'We need all the help we can get from London – particularly here at the medical practice. We treat the wounded from a number of other resistance networks in the Paris region. Need morphine, syringes, proper bandages and so on. Urgently.'

'"We"?'

'Yes, I've a partner, downstairs.'

'Oh yes, the other name plate I saw: Dr Langlois.' The common French name had meant nothing to Léonie then and no more now.

'Yes . . .' He looked at her pointedly. 'Though of course you don't know that name – or mine. You've never seen or heard of either of us in your life.'

'Of course.'

'You'll be staying on in Paris?'

'Yes.'

'With your own SOE circle over here?'

'I don't know yet. I have a "safe house" – not far away from here, in fact. But I'm to collaborate with you, if you need anything, until I get further instructions from London.'

'Good. I'm glad of that. You can contact me here any time, of course, simply as my patient. And if I need you?'

'There,' Léonie said, pointing at the window looking out over the Avenue Foch. 'Stick a white envelope on the glass there. I'll pass by most days, and come straight in, if I see it.'

'Excellent. So you'll tell them in London at once then – that all's well with the Passy circle?'

'Absolutely.' She left, returning to the apartment on the Avenue Henri Martin.

Furnished in the heavy Louis Quinze style, it was a large, gloomy place on the fourth floor – made all the more gloomy by the fact that it had been shuttered up when she arrived and she had to keep it so, in order not to call attention to her occupation there. There were three bedrooms and a heavily ornate salon in front, divided in two by sliding doors giving on to a dining room, a kitchen beyond that leading to a small servant's bedroom, with narrow back-stairs running down to the ground floor and basement cellars, with an exit leading out behind the apartment block, giving on to the cemetery – an ideal escape route which old Madame de Sertigny had told them about in London.

Léonie lived in permanent shadow now, creeping about under the yellow light from chandeliers through the untidy rooms – hurriedly abandoned by the two women nearly three years before, in June 1940, when they had joined the hordes of panic-stricken Parisians rushing southwards.

The whole apartment had the musty, decayed air of a vault, where very little had been touched or moved or cleaned since that summer day in 1940. The contents of half-packed bags and suitcases, clothes – papers, silver, knick-knacks of all sorts – were still strewn in corners covered in dust. The heavy gilded furniture was draped in cobwebs. Drawers and cupboard doors in the bedrooms had been pulled open, shoes and clothes scattered about, silk lingerie tossed over the beds, bottles, cosmetics and lotions lying on the carpets.

Yet the gas and electricity had not been turned off, nor had the place been entirely unoccupied since 1940, as Léonie soon discovered. The spare bedroom at the back, not used by the two women, was more or less entirely in order, clean sheets on the divan and a pile of newspapers on the floor. Léonie had inspected the dates carefully. There was an intermittent regularity about these. The newspapers showed a sequence of visits to the apartment over the previous year or so: every eight or ten weeks, for two or three days. The last newspapers were dated three weeks before, in early March. At this rate, if Madame's brother-in-law Edouard de Sertigny maintained his regular habits, he would be due here again some time in mid-May – to pay the apartment bills, see his friends or whatever in Paris. So she had a minimum of six weeks, she thought, before he arrived again.

Meanwhile Léonie took over Yvonne's bedroom, where there were all the clothes and shoes and hats she needed – only a little too big for her, which she took in or adapted, not even needing the sewing kit she had brought with her, soon finding all that, and more, in the eerie apartment where the two women had spent fifteen years of their life together before abandoning everything, not only their possessions but in Yvonne's case her career.

Lifting the lid of the Pleyel grand piano in the salon one morning, Léonie found a book of pencilled-in scales on the stand, no doubt used by Yvonne in a last lesson with one of her pupils. Behind, lying on the strings, were stacks of music books: Saint-Saëns, Fauré, Mozart, Chopin, together with a number of piano parts from operas – including *Madame Butterfly*.

This discovery came as a shock to Léonie. Seeing Puccini's well-remembered music in front of her, she felt a sudden echo of Hetty – her voice, her spirit, present again in the claustrophobic salon: a voice of youth and old love clear on the musty air, in the passionate duets they had shared together years before from this opera. '*Te voglio bene . . .'* Léonie fingered the notes of the music noiselessly on the keys in front of her . . .

What had happened to Hetty?

She realized then why she so rarely thought about her. Dermot had told her, some years before in England, how Hetty and her husband no longer lived in Summer Hill, how they had left the house in 1939, settling in France somewhere; with the arrival of the Germans in 1940, everyone at home had lost touch with them. And that was one reason why Léonie did not think about her. It was difficult to think of someone who had so entirely disappeared into the murderous gulf of war, who was quite lost, imprisoned perhaps, or even dead. Hetty had gone from her life beyond any possible redemption. Léonie closed the piano quietly and forgot about her once more. She had other things to think about. And besides it was Jenny, not Hetty, with whom she must now keep faith.

She had contacted Louise, the SOE courier in the café by La Muette. A message was sent to Baker Street, and the Passy circle had been entirely cleared. In return, via Louise a week later, Léonie had received instructions from London to maintain the 'safe house' on the Avenue Henri Martin for other SOE agents in Paris or those who might arrive there in the future. She was as well to act as courier between Michel's Passy circle and Louise's SOE network outside the city, principally to help Michel get his messages through to London, something which he was finding more and more difficult with detector vans increasing everywhere in the capital.

So it was, in the ensuing weeks, that Léonie came to see Dr Vonnot quite regularly, watching for the white envelope in his window as she passed up the Avenue Foch each day. So, too, as part of her instructions from London, she told Dr Vonnot the address of her 'safe house' in the Avenue Henri Martin. The apartment was never to be used for radio transmissions, and only Michel in the Passy network was to know of its existence. But Colonel Buckmaster, recognizing this now-secure and vital Passy circle again, was anxious to give Michel as much support as possible – and the use of this 'safe house' in emergencies was intended as a major token of this endeavour.

The apartment was, of course, ideally suited to all their needs – since it could be left or entered, undetected, from the rear, by walking through the Cimetière de Passy, climbing a wall at the end, then in by the back entrance to the apartment block and up the servants' stairs – a route which avoided the concierge's office entirely. Léonie was pleased with herself and her work. Only the possible sudden arrival of Edouard de Sertigny gave her qualms.

12

Food was scarce in Paris – and meat was a great luxury, not always available even on the black market. But Hetty, in league with the local butcher, the café proprietor and one of his trusted customers who had a cousin with a farm to the west of Paris, had taken shares in a whole live pig, which had been led to the outer suburbs and then, surreptitiously and with considerable difficulty, moved across town concealed in a vélo-taxi and then a horse-drawn van to the *boucherie* where it had met its fate and been quartered.

So that on that warm spring evening, in their apartment on the Avenue Mozart, Hetty, knowing this was one dish which could not be spoilt by the irregular gas supply, had made a splendid Cassoulet de Toulouse –

with ribs of pork, white haricot beans, some precious Toulouse sausage, garlic and a *bouquet garni* – which she and Pierre, together with André Vonnot and his wife Eve, ate that evening, celebrating Pierre's forty-fifth birthday with a bottle of Gevrey-Chambertin and a box of Turkish Delight both preserved from before the war.

Afterwards they danced to some popular songs on the gramophone – Jean Sablon's 'Je tire ma révérence' and Léo Marjane's 'Je suis seule ce soir'.

Hetty, holding Pierre firmly for he was an inept dancer, whispered mischievously in his ear, 'I'm not alone . . .'

'Shouldn't be playing that woman's songs at all – something of a collaborator herself, singing for all those Nazi officers in the cabarets.'

'Oh, Pierre! It's your birthday! *Some* pleasure – before you have to go out again. Why did you have to have a surgery this evening of all evenings – on your b-birthday?'

'I'm sorry—'

'And the curfew, it worries me.'

'Doesn't apply to me. But I'll be back before that in any case.'

'This b-bloody war.'

'Yes.' The record stopped. Pierre took off his glasses, rubbed the lenses, looking abstracted, hair on end. 'Yes – just that.'

Ten minutes later, putting his jacket on, he started to leave the apartment, talking alone with André in the hall for a minute.

'Look after Hetty, won't you? – if I'm not back. I'll stay overnight if I'm delayed – won't risk the curfew.'

'What do you have tonight?' André whispered.

'Bullet wounds, I gather. Someone from the Montrouge network. I don't know when they'll bring him in – if they manage to get him up to me at all.'

'There's some morphine in my chest upstairs.'

'I still have some from the last lot we got – that drop near Beauvais.'

Hetty arrived, fetching a scarf for Pierre. 'Must wrap up.'

'It's not cold. Windows are open.'

'Still . . .' She looked at him, with longing. He kissed her and left.

'Come on then, Hetty,' André said. 'Now at last you can dance with *me*!' He dragged her back to the drawing room, put a record on, then did a tango with her, holding her close, making exaggerated steps to and fro, bending right over her, pulling back, holding their arms dramatically high, ogling her like a café gigolo.

'See!' he told her. 'Rudolph Valentino . . .'

'You're better, André! I danced with him years ago.'

The three of them laughed uproariously.

Leaving the apartment block, Pierre heard the music faintly from the open window above him. 'Je suis seule ce soir . . .' The traitorous Léo Marjane, he thought – and people like her. They were never alone. They had friends everywhere in Paris.

Behind him, some fifty yards down the avenue, two figures stood in the shadow of a doorway. One, a sullen little man, was a neighbour of Pierre's living in the same block – the other a member of the hated French *milice*.

'There! – there he goes,' the smaller man said. 'The dirty Jew! You see if I'm not right.'

The second man, saying nothing, stepped from the shadows, following Pierre. As he did so he signalled to a black Citroën some way behind at the kerb, which drew away quietly, following him.

Hetty was upset when Pierre failed to return that night. But André reassured her. Even though, as a doctor, he was immune from the curfew regulations, he had obviously decided not to risk travel during it and had stayed the night on the couch in his consulting rooms.

'Why didn't he answer the phone then? – when we rang.'

'Busy with a patient, maybe – the receptionist doesn't come in in the evening. Or maybe he'd just left the room. Don't worry – Eve and I will stay here the night. And I'll go round to the Avenue Foch first thing tomorrow.'

But when André got there early next morning he discovered Pierre was not in his own rooms. Nor had he been there the previous night. He would have cleaned up all his surgical equipment. But there were no swabs or dirty bandages in the secret disposal bin they kept for such clandestine medical work. Pierre had never seen the wounded man from Montrouge – had never arrived in his rooms at all.

He must have been picked up *en route* to the Avenue Foch – by the French police – or the Gestapo. And there could surely be only one reason: they suspected or had evidence that he was with the resistance. As his partner he was at risk now, too – and so were Eve and Hetty. It was the last thing he wanted – to break, to go to ground. But he would have to – until he found out exactly what had happened to Pierre. If the Gestapo had taken him, well, it meant he had twelve hours or so to get clear. And of course he would have to take Eve and Hetty with him.

He had a contingency plan for just such a turn of events: a retreat to Yvonne's safe house on the Avenue Henri Martin. He returned to Hetty's apartment at once.

Hetty and Eve, knowing nothing of André's resistance activities with Pierre, were astonished at André's urgent directions that they must all leave at once for another apartment near by. 'I can't explain now,' he told them. 'Later, when we get there.'

When they reached the apartment block on the Avenue Henri Martin, they entered it separately, at five-minute intervals, taking the lift up to the fourth floor. André had his own key. The place was deserted when they got inside. Léonie was out.

'What in God's name is happening?' Eve demanded. André, turning on the chandelier in the big salon, explained. The two women were even more astonished and upset.

'Not that I don't agree with what you've both been doing. But surely you could have taken us into your confidence?'

'You least of all—'

'But wha-what about P-Pierre?' Hetty interrupted, not concerned with this deception. She was shaking with anxiety and her stammer had returned.

'We have a contact inside the Deuxième Bureau on the Quai des Orfèvres. He'll be able to tell us if Pierre was taken by the French police. And, if he wasn't, he can usually get information on who's been arrested by the Gestapo from their headquarters on the Avenue Foch. I'll go and see him now.' He got up. 'You two stay here. I'll be back by midday, or sooner.'

'What, are we just to stay cooped up here indefinitely?' Eve demanded again.

'Who owns it? Who lives here?' Hetty asked, pacing the dusty salon nervously.

'I told you – it's a "safe house", presently being used by a British agent in Paris. She's out this morning.'

'Who is she?'

'You don't need to know—'

'What's her name?'

'No idea what her real name is. She has a code-name here. And you don't need to know that either – the less you know the better. If she's back before I am, just explain what's happened. And, remember, she's here to help – if the Gestapo are looking for us – help us all get out of Paris, which is what we'll have to do at once.'

Hetty, wild with worry now, almost shouted. 'I'm not leaving P-Paris. Not until I know what's happened to P-Pierre. And I'll go down myself to the Quai des Orfèvres or the Gestapo headquarters and find out what's happened to him. They can't touch me – I've an Irish passport, a neutral country!'

André sighed. 'They *will* touch you, and worse – neutral passport or not – if they think they can get anything out of you about Pierre. The Gestapo don't abide by the rules of the Geneva Convention. So just wait here. I'm sure I'll have news of Pierre when I get back.'

After he had left, Hetty, unable to sit still, paced the salon in a barely suppressed frenzy of agitation. She moved through the bedrooms, finding Léonie's night clothes on the divan in Yvonne's room – seeing the vague shape of her head on the pillow, putting her head down on it, sniffing. There was a faint yet somehow familiar smell of violets coming from the pillow and sheets – a perfume remembered from somewhere or someone. But she could not place it. She picked up a novel on the bedside table which the woman had been reading, with her name in it, 'Yvonne de Sertigny' – one of the 'Claudine' novels by Colette. *Claudine in Paris*. Flicking through the pages, she found a book marker half-way through, and glanced at the first paragraph there.

Strange, she thought – a British agent with a taste for Colette, for these amorous goings-on between Claudine and her girlfriend in the Paris of the Belle Epoque. These sensuous feminine images, and the memories they brought, upset her now and she slammed the book shut. It was Pierre she wanted – Pierre, only him. She returned to the salon almost in tears. Eve tried to comfort her.

André returned just after midday. He was not happy. But things could have been much worse, as he explained to Hetty. 'Pierre was picked up by the local *milice* last night. But nothing to do with the resistance. Because he's a Jew . . .'

'A *Jew*?' Hetty was breathing hard.

'Yes. We should have thought of that. Someone informed on him. One of his patients. Or a neighbour in his apartment block.'

'Where – where is he?'

'A camp at Drancy, outside Paris, near Le Bourget.'

'But that's terrible!—'

'It may not be. We can probably get him released.'

'What happens – at this camp?'

André had confirmed what happened there from his contact – whenever they had sufficient numbers, every week or so, they took these French Jews off in cattle trucks to forced labour camps in Germany. They did not come back. But he would not tell Hetty this. 'They hold them there – interviewing them. Some they release. Some are sent to prisons in France—'

'That's not true, André! They take them off to Germany, one of those labour camps—'

'No. It's not certain.'

'I am! I have to get to him – at Drancy.'

'No, Hetty! You stay here. The last thing you should do is to go out to Drancy now – or back to your own apartment. Because they may be waiting for you there. You're his wife, and partly Jewish, too, remember. And the Gestapo won't worry a damn about your neutral Irish passport – they'll just take you as well. So stay here till I find out how the land lies. There's a good chance, with my contacts, I may be able to get him out of Drancy myself. Now I have to get back to the surgery. They'll wonder where I am—'

Eve interrupted him, with her own urgency now. 'If you and I are in the clear, André, I should get back to our place, too. The cleaning woman's there this morning. She'll be worried – seeing we've not been at home last

613

night, and no sign of us this morning. She may call the police.'

'Yes. Do that. And bring back some food while you're at it. Seems to be none here.' He turned to Hetty. 'I'll be back this evening – or sooner. Just stay put. You'll be perfectly safe here.' With this last reassurance they left Hetty alone in the apartment.

It was Tuesday, the day for Léonie's weekly meeting with Louise. They changed their meeting place every week now, choosing a different café, Métro station or shop. Today she was to meet her at the Café des Roses on the Place de Passy. She had been out all morning and now, as she approached the café, she checked everything – stopping at shop windows, watching the view behind her reflected in the glass, doubling back along the crowded pavements, crossing and re-crossing the road, to see if she was being followed, to drop any possible tail.

Eventually she entered the café, took a table and waited. Louise arrived late. But what business they had was soon completed and Léonie, to her relief, was able to get away early. She was hungry, but had managed to buy half a Camembert cheese earlier. It was hot and she had been walking all morning. Today, at least, she really looked forward to lunch in the cool of the shuttered apartment.

So perhaps, after she left Louise, she was not so thorough in her manoeuvres about the streets as she might have been. The man who had been standing at the bar of the Café des Roses with a friend all the while during her meeting with Louise had little difficulty in following her back to the apartment block on the Avenue Henri Martin.

Waiting in the hall after Léonie had taken the lift up, he watched its progress as the counter-weight descended, then stopped. The woman had left it on the fourth floor.

He was well accustomed to judging such matters, out on many such stalking missions about the city. Though he had no air of this whatsoever, he was a Gestapo officer.

Several days before, he had been informed by a Gestapo colleague stationed in the Seine-et-Oise region about a woman suspected of being a courier with one of the resistance networks there – a woman who travelled up to Paris every week, who met another woman then in one of the cafés near La Muette. This colleague, having followed the first woman up on the train that morning, had identified the second woman for him in the Café des Roses. He was to follow her, see where she lived in Paris.

Now he had done just that and it would be up to his superiors to decide what action should be taken. He hurried away to the Gestapo headquarters in the Avenue Foch. They would want to pick her up at once, he thought, while she was back at her apartment – having lunch. He had seen the Camembert in her string bag.

Léonie, who, every time she left the apartment, dusted the door handle with powder from her compact, knew someone had tried to enter the place that morning – someone who might well be inside waiting for her at that moment. Dr Vonot – or Edouard de Sertigny? Or someone even less welcome?

Alerted at once, she went back along the corridor to the servants' entrance. Using her other key in the oiled lock, she went into the kitchen, took her Beretta automatic which she kept hidden there, before tip-toeing silently along the corridor towards the salon.

Peering round the open doorway she saw a woman, a total stranger, back towards her, sitting beneath the yellow light from the chandelier – no face, just a toss of greying hair, head bent forward in her hands, shoulders throbbing, as if the woman was trying to contain some intolerable emotion. The gun was unnecessary. Léonie stepped into the salon.

'Who . . . who are you?' she asked gently.

Hetty nearly jumped out of her skin.

They recognized each other at once – but then immediately refused to believe the evidence of their eyes. Hetty gazed at the figure in the doorway.

'Léa? But it can't be . . .'

'Hetty?' Léonie was equally uncertain. She came forward. The two women faced each other under the jaundiced light from the chandelier, at last having to recognize the truth of their vision.

Hetty finally broke the silence – but was still so stunned that the words she found seemed irrelevant. '*Now* I know – that scent on the pillow, violets – it was always yours.' She wiped her eyes and tried to smile, but could not. 'How could you be . . . the British agent?' she demanded instead, annoyed, as if this was some cheap deceit on Léonie's part.

'How could you be *here*?' Léonie was equally put out, almost curt. Each woman, still unable to come to grips with the other's presence, spoke now in tones which suggested some possible outrage or betrayal in this meeting, as if life, in contriving it, had played one more disagreeable trick on them. And this wary, indignant tone persisted as they sat down, keeping their distance, starting out on their long explanations.

Léonie felt she should withhold herself, the details of her work at least. She would need confirmation from Dr Vonnot for all that Hetty began to tell her now. But Hetty became more animated in the telling.

'It's true,' she said to Léonie again. 'It's all *true*! I've known André for years. Though I only understood this morning that he was in the resistance, when we got over here. And now to meet you!' Hetty, becoming accustomed to the reality of her old friend, could no longer restrain the growing warmth she felt towards her. 'Oh, Léa, it's wonderful! If only it weren't for Pierre. I don't know what to do . . .'

Léonie saw her pain and despair. She recognized the feeling. It had been her own, when Jenny had gone. And now, seeing Hetty's agony, she warmed slightly towards her. 'I'm sorry about Pierre. I know how you feel. I lost someone in the war, killed in the blitz in London . . .' She paused, as if weighing some hard decision. Then she continued hurriedly. 'The woman I lived with, after I left Robert. Jenny,' she added with abrupt finality, fearing she had said too much, that Hetty might be unsympathetic towards the idea of this other woman, this later passion.

But Hetty was not. In seeing Léonie again – beginning to savour the reality of this once-so-loved woman – she began to change her mind about such love, the loves of Claudine, and of Léonie. It no longer upset her. She did not feel at all betrayed by Léonie. She felt instead – she was unable to deny it – a tenderness towards her, an envy even, for this constancy in her nature.

'Jenny?' she asked gently, with all these feelings in her eyes. 'Who was she – what happened?'

So Léonie explained about Jenny, suddenly unburdening herself, telling Hetty everything, feeling that here, in her old friend, was the one person who would understand all her agonies at this loss.

'Oh, Léa, I'm so sorry,' Hetty said at the end. 'I wish I could help.' She longed for more than this. 'I wish I could make it up to you somehow. For her. For me as well. I still feel so bad about the way I behaved, years ago, to you, and when we last met in Dublin, that awful prison. I was so dismissive, so cold. Sick perhaps. But not that sick. I just couldn't face the idea of my being responsible for you and Robert coming apart again—'

'We'd have come apart anyway—'

'No! It was me – just like that first time in Egypt . . .' She shook her head in pain at the memory. 'If only I hadn't tangled up both your lives. All those crazy, destructive feelings I had before I found Pierre. And I so regret it. I just *wish* I could make it up to you,' she added with a force that surprised Léonie.

'You don't have to feel that any more – and certainly not about Jenny. You had nothing to do with her. Besides, it's not me but Pierre you have to worry about now.'

'Oh, I'll get him out of that camp – I've quite made up my mind about that – one way or another.' She paused, her confidence subsiding for an instant, before she resuscitated it. 'And, if I can't, then I'll join him there, go where he goes, some forced labour camp or whatever. I'm not going to leave him – I'd be nothing without him . . .'

Léonie nodded. 'I felt exactly the same about Jenny. But don't be a martyr – I learnt that too. Live for Pierre, don't die for him.'

'Die? Why should I die? They've no idea Pierre's in the resistance – just that he's a Jew. As I am, partly. And it's only a labour camp they send them to. Anyway, I'm going to stay with him. I owe him – I owe you – a life.'

'Not me, Hetty.' Léonie was touched by these admissions of Hetty's – this concern for a past between them which was quite dead for her.

She looked at Hetty – transformed once more. Hetty, despite the repeated disasters of the years, had found that grace again, that true character which was transcendant in her now. Hetty possessed again all those qualities which Léonie had loved in her years before, a radiant spirit, all those destructive emotions she had spoken of, quite sunk away.

And Léonie suddenly sensed that her past with Hetty was not dead. She felt a vague tenderness towards her.

'No, you don't owe me anything,' she said. 'What's done is done between us, good and bad, years ago. That account's closed. You owe Pierre all these things now. With me, Hetty – we can just be friends, when the war is over . . .' She stood up hurriedly, turning away, thinking she might have said too much.

'Oh, Léa! If that could happen – I'd be so happy!' Hetty was enchanted by this token of forgiveness. And suddenly, in her despair over Pierre, she longed for consolation. She stood up, went to Léonie through the gloom, and put a hand on her shoulder. Then, before she knew quite what she was doing, she had kissed her, and Léonie had responded, kissing her with a moment's sudden passion in return.

They broke apart, both shocked at this old love of theirs come to life for an instant, that shared nature which Hetty had thought quite dead in her, rising like a genie from the lamp, so that they both tried to deny it at once.

'I'm sorry . . .' Hetty said limply. Léonie took the initiative. 'Listen,' she said breathlessly. 'I have to go out. I've an appointment I can't miss, down on the left bank. I'll be back – this afternoon.'

'Do stay!'

'I can't!'

She hurried out of the apartment, taking the kitchen entrance so that she could hide the automatic there. And it was she who felt she owed something to Hetty then, she who had let her down. She had no appointment. It was simply that she had not trusted herself to stay another minute in the apartment alone with Hetty.

Half-way down the narrow servant's stairs, Léonie heard the clump of boots running up the marble staircase just beyond the dividing wall. On each floor there was a small connecting door leading out on to the main staircase. Opening one of these a fraction she glimpsed a swastika armband, jackboots, the black uniforms of several SS officers with a Field Security Patrol – rounding the balustrade, making for the top floor. There was little doubt where they were going – to the de Sertignys' apartment. Someone had betrayed them. The 'safe house' had been discovered.

Hidden behind the door, Léonie hesitated. If she had brought her automatic with her she would have run back upstairs and tried to fight it out with them – just to try and save Hetty, for she was stricken now at her fate. Perhaps she should return as she was, unarmed? – expose herself as the woman they were looking for, and hope to get Hetty released. But the Gestapo would never believe Hetty had no part in the business. Both of them would be simply taken then. Léonie remained horrified at this desertion. But she saw she had no alternative. She had to get away herself, to warn the others, André and Eve, not to return there. They were due back at the apartment later that afternoon; the Gestapo would certainly be waiting for them. And if they took André the whole Passy network would very likely be betrayed.

She knew she had no choice. She must get away as quickly as possible. Moving silently down the rest of the narrow stairs, she turned the last corner – only to be confronted by the concierge, Madame Bonnot, her back against the small door, blocking her escape out the rear entrance. It was clear to Léonie what the woman was about: it was she who had betrayed them, so that seeing the Gestapo rushing up the main staircase, and knowing of this hidden servant's exit, she had thought to take the chance of catching some prize for the Gestapo herself. And though she must have been in her fifties, she was far from frail – a big woman, weighty in all the right places.

But Léonie did not hesitate. Hurling herself down the last flight of steps she threw herself at Madame Bonnot, first clapping a hand over her mouth and pulling her from the doorway, then locking her right arm in a fierce grip round the back of the woman's neck, smelling her garlic-filled breath for an instant, before she swung her right round, increasing her hold on the woman's windpipe now as she drew the woman towards her.

Madame Bonnot fought furiously, grunting and gasping, trying to cry out. But Léonie, all her unarmed combat training coming into play now and spurred on by the guilt she felt in so abandoning Hetty to her fate, was far more skilled and vicious. Almost unaware of the strength she was exerting, she held Madame Bonnot from behind, one hand over her mouth, the edge of her wrist on her throat, in an ever-tightening embrace. Suddenly it was all over. The concierge lay at her feet, silent and quite still. Léonie escaped out from the back of the apartment block then, over the wall and into the cemetery, before getting clear away from the area into the busy Trocadéro.

She called André at once from a café, giving him the news. 'So you must warn Eve, at once,' she added. 'Not to go back there—'

'Yes, she hasn't left our place. I spoke to her a few minutes ago. You meet me there, too. All three of us – we'll have to get straight out of Paris, go to ground. Hetty has no training in this business – she won't last long with the Gestapo. We've probably only got an hour or two before they know all about us.'

'So, Mademoiselle, you refuse even to admit your real name – quite apart from your code-name, of course. Or the names of the others in your network,' he added as if this was a matter of lesser importance.

Standartenführer Helmuth Knocken, Chief of the Paris SS, looked across his desk on an upper floor of his headquarters in the Avenue Foch. Hetty sat opposite. They were alone. The Colonel's French was cultivated.

So were his pale features. He had a generally benign and civilized air. Standing up, he offered her a cigarette, which, sitting bolt upright in a high-backed chair, she did not even look at.

'Well, it hardly matters,' he went on lightly, moving over to the window. It was cool at last after the unseasonable heat of the day. He returned to his desk, picking over some papers, which the Gestapo had found earlier in the apartment. 'It's perfectly clear – you are Yvonne de Sertigny. These papers, letters of yours, this book with your name on it: "Yvonne de Sertigny" – you live in the apartment. I wonder why you won't admit it . . .'

'Yes, yes – I'm Yvonne de Sertigny,' Hetty said at last.

She had not wanted to admit this too quickly. But once the Colonel had given her this identity, which she knew now to have been Léonie's alias in France, she had thought immediately to adopt it as her own, to take Léonie's place. It was obvious – the man had played into her hands: in this way she could protect Léonie, as well as André and Eve. In her role as Yvonne de Sertigny she could protect them all, including Pierre. And that was the most important thing: now that she was Yvonne de Sertigny, branded as a member of the French resistance, they would never know her as Pierre's wife. And since he was only being detained for being a Jew – well, if she survived in the Avenue Foch, they might survive together, for she would very likely be sent to Drancy as well, before being deported with him to some labour camp in Germany.

Yes, there was a chance they might meet up in this way. But for this to come about, for her to see Pierre again, she must say nothing of the others. She must resist everything, whatever they might have in store for her – since to give them Léonie's or André's name would almost certainly result in their taking Pierre on a much more serious charge, not simply being a Jew but as a member of the resistance. Either André or Léonie might break under torture, admitting this. Would she break herself? If she did, it would almost certainly cause the deaths of Pierre and Léonie, the two people who meant most to her in life. Her own death, by comparison, was much easier to contemplate. For them to survive, she was quite prepared to die. After all, as she had told Léonie only that morning, she owed them both a life.

'Good! – Mademoiselle de Sertigny.' The Colonel was pleased at this final admission of hers. 'I can't think why you should want to deny your real name, at least.' He fingered through Yvonne's papers again, picking up the 'Claudine' novel. 'An admirer of Colette, I see. Excellent!' Then he picked up the Beretta automatic. 'Which brings me to this – and your other, your clandestine, identity.' He flourished the automatic an instant. 'You are part of a French resistance network, of course . . .'

Hetty said nothing. The Colonel gazed over the gardens again. Then his attitude changed. He was not harsh, simply more serious, concerned, a note of regret almost in his voice. 'Mademoiselle de Sertigny – it's also perfectly obvious: you were waiting in your apartment today for another member of your circle. We know that for certain. One of our officers followed this woman, to your apartment. You met her there. She clearly left just before my colleagues arrived – we found the concierge . . .' He took up a fountain pen and fiddled with it. 'We must know who that woman is. And the names of the others in your circle. Will you tell me?'

Hetty remained silent.

'No, I suppose not. Part of your job, as you see it. But, I have to tell you, we *will* find out, either from you, or from your colleagues, when they return to the apartment. It's a "safe house" obviously. And some of your friends won't know we've been there – and we're watching it, of course.'

He gazed at Hetty intently then, before she finally spoke, equally even and polite in her reply. 'Yes, no doubt you are watching the apartment. Part of *your* job. So perhaps you will find out who these people are. But not from me.'

'Indeed.' The Colonel was brisk now, as if they had at last concluded some mutually satisfactory agreement. 'Well, we shall see. I simply thought to save you . . . trouble, if you told me now. I give all resistance people this opportunity when I first interview them. However, you will appreciate . . .' He seemed genuinely apologetic now. 'I'm a busy man. I don't have time to conduct every interrogation here. But my colleagues in the Gestapo, under Hauptsturmführer Puetz in the basement, though equally busy, I believe are not so considerate – or patient. Well? What is the name of your friend, the woman who came to see you this morning?'

He waited, in case Hetty should say anything. She did not. He picked up the telephone. Hetty was taken away a minute later, downstairs to the basement.

The Passy circle went to ground. André and Eve, together with Léonie, had escaped the city that same afternoon – Léonie and Eve taking separate trains south from the Gare de Lyon, André moving in the same direction, by local trains at first, before taking an express on the main line to Clermont-Ferrand. Late that night they all met at a farmhouse, way up in the hills of the wild country, to the north-east of Clermont-Ferrand. Here, taken in care by the chief of the local resistance, they would lie low, before André regrouped elsewhere in France, while Léonie would try to contact Baker Street, tell them the news and wait for further instructions.

But Léonie had no thoughts for any such future resistance schemes that night as they ate some coarse bread and ham, by the light of an oil lamp in the farmer's kitchen. Thinking of Hetty, then speaking of her, she could barely eat at all.

'You did the only thing you could,' André told her once more. 'You can't blame yourself.' Then, perhaps a little tactlessly, he was rather more blunt with the truth. 'Hetty knows very little about our circle, almost nothing. But, if the Gestapo had taken you, then they would very likely have had me – and the lives of *dozens* of others would have been at risk.'

'You don't seem to understand – Hetty, she's a great friend of mine.'

'Yes, I do understand that. But she's just as much a friend of ours, Yvonne. I promise you. We feel just the same about her.'

'But what will *happen* to her?' Léonie, though she was certain of the answer, could not stop herself from voicing her concern, her agony at Hetty's likely fate.

André said quickly, 'You mustn't torture yourself—' He stopped, aware of his gaffe. There was silence.

Before Hauptsturmführer Puetz started to interrogate Hetty that night at the Avenue Foch, his men took rubber truncheons to her face, threw her to the floor, drove boots into her kidneys, so that soon one of her eyes was closed, blood streamed down her forehead and her lips had become ugly swollen lumps. Each time they dragged her to her feet, they knocked her down again, as if to some juvenile formula.

And indeed all this was the usual practice – the preamble to most Gestapo interrogations: break the prisoner's nerve at once, hurt, daze and humiliate them with these violent tactics, knock them off balance, physically and mentally, so that when the actual questioning began their victim would be at a total disadvantage. Prisoners rarely regained their nerve after such a violently capricious introduction. Finally, they dragged Hetty,

625

bruised and bleeding, to a chair and sat her down against a bright light.

Captain Puetz, in a grey uniform, black riding breeches and top boots, arrived in the room then, to take charge of the proceedings. A pedantically fussy little man, he spoke to Hetty in much less certain French, referring back to a memorandum on his desk all the while he addressed her, as if from the text of a play where he was uncertain of the lines. Yet what he apparently lacked in memory, he made up for in volume. He increasingly harangued, he shouted, he *snorted* at Hetty in a nasal voice. There was not even the sense of a ham actor here, but of someone much further adrift from reality in these fantastic histrionics. The man was quite unreal and yet had not the least inkling of this.

'So, Mademoiselle de Sertigny, my colleague, Standarten-führer Knochen, managed to get nothing from you, I see.' He spoke dismissively of the senior SS officer in overall charge of operations at the Avenue Foch. 'Be assured that we in the Gestapo will not be so superficial in our enquiries. The name of the woman you met earlier today – who was she? And the others in your group. What are their names?' He gave a final snort, resting his case.

Hetty, though her lip was bleeding and badly swollen, knew she could still speak. But she said nothing. However, she could not prevent herself from shaking, with shock and pain – and fear.

The Captain noticed her shaking. 'Cold, Mademoiselle?' Then, maintaining his bad French, he spoke to one of his men standing by the door. 'Obersturmführer, be so kind as to get something to warm Mademoiselle de Sertigny.'

The lieutenant left the room, and went to the end of the corridor. There he prepared a blow-lamp, igniting the methylated spirits first, allowing the burner to warm, then pumping the pressure up before opening the nozzle and setting a match to it. A bluish flame jetted out with a roar. Captain Puetz interrupted his work a few minutes later.

'No, you idiot! What are you trying to do? – burn her alive before we've had a word out of her? By *degrees*, Lieutenant. The matches first. The blow-lamp is a last resort, you incompetent fool . . .'

In the days that followed at the Avenue Foch they questioned Hetty, stupidly and aimlessly for the most part, about clandestine matters of which she had absolutely no knowledge – so that, unable to reply, they increasingly assumed she was hiding vital information and tortured her progressively more brutally. They stuck sharpened matches up her nails, lighting the phosphorus at the other end. They dipped her, head first, repeatedly, into a tub of ice-cold water, pulling her out each time only at the very last moment, nearly asphyxiated, before applying artificial respiration – leaving her then, in her soaking clothes, overnight in a cell. Electrodes were attached to her feet, her ear-lobes, finally her nipples, before the current was turned on. They handcuffed her wrists behind her back, slipped a hook into the cuffs, then dragged her up by a pulley, leaving her suspended until her arms were almost dislocated and she fainted. Finally the blow-lamp . . . It had started to sear the skin off her forearm before she fainted again.

She was unconscious for increasingly long periods. But each time she woke, floundering about through curtains of livid pain, she always discovered a vision of Pierre, or of Léonie and the others – seeing them clearly, in some remembered happy site or circumstance, a spring morning over coffee with Pierre, before he left for work, at the window of the apartment in the Avenue Mozart, an autumn day years before up in the orchards of Summer Hill with Léonie.

So that when the next obscenity faced her, a repetition of the cold tub or the pulleys, she kept these visions firmly in mind, expelling every other thought; soon, finding some knack in this, her own spirit seemed to leave her, joining these others, leaving only her empty, tortured body behind.

Just as years before, at the American hospital in Neuilly, with Dermot watching over her, when she was dying and had felt herself rise up out of her own body, floating about the ceiling, looking down on herself and Dermot, so now she found the same strange release – floating away from herself, as the pain overwhelmed her, so that even her fearful shrieks seemed to her then the cries of another woman.

This transference, this stepping into a quite different dimension, other lives, into the lives of her friends – like an actress completely taking over, inhabiting a new role – probably saved her, for the pain was blotted out, was suffered by a former and now discarded person.

The only thing that nearly undid her was the pain of others. One evening, while not being tortured herself, she was forced instead to listen to the muffled screams of someone, a man being tortured in the next room. Captain Puetz stood over her. 'Your *husband*,' he told her. 'Oh yes, we found out. Not "mademoiselle" at all. You're married. We picked up your husband the other day!'

She listened to the appalling screams. Was it Pierre? She could not decide. Yes! – No, they were bluffing. But *was* it? Could it be?

'*Now* will you give me those names?'

She very nearly told him then. Until she thought – if it really were Pierre they would have tortured him in front of her, not in the next room. She told them nothing.

After a week of this Colonel Knochen spoke to Puetz.

'No one ever showed up or returned to her apartment. It is just possible this woman has nothing to do with the resistance – and that the other woman was just a friend of hers.'

Hauptsturmführer Puetz snorted. 'Innocent? – of course not! Anyone we arrest must be involved in *some* subversive activity. It's just a matter of time with this woman – before we find out what it is.'

'In time, Captain, she will simply die . . .'

'What matter is that?'

'You will still have found out nothing.'

'We should continue our interrogation. And, if we discover nothing, then simply . . . get rid of her, like all the rest.'

The Colonel gazed at the little man. How cocksure, how ignorant he was. He would go on torturing this woman just on the off-chance that she might know something – and the woman would be dead, when Puetz still would not admit that she had nothing to tell them at all, that she was, indeed, probably innocent. It was all so clumsy and unintelligent an approach. The Colonel was suddenly, if silently, furious with Puetz. At the best of times he hated dealing and compromising with these Gestapo thugs, drawn from the lowest riff-raff all over Germany. But now he would put his foot down, certain that in this instance Puetz was wasting everyone's time. He would show his authority in the matter.

'No, Hauptsturmführer – this is not an abattoir. And to kill *everyone* we interrogate is simply an admission of defeat. Headquarters in Berlin will not like that, when they see the monthly figures – nothing but invariable deaths in the Avenue Foch. And, besides, this woman is not worth any more of your time. Send her to the camp at Le Bourget, have her deported, along with all the other . . . undesirables . . . up there.'

Captain Puetz, seeing some sense in this, agreed. He

had, indeed, other pressing work – a number of new prisoners to deal with. And it was a point – a few, at least, of these French resisters should be numbered among the living when they left the Avenue Foch. Berlin might complain of the continual imbalance in the figures sent to them every month, possibly suspect him of getting too casual in his work – if the figures were all in the red, so to speak. They were fussy over little things like that in Berlin, figures . . . None the less, when next he had occasion to send a memorandum to Colonel Eichmann at Prinz Albrecht Strasse, he would insinuate his doubts about Colonel Knochen. There was something not entirely reliable about him . . .

Hetty was sent to Drancy. It was a makeshift transit camp, part of what had originally been a public housing development on the outskirts of Paris – a collection of grim four-storey apartment blocks, huts and desolate open spaces hidden from the general view, yet conveniently near the main railhead east at the station of Le Bourget. Now it was filled largely with French Jews. And, since it was so obviously a transit camp, without any proper facilities, most took heart from the frightful privations and discomforts here, which could not be other than temporary, and so were the more encouraged in their belief that they were about to be sent to appropriately equipped and staffed labour or resettlement camps in Germany, or even the Tyrol perhaps – on decent trains, they assumed, which they had never actually seen, but which arrived for them every week at sidings near the station half a mile away.

However, there had been no transports out for nearly three weeks, so that the camp was filled way beyond capacity, with nearly four thousand deportees in a space built for 1,200 – men, women, and many young Jewish children, orphaned or taken from their parents –

crammed together in the bleak open spaces behind the barbed wire. A few optimistic people milled about feverishly, expectantly by the gates, suitcases packed and ready to return home, certain there had been some mistake in their arrest which would at any moment be rectified. Others, wiser and more numerous, slumped on the ground or against walls, careless of their meagre belongings, with the vacant, hollow-eyed expression of people quite aware that a hideous nemesis had overtaken them, against which there was no appeal, which had already condemned them to some nameless fate.

The conditions, exacerbated by the very hot weather that summer, were quite appalling when Hetty arrived there, more dead than alive, pushed off the back of a truck, among a dozen others, like so much garbage. The deportees were packed twenty or thirty to each small room, where there were wooden bunk beds for only a dozen. There was no food, apart from a thin cabbage soup and some stale bread once a day, together with what the prisoners had managed to bring with them. And the only water came from four street hydrants dotted around the camp, some close to the overflowing cesspits and latrines already infected, so that dozens of people, contending for the few straw-filled mattresses, laid out in the rooms and long corridors, were ill or dying with typhoid, dysentery and enteric fever.

The camp, too, was infested with vermin, lice and fleas – so that infection spread like wildfire. In both the men's and women's blocks suicides were a daily occurrence, several people slashing their wrists or throwing themselves from the rooftops. Worst of all were the mothers who, suspecting the worst possible fate for themselves and their children in Germany, flung their offspring from these same roofs before following after them. Early every morning a special squad of prisoners took the dead away in handcarts. The place was an inferno – of sickly odours, illness, death. And yet for Hetty, after her days and nights of torture in the Avenue Foch, the camp seemed almost a happy release.

Soon discovering that there had been no transports out of the camp since Pierre had been arrested she would have been happier still – if she could have found him. But among the thousands of people there was no sign of him. And then, worse still, on the second morning, having struggled about the camp all the previous day searching for him, she fell ill herself, overcome with fearful stomach cramps, back pains, a raging headache. She thought at first these must be due to the Gestapo's attentions or the result of some infection in the camp. Then she recognized the symptoms. Of course, it must be her syphilis. Long dormant through the good years with Pierre, it had returned with a vengeance.

She was furious at this turn of fate. She had survived everything in these last years, even the Gestapo. Was her far-distant past to catch up with her once more, all her old mistakes and stupidities, paying her out one last time? For it was perfectly clear to her from what she had already seen and heard: there were only two future alternatives here. You either left the camp eastwards, on the transports, or were carried out dead on a handcart.

No longer able to move, she lay flat out on the floor at the end of a long corridor in one of the women's blocks, among scores of others in the same or worse condition – pregnant women, a cripple who had just miscarried, a paralysed woman screaming on a stretcher, old women, blind or deaf; women dead or dying. This, surely, was the end, Hetty thought. She had survived the Gestapo, survived so much before that, only to fall victim of her own inherent faults of character. She supposed it was fair, being finally paid out like this for her idiocies, all the arrogance and crass ambition of her earlier life, which had led to her marrying Craig, who had given her this disease . . .

She had done her best to atone for all this in the latter years. Above all, against the worst the Gestapo could do, she had kept faith with her friends. She had not betrayed them. And so, too, she had finally made it up to them – Pierre and Léonie. The life she owed them would be theirs soon. Her own life was not now to emerge, by some final act of bravery or renunciation, on any further brighter course. She was beyond everything then – had had that portion allotted to her of fine, bright things. She closed her eyes, not expecting to open them again.

Someone woke her, a dark-haired youngish woman, toughly built, fat, with a small pug face, but with tender gazing eyes. 'I'm Rosa,' she said, bending down, wiping the sweat from Hetty's brow with a soiled handkerchief, offering her a little water in a tin mug. 'Drink it,' she said. 'It's been boiled.'

Hetty, struggling to consciousness, tried to sit up, but could not until the woman lifted her head very gently with one arm, giving her the mug with the other. She managed to take a sip, then some more, feeling slightly better after a few minutes – as much from the tenderness of this huge woman with the small nut-brown face as anything else.

She managed to finish the water. Rosa wiped her face again, gently avoiding the awful cuts and bruises. 'Gestapo?' she asked. Hetty nodded. Rosa shook her head, unbelieving. 'In the resistance?' Hetty did not reply. 'You must have been. The brutes don't go that far even with us Jews – I was just a schoolteacher. There's a doctor in the camp. He tries to see some of the worst cases. I'll see if I can get him to come—'

Hetty's heart leapt. 'Oh, please – please do!' she told her. Was it Pierre? Could it be?

Hours later, in the fetid afternoon heat, with people

groaning all round her, Hetty saw a figure coming through the door at the far end of the corridor. He bent down, examining someone on the floor. The doctor! But was it Pierre? Her eyes were blurred, and the man was too far away for her to identify him.

Gradually, tending one person after another, he drew nearer. Yes! It must be him. Then, equally sure, she knew it was not. Like a mirage the figure hovered in her fevered vision, appearing, disappearing, bringing hope, then despair. So that she was driven wild with frustration as she waited.

Finally, after what seemed hours, she saw the shock of thick hair, the spectacles, the green shirt, all tattered now, which he had been wearing that evening on his birthday ten days before.

It was Pierre.

She wanted to shout out for him then, to roar her head off with joy. But even if her swollen lips, her cracked voice, would have allowed this, she dared not. There were sure to be *agents provocateurs* about the camp – and no one must know they were married.

It was another ten minutes before he got to her at the end of the corridor – and when he saw her he could not restrain his shout.

'Hetty!'

She at once put a finger to her lips as he rushed over to her. 'No, not Hetty – pretend you don't know me – no one must know I'm your wife.'

He saw her burnt arm then, the cuts and bruises all over her face, how aged and hurt she was with the pain of the past ten days. 'Hetty, what? . . . what's happened?' He was appalled. 'What have they done to you?' He wanted to do everything, anything for her. But again she restrained him.

'*Whisper*, Pierre darling. And don't do anything

unusual. I'm just a stranger. Bend down, whisper, and I'll tell you everything.'

He bent down – and whispered then, 'I can't believe it . . .' Then, despite her warnings, he kissed her.

'So you see,' she told him later. 'I'm "Yvonne de Sertigny" – they think I'm with the resistance. And you're just here because you're a Jew. So no one must know we're married.' He nodded. 'Not for the moment anyway, while we're still in the camp here. If they discover we're married they'll take both of us back for more interrogation. When we get to the camp in Germany, well, it certainly can't be as bad as this. Things'll be easier there. They won't care if we're married then. You'll see! This is hell – but, once we're out of it, we can be properly together again – working some potato patch, or whatever it is, in Germany . . .'

The transports finally arrived a week later. Hetty, under Pierre's attentions, and with the food, drugs and bandages he had managed to obtain from the thriving black market about the camp, had improved considerably. But most of all she was better for seeing him alive and being with him. Early one broiling afternoon, lined up in columns, some 1,200 deportees, including Hetty, Pierre and some hundreds of unaccompanied children, were led out of the camp by French police and taken to the marshalling yards at Le Bourget.

Here, to the surprise of many, instead of passenger carriages, a long line of cattle trucks awaited them. The police herded them on board like the beasts the wagons were intended for – eighty or ninety people crushed together into each airless, windowless truck, including a dozen or so of the children, carefully inserted into each wagon, so that onlookers, any local inhabitants or railway officials, would believe they were travelling with their parents. Inside there was nothing but dirty straw to ease them, no water, and barely any ventilation or sanitary facilities. And here they were left to roast under the hot afternoon sun for nearly three hours before the train finally left just after six o'clock.

But again Hetty, with Rosa who had become her friend now, did not complain. Nor did the others in the wagon. It was just a temporary discomfort, many of them agreed, like the camp at Drancy. They soon regained their earlier optimism, even a sense of humour. 'You know what French trains are like these days! . . .' 'The decent trains have all been commandeered by the Wehrmacht . . .' 'They've all been bombed by the allies!' 'At least there's straw and a slop-pail!' Germany was only an overnight trip, they continued more seriously. And things were much more efficient there, at least – everyone knew that. They'd be transferred to a proper passenger train, or would have arrived at the labour camp by then, perhaps in the Tyrol, where there'd be space and air and it would be clean. Everyone knew how things like railways and camps of any kind were much better run in Germany.

'You fools!' one older Jewish woman shouted. 'They mean to kill us! – machine-gun us all as soon as we get off the train – at some rail siding or in the middle of the woods.' No one else agreed. They told her to shut up. Someone opened a bottle of wine they had managed to bring with them, while others started to share out their meagre provisions – tins of sardines, some cheese, even some sweet biscuits – so that soon there was almost a picnic atmosphere in the truck.

Hetty, having experienced the Gestapo at close quarters, was tempted to believe the old woman for a moment. Yet she vigorously repressed the thought. This cattle truck, like the camp at Drancy, was simply a temporary aberration. Above all, Pierre was on the same transport – that was the great thing. She had been terrified of being separated from him. But, no, he was with her. He had been walking twenty yards ahead of her in the column to the station. She had seen him pushed into one of the first cattle trucks. He was there, with her, a few wagons up towards the engine, and she was happy.

It had all worked out, just as she had planned and hoped. She had been given a reprieve. She could change her life once more – for surely the worst that could happen to them now would be an interlude, grim enough no doubt, digging potatoes or some such, until the war ended in victory for the allies, as it obviously would. With her new friend Rosa, the tough, quick-thinking Rosa who had forcibly commandeered a corner of the truck, she settled down in the straw, counting her blessings.

The journey was a nightmare.

The pitch-black interior of the truck, with everyone so tightly crushed together that many had to stand bolt upright, soon became intolerable. It was dark, airless, increasingly hot. The picnic mood vanished completely, along with every previous optimism, as the slop-pail, soon filled to overflowing, tipped over and people began to relieve themselves where they stood.

The air stank. The children whimpered, then began to cry. People started to quarrel for space, some to fight. They shouted then, trying to attract the attention of the guards, hopelessly. There was no water and soon all the food and drink they had brought with them was gone. A woman, a cultivated Jewess, who had taken charge of two attractive boys on their own, disciplined them gently. 'You mustn't complain – you're disturbing the others . . .' and Rosa tried to comfort Hetty. 'Never mind,' she told her next morning. 'It can't be far now. They'll let us out soon – must be in Germany. We'll soon be at the camp.'

They were indeed in Germany by then. And the train did stop, but only to take on coal and water for the engine. No one was let out. And in the silence Hetty heard the cries rising from all down the train, taken up by one truck from another, carried on the stinking air – cries which had only a vague tone of protest to them now, which seemed to Hetty much more like a keening over some vast funeral cortège.

They travelled on for nearly another two days. By the time they finally stopped two elderly Jews in Hetty's wagon had died, and she had long before ceased to count her blessings. Instead, numb with cramp, filthy dirty and almost suffocating in a space that was now layered inches deep in excrement, she saw the bright lights sweeping through the chinks in the wood as the train pulled to a halt and the doors were finally opened.

'*Raus! Schnell! Los – los!*'

She heard the guttural orders barked in German. Tumbling out of the wagon with Rosa she felt the cool night air on her face like a balm, breathing it in deeply. The feeling of release was unbelievable. The other deportees were gathering now, from all the trucks, on a long wooden platform, brightly lit from floodlights on tall pylons, surrounded by SS guards with snarling Alsatian dogs.

Yet the dogs did not bark, nor did the guards shout again. There was an air everywhere of thankful release, of calm and good order as the deportees were made to form up in long lines down the platform. The only stir was caused when people tried to take their luggage with them from the wagons.

'No,' Hetty, who had no luggage herself, heard an SS officer say to an elderly couple behind her. 'You don't have to carry your own luggage here. We have porters for that,' he continued agreeably. 'Just make sure you can identify your bags afterwards, at the luggage bureau in the camp – after you've had your decontamination and hot shower bath.'

The old Jewish couple, almost at the point of total exhaustion, were grateful for this, setting down their threadbare bags, patting them gently, settling the labels neatly, making a studious effort to memorize these objects already so familiar to them. Hetty, too, was heartened by this consideration on the officer's part. Things could not be too bad here at all.

She was surprised only when she saw the 'porters' – rake-thin men, hollow-eyed and -cheeked, the skin drum-tight everywhere, with shaven skulls in striped pyjamas, moving like wraiths among the crowds, stumbling up into the wagons, pulling out what luggage there was. Porters? They were more like victims – victims of some punishment, she supposed, the unlucky ones who had been caught stealing potatoes or some such. They were strangely silent, too, she noticed, saying absolutely nothing when asked, as they were, where the train had arrived.

Still, she had no time to worry about them. She must find Pierre. Stumbling up the platform towards Pierre's truck she suddenly saw him, the shock of dark hair sticking up against the bright floodlights, as he helped an old woman down from the truck. He was alive and well, though as filthy and bedraggled as she was. She longed to embrace him, but did not dare. Instead they exchanged a few whispered words.

'All right?' he asked.

'Just about. It was *awful* – where on earth are we?'

'Poland. One of those porters – I heard him speaking Polish.'

'But *where*?'

'Some place called Oswieckiem, I heard someone say.'

'It can't be too bad. I heard one of the SS officers say we were all to have a hot shower bath. And they're even carrying our luggage—'

Rosa had come up behind them then as they were

interrupted with more commands. The line down the platform, finally formed, was now moving forward slowly towards the head of the ramp, where a group of SS officers were standing under a floodlight. And beyond them, to her relief and astonishment, Hetty saw a line of military trucks drawn up, but each of them with a large red cross emblazoned on the side.

'Look – the Red Cross!' she said to Pierre, just ahead of her now in the line. 'We can't be in any danger here.'

The column moved slowly forward. And soon, nearing the head of the platform, Hetty saw who the Red Cross trucks were for. All the elderly, the infirm, the ill and all the children among the deportees, separated from the others by an SS officer as they reached the head of the line, were being helped on board the trucks and taken away.

'God! I hope we can get on one of those trucks!' Hetty told Rosa. 'I can hardly walk.'

'Oh, I couldn't bear to be cooped up again,' Rosa said. 'Can't we walk? – with the others.'

She gestured towards a much smaller contingent of younger, able-bodied people, now being formed up in another line beyond the SS officers.

'Oh, Rosa, let's not. I'm really finished. Let's take the Red Cross trucks. I can very well pretend I'm old and doddery. At least, if Pierre goes in the trucks, I will. I do hope he does.'

'All right, if you want.'

They were nearly at the head of the line where the column was being divided, with Pierre just in front of them. When his turn came to confront the officer he was waved aside to the left at once, away from the Red Cross trucks. And Hetty had to change her mind then. 'All right, let's not. We'll pretend we're fit as fiddles. We'll walk with Pierre.'

Hetty, when she and Rosa faced the officer, braced

herself purposefully, smiling confidently. The officer gazed at them for a moment, then waved them aside, to the left, with Pierre.

But, just before they moved off, Hetty saw the cultivated Jewish woman, with her two young boys still in her care, who had all been ahead of them, all being helped up into the back of a Red Cross truck before it drove sharply away. She waved at the two boys. One of them took out a handkerchief to wave back at her, smiling broadly.

The officer, noticing Hetty's gesture, attempted a brief smile himself. 'Don't worry,' he told her in passable French. 'You'll see them again, when they've had their shower bath.'

'Oh, they're nothing to do with me,' Hetty said quickly. 'Just friends I met on the train.'

She was suddenly comforted by this last phrase, the casual, everyday words, as if all of them, setting off on a vacation and having come through an expectedly difficult journey, were now at last entering the holiday camp.

Fifteen minutes later, with Pierre and Rosa, she was walking off into the cool night, away from the ramp, flanked by soldiers, along a track among trees. There were fewer than a hundred of them now remaining, separated from the many hundreds more who had gone off in the Red Cross trucks. Again Hetty breathed the cool night air and was thankful, though she was still exhausted and aching everywhere, still wishing she had gone in one of the trucks. They would have had their hot shower baths that much sooner. She longed, above all else at that moment, for a hot shower.

A young soldier, marching ahead of her, dropped back and said to her in bad French, 'I'll give you a cigarette – if you let me screw you.'

'*One* cigarette?' She turned to Rosa. 'That's a pretty poor rate. Or else cigarettes must be priceless around here.' She turned back to the soldier. 'No, thanks. But where are we going?'

'Labour camp. But you'll be all right. Don't worry. Two cigarettes?' Hetty shook her head and the soldier moved on ahead of them.

'It's strange,' Hetty said after another ten minutes' walk, as they came out of the trees, seeing a bare flat expanse of land ahead of them, illuminated by distant flood and search lights, set at intervals round what was obviously a huge perimeter fence. 'It's only two o'clock, so it can't be the dawn. But look – that red haze on the horizon, to the right, over the camp there.'

The two women observed this strange phenomenon which, as they drew nearer, materialized not only as a red glow, but as several smoky cones of fire, spiralling upwards, a ruddy apocalyptic vision against the clear night sky.

'Factories, I suppose,' Rosa told her. 'Furnaces. Working all night. Where we'll be working, I suppose.'

'Pity. Fields and gardens – I'd hoped we'd be doing something like that . . .'

Then, as they approached the floodlit perimeter fence, with a sentry block and high-arched gateway in the middle, a drift of air passed over their heads, a sudden sweetish smell in a change of wind that was gone in a moment. But as it passed their nostrils the message it left was unmistakable.

'*Meat?*' Rosa said in astonishment. 'Who could be roasting meat at this time of night?'

'Why not?' Hetty smiled. 'Food! We've not eaten for days – and they've got to *feed* us here, at least, haven't they? – if they expect us to work. Red Cross probably insisted we got something hot to eat, when we arrive . . .'

They came to the arched gateway. Above it, picked out in iron letters in a semi-circle round the arch, was the legend: 'ARBEIT MACHT FREI'.

'What does it mean?'

Rosa, the schoolteacher, looked at it. '"Work – work gives you freedom", I think.'

'Oh good,' Hetty said. 'Thank God we're here, in some proper camp at last. After the hell of Drancy and that terrible train journey this place is bound to be better – all round.'

'Yes,' Rosa said, as the column entered the gates and disappeared into the vast camp.

13

'What *would* have happened to Hetty, though – in one of those camps?' Olivia spoke to her father on the porch after lunch at Summer Hill. It was a glorious summer afternoon in 1945. Robert, back from the war – back a few months before from Dachau where, as one of the allied journalists present, he had seen exactly what had happened in these camps – did not reply at once. 'Did no one survive, Dermot?' She turned to her cousin, in another wicker chair – Dermot, retired at last from the Army, over at Summer Hill and living there now.

'I really . . . don't know exactly . . .' He prevaricated. Olivia was only nineteen. Surely, he thought, she might be spared the details of these horrors, which he, like Robert, now knew all about.

Olivia impatiently ran a hand through her thick, glossy-dark hair and turned back to her father. 'Well, somebody must know what happened to Hetty and—'

'Some people survived, *yes*,' her father spoke at last, almost brusquely. 'But very few. Most that weren't – incinerated – were driven out of the camps just before the Allies arrived and taken on forced marches, in the freezing snow, and most of them died, too.'

'So, Hetty . . . went that way?' Olivia's curiosity would not be denied. 'And what about Pierre, her husband – the same thing?'

'Possibly—'

'Or were they just burnt?'

'I – we simply don't know, Olivia,' he said impatiently.

'Or could they have *survived*?'

Robert, frustrated, stood up. 'No. No chance. The camps were opened up several months ago. Only a very few – a few thousand among *millions* – got out alive. And neither Hetty nor Pierre was amongst them. If they had been, they'd have turned up somewhere by now. So let's leave it at that, shall we? They're both . . . dead.' He moved to the edge of the porch, looking over the pot-holed, weed-covered gravel surround – Lady Cordiner's elaborate pleasure garden beyond, which Hetty and Pierre had so painstakingly restored before the war, now quite gone to seed again.

'All right,' Olivia said, a little put down. 'I didn't want to make a thing of it. And it is absolutely *awful* about Hetty and Pierre – terrible and sad, even though I never met Pierre and hardly remember her at all. But the thing is Mummy won't talk about it at all. And I'd like to know. After all, it is their house we're living in now.' Shading her dark eyes against a sudden burst of sunlight, she stood up and joined her father.

'I'm sorry,' Robert told her. 'It's just the whole concentration – no, *extermination* – camp thing is, well, it's all so horrifying I haven't really taken it in yet.' He shook his head. 'It simply wasn't believable. Dachau, when I saw it – the gas chambers, the ovens, those huge crematoria – it just didn't make any sense at first. One of the American officers told me, when he first saw all these ovens, he thought for a moment they might have been *bread* ovens, couldn't understand why they needed so many bread ovens, especially since the few survivors obviously hadn't eaten properly in years, sheer skeletons. So, let's not dwell on it now, that's all. It'll take years to make sense of it, if we ever do.' He turned back. 'More coffee, Dermot?'

'But Mummy – what are we to do about her?' Olivia followed her father.

'All we can – all we have been doing. The doctor in London said rest. And that's exactly what she's getting here. She was recovering, too – forgetting, until she saw all those newspaper and newsreel reports on the camps.' He spoke more to himself than to the others. Pouring Dermot more coffee, he looked up at Olivia. 'You see, for her it's all so much worse – Hetty taking her place in that Paris flat, when the Gestapo arrived. If it hadn't been for Hetty, Mummy would almost certainly have ended up in one of those camps. That's the problem for her now. And, when she saw what the camps were like, what really happened there – well, it sort of sent her over the edge. Shock, depression.'

'Yes.' Olivia considered it all. 'Hetty saved her life then, didn't she?' Robert said nothing. 'And saying nothing to the Germans when they tortured her – as those French people told you. That was so brave. Will they give Hetty a medal, like Mummy's getting? – they do, don't they, even after they're dead, sometimes?'

'I don't think so. Hetty's reward . . . will simply have to be here.' He gazed across the lush valley towards the purple shoulders of Mount Brandon. 'That's what she and Pierre would have wanted – to keep this place going, set in some order again, which is why we've come back to live here. Hetty was very fond of Summer Hill.'

'Yes. Like we all are—'

'Go up and see if Mummy wants anything. She may be asleep, but just see.'

Olivia, in a pair of old slacks and a tattered blue pullover, stretched her arms high above her head, arching her back, yawning. 'God, I'm still so tired after that awful journey over. But I'm so glad to be here. Because I loved it here – remember? – when we lived here before. Can we get the swing going again, up on the big maple?'

'Yes, if you can get near the tree with all those briars . . . But aren't you a bit old for swinging?'

'Certainly not! And the river,' she rushed on excitedly. 'We'll get the boat out again, won't we? It's still there, in the boat house, I saw it this morning. And go for trips on it like we used to do. And the otters! You will come with me – and Dermot – on the river? Because I'm so glad to be back, and having a whole summer here before I go to Trinity . . .' Olivia rushed on, a child again in her enthusiasm for this return, to this place where she had been happy as a child, which she had thought entirely lost to her, a world now regained. 'I really *do*! – like it all so much better over here than dreary England. Simply couldn't stand any more of that powdered egg and margarine and *Spam*. All the fresh eggs and bacon and *butter* we had this morning for breakfast – couldn't believe it. So you will come and do things, before you go back, Daddy? – like we used to do, on the river and things.'

'Yes. And I've talked to Jack Welsh – we'll get the pony and trap out and going again. Have to. Pierre's old Wolseley is still in the coach-house. But not a drop of petrol for it anywhere.'

'I wish you weren't going away again so soon. And why *Germany*, when you've only just come back from the horrible place?'

'Paper wants some articles: "The Post-War Scene" . . . But you'll be here with Mummy – and Dermot and Aunt Emily and Elly and Jack. Almost a whole household again, as it used to be . . . And I'll be back soon enough. Do go up and see if Mummy's all right.'

'And that's be-best of all . . .' Olivia had stopped by the hall door, half-turning, her slight stammer returned for an instant. 'Us three together again, isn't it?' She made a move towards him, head to one side, quizzical, half-smiling, hesitating, running her hand through her hair again in a nervous gesture.

'Yes,' Robert said lightly. 'That's best of all.' Olivia turned then, doing a small skip, as she disappeared through the doors.

'Yes . . .' Robert turned to Dermot after she had gone. 'I never thought it would turn out like this. Back here – with Léa, again.' He sat down, gazing into his cup. 'And it wouldn't have happened, but for Hetty going like that . . .'

Dermot nodded. '"An ill wind" . . .'

'Léa always had such hidden steel in her, over things – with Hetty when they were young, and her friend Jenny when she died – then joining the SOE and all that. But, after Hetty went, and her father dying last year – she started to break up. Then reading those reports on the camps, and the newsreels – that was the last straw.'

'Yes. She and Hetty were close, of course, over the years . . .' Dermot, as usual, left the nature, the degree, of this intimacy undefined.

But Robert, thrilled by Léonie's return to him and so forsaking his usual reticence, was happy to talk to his oldest friend, about things he could not have begun to talk about with anyone else. 'More than close. It was Hetty who always stood between Léa and me. You remember . . .' He smiled a fraction.

'Yes—'

'As long as Hetty was there I was always to play second fiddle.'

'I see.' Dermot did see, but did not care to comment further.

'Oh yes. That was exactly the problem between us. No other. And I couldn't help Léa – then. Hetty was always an *idée fixe*, an obsession with her. So that, when Léa saw those press reports and finally had to accept that Hetty couldn't have survived the camps, that she was dead, she couldn't face it. Because she had to accept that she was responsible for her death in a way, by running out on her when they met that time in Paris.'

'Running out? I didn't know – just that they'd met there, before the Gestapo arrived.'

'Yes, Léa left her – she told me. She was frightened of staying with her . . .'

'Frightened?'

'Of their old feelings for each other.'

'I see.' Dermot remained brief.

'So you do see, don't you? – what a long way Léa has to go. The guilt . . .'

'It's hard, yes.'

'And now she sees her agony as some sort of punishment for her earlier life with Hetty, her feelings there.'

'And how do you see it?' Dermot asked, by way of changing this, to him, delicate topic – the tragedy, always implicit, as far as he was concerned in any aberrant nature.

Robert drained his cup. 'Well, I loved them both. Now there's only Léa. So it's easier.'

'No longer in the middle.'

'Yes . . .' Robert paused, made aware, once more, of all the pain there had been in this triangle. 'But at least I can help Léa again now, as I've always wanted to. Because now she'll *let* me help her. The quite appalling thing is that it's taken Hetty's death for me to do this, for us to come together again.'

The two men looked out over the ruined demesne,

hearing the tall, dry summer grass rustle over the buried pleasure garden.

'It's really quite terrible about Hetty . . . But Léa will surely recover at Summer Hill,' Dermot said at last, emerging from his guarded mood, renewing a theme which had always absorbed him about the great house. 'Because you know there's something about the place – felt it almost as soon as I got back a month ago – something hopeful in the air, even when everything has gone to seed again.' He leant forward, finding his stride with a quite unusual enthusiasm. 'I've always felt, even when things were at their very worst here, in the old days, with old Lady Cordiner and Frances fighting and then all the terrible rows between Frances and Hetty, and the fire and the Black and Tan horrors – always felt there was a future somehow brewing in the ruins of things, under the dust-sheets, a phoenix in the ashes! Felt that people here – I used to say this to Hetty – could and would one day be unimaginably happy at Summer Hill. I can't account for the feeling, because so much *has* gone awry, and so often things have turned out for the very worst. And with Hetty and Pierre gone like that – what could be worse? The last straw, you'd think. Yet now there's you and Léa and Olivia here again. So once more – out of the blue, or the dark – there's a future for the place. How can one account for it all?'

'I can't really. Except that the house always seems to be there for saving people.'

'Or destroying them – like Frances and her mother. And poor Bunty.'

'Yes. Well, then, it's always saving *itself*, for something or somebody, for the *right* something or somebody.'

'Some sort of strange musical chairs.'

'I don't know what it is exactly,' Robert now took over Dermot's earlier passion. 'But I've felt something as you have here – the feeling of dead lives – old Lady Cordiner,

Frances, Hetty now, and dozens of other Cordiners in the past – all influencing us. People who loved Summer Hill, or hated it, or the people in it, who lived out their dramas here with such passion that their imprint is still on the house somehow. *They're* still here – pushing us, to keep the place going, or maybe to live their lives for them, make up for their failures, faults, stupidities here, set the record straight, once and for all. I don't know . . .'

Robert gazed around him, searching the empty porch, as if trying to identify a whole host of ghosts. 'Everyone's still very much still here, aren't they? – sitting on the porch with us – as in some stiff Victorian family photograph. All of them. And they're all *watching* us – criticising, encouraging. Above all expecting us to get on and *do* something. Very Victorian, that. That's the feeling I have.'

'Yes, exactly.' Dermot lit his pipe, a drift of tobacco passing on the summer air. 'So, we'll have to do that then – try and put the place to rights again.'

'What is the situation, with Hetty and Pierre – and Summer Hill? I only had the rough details from you on the phone.'

'Hetty left no will, as far as I can ascertain. And in any case, as you know, Summer Hill never actually belonged to her or Pierre. All left to her, for use during her lifetime, by an "admirer". And I've told you who I think that is, the present Duke of Windsor. But I spoke to Mulrooney, the solicitor in Dublin, as soon as I got over – the man who dealt with the whole business originally. His "client", he told me, is quite willing that I should continue to have the legal administration of the house and estate, pending Hetty's possible return. And that if, after a period of five years, she doesn't show up, then we will reconsider the matter. And at that point his "client", he says, will very likely accept my recommendation as to who the place should go to then. Well, of course, I have and I shall recommend that you and Léa – and Olivia – have it at that point. Meanwhile, as the administrator now, I hope you and Léa *will* live here – and won't mind my living here, too!'

'Nothing would please us more, as you well know. But how should we arrange things – financially? What's the situation there?'

'Hetty had no bank account herself – she remained an undischarged bankrupt technically. I've had all the administration of the funds, some of it my own and Mortimer's money and what remained of Mulrooney's "client's" money after he bought the place back from Kennedy. There's presently only some £3,000 remaining at the bank here – pays Jack and Elly and Bridget. And the rates. And not much else. So we'll have to think about that. The roof's all right, that's the great thing – no damp or rot to speak of. But there will be soon. It's my idea that you and I share expenses here fifty-fifty—'

'Certainly not! Your share shouldn't be more than twenty-five per cent at the most.'

They discussed these business affairs for five minutes longer. But in their enthusiasm for what lay before them – the restoration, once more, of this house which they both loved – the matter was hardly important to either of them. They would have enough money, together, to effect some immediate repairs on the house, and to maintain it. And that was all that mattered. They could live here now – start to rescue something from Hetty's death, rescue other things from the wreck of the war: a marriage for Robert, a happy retirement after nearly fifty years in the Army for Dermot. What Robert and Dermot had always seen as a world elsewhere for them was theirs now, willy-nilly, in this cast of fate, the ill wind that had blown them great good. They had both been away, estranged in heart and by distance from Summer Hill. Now they had come home.

Cabbage whites and red admirals zigzagged over the tall ragwort and wild grass which had practically obliterated all the paths. Swallows, darting and swooping over the ivy-choked walls, fed on the listless air, where midges and thunder flies formed a continual feast. The high-summer afternoon was dead-still and hot as Robert and Léonie pushed their way through the heavy undergrowth in the vegetable garden, searching the paths out with their feet, explorers in this jungle.

'Look, those lovely tall yellow flowers,' Léonie remarked, 'in the *vegetable* garden?'

'Must have seeded themselves here – Evening Primrose. *Oenothera*,' Robert added, his old passion for natural history returning now, in the place where he had learned these things. Léonie fingered the floppy, tulip-shaped flowers. 'They smell – in the evening,' he told her, swatting at the midges swarming above him.

Coming to the old vine house in a corner of the garden they found it collapsed at one end, glass broken, tendrils of vine spreading out all over the top, falling down in an arbour over a broken water barrel.

'Wonder if there are still any peaches inside?'

They pushed open the arched, diamond-paned door. A blackbird, disturbed, flew upwards against the glass, battering itself for an instant, before retreating, hiding among a collection of old apple boxes.

'Endless things to be done,' Robert said encouragingly.

'Too much . . .' Léonie was tired suddenly in the heat under the glass.

'We can do it. By degrees. We'll get a gardener. And help from the village.'

'Never was much good at gardening.'

'Doesn't matter. I like it.'

They walked down the central aisle, among nettles, the decayed entrail-like remains of long-dead tomato plants. Then they found the peaches on the wall at the end, more than half a dozen of them and ripe enough. Robert picked her one. The juice spilled down her chin as she bit into it.

'See! The peaches are still OK. We used to steal in here, eat them—' He stopped, for it had been he and Hetty, not Léonie, who, as children, had come in here, early on summer mornings years before, to do just this.

But Léonie knew this, too. 'You needn't stop,' she said. 'It was you and Hetty – who stole in here and ate them.' Her eyes flickered a little as if she were trying to clear them of something. 'You mustn't think I – that I can't bear the thought, the mention of Hetty.' Then, as if suddenly deciding something, she reached up, stretching far up the wall, for another peach which she gave to Robert. 'I can bear the thought of her – with you. What I couldn't bear was neither of you, I suppose. And the way I behaved to you, before the war – well, there was no reason for you to be kind to me, as you have been, after it. I misjudged you.'

He bit into the peach. 'No, I don't think you misjudged me. Just, neither of us could deal with each other – while Hetty was alive. We both loved her. Now she's not here, we can. I hope.'

'"Deal with each other" – sounds like a business! I hope it needn't be like that with us, Robert . . .' Some irony, a touch of life, had returned to her voice at last.

They took the other peaches back to the house. Robert had counted them. 'Just one each for everyone – Olivia, Dermot, Aunt Emily, Jack, Elly and Bridget.'

They smiled at the idea of how exactly the peaches had divided themselves up. For both of them it seemed a happy portent, this rediscovered bounty in the ruined vine house. There was promise here in the late sunlight over the garden, the smell of peaches, in the hem of Léonie's dress which she held up now like a dancer, cradling them. They had rescued something wonderful in the dust.

Certainly things changed for Léonie in the vine house that afternoon. She began to rise a fraction from her dead level. She went out with the others on the river that evening, trailing her hand in the black water by the over-hanging willows. And, gradually in the days that fol-lowed, she took to life again in the old house, unpacking, settling things, storing, exploring.

She never, though, found the courage to enter Hetty's primrose bedroom. Elly took on the job there, of sorting and putting away Hetty's things – her clothes, books, knick-knacks, papers – packing them before they were sent to join so much else of the same sort belonging to earlier Cordiners, up in the attics. Only one thing she kept aside, found in Hetty's bureau: the snow-dome with the ivory miniature of Summer Hill inside, the little paperweight which on Frances's instructions, nearly fifty years before, she had thieved from old Lady Cordiner. Gazing at it now, she decided to return it, in her own person, just as she had taken it all those years before – replacing it where it had always been in Lady Cordiner's time, in the centre of the drawing room mantelpiece.

One afternoon a few days later Léonie noticed it, recognizing it at once – as Hetty's most special charm, always kept by her bedside in their Dublin days together, taken with her everywhere when they had toured Ireland with Fonsy O'Grady's troupe.

How had it got there? She dared not ask, thinking this might break the magic of its sudden appearance. Instead, tumbling the snow inside so that it frothed over the miniature chimneys, she watched the flakes circle round the aerial chamber, falling lightly then, soon smothering the roofs and gables. How often before had she seen

Hetty do just this, in a despondent moment, as a balm, a cure.

And she could not restrain her tears then, alone in the drawing room, gripped once more by the guilt of a terrible emotion – for a life that could not be returned and set before her, like the snow-dome.

She buried her face in her arms, unseeing, leaning on the mantelpiece. Behind her, as the snow settled everywhere in the glass dome, another special toy of Hetty's had started to move. The zoetrope, the magic Wheel of Life, was very slowly circling – the cow, vivacious again, about to renew its endless hurdles over the moon.

Robert found her, face still buried in her arms, a few minutes later. He saw the snow-dome in front of her, recognizing it, knowing its meaning, the emotions it contained – for both of them. Picking it up, he set the flurry going again, re-animating it, holding it up briefly in front of him. Léonie had turned to him by now, watching his attentions here, to this object held between them now, shared, understood.

'It's all right, Léa,' he said quietly. 'She's gone. But she's still here.' He put the dome back in the centre of the mantelpiece. 'And will be,' he added, a sudden bright timbre to his voice. 'Because *we're* here, you and I, together again.' He gazed at her in the hot afternoon silence. 'We can start again now. We really can.'

'Yes . . .' she said. '*Yes*', she repeated with much more conviction as she walked towards him.

14

'This place doesn't look to have been bombed at all.' Robert, after a first week on the road, touring Germany, spoke to the Army press liaison officer beside him, driving into the outskirts of Dortmund in Westphalia.

'Oh, Dortmund was bombed all right!' The Captain was derisive. 'Wait till you see the centre.'

Ten minutes later, leaving the practically untouched suburbs of heavy Prussian villas, they arrived at the centre, in one of the main streets. And now the view had changed completely. From end to end of the long straight thoroughfare, and all about them, the scene was one of utter desolation. Almost every building had been razed to the ground, collapsed in huge mounds of uncleared, blackened rubble, with a few houses left standing – but with only a single wall and chimney, windows open to the sky, cardboard cut-outs, standing free against the grey clouds, clotted with smoke from small fires everywhere, watched over by tattered figures cooking on open braziers amidst the ruins.

A vision of the underworld, Robert thought. Nobody could live here, surely. And yet it was crowded with people that afternoon. They were everywhere, as if this was an ordinary town, yet all engaged in the most unlikely metropolitan things. Old women brewed up kettles in front of sackcloth shacks set up in front of grandiose ruined steps and porticoes. Others, like worker bees, clambered up and down the huge mounds of rubble, unceasingly, carrying things, going to and from the wrecked houses. A majority, it seemed, pushed handcarts piled with broken furnishings up and down the narrow central aisle of the street. All of them, at a glance, seemed full of purposeful life.

Yet on closer inspection it was clear that they were

doing very little. They went – but they always returned. They were driven, yet aimless. And, as soon as they saw the military car, their attention was immediately diverted – crushing up against the windows, asking for something. A lift? Food? Money? It was not clear. And they did not insist. This vast collection of humanity – waiting, going, trudging, imploring, pressing against the car windows – all were strangers to life, with the sunken, expressionless faces of the mad, completely, obsessively absorbed in their own aimless acts.

'What are they all doing?'

'Watch out, Corporal!' The Captain leant forward to the driver. They had narrowly missed running down an old woman pushing a handcart from a side-street.

'What are they all doing?' The Captain sat back, lighting a cigarette casually.

'Yes. All this moving about. The bombing must have stopped months ago here.'

'Oh yes – that. These people, they stay in their houses till the bitter end, till the place literally falls down about their ears. Then they move to the cellar, before it finally collapses on them. They get these handcarts then and try and move in somewhere else nearby. Determined to stay close to home, you see. That's the whole point. Their only chance as they see it, if they're to be reunited with their families, is to stay close to home – hoping for a son back from the war – long dead of course on the Russian front. Or a daughter from Berlin, most likely raped and killed by the Russians during their last assault there. That's all these people have in mind now – to try to get the family together again.'

'My God . . .' Robert, thinking of his own family, of Summer Hill, thought the Captain brutally insensitive. No doubt he had seen it all before. It had hardened him. He was a realist. Yet for Robert in some ways Dortmund was as bad as Dachau. Here the people had survived, only to live in hopeless hope, a living death.

'Yes, that's Dortmund,' the Captain said dismissively as they left the ruined city. 'A lot of people pretending they still have their homes. The D.P.s are better off in a way – you'll see this evening. At least they know they've lost everything. Can only start from scratch – if they start back at all. Should get to their camp in an hour or so. Luckily it's just beyond our 21st Army Group H.Q. at Bad Oeynausen. So we can put up there for a night or two. Get a decent meal – a wash and brush-up. Could do with that.' He sighed, taking out a very clean handkerchief, dabbing his face and neck. 'My God, the dirt of these towns. And the *people*. Soot and smuts, gets everywhere.'

A few hours later, coming over a rise, they suddenly found themselves in a quite different world: a group of absurdly ornate, nineteenth-century gingerbread villas, set in a landscape of immaculately kept grass, between groves of exotic trees. They had arrived at Bad Oeynausen, a large health resort once, built in the times of the Kaisers, long emptied of all its patients, where every villa and *kursaal* had been taken over now by the British occupation forces, as their Army headquarters in Westphalia, so that the only things which marred this idyllic vision were the military notices everywhere – ARE YOU ARMED? – and the endless coloured wires of the Signal Corps running from one building to another.

'Where's the Displaced Persons' camp?'

'Over there, beyond the church, down the hill. They've a hospital there as well, in the old gymnasium, I think.' He snorted. 'Hospital, food, every comfort – all laid on. These D.P.s are too damn lucky really, ending up here. And some of them are sure to have been collaborators. Hardly deserve it . . .' He straightened his cuffs, his tie.

'They're not Germans, though, these D.P.s,' Robert said rather sharply.

'No. Poles for the most part. A few Russians.'

'Allies of ours.'

'All the same . . .' The Captain grimaced, remaining disgruntled at this largesse extended by the British occupation authorities. 'You should see them . . . Quite beyond everything really. And still coming in by the truckload. *Filthy*.'

An hour later Robert, accompanied by the supercilious Captain, walked over to the D.P. camp behind the health resort. The grey clouds had gone and a faint, hazy sun had appeared. The afternoon was very still as they moved beneath the lemon-yellow trees. Passing by the little Gothic church Robert heard the organ music, the sound of voices. He was startled by the familiar tune, the words, the strong male voices drifting out from the open porch doors.

'We plough the fields and scatter,
The good seed on the land . . .'

He thought of autumns at Summer Hill with Hetty years before, this very hymn heard so often in the family church beyond Cloone. And suddenly he was struck by an emotion so strong, so eerie, that he shuddered, as if someone was walking over his grave.

'Yes,' the Captain told him, noticing his surprise. 'Harvest festival obviously. Army choir rehearsing. Next Sunday.'

'What harvest?' Robert asked, astonished.

The Captain was surprised now. 'Well, the usual harvest, of course. It's August, isn't it? Or next month?'

They passed on. This would make a paragraph in one of his articles, Robert thought. A harvest festival – in this ruined, famished land. How quite extraordinary the English were, he thought, his realistic colonial blood beginning to boil: celebrating harvest festivals here, as if nothing had happened, as if there'd been no war at all, no complete desecration – only an hour away, in cities like Dortmund, where they were starving. And he'd hope to get this arrogant, ignorant Army captain into the same article.

Moving through the sentry gate at the barbed wire perimeter fence and going on down the hill along an avenue of acacia trees, they came to another barbed wire fence with sentry posts, and behind it the heavily ornate granite gymnasium which housed the D.P. hospital. A medical orderly met them in the vast marble hall with its dry fountain in the centre.

'Robert Grant, of the *Express*, to see Surgeon-Major Fields,' the Captain told the man brusquely, stamping his boots as they waited.

Major Fields appeared beyond the central fountain in a white coat – a tall man, hawk-nosed, with a neat moustache. He took Robert's hand warmly.

'Mr Grant – very good of you to come all this way to see us.' The words were expected, formal, precise. But there was warmth in his precision. 'Always appreciated your articles in the *Express*. Particularly your Western Desert reports. Superb. Nothing so dramatic here, I'm afraid. Though there are one or two things may interest you . . .'

'I'm sure, Major. Though it's not really war – it's the people that interest me, us . . .' They understood each other at once.

Moving from the huge hall they found themselves in an even larger and more ornate space, with marble pillars and friezes decorated with hefty Teutonic nymphs and fauns bathing, disporting themselves among waterlilies and bulrushes. For this was not a gymnasium, as the Captain had said, but the largest of the old *kursaals*, a long, gently-sloping swimming pool, empty now, but filled instead with a score of hospital cots.

'Rather makeshift,' the Surgeon-Major told him. 'But we've just had a lot of new arrivals this morning, terrible condition many of them. We've had to put some of them in here temporarily.'

Stepping down into the shallow end of the pool Robert moved among the patients, wrapped in grey Army blankets, two medical orderlies attending them; there was a smell of ether, of some strong disinfectant, in the air. He gazed at the wan faces – old peasant men, crones, some young children, all with the same quite vacant, uncomprehending faces – incarcerated, terrorized by the Germans for years and now once more imprisoned by the liberating forces. These people no longer had any idea of where they were or what was happening to them. They were worse off even than the citizens of Dortmund. These people no longer knew what life was about at all, had lost even the obsession of aimlessness.

'Where are they from?'

'Slovakia mostly. Had a rough time. First with the Germans, then the Russians. And then a long journey – taken them months to get here. But these are the few lucky ones . . .'

They moved down the gentle slope towards the deep end of the pool. Robert saw an old peasant woman, still wearing a spotted headscarf, out of her cot, kneeling, apparently praying over the cot next to her, where a huddled shape lay, the face invisible.

'Now here's an interesting case I'd like to show you – just came in this morning – give you an idea what these people have been through. A woman from one of the Nazi concentration camps. We'll get the interpreter. Corporal?' He turned to one of the orderlies. 'Where's that Slovak interpreter? Should be with us. Can you find him, please?'

'A concentration camp – that old woman kneeling?'

'No. The younger one beyond. That's her friend Anna with whom she came in. We don't know who she is – seems to have lost her memory. Doesn't speak any Slovak – doesn't really speak at all. Except a few words of English – that's the strange thing. Here, I'll show you – the tattooed number mark inside her arm, the first we've had here, certainly from one of the concentration camps.'

They moved over to the far cot. Robert saw the shape beneath the blanket, an arm lying over the top, but the face invisible, turned away to the side.

'No need to wake her,' he told the Surgeon-Major. But, as if at the sound of his voice, the woman turned her head slowly round, her greasy, matted hair twisting over the pillow, neck thin as a swan's, a death's head staring up at him.

It was Hetty.

Robert's head began to buzz, the swimming pool walls, at the deep end now, beginning to shift and tilt, as he heard the voices again, the brash soldiers' choir belting out, 'We plough the fields and scatter . . .' He started to sway, so that Major Fields had to steady him.

'All right?'

Robert, regaining control, at once knelt down by the cot. 'Hetty?'

Her big blue eyes were the only really recognizable thing left in the wreck of her face, which was scarred, pock-marked, grey, the skin drum-tight over the sharp bones. And she seemed to recognize him, but with a quite unexpected anger in her expression, a malignancy which astonished him.

'Hetty?' He repeated her name more urgently.

'Yes,' she said finally, faintly but with a bitterness that made him shudder.

'You see,' the Major said enthusiastically. 'I told you – she speaks some English. Extraordinary.'

15

'Ask her how the other woman got to Slovakia.' Robert, sitting with the peasant woman, the Slovak interpreter and Surgeon-Major Fields in his office, waited while the man translated his question, listening to the woman's response, before the interpreter turned back to him.

'The woman here, Anna – she was a farmer's wife. They had a hill farm in northern Slovakia, east of Cadca, way up in the Beskid mountains – that's part of the Tatras. This other woman – she calls her Eva, the "French woman" – arrived one day at the farm last February, she thinks it was, dying – of cold, hunger. Said she'd escaped from a German camp at Oswieckiem, fifty miles north of the border, in Poland. Anna and her husband took her in and hid her in the hay store – hiding her from the German patrols and the Slovak quislings, the Hlinka Guards. She got better gradually, very slowly . . .'

'And then? What then?'

The interpreter resumed his work before returning to Robert. 'Then the Russians came into Slovakia – from the east and the north. Fighting, raping, pillaging. There was panic everywhere. The Russians went up into the hills, the Tatras, pursuing fleeing Germans, Slovak collaborators, the Hlinka Guards. A group of these Guards had forced themselves into Anna's farmhouse, taking refuge. A Russian patrol tracked them there. There was a fight, a lot of shooting. The Russian patrol overwhelmed the place in the end – and of course assumed this woman and her husband, along with Eva in the hay store, were Nazi collaborators as well. They took them all down to Cadca – beat them, imprisoned them, tortured them. All the men were finally killed or executed. But the two women, Anna and the "French woman",

Eva, were spared. Just raped, very badly treated. Eventually they escaped, when the Russian troops moved on from Cadca. The two women, with a group of other Slovaks, moved west into Bohemia then, finally getting over the border into Germany, first to a D.P. camp in Swabia and then here.'

'And the French woman's husband? She had a husband – what happened to him?' Robert asked. 'Ask her.'

'He died, she told her, during their escape from Oswieckiem,' the interpreter said after a further few minutes. 'She told her they'd run into a German patrol, north of Zywiec. They were crossing the Sola river. The Germans fired at them as they dodged over the ice – they hit him, but missed her. She fell into the water and got across. That's what she told Anna here. They could only speak in bad German, both of them, so she's not certain if she's got it right.'

'Thank her, will you?' Robert said to the interpreter. 'Thank her very much for looking after my friend. And tell her I'll make arrangements – with the Major here – for her to be properly resettled, and have money, when I get back to London.'

'Oswieckiem,' Robert said to the Major after the interpreter and Anna had left the office. 'That's Auschwitz.'

'Auschwitz? I thought no one had got out of there alive, let alone escaped from it.'

'How ill is she, Major?'

'Not one thing, more like half a dozen. Malnutrition, exhaustion. Remains of frostbite on her toes and fingers. She's also suffering the after-effects of smallpox. You can see those pock marks. Not to mention the cuts and abrasions everywhere, barely healed. And then of course, what with being raped and all the other appalling treatment, there's the mental trauma. She can't really speak, as you saw. And she's lost her memory. It's lucky you found her here. And recognized her. I'd never have known who she was or what to do with her. She'd just have ended up in some German lunatic asylum, never to be heard of again. As it is, she's alive. And thanks to you, now that we know about her, she's curable – with proper attention.'

'London?'

'Obviously. But there's no chance of our getting her there—'

'I think I could get her flown out, with the RAF.'

'Perhaps, with your contacts – at the *Express*. What an extraordinary story you have there – if it's true. An Englishwoman, escaping from Auschwitz. What did you say her name was? I'd like it for my records.'

'Cordiner. Henrietta Cordiner. And Irish, not English. You might have known her better as "Laura Bowen". She was a big cinema star twenty years ago.'

The Major searched his mind. 'No, can't say I do. But then I'm no great cinema-goer.' He looked out of the window at the line of acacia trees bordering the long avenue, their branches stirring in a faint breeze, a few leaves dropping, swirling up again in the wake of a jeep tearing up the hill. 'More interested in facts – in my work.' He leaned back in his chair, thinking. 'And they're really more interesting – aren't they? – when you think of your friend's escape . . .'

Robert walked back up the avenue alone five minutes later, passing through the perimeter fence and sentry post back into the main Army camp. He stopped at the little Gothic church, hesitating a moment before going inside.

The choir had gone. But the organist was still there up in the gallery, invisible, playing a Bach organ prelude, the sound gradually swelling up, before reaching dazzlingly repeated crescendoes, so that the windows shook and the church seemed about to burst apart.

He stood there, at the back beneath the gallery, the evening sunlight, low down now, flooding directly through the open porch door. He sat down and listened to the triumphant music.

He had not taken it all in yet – not at all. Ten days before he had confirmed everything, a fresh start with Léonie, just the two of them, a whole future for them both at Summer Hill. But now there were three of them again. Was he at the end of something? Or the beginning? Or was he – as so often before with these two women – at an end and a beginning, a fearful balance, inextricably held between them, all three once more forming a precarious cat's cradle?

Hetty stayed on at the D.P. hospital for another few weeks while Robert completed his work in north Germany. Then, returning to Bad Oeynausen very briefly, and finding how she had recovered a little of her memory and health, he arranged to have her flown to London with the RAF, before he hurried on to Berlin and then Munich for the final two weeks of his assignment. Meanwhile, unable to telephone Summer Hill, he had sent a cable, and then a letter, to Léonie and Dermot, telling them the astonishing news, without hearing anything back from them as he continued his travels.

So it was, returning to London and going straight to the Royal Free Hospital without calling at his flat down the road in John Street, that he found Léonie, alone with Hetty, in a private room there. He seemed to have interrupted some intimacy as he opened the door – Léonie sitting on Hetty's bed, leaning away from her quickly.

'Darling!' Léonie jumped up. 'Here at last – we've been so waiting for you.' She stood up, embracing him, while Hetty, propped up on her pillows, looked at him with perhaps not quite so joyful an expression. He had

666

brought a spray of pink and mauve chrysanthemums for her at the corner of High Holborn. But he held them now, absentmindedly, at a loss. Quite expecting to see Hetty alone, he felt an intruder, at a disadvantage – Hetty already much-visited, obviously by Léonie, surrounded by little gifts, cards, books, even a half-bottle of champagne – whereas he was a late-comer at this celebration. He made the best of it, giving Hetty her flowers, kissing her forehead.

'So,' she said, echoing his thoughts, 'late for the p-party! We were waiting. Now we can open the champagne.' He noticed at once the very slightly tense and petulant tone to her voice.

'I couldn't get back from Berlin any sooner—'

'Never mind – you're here! That's the great thing.' She looked up at him. There was a haughty self-sufficiency in her expression. She had recovered in an extraordinary way – mind quite restored but in a pert, sharp, dismissive manner.

'You certainly look better.'

And she did. And so did Léonie, even more so. She was alight, alive in a way Robert had not seen in her for years, all her long depressions lifted in this miraculous return of her friend. Hetty was still dreadfully thin, scarred, pock-marked. But there was a strange fire in her eyes – that bitter dominant look which he had first noticed in the hospital at Bad Oeynausen, increased in the interval. Yes, despite – or was it because of? – the appalling physical punishments she had undergone, there was about her now, in her set, harsh expression, something which he last remembered seeing in her years before, as a wilful child, a young woman, when she had been a great picture star, that time in Egypt.

All her old domineering arrogance had returned, Robert saw. At Bad Oeynausen he had put it down to that temporary feeling of elation, of *Schadenfreude*, which

667

survivors of great tragedies often feel. But now he saw it was no temporary characteristic. Hetty, abandoning all her reforms, had changed once more. And so, too, as part of this change – and because Léonie owed her life to her – Hetty held her once again in thrall.

Robert sensed this clearly. It explained his sharp initial feeling when he had first arrived in the room, of being an intruder. It was all perfectly clear – these submerged longings between the two of them, lying on the air, an air of celebration, warmth, joyous renewal – where he was loved, but not essential, where Hetty, always the survivor, the joker come up once more untimely, had returned to trump his suit and regain Léonie. He might as well have walked out of their lives there and then, he thought. But he did not.

'Oh yes!' Hetty said a few weeks later, when all three of them, with Dermot, were back in Summer Hill sitting by the first of the autumn fires in the big drawing room. 'It was *Madame Butterfly* that saved me!' She looked over at Léonie. Then she turned to Robert, with that same bright dizzy look which he had noticed in London. But now it was more obvious. There was madness in her eyes. 'Wouldn't have survived otherwise, not a chance. It was that first week, after we arrived. The *blockowa* – our block chief, the bloody Polish bitch – said was there anyone among us new arrivals who sang or played music? I put my hand up. So did Rosa – she played the accordion. It was for the camp orchestra, can you imagine. So we were taken over to another block, warm, much more comfortable, where the *kapo*, the head of the women's orchestra, Alma Rose, auditioned us. I was shaking with fear, no idea what to do. Then it came to me: *Madame Butterfly* – of course! Those duets, Léa, we used to do here – you remember? "*Te voglio bene . . .*"'

'How could I forget?' Léonie looked at her happily.

'Well, I did it – sang and played it, doing both voices. And they took me. And Rosa. And from then on it was much easier. We had fairly decent clothes and *shoes* – you've no idea how important a pair of even half-decent shoes were there. In the winter – you were dead in a week without them. Anyway, from then on we played every morning and evening, on a sort of bandstand by the main gates of Birkenau, while the labour details marched in and out. And then there were the formal concerts, every month, for the SS officers. Hoess, the head of the camp, usually came, and his deputy Aumenier and Dr Mengele and our *Lagerführerin* Mandel – these *savages*: they had to have music, can you imagine? Classic and *schmaltz*, Beethoven and the Beer Barrel Polka. And it all had to be done *perfectly*. And they had to have new music, new songs at every concert. So the copying was a frantic business. Orchestrating it, getting all the parts out, absolutely endless business, sixteen, eighteen hours a day. Rosa did a lot of that . . .'

'And all this, while the others – were going up in smoke?' Robert asked quietly.

'Oh yes, we knew all about *that*,' Hetty said off-handedly. 'Almost from the word go. The chimneys, the absolutely foul smell when the wind changed. But no one talked about it. You didn't talk about that in Birkenau. If the *kapos* or the SS heard you mention it – you were off into the ovens yourself. So you just did everything, but everything and *anything*, to stay alive, to make sure you weren't in the next selection. Or that you didn't get a note wrong at the next concert. Because if you did, Alma Rose – well, you'd be sacked from the orchestra. And that meant back to the labour blocks. And people didn't survive there for more than a month or two. And then there was always the rumour that Hoess was going to close down the orchestra. And that would have been sure death for us, as well. So you forgot about the others,' she said casually. 'You just thought of your own survival, nothing else.'

Robert was surprised, even horrified, by Hetty's insensitivity over all this. So, he saw, was Dermot. He was not sure about Léonie. Hetty had certainly changed completely. Hers was not the natural elation of the survivor at all. This heartlessness was the reason for her survival. Hetty had survived Auschwitz because she had regained all that steel-hard domineering need to win, that riding rough-shod over people, which had often characterized her early life and made her a great picture star. It was obvious: a matter of sink or swim in Auschwitz, Hetty had rediscovered all those quite ruthless characteristics of hers, abandoned before in her various renunciations and reforms – had swum, while the others, in millions, had gone up in smoke.

She continued her story in the same almost lively vein until she came to the events leading up to her escape, when some of the fire went out of her voice and she paused. 'Perhaps we wouldn't have gone through with the escape, if we'd known how close the Russians were getting to the camp. But the orchestra was about to be disbanded, we'd heard. And Pierre was getting desperate. He'd survived well enough in the early months, as a doctor in the main camp, and he could move around fairly freely – he had a black triangle – so I saw him quite often. But then Mengele got on to him, forced him to work in his "surgery" . . .'

She paused, as if about to comment on this Mengele's operations. But she dismissed the idea, as not part of her story, continuing in her bright, increasingly exalted mode. 'Anyway, it was my idea, getting away, because I suddenly had the opportunity. One of the senior SS officers, Oberscharführer Linz he was called – something different from the rest, educated, been at university in Bonn, though he was still a brute – he took a fancy to me. I got to know him – he had the overall responsibility for the concerts, had a house next the camp. He wanted to sleep with me, said his wife was going to be away. I agreed – on one condition, if he beat me in a fencing duel . . .'

'A duel? But why?'

'I'd seen the scars on his face – knew he'd gone in for that sort of thing as a student. It was our only chance. I'd spoken to Pierre about it. We needed his uniforms, you see. The vain brute – he had dozens of them, in the house. So when his wife went away and the servants were out for the evening – that's what happened. He agreed. Said he'd arrange the swords – the *Schläger* sword the students use there.

'The plan was simple enough. If I won I'd kill him – and take the uniforms. Get dressed in one and take another back for Pierre. And then we'd simply walk out of the main gate that same night. Pierre spoke German fluently. And I'd have little or nothing to say. After all, we'd be two senior SS officers leaving the camp – none of the guards would dare question us. And I'd fixed up all the make-up for myself, no problem playing the part. Then we'd have the civilian clothes which we'd got together – beneath the uniforms. If it worked it'd be because of the sheer simplicity of it all. Quite a few others tried to escape – and one or two succeeded. But they were always caught, either before they got out of the camp at all or a few days later. And usually because their plans were too difficult, complicated. They hid out after evening roll call, between the two perimeter fences, in a big wood pile several times. But the dogs got them. Nobody had ever even tried just walking out of the main gate – and one reason was that no prisoner could ever get hold of or hope to mock up a complete senior SS officer's uniform. But now I had the chance of doing just this – and I took it. Nothing to lose. We were both of us desperate. We knew we'd certainly be killed, one way or another, if we stayed in the camp. The orchestra was definitely going to be closed down. And they wouldn't have let Pierre survive, after what he'd seen of Mengele's work. They were gassing and burning more than ever that winter, furiously, knowing the Russians were closing in on them. And I'd recovered. I was quite fit. We got special food in the orchestra. And I'd been practising with a stick for several weeks beforehand. This was our only chance. And far better to die fighting than being pushed into the gas chamber.' Her eyes were alight with a manic energy, living again now all the risks she had lived through then.

'But the Colonel?' Robert asked. 'Had he no suspicions – when you suggested this duel?'

'No. I told him I'd done it in France, with foils, when I was young. He liked the idea, in his twisted mind – quite certain he'd win and then have all the more pleasure in taking me afterwards. He was thrilled by the idea really. And he should have won. I'd never fenced with those broad *Schläger* swords before, like a bayonet, with a great soup plate thing as a hand guard. You chopped with it, more than parried or lunged. But I *did* win – he was just fighting to sleep with me. I was fighting for my life – and Pierre's.'

'What – what happened?'

'We fought in the basement of his house, alone. He'd sent the servants out beforehand so as to have me at his leisure afterwards . . .' She paused, an ugly look in her eyes.

'So – tell them what happened, Hetty!' Léonie, who had heard all this before, was anxious that Hetty, her protégée now almost, should display the full extent of her prowess.

'He laughed – that's what happened, which infuriated me. And he took it all too easily. To begin with. He wasn't used to lunging – that's not the German way – just parried my blows and chopped back now and then, not very seriously, playing with me. I knew he wouldn't be prepared for the lunge himself, so I held it back, my strong card. And when it came – well, he'd left himself open, tip of the sword went straight through his shirt. Then he started to fight, furiously, and it was touch and go for a while. But the first wound, you see! He was bleeding badly. He was too late . . .'

Hetty paused on a note of triumph. 'It was all fairly plain sailing then. Absolutely no trouble getting out of the camp – they just saluted us sharply. And we got right down near to the Slovak border all right, in about a week, travelling only at night in the freezing cold, until we had to cross the Sola river – when we ran straight into a German patrol. They were in the bushes on our side, resting, smoking. We more or less crashed into them. They were so surprised we were able to get away across the river, over the ice on one side, until they shot Pierre. They were shooting all round us, but wildly in the dark. They missed me. I stayed with Pierre, tried to pull him with me into the water, hoping he was only slightly wounded. But he wasn't, just pretending to be – kept shouting at me to go on, pushing me into the water. I fell into it. The current took me away down-river. I got to the far bank somehow – about half a mile downstream. Got clean away then. The dogs couldn't track me in the water. It was terrible.' She ended her story suddenly, curtly, almost viciously, then completely dried up, staring round her in a vacant, chilling way.

In the autumn days that followed at Summer Hill, as
Hetty slowly recovered and now that she was safe at last
in her old home, something snapped in her mentally.
She was either quite silent or else her manic ramblings
increased. Her mind began to wander – bitterly, horrify-
ingly – among vile things.

Now that she was no longer under the daily threat of
extinction, a pus of anger broke from her, which she
fingered through, haphazardly resurrecting all the
repressed memories, the horrors she had undergone, and
much more witnessed, in the camp.

Walking with Dermot slowly down the old monkey
puzzle avenue, or with Robert and Léonie on the porch
steps, or with Léonie alone, back in her primrose bedroom, she would suddenly come out with, and elaborate
on, some spectacularly brutal detail, speaking of it not
with sanity or sympathy but with cruel emphasis, as if
she had taken on the role of one of the SS guards herself
– the vivid, bloodied images intruding on the lovely
autumn air around Summer Hill like visions from hell.

'. . . they brought back the two who'd escaped a few
days later – the dogs got them of course. The SS had
their drums out as usual, all of us paraded in front of
Hoess and Auminer. Then they were strung up on the
gallows, with only a six-inch drop. They struggled for
minutes on end, gasping for breath. We had to stand
there for a whole hour, watching them sway . . .

'He was called "Ivan the Terrible", a huge man, one
of the Russian *kapos*. He and two other of his *kapo* friends
used to have competitions to see which of them could kill
someone with just *one* blow. They'd choose just anyone,
any group they happened upon. Ivan always won . . .

'Down at the ramp once, with a transport just in – we

had to play there that day for some reason: the SS guard took the baby from the woman's arms – the baby'd been crying – and just dashed it to the ground. The dogs started to eat at it.'

All these vignettes were made the worse by being offered so casually, coldly, objectively – or else in a voice of rising frenzy, eyes wide and staring, as she bunched her hands, and cracked her finger joints. And when Robert tried to soften her approach to these memories, to calm her tortured spirit, she laughed at him.

'You – you've no idea! You weren't there,' she spat at him. 'You can't understand. No one can, if they weren't there.'

'Yes. But now it's over, Hetty. You're back, safe—'

'It's *not* over!' She was angrier still. 'Never! It never will be.'

Robert spoke to Dermot one morning, as they walked along the river drive on a squally September day. 'I suppose it's obvious,' he said. 'All a reaction. Now that she's survived she feels desperately guilty – about all the others who didn't. Can't face her own survival. And it shows up in this mad way – almost relishing the horrors, trying to immerse herself in them now, punish herself – suffer now for all that she didn't suffer herself at the time. And then there's Pierre. You notice? – apart from that first time, she doesn't talk about him at all. Hasn't really begun to think about that, accept his loss.'

'She needs attention.' Dermot looked out at the stormy water.

'Yes. Just the sort she had from Pierre. And Pierre isn't here any more.'

'Someone then.'

'Yes. But who? Léa and I – we'll have to go back to London soon.'

'I'm not much good at that sort of thing. I'll try . . .'

Robert and Dermot understood the apparently

hopeless situation. But Léonie, when Robert talked to her alone, was much more optimistic.

'So you do see, don't you?' Robert said. 'What's happened.' And he repeated his diagnosis of Hetty which he had given to Dermot.

'Yes, of course I see all that,' she replied sharply.

'You don't seem to have seen it. You seem to go along with her, when she talks in this mad cold way—'

'I *do* see!' she interrupted him vehemently. 'I know her better than anyone else. She's suffering all the horrors now that she didn't then, and all the guilt. Of course! But she doesn't need another doctor or psychiatrist. She needs *me!*'

She looked at Robert defiantly. And he thought, yes, he'd been right in his initial intuitions at the London hospital a few weeks before. Once more Hetty had come between him and Léonie. Once more Léonie was about to be dragged into the maelstrom of Hetty's life. But this time he mustn't let it happen. He had made things up so well with her – this time he wouldn't lose her. He would fight – for Léonie's life, for his. And Hetty, however much he understood and sympathized with her, would have to take second place.

They were picking their way through the overgrown rock garden, the paths wild with blackberry briars. Léonie stopped to pick the over-ripe fruit, suddenly unconcerned with Robert. He watched her – the slightly chunky figure in a patterned smock dress, still with that lovely toss of silk-fine hair, greying now: an air of abundance about her, fruit-filled, almost as he remembered her that time they had first met in Paris, in the hall of her father's house in Passy, when she had looked at him, with such candour, as if certain then of all the happiness that was to come to them – as it had, as it could have gone on coming, but for Hetty. Yes, he would fight for her.

He said to her in the heavy silence, with no fight in his attitude or voice, speaking evenly, calmly. 'Léa, if you go that way with Hetty again – you'll never escape, not this time. You know that . . .'

Léonie swallowed a blackberry, offered him one. 'Oh, Robert, what do you mean?' she said lightly, equally reasonably. 'She *needs* help. And how could I not, after what she did for me – taking my place with the Gestapo in Paris, and in that terrible camp. There's no question.'

'Let's not go through all that again. You know perfectly well what I mean. Helping her is one thing. But you want her again as well –'

'It's *you* starting all that again, not me. Starting the old jealousy thing.'

'No. It's not jealousy. Just I know you too well – when you get involved with Hetty it's all or nothing. Seen it before. The obsession. You lose touch with reality. You two together – you won't have time for anyone else.'

She turned and faced him, herself calm still, a touch of pity for him in her expression. 'Anyone else? You mean you, don't you? As if *you* couldn't be included. As if one can only love one person at a time. But don't you see – if not jealous – how small-minded that attitude is? Always told you that. It needn't be either/or. It can be *all* of us, here at Summer Hill. You and I. And Hetty. And Olivia and Dermot . . .'

'So you've always said – making a crowd of it. But it'd really only be you and Hetty in the end.'

'It's just your immaturity that stops it, Robert. I've always known that, too!'

They were arguing now – a deep anger, all sorts of bitter emotion, rising in them. They were back where they had left off, when they had parted nearly ten years before in Hampstead. But Robert regained his control.

'It's not immaturity, Léa. Temperament, yes, mine and yours. And they're different, that's all. Of course we should help her – and I don't object to your loving her. But I'm just not interested – never have been – in sharing you with her.'

'Ah!' Léonie could not restrain the sneer in her voice. 'Not *able*, you mean.'

He shook his head. 'You see, you're losing touch already. Because a person doesn't want something it doesn't automatically mean that they fear it, or aren't capable of it. It can just as well be because that "thing" runs quite against the grain of their nature. It doesn't run against your nature. But it does mine. It's not a question of weakness or strength, nor even morals. It's just a fact: your inclinations are not mine.'

She listened. Or rather she half listened, half agreeing, half not. She was on a knife-edge of impending decisions, and she hardly knew this either. As regards Hetty, she had given herself over once more to what she simply felt.

'And can we ever really change our character?' Robert went on. 'I doubt it. Look at you. Look at Hetty – back in all her old domineering ways again. Oh, this time she has a real excuse for it. But that's really part of her true nature as well – the need to dominate, exploit, hurt, for all that happened long ago to her. And that's what's happening now. She's hooked you again, with this cast-iron excuse of her terrible suffering. And that I can't live with in you – your hidden, obsessive thing again for Hetty. I can't live with that. That's too much against the grain.'

Léonie, refusing to admit the truth of any of this, as she always had with Robert, made no answer. Instead she changed the topic to one in which she could be sure of her ground and could thus renew her attack. 'And you? What about you and Hetty? You see nothing hypo-critical there? As if you don't . . . as if you hadn't loved her?'

'I did. And I do. But it's not that sort of love. I have

that for you now. Why won't you see that, before it's too late, and come with me?'

They had pushed on through the jungle of the rock garden, pulling briars aside, but now they had come to an impasse in the wilderness. Léonie turned back, taking a thorn from her hand.

'You're making it either/or again.'

'Yes.'

'That's blackmail!'

'No – I've tried to explain. It's just fact.'

Returning to the high lawn, they stood beneath the cedar tree, looking over the valley in the late sunlight, the house beneath them, covered in Virginia creeper, golden-yellow above the porch: the house, full of warmth and promise, where everyone could be happy.

Robert picked at the bark of the cedar, taking a bit in his hand, putting it to his nose, smelling all his years at Summer Hill. He was not just losing Léonie then, he knew. He was losing this house, his home, as well. And it was this that finally made him angry – this impending loss of his birthright – when Léonie said to him, 'Fact or blackmail, it amounts to the same thing.'

'For you. Not for me. And that's really what it's all about, isn't it? Always was, when you and Hetty get together. Always is with lovers. They just can't get to see anyone else's point of view.'

He put the bit of cedar bark in his pocket and started to walk down the wild lawn, back to the house.

'You don't love me!' she shouted after him. 'If you did, you'd *see* my point of view – over Hetty.'

He turned to her briefly, bitterly. 'It's not a point of view, Léa – it's just a blind obsession.'

He walked on alone towards the house.

He had lost Léonie, he thought, as he sat in a window seat, taking the train back to Dublin next morning. He had tried to make a fight for her. But you could not regain someone in the grip of such a fierce emotion – the need to sacrifice, to love, the need to return to their real nature. He had lost her, Hetty, Summer Hill. Or as good as lost it all. No doubt he would visit from time to time. But he would be a supernumerary now in the house. Hetty had regained her home once more, and that was right. But *he* had lost his home – and his wife. And that seemed atrocious.

He had hinted at nothing of this to Hetty when he had spoken to her alone before leaving. 'It's simply . . . I have all this work to finish in London. These German articles. And I must see Olivia in Dublin, before she gets started at Trinity.'

'Yes, well, you might have stayed on here a bit. Still, I don't know what would have happened to me – if you hadn't found me at that D.P. camp. I'd lost my memory, everything. Never have got back here at all. Or my wits back. Thank you . . .'

He had found it difficult to look at Hetty then, appalled by the brazen expression on her face, which quite belied her last words. Yet he did not think she was taking any victory from his departure, any triumph in having regained Léonie once more. Her expression was entirely self-serving – a busy, frustrated look, with something malign about it. Her face had reminded him of her mother's then. Frances had had just the same sort of embittered, self-justificatory look in her eyes, so often towards Hetty herself, when they had been children together at Summer Hill. And now that same expression, years later, had come to be levelled at him.

He looked out of the train window, at the stooks of corn piled up in a field, carts taking it away to a threshing machine and a smoking traction engine in the distance, a plough pulled behind a tractor in another field, the earth turning black in long furrows. 'We plough the fields and scatter, the good seed on the land,' he said quietly, remembering the choir at Bad Oeynausen six weeks earlier. And now he knew why he had felt that appalling emotion, when he had first heard the hymn outside the church – the feeling of someone walking over his grave. The message there had not, indeed, been one of celebration for harvest home. It had been a foretaste of the bitter harvest he was to reap, in finding and rescuing Hetty half an hour later – which would lose him his home.

In Dublin he met Olivia, just about to start her first term at Trinity, his old college. As a treat he took her to Jammets, near the front gates of the College, a French restaurant, done out in the belle époque style, all gilt, velvet and mahogany, where they had a table under a great mural of Diana the huntress, flying across the blue empyrean, bow in hand, pursuing a golden hind. Olivia, in a new tweed skirt and fine cotton blouse which she had bought out of money her father had given her, at Brown Thomas's store up the road, was beside herself.

'Oh, Daddy! This is such fun. I've not seen a place like this – ever, I think. And certainly never eaten like this!' She scanned the menu dizzily, unable to take it all in.

'Yes. It's good. Used to eat here. Oh, just once or twice when I was up at Trinity myself and in the money.'

'Did modern history, didn't you?'

'Yes. But modern languages will do you even better. Especially since you already have such good French. I'm so glad you're here . . .' He smiled at her, but it was not as full a smile as he would have liked.

At first, putting a good face on things, he gave only the merest hint as to what had passed at Summer Hill. But Olivia, knowing all too well the problems between her parents, and older and wiser in years thereby, soon sensed what had happened – soon realised how broken her father was behind his welcoming façade. And, loving him, she was hurt by his hurt. Yet, sharing some of his restrained temperament, she hoped not to show too much of her feelings over this – or to show them, at least, but not in too obvious a way.

So she said, looking through the elaborate menu more carefully, 'Daddy, I've never seen anything like it! Oysters and duck *à l'orange*. Can it be real? – after years of Spam and dried eggs?'

'It's real. Though I've forgotten it all myself.'

'Well, you must eat it, eat it *all* then!'

'Olivia—'

'No. I mean treat yourself as well as me. You like food, don't you? I remember—'

'Yes, but not to make a pig of myself.'

'Well, let's *nearly* make pigs of ourselves. You deserve it . . .' She looked at him tenderly.

Her ploy had the desired effect. Robert did like good food, had tasted nothing of it in nearly six years. He brightened under the idea of being a bit lavish – but more particularly under his daughter's warm yet concerned gaze.

They ordered Galway oysters, pâté de foie gras, the duck *à l'orange* and a bottle of vintage Moët to go with it all. He gave the menu back to the elderly waiter in a wing collar and rather threadbare dark jacket. The food, the mood, were both supremely French. But not the waiter or his accent. He spoke in the broadest, sprightly Dublin tones when he said, 'Ah, that'll be fine, sir. I couldn't have chosen betther meself.' Robert smiled at Olivia after he had left.

'It's wonderful, isn't it?' she said. 'Dublin. And three years here. I couldn't be happier. But you must be, too, Daddy . . .' And, when the champagne came in its cooler and the bubbles frothed a little in their glasses, she lifted hers and said, 'It's all somehow . . . so jaunty here in Dublin, isn't it? Everyone, the people, the mood. Not like dreary England. Let's be jaunty from now on, Daddy.' And they were.

But later, before the coffee, she asked him – she could not restrain herself – for more details of what had happened at Summer Hill.

'It's Hetty, isn't it? That's the real reason for Mummy staying down there.'

'Well—'

'Of course it is. Mummy's like that, isn't she? It was just the same with her friend Jenny. I know it now. I didn't really understand it before.'

'Well, Hetty and your Mama were always very close – the closest friends, long before Jenny.'

'Yes, but you and Hetty were even *closer* friends, long before that – before Mummy ever came on the scene – on that island, as children, weren't you?'

'Oh yes.'

'So it's *cruel* of Hetty. Taking Mummy over like that again. Because that's what she's doing, isn't it?'

'In a way, yes.' He made a hopeless gesture. Then he reminded himself how they were to be jaunty. 'But you have to remember how much they owe each other. Mummy would almost certainly have been in that camp – and dead now – but for Hetty.'

'And Hetty? – what does she owe Mama?'

'Oh, everything – long before, when they were close. Everything. I don't think Hetty would ever have become the person she is but for Mama. Her support.'

'But Hetty's become *awful* – by all accounts!'

'So might you – if you'd been through Auschwitz. Anyway, there's nothing to be done about it.'

'Isn't there?'

'No. I've tried, often enough. And this time it was all the more difficult. Because now they've finally proved how right they are for each other, and how right they were all along. Fate. The other two have gone – Jenny and Pierre. So now it's obvious to them – they were made for each other.'

'But that's nonsense! This "fate" business – because what about you and me? And us? All three of us. Isn't all that more important to Mummy? We're not "fate". We're real. She's still married to you, still my Mama. What can she *think* she's doing – giving all that up?'

Olivia was angry now, startlingly angry. Robert tried to calm her. 'She doesn't think she's given it all up. She thinks I've done that. Running away. And I haven't. It's just I can't live with Mummy *and* Hetty at Summer Hill. So *I'm* the one to blame, in her eyes.'

'Well, that's worse nonsense on her part!'

'So it seems. To us. But we're not her. It's nonsense to us. These . . . obsessions . . . always seem so, to outsiders.'

'Obsessions? Sounds more like an illness to me.'

'Perhaps.' He shrugged. 'So perhaps they'll cure each other . . .'

Olivia slumped back on the velvet banquette, sighed, fiddled with her napkin. 'It's still nonsense. You're just being kind about it all, about Mummy.'

'What else can I be? I've been angry about it before. Oh yes. But that didn't help anybody. So that's all there is to be now – as kind as we can about it all.'

He did not say anything more for a moment. But then, seeing Olivia's wan face, he reached across and took her hand on the table cloth. 'Come on, don't be sad. You and I – remember? – we're going to be jaunty.'

She said nothing. But then suddenly, waking up and smiling a bit, gripping his fingers, she said, 'Yes, we will be. And if there isn't you and Mummy – there'll always be you and me.'

And with this Robert was bright at last. And they both had proper smiles for each other. And later, when the coffee came, he said, 'Would you like to try a special

Irish whiskey? They used to do one here, thirty years old or some such . . .'

'Yes,' she said, leaning back on the red velvet again, this time holding her head high. 'But Irish whiskey – in such a French restaurant?'

'Oh, they have everything here, in Ireland.' For a moment, after he had said this, he felt a spasm of sadness again. For he was losing everything in Ireland. But no, that was not true. Olivia would be here. He would see her, now and in the future. He had lost his home, his wife. But he had truly gained his daughter.

Robert was right. In the ensuing months, and the years that followed, Hetty and Léonie cured each other – for all their losses. At first it was a slow process. Luckily Hetty was still too frenzied then, with her violent memories of Auschwitz, to take in how she had, once more, destroyed Robert and Léonie's marriage. While Léonie, just as Robert had said to Olivia, reassured herself on this score by thinking how it was Robert, not she, who had broken things up.

Could he not see, quite objectively, how she *must* stay and help Hetty? – how Hetty's punishing daytime visions of the camp, her wicked commentaries on it and the far worse nightmares she suffered then and for years afterwards – how all this was directly due to her having abandoned Hetty in the Paris apartment? Could he not see, too, how she owed Hetty her life? For she doubted, even with all her SOE training, if she would have survived the Gestapo interrogations or the camp. Hetty, in doing both these things, had, as always, found a stronger heart than hers – found reserves, an extraordinary resilience against the worst life had to offer. Could Robert see none of this? Was he so morally and emotionally blind – so selfish?

And then on another, deeper emotional level Léonie returned to her old opinions about Robert. Why could he not have accepted her affection, her love for Hetty – and the fact that she loved him as well? Why could he not share in this loving? Robert, just as he had before, had broken this happy combination, when all three of them could have lived on at Summer Hill contentedly, had destroyed this obvious future in a house they all loved.

And this was simply his immaturity. Or his ridiculous puritan notions. Or both. She had not misjudged him, as she had told him in the old vine house. Unfortunately not. She had been right about him all along. People, she had to admit now, did not really change. And certainly she could not change herself now. She had remained true to her nature, had been quite prepared to love them both. But if Robert refused this natural scheme of things – well, then, that was his look-out. She would love Hetty alone.

And she did. As the months passed, autumn turning to winter, Hetty found a cure in this loving, her fevers and nightmares gradually subsiding, her health improving, memory and balance returning. So that soon, when the topic came up, she was able to talk quite rationally, as she and Lèonie thought, of Robert's defection.

'I suppose it's just his . . . childishness,' Hetty said one winter afternoon, echoing Léonie's thoughts. They were in the basement still-room, sorting through boxes of Cox's orange pippins, wrapping them in newspaper, before storing them away on racked trays, so that the air reeked of apples, a crisp autumnal fulfilment. 'You see,' Hetty went on, 'you have to remember, losing both his parents, he has this terrible need to possess things, undivided possession, of a house or a person. That's the feeling that secretly dominates in him: possession.'

'But why? When, really, he had both of us?' Léonie threw a bad apple away.

'Men find it difficult to share things,' Hetty said easily.

'Learnt that long ago, with Craig. And I lost that sharing feeling myself in the camp. We were like men there, most of us. Had to be. You took everything, anything *for yourself*. If you didn't you were dead. But with you . . .' She paused, an apple in her hands, smelling it. 'With you I'm getting back to the real me, getting back what I lost, in the camp, losing Pierre.' She wrapped the apple up and put it on the tray; the two of them like squirrels in the dark room preparing for a long hibernation. 'Sharing . . . whether we learn this, or just have the gift more naturally as women, I don't know. But we do. We have to share . . .'

'It's such a pity, though. About Robert.' A note of passion had come into Léonie's calm voice. 'Because we could both have shared things with him, too. Especially him,' she added bitterly.

Hetty looked at Léonie quizzically, noting this urgency in her voice, sensing how it reflected a real love she still had for Robert, when a stab of jealousy rose in her. But was she jealous of Léonie, whom she now possessed so completely once more? – or of Robert, recipient of this love, as she suddenly felt a pang of her own old love for him. And the thought, a possessive masculine thought, which remained, even now, part of her character . . . intruded on her next words.

'Yes, especially him. But, Léa, perhaps it's not so easy sharing, when it comes to it. Perhaps it's better when there are just two of us?' She gazed at Léonie anxiously, in that old way of years before, when she had wanted her exclusively, needed to dominate and possess her completely.

And Léonie saw this and, fearing loss, said at once, 'Yes, perhaps it's easier that way.'

They finished storing the apples and went upstairs, where the maid Bridget – now that Elly was getting slow on her feet – brought them tea by the big log fire in the drawing room. Aunt Emily mostly took tea in her room now, with her oatcakes, and Dermot was out for the day, shooting with some of the neighbours.

'Whatever about Robert,' Hetty said, leaning forward, settling a log, 'people's real feelings are so . . . difficult. And one just has to get on with things. We have to.' She looked up at her with such a vulnerable expression, that Léonie knew that everything she had done, everything she had decided, in losing Robert – all this had been worth it. She was right to be linked with this woman for as long as life was. 'We have a l-l-life together here, don't we?' Hetty went on. 'You and I. And Dermot and Aunt Emily. And Jack and Elly.' Léonie nodded.

And they did. What they had both shared in so passionately – in Dublin years before and with Fonsy O'Grady's troupe and momentarily in Egypt – was now returned to them as a permanence at Summer Hill: a life together – the two women regaining all that was lost between them – love, companionship, dependency, touch. So that sleeping or waking, with each other or apart, they wove as the years drew on those silken threads, the unique lines of the heart which can grow between people who are, indeed, made for each other.

Hetty no longer had to act parts to her old friend. She had lived all those parts now, and more. She no longer, in her old petulant ways and means, had to dominate her. She had done this already, with so many people, won out over so many things. She was a survivor. She had survived everything. And this was almost enough to satisfy her. But not quite.

As Robert had said – people never really change their deepest characteristics. And this was true of Hetty. There remained – indeed after her full recovery six months later it became a disruptive itch – some of her old arrogance, a frustrated ambition to create, to succeed, to dominate in one sphere or another. And this urge she could not repress indefinitely. It came to intrude now and then, upsetting the balance of their lives – in rows, misunderstandings. So that recognizing this, and seeing how, just as before, it could come to erode and destroy her relationship with Léonie, Hetty knew she must find some other outlet for this vivid, dangerous spirit of hers.

And she did. Going through all her old books and papers in the attics the following spring, she came across the novel she had begun years before, *Aquamarine*, the story of her early life in Domenica and Summer Hill. She took up the book again and by the autumn had completed it. She sent it to a London publisher who at once accepted it.

'How marvellous!' Léonie said when Hetty showed her the letter, the two of them sitting out on the porch after breakfast in the golden weather. 'Now – now we have everything!'

And they did.

epilogue

Robert, before the servants Pietro and his wife Maria came, and with nothing much better to do on the morning of his sixty-fifth birthday, went to his study desk in the Villa Serena and opened his journal, in which he wrote sporadically, remembering events in a jaunty way and generally bringing himself up to date by naming things, so to encourage the sense of his own otherwise rather isolated existence. The villa, designed to hug the almost sheer cliff-face, was built on a haphazard succession of different levels and extensions – not broad or tall but long, rather in the Spanish style, with a colonnaded serpentine terrace all along the front, set high up on Monte Marcello, facing the Poet's Gulf just south of Lerici on the Ligurian Riviera. He had bought this lovely maritime folly over fifteen years before, as a holiday retreat, just after he had married Catherine. But now she was gone, just a year before, and retiring from London he lived here on his own. Opening the ruled pages of the Italian school exercise book, taking out his old fountain pen, he started to write.

'*Crostini di Mozzarella, fritelle di Bel Paese, crostini di Mare, pizzette*,' I muttered first thing when I woke this morning, invoking Lucullan spirits, a litany of hot and cold *antipasti* running through my mind. The hot ones first – little rounds of baked bread and fritters garnished with seafood – for, though I saw from my window it was going to be midwinter warm today, it might start to cool early and it would be as well if Pietro and Maria had lots of piping-hot tit-bits on hand, along with the cold side dishes, of course: '*Prosciutto di Parma, Prosciutto di San Daniele*,' I addressed the sunrise, '*Salame di Felino, Lingua con Salsa Verde . . .*'

Splendid. I'd consider the other birthday dishes later, turning on my pillow – and it was only then that I felt the sick headache and remembered the nightmare. God! And I'd hoped that everything was going to be cloudless today, especially today, especially with so few complaints recently.

I've been pretty well lately, body and soul. So the headache and the bad dream surprised me. Perhaps I've been more worried than I care to admit by Olivia's not being here yet. She was due out on the Genoa flight yesterday. But fog had closed Heathrow down and she'd called to say she and William and Lottie hoped to get away first thing this morning, taking a hire car straight down as soon as she arrived. With any luck she'll still make the lunch party. Still, I suppose I wanted to be certain of her being here well beforehand, a little familial support against the impending crowd. Not that I'm expecting many outsiders. I think only Matteson, the consul in Genoa, and his pretty wife – and some stringer with *The Times* who said he *had* to interview me. The cheek of it! A paper I never much cared for – now gone quite to seed.

The other guests will be old friends. Hugh Latimer, of course – my publisher – amongst them. He and Molly spent Christmas in Rome, before going on to see Vesuvius – for some unfathomable reason. They're coming up on the *rapido* from Rome this morning. Of the rest of the guests – well, a dozen or more, English and Italian, people Catherine and I have come to know in this Lerici area, a few others I've come to know myself in the last year, having more or less retired here full time. Not that I mind living alone . . .

All the same, I'd like to have been sure of Olivia. She's had a difficult time this last year – what with her divorce and having to cope with the two children on her own. Still, that'll be another treat – seeing them before they go back to school. And lucky, too, that my bank account is fairly healthy, what with the royalties on that last African book, so that I was able to send Olivia a good whack of money this Christmas – which will more than cover all their air fares and so on. And then again I'll have all three of them with me out here afterwards to myself for nearly a week. No, Olivia could hardly have accounted for the nightmare.

Perhaps I'd slept with a crick in my neck all night, unable to right myself in the bed, like a sheep stuck on its back? That's possible. There's a stiffness about the top of my shoulders this morning. I'm sixty-five. No avoiding the fact.

But I shall certainly avoid it – and think about the celebratory wines instead. There's some quite decent champagne, though I've never really fancied that drink. Makes me burp, like an infant. Much better is the Barolo Classico I've been keeping – a lovely deep red-brown now, a 1955, just right at nearly ten years old. As for the white wine, I've tasted nothing better than Bertini's Frascati which I got half a dozen cases of before Christmas, a dozen bottles already chilling in the fridge. Pietro stacked them away there yesterday. At least I hope he did.

A sweet wine after the zabaglione? Well, I've never much cared for the local Cinque Terre, the famous Sciacchetra – liqueur-sweet, almost oily. And, besides, Pietro has got me something wonderful from Sardinia: an old Vernaccia – pale, gold, soft, but nothing cloying. Superb. Elixir of youth . . .

Yes, I'm far from being on my last legs. Though I sometimes find it a task to climb back up all the steps from the little bathing cove at the bottom of the cliff here. But I can still easily manage the shorter flight leading to the road above. I can even walk to the town if I've a mind to – and back. No trouble. After all, I crossed Africa only a few years ago, coast to coast, and quite a bit of it on foot. (Well, no, I mustn't lie – probably less than fifty miles actually on foot . . .) So, yes, I'm fit enough and don't believe I slept with a crick in my neck all night.

So why the bad dreams? No, let's be exact again: why the grotesque, excruciating, grinding nightmare? I thought I'd

done with that sort of mental agony years ago, that the
spirit on this last run in was finally calmed. And, yes,
it *has* been calmed. After Catherine died, a year ago,
things were difficult certainly. The dying, of course, though
it was quite quick and mostly painless – and the missing
her, which I don't suppose I have, or ever will get over.

But latterly, and apart from this, there's been a lot of real
peace for me out here this last year. Olivia divorced –
painful no doubt, but seeing the better side of it now,
because she really is better off without him; my
'memoirs' written – published in London today, in fact
to coincide with my birthday. And then, of course, last but
not least the knighthood! What a laugh! But a surprise,
too. I had that OBE after the war – services rendered
as a war correspondent and so on. And I'd thought that
was it. So yes, I was surprised – and moved, I suppose. Not
because I felt I deserved it (don't think I did), but because
I wished Catherine had been here to share it with me.
Though in fact, remembering her droll honesty in
everything, she might well have dissuaded me from
accepting it. ('Oh God, Robert! – not that. You know it's
all nonsense: a tin medal and a doll's ribbon, all
frou-frou and pink satiny in a box, a clout with a phoney
sword, gracious murmurings with HRH in that *heavy*
throne room, band of the Grenadier Guards crashing
through "Tales from the Vienna Woods" in the
background. Not you at all . . .') But I did accept it –
and no doubt will have to go through exactly the sort
of ceremony Catherine would have envisaged. Still, that
will be one more nice way to remember her, a
confirmation of her sudden nicely malicious wit – almost
Irish in that way. Though no one could have been more
English: the proverbial rose – small, compact, sweet,
peach-cheeked, that unflawed, creamy skin, so reserved
on the surface – which made her quick words and wit,
her sensuousness, all the more unexpected. I miss her.
Badly.

Still I have found peace out here at last. And perhaps I've

finally managed to come to terms with all my earlier
life, with Hetty and Léonie. Come to terms with Summer
Hill – with all that was won and lost there. I used to
think it was only these two people, this house, that could
ever give me real happiness. I was wrong. I was lucky
to find an even greater happiness with Catherine out here
at the Villa Serena – quite forgetting all the
disappointments, horrors, nightmares of the old days.
Yes, because of Catherine – but also in myself, finding
that jauntiness of spirit – the very word Olivia
recommended to me that evening together in Dublin, just
after everything had come apart for me at Summer Hill.
Yes, all that old *sturm und drang* was finally settled out here
in Italy, over the last fifteen years. So that I came to see
all that past with the two women and Summer Hill as
another man's life.

So why the horror again last night?

Have I, in my mind and scribbling my 'memoirs' out here
on the terrace in the sun these last years, simply
repressed all this painful past, conveniently forgotten
about it? It's true that I've written almost nothing about
Hetty and Léonie or the great house in these 'memoirs'
which are intended as a professional, not a personal,
account: my life as a reporter, war correspondent,
columnist, travel writer, author of sorts, all over the place
in the old days. Fine. But did I in fact keep out everything
in this autobiography that *really* mattered? No, surely
not. Autobiography must reflect one's *nature*. I'm simply
not a heart-on-the-sleeve sort of person. Not at all.

Now, let me think again about the party arrangements:
Pietro's *pièce de résistance* today – *Tartufi Bianchi*! That
wonderfully pungent, penetrating flavour and scent of
those rare white truffles he's managed to get hold of
from Turin, big as tennis balls, which he'll cook as *Filetti
di Tacchino Bolognese*, the truffles sliced very finely over
turkey breasts and ham, then cooked gently in butter
and the best grated Parmesan. This really is something.

Pietro did it for Catherine some years ago, as a special treat on *her* birthday . . .

But I must stop thinking about Catherine all the time. An indulgence. I could think of her most of the day without any trouble. Her and the happiness – and her not being here any more. Oh yes, I've faced the facts. The pain, the loss. It's simply that I won't beat my breast about it – not that I'm cold or that I've repressed things.

Anyway, when I finally got out of bed this morning, I felt better. The view out of the window – sharp blue sky over the bay, the Gulf a darker azure beyond, sunlight glittering on the white horses riding further out to sea. A day with an intense winter sparkle to it, the sort of atmosphere, so keen and bright, that you felt you could reach out and *touch* it – though that's the sort of sensuous idea and expression which would come much more naturally to Hetty than to me . . .

Robert paused in his writing. Here he was thinking of Hetty again, out of the blue, for no good reason. He got up and went to the kitchen, making himself a pot of coffee. But Hetty remained on his mind. Was this what the nightmare had come to tell him? – how he had avoided all the real issues, both in his life and his memoirs? But surely, he sought to persuade himself again, he was doing himself an injustice? He had never been that kind of writer. He had always dealt in facts, where there was some literary skill in their presentation no doubt, but little or no invention – he hoped. Nothing to be ashamed of there, he thought.

Yes, indeed, why should he ever have embarked on the treacherous slopes of 'truth telling' – the usually quite imponderable motives of private lives: all that dizzy confusion of high emotion when people, losing their heads, came to deal out hate and love like cards in a wild gambling game. He'd never been interested in that game. He'd had to play it with Hetty and Léonie long enough – had suffered it, and that was surely sufficient. Taking his coffee with him he returned to the study and his journal.

'No,' he continued these thoughts in the school exercise book.

I never enjoyed these sharp contradictions of emotion, as the other two seemed to. I've always believed that life should be susceptible to reason. The other two ran freewheel. I tended to keep in gear. Chalk and cheese. Though this didn't stop us from getting on in the old days. I have to admit – from falling in love and goodness knows what else. Rather the reverse: attraction of opposites, no doubt.

Well, all the confusion, this hot emotion, was in my 'lived' life, with them, not my written one, my 'memoirs'. And that, surely, was more than enough. Writing for publication in any sort of personal, intimate vein simply wouldn't have been me.

And there is another point: Hetty has done a lot of this 'truth telling' already, in her own writing, in many of her novels. She's just the sort of writer I'm not. That's always been her gift as a fine, intuitive novelist: fiction, where I've always worked with the facts. Yes, she's written extensively about all three of us, here and there throughout her novels – lightly or heavily disguised. But it's perfectly clear, to me at least, that it's us. We're all there, in our messy acts and emotions – the way we lived together, then didn't live, and lived again, and finally parted from each other.

Oh yes, at a distance, for Hetty, and Léa too, I've always remained the necessary third in that triangle – I can see that – necessary to support the other two corners, so that they've both kept in touch with me over the years, Hetty with her novels suitably inscribed – books to show me where I went wrong with them no doubt, all that I missed out on by not being more emotionally co-operative with them both. Books in this way as a sort of literary revenge? It's very possible. Or am I just being cynical, still hurt by it all, in my heart of hearts?

Perhaps this is true, for some of the dedications are full of real emotion towards me. However, the novels themselves – and this is what I'm really getting at – are filled with barely disguised incidents from my life with her, in Domenica, at Summer Hill, right up to my finding her in Germany after the war. And the same is true of the details of my life with Léonie, which Léa must have talked to her about in their years together. Hetty, though she has so much herself, always needed to feed on other people, for her insecurities, her imagined failures. She's a very autobiographical novelist.

So it's obvious – Hetty has written this personal part of my life for me in this way. And if anyone, some nosy biographer, ever thought it worth it, they could easily find me there, in her novels, along with Léonie, rising to the top in this manner, like cream in a dairy pan. Or perhaps, more honestly, like the fat you take off a stew, which you discard. For I've sometimes wondered how much I ever really meant to either of them – in terms of anything reasoned or reasonable – so obsessed have they always been with each other.

Or, again, is it me who's being unreasonable? Cynical? Hurt? For I did love them both – at different times, together. Can't deny that. Yes, there was love, on all sides, in different ways, times, places. What a strange nonsense it now seems. The three of us made up a droll caravanserai of love, each laden down with precious bales, deviously sold or bartered or swapped en route. Or wantonly lost in the sands, sometimes miraculously discovered again on a later journey. For years we all traded in emotions, haggled over its weights and measures, ran the silk road of kisses . . . But in the end – what disasters! So that I've come to think that the real urge we feel in love – is to end love, to be released from it, which is what I did out here at the Villa Serena:

released long ago from those two women who made my life so happy, yet finally agonizing.

So why the nightmare? Why shouldn't I just be happy now, freed from both of them at last, free from all the terrors, hopes and despairs of that past, free to enjoy what I've rescued from it all, by myself and with Catherine. And I've rescued a lot: Catherine, and a daughter I love dearly coming today with my two grandchildren, along with my old friend Hugh, and Molly, and the others. A knighthood, undeserved (but why worry about that? – someone has to get them); a lunch party with *Tartufi Bianchi* and Bertini's Frascati. Sixty-five, fit enough and still with my marbles. What more could one ask for?

What luck – if I were to die tomorrow – to have had all this life here at the Villa Serena, living high up, like a bird perched on this steep, bare cliff – a cliff that fists out and then subsides, running into this Poet's Gulf where Shelley drowned but which cradles me. Yes – and today so particularly to be grateful for: a midwinter sun still promising me things as I start out on my own midwinter. What more could one ask for? A small future, with few painful memories, no nightmares. 'Old men forget.' So be it. So very much be it.

He sipped his coffee. It had gone cold. He made another pot in the kitchen and took it out on to the terrace, warming in the sun now, the wicker chairs and table sheltered behind a tall glass windbreak. He sat down, gazing out over the bay. Small boats were returning after their night's fishing, the acetylene lamps doused on their bowsprits. 'Home is the hunter, home from the hill – and the sailor home from the sea,' he said to himself pleasurably.

Yet still he felt unsettled, nervy. And he knew why. He had avoided the crucial issue in his journal this morning – cleverly worked round it in every possible way. He had quite failed to face, to define, the nightmare itself. Here at least he was certainly avoiding an issue. This ghost, returned untimely, would have to be laid. Unwillingly he returned to his study desk.

'The nightmare,' he wrote. Then he felt the pain of it all over again, so that he paused. Then he hardened himself for the task.

> It was quite short, simple even. It was its grinding repetition that made it awful. Hetty's words – her much younger face and voice, fourteen or so, when she was hardly more than a child, leaning over me, the words stammered out again and again: 'You're n-not going to g-get out of it so easily! You're not going to g-get out of it!'

> But out of what? – for I wasn't *in* anything at that point. Both of us were in some open, quite unrecognizable space, a surrealist landscape, absolutely flat desert, with a highly coloured, enamel-blue sky. Hetty was standing above me. I was flat out on the bare earth, being pressed into it by some flimsy transparent material, thin gauze paper, the sort used in old flower presses. And these sheets were falling on me, one after the other, like great snowflakes, so insubstantial that I felt I could easily throw them off. But of course I couldn't, I was helpless, being suffocated by them, the sheets (pages from an empty book?) gradually pressing me underground – with Hetty's face then, that lovely wide brow, big oval blue eyes, locks of jet-black hair, becoming less and less clear, as she disappeared then, up into a flaming sky, but with her repeated words loud as ever: '. . . not g-going to g-get out of it, g-get out of it, g-get out of it!'

> Then she disappeared altogether in the flames and I was deep underground, forced down by these innumerable leaves of paper which, like papier-mâché, were now solidifying all round me and I was fighting not to be buried alive, the paper rapidly hardening like stone, so that I would soon be a fossil myself, dead and embedded in the earth forever.

Well, there's the nightmare. Seems pretty inconclusive, to say the least. Does it mean anything? Well, that Hetty always liked to tease and hurt me, at that age, when we were adolescent – there's that, obviously. But what was I not going to get out of? There's the question. Some responsibility to her? Or to Léa? Some sort of unfinished business there? That *I* have failed to finish – as the guilty party? Can't be. I did everything I could then, to keep Léonie, to hold her. I wanted her with me then. We'd just made things up. I loved her. It was she who insisted on going back to her old ways with Hetty.

Or is it some long-lost debt I owe *Hetty*, something unfulfilled there? – going right back to our childhood? Dreams, bad dreams especially, are often about this, aren't they? – traumas from childhood, unresolved. Well, the only thing unresolved between us then was my loving her. And I can't be blamed for that. The blame was hers, if anybody's, in that she didn't love me in return. Or, at least, she didn't then. That was much later, up in the children's garden, and by then it was *too* late. I was with Léonie.

And what of the fire? Why did Hetty disappear, like the Virgin in some cheap religious painting, clouds of fire, ascending heavenwards? What's one to make of that? Just a reflection of how much I idolized her, I suppose, the infatuation I had for her when we were young. So the whole dream is simply a reflection of how much she once meant to me, that's all – a reflection of all the pain that long infatuation brought to me. Yes, that's it. Just a confirmation of that. So obvious really. All over and done with now. I've faced it, written it down. Now I can sleep easy . . .

Pietro and Maria arrived ten minutes later, meeting Robert in the kitchen, profuse with birthday greetings and a bunch of red hothouse carnations. Some of the food for the birthday party was up in their car at the top of the steps. Robert, still in his dressing gown, helped them down with it. And soon, with this bustle about the Villa, he began to feel better – and better still when he had bathed and dressed.

Afterwards he looked at himself in the bedroom mirror: the old linen tropical suit, almost Edwardian in cut, a red carnation rampant, one of the last of his tailored, Egyptian blue cotton shirts, a nicely faded silk polka dot tie, the comfy brown brogues which Duckers in Oxford still made for him . . . Quite the English gentleman, he thought, adding simple gold cufflinks and a dash of Trumper's cologne about his temples. No one would know him now for the rough colonial boy, brought up and orphaned on a ruined citrus farm in the West Indies, a boy from nowhere, an island, a mere speck, lost in the middle of the wide Sargasso Sea . . . Quite the gentleman? Quite the Knight, he might rather say. Sir Robert Grant . . . it didn't really sound too bad. A lot of nonsense and vanity, of course. All the same, he felt very much better now, the headache dissolved, the bad dream quite forgotten. He moved out on to the terrace then, with the post which Pietro had brought up from his box in Lerici.

There were quite a few Christmas cards and letters from various people – all of it delayed in the terrible Italian posts. He glanced through the letters quickly, picking a few out for more careful consideration later – until suddenly he started. The envelope in front of him was from Hetty. He saw the Irish stamp, and the postmark dated well before Christmas, addressed in that hurried, assured yet somehow naïve scrawl of hers – the hand of an Edwardian *grande dame* full of natural hauteur which, if you had not known the woman, would have suggested someone cold, arrogant, ruthless.

And how real these qualities were in her, he thought, as he fingered the envelope gingerly. And yet they were only facets, he well remembered, among so many other quite opposite qualities, her grace, beauty, that sweet wit sometimes, above all that stammering vulnerability which could so easily overwhelm her, so that one knew how wonderful a person she was at heart – if only she could find and inhabit that lovely realm of her spirit as a permanence.

Robert's hand shook slightly as he opened the envelope with his tortoiseshell paper-knife. My God, he thought, so long since he'd first met her, since it had all been over between them – yet still there was the vague excitement.

Henrietta had written at length, the difficult script pushing right up to the margins of the notepaper. He wished she had used a typewriter. But she rarely had, even though latterly, the effects of her syphilis bringing an early arthritis, this would have made writing so much easier for her.

But, no, she had once written to him about the thrill of ink running over fine paper, the joy of her old Mentmore fountain pen. Or writing in pencil – that was wonderful, too, she had said, for then there was the added pleasure in the dry-sappy pine smell when you sharpened them, especially in bed, where she usually wrote in the mornings, surrounded by half a dozen soft-leaded artist's 'Imperials', their wafer-thin shavings curled into little crowned trumpets all over the patchwork quilt.

That was how he had last seen her, indeed, sitting up in the four-poster – moved near the window so that she could look straight out over the demesne and the river valley – when he had gone to Summer Hill three years before for Dermot's funeral. Since then he had only had messages on Christmas cards. What could Hetty want to say now – in this obviously long letter? What explanation, demand, justification? What was to be invoked now of all that he had won and lost at Summer Hill? His hand still trembled slightly as he opened the sheets of paper.

18 December 1964

Dear Robert,

Out of the blue for you once more, like that first time all those years ago when I landed on your family hearth in Domenica, a screeching bundle from nowhere, as I imagine. And this may be just as unexpected and possibly disrupting an arrival, though I hope not.

I want to ask you if you would look after all my papers, manuscripts, letters and so on – be my literary executor when I'm gone. I really don't want them getting into the hands of the nosy literary folk who've been at me already about them – these new gossipy biographers, dull academics, booksellers, auctioneers, libraries in Texas. I've heard from them all, and worse, seen some of them at the door, too, and don't really want any of that. Yet I want to preserve them none the less from the ruin that Summer Hill is likely to become when I'm gone. So I've had most of these papers packed in boxes and had Ronnie Ryan, my solicitor here, take them to the bank vault in Kilkenny.

I've kept them for you – really no other reason. You were always to have had them, if you survived. And you have, and will I'm sure, longer than me. But somehow I could never bring myself to talk about this, or give you these papers, face to face – since I felt you would too easily refuse or talk your way out of it in your clever old logical ways.

So I write, where you can't overwhelm me with your voice – where I hope, please, at this distance, you will think about it all calmly and accept the commission. You, together with Hugh Latimer of course, who publishes us both. You are the two trustees and literary executors named in my will. Future income (if any) from all my books is to be divided between you and Olivia, after 10 per cent of these royalties go to the Royal Literary Fund. It's all in the will – with Ronnie Ryan, if I keel over tomorrow!

Robert paused in his reading. There was something

missing in Hetty's résumé of her will. Of course! The house and lands of Summer Hill – and Léonie. No mention had been made of either. He supposed that Léonie was to have the house and estate, if she survived her, but that Hetty had been embarrassed to say so in the letter, knowing how he would feel, seeing this as a further betrayal on her part. Well, it would be, he thought, resuming his reading in a colder mood.

So you will think nicely about this imposition, won't you? At this distance it should be easier for you to do so. In writing like this we can surely stand back from each other a little, can't we? (Before we recede from each other altogether!) In writing, too, perhaps I can make up for some of the pain which I – and Léonie, too – have caused you over the years. This may be more difficult. Words, since they've been our profession as well as our expression, have always been a bit of a problem between us. We were often too good at them, so that feeling was lost – wordy battles that go back such a long way!

I was at church here the other day and remembered how it was when we were children there: the one place we couldn't argue the toss, as we so often did then. Yes, I was reminded of all that, sitting in the same pew where we sat together years ago, bored and fiddly children, through so many Sunday mornings of enforced speechlessness. For it was in this church, I'm sure – during one of Canon Bradshaw's gracious, soft-voiced, interminable sermons – that for want of anything better to do we first calmed down and thought of each other properly, saw ourselves as other than nursery rivals contending for a 'parent', realized that we were not for ever to be fractious children, permanent 'orphans', but sensed that one day we might find safety together – love even – which we did, however briefly.

Yes, when you and I couldn't speak and weren't arguing, we had the gift, I felt, of *looking* at each other properly, and finding truths there which had been quite lost with words. So look at me now, in your mind, when you consider this request, and I feel you may agree with it then. You may agree, too, because so many of these papers reflect Summer Hill, in one way or another, a place I know you've loved. As I have.

Latterly, I'm sure, you've wondered why I've spent so much time and effort and money I didn't really have in keeping up the house. Well, apart from loving it, I've tried to look after it because the house and family here reflect qualities of independence and spirit now sadly lacking in this for-so-long tyrannized, frightened and conformist country: qualities of plain speaking, of concern, of national and neighbourly involvement, as well as all that old wit-and-elegance-of-the-Anglo-Irish bit.

I saw these things as my own Irish inheritance and have wanted to maintain them – so continuing to 'protest', to ask embarrassing questions, long after most of my Protestant co-religionists in the Republic have disowned that spirit and took to large helpings of humble pie. It's certainly made me unpopular with them, just as the same sort of questioning has with my Catholic and republican neighbours. Though I'm as Irish as they are . . .

Forgive these asides. It's simply my instinct that you'll accept this request. Or is it just that I still have a small residue of vanity – in thinking you may still be interested in me, in what will survive of me at least, in these papers? Possibly. Though you can't deny your qualities as a memorialist. I've often noticed this in your columns, your books. (Yes, I read them, each time they arrive, with your neat, non-committal inscriptions.)

People like you who remember things in such detail, who want to get that detail on paper at all costs, are essentially memorialists – spies on time, old money-lenders fingering the days. You may not like to think of yourself as such. But I know it – know what lies behind that often brisk and literal, here-and-now façade of yours, when you've made out your gifts were aimed at nothing more than a deadline in Fleet Street.

I suspect you see yourself as a less creative writer than me – just a journalist, travel writer or whatever. But with your knowledge (as opposed to my intuition) about what *really* matters you've been just as creative as I. People, places, events in your books – even the near trivia you've sometimes dealt with in your journalism – all this in your style, your heart, you've set against the clock of life, the larger fates. That's been your great distinction – the unpretentious way you've set the transient against a background of last things. There's always been that light yet grave tone in your work that I've longed for in mine – which has been too unrelievedly in the wild laughter and tears-before-bedtime mode: romantic where you are classic, if you like.

So I do hope you will look after these papers. And read through them, for there are letters, diaries and so on, things you've never seen – not, with your own so independent spirit, in search of, or in any need of, me after I'm gone, but as evidence of my mind, the way I've seen all three of us, our lives, problems. And the way I've seen just you and me, from the beginning in Domenica: the people we were together then, or the couple we might have been, for there are comments on this as well. The children's garden . . . You, with your logic, your energy, have always been one for completing things, I for leaving them undone. Perhaps these papers will make some amends for that.

Of course, this idea of your needing me in this mental way: you may well feel just the opposite – that it is I, in this rather enfeebled, reclusive life in Ireland, now and when I'm gone, who might need you. But I have you in thought – in faith, if you like. Just as you were always so much 'there' for me when we were children, so you are still, even though *you* may not feel this now. And indeed I often gave you good reason for feeling this . . . I'm sorry. Anyway, knowing your doubts, your unhappinesses about me in the past, these papers are for you – as an explanation I hope of the many things I didn't or refused or wasn't able to tell you in the past, about me, about Léonie – and about *us*, that uniquely 'you and I' part of both our lives.

You know that aside from a few trivial pieces I've never published any autobiography. But I've written one all the same – and you'll find it among the papers, too. It's for you. Perhaps in reading it you may find that it completes our life somehow, makes the relationship whole; that we live together, as we once wanted to, live now what was unlived then. An impossible idea? I don't think so – simply two people sharing their true, their full shape and potential, which can only surely happen in thought – in words, not action.

You may feel of course that a good deal of you and I – our trials, tribulations together – already exists in some of my novels, which you tell me – if you tell me no more! – that you've read. But we've both been necessarily filtered and changed through the fiction there: me especially, changed completely – re-inventing myself, becoming so many 'others' in each story I wrote.

Who was I? Of course for many years I didn't know who my real father was. But I think that my temperament was such that I was never likely to understand my own nature in any deep sense anyway – just acted boldly, usually rashly, in accordance with what I *thought* it to be. My acting first and my writing later always took me away from myself, which was exactly the point of both these exercises! – to escape what I didn't know about, what I feared in myself: the emptiness there. But perhaps, if when you read this 'memoir', you will be able to fill that void suitably and know who I really was – you if anybody.

The autobiography isn't fiction. It's as true, warts and all, as I could get. But I know it isn't any ultimate reality either, the absolute truth about myself, or about my

feelings towards you. The words here must always be
tentative, unfertilized, hooks without eyes, I'm afraid:
one side of a written dialogue waiting to be voiced,
where you alone can play the other role. For the truth
about us both is only ever likely to exist in some mid-way
meeting of our thoughts, in the air between us as it were,
a co-operative verity, which we failed to produce in fact
but which I hope may be established now, when you read
the autobiography – so that when you do, thinking of me,
I'll be thinking of you. Be sure of that. And that's really
the whole point, isn't it? – in life or death: it's the
thought that counts!

My love,
Hetty.

Robert put down the letter. His hands were still shaking. But it was more from anger then, not excitement:
anger at the thought confirmed – how this ghost, which
he thought so well laid, had now returned. And then
there were some of the details, phrases, which annoyed
him. This talk of their meeting in mid-air, a 'co-operative
verity', their living in her memoir 'all that was unlived
then'.

It annoyed him because he knew well how, if Hetty
had only thought like this years before, they would never
have had to meet in mid-air. They could have met, could
have lived and loved together in fact, not fancy, for he
would not have married Léonie then. Almost everything
she had said in the letter was perforce – the results of
her own whims, choices, her own wildly swinging and
divided nature. He had never wanted it that way – any
mid-way, mid-air thing between them. He had just
wanted her, in reality. And he knew that again now,
astonished at the wave of emotion that swept over him.
He could have calmed those ills of hers, restored those
losses, balanced her divisive nature, just as much as
Léonie ever had – if he had ever been given the chance.

But Hetty had never given him that chance at all, all those years ago. Had she done so – why, they could both have been living together for years now at Summer Hill, happy in their old age . . .

My God, he thought – his earlier idea that morning that he had quite got over Hetty! Yet here he was trembling with rage and emotion: all the old poisonous frustrations and obsessions returned. And, worse still, here she was telling him how, with this autobiography, he was going to have to live all his experiences with her over again, all the pain, the loss.

He re-read bits of the letter, grudgingly acknowledging the praise she gave him, the affection she confirmed. Yet still, in his annoyance, he refused to see the essential message there – how she was apologizing for all her behaviour towards him, her behaviour alone – and hers with Léonie. He failed to see, clearly intimated between the lines, how fond she still was of him, how she was asking his forgiveness. Instead what he did notice was the mood of doom in the letter, Hetty sensing her end. And this surprised him. It was Léonie, as he knew from Olivia who saw her fairly regularly, who had been ill earlier the previous year, with stomach cramps, pains in the abdomen. Hetty, when he had last seen her, had been arthritic, with sporadic aches, but otherwise well. And her few messages to him since had confirmed her health. So why the leitmotif of 'last things' in the letter? Well, he wasn't going to worry about it now. A whiff of some herb blew out on to the terrace – rosemary, he was sure. And the smell roused him. Hetty's letter could wait and so could the others. He would go into the kitchen and chat with Maria, get in her way for a minute or two. The kitchen – cure for all ills . . .

When he got there Maria was taking a tray of little *pizzette* out of the oven.

'Rosemary?' he asked her.

'No. Oregano.' She was very busy.

'Oh, that's funny. I could have sworn it was rosemary – "Rosemary for remembrance".'

He returned to the salon where Pietro had just come up from the small cellar and was organizing the drinks.

'Warm enough to have it all on the terrace, I think, Pietro.'

'*Si*, Signor.'

He helped Pietro move the bottles and glasses out into the sun, lining them up on a table. Then he started to polish the glasses – anything to forget Hetty and her letter.

'Ice?' he asked Pietro. 'For the gin and tonic, if they *have* to have it.'

'*Si*, Signor.'

'And you have the Frascati well chilled, in the fridge?'

'*Si*, Signor.'

Pietro was no conversationalist. His wife usually more than made up for him in that way. But Robert decided he could not bother her again so soon. Instead he went back into the salon, thinking to tidy the place, before he saw how tidy it was already. He fidgeted about a bit, moving furniture, then replacing it. He went to the mantelpiece. But that was all perfectly tidy as well. Except – what was it? Something was wrong. Of course – the two small Chinese famille rose vases, which were always kept at either end of the shelf, were right next to each other now.

Had he or Maria moved them recently? He thought not, but could not be sure. As he returned them to their proper places, a smell of violets flooded the air. It made him start. He raised the neck of one of the vases, putting it to his nose. There was no doubt – it reeked: a deep, oily essence of violets. Léonie's violets. Her smell.

These were two Daoguang vases, Cordiner family heirlooms, which Henrietta – on behalf of Léonie, too – had given him as a Christmas present, over there, ten years before. But they were strange vases, since one or other of them – and neither had ever held flowers or perfume at Summer Hill – would offer from time to time, but only to certain people, this intense odour of violets. Hetty could smell it – and Robert, too. But for almost everyone else there was absolutely nothing there – as indeed there had not been for Robert in years. But now this morning, with this unmistakable odour, Léonie had returned, was in the room with him, just as Hetty had been half an hour before in her letter. But the presence of this new *revenant* disturbed Robert even more deeply than the nightmare or Hetty's letter; this sweet smell of Léonie returned to him, essence of their bed together in many places, of a woman who, despite everything, he knew he had once loved just as much as Hetty.

His hand was shaking again. He decided he needed a drink, a mid-morning whizzer. Even better, he would get it from the kitchen drinks cupboard – which would give him the excuse to bother Maria again.

The *pizzette* were delicious – the *Tartufi Bianchi* superb. The guests drank well and had a merry time. Hugh Latimer proposed a birthday toast, adding a few gracious words, to which Robert responded with equal brevity, before offering a toast to Pietro and Maria for the splendid feast.

Molly Latimer talked to Robert later. 'It's all so *nice*,' she said, head to one side, smiling, quizzical. Robert was as fond of her as of Hugh. He raised his glass of Frascati to her.

'And *you* are so nice.'

'I'm only sorry about Olivia.'

'She called from Genoa, flight was delayed. But she'll be here before we finish – plenty of time yet. Here, do get rid of that gassy champagne and try some of this Frascati . . .'

The British Consul from Genoa bearded Robert then and he switched to a more formal mode. The man congratulated him on everything – for the second time, for he and his pretty wife had done all this on arrival. Hugh Latimer, the more adept diplomat, finally rescued him and they went out together on to the terrace.

'A splendid review in the *Telegraph* already. I've a copy for you – got it in Rome. And both the Sundays are giving it lead reviews – I called the office. And an excellent subscription. I couldn't be better pleased – with your "memoirs" . . .' His eyes twinkled.

'My apotheosis . . .'

'I hope not! You'll write something more, won't you?'

'About what, dear Hugh? Can't really slog around the wild places much any more. And I'm not one for the vine-and-olive-grove Tuscan book, old British gent in a ruined *podere* squelching grapes with his bare toes in a vat. Not really my style – least of all living on this bare rock.' They gazed out over the Poet's Gulf, sipped their drinks.

'What will you do then?' Hugh asked.

This gave Robert his cue. And he took it, rather unwillingly. 'I had a letter from Hetty this morning, delayed in the post.'

'Yes?'

'You must have had the same request. She wants both of us to be her literary executors.'

'Yes. I had a note from her about that.'

'Well, that might keep me occupied for a bit – if I don't go before her, which is quite possible. She was fit enough when I last saw her.'

'Yes, she is. Saw her last autumn. She came over for her new novel.'

'But what do you think – about her papers? Lot of

715

work there, I imagine. She should leave them all to that manuscript library in Texas, get a handsome price for them there, too, I imagine.'

'She doesn't want that. She said in her letter to me – she wants you to have them, particularly.'

'Yes, I know.' Robert was downcast. 'And that's the problem. I don't want to have to – well, live my life with her all over again.'

'No.'

'And of course I would, because she's written a proper autobiography as well, warts and all. She told me.'

Hugh perked up at this. 'Oh, I didn't know. That must be absolutely fascinating. *Her* life – my God.'

'Yes. But she may not want it published. She didn't say. Just left it to us, I suppose.'

'To you, Robert. You'd be the person to decide. Chief executor as it were – which you surely are, in truth.'

'I don't know, Hugh . . . I'm not keen on the whole thing, honestly. I'd sooner not be involved – far too much water under that bridge. I'd really prefer if you handled it, when it comes to the point—'

Just as he said this a searing pain shot through his head, the early-morning headache, after the nightmare, returning suddenly with a vengeance – like a needle passing through his skull. A further message from Hetty – just as he had denied her? He had had these strange intimations all morning. Of course, he did not believe in it all, the psychic thing, messages through the ether. Nonetheless he was unnerved by it, thinking he might as well amend his last statement. 'Well anyway, Hugh, I suppose I can't actually turn her down. I'll do something. I'll write to her.' As he said this the pain quite disappeared. Then Pietro came out on to the terrace.

'Telephone, Signor.'

Robert had taken several congratulatory calls already

that morning and was tired of them. 'Tell them to leave a message, Pietro.'

'It's a long-distance, from Ireland, Signor. The man said it was urgent.'

'The *man*?'

'*Si*, Signor.'

Robert looked over at Hugh. 'I don't think I know any man in Ireland these days – just women. Unless it's the *Irish Times*, looking for an interview.' He stood up, finishing his Frascati. 'A few words of wisdom from the old sage at the Villa Serena? Can't be. I haven't won the Nobel prize. And I'm not Irish either.'

He pondered these last words as he went to the telephone in his study. Of course he supposed he was Irish, if he was anything. It was there, in Ireland, at Summer Hill, that almost everything that had really mattered in his heart had happened. Hetty's letter, and all the other strange intimations of the morning, were more than enough to confirm that emotional nationality. He picked up the telephone.

'A *what*?' Robert asked again. The line was crackling badly. Then it cleared.

'A *fire*, Sir Robert – at Summer Hill,' the voice shouted.

'Who's calling?'

'Mr Ryan – Ronnie Ryan – Miss Cordiner's solicitor, from Kilkenny. The point is—'

'A fire? Where? When?' Robert was still confused.

'Last night, or the early morning. Some of the bedrooms in the south wing, the landing above the hall. Started in Miss Cordiner's bedroom apparently. Luckily, Jack Welsh downstairs smelt something, got the brigade out, and they had it under control in an hour or so. But the point is, Mr Grant – Miss Cordiner is all right, a few bruises, superficial burns – but Miss Straus, I'm afraid she died in the blaze. They couldn't get her out of the bedroom and—'

The line, which had cleared for a minute, was now crackling again and Robert did not hear the end of the sentence.

'Léonie?' he shouted.

'— Cordiner, she asked me to call you, so—'

The static was bad now. 'Of course—'

'— the funeral — Friday — been snowing heavily — I'm making the arrangements. Miss Cordiner asked me—'

'Yes, yes. Tell Miss Cordiner I'll be over right away. I'll fly over as soon as I can.'

'Fine. I'll tell — arrangements for Friday, at the house, so—'

The static returned and Robert heard no more, finally putting the telephone down. How much clearer the earlier messages from Ireland that morning had been – the fiery nightmare, the searing headaches, the whiff of rosemary when it was oregano, the smell of violets. And now their meaning was at last quite clear to Robert. Above all the note of doom in Hetty's letter made some sense now. But what sense? What exactly had happened? He returned to the terrace, taking Hugh aside, telling him of the call.

'Oh, my God – how quite appalling. Of course I'll come over with you.'

'What puzzles me though is how the fire started, mid-winter, with all that Irish damp and wet. And the solicitor said it had been snowing heavily over there.'

'These old houses, fires in the drawing room – a log, a spark – after they'd gone to bed.'

'It started up *in* one of the bedrooms, though.'

'Faulty wiring?'

'They only had the electricity put in ten years ago.'

'Dear me, so all Hetty's papers gone, too. She worked in her bedroom.'

'No. I didn't tell you. She had all her papers and manuscripts packed up and sent to the bank. She wrote to
me . . .'

As he said this something struck Robert. The note of
doom in the letter . . . And then he thought he saw
it: had Hetty sent all her papers away, intentionally, in
advance of the fire? Was there something prepared in it
all? No, it couldn't be. That was nonsense.

'We've got seats on tomorrow afternoon's flight from
Genoa. Come back with us on that.'

'Yes. But let me wait and see what Olivia says when
she gets here.'

Olivia arrived, with the two children, ten minutes
later, the hire car skidding to a halt at the top of the Villa
steps where Robert, seeing some other guests off, was
waiting. Lottie and William, cooped up in the tiny Fiat
for hours, jumped out all agog. Olivia got out on the
other side much more slowly, leaning on the roof, looking
at her father a moment, sighing, cradling her head in her
arms.

'Oh – oh oh!' she groaned in mock dramatics. 'This
awful little car.' She thumped it on the roof. 'Stalled on
the autostrada. And now I've missed everything! You
drunken, foody lot, you!'

She hurried round the car, rushing into her father's
arms, embracing him. Then, hands on her shoulders, he
held her apart from him for an instant, gazing at her: the
same silk-fine, dark hair riding the high brow, something
of the chunky build, same blackberry eyes, the very
slightly pouty, sensuous lower lip – so little of her father
in her looks, he thought, so much of her mother. And
then, for the first time that day, Robert felt real pain as
he hugged her again.

Huge moist flakes of snow fluttered through the air, icing
the stone pineapples on the gate pillars, drifting across

the fretworked gable-ends and diamond-paned windows of the little Gothic lodge: a Christmas card scene as Ronnie Ryan drove Robert and Hugh and Molly through the main gate of Summer Hill, Olivia with the two children in another car behind them. The funeral was in an hour's time.

They drove up the avenue. In the white drifts nothing was visible beyond the line of tall beech trees. The demesne was foreshortened everywhere, without length or breadth, in which none of the informal eighteenth-century landscaping showed, curtained by the gentle spirals of snow which muffled every sound. The car ran noiselessly over the spongy flakes, so that they seemed to be moving through a huge crystal ball, a vast toy, a glass ornament shaken out of its liquid, translucent peace, the snowflakes dancing in the orb; soon the travellers would reach the centrepiece of this conceit, the pinnacles and domes of some fairy-tale castle . . .

But the house when it came in view at the top of the rise was a sad sight. The east façade which gave out over the valley was grimed and blackened. Tongues of soot rose up the walls from gaping windows, the glass and casements were shattered, all the way up to the roof. A debris of snow-covered brick and plaster lay on the lawn in front. There was an air of something freshly killed about the house – still bloodied and warm, a body whose intimacies had been laid bare.

Ronnie Ryan – benign and portly, balding, in a dark suit and Homburg hat – looked up at the house as they rounded the old pleasure gardens, the astrolabe still there, its ribs, skeleton-like, rimmed in snow. 'A bad business – very bad altogether.'

'Which room exactly did the fire start in?'

'The primrose room – Miss Cordiner's room. Between twelve and one in the morning, they think. Jack Welsh, at the back, was awake – smelt something. Luckily his daughter Mary and her husband Seamus were staying, over from Birmingham last week. Seamus got upstairs quickly. But the whole landing was engulfed, smoke and flames. He only just managed to drag Miss Cordiner out of her room. Of course . . .' Ronnie Ryan paused. 'He'd – he'd no idea that Miss Straus was in the same room.'

Robert said nothing. The car drew up some distance from the portico. It had to. Mounds of snowy debris lay between them and the hall door. They all got out, as Olivia and the children arrived in the car behind. Robert, moving slowly through the thin flakes towards the house with his daughter, started to pick and poke vaguely over the mounds of burnt rubbish. Bits of charred furniture stuck out from the snow, sodden books, ice-encrusted carpets. The remains of a leather chesterfield sofa crouched beneath the snow.

'Look,' he said. 'That's the canterbury Hetty kept her books in, next to her bed.' He examined the smashed and charred antique. 'And there – that pembroke table. We did lessons on that, as children.' Moving on he came to a pile of sodden books. Lifting up one, he dusted the snow off it. *The Boy's Book of Railways* – that was mine.' Beneath were a red-bound copy of *Punch* for 1898 and an old Victorian manual on beekeeping.

'Come on, Daddy, let's go in.' Olivia took his arm and they walked up the steps. Elly and Jack Welsh, a very elderly couple now, were waiting for them. They all went into the hall. The debris here, which had fallen from the walls and down the stairwell from the first-floor landing, had been almost entirely cleared away. But Robert's shoe squeaked over something on the floor. Bending down he picked up part of a broken crystal pendant, holding it for a moment, so that it glittered faintly in the snowy light from the open hall door. Then he looked up. The great Waterford chandelier, which had always hung right down through the house from the top of the stairwell, had gone completely. He put the piece of glass into his pocket. He felt he had come into a time of last mementoes for Summer Hill.

Then, turning, he suddenly saw Léonie's coffin, on trestle stands to one side of the hall, by the long Flemish tapestry. It was surrounded by laurel, ferns, holly, garlands of simple winter greenery. He moved towards it, stood there an instant, but could think of nothing – except of how much colder she must be than he was.

'Come into the drawing room, Daddy. There's a fire . . .'

'And Hetty?' He turned to Olivia who had been talking to Elly.

'She's upstairs, in another bedroom. Elly says she doesn't want—'

'I should see her.' Robert, as if pursued by something, was anxious to see Hetty, attend the church – complete all his business in Summer Hill as soon as possible and get away.

'No. She's not coming to the funeral. She doesn't want to see anyone till after it.'

Robert reluctantly joined the others in the long drawing room where there were sandwiches and whiskey – and a fire, two small electric fires. Robert huddled close to one of them, barely nibbling at a sandwich, sipping his whiskey, still numbed. Outside the tall windows the snow drifted lightly down, a soft shroud over the world.

An hour later the first of the mourners arrived, cars gliding silently up the long avenue, being parked in the yard, the people walking round, beginning to congregate under cover on the porch steps in greatcoats and scarves, stamping the snow off their shoes.

And, half an hour after that, Robert with Olivia and the two children were in the first of the hired cars, following the hearse down the avenue, before they turned right outside the front gates and started slowly down the narrow twisting hill road into the village of Cloone.

The snow had thinned in the early afternoon and the hill had been specially gritted beforehand. But even so the chauffeur nearly ran them into the back of the hearse, giving its bumper a sharp clip as their car skidded on, before almost colliding with a group of villagers paying their respects, hats off, standing in front of one of the old terraced estate cottages on the steep corner.

'Just the thing – at an Irish funeral: mourners up on a manslaughter charge . . .' Robert hoped to lighten the mood, without success.

But the service in the little church across the river, with Cranmer's vivid words and the hymn 'To be a pilgrim' played by the organist and a small choir out from the cathedral in Kilkenny – all this was beautiful, appropriate, moving.

Yet Robert, at one end of the front pew where he and Hetty had fiddled with boredom nearly sixty years before, found himself quite without emotion. Though he wanted to feel for this woman, cold beside him now on trestles a few yards away, who had once meant so much, had been so warm and close to him.

Why could he not feel for her now? It was surely nothing to do with all that had happened between them years before, her staying on with Hetty finally. He had long got over that. Why was it then? Just his restrained temperament once more? Surely not. Surely, at least at such times like this, he was capable of having, even showing, some emotion.

Then the thought suddenly struck him – perhaps it was because Hetty was not here, ever that vital third in his relationship with Léonie. A crucial player in this mourning was missing. But then had he really needed Léonie because he had failed with Hetty? Had he taken Léa on because, as her greatest friend, that was as close as he could get to Hetty – taking revenge against Hetty at the same time, for her coldness to him, by stealing Léonie from her?

Could his feelings for these two women have been so twisted? It was possible. He prayed he had not been so perverse, so immature, so selfish with them. He literally prayed then, something he had not done since he and Hetty had been children together sitting in this same pew.

'I have lifted up mine eyes unto the Lord and seen my salvation! . . .' He listened to the anthem, with the choir. Had he, he wondered, ever seen anything of the sort? Had he denied his salvation somehow? – a man incapable of any simple natural emotion, with a heart as cold as the white weather outside. He prayed – for some ordinary human feeling for this woman, once so loved, lying dead almost next to him.

Then, kneeling a few minutes later, he glanced over at Lottie and William at the end of the pew, bent right down, hidden beneath the wood, heads together, up to some vital business. They were bored – fiddling, whispering, disputing a hassock, pulling it one way, then another – lost in a secret world, see-saws of argument, affection, spite and making up. Children.

And at that moment the emotion he had hoped for suddenly swept over him, for the two children in their own right, and because they were him and Hetty years before in just the same place, and for Léonie finally, because she, whatever else, had become that vital third in their world, all those years ago at Summer Hill – a world she was leaving for ever now. So that now he could feel for her completely.

And he saw then, with awful clarity, how there had been, and must still be, essentially three of them in the equation of their lives, that cat's cradle difficult – for him impossible in the end – to maintain, but which nonetheless contained the truth of all their lives: for him an unattainable truth.

And he could mourn that too, now – how for his own good or bad reasons he had refused to be part of that equation in the end, had abandoned the two women, had destroyed what might have been meant for them all – a life together, for the last twenty years, at Summer Hill.

Now he felt too much – a sense of guilt as well as love towards Léonie, a longing to make things up to her for betraying her in this way. So that he found the short journey through the snow, walking behind the undertakers carrying her coffin to the Cordiner family vault, almost unbearable.

'In sure and certain resurrection . . .' the rector intoned. But Robert could not look into the vault, bright from the reflected snow, as they put her among all the Cordiner ancestors, returning her here as well to what was her true home, from which, once more, he was excluded. When the vault door finally clanged shut he longed to be out of the whole place, back to the hotel in Dublin, a flight to the Villa Serena.

Afterwards, when most of the mourners had struggled purposefully back to Summer Hill in the snow, there was a reception, a funeral 'tea' – largely composed of strong drink – in the drawing room and hall.

After half an hour Robert could stand it no more. He would simply have to force himself on Hetty upstairs, offer condolences – then leave. He strode into the hall. Luckily Ronnie Ryan, just coming downstairs, met him there. 'Miss Cordiner – she wonders if you would like to go and see her now.'

Robert went upstairs with Ryan, along the corridor of the west wing, not touched in the fire. The solicitor stopped at one of the bedroom doors. With a moment's trepidation now, fearing the worst, emotionally and visually, Robert went inside.

He was astonished by what confronted him.

It was a large room – it had once been the best of the visitors' bedrooms. But now nothing of its old furnishings remained. It had been done up recently, completely and expensively redecorated, transformed, with two new large divan beds, loose-weave white wool counterpanes, white cane furniture, pretty wallpaper – a bathroom, he saw, built *en suite* into the next room: a bedroom with every modern comfort, warm and bright, the flowery curtains still open, giving out on to the snowy gardens.

Hetty sat on a high cane chair, next to a glass-topped table, covered in books, new novels, magazines, papers, with all her pens and pencils at the ready – a handsome new electric fire aglow at one side. But what astonished Robert most was her demeanour. Dressed in a smartly-cut tweed skirt, fluffy white cotton blouse and an embroidered sleeveless Russian waistcoat that he remembered her in years before, Hetty – apart from a slightly black eye and a light bandage round her forearm – looked formidably handsome, composed, a woman quite in charge of things. Robert had fully expected someone in bed – enfeebled, distraught, unhappy. Hetty in one of her most collapsed modes. Instead, here was a woman dressed, and against a background, straight out of an advertisement from *House and Garden*.

'Hetty . . .' He could not hide his surprise.

'Robert! – at last. How l-lovely.' She spoke casually, smiling faintly, rubbing her nose with one of her artist's 'Imperial' pencils.

'I – I thought you'd be in bed. Or something.'

'Yes, they all think that. That's the general idea. Just I can't be-bear funerals. Almost as b-bad as seeing people off at railway stations.' She looked at him in her old quizzical, haughty manner. 'You're surprised? Shouldn't be. Why should I have to face up to all that dreary chilling business in the church, coffins and things? Or that nonsense downstairs now. Nothing to do with Léa. All that I feel for her is up here.' She touched her head. 'Or down there.' She dropped her hand to a typescript on the glass-topped table. 'I won't be made to mourn people their way. Only mine. And mine's be-*better*,' she added tartly.

'Yes.' But Robert remained perplexed. He took the other white cane chair near her at the table. 'It's just – I hadn't expected you here.' He looked about the smart room.

'Oh, I had this done up all frou-frou and silk satiny for my American publisher and his wife when they come to visit. Harry Jacobson and Mary-Ann: they couldn't bear the cold in the other rooms. Overheard them talking one m-morning a few years ago. "Harry," she said, "I didn't just lightly fr-freeze in bed last night. I was *solid*." So I thought if he was going to go on publishing me I'd better do something about it.'

There was silence after this. Robert did not know quite what to say, so he said 'yes' rather inconclusively. Then, by way of changing the topic, he said, 'I got your letter, just a few days ago. Delayed in the Italian posts.'

'Good. I'm glad. I wondered – not hearing from you. I hope you weren't too p-p-put off by it?'

Now, for the first time there was a note of doubt in her voice, a feel of genuine, not breezy emotion. And Robert, unable to take much more of the latter, took his cue from this changed approach.

'Hetty, what really happened?' he asked. 'With you and Léa – and the fire. I've only heard the vaguest details from Ronnie Ryan.'

She looked away, raised her head, as if seeking inspiration from the pretty wallpaper. Then she looked back at him. And now there was a real emotion in her face. 'I thought you might guess it all from my letter.'

'Guess what? Apart from rather a note of doom in it all—'

'Exactly.'

'But why? You're looking so well – you weren't going to die.'

'No. But Léa was. We both were,' she added decisively. 'That was the whole point.'

'What point?' he asked, fearing his worst suspicions were going to be confirmed.

'Léa hadn't been that well this last year—'

'I knew that, stomach pains, but nothing serious, you all said.'

'That's what we all thought. And the doctors. Nothing really wrong at all. But then a few months ago – it was all very quick. She had cancer, of the womb. And it was too late. They couldn't operate, they said. It had spread all over. She was in pain, and it got worse, even with the drugs – unbearable. Now do you see the p-point, of the fire?'

'No—'

'And why Léa was in my bedroom when the fire started.'

And Robert was forced to see it all then. 'No, Hetty . . .' He paused. 'You, too.'

'Yes. I started it. Just bad luck – that Jack Welsh smelt the burning. And that Seamus was staying here. Dragged me out of the room. But didn't see Léa – didn't know she was in the room at all.' She picked up one of the new novels on the table. 'Review copies, what a chore. I was hoping not to have to do any more of them.' Then she looked at Robert quickly, just as he was about to speak. 'You don't have to ask me why.'

'No.'

'Twenty years with her here. And all that went before. I wanted no more of it, alone. We'd agreed a month

728

ago – said when the pain got too bad. After Christmas, we thought.'

'Yes.'

'She'd seen Olivia in October when she was still OK. They all had a lovely long weekend here together, Olivia and the children. So we'd said our goodbyes, all my p-papers in the vault, the letter I wrote you and Hugh. And then there was Christmas – which we managed. It was all as neat as it could be. Then last week, last Sunday, she could stand no more. It would have been the happier solution. For both of us.'

Hetty had regained some of her composure as she spoke, in all but her eyes which were frightened.

'I am sorry,' was all Robert could say.

She picked up the old snow-dome, using it now as a paperweight on the table, with its miniature of Summer Hill inside – starting to turn it slowly, so that the flakes began to drift over the tiny chimneys and gable-ends. 'Now, I'm back where I started,' she said. 'Wherever that is.' She gazed vacantly into the crystal.

Robert who, until that moment, with the others waiting for him downstairs, had been anxious to leave, suddenly found himself staring at the dome, transfixed, seeing the house complete inside it – inviolate, perfect, a glittering ageless emblem. And it struck at his heart then – feelings of all sorts of desertion. But he must leave. He had to.

'You're not rushing away at once, Robert?' She had read his thoughts.

'We have to, Hetty – the bad roads – before the light goes.' He glanced at the window. The light had not yet gone at all. Indeed it was rather brighter than it had been, the snow clouds lightening, the weather passing on, leaving a soft white glitter over the gardens.

'Oh, do stay the night. You're all expected. Biddy has made beds up all along this landing, there's food. Go tomorrow.' She glanced at him, still fingering the crystal dome. 'Or why go at all?' she added in just the same casual tone. 'Why not stay here, Robert?' She looked into the orb. 'Always your home – just as much as mine.'

She set the dome back on the table. The flakes started to settle gently over the house. She glanced up at him in the silence. 'Why don't you stay, Robert?'

The funeral party finished early, most of the guests equally anxious to get away in the bad weather. Olivia was with Molly Latimer in the drawing room. They had just finished helping Biddy, and two other local women in for the day, to clear away the tea things.

'Papa's so keen to get off,' Olivia said. 'We really should stay the night. Leaving Hetty on her own, just with Jack and Elly . . .'

'Yes.'

'I suppose she'll be all right. Such a strange house.' Olivia looked around the room, where the lights had not yet been switched on. 'That it doesn't give you the creeps at a time like this – half-burnt, fires, deaths, funerals. Yet there's still an air of – what is it? – safety, welcome?'

'Yes,' Molly said. 'It's always had that, whenever I've come over with Hugh. But then Irish houses nearly always do, don't they? That feeling of warmth – even when it's *freezing*.' Molly shivered.

They left the room and went into the hall. 'Better get our hats and coats together. It'll certainly be freezing in the car. And where on earth have the children got to?'

Lottie and William were at the top of the house, on the old nursery landing – which had been strictly forbidden them on earlier visits, as the boards were thought to be unsafe. It was gloomy since they dared not put on the lights, tip-toeing along, the floorboards creaking, exploring. A door was ajar. They pushed it open – then nearly jumped out of their skins.

A great crocodile stared up at them, its mouth a snarl of vicious teeth. Recovering from her fright, Lottie ventured into the room. William hung back. 'Come on, you coward! It's nothing. Just stuffed.' They moved further in. The room was filled with rubbish. But when they came to inspect it all more closely they were fascinated.

'Look! Bits of an old gun!' William said in wonder. 'A *real* gun, a rifle!'

'And all those other strange animals next door, do you see?'

They had come to the threshold of the adjoining room, gazing at the strange animals in the glass cases – the lemurs, the porcupine – ghostly beasts in the white gloom.

'What a place!' William said. But he was still a bit frightened. 'If we're caught we'll be for it, though.'

'You're just a coward,' Lottie said. 'I *like* it here.'

'So do I, but—'

'Look!' Lottie had found the long skeleton of a snake in an old tea-chest. Pulling it out, she shook the stringed vertebrae suddenly, rattling the evil thing in his face.

'Don't!' he yelled.

'Shush! – they'll hear us, cowardy.'

'I'm *not*!'

Returning the skeleton to its chest, she relented. 'Nice if we could play here.'

'Yes. But we can't. The floorboards aren't safe. And we're all going back to Dublin now – Mummy said, to the hotel.'

'Yes. Pity . . .'

'Come on then, or we'll miss the car.' He fingered the remains of the old Winchester rifle lovingly an instant before they left the playroom.

Hugh Latimer was in the library with Ronnie Ryan. They had been talking of the future. 'So what will happen now, do you think – the house, Miss Cordiner?'

'She shouldn't stay here on her own – that's certain. Take a service flat in Dublin.'

'Exactly. But do you think she'll *want* to stay on here?'

'Yes, I'm sure she will. That's the whole problem. Always seen it in her. Absolutely attached to the place. It'd be the devil's own job getting her out of here. No question. Won't be told – you know Miss Cordiner . . .'

'Yes, I know. Could she get any sort of a companion?'

Ronnie Ryan shrugged. 'Unlikely. Stuck way up here on the hill in this great place. And who could possibly make up for the last one, Mr Latimer?'

'No . . . I don't want to pry, but has she the money to keep the place up here?'

'Probably. Just about. But that's not the real problem – just keeping it up. The fact is that she could never live here on her own. Always a great one for *company*, Mr Latimer. And then, as far as money goes, there *is* the problem now. If anyone's to live here there'd have to be substantial repairs to the east wing, the landing, the hall. I don't suppose she'd see much change out of fifty or sixty thousand these days for that. No, my advice would be for her to get out of the place, before the roof comes off, get herself a nice warm service flat in Dublin. This place . . .' He sighed. 'It's beautiful. But it's done its turn, Mr Latimer. Gardens all gone to rack and ruin, the house itself half gutted in the fire. And the roof will be next – always is in Ireland. To keep it going now, well, it'd be flogging a dead horse.'

'Yes, I suppose so. A pity . . .' Hugh gazed around at the books, the old leather-bound volumes, ancient folios, set everywhere around two walls, as many modern books against the other two. 'I suppose we'd better be thinking of going – weather may turn bad again. And I should see Miss Cordiner before I leave.' Hugh looked out of the window. The snow had stopped, the cloud quite passed on, so that now, in mid-afternoon, there was still no need of the lights, a bright white glitter reflecting off the snow, shining into the library.

They stood up, moving to the door. But Hugh stopped suddenly, seeing a pile of artist sketch-books on the floor next to it, used as a door-stopper, it seemed. He picked one up, opening it. It was dated '1902', the numerals set in a wonderfully elaborate mock-Gothic scroll. Turning the pages he saw the pen and ink and water-colour drawings – the perfect draughtsmanship, vivid, beautiful, witty, all quite original, with an accompanying text on each opposite page: an illustrated journal of life at Summer Hill, its routines and eccentricities, landscape, flora, fauna, its even more abundant and bizarre human life. The other sketch-books, he saw, were just the same. It was a startling collection.

'Oh, yes – Miss Emily's drawings,' Ronnie Ryan told him. 'A remarkable woman, sister of old Sir Desmond—'

'Yes. I met her briefly, years ago, just before she died. But I'd no idea – of all this!'

'Ah yes, just a few old scrapbooks, drawings and things. Kept her out of mischief, they said. She was, well – ninepence in the shilling.'

Hugh flicked through the pages again, his publisher's eye alert now. 'Worth a lot more than that, Mr Ryan, I'm certain. The whole story of a great house, over several generations, in words and pictures. Absolutely marvellous. Never seen anything like it.'

'You mean, there's money in it?'

'I should say so, yes. Thousands . . .'

They went back to the hall, meeting Olivia and Molly, getting their things together. 'Where *are* those children? We really should see Hetty – and leave before it gets dark.' Olivia was worried. 'What *is* Daddy doing up there?'

The group looked up the great staircase, waiting for him, wanting to go.

★

The daylight went quickly then. The snow lay thick and still about the house in the sudden dark. But the two hire cars, which had been engaged that morning at Dublin airport, stayed where they were on the gravel surround. Then one by one the lights came on in rooms about the house: in the drawing room, the library, the dining room – where Bridget started to lay places for eight on the long table – then in three of the other bedrooms in the west wing, the house gradually coming alive again in the strange airless calm of the night. The snow dazzled now, a myriad of tiny pinpoints reflecting the light from a half-moon over the silent valley.

Robert, having taken his overnight things upstairs to a bedroom next to Olivia's, spoke to her alone as he unpacked his few clothes.

'What happened? You'd been so mad to get off back to Dublin!'

'Yes.' He took his reading spectacles out of his pocket and put them with a book on the bedside table. 'I'd absolutely no intention of staying.'

'What changed your mind?'

He told her of his earlier conversation with Hetty, how she had asked them all to stay the night, at least – and then how, as an afterthought as it seemed, had said to him how Summer Hill was as much his home as hers.

'And?'

'Well, she'd been so casual about everything, the invitation, about telling me the place was mine as much as hers – no dramatics. So I thought I'd just tell her we'd stay overnight, the bad weather and so on. But I didn't say this. Because it was obvious what she really meant – which was that I, you, all of us, should live in the place with her, as a permanency. Obviously. You know that little snow-dome of the house, used to be kept on the drawing mantelpiece? – she was fingering it, gazing into it. It was quite clear what she meant.'

'And?' Olivia was on tenterhooks.

Robert took his dressing gown from the bag. 'So I said, I told her – the words just came out as if someone else was speaking – that we, I at least, would stay on for a bit. Nothing permanent, I thought. Just a week or two. Help her get things settled, see what she wanted to do, a flat in Dublin or something. Anyway, at that point, after I'd said I'd stay, her calm casual air quite vanished. She broke down, started to sob . . .'

Robert searched his coat pockets now for something. 'Everything she'd been repressing, about Mama, about me, I suppose, the future of the house – it all came out in a fearful rush.' He found some pipe-cleaners at last, putting them with the book and spectacles on the bedside table. 'So I will stay. More permanently, and of course I told her that then, seeing how she was, weeping over that frightful glass-topped table she got in to please her American publishers. Told her I'd stay – and help her put the place back in order a bit. What do you think?' He looked up at Olivia doubtfully.

'I think that's fine!' She smiled, came over and kissed him on the forehead. 'But I'm astonished . . .'

'Yes. But what else? Hetty's right. It was my home. Though I certainly shan't stay here in the winter,' he added quickly, shivering. 'Winter at the Villa Serena. But we could spend the summers here . . .'

'"We"?'

'Why not? The children at least. And whenever you can get away from London.'

'Why not indeed!' Olivia was excited at the prospect. 'The children love it here. And I've always loved the place. Except, well, I've never been entirely easy here, just visiting Mama, with Hetty – knowing how you've felt about them both. Now it'd be different.'

'Yes, it would.'

That third in the triangle had gone, he thought. Things

therefore could not but be easier for him in one way, if sadder in another. There was a strange justice in it all. He was back where he had started with Hetty, more than fifty years before – where he had always wanted to be, alone again with her at Summer Hill. He had lost everything. Now, at the very last moment, he had regained it all.

They went down to supper half an hour later. Hetty joined them – Robert, Olivia, the two children, Hugh and Molly, Ronnie Ryan. Hetty, despite the fire, insisted on bringing out the two candelabra, lighting them. The occasion was not breezy or convivial. It was calm and sober, but filled with all sorts of secret or unspoken thoughts.

'We'll be able to play upstairs now as much as we want,' Lottie whispered to William over the chicken broth. Their mother had told them how they would be here much more often now.

'Those sketch-books of your great aunt Emily's – I've been looking at them in the library,' Hugh said half-way through the meal. 'They're absolutely wonderful. Do you think we might publish them – the best of them? They'd make a wonderful book. A series of books.'

'Yes. If you think so. But would anybody b-buy them?'

'I'm sure they would – great nostalgia for all that now, Edwardian country life and lives.'

'You mean – they'd really pay *money*?' Hetty asked, a little jealous now to hear of this other hidden literary bounty in the house.

'Yes, I'm sure—'

'And what of my "memoirs", Hugh? Will you p-publish them? You've just done Robert's.'

'Yes, Robert told me – I'd no idea you'd written anything like that. Your life, Hetty . . . That would be a *real* bestseller . . .'

'Enough, with Aunt Emily's sketch-books, to repair the east wing?'

'More than enough, I should say – and put the rest of the place in order, too.'

Hetty smiled, lifting her glass. 'Well, to all of us, then – a future.' She looked round the table. 'And to absent fr-fr-friends . . .' She raised her glass to the portraits of all the Cordiner ancestors, who once more seemed to come alive in the flickering candlelight – and kept it raised a moment for the others in her mind then, for all the Cordiners in the family vault across the river, with Léonie.

The snow had quite moved away by morning, bringing a day of brilliant blue sky and sun, almost hot, which soaked down on the landscape – an enchantment of pearly folds and meringue twists, a crisp glitter on the garden terraces, creamy glaciers running down the lawn to the river gorge where the trees were canopied in powdery foam. It was a day so unexpected in an Irish winter – buoyant, tingling, fine, where land and sky made one vast empty canvas and there seemed no end of things in the air.

Robert, taking Hetty's arm, went for a short walk with her, down the porch steps and out over the gravel surround. Their boots crackled, pushing through the crisp surface, leaving deep footprints in the virgin snow as they moved between the white hillocks of debris from the fire. He came to the pile where he had found the old books the previous afternoon, digging about in it again now, rescuing the bound volume of *Punch* for 1898, then the Victorian manual on beekeeping. He rubbed the snow off it.

'Now there's a thing,' he said enthusiastically. 'Bee-keeping. I've often thought of it: we should really keep some bees here, Hetty – at Summer Hill.'

Inside the great hall, with their mother beyond the green baize door in the back regions, talking to Jack and Elly, and the Latimers still upstairs, the two children wondered what to do, how to make best use of their sudden freedom.

Lottie gazed at the long Flemish tapestry. Then anchoring her arm about one of the hall pillars, she let her body swirl slowly round it, so that, as she turned, the stories in the weave came alive, a panorama of fearless hunters and their prey, of wonderful mediaeval courts, of invulnerable Kings and Queens.

'"The King was in the counting house counting out his money – the Queen was in the parlour eating bread and honey" . . .' she chanted to herself. She wondered where a house like this could ever end, there was so much of it – rooms and corridors, nooks and crannies – all unexplored, all waiting.

'Here, come and look at this!' William said, kneeling on the window box over on the far side of the hall. He was gazing at a small pane of stained glass set at the bottom corner of the tall window. It showed a yellow-eyed eagle, perched on an old helmet – with some writing beneath, the morning sun streaming through it all – illuminating the colours vividly. 'There's something written there,' he said when Lottie arrived. '"Audaces Fortuna Juvat" . . .' He made a rough stab at the Latin. 'What does it mean?'

'Oh, nothing – I don't know,' Lottie was forced to admit after a minute's inspection. 'Come on – there's much better things to do than look at that! Let's do something *really* brave and risky.'

'What?'

'There's another room upstairs in the attics, beyond the one with the croc. It's *locked* . . .'

'I don't think—'

'Come *on*!'

They tiptoed away, starting properly to explore the big house.